River

DISC...

✓ W9-ACF-092

the Confederate Gun-Boat "ARKANSAS"

MAP of
the LOWER
MISSISSIPPI

LAKE PONTCHARTRAIN

LAKE MAUREPAS

MONROE COUNTY

ORLEANS →

By Valour
and Arms

By Valour
and Arms

by
James Street

THE SUN DIAL PRESS
Garden City   **New York**

**For
Mother**

By Valour
and Arms

Chapter One

EVEN at dawn the heat was stifling and clammy, and Wyeth Woodward ran his hand across his forehead and over his eyes, then peered into the mist that was boiling from the Mississippi. There was no sound out there and nothing was moving except the river. So he leaned against a water oak and waited. He knew how to relax and wait.

The mist was in layers, pressed down by the heat. It clung to the leaves and formed dirty little blobs that, surrendering to their own weight and the law of gravity, rolled off of the trees and vanished in the brown, scarred bluff that kept the river away from Natchez. Behind Wyeth and to the East, the town lay panting and gasping, stewing in its own sweat and perfume.

There should have been a breeze. A northeast wind, born in the Tennessee mountains five hundred miles away, usually preceded the dawn. It always had and it would come again unless nature, too, had deserted the South. So Wyeth waited patiently, confident that the breeze would come and help him.

He wiped the moisture from his eyelashes, stared down the bluff, and selected one leaf on a huge magnolia and watched it, knowing it would signal the approach of any wind that dared creep into the valley. The leaf was drooping listlessly while the mist formed pock-marks on its broad green face. Wyeth didn't like magnolias. Their blossoms were too sweet and the trees were too green and complacent, never changing except to grow greener and bigger and more aloof from their fellows. They stole food and water from the other trees, too, and choked them. They were fat and rich and thrived in this fat, rich land. They preened during the day and stood guard at night, guarding only themselves and caring nothing about the smaller trees that struggled for a chance to live.

No, Wyeth didn't like them, but they belonged in this bloated valley where life was too easy for some men and too hard for others. He didn't like the Natchez country. The rivers were too big and the land was too green, and never changed.

It got hot up in Missouri where he was born, but things changed. It got cold up there, too, and nobody had much, but everybody had something. He had seen it change during the twenty-four years of his life. Natchez, however, looked and behaved exactly as she did when he first saw her that time his father brought him there to meet his old friend Sam Dabney. Well, Sam Dabney was dead now and so was his father and the Union they helped build was on its death bed, for it was the summer of 1862 and the Confederacy was in its prime, defiant and apparently unconquerable.

The leaf fluttered slightly and swayed. The breeze was coming. Wyeth turned his face to the northeast. The breeze cut a path through the mist and the spire of St. Mary's Cathedral was visible for a second and then the mist closed in again. He felt the wind on his cheeks and faced the river. A dog barked across on the Louisiana side where the flat gumbo land poured out its wealth for the Natchez planters. A bell tolled over there and his pulse quickened. The sound, however, was too heavy and melancholy for a ship's bell and he realized it was a plantation signal calling the hands to the fields. God! what a day to work men and mules.

The work gong still was ringing when he heard the cheerful tingling of another bell, and he straightened and leaned over the bluff. All the leaves were rustling and dancing a welcome to the breeze that slipped under the mist and swirled it, prying it up from the river.

Wyeth saw the ship then, anchored near the foot of the bluff, and the muscles of his stomach tightened. Her guns were run in and only a wisp of smoke floated out of her stack. By her lines, he knew she was the *U.S.S. Iroquois,* the steam sloop that had conquered Natchez.

without hurling a shot. Her fires were banked. Her commander, J. S. Palmer, wasn't wasting coal, inasmuch as he was two hundred miles from his base at New Orleans and almost a hundred miles from the mouth of the Yazoo River, just north of Vicksburg, where Flag Officer Farragut's squadron of six ships-of-the-line was rendezvousing with Commander Dave Porter's mortar flotilla and Davis' Upper River Fleet of rams and ironclads.

The *Iroquois's* nose was upstream. To her starboard, between her and the bluff, was a mortarboat whose huge fat gun was pointed toward the town. The mouth of the gun looked like a dead volcano's crater. Wyeth scarcely noticed the mortarboat. Like all the others, it was a clumsy thing that had to be towed. The *Iroquois* fascinated him, however, for he was a sailor without a ship, a gunner's mate of the Confederacy, fighting for a nation that had no fleet except a few tubs and privateers.

The steam sloop was changing her watch and he saw men in fresh blue uniforms salute the quarter-deck and go to the relief of their sleepy comrades. Wyeth glanced down at his own muddy boots and tapped his feet against the trunk of the water oak, dislodging some of the mud. He was wearing black broadcloth trousers and a black coat, gifts from a Confederate sympathizer in Vicksburg where he had changed his light grayish blue uniform for civilian clothes, a change, incidentally, that meant death if he were captured and identified in enemy territory. And the presence of the *Iroquois* meant the Yanks were still in Natchez.

Wyeth inhaled deeply of the clean air up there on the bluff, took one parting look at the ship, then walked toward the muddy road that ran from the bluff down to Natchez-Under-the-Hill. Even the mud stunk, and a blast of fetid air choked his nose as he passed the first dwelling under the hill. The blinds were drawn and a dog walked from under the porch, sniffed Wyeth's legs and went away. A girl called to him from a shack across the road. She was standing by the blinds and when he turned and looked at her she opened the blinds and he saw that she was naked. He shook his head and walked on and she cursed him. Then she closed the blinds and forgot him.

There was no reason for her to remember him, for there was nothing about him to attract attention. He was of medium height, thin and wiry. The damp air caused his chestnut hair to curl, but in dry weather his hair was straight and almost coarse. It was bushy around the nape of his neck and on his temples.

His eyebrows were bushy, too, and strangers always noticed his eyebrows and seldom his eyes, which were bluish-gray. Captain Isaac N. Brown, his commander, said Wyeth had the best pair of eyes in the Confederate Navy and could see a Minié ball coming. That, of course, was exaggeration. His eyes and the scar on his face were the only things that set him apart from a thousand other men who were born and reared on the Missouri frontier. The scar ran from the end of his left jawbone to the cleft in his chin, a tiny cleft that his mother had called a dimple. The scar wasn't noticeable except when the blood rushed to his face and then the scar stood out, white and livid.

There was a story in the Dakota country, where Wyeth trapped before the war, that the scar was a result of a fight over a squaw. He never had fought over a squaw. He *had* killed a man for stealing pelts, but squaws were plentiful in the Dakota country and pelts were valuable. The scar followed a wound he suffered in his boyhood when he fell against a capstan on his father's little freighter up on the Osage River in Missouri, and Wyeth hated it because it betrayed his emotions by showing white when he was angry. And it kept him from growing a beard. Hair wouldn't grow on the scar and he was ashamed of his beardless face.

He reached the landing at Natchez-Under-the-Hill and looked back up the bluff that towered above him. The mist was melting rapidly and he felt the sunrays stab through the mist. Even at that early hour the heat made him dizzy. The sun sharpened the odors of the filthy village that sprawled under the bluff, a haven for harlots and gamblers, a nest of the vilest dives between Quebec and Texas.

The *Iroquois* stood out sharply in the sunlight and Wyeth wondered how many of her crew had shore leave. Then he turned up a path that ran parallel to the river, walking slowly until he came to the house he was seeking, a two-story unpainted dwelling that had a second story gallery and dilapidated banisters. He knew that the lookout on the *Iroquois* was watching him, so he didn't hesitate, but stepped quickly to the door, as though he knew his way. The door was locked and he rattled the knob.

A mulatto girl of about 15 opened the door and he stepped into the dank, gloomy hall.

"Your mistress, please," he said to the girl.

"She's in the back. I'll show you."

He followed the girl to the tap room. Standing near a window was a tall woman, wearing black silk. Her clothes didn't surprise Wyeth, for most Southern women were down to their Sunday best because their everyday clothes had long since worn out and couldn't be replaced.

She turned slowly and looked at him and he remembered what Ves had told him. "You'll know her. Don't worry about that. When you see those coal-black eyes and that yellow hair, you'll know her. Even if she is my cousin, she's as pretty as a sunset in a snowstorm and just as unusual." That's what Ves had said, Vespasian Gillivray, the Cajan who had followed traplines with Wyeth from Gitche Gumee, the Big-Sea-Water, as the Ojibways called Lake Superior, to the far reaches of the Dakota country.

He would have known she was a Cajan even if he hadn't known Ves. Only Cajans could have produced such a woman. Her eyes proclaimed her Indian blood, the eyes of Sehoy of the Creek Clan of the Wind, a princess of the Alibamu. Her skin showed her Spanish strain, maybe Portuguese, maybe African Moorish. Her hair was her Scotch heritage, for she traced her line back to old Lachlan Mac-Gillivray, the Scotch merchant who settled among the Creeks a hundred years before, made his fortune, married Sehoy and bred as a gentleman should. No one knew all the blood lines of the Cajans. They had no connections whatsoever with the French Cajuns of Louisiana. None knew exactly whence came the swamp Cajans, for they were an isolated people who lived in clans along the rivers of South Alabama and Mississippi. Some thought they sprang from sailors wrecked along the Gulf, or from the buccaneers who fled there from the Spanish Main. However, the Cajans enjoyed a medley of breeding and freedom, and every so often a brown child appeared. They were never accepted into Southern society, and never wanted to be.

The melting pot really had melted to produce this woman. Wyeth assumed she was a lady and was determined to treat her as such although she was not a lady by the inflexible standards and

[7]

castes of the age. He knew she didn't belong in Natchez-Under-the-Hill and that only devotion for her native land could have driven her to operate a tavern in the Sodom of the South.

Her hair wasn't as yellow as he had expected it to be. It really wasn't yellow at all, but was the color of burnished copper. Her skin was tawny, almost olive. She was watching him, casually. Too casually. Her bearing was languid. Wyeth, however, saw a slight frown pass over her forehead, just a suggestion of a frown, and saw her eyes veer for a second toward two men sitting at a table.

He sized the men up quickly as cotton speculators, for now that Northern blood had won the lower Mississippi Valley, the leeches were coming, Yankee buyers and Southern sellers. What they couldn't buy and sell, they stole; and they were swarming on the country like locusts, stripping it.

Wyeth scraped his boots on a chair leg and mumbled, "I haven't seen any cotton yet that's worth tramping through mud for. I'm going back home."

The men assumed he was a speculator, too, and one asked, "Where is home?"

"Missouri. Now laugh, damn you."

They did, and so did Wyeth. The woman moved from near the window and walked to the end of the bar.

"Any luck?" the men were curious.

"Twenty bales," Wyeth said. "The Yanks burned out some Reb just north of town last night. It seems he fired on the *Iroquois*. Or threw a brick at her, or something."

"How much?"

"I gave the lieutenant a quart. He approved the papers consigning all the cotton to me and I agreed to handle a few bales for him. I've been out all night."

"What about the government stamp? Uncle Sam is supposed to get that cotton."

Wyeth laughed again and the men joined in.

The woman moved behind the bar and approached Wyeth. "What is your pleasure, sir?"

The men at the table winked at him and one said, "Tell her, Missouri. Tell her what's on your mind."

Wyeth looked at the woman, then over at the men and said, "If these men are annoying you, Miss . . ."

She shrugged her shoulders. He saw that slight frown again and checked his temper. "They're drunk," she said.

Wyeth watched her eyes. "You are up early. You are much too beautiful to have been up all night as I have."

"Sleep is a thing I have not enjoyed much since the war started. I see the stars fade every morning." She said the words slowly. "But if you have been up all night you must be thirsty."

"Yes. Brandy." He caught her look. "Grape brandy. Grapes from the Valley of Sharon."

She put her hands on the edge of the bar and he noticed her long fingers and the halfmoons of her nails. Quickly, he put his left hand on the bar. "I am sorry, sir," she said loud enough for the men at the table to hear her. "I have never heard of such a brandy."

She moved her hands and Wyeth followed them and she pointed under the bar to a pistol and a long knife.

"I see," he said, and nodded slowly. "Then any good brandy will do." He turned his back to her and faced the men. "If I spoke hastily a minute ago, I ask your pardon."

"Aw, forget it. But just where is this place that was burned last night?"

"Out the Natchez Trace about six miles. I hope you're not going out there today. It will be too hot to move in an hour or so. It was hot as blazes last night. I never saw such a night. Even the stars threw heat, and every star was out."

"There may be a thunder storm today," the woman said quickly.

The men pressed Wyeth for exact directions and he told them. He had seen the place burning as he rode in last night and knew what had happened. The men hurried out and Wyeth was alone with the woman.

She put a bottle of brandy on the bar and smiled at him. "I am Sharon Weatherford. You are Wyeth Woodward. I have been expecting you."

"Is he here?" Wyeth snapped, forgetting his manners, a thing he seldom did.

"Who?" She realized immediately just how silly her question was.

Wyeth's temper, usually placid, for he was a stoical man, surged and the blood began pounding through his face. "Do not play with words, Miss Weatherford. You know very well who I mean. . . ."

"Mr. Granville?"

"Mr. Simeon St. Leger Granville." There was a trace of sarcasm in his voice as he rolled the words on his tongue.

Sharon glanced out of the window where the heat was simmering and dancing above the steaming earth. Then she looked back at Wyeth and said softly, "Yes, he is here. Up stairs. How is Ves?"

"Ves is all right," Wyeth said impatiently. "He is up at Yazoo City waiting for Mr. Granville and me to get back and be about our business. Now, if you will show me the way up stairs . . ."

"He is asleep, and he needs the sleep."

Wyeth felt his temper rising again. "How long has he been drunk?"

"A week."

"Is that all? Just how drunk is he?"

"I don't know." She sighed and there was compassion in her eyes. Wyeth was annoyed and a bit alarmed. He didn't like the looks of things. When a woman shows compassion for a drunk man it usually means an affection that is deep enough even to tolerate his errors. He cursed Granville under his breath. Sharon said, "I can't tell how drunk he is. I can't tell much about him. He has been here a week and I know less about him now than when he first came."

Wyeth smiled in spite of himself. Then he realized she was looking at the cleft in his chin, the dimple, and he blushed. The blush brought out the scar. He drank his brandy to hide his confusion. "You will never know anything about him. Ves and I have been with him for three years and he is still a mystery to me. But you're right. If he is asleep, let's let him sleep. We've got to get him sober."

She called the slave girl who had opened the door for him and the girl set a table and brought corn fritters, bacon and coffee. He ate slowly, enjoying the last full measure of the food. It was the first good coffee he had tasted in months. Already, coffee and salt were at a premium in the South. He nodded toward his coffee cup and Sharon understood the gesture and nodded toward the river where the *Iroquois* was riding. Her gesture told him that the coffee came from the Yankees. She put the brandy bottle on the table by him and sat down.

"I will give you some coffee to take back to Ves," she said.

"You're very kind."

"Why does Mr. Granville fight for us? He is not a Southerner."

Wyeth pushed the brandy bottle to one side and sent the slave girl for another cup of coffee. "Oh, I don't know why he does it. Maybe because Ves and I are fighting, and we're friends. Maybe because he thinks the South is the underdog. Maybe because he just likes to fight." He shrugged his shoulders and accepted a cheroot from the slave girl and watched her move away to be about her chores.

"He hates slavery," Sharon said, trying to attract Wyeth's attention from the girl. "I heard him say so."

"Many Confederates hate slavery," Wyeth said. "Mr. Granville says slavery has produced a barren culture down here. But he hates most Abolitionists as much as he does slavers. He says this is a war between Yankee money and Southern money and that most of the Yankees care nothing about Negroes, but use their bondage as an excuse for a crusade to arouse the Northern people."

Sharon didn't understand such talk. She owned a slave and thought nothing about it. Wyeth never had before, although he had heard his father rail against the peculiar institution. Wyeth, born near the border of free territory, was fighting for the South because she had been invaded. So were most Southerners, poor men who hated the planters and had no stake in slavery.

"Where did you meet him?"

Wyeth really was annoyed at her persistency. Had she not been Ves' cousin he might have told her to mind her tongue and stop pestering him with questions. However, he puffed the cheroot, then said, "In the Dakota country. Ves and I were running some traps near the Canadian line and found him in a squaw's lodge. He was drunk as a lord, which some folks think he is. He went back to the post with us only for more rum." Wyeth began smiling as he recalled the incident.

Sharon was leaning forward, hanging to each word. "Yes. Go on."

"That's about all. We knew he was an Englishman. He blabbers about England when he is drunk. Ves and I finally got him sober and he worked up to be the *bourgeois,* the overseer of the post. Ves and I were *voyageurs,* and he often ran our lines with us. We were on Shonkin Creek and there was a *chantier,* a shipyard, at the post. That's when I learned that he knows just about all that's to be known about ships. Guns, too."

He drank the last swallow of his coffee and looked up toward the stairs that led to the second floor.

"But that's not all," Sharon said eagerly.

"Why are you so interested? I am indebted to you because you are working with us, but must you pry?"

Her smile was her best visible weapon. "I could be a silly woman and say I'm interested because he is a friend of my cousin."

"That would be silly." He crossed his legs and yawned and begged her pardon. "I rode all night, and am sort of tired. Well, anyway, when the war started Ves and I decided to fight for the South. Mr. Granville said he would, too, if we joined the Navy. That was all right with us. So we did."

"You were at Memphis?"

"Yes. And at Island No. 10. We were on the *Jeff Thompson* at Memphis. The Yanks beat us, you know. We lost our ship. The *Queen of the West* hit us." A heavy frown passed over his face and the white scar showed again. Then he began smiling. "That's when Ves flagged a Minié. He was bending over the breech sight of our gun. Mr. Granville wanted a *curvated ricochet*. The distance was 220 yards and our elevation was 7 degrees, 30 minutes." His eyes began dancing and he used his arm to show the elevation. Then he checked his words, realizing she was bored. "Anyway, Ves wasn't hurt much. He still sleeps on his stomach. Got in the habit, I reckon."

"He sent me word that he was all right. Then what happened?"

"We signed on the *Arkansas*. There was no *Arkansas* then. Only a keel. But there's going to be an *Arkansas* if we can get metal enough to build her."

She leaned over and put her hand on his. Her hand was warm. It was a friendly gesture and nothing more. "You will build her. Come with me."

He followed her to a back room and she unlocked the door. When Wyeth stepped into the room his heart began pounding wildly. There were nine kegs of bolts in the room and the floor was littered with railroad iron. Iron was selling at $1300 per ton in the South where there were only a few rolling mills capable of turning out a 2½ inch iron plate.

"My God!" He said it reverently.

She pointed toward six more kegs and whispered, "Powder. And I have five hundred percussion caps. You will build the *Arkansas* and she will fight."

Powder was selling at $1.50 per pound and percussion caps were worth their weight in gold.

Wyeth stared at the valuables. Then, impulsively, he took her hand and kissed it. She laughed and offered her cheek and he kissed that, too. "For Ves," he said. "But how are we going to get this stuff to Yazoo City? That's where we're building the *Arkansas*."

"That will be arranged. The Yankees will haul it for you. And now back to Mr. Granville."

"I've told you all I know. He never talks about himself."

"Who is Dolly?" She didn't look at him when she asked him.

Wyeth's eyes lit up and he arched his bushy brows and his eyes shone under his brows. She glanced at him and realized then just how piercing his eyes were. "Oh," he said, "so you know about Dolly."

Red showed on her olive cheeks and her lips, naturally red and full, suddenly were white. "He has mentioned her several times during the spree. He drank a toast to her the other night. Is she beautiful?"

"Very."

"Has he known her long?"

"Less than a year. But he loves her very much. You must know that."

The pupils in Sharon's eyes came to a pinpoint and she compressed her lips. Wyeth had seen Ves's eyes do the same thing. His eyes always looked that way when he was fighting. Those Cajans. They laughed most of the time, but their anger was a cold thing and their hatred was deadly.

"What does she look like?" Sharon asked. "And does she love him?"

"She must. She does everything he expects her to do."

"Enough of that." She turned on him fiercely and Wyeth thought for a second that she was going to scratch him. "Answer my question. What does she look like?"

He went over to one of the kegs and looked at the bolts, teasing her by the delay. "Yes, she's very beautiful. I love her, too. She weighs 9,200 lbs." He glanced her way and saw that Sharon was amazed. He was enjoying himself immensely. "She is a deadly old lady and gulps 13 pounds of powder when she's hungry and throws a 93-pound shot or a 70-pound shell. Her bore is 107 inches. . . ."

"A rifle!" Sharon exclaimed.

"A gun, madam. Dolly is a Dahlgren gun. She was cooled from the exterior when they cast her and the metal around her seat is a little larger than the diameter of her bore. Her chase tapers rapidly and her chamber is of the Gomer form. . . ."

"Stop it." Sharon was laughing. "What a dunce I was."

But Wyeth was very serious, hiding his mirth. "Mr. Granville and Ves and I often sleep near her. Ves was leaning over her breech when that Minié hit him in the breech."

"Stop it, I say. . . ."

"She was on the *Jeff Thompson* and we saved her. She will be on the *Arkansas*. We will use these bolts to hold her down and to fasten the plates that will protect her. And all we don't use we will throw down her mouth and let her spit at the Yanks."

Sharon was still laughing when they left the room and went to the front of the house. The day was well under way. Wyeth opened the front door and looked out at the *Iroquois*. A few men were lolling on deck and her fires were still banked. The river was steaming and its dirty muddy water threw off blankets of heat. Wyeth felt sweat seeping through his clothes although he scarcely had exerted himself. He closed the door and glanced toward the stairs again. And from above, in thick accents without much melody, he heard the chant. A boot was being pounded on the floor in time with the song.

The echo rolled down the stairs:

> "*Dans mon chemin j'ai rencontré*
> *Trois cabalières bien montées,*
> *L'on, ton, laridon danée*
> *L'on, ton, laridon, dai.*
> "*Trois cavalières bien montées,*
> *L'une à cheval, l'autre a pied.*"

Sharon suddenly was excited and Wyeth said, "A song of the *voyageurs*. Mr. Granville apparently is awake. I'll go up."

"Just a minute please." She called the slave girl. "Get warm water and towels and take them to our guest. And mind you, don't stay in there too long."

The girl giggled.

"Give him time to collect his thoughts," Sharon said to Wyeth. "Then I will go up with you."

"I will go alone."

"You won't be too harsh on him? He can't help it. I know he had a duty here. It was my fault. I gave him a drink the night he called. It was raining that night and when he saw me he said he wanted wine from the Valley of Sharon, but that he much preferred a kiss."

"I assume he got only the brandy." Wyeth was walking toward the stairs. "But you need not worry. I won't be harsh on him. Sometimes I feel like breaking his neck, but if I raise my voice to him he will throw me down these stairs. Head first."

The slave girl came out of the room just as Wyeth reached the door. She was giggling again and he slapped her buttocks as she passed him. Then he opened the door and tiptoed into the presence of Simeon St. Leger Granville, once a lieutenant of the Royal Navy and now a master gunner for the Confederacy.

The Englishman, a bit taller than Wyeth and just as thin, was standing by the window, staring at the *Iroquois*. His back was toward the door and Wyeth started to speak to attract his attention. Then he assumed that Granville was thinking and not daring to interrupt his thoughts, he leaned against the doorway and waited. He had expected to find his friend messy, as he usually was during a protracted drunk. Granville, however, was immaculate even at that early hour, evidence that he hadn't been as drunk as Wyeth had feared.

Always the dandy, the Englishman was wearing Wellington boots over which his gray trousers fitted tightly. His waistcoat was of cream-colored silk, lined with white, short in the waist and snug. His cravat was a piece of gay silk tied loosely at his throat. He was one of the few men in the South who still had silk and linen. His white beaver hat was on a chair by the door.

Wyeth studied his back for a second, wondering how any man could live such a life of dissipation and keep his strength. Granville always reminded him of a polished silver spring, tightly wound. His hair was black with a trace of white showing through the heavy mat that fell over his neck and to the rolled collar of his waistcoat.

Granville's hair was deceiving. The white strands usually led strangers to think he was older than he really was. Wyeth didn't know his age and had guessed it variously from 35 to 45. Once

Granville, in his cups, told Wyeth that he was an apprentice in the British Navy when the *Great Western* sailed from Bristol on the voyage that revolutionized ocean travel. That was in 1838. British apprentices often were as young as 14. Wyeth used that date to estimate that Granville was born in '24. So he must be at least 38. He had heard him speak of the potato famine in Ireland in '47 when 200,000 persons starved to death. He was in the Royal Navy then and helped take relief to the 730,000 families that lived only by government help.

However, he fought for Denmark during the revolts of 1848. It was obvious to Wyeth that he left the Royal Navy late in '47 and he assumed, quite rightly, that rum was responsible. An officer had to consume quite a bit of rum to lose his place in the Queen's Navy. It simply never entered Wyeth's head to ask Granville how old he was or why he left Her Majesty's service. If he had, Granville might have told him that he was discharged dishonorably for drinking, and he certainly would have told him that he was 39.

Wyeth saw him reach into his waistcoat pocket and knew he was twirling his watch chain, a habit he humored while thinking. It was a thin watch chain, a gift from the French government for his services as a sailor-of-fortune at Sebastopol. The charm on the chain was a tiny dragon carved from ebony.

He turned around then, still twirling the chain, and his face showed no surprise when he saw Wyeth. "Hello," he said casually. "Have a drink?"

"Is there any left?" The man's nonchalance always irked Wyeth, yet he envied his friend's traits.

Granville adjusted his chain and straightened his waistcoat. "Only a very wise man can afford to be sarcastic. Where's your horse?"

Wyeth walked to the center of the room and sat on the bed, deliberately taking his time. Granville's eyes were red, the only sign that he'd been drinking. His eyes, however, were not puffy, and his hands were steady. His beard, a tribute to his vanity, was neatly trimmed and he smelled of Eau de Cologne, as he always did after shaving. The beard was the envy of the Confederate Navy. His mustache turned up and the beard began at the corners of his mouth and grew to a sharp point, leaving his cheeks bare. The smooth black hair was sprinkled with white. His sideburns were bushy and the hair just over his ears was almost wholly white.

"I ate my horse." He knew that would annoy Granville and it did. The Englishman's light gray eyes flashed and Wyeth was delighted, knowing Granville had all of his faculties in hand.

"I will warrant that it was the best meal you have had since the war started." Granville took one more look at the *Iroquois* and then sat down facing Wyeth. "But I am serious. Unfortunately, war is a serious business and inasmuch as my life depends on you I want to be sure you have not been foolish."

"I killed my horse. There was nothing else to do. They might have traced me through the horse. But now we are safe, Mr. Granville. So far, so good."

Granville laughed and it always was good to hear him laugh for he had a way of throwing his head back and to one side and laughing as though he enjoyed it. He went over to the washstand, reached into the water pitcher and pulled out his binoculars. They were wrapped in India rubber. He handed the glasses to Wyeth and nodded toward the *Iroquois*. "Take a look."

"I've seen her."

"She has been out there for a week and I've been cooped up in this room not daring to show myself. The United States Navy employed me once to design a gun-carriage. Then I got drunk, but not before I argued with half the officers at the shipyard and drank with all the men. Half of the crew of the *Iroquois* probably knows me. We are in civilian clothes, Wyeth. When I hang, I want to hang to a yardarm, not to one of these trees down here."

"If you shaved that grass from you face they might not recognize you."

Granville looked at him scornfully and didn't reply to such a preposterous statement. "You must take some information back to Captain Brown. In your head, Wyeth. Can you remember what I tell you?"

"Of course."

"Tell Captain Brown that Farragut, Davis and Dave Porter have joined their fleets at Vicksburg. Now do not confuse Dave Porter with his brother, Bill Porter who is on the ironclad *Essex*. Bill Porter is a fool, a conceited blow-hard. . . ."

"I know all of that," Wyeth aid impatiently. "So does Captain Brown. He served in the United States Navy with both Porters and Farragut. He was at Annapolis with many of the Yankee officers."

"Please do not interrupt me," Granville said. "Report to Captain Brown that Dave Porter has at least 16 mortar-schooners. Davis has at least three gunboats with him and nine rams. Here are the iron-clads." He reached for his chain again and began twirling it, staring at the ceiling as he rattled off the names. "—*Corondelet,* 14 guns; *St. Louis,* 13 guns; *Essex,* six guns; *Benton,* 16 guns—" And on and on. It taxed his memory to list the ironclads of Davis' Upper River Fleet and Dave Porter's mortar-schooners. Then Granville began naming the rams of Davis' fleet. "—*Mingo, Lancaster, Monarch,* and our old friend, *Queen of the West. . . .*"

Wyeth shuffled his feet and whistled softly. "Is that all?"

"Good God, no! I haven't mentioned Farragut's fleet, all ships-of-the-line. *Hartford, Richmond, Iroquois, Brooklyn, Scioto, Oneida. . . .*"

Wyeth whistled again. "Anything else?"

"The Yanks have enough strength on the river to challenge any fleet, even England's, but they will never take Vicksburg by a river siege. Vicksburg is a task for the Yankee Army, but they don't know it—yet."

He was right. In the summer of 1862, Vicksburg was held by a handful of Confederates under General Van Dorn. The South had no naval power there. Not then. But a giant was coming. The *Arkansas* was only a dream in the mind of Captain Brown, her master, a rusty keel lying in the Yazoo River almost under the bows of the crack ships of the United States.

Granville kept listing ships of the fleets. Then he paused and took a long breath. "More are joining the Yanks every day," he said. "There are six steamers with the mortar fleet and about 20 supply ships. The Yankees have established three miles of batteries just across the river from Vicksburg. Including the army and navy, there may be 10,000 Yanks at the rendezvous and God knows how many guns." He quit playing with his chain and the little ebony dragon lay on his knee. He was watching Wyeth. "The *Arkansas* will have 10 guns and maybe 200 men. How do you like the prospects?"

"I don't like them." There were no heroics about Wyeth, no

flamboyancy. Granville had enough for the pair, but it was a flamboyant age, an age of stilted words and flowery speech.

"Neither do I. But we'll have a good ship and a good crew. And Dolly." Granville poured a drink, the first since Wyeth entered the room. He smacked his lips and ran his long fingers over his beard, smoothing it to a point. Then he twisted the ends of his mustache between his thumb and index finger. "As long as the *Iroquois* is here I can't show myself. You will have to do some of my work."

"I expected that." He picked up the bottle and estimated that only two or three drinks were left. "You might as well drink this now, Mr. Granville. You're not going to have any more."

The Englishman suddenly was sullen and began reviling the young Missourian. Wyeth, however, sat calmly on the bed stroking his chin. He had heard it all before. Then Granville's temper passed and he was calm again. "All right, you damned nursemaid. It's a promise. My word as my pledge."

"Your word is no good in this case, Mr. Granville. You will have no more drink today. After supper you may have a brandy flip. . . ."

"Oh, for God's sakes, Wyeth. Make it at least two."

"One flip. Maybe a little beer."

"If my word is no good then how can I assure you and get rid of you? I can't have you on my coattail all day. You've got work to do."

"Your oath, Mr. Granville."

"Very well." Then he swore by his friendship for Wyeth Woodward and Vespasian Gillivray.

"Now what do you want me to do?" Wyeth went to the window and watched the *Iroquois* through the binoculars.

"I've been watching Yankee ships pass here for days," Granville said, "and I am going to stay here until all the ships have passed. You must see to getting the iron to Captain Brown."

"Have you seen the store of iron and powder in this house?"

"You mean the wealth of the Incas?" Granville closed one eye and grinned at him. "Sure, I have seen it. And there is more in Natchez. The Confederates have an amazing organization here. Most of the members do not know the others. You are to get in touch with certain people. I do not know them. They will help you get the iron to Captain Brown."

"And you?"

"Perhaps I will meet you in a few days. If I do, I will report to Captain Brown. If I do not, then you report to him about the fleets." He reached for the bottle again. "All right?"

Wyeth nodded and Granville poured a drink. He held the bottle up between him and the light, mumbled in surprise and disgust, then emptied the bottle.

He scarcely had downed the last of the brandy when a tapping at the door startled him. He wrapped the binoculars in the rubber covering and put them back in the pitcher. "You are a cotton speculator."

"I have been using that story since I left Vicksburg. Shall I open the door?"

"Yes. It might be anybody."

"Miss Weatherford would have warned us."

"That depends. She wouldn't lift a finger to warn us if it would jeopardize the organization. Open the door. If there is a fight, don't let them scream."

Wyeth tried to appear unconcerned when he turned the knob. Then he laughed in sheer relief when he saw Sharon standing there. She had changed her clothes and was wearing a dress of India muslin with broad ribbon stripes. Her mantilla was edged by embroidery and she held her leghorn Pamela in her hand. The hat had a low flat crown and a drooping brim.

"Am I intruding?" She was speaking to Wyeth but was looking at Granville.

"Yes," said the Englishman bluntly. He never fawned over women and seldom flattered them.

"I thought you might need something. . . ."

"No more drink, Miss Weatherford," Wyeth said. "Is that clear?"

"That is right," said Granville and went to her side and escorted her to a chair. "No more drink. Shame on you, Sharon. Your wine made me drunk and your beauty makes me drunker. Why all the finery?"

"It is all I have. I have been up town."

"Hot?"

"Scorching." She sat down and smoothed her dress.

Wyeth sat on the bed and Granville stood by the window. "I have told my puritanical young friend here that he must take over some of my work. Now you take him in hand."

"It will be a pleasure." She fanned herself with her hat. "Where is your baggage, Mr. Woodward?"

"You know I have no baggage. . . ."

"Oh, that's right. A group of Rebel bushwhackers saw you near that burning house last night and robbed you of your baggage. Your horse, too. When you leave here go straight up the hill to Broadway Street. Then walk up Franklin Street for four blocks. If anyone stops you, you are looking for a store to buy baggage. Just walk along looking in the windows. Keep your wits about you. They will find you. The passwords are the same."

Wyeth looked from her to Granville. The Englishman shrugged his shoulders. Wyeth said, "Is that all?"

"That's all." She arose and walked toward the door. "I will have your breakfast sent up, Mr. Granville."

"Thank you." He watched her walk away, a slow tantalizing walk. When she got to the head of the stairs she looked back at him and smiled.

Wyeth was disturbed. Granville went over to the washstand and ran a comb through his hair. Wyeth removed his coat and began cleaning up, too. He dashed cold water on his face and borrowed the comb from his friend. He was thinking deeply and when he found the words he wanted he said, "Mr. Granville, you know that she is Ves' cousin."

"About fifth cousin. That is no kinship."

"It is among the Cajans," Wyeth said slowly. "They are a proud people, and clannish. When they hate, Mr. Granville, they go all the way. To them, hate means killing."

"And when they love?"

"They go all the way again. And they are sensitive and touchy about their honor and their women folks. I just thought I'd tell you, knowing you are Ves' friend. So far."

Granville didn't reply. He touched up his beard again, then went to his bureau for cigars, and handed one to Wyeth. "My God, but it's hot." He ran his hand across his forehead. "The marrow in my bones is boiling. I thought India was hot."

They both stepped to the window, hoping for a breath of air.

The world seemed to be holding its breath. The sun gleamed on the starboard guns of the *Iroquois*, huge Columbiads. The flag flopped on the mast, for there was no breeze to arouse it. Gulls that had followed the ship from New Orleans perched in the rigging, their heads drooping. High above, a lone buzzard circled and nothing moved except the river and the buzzard.

Wyeth watched the bird, then said, "I wonder if it's cool up where he is?"

"I don't know how it is up there, Wyeth. And I have a feeling I never will find out."

The buzzard wheeled and started down.

"Uh oh!" Wyeth said. "They are burning another planter out, and his stock has been killed."

Chapter Two

THE heat almost suffocated Wyeth when he left the tavern and walked slowly back up the hill to Natchez where a breeze scattered the miasmal mist that seeped from the swamps. The town looked down on everything around it, figuratively and literally, and because a few persons there escaped malaria and yellow fever it was considered a healthy place for those able to live among its magnolias and moss.

Of course, no one escaped all the ills of the land; chills and fever, rheumatism, ague, pellagra and a hundred other curses that came from the rich soggy acres that made the Natchez plantations the envy of the cotton world. There were no plantations in the town. The planters lived on the hill and their slaves farmed the muck over in Louisiana and even the loess land that spread to the base of the towering bluff which the river had formed just south of town and which, rising and falling as a sea wave, loped as far north as Vicksburg and the mouth of the Yazoo River.

It was easy to grow cotton in such a land, and simple to float the cotton down the bayous to Natchez and the Mississippi, where it was loaded, usually for New Orleans, but often direct for Liverpool.

Wyeth paused at the summit of the hill. He was panting from the exertion of the climb. He stood there a minute cursing the heat and the town that languished under the cobalt sky. Natchez was neither

American nor European, Northern or Southern. It was Natchez. Only men of courage and stamina could survive such a land, but Wyeth hated them. They wanted the *status quo*. They wanted to eat their syllabub and have it, too. The leading planters were old line Whigs, compromisers who sought to hide behind the ambiguity of the law and save their slaves and silver. The Confederacy was attempting revolution and Natchez didn't like revolutions. The war had put guns into the hands of the common people and the common people were poor. The Natchez planters had more vision than the politicians and preachers who beat their bosoms for Southern sovereignty. The planters realized that the poor were fighting the war and that the poor hated slavery and that, should they win against the Union, they would turn next on the planters.

The land-owners didn't want things to change and war often brings change. Natchez had become all things to all men. Her spokesmen had voted against secession and although their sons had hurried into the Confederate Army, the fathers played both ends against the middle and were trying to save their fortunes by accepting Yankees into their drawing rooms. Expediency was the chosen god of Natchez and *noblesse oblige* was her code.[1]

The ease with which the North had conquered Natchez only a few weeks before, on May 12, 1862, infuriated Wyeth. True, the town was of no strategic importance since New Orleans and Memphis had fallen, and had been defended by only two cannon, one a relic of the Battle of Saratoga in the Revolutionary War.

The Union Navy had swept up from New Orleans and covered Natchez with a hundred cannon, but didn't fire. Then for some reason, perhaps because Farragut understood the planters, the fleet proceeded north to Vicksburg, leaving the *Iroquois* to deal with the gem city of the Confederacy.

Only fourteen Natchez men volunteered to defend their town. Others, including a preacher, refused flatly to help. The preacher went so far as to decline to pray for Jefferson Davis. Nine men, under Adjutant William Lyle, marched to the river to repulse any landing party or to accept an invitation for a military conference. That was the polite and proper thing to do. Had the Yankees been polite, they would have sent a flag of truce to Lyle and demanded surrender. But they ignored Lyle and sent a message to the civil authorities who surrendered the town, bag and baggage, to save their homes from bombardment. The South was disgusted. The Confederate defenders arrested a few citizens and retired, mouthing threats and curses. They were sorely angry, not so much because the town had fallen, but because the Yankees had ignored them.

Wyeth smiled in spite of himself at the idea of nine men lining up along the Mississippi to defy the United States Navy. He glanced back at the *Iroquois* and frowned, for many of her sailors were getting shore leave. Down at the landing, almost in the shadow of the man-of-war, a cotton barge was being unloaded by Irish laborers. Natchez didn't use her slaves for such dangerous work. A slave was worth $1500 and Natchez was too practical to risk valuable property when Irishmen were available for a pittance.

The cotton had been purchased at a premium by the United States from sympathetic planters. Again Wyeth cursed and walked away toward Broadway Street as Sharon had instructed. Six blue-jackets from the *Iroquois* passed him. Officially, the ship was linger-ing at anchor to preserve order. Her presence wasn't necessary, but the food and wine of Natchez were good and the women were pretty and friendly.

Mule teams from the outcountry were hitched to racks along Broadway Street and stood there swishing flies and shifting their weight, their heads lowered. They, too, were hot. Wyeth turned up Franklin Street and paused at a store front to get his bearings. He tried to appear casual. The town still was governed by its civil au-thorities who were cooperating with the Yankee invaders within limits of the terms of surrender. Two drunken tars, escorted by a friendly policeman, passed him. He gave his attention to the store window. A price list was posted there and the abundance of food amazed the Missourian. Bacon was selling for 25¢ a pound. Beef was 10¢ a pound. Salt, however, was $15 per sack and quinine was $10 an ounce. The quinine was worth $50 an ounce on the Yazoo River where Confederates, working waist-deep in mud, were building the *Arkansas* out of scraps.

Convinced that his presence was attracting no attention, Wyeth wandered up Franklin Street until he saw a group of men gathering around a corner and talking excitedly. He stood on the edge of the crowd, peering over the men's heads. One of them, a pudgy little

Scotchman whose thin white hair showed from beneath his floppy straw hat, was reading aloud from a printed document, gesticulating as he read.

"It's the damndest thing I ever heard of," the little Scotchmen said and the men nodded agreement.

"Where did you find it, Wall?" The question was asked by a tall man who was standing at the Scotchman's elbow.

"It was nailed to my door when I opened my store this morning. You notice they put it on *my* door. They know a good store. Hoab Dabney doesn't want any truck with Jews." The little man looked up at the tall man, and the crowd laughed.

"Read it all, Wall," somebody shouted. "Looks like old Hoab Dabney has finally loaded his gun."

Wall MacKenzie read the document slowly. It was formal notice that Hoab Dabney, son of old Sam Dabney and master of the County of Lebanan,* was organizing an independent republic over in the valley of Bogue Homa, and was seceding from Mississippi.

Lebanon was about a hundred miles east of Natchez, in the wilderness of south Mississippi, and had been the home of the Dabneys since Sam Dabney went there after the battle of New Orleans in 1814. Sam Dabney ruled Lebanon during his lifetime and then Hoab Dabney assumed mastery. Hoab was a shouting Abolitionist who hated slavery and the Confederacy and had led his county into open defiance of Mississippi. Now he was giving notice that Lebanon was seceding from Mississippi and ready to fight for its independence.

The news did not shock Wyeth although he was surprised at the audacity of the plan. He had never met Hoab, but had heard his father mention him and Wyeth respected him because his father had. Wyeth reasoned that Lebanon had as much right to secede from Mississippi as Mississippi had to secede from the United States. It was Hoab Dabney's business, and that was that. However, he wondered what would have happened if Sam Dabney were alive. The elder Dabney was Mississippi's trail blazer, her oracle and patriarch. It was good that he didn't live to see his state leave the Union, and see his county leave his state.

The crowd muttered in amazement when Wall MacKenzie finished reading the proclamation.

* See TAP ROOTS.

[26]

"It's fantastic," Wall said. "The Confederacy will hang Hoab Dabney and all of his followers. The Confederacy cannot tolerate a backyard rebellion."

The tall man shrugged his shoulders. "Don't underestimate Hoab or any of the Dabneys. He is calling for volunteers to join him against the Confederacy and he will fight. He has Keith Alexander with him."

Again, the crowd muttered. They all had heard of Keith Alexander, the hard riding and morose melancholiac whose contempt for life had earned him the sobriquet, "The Black Knight of Vengeance." He was the most feared man in Mississippi; shameless, ruthless and bitter. The bastard son of a Confederate leader, he hated the Confederacy because his bachelor father loved it. He hated the Confederacy almost as much as he hated his father.

"Keith Alexander is worth a regiment to Hoab Dabney," a bystander suggested. "His two pistols are as good as a hundred rifles. How many men has he killed in duels?"

"God knows," said another. "Maybe seventeen. Maybe twenty. I'd hate to have him mad at me. Wonder why he threw in with the Dabneys?"

"Maybe he loves liberty," Wall MacKenzie said, and laughed.

"It's not liberty he loves," said another. "It's old Hoab's daughter. It'll be quite a come-down for the Dabneys if their daughter marries a bastard."

Several sailors from the *Iroquois* joined the crowd and Wyeth stepped back from the sidewalk to a building and leaned against it, watching the Yankees. Wall MacKenzie noticed them, too. The grizzled little Scotchman seemed to notice everything. His eyes roamed over the crowd, and his gaze fastened on Wyeth. Then he looked from Wyeth to the sailors.

"What is all the excitement about?" one of the sailors demanded.

"Oh, nothing much," Wall said. "A county east of here has jumped the traces and is throwing in with you Yanks. Do you boys want something?"

"We are looking for Nathan Frome's store. We heard he has rye whiskey for sale."

The tall man stepped out of the crowd. "I am Frome. My store is up the street a few doors. I have some good whiskey. Brandy, too."

Wall MacKenzie began sputtering his indignation. "Soliciting business on the street. Now that's a Jew trick." He brushed past Frome and confronted the sailors. "My store is right yonder. The first door. I sell whiskey, too. Frome will rob you. All Jews are robbers."

"Oh, for God's sake, MacKenzie, don't start that again," Frome said impatiently.

The crowd gathered around the two men hoping for an argument.

"It's true," Wall said. "The Jews are responsible for this war. Everybody knows that. The biggest slave dealers in New Orleans and Virginia are Jews. If the Jews hadn't sold slaves there wouldn't be a war. . . ."

"Oh, for God's sake." Frome tried to move off, but Wall grabbed his sleeve. The crowd pressed closer.

"Who is Jefferson Davis' right hand man?" The little Scotchman shook his finger in Frome's face. "Judah P. Benjamin. A Jew. A foreigner, too. I'm sick and tired of foreigners running this country."

Nathan Frome looked down at his competitor. "Foreigner? I was born right here in Mississippi. You were born in Scotland. My father and Sam Dabney built the Three-Chop Way from Georgia to Mississippi.* And you call me a foreigner."

Wall got red in the face. The Yankee sailors were enjoying themselves. They always enjoyed hearing Southerners squabble among themselves. Wyeth, however, was disgusted. Anti-Semitism was rampant in the North, as was anti-Catholicism, and both the plagues were seeping into the South. General Grant had barred Jewish sutlers from following his army, contending that they were waxing rich on the poor soldiers. True, President Lincoln had overridden Grant's orders as discriminatory. But Grant's orders showed the way the wind was blowing.

Frome shook his arm free from Wall's grip and walked away toward his store. One of the sailors followed him. The others waited for Wall. The Scotch merchant wiped his face and mumbled curses after Frome. "Christ-killing robbers! We ought to run every one of them back to the Valley of Sharon where they came from."

Wyeth's throat suddenly was dry. Wall brushed past him, then stopped. "Isn't that what you say?" He glowered at Wyeth.

* See OH, PROMISED LAND.

[28]

"I have no feelings about it," Wyeth said, watching the sailors. "I'm a stranger here. A cotton buyer. I got in last night."

"Just a minute, sailors," Wall said. "This stranger looks like a customer. I sell a little cotton. I was out last night looking at some. Never saw such a night. Hot as the hinges of hell and the sky was as clear as crystal. Every star was out."

"So I noticed," Wyeth said. "Maybe the weather will break soon. There might be a thunder storm today."

"That's right. They come up quick down here. And you'll need boots if you're going out looking for cotton. Step right into my store and I'll fix you up as soon as I wait on these sailors."

Wyeth followed the sailors and Wall into his store. The tars bought two quarts of cheap whiskey and took their leave. Wall offered his hand to Wyeth then. "So you are Wyeth Woodward. I thought I spotted you when you walked up. Sharon described you. Have you any baggage?"

"Not a bit."

"They never have. And that's bad. You can't go to a hotel without baggage. It's too risky." He went to a back room and returned with a carpet bag. "It's full, but don't use any of the stuff. See that I get it back as I will need it again. You're sleepy?"

"Very. I traveled all night."

"Go to the Natchez Hotel. Use your right name. The password changes at noon today. The challenge is, 'It's time for a new moon.' And the countersign is, 'The old moon was good enough for me.' You will hear from me later."

Wyeth, at the point of exhaustion from his long trip and in a vile humor, was not impressed by MacKenzie. He didn't like the way the little man gave orders and he thoroughly disapproved of the merchant's public tirade against Frome. He put down the carpet bag and said slowly, "Mr. MacKenzie, there is something on my mind."

"I hope so. There had better be a heap on your mind if you expect to live long."

"I am being treated as a child," Wyeth said.

Wall looked him over and a wry smile played around the corners of his tight little mouth. "I can't imagine any sane man treating you as a child."

"I came here on orders from my commander. I still do not know what I am supposed to do. I thought a friend of mine. . . ."

"You thought Mr. Granville was drunk and that he might mess up the mission on which Captain Brown sent him," Wall said quickly. "Granville has been drunk. But not as drunk as most folks think. We told Brown to send another good man down. We need two. So he sent you. Brown doesn't know why we need you. What were your orders?"

"To report to Natchez. Find Sharon Weatherford and Mr. Granville. And then do anything possible to hasten the building of the *Arkansas.*"

Wall picked up the carpet bag and removed it from sight as they talked. "Exactly." He put his arms above his head, stretched and yawned. "I was out all night, too. But not stealing cotton. This war is turning me into a confirmed liar. Take it easy, Mr. Woodward. We, too, are trying to build the *Arkansas* and we need your help."

"Doing what?"

"I will not tell you. I will tell you no more than is absolutely necessary. Of course, I trust you. But you might be captured and the Yanks might squeeze some information out of you. If you do not know anything, then you can tell nothing. Your friend Granville doesn't know all the plans. It is best that way. This town is full of renegades and Unionists who would turn you over to the Yanks. And you are being watched, have no doubt about that. Every stranger is watched."

"Will you meet me at the hotel?"

Wall shook his head. "Great God, no! I will not be seen in public with you at all. You just do as you're told and we'll help you build your boat. Now go on to your hotel and get some sleep."

Wyeth picked up the bag again. "Just one more thing. It is none of my business, but I do not hold with you in what you say about Jews. There is too much of such talk. It is spreading disunity."

"Well, I'll be damned." Wall leaned against his counter and stared at Wyeth. "So you don't agree with me. You don't want me to give old Frome all the hell I can. Don't deny me that pleasure, Mr. Woodward. If a merchant can't cuss his competitor, then the world has come to a pretty state of affairs. Now, away with you. And watch your step. I'd hate to see you lose your neck, but mostly I'm concerned with my own, and a few more. My neck escaped the

Mexicans and I'll be damned if I want the Yankees to break it."

There was a broad smile on the old man's florid face as Wyeth left him and walked over to the Natchez Hotel. The Confederate sailor still was bewildered and his temper was sharp. He registered from St. Louis, a town he knew well, and noticed the clerk peering at his luggage. Then the clerk said, "You look tired, sir. There is a bath tub on the third floor and I can send you a barber."

"Fine. Call me at four o'clock this afternoon."

"Four?"

"That's what I said. Four."

"Very well." The clerk reached under his desk. "And here's a copy of the latest issue of the *Natchez Courier*. It will entertain you while the barber is at work. I will send a porter for your clothes and he will brush them and clean them up."

Wyeth went to his room and put the carpet bag under his bed. Then he walked down the hall to the bathroom. A Negro brought hot water, soap and towels and volunteered to help Wyeth cleanse himself. The young man sent him off, however.

The bath refreshed him and when he returned to his room the barber was there; a free yellow Negro who asked no questions, but who answered many. Wyeth was surprised to learn that the Negro owned slaves, a Bantu and a Krooman who helped in the barber shop, and nine Gullahs who farmed the barber's land. The Negro was a rabid Confederate and wished it were possible for his sons to fight in the Southern Army.

Alone and completely relaxed, Wyeth stretched on his bed and began reading the *Courier*. The paper contained many little poems and recipes, but little news. Only one column was devoted to the war and as he read it the blood rushed to his face and his scar showed white. He cursed the Confederate leadership that was neglecting the Mississippi Valley and pouring the South's resources into Virginia.

On the Northern front, along the rivers and railroads of Virginia, the Confederates were blocking every attempt to take Richmond, and Joe Johnston and Robert E. Lee were mauling McClellan in the Peninsular Campaign. The Confederacy's strategy was to fight for a stalemate, hold Richmond and wait for recognition and aid from Europe. And the Virginia crowd, blind to anything beyond Virginia, thought the strategy was working. Wyeth, however, knew otherwise, as did every Confederate fighting in the Mississippi Valley.

The valley was the heart of the new republic and the Mississippi was its backbone and jugular vein. The Confederacy was losing the valley. Virginia, poking out like a sore thumb, was draining the life blood from the heartland. A few Confederates realized the folly of saving Virginia and losing the valley, but their voices could not be heard among the babblings of the Tidewater crowd.

Jefferson Davis, a better military man than many of his generals, was well aware that loss of the valley might be fatal and was doing his best against a hopeless situation. Mississippians, Arkansans, Texans and all soldiers from the West and deep mid-South were willing to fight in Virginia, for they were Southern nationalists who put the Confederacy above their states. But Virginians were Virginians. Imagine Robert E. Lee leading an army at Vicksburg!

And Vicksburg, bleeding behind a bluff that bristled with cannon, was the only spot along the Confederacy's backbone that was free of Yankees in the summer of 1862, New Orleans was gone and Farragut's fleet had pushed up past Vicksburg to the huge lazy S formed by Milliken's Bend. Vicksburg was to the south of the bend, where the river swept around a huge toe of land.*

From the North, the Upper River Flotilla of United States ships had pounded its way down to Milliken's Bend and united with Farragut. In the early summer of 1862, not a Confederate ship of any size was on the Mississippi, and Vicksburg suddenly became of tremendous importance. Not only did the town, in Confederate hands, prevent free flow of Yankee goods from Illinois and the Ohio River Country to New Orleans and the Gulf, but Vicksburg was one of the most important railroad junctions of the South whose life depended on her railroads and rivers.

A little railroad ran from Vicksburg over to Monroe, Louisiana, on the Ouachita River (pronounced Washitaw). The Ouachita flows into the Red River, which waters the richest lands of Louisiana, and then the Red flows into the Mississippi between Natchez and Port Hudson, a village that was to become one of the most strategically important spots in the United States. Supplies from the Red River Valley were moved up the Ouachita to Monroe, thence over

---

* The Mississippi changed its course after the Civil War and Vicksburg no longer is on the toe. The city now is not even on the Mississippi, but is on a canal.

the little railroad to Vicksburg. East from Vicksburg a railroad ran through Jackson, the state capital, and Meridian to Demopolis, Alabama, on the Tombigbee River, which flows south to Mobile and open water.

So Vicksburg was more than a community sleeping behind the bluff. It was the hub of the Confederacy from Georgia to Texas, and from Kentucky to New Orleans.

That's why the two Yankee fleets were ordered to join at Vicksburg and lay siege to the town. Farragut didn't like the idea. His lines of communication were stretched too thin and he believed that Vicksburg could not be reduced by naval strength. But Lincoln told him to try.

The South was sending reinforcements to the little garrison there as rapidly as possible and the first siege of Vicksburg already was a standoff. The Yankee ships threw shells into the fortress and the Confederates replied. It might have gone on forever.

Farragut was nervous, however. For vague reports came to him that somewhere up the Yazoo River the Rebels were building an ironclad, dedicated to lifting the siege of Vicksburg. Many Yankee naval men scoffed at the idea of Rebel landlubbers building a man-of-war in the wilderness but Farragut didn't underestimate his fellow-Southerners, now his enemies. His information was that the mystery ship was named the *Arkansas* and that her batteries were superior to the *Virginia's,* erroneously called the *Merrimac,* which had frightened the North so badly at Hampton Roads. But that's all Farragut knew—that such a ship was being built somewhere up the Yazoo, and that Isaac N. Brown was in command.

There were vague hints in the *Courier* about the *Arkansas* and Wyeth smiled when he read them. The newspaper said the ironclad was two hundred feet long, and a monster. The editor was joshing the Yankees.

Wyeth folded the paper and used it as a fan. He was dripping sweat. Well, he would take another bath when he woke up. He lay there staring up at the high ceiling, wondering when and where he would see Granville again. Then he began thinking about Dolly and Ves. That brought his mind to Sharon. He fell asleep thinking of her and Granville, and his sleep was disturbed by wild dreams.

The sun was dropping over the Mississippi when the porter came and aroused him. He was lying in a pool of sweat, but jumped to

[33]

his feet and, shaking the sleep from his brain, hurried to a window. He couldn't see the river and turned to the porter. "Is she still there?" he demanded.

"Who?"

"The *Iroquois*, you ninny."

"She ain't gone nowhere."

Wyeth bathed again and put on clean clothes that the porter handed him. While he was dressing, a waiter brought coffee and food. Wyeth had no idea of the time and was furious when he went downstairs to the lobby and saw that it was six o'clock. He turned to the clerk and growled, "I told you distinctly to call me at four."

"Did you say four?" The clerk scarcely noticed him. "I thought you said six." The lobby was crowded with guests and the clerk turned his back on Wyeth.

That was too much. "You know damn well I said four," Wyeth muttered.

"Did you have your bath, Mr. Woodward? I hope you enjoyed it. Nothing is as refreshing as a bath in such weather. I fear the weather will get hotter. It's time for a new moon, you know."

Wyeth gulped in surprise. He wanted to smile, but didn't dare let the other guests see any change in his mood. "The old moon was good enough for me," he grumbled and walked over to buy cigars.

The clerk followed him. "The party you were expecting has arrived. This way, Mr. Woodward."

They walked to the front of the hotel and there, waiting in a buggy, was a girl who was frowning politely at him. "You kept me waiting, Mr. Woodward," she said. "You told me to meet you at six. It is ten minutes after."

"I am sorry," Wyeth said, wondering what to expect next.

The clerk stepped to the buggy with Wyeth and whispered, "This is Miss Laurel MacKenzie. She is Wall MacKenzie's daughter. Do as she says."

"Gladly," Wyeth smiled at her. She smiled, too. The first things he noticed were the few freckles around her nose.

"They just come in the summertime," she said. "They go away in the winter."

"Oh." Wyeth was flustered. He didn't know she was conscious of his stare. He didn't look at her then, remembering his manners. And he wanted to stare at her. He didn't know why, but he just wanted to stare. Perhaps it was because she looked cool and gay, and he was hot and worried. She was the most refreshing sight he had seen in Natchez and looked like she didn't belong there. Sharon, exotic and mysterious, belonged in Natchez. But this girl reminded him of frosty mornings back in Missouri. She looked tiny up there on the seat. However, she held the reins competently and steadied her horse.

The clerk was smiling at both of them. "One more thing, Mr. Woodward. Because you're a stranger here the authorities will expect me to search your baggage. Is there anything you don't want me to find?"

"No. And I'm sorry I was abrupt. I am glad you didn't call me until six."

"I had no intention of calling you until six. It would be risky for you to wander about Natchez, and young couples here always go riding at six. There is nothing strange about a young lady and a young gentleman riding around in the cool of the afternoon."

Wyeth climbed into the seat and made himself comfortable beside Laurel. "Where did we meet before, Miss MacKenzie?"

"In St. Louis, sir. Don't you remember? I was in school there. Just in case any nosey person asks you. We have been friends for years."

"I am a poor liar. I hope we are friends for years to come."

She looked at him quickly. "Papa knows many Yankee speculators. So folks will not be surprised to see me with you. I will take you to Papa. You take the reins. But don't use the whip. Don't take it out of its holder. There's a dirk in the holder. If we are stopped and you are trapped, then use the knife. I will swear you were defending me."

Chapter Three

WYETH grasped the reins with a heavy hand, for he was not a good horseman. The mare tossed her head indignantly, shied a few steps, and moved off, snorting and prancing. That embarrassed the sailor. He always had regretted his ignorance of horses and was irked because the ignorance was showing itself at a time when he wanted to impress a young lady.

Manlike, he tried to alibi for his own shortcomings. He flipped the reins clumsily and said, "I've been on the river so long that I've lost my touch with horses."

The girl nodded. "This horse is used to a very light touch."

"Naturally," Wyeth said, "I'm used to a man's horse." He didn't realize just how silly that sounded. "You've got a lady's bridle on this mare. I'm used to heavy stuff."

"It's a French bridle," Laurel said simply. "The weight of a bridle has nothing to do with its performance. That bit is very mild, but it is the most efficient bit in the world. Notice that the bridoon is a double jointed snaffle and is attached to the headstall by toggles. It weighs less than two pounds. Only the French are delicate enough to make such a bit."

Wyeth turned and looked at her. He didn't know what toggles were. All he knew about bridles and bits was that he put the bridle on the horse's head and the bit in his mouth. "I prefer the American bit," he said. "It's good enough for me."

"Which American bit?" Then she realized she had trapped him and laughed. "Most Americans use the Shoemaker, Mr. Woodward. It's a cavalry bit. Papa and I simply do not like the Shoemaker. The French bit is just right. The German one is lighter still. I'm not trying to show off my knowledge, but Papa used to be in the horse and mule business and I grew up in the trade."

Wyeth still wouldn't give up. "That's a mighty fine mare." He shook his head gravely as an expert should and turned the beast toward the river.

Womanlike, Laurel tripped him again and seemed to enjoy it. "As a matter of fact she is not a very good mare. She has been bishoped."

She knew Wyeth was looking at her and she looked straight ahead. He was silent for a second and then he said, "Miss MacKenzie, just what is a bishoped horse?"

She tilted her head a bit and laughed. "Now that is more like it. I know you're not a horseman. A bishoped horse is one whose teeth have been doctored. It's an old trick of Irish horsetraders. The idea is to fool the other fellow. When Papa traded for this mare he knew she had been bishoped. But I wanted her for her gait. She suits me as a buggy horse."

Wyeth was subdued and felt almost light hearted, handling the mare. It was a good feeling, sitting in a light spring buggy and driving along with a pretty girl at his side. He wanted to take the whip and flick it as he had seen dandies do. He took off his hat and put it beside him and let the breeze cool his brow. It was the gesture of a sailor. A Natchez nabob never would have removed his hat while riding in a buggy except to greet a lady. But Wyeth didn't know that. Laurel looked at the hat and then at him and smiled again. She was glad for what he had done. She didn't like Natchez dandies and their stilted manners. But this man appealed to her. Wyeth faced her and returned the smile.

Aware that he must not stare at her, he took in her features bit by bit, stealing glances at intervals. First, he looked at her light parasol and remarked that it was a very pretty parasol. Then he glanced at her bonnet, a saucy little thing made of white tulle with red poppies on the brim. He said it was a very pretty bonnet and Laurel thanked him and smiled again. Natchez gentlemen didn't comment on a lady's bonnet at their first meeting. A bonnet was a personal thing. Wyeth used the bonnet as an excuse to look at her face, and was impressed. Her eyes were gray. He had seen a hundred eyes just as gray, but these were different because they laughed even when her face was serious. Her hair was brown and rather wavy and showed from under her bonnet. He was glad she didn't wear her hair in tight curls around her neck or in ringlets. Her hair was done into a graceful roll at the back of her neck. Her arms were bare, in keeping with the style of the day, and her dress was cut low in front, accentuating her bosom. It was a tantalizing age when women hid their legs and showed their breasts, covered their hands with long gloves and showed their shoulders.

Wyeth's nimble eyes took in every detail and he thought his glances were casual and discreet. She watched him and then looked away. "And I am 20 years old, Mr. Woodward. I weigh 108 pounds. I am not betrothed and probably never will be unless this war sends me a lover. Men are very scarce now."

"Oh!" Again he was flustered. The blood left his face and the scar showed. He put his hand to his cheek as though to hide the scar and then said, "It's like your freckles. It comes and goes."

"I noticed that," she said. "You're sensitive about it. That's a man's vanity. Did you get it in a fight?"

Instead of telling a tale of derring-do, Wyeth told the truth. "It is not an interesting story." He ran his finger over the scar.

"It is an interesting scar," she said.

"Your freckles are interesting, too."

"All right, sir. You forget about my freckles and I will forget about your scar."

"It's a deal. But I like freckles. Honest. I don't know why. I just like freckles." He slapped the mare with the reins and at Laurel's direction turned toward Clifton Street and the old King's Highway. "Go along, horse," he commanded, and the animal lifted her head and broke into a trot. "By the way, Miss MacKenzie, what is your horse's name?"

"Horse."

"I mean her name."

"Her name is Horse."

"That's no name."

"That's her name." She wiggled to adjust her hoops, then smoothed her dress.

[38]

Wyeth was grinning. "Did you really go to school in St. Louis?"

"Yes."

"Did you pass?"

"With honors." Their eyes met and they laughed again. Hers was an unhampered laugh, not at all ladylike. Ladies were not supposed to enjoy laughing, but she did. And Wyeth shook his head from side to side and laughed in his throat and then in his belly.

"Maybe I am the looney one," he said. The buggy ran over a rough spot in the road and they bounced and Wyeth found himself closer to her.

"I suppose it does sound looney, naming a horse Horse. When I was a little girl and Mama was alive we had a picture book and she taught me to say horse by looking at the picture. So every time I saw a horse I called him 'Horse.' I had my first horse when I was five and named him Horse because that was just natural. Since then I have named all my horses Horse."

"Isn't that a bit confusing? For the horses?"

"Not in the least."

Wyeth ran his fingers through his chestnut hair. "But suppose you had two horses?"

"I have four horses."

"Now wait a minute, Miss MacKenzie. This has gone far enough. How in the blazes do your horses know their names? How do you call them? How do you drive them?"

"I only drive one at a time and only ride one at a time. It's very simple."

"So am I." He readjusted his position, having felt sweat gathering on the buggy's leather seat. "You didn't happen to have a picture of a man in that book, did you?"

She nodded and twirled her parasol. "Uh huh. I didn't like the man. He looked so little beside the horse."

"Sort of useless, huh?"

"Exactly. Mama said that when she pointed at it and told me to say man I bawled."

"Were you afraid of him?"

"No. I suppose I felt sorry for him. The same thing happened to him that happened to the horse. After that, I called all men Man. Even Papa. He finally broke me of that, but sometimes right now I forget myself and call him Man instead of Papa. Silly, isn't it?"

"You want the truth?"

"No. A woman never wants the truth."

"Then I will lie. I'll say I think it's clever. But really I think it's batty. Besides, I don't like clever things."

"Neither do I."

Wyeth gripped the reins tightly again and said, "Get along, Horse. Man is going crazy."

"Now you're being smarty. You can take the whip out of the holder and get that dirk. Nobody's looking."

He removed the whip and found the knife, a long thin blade with a bone handle. He fingered the blade and whistled softly. "I don't like knives."

"I thought all men liked knives. Knives and war and killing."

Again the scar showed on Wyeth's face and his jaw was set. "I hate wars." There was no shame in his voice. He didn't look at her when he said it, but looked at the blade and then put the knife away at his side.

"I hate wars, too," Laurel said. "When I think. And yet, there's something noble about war. You know, Mr. Woodward, most women like war."

"Why, women hate wars."

"No, they just say that. In my brain I hate wars, but in my heart I'm thrilled. Most women are that way. War is exciting. Unless a woman has a son or a husband or somebody close who is in danger she usually is thrilled at the idea of men fighting. She likes parades and the presence of strange men who strut before her. War tears away certain barriers, too. Conventions are forgotten. Women do many things they want to do and people forgive them because war is what it is. That's a fact."

Wyeth balanced the buggy whip in his hand, flicked it inexpertly and put it back in its holder. He reined the horse to a slow walk and gazed at Laurel, watching her eyes. "Now I know you passed your school with honors."

"Thank you, Man."

"You're welcome, Woman."

Neither felt like talking then and they moved out of Natchez along the highway that flanked the river to the north, the old Spanish Road that ran past the cemetery and out along the Mississippi's bank. She broke the silence. "We're out of town now. Look the other way."

He did as he was told and heard her dress rustling and realized what was happening. The thought made his blood pound. He wished she would get tangled in her hoops and need his help. An almost overwhelming urge to fake an excuse and look at her came to him, but he knew that such a cheap trick would disgust her.

"All right," she said. "Here, take it." She put a pistol in his hand. The metal was warm and he knew it had been next to her flesh. That thrilled him, too. "It was very uncomfortable." She readjusted her dress. "I couldn't give it to you in town."

"I almost peeped," he said boldly, childlishly, then wished he had bitten his tongue.

"I'm glad you didn't, Mr. Woodward. I hate men who peep. An honest look is one thing, but a peep is disgusting. Can you use that pistol?"

"If I have to. But I am not a good shot. I am fair with a rifle. A pistol is not my kind of gun."

"I thought not. You just don't look like a man who handles a pistol. Or a knife. Do you know what I mean?"

"No."

"I can't explain it." She lowered her parasol and took off her bonnet, peering up the road the while. "Your friend, Mr. Granville, is a pistol man, isn't he?"

"The best. How did you know that?"

They rounded a bend and far up the road on a ridge was a cabin. Wyeth saw the cabin, saw every detail, and gave it no heed. Laurel was staring toward the cabin, her eyes crinkling in the sun that was rolling down rapidly beyond the rim of the world. "Oh," she said, still watching the cabin. "That's what I mean. Mr. Granville just looks like a pistol man. Sort of gay and reckless and unreliable. A pistol is unreliable."

"I still do not understand you."

"I suppose you never will. But you look like a rifle man. Mr. Granville looks like a pistol man. That's all there is to it. Papa looks like a shotgun man."

"What about Mr. Frome? You know him."

"He looks like a rapier man. Now am I making myself clear?

General Grant looks like a saber man. General Lee like a javelin man."

"And President Lincoln?"

"A slingshot man. Mr. Lincoln is the kind of man who will pick off his enemies one at a time."

"I think I see what you mean. Say, you keep watching that cabin. Why?"

"Had you noticed it?"

"Yes. It's a dogtrot cabin, unpainted. There is a muskrat pelt nailed to the wall. . . ."

"Can you see all of that from here?"

Wyeth was very proud of his eyes and did a little showing off. "That's nothing. It has two windows in front and six stumps along the front walk. There is a clothes boiler to the right of the house and a clothes line. Somebody has been washing because there is a linsey shirt on the line."

Laurel reached over and grabbed the reins, then wheeled the horse to the right, into some woods. Wyeth was too surprised to ask questions, and, besides, he was used to unexpected developments. Laurel made sure they were out of sight of the road and quieted the horse. Wyeth reached for the pistol. "Your eyes may have saved us," she whispered. "Do you hear anything?"

He cocked one ear toward the road. "Some horsemen are coming."

"That linsey shirt was a signal for us to hide."

A group of horsemen clattered along the road and soon was out of hearing. Laurel drove the horse back to the road and Wyeth looked at the cabin and saw that a linsey dress was on the line. He reported that fact to Laurel, and she nodded and they drove on. "Now, where were we?" she asked.

"We were talking about pistol men and such. Mr. Granville is the best pistol shot I ever saw."

"Then you never saw Keith Alexander."

"Do you know him?" Wyeth accepted the reins from her.

"I've met him. Papa does business with him, sometimes. Mr. Alexander sells things to both sides. He is getting rich out of the war. He fights against the South but sells iron to the Confederates. He has no feeling for anybody, and, yet, I sort of feel sorry for him. He is very handsome and seems so lonely. . . ."

"Why is he lonely?"

[42]

Laurel shrugged her shoulders. "He's in love. He loves Morna Dabney and she doesn't love him. At least, I don't believe she loves him. She loves a Confederate officer who is married to her only sister. The Dabneys, in fighting the South, are fighting their son-in-law and Mr. Alexander is helping them because he loves Morna and hates the Confederacy, and he hates the Confederacy because his father is a big man in Richmond and Mr. Alexander won't bear his name. You see, Mr. Alexander's father and mother were not married and he hates his father for disgracing his mother and leaving him nameless. It's all very confusing."

"So it seems." Wyeth wasn't interested in Keith Alexander.

"It's sort of sad, if you think about it."

"Then don't think about it."

"I can't help it," Laurel sighed. "Everybody in Natchez talks about it. Mr. Alexander is very romantic. . . ."

"I'm not so sure right now that you passed that school with honors." He said it curtly.

Laurel laughed again. "I don't know why I am interested in him. He is a rascal, but he fascinates me. It's the mystery of him, I suppose. He worships Morna Dabney. Morna was betrothed to her childhood sweetheart and then she got sick and he married her sister. Papa says Keith Alexander will marry Morna Dabney yet, that he always gets what he goes after."

The sun eased down behind the horizon and then plopped out of sight, sending out a reddish glow of farewell. Then there was darkness, the quick total darkness of the deep South which has no twilight. Stars popped out and stared and a light breeze came. It still was stifling, however, and instead of cooling things the breeze only teased the land. Wyeth scarcely was giving any heed to Laurel's ramblings, knowing that she was talking just to make conversation and to prevent him from asking any of the dozen questions on his tongue.

"Well, anyway, I wish Mr. Alexander luck," Wyeth said, mostly to be polite. "However, if he's looking for trouble I'd like to see him cross Mr. Granville's path."

The mare was picking her own way along the road. The night things were out, buzzing and croaking. Mosquitoes swarmed about them, and down along the river a thousand frogs bellowed their welcome to the night. The mare came to a fork in the road and stopped. Laurel, without speaking, took the reins and headed the mare up the right fork toward the cabin, scarcely visible in the darkness.

"Morna Dabney is the most beautiful woman I ever saw." She took up the conversation and her voice betrayed her tension in spite of her efforts to appear calm. "I like all the Dabneys even if Mr. Hoab Dabney is leading a rebellion against the South. There is something fine about him and his little clan defying the Confederacy and seceding because they don't believe in slavery. Do you approve of slavery?"

Wyeth's eyes had become accustomed to the darkness and the path was clear to him. He was watching the trail closely. There was a trace of annoyance in his tone. "I knew we'd get around to that sooner or later if we just kept talking to hear our own words. Few people really approve of slavery but it got fastened on the South for economic reasons and now it is a stone around our neck but we can't agree on how to get rid of it."

"You talk like a school master."

"That's rather far-fetched. You ask about slavery. Well, I do not approve. But it's the law of the land. If a law is wrong it should be changed. The United States Government is not trying to free slaves. It is denying the South the right to follow a government of her own choosing. The South wants its own government. The North doesn't want her to have it because the North needs us and that's all there is to that. Most Southerners I know are against slavery, but what can they do about it unless they revolt against their own states? Slaves represent several billion dollars worth of property and men don't give up property without a fight. Only two groups in this country are consistent in this fight. The Abolitionists, a minority, are determined to abolish slavery even if they wreck the country. The slavers, another minority, have set their heads to keep slavery regardless of the consequences. And the majority is between two fires."

Laurel reined the mare to a stop and listened. Then she touched the horse lightly and they moved on. "Did you pass your school with honors?"

"I got by as far as I went. But I left school when I was a boy and began steamboating with my father. He owned two slaves. He freed one of them and the other one died and he never bought any more."

"We have one. An old woman. She reared me when Mama died. I have to sort of nurse her now. I never thought much about slavery until the war started. I know it's wrong, but I think the Yankees are hypocrites about it. Don't you?"

"Not all of them. Most of them don't give a continental one way or another. But they will before this war is over. The North needs a crusade to win and slavery offers that opportunity."

A rifle shot sounded to their left, over along the river and Laurel looked at him quickly. She halted the horse and they waited, listening. She was so nervous that she whispered and her voice was hoarse until she cleared her throat. She was saying anything that came to her mind, anything to keep her spirits up. "Since you do not believe in slavery and are a Missourian, then why are you fighting for the South? Missouri's neutral."

"So neutral that just about every able bodied man in the State is on one side or the other. Brushing aside all the flimflam, the Yankees invaded the South. They marched in on us. When a man comes to my door with a gun and demands to get in and rearrange my house, then I'm going to shoot. That's all there is to it."

She waited a minute then said, "We will get out here. And I want to thank you. It has been a pleasant trip and you have been very considerate. You might have asked many questions that I should not answer. But I might have answered them."

Wyeth got out of the buggy and helped her out. "We certainly have talked around the bush about everything in the world. What is next on the menu?"

When she stood by him he realized just how tiny she was. He was glad he could see so well in the darkness, for he saw that her eyes were calm now, and sparkling in the starlight. She left her parasol in the buggy and stepped to the side of the path. "That cabin is the home of Mort Kincaid. He is one of us. He used to be a mule skinner for Papa until he took to the river. He put out those signals. That linsey shirt meant that strangers were around, and the linsey dress meant that all was clear."

"So now we look for Mort?"

"No. He will come to us. You won't approve of Mort. He is a bushwhacker, a guerrilla. A couple of Yankees working with some Union bushwhackers came this way several weeks ago and stole Mort's horses. He wasn't at home. The excitement killed his wife who was sick from the lung fever. His boy showed fight and they shot him. Then they tried to hide the murder. They tied weights to the boy's body and threw him in the river. The body caught on one of Mort's fishing lines. I think you see what I mean. I have an idea that Mort fired that shot a few minutes ago and that by now some Yankee or renegade is floating down the river."

Wyeth didn't reply. There was nothing to say, so he said nothing. His nerves were on edge and he was weary of chatter. He didn't approve of guerrillas, but accepted them as necessary evils of war. His observation had been that guerrillas, North and South, were needlessly brutal. She touched his arm and then led the way up the ridge to the crest and they looked down on the Mississippi, silent and ghastly in the starlight. The few lights of Natchez glimmered to the south and from that distance Wyeth recognized the *Iroquois,* swaying at anchor, her harbor lanterns gleaming.

"It is very nice up here," he said. "Nice and quiet."

"I must do something very silly and you are going to laugh at me. I must bay like a dog."

"A big dog?"

"A hound. Can you bay like a hound?"

"If I could, I wouldn't. I want to hear you."

"Here goes." She cupped her hands and made a long cry, a melodious cry, the bay of a hound. It was a sad sound; mournful. It rolled down the ridge and Wyeth smiled and she began laughing.

"Was there a dog in that picture book?"

"Yes. But I never named dogs. Mort taught me to bay like that."

A reply came from down along the river, another long bay and two short yelps. Laurel said, "That's Mort."

"He sounds like a bloodhound. What kind of man is he? Pistol, rifle, slingshot? Or does he just chunk rocks?"

"Wait until you see him and then you tell me what kind of man he is."

The Missourian heard Mort moving through the underbrush and was expecting a gaunt, taciturn riverman just because most rivermen were gaunt and taciturn; gaunt because the river bred tall men and taciturn because they usually lived alone. So when the little man stepped out of a clump of bushes and sidled up to him, Wyeth was startled. Morton Kincaid looked like a gnome, about five feet tall and with a big head and a pot belly. His gun was taller than he.

"Good evening, Laurel." He was looking at Wyeth. "I reckon this is Mr. Woodward?"

"That's right." She introduced the men and Mort scratched his stubby beard and said, "He looks all right. By God, Laurel, he looks all right. Like he's got salt in his craw and iron in his innards. How are you, Mr. Woodward?"

"Sort of mixed up."

"We'll straighten you out." He led the way back down to the buggy and propped his rifle against a wheel and began unhitching the mare.

Wyeth leaned over and whispered to Laurel. "He's a butcher-knife man."

"That's fair enough." She whispered too. "He uses a knife and a rifle. And his finger nails and teeth."

Wyeth watched the little man unhitch the mare and lead her into hiding beside the path, calming her with a few words. Then Mort removed his gun, leaning it against a stump, and began maneuvering the buggy into some high bushes. The sailor offered to help, but Mort shook his head and Wyeth walked toward the stump to examine the rifle, a valuable Whitworth Snipper piece with a telescope fastened to the barrel. Vespasian Gillivray had such a rifle and Wyeth longed for one, for the Whitworth was the envy of every marksman in the world. It was made in England and sent to the Confederacy on blockade runners. There were only 300 such guns issued. It had a hexagonal bore and was of .45 calibre. It used a long bullet that was cast and then swaged to the shape of the bore. The rifle was accurate at half a mile and was responsible for the death of many Union officers.

"Hey. What are you doing?" Mort called sharply to Wyeth when he reached for the rifle.

"I want to look at your rifle."

"Leave it be, Mr. Woodward." Mort stepped to the stump and put the rifle across his shoulder. "It's a Whitworth."

Wyeth didn't like the idea of being rebuked, especially in Laurel's presence. "I'm quite aware of what it is. It's all right for special work but I prefer a .69 calibre Plymouth, made by Eli Whitney. That's regular Navy issue. To the Yank Navy, of course, but we have managed to pick up a few." He was anxious to establish his knowledge of rifles, hoping it would please Mort and impress Laurel.

"For snippers, give me the Langdon. The Langdon has never been beaten at moderate distance, and in the Navy you get close to your enemy."

Mort laughed and the laugh showed that several of his teeth were missing and that his remaining teeth were yellow stubs. "No offense, Mr. Woodward. My gun still smells of powder. Now just suppose some Yank stopped you and asked you about my gun and your tongue slipped and you said you smelled powder. That would be rightly bad for me. I just killed a Yank. As it is, you can't prove that my gun has been shot."

"We heard the shot," Wyeth said.

"The light was pretty bad." Mort took the heavy ramrod out of his gun and began cleaning it. "I gen'ly get one along about dark every day. That's when they go up and down the river buying or stealing cotton."

"It sounds like interesting work."

"I like it. I stretch out along the bank and wait for them to come by."

Wyeth looked down at the little man and then up and around at the trees. "Have you picked out the limb that you want to die on?"

"Uh huh. A little limb on a tree back up near my cabin. It won't take much limb to hang me if the Yanks catch me. I ain't so big. Used to be a jockey up in Tennessee. Have you picked out your limb? If they catch you out of uniform they'll jerk you higher than a cat's back."

Laurel was not pleased at the turn of events, realizing that Wyeth instinctively disliked the runty river man. She was fond of Mort in spite of his shortcomings. Up in Maury County, Tennessee, where her father used to buy mules, Mort had worked for them. He really was a jockey in his youth, then a trainer and eventually a stableman. His little body was scarred from a dozen accidents. Laurel liked him simply because he had been loyal to her father. He was ignorant, superstitious and dirty. He was *white trash,* a phrase that was just coming into use in the South. Laurel touched Wyeth's sleeve and looked at Mort and said, "Let's be on our way. You two can wrangle some other time."

Mort grunted and walked away toward the north. He stooped as he picked the way through underbrush and Wyeth noticed that his right foot was twisted, causing a limp. The girl followed him and

Wyeth brought up the rear, stepping gingerly. The contrast between Laurel and Mort startled him. They were about the same height, but she was trim and he was sloppy, almost repulsive. It came to Wyeth then, just how many elements made up the Confederacy. Mort and Laurel had nothing in common except their love for the land they were defending. Even then, the South was not a unit, politically, economically, racially. Virginians and Texans had only one common problem, the defense of their land. Some people thought slavery bound the South together, but Delaware was a slave state and it was Yankee. Picking their way up the ridge, Wyeth realized that each of them was the product of a different way of life, and yet each was a Southerner. The thought disturbed him. The whole conflict disturbed him, for he didn't understand it and he wondered again why men do the things they do. In the complex categories of the South, Mort belonged to the lowest class, scorned even by the Negroes. Laurel and Wyeth were upper middle class, the backbone of the Confederacy.

He was deep in his own thoughts when Laurel turned and put her hand on his arm. "Careful," she said. "Watch your step."

"By God, you'd better watch it." Mort had paused at the brink of an enormous black hole in the bluff. "This here is the Devil's Punch Bowl, and if you slip you'll fall plum' to China."

Wyeth checked himself suddenly and was frightened for one of the few times in his life. The hole spread before him, a huge black blotch, awesome in the darkness. He had heard of those mysterious formations along the lower Mississippi but never had seen one before. The top of the hole was more than a quarter of a mile wide, and the opening was so deep that its bottom could not be seen even in sunlight. He peered over the brink and below he saw the tops of trees and heard the wail of winds, crisscrossing through the trees.

"What caused this thing?" Wyeth whispered.

"The Devil," said Mort. "The Devil built it. There are a heap of them along here, each deeper than the other. Back in the days of the Harpe Boys and other river pirates they used to hide their boodle in these durn things. You can put St. Mary's Cathedral, the courthouse and two or three mansions in this thing and never find 'em."

Laurel held tightly to Wyeth's arm. The formations always frightened her. "No one knows what caused them. The bluff here is mighty high and these holes go straight down, lower than the river. Men have been lost in them. I suppose the river formed them, or an earthquake. There are trees all up and down the sides. I don't like them. They scare me."

Actually, the cone-shaped holes in the bluffs were caused by spasms of the earth and by time. The bluffs along the lower Mississippi are formed partly of a peculiar loess foundation, a brown dust, a rock flour, blown millions of years ago from the Mississippi basin. The river, cutting through the land, heaved up towering banks along the east side and the loess dust covered the high banks to a depth of 40 feet. Then came jungle-like vegetation. Wind and earthquakes shook the bluffs and in spots they sloped off evenly, but at intervals they rose in sheer precipices, making a wild contour that, from a distance, gave the appearance of frowning castles and brown forts. Some of the bluffs cracked into bowls and erosion closed their doors to the Mississippi River, leaving them alone in the bluffs, gigantic holes as large as the craters of volcanoes, matted and tangled with vines and trees.

Wyeth felt himself glued to the spot, staring down into the black maw. Laurel tugged at his arm and he turned and followed her and Mort around the brink and down the bluff to the river's edge. The moon had come out and the river was yellow and silent. Mort walked up the bank and called to them. Wyeth helped him move a pile of green boughs and underneath was a skiff.

The riverman pointed to some rags in the bottom of the boat and told Wyeth to muffle the oarlocks. The sailor was tying rags around the locks when he saw a body float into view and bump against the bank, about 10 yards ahead of them. He pointed before he spoke, and then, frightened again, said hoarsely, "It's a dead man."

Laurel turned her head. Mort, however, jumped out of the skiff and ran toward the corpse. "It's my Yank." He stopped and stared at the body. "A nigger." There was contempt in his tone and no remorse. "A burr-headed nigger in a Yankee coat. If I'd known he was a nigger I'd have cut his throat and saved a bullet."

"We can't leave him here," Wyeth said.

"He'll wash away by morning." Mort leaned over and pushed the body away from the bank. "I reckon you think we oughta take time to bury him."

[50]

"Such things have been done," Wyeth said. "There's nothing dishonorable in burying your enemy."

Mort spat and wiped his mouth with the back of his hand. "This here is a nigger. I don't like niggers. He was helping the Yanks. Let his soul rot in hell."

Laurel heard some of the conversation and when the two men returned to the skiff she rebuked Mort. "It seems to me that you enjoy killing Negroes."

"I do. I don't like 'em."

Wyeth bit his lip, but Laurel said, "What about old Charity? She nursed you at our house."

"She's different. I know her. I'd do anything for her. And for Brutus Williams, the barber. He's a free nigger and we're friends. And old Big Willie, the Vidal slave. I know 'em."

Wyeth knew the futility of arguing with Mort. The riverman belonged to that class of whites who appreciated Negroes as individuals but who hated their race. Such men were victims of a maddening bigotry born of ignorance, superstitution and economic fear. The sailor shared none of that hatred. He disliked many Negroes as individuals, but gave the race only passing thoughts. He was a bit contemptuous of the race as a whole, however, for being so docile. He and many other Southerners wondered why the slaves didn't use the war as an opportunity for a general revolt against their masters. True, Negroes were revolting in isolated incidents. Most of them, however, were loyal to their masters, while others pretended loyalty until the Yanks arrived.

"Let's go," Laurel said. She didn't want Wyeth and Mort to begin arguing the Negro question, knowing that they could never agree. Of the six million white people in the South, only a few agreed on anything.

Mort grunted as he pushed the skiff from the bank. "Niggers! I get sick of all this talk about how come we're fighting this war. We're fighting to keep the nigger in his place. If we ain't fighting for that, then what are we fighting for?"

They didn't answer the truculent old man. Wyeth was anxious to be away from him and Laurel was nervous. Mort, however, seemed to be enjoying himself. He took the oars, dipped them silently and they moved up the river, just off of the east bank.

"Now listen, young man," Mort said. "If any Yankees or niggers or bushwhackers jump us, you take the one on the left and work in. I'll start from the right. Use your pistol and then go after 'em with your knife. Laurel, you hit for the river, get ashore and hide."

His warning brought Wyeth back to the realization of their danger and he sat in the stern of the boat, his pistol in his lap. About a hundred yards up the river the wind began moaning. Laurel looked back at him and said softly, "The Devil's Punch Bowl is right over there. The wind is playing tricks among the trees. It is as still as death out here on the river, but there always is a wind down in the Bowl."

They proceeded up the river almost a mile and Mort turned toward a bluff that came to the water's edge and towered above them. "This is it," he mumbled. He leaned out of the boat and parted a cluster of saplings and willow branches. Then he forced the boat between the trees and Wyeth thought they were going into the bluff.

"There is another bowl back in this bluff," Laurel said. "We are going there."

Wyeth looked back and the river was out of sight. They were on a narrow canal, or sluice. Wyeth's eyes actually bulged. The canal had been dug from the river into the bluff and back to the bowl and the bottom of the bowl was flooded. Small barges, piled with cotton bales, lined the canal and the waterway was so narrow that the skiff scraped between the bank and the barges. They passed six barges and were into the bowl before Wyeth was aware of just where he was or what he was seeing.

Part of the bowl was covered by timbers and logs and back under the covering, far in the recess of the bluff, two forges were going and there was a ringing of hammers and a glow of fires. Piles of iron were along the canal and men and women, white and Negro, were putting the iron into cotton bales, pressing the fibre back into place and weighing the bales before they were swung aboard the barges. There were long dancing shadows in the bowl and the faces of the workers were red in the glow of the fires. Even the Negroes looked red. There was an odor of sweat and hot iron, rust and stale water. Wyeth's heart began pounding.

Mort steered the skiff to a little landing and Wall MacKenzie was waiting on the landing. Behind him was Nathan Frome.

"So you made it." Wall took his daughter's hand and helped her ashore. "Glad to see you again, Mr. Woodward. I believe you have seen Mr. Frome before. Nate is sort of the ring leader of this business."

Wyeth just gulped. Frome said, "Glad to know you. I saw you today." He offered his hand and then waved toward the forges and barges and workers. "This is for the *Arkansas*."

Still Wyeth didn't speak. Mort pulled the bow of the skiff onto the sloping bank and stood by the sailor, peering up at him. "Yep, by God. This here is iron for the *Arkansas*, and me and Laurel are going to see that it gets to the Yazoo. You and your English friend are going to help us and then you can build your durn boat and chuck some of this iron back at the Yanks."

Workers began gathering around the young Missourian. They came from back in the bluff, from the bowels of the earth. They were dirty and weary. But their eyes shone at sight of a sailor from the *Arkansas*, the hulk they were determined to help turn into a man-of-war. Wyeth stared at the workers and nodded. Then he looked at Frome, at his lean face and tired eyes. His gaze wandered to Wall MacKenzie, thence down to Mort. Finally, his eyes found Laurel, and she was smiling at him.

Wall MacKenzie saw the light in his daughter's eyes and looked quickly at her and then at Wyeth. He was a very wise old man.

Chapter Four

Nate Frome and Wall MacKenzie guided the bewildered Missourian on an inspection tour of the underground workshop and Wyeth resolved then and there never again to form an opinion of persons without knowing all the facts; a resolution that he didn't keep, naturally.

He was rather ashamed that he had misjudged Wall and wanted to tell him so when the opportunity presented itself. Two women took Laurel in hand and escorted her to a tunnel far back in the bluff. There were cots back there and a dressing room and the women made Laurel go to bed. Mort went to a section of the shop where harness makers were working and began helping them.

From a pile of dry fagots, Frome selected a pine torch that had been wrapped in cotton and dipped in turpentine. He lighted the torch and Wyeth and Wall followed him around the shop. The heat was almost unbearable, but nobody complained. Workers fainted often, however, and were stretched along the canal to revive. The workers did not talk much. They were too exhausted.

Back at the forges, the iron was molded into plates and bolts, or cut into bits. Then it was lugged by hand to the edge of the canal and hidden in cotton bales. Roustabouts carried the bales aboard the barges and stacked them in orderly fashion.

"It is the most amazing thing I ever saw," Wyeth said. "It just beats all."

"Thanks." Frome was very proud of the shop and his organization. "Wall did most of the hard work."

"Now wait a minute, Nate." Wall was examining a hunk of rusty iron. "Modesty doesn't suit you. We had to have a head, so we chose Nate. He's a good organizer. Building this shop wasn't as difficult as it looks. The bowl was here. We dug that sluice to the river and let the water in. Then we dug back into the bluff and made the tunnels for the forges and all that. We put a roof over part of it so the fires couldn't be seen from above. That's all there was to it."

"Do the Yankees suspect anything?" Wyeth asked.

"We don't know," Frome said. "But it's not the Yanks we worry about so much. The Yankee sympathizers in Natchez are the big danger. If they get wind of this thing they'll tell the Yanks and then there'll be a wholesale hanging bee."

Wall began grinning. "Farragut scared hell out of us one day. He anchored his flagship right out yonder near the mouth to this bowl. He stayed there all day. Then he upped anchor and went on up the river. You can bet that after that we put more trees, especially willows, around the opening."

Wyeth watched a Negro lug a bale onto a barge and marveled at his skill in handling the heavy load. "May I ask questions?"

Frome said, "There's no law against it. But there's no law that we've got to answer. There are some things about the organization that no persons know except Wall and me."

"Where did you get your iron?"

"Oh, round and about. We picked up stuff here and there and smuggled it in here. Sharon Weatherford's iron was brought in tonight. She traded drinks for it. But we bought most of the stuff from Keith Alexander."

"Him again, huh?" Wyeth dipped his hand into the canal and wet his face to cool it. Even the water was warm. "Every time I turn around I hear his name. So he's in the iron business, too."

Frome and Wall laughed. "Alexander never allows his sentiments to interfere with a profit," the little Scotchman said. "He is with Hoab Dabney and against the Confederacy, but he sold us iron. We bought it through an agent and after the agent completed the deal we saw to it that he went to Mexico."

"Where did Alexander get the iron?"

"From the North. He had an arrangement with a Yankee skipper

[55]

to bring down iron and swap it for cotton. Alexander made a tidy fortune until the skipper got caught."

"I'll say he did," Frome broke in. "I handled the business from this end. Don't ever let anybody tell you that a Jew is sharper than a Gentile in a trade. Alexander held our feet to the fire."

"So far, so good." Wyeth unloosened his shirt and ran his hand around his neck. When he breathed the heat seemed to sear his lungs. "But how are you going to get the iron up the Yazoo River where the *Arkansas* is? That's a hundred miles from here."

Frome ignored him for a second while he instructed a worker to hide a handful of bolts deeper in a bale. "Excuse me, Mr. Woodward, for the interruption. The Yankees are going to take the iron part of the way for us. Up to Grand Gulf, anyway, a village near the mouth of the Big Black River."

"And from there to the Yazoo?"

"You will get your orders at Grand Gulf."

"Me?" Wyeth looked from one to the other. "Where do I fit into the picture?"

"Why do you think we asked Captain Brown to send you down?" Wall reached into his pocket for his pipe and clamped it between his teeth, but didn't light it. "You are a cotton buyer. A Missouri speculator. There is a ring of Yankee speculators around Natchez. I have a feeling that General Ben Butler is in on it. If he's not, then it's the only bet he's overlooking down here. He's stealing everything else in sight."

"But what has all of that to do with me?"

"Just hold your horses, young man. Me and Nate have promised some speculators a heap of cotton tonight. We'll run those barges out on the river and sell it to them, lock, stock and barrel. We'll use the money to buy more iron, incidentally, and have the laugh on Keith Alexander. We have told the speculators that you're at Grand Gulf ready to pay a whopping price for the cotton, no questions asked."

Wyeth pursed his lips and whistled softly at the daring of the plan.

Frome said, "The speculators have a tie-up with the Yanks. They can get two or three tugs and push the barges to Grand Gulf. We have pointed out the danger of guerrillas waylaying them. That puts us in the clear. But they'll take the chance because they think you are waiting at Grand Gulf with a satchel full of money."

"So I'm the bait?" Wyeth said. "All well and good, but what happens at Grand Gulf?"

"You'll see," Wall said. "If everything goes all right nobody will get hurt. But if things go wrong, you start shooting. And shoot the speculators. Don't shoot the guerrillas because your friend, Mr. Granville, will be among them."

"Where is he?"

"Right now he is over around Washington, a little town just east of here. There is a Confederate camp there and he is recruiting men. That's all we can tell you now. You're going to pull out of here before dawn tomorrow in a wagon train. Mort will go along. So will my daughter." He looked sharply at Wyeth.

The sailor was conscious of the look. "It's a dangerous undertaking for a girl."

"War is dangerous. Frome and I can't go. It would be a dead giveaway if we were absent from Natchez at such a time. Laurel knows horses and mules. Any other questions?"

"I suppose not." Wyeth was skeptical. He didn't like the idea at all. But Captain Brown had told him to get his orders in Natchez.

The three men walked back into a tunnel and sat down. Wall sent a Negro for some brandy. The drink relaxed Wyeth and made him hungry. Another Negro brought food and he ate it with his fingers. Then he lay down and closed his eyes. He felt that Wall was watching him and when he opened his eyes he saw that the Scotch merchant was staring at him. Frome was looking from Wall to Wyeth and smiling slightly.

"You know." Wyeth sat upright. "I owe you an apology, Mr. MacKenzie. Back in Natchez this morning I didn't realize that your tirade against Mr. Frome was a blind."

"It wasn't," Wall snapped.

"Oh, for God's sake, Wall," Frome said. "This young man is confused enough. Of course, it was a blind, Mr. Woodward. The folks in Natchez think Wall and I stay at each other's throats."

"I am glad it's that way." Wyeth was relieved. "There's too much talk in the South about Jews."

Frome opened a small silver cigar box that he carried in his hind pocket. He selected a cheroot and offered one to Wyeth. "Don't worry too much about that. The South will never be really anti-Semitic so long as we have the Negro to blame for our troubles."

"I never thought of it that way," Wyeth said. "All I know is that in the part of the North I've seen the folks are dead set against Jews and Catholics. I know a lot of members of the Know Nothing Party who were pledged to support only native Americans. The party joined with the Republicans, you know, and backed Mr. Lincoln." [2]

Frome, an authority on the politics of the times, hid his smile behind his hands. But Wall didn't. He was amused at Wyeth relating a fact that Frome already knew, that every informed Southerner knew. "You'd better stick to fighting and forget politics," Wall said.

"Leave the young man alone," Frome said. "What he says is true. You see, Mr. Woodward, the whole situation is crazy. They call President Jefferson Davis a rebel. He's no rebel. He's a fundamentalist, a hide-bound Constitutionalist. Actually, Mr. Lincoln is a rebel. Southerners are the stand-patters and Mr. Lincoln's crowd wants to change things. Don't allow yourself to get all tangled up in side issues. The time has come when the industrial North, built on wage-slavery, and the agrarian South, built on body-slavery, cannot live together in the same family. Both systems are vicious. To me, the Southern system is the lesser of two evils because, sooner or later, the South will free her slaves simply because they are unprofitable. But wage-slavery is another matter."

Wyeth liked to hear Frome talk and instinctively developed an admiration for the man. "Another thing bothers me, Mr. Frome. Why should you support the South? I thought Jews hated slavery."

"I am a Southerner," Frome said. "The main issue to me is the effort of the North to dominate the South. My Semitic blood has nothing to do with it. Jews are no more a united people than your folks are."

Wyeth said, "Well, there are not many Jews and foreigners in the South. . . ."

"Whoa!" Frome put his hands to his head and rocked it from side to side. "You're wrong, Mr. Woodward. Nothing is quite as far-fetched as the South's boast that her population is overwhelmingly native-born American. It's one of the silliest myths of this war."

"I don't get that," Wyeth protested. "The Confederate Army is made up almost entirely of Southerners."

"Is Patrick Ronayne Cleburne a Southerner?"

"No, not exactly," Wyeth said. "He was born in Ireland, but he lives in Arkansas.

Frome laughed. "And he is a major-general. So is Camille Arnaud Jules Marie, the French Prince de Polignac. Name any nation and I can name her officers in the Confederate Army. William Browne, an Englishman, is President Davis' aide. General Selkirk McGlashan is a Scot. General Wagener is a German. And on and on."

Wyeth was stunned for he, too, had believed the stories that native-born Southerners were fighting alone against European mercenaries imported to the North. Many Northern soldiers, mostly Irish and German, were mercenaries, but the Confederate Army had whole regiments of Irish, and companies of Germans, French, Poles and Mexicans. Hungarians, Russians, Cubans, Persians, Danes, Chinese and Maltese fought for the South. Many of these were naturalized but others, including that incredible Turk, Hobart Pasha, fought for the Confederacy for profit and glory. There was scarcely a company, except from Alabama and North Carolina, in which there were not foreigners. Texas was one of the strongest German states in the Union. New Orleans, a melting pot, was known to have many foreigners, but most Southerners never stopped to think that Savannah, for example, had a foreign white population of twenty per cent. And Memphis, land locked Memphis, was the home of 4,000 Irishmen and 1,000 Germans. More than thirty per cent of Memphis' white population was foreign.[3]

Sitting there with Frome, Wyeth learned more about the South and her army than the average enlisted man ever learned.

"Have you any sons?" he asked.

"I had two. One is at the Confederate Naval Academy. The other was killed at Fort Pillow."

Wall changed the subject. "Did you hear about that French prince? The general over in Louisiana?" The Scotchman began laughing. "He rode up in front of his men, a bunch of wild loonies from Arkansas and the piney woods, put his hand over his heart and said, 'Soldiers, behold your Polignac!' Just like he was talking to the Frenchies."

"What happened?" Wyeth was smiling.

"The Secesh boys were pop-eyed at first and then they began whooping and hollering. They are hog-wild about him now."

Frome said, "Tell Mr. Woodward about the shebang."

"Well," Wall almost doubled up with laughter. "One day a boy just back from furlough went up to this French general and said, 'Cap'n I just got back to this here damn army and I'm rightly mixed up. I belong to Colonel So-and-So's layout, but I don't know where it is. Where might it be?' Well, sir, the prince's eyes popped out like fried eggs and he said, 'You belong to what?' "

Frome interrupted the story with an outburst of chuckles and Wall was laughing so hard that tears showed in his eyes. Finally he found his voice. "The boy looked at the general as though he thought he was crazy and said, 'Colonel So-and-So's layout. You know, his layout belongs to your shebang.' Polignac put his hand to his head and started groaning, 'Well, damn my eyes to ze deep blue hell. I have been militaire all my life. I was educated for ze army. I have heard of ze compagnie, ze battalion, ze regiment, ze brigade, ze division, and ze army corps, but damn my soul to ze hell ef evair I hear of ze layout or ze shebang before.' "

Frome's chuckles grew into raucous laughter and Wyeth laughed mostly because they did. He didn't think the story justified such mirth, but then he didn't understand the wit of the lower valley, where exaggeration was a way of humor. "Speaking of this prince," he said, "What is there to the report that the United States has offered Garibaldi a commission as major general?"

"Secretary Seward has made the offer," Frome said. "But Garibaldi hasn't accepted. Maybe he won't. Garibaldi lived in the United States for four years but the chances are he won't fight against the South. His aide, Major Bausenwein has accepted a commission from the Yanks. So have the Count de Paris and the Duc de Chartres."

Many foreign soldiers were attaching themselves to the Union Army as aides and observers, and thousands of bounty soldiers from Europe were filling the ranks. However, the Confederacy was missing no tricks to get recruits. Southern envoys at the Vatican and among the Catholic populations of Ireland and Germany saw to it that tales of Yankee anti-Catholicism were spread. Many of the stories were out of proportion to the facts, but the smart Rebels made the most of the record that at least one Catholic Church had been burned by a Northern mob.

The Confederacy's Conscription Law, drafting men between 18

and 35, had gone into effect, but only comparatively few Southerners waited to be drafted in 1862. They flocked to the colors as rapidly as equipment was available. Many joined to escape the odium of conscription and to get the $50 bounty paid by some companies to each volunteer. By and large, however, the average Southern soldier was a volunteer who was determined to throw the invaders out of Dixie. The South had 400,000 men in the field and was riding the tidal wave of her power.[4]

Wyeth was getting sleepy. He tried to stifle a yawn. "It look likes this is a war of foreigners. Maybe a lot of them are with us, but the Yanks have at least one whole corps of Germans."

"That's true enough," said Frome. "And we can handle anything the North throws at us for a couple of years. But if we haven't won by that time then we will be in a mess. Now you get some sleep."

The two merchants walked away. There still were many questions that Wyeth wanted answered, but he decided they could wait. He simply was too tired to concentrate on questions. He removed his boots and wiggled his toes, wishing for a bath. Then he stretched out and a good tired feeling moved up his legs. He sighed deeply and closed his eyes. His body was relaxed, but his mind was active, jumping from one thought to another. Mostly, however, he was thinking of Mr. Granville and Sharon. Knowing his friend so well, he was convinced that the Englishman would seek any privilege that a pretty woman might allow and a woman in love will allow anything. The thought frightened him. Granville was a rake. But this time he was not concerning himself with a squaw in the fur country, or with a lonely widow. This time it was a Cajan, the cousin of Vespasian Gillivray. And Granville, and Ves and Wyeth were like brothers.

He heard workmen shouting down near the landing and then he heard a rasping that made his flesh crawl. He didn't know how long the rasping continued, but next he heard the happy shout of Mort Kincaid and the wizened old man was yelling, "Gar! By God, Gar."

When Wyeth woke up he thought at first that he was back up on the Yazoo, near the *Arkansas*. The rasping might have been a boat builder filing his tools. Then he remembered where he was and sat up, reaching for his boots. The rasping stopped and Wall Mac-Kenzie approached him, a torch in one hand and a cup of coffee in the other.

"Feel better?" Wall sat down beside him. "It's about three o'clock in the morning."

"I still feel groggy." Wyeth took the coffee and thanked him. "Is it time to go?"

"Just about."

The sailor rubbed his eyes and stretched. "You say your daughter is going, too?"

"You are going with her." Wall stuck the torch into the ground. "You are going in her buggy. I know she'll be all right."

Wyeth said, "She'll be all right."

Wall looked at him steadily and was glad he didn't say any more or that he didn't vow on his honor that Laurel would be safe. Pledges of honor annoyed Wall. "I like the way you talk, Mr. Woodward. I also like the way you don't go around asking questions. There's not much I can tell you."

Then he told him all he knew. The barges of cotton would go up to Grand Gulf by the river. Two Yankee tugs would handle them. Four empty wagons would go overland to Grand Gulf. "The wagons will be a mile or so apart so the Yanks, if you see any, will not suspect that it's a wagon train. You and Laurel will sort of ride herd on the wagons, going from one to the other to see that everything is all right. Each driver has a story in case he's stopped. Laurel's story is that she's going to Vicksburg to visit a friend. She really is."

"Why don't you send the iron by wagon instead of hiding it in the cotton bales and going to so much trouble?"

Wall said, "I knew you'd ask that question. We haven't enough wagons. That iron is heavy. Besides, there are marauders between here and Grand Gulf. The only reason we're sending wagons at all is because they'll be needed at the other end to haul the iron to the *Arkansas*."

Wyeth put down the empty coffee cup. "What do I do in Grand Gulf?"

"You go to the McGill House. It's a boarding house. That's all I know. I'll swear. Nate made the plans and didn't tell me. You'll get instructions at the McGill House."

"All this is too damned mysterious to suit me." Wyeth was smiling but he meant what he said. "Where is Mr. Frome?"

"He's gone. The last of the barges was loaded about midnight. All the barges are out on the river now and Nate is waiting for the Yankee speculators and the tugs to pick 'em up. Laurel is gone, too. She'll meet you at the buggy."

The rasping began again and Wyeth shuddered. "If the men are not still working, then what is that? It makes my flesh run up and down my back."

"That's Mort. He's sharpening his knife. He and Gar won't be satisfied until they can split hairs with their knives."

"I don't know Gar."

"You will. Gar is a Negro. A contraband slave. He and Mort make a team. . . ."

"Friends, huh." Wyeth laughed. "Just last night Mort was yelling about how much he hated 'niggers.'"

"That's Mort for you," Wall said. "He's always talking about how he hates 'em. But you see, he knows Gar. That Negro was a stable boy up in Tennessee when Mort was a trainer. Mort sort of brought him up. They think the world and all of each other now. Gar will handle one of the wagons."

"Who owns him?"

Wall reached for the torch, indicating that it was time to go. "Nobody owns him. It's the damndest thing you ever heard of. Gar belonged to old man Taliaferro up in Memphis." He was careful to pronounce the name Tolliver. "The Yanks took Gar as contraband and old man Taliaferro died. Then Gar escaped and came down here to me."

Wyeth got up, too, and followed Wall. "What's so unusual about that?"

"Old man Taliaferro didn't have a relative to his name. If he had, then Gar would have gone to the kinfolks. But since there are no kinfolks, he's a free slave. He can't go to court and sue for his liberty because he has no standing in court. So he's a slave without a master. The legislature could free him, but it's too busy with the war."

"That's a funny one," Wyeth said. "So the man is legally a slave, but actually he's free." They reached the canal and Wyeth wet his face and washed his hands. Then he began feeling the heat again, and was limp.

"And that ain't all." Wall splashed water on his wrists. "Old man Taliaferro buried $3800 before the Yanks came. Gar dug it up. The money belonged to the estate and so did Gar. He is the estate. I have the money. Gar has no idea how much it is. He can't read a lick or add two and two."

"That's too much," Wyeth said. "A free slave with money and no master. Contraband that walked off from the Yanks and now is helping us. Sometimes, Mr. MacKenzie, this war just doesn't make sense."

They came to the landing and Mort and Gar were squatting there honing their knives. Wyeth stopped and gazed at the Negro. Never before had he seen such a man. He immediately recognized him as a Wolof, a member of that proud African tribe that was sold into slavery almost to a man. He was as thin as a pine, and supple. His hands were huge, out of proportion to the rest of his body and his fingers were as long as Ves' who had the longest fingers Wyeth had ever seen. Gar had a beard, a black woolly beard that tapered to a point. His chin came to a sharp point, too, and his mouth protruded, making a tight bow. His teeth followed the shape of his lips and his mouth actually resembled a snout. His nose looked like a wrinkled leather button. The man was hideous.

Wall whispered, "His mother named him Gar because he looks so much like an alligator gar."

The alligator gar was a predatory fish of the lower Mississippi Basin, a long pikelike fish with hard shiny scales and long narrow jaws. The Negro did look like a gar.

Mort glanced up, saw the two men and jumped to his feet. "Morning, Mr. Woodward. This here is Gar."

Gar stood up, too, and looked at Wyeth. He didn't grin. He just said, "Howdy, Mist' Woodward. Mist' Mort's been telling me about you."

Wyeth mumbled that he was glad to know Gar and then looked down at their knives. The Negro's knife was a long keen blade, its handle wrapped in leather. But Mort's blade was a genuine Bowie. Wyeth had seen many imitations but never before had he seen an original. Gar noticed his interest and picked up the blade. "Mist' Mort's got the best knife along the river. And the best rifle. When he dies, I get 'em. Huh, Mist' Mort?"

"That's right." Mort took his Bowie from his friend. "Cep'n

being black you can't own a rifle. Not if you get caught." He handed the knife to Wyeth. "Rezin Bowie made that one."

The sailor balanced the blade in his hand, admiring it. The Bowie knife was famous all along the river. The first one was made by Rezin Bowie who used it to kill wild cattle. Later, he made one for his brother, James Bowie, who wielded it at the Alamo. The knife had a ten-inch blade and was single edged. The model eventually fell into the hands of a Sheffield house and thousands of Bowie imitations were made. Mort explained that he got his original from a riverman who traded it from Jim Bowie back when the famous warrior visited Natchez before the Texas War.

Wyeth returned the knife to its owner and Mort jabbed it into the earth several times, cleaning it. "Gar borrowed it about a month ago and brought it back last night. I didn't know Gar was around here. Thought he was up around Memphis."

"I thought you hated 'niggers.' " Wyeth couldn't resist the taunt. Gar looked down at him and again he didn't smile. Then he looked at Mort and picked up his own knife.

"Don't call Gar a nigger, you ninny." Mort straightened his wretched little body. "Gar is a Wolof. Niggers are from the Niger River Country. I've known Gar since he was a bare-butted young'un up in Tennessee. He used to hang around my stable. Ain't that so, Gar?"

"Most ever'thing you say gen'ly is so, Mist' Mort."

"I nursed him when he had croup," Mort said. "He was the damndest young'un. Always messing around. Lazier than hell. Always drawing pitchers on the walls of my stable. I used to slap him flat, but he kept on drawing pitchers. Remember that, Gar?"

"They made the stable look pretty," Gar said.

"Pretty, hell. I had to whitewash 'em off every morning. He used to dip a nail in ink and draw pitchers." Mort began laughing at the recollection. Gar laughed, too. It was the first time Wyeth had heard him laugh and he was glad for the laughter. Gar was a serious man and Wyeth didn't understand serious Negroes. They gave him an uneasy feeling.

Wall walked away and Wyeth followed. They went to the tunnel where Laurel had slept and Wall pointed to a small turtleback trunk. "Mort and Gar will help you get that to the buggy. Be careful with it." He opened the trunk and the top tray was filled with

Laurel's clothes. He removed the tray and bottles of medicine were stacked neatly in the bottom of the trunk. Wyeth recognized aloes, belladonna, ginger, aconite and many other remedies used for horses and mules. Then he saw quinine and morphine.

Wall put the tray back in its place. "Laurel knows how to use the horse medicine in case something happens along the road. If nothing happens she will leave the horse stuff at Vicksburg and you will take the quinine and morphine on to the *Arkansas*."

"I'll take the trunk back to the landing," Wyeth said.

"I'll take one end and you take the other," Wall said.

They bent over to lift the trunk and from down near the canal came a mournful singsong chant. Wyeth straightened suddenly. "It's that Gar," he said. "He gives me the creeps."

"That's Mort," Wall said. "That's the way he sings. First time I've heard him sing in days. Reckon he's happy because he's with Gar."

"They sound so much alike I thought it was Gar."

The chant came:

> *"We cannot bear your scorn and pride,*
> *Your malice and your taunting,*
> *That have for years our patience tried—*
> *Your hypocritic canting.*
> *We will not bow our necks beneath*
> *The yoke that you decree us;*
> *We will be free, though only death*
> *Should have the power to free us!"*

Wyeth reached for the trunk again. "Wonder where he learned that one."

"It's pretty popular hereabouts," Wall said, and lifted his end of the trunk and they walked toward the landing.

Then another stanza of the song echoed through the cavern:

> *"We loved our banner while it waved*
> *An emblem of our Union;*
> *The fiercest danger we had braved*
> *To guard that sweet communion.*
> *But then it proved that 'stripes' alone*
> *Were for our sunny South,*

And all the 'stars' in triumph shone
Above the chilly North."

Wall glanced over at Wyeth. "That's Gar."

"How do you tell them apart unless you're looking at them?"

"Most folks can't. I just happen to know 'em so well. They talk exactly alike. Both are illiterate and both love the river and horses. One is a white runt and the other looks like a gar. About the only difference between Mort and Gar is that one is white and the other is black."

That disturbed Wyeth, too. He didn't know why. They reached the landing and put the trunk aboard the skiff. The workshop was almost deserted. A few workers were sleeping near the landing. Gar took the oars. Wall offered his hand to Wyeth. "These men will take charge of you now. I'm staying here. I'll be seeing you, Mr. Woodward."

Gar dipped the oars silently so as not to disturb the sleepers. They moved down the canal where the barges had been and onto the Mississippi. Mist was rising again, hovering over the river. A blast of heat struck Wyeth and he gasped for breath. The land and the river were in the grip of a torpor. Gar, however, didn't seem to mind. Far down the river a bell sounded. The *Iroquois* was changing her watch. The barges were down the river, too, loaded with iron for the *Arkansas*. Wyeth let his hands trail in the river, but the water was tepid. Dawn was about an hour away.

Gar rowed about four hundred yards and then they hid the skiff and Wyeth and Gar lifted out the trunk. Mort led the way, his snipper rifle in the crook of his arm. They climbed to the top of the bluff, pausing often for breath. Wyeth was ringing wet with sweat. Gar kept looking at him as though he felt sorry for any man who couldn't stand a bit of heat. Finally the Negro said, "You are about whupped, Mist' Woodward. I'll tote the trunk."

"Don't worry about me," Wyeth said testily. "I'll handle my part."

Laurel was in the buggy on the path by Mort's cabin. She greeted Wyeth and he heaved a big sigh when he put the trunk down and spoke to her. She was wearing the same dress of the day before. Mort and Gar strapped the trunk to the back of the buggy. "We'll be going now," Mort said. "Give us about an hour's head start."

The two rivermen disappeared into the night. Laurel said, "Their wagons are just over the way. Mort will lead off and Gar will follow in fifteen minutes. The other wagons will move at intervals. We go last."

"Then there's nothing to do but sit here and wait," Wyeth said. "That's the most pleasant job I've had since I arrived. Why don't you take a nap?"

"I will." She moved around until she was comfortable and then put her head on the back of the seat and relaxed. Wyeth took off his hat and let his head rest on the back of the seat, too. He was looking up at the sky and then was aware that Laurel was glancing his way. "Why, Mr. Woodward. Your hair is curly. The damp mist has made it curl."

"Yours is curly, too," he said. "I noticed it when I first came up."

"We will have to reach the Oliver Place by nightfall." She changed the subject quickly. "They're expecting us and if we're not there by dark they'll start looking for us." She closed her eyes and they both were silent. Then she opened her eyes quickly, "Oh, I forgot. I'll bet you are hungry." She reached into a box and brought out some hard boiled eggs and fried chicken and gave them to him.

Wyeth ate slowly and Laurel went to sleep. When he finished his breakfast he went up to the well near the cabin and drew a bucket of water. He drank his fill and took a dipper of the cold water to Laurel and waked her up.

"Dawn is coming," he said. "It's time to go."

"Yes, I reckon we'd better be on our way. I will drive first because I know the trail. You can see Natchez back yonder. She is just waking up. You'd better take one last look at her. You may never be this way again."

Wyeth turned around and looked down the bluff at the sprawling old town. Then he saw the *Iroquois,* lazying at her anchor. "I'll see her again some day."

"Natchez?"

"The *Iroquois.* I'm going to rake her with hotshot one of these days. And I'll see Natchez again, too."

"Are you sure?"

"I'm sure. It is your home and I'll be this way again."

He didn't realize that his words thrilled her, but it thrilled him just to say them.

Chapter Five

T HEY left the trail along the bluff and reached the main river road by the time the sun gathered all of its strength and began cooking the land in a slow even heat. Wyeth held the mare to a conservative gait, but the horse sweated and foamed under her harness. The land was intolerably still, blazing white along the road and green in the woods. The horse kicked up tiny clouds of dust and the dust spread and settled.

The Missourian was rather glad to be away from Natchez. The place depressed him, for, in spite of its money, Natchez was barren. Capital of the new, raw get-rich-quick South, the town paid homage to the gods of materialism and thought that silver doorknobs, damask and mansions really were important and proof of culture. Yes, he was rather happy to be away and heading for the war again. There is something clean about battle.

Laurel and Wyeth talked enthusiastically for the first hour or so and then their conversation dragged and they sat there in the buggy, limp and spiritless. The leather seat was wet and sticky, but the dashboard was hot to the touch.

The morning was about half gone when Wyeth let the mare increase her pace and overtake the first wagon. The driver ignored them until Wyeth said, "Where you going?"

The driver looked up. "To Bruinsburg. Got to get a load of corn."

Then they all laughed. It was the story he was to tell the Yanks if the occasion arose. He stopped his team and Laurel got out and looked at his mules, and then waved him on. They passed the next wagon about ten minutes later and all was well.

Wyeth knew they were approaching Gar, for he heard the Negro singing. Even the man's songs disturbed him and aroused within him a strange feeling of melancholia. It was something he didn't understand. He didn't feel sorry for Gar. Yet it seemed to him that the ugly man with the tapering beard was the embodiment of all the Negroes he had known. Many Negroes sang happy songs, but Gar's songs had a yearning about them, a plea. A bit of defiance, too. And they were proud songs, a challenge for a chance. The dignity of the man upset Wyeth. Yet this time he was singing:

> *"We're free from Yankee despots,*
> *We've left the foul mudsills,*
> *Declared for e'er our freedom—*
> *We'll keep it spite of ills.*
> *Bring forth your scum and rowdies,*
> *Thieves, vagabonds, and all;*
> *March down your Seventh regiment,*
> *Battalions great and small.*
> *We'll meet you in Virginia,*
> *A Southern battle-field,*
> *Where Southern men will never*
> *To Yankee foemen yield."*

Wyeth and Laurel rounded a bend and Gar's wagon was in sight. He was holding his mules in check, nursing them to save their strength. The Negro looked back when he heard the buggy coming. He didn't smile, but said solemnly, "Good morning, strangers. My name is Gar and I'm going to Rodney for a load of cottonseed." Then he smiled, a slow toothy smile. He wasn't so hideous when he smiled. "Ever'thing is all right, Mis' Laurel. My mules are always all right. I sees to that."

"We heard you singing," Laurel said. "Do you know the latest parody on *Dixie?*"

"How does it go?"

Wyeth reined the mare alongside Gar's wagon, and Laurel tapped her foot against the dashboard, then sang:

> *"Oh! have you heard the latest news*
> *Of Lincoln and his kangeroos;*
> *Fight away, fight away, fight away for Dixie's land.*
> *His minions they would now oppress us,*
> *With war and bloodshed they'd distress us!*
> *Fight away for Dixie's land.*
> *Abe Lincoln tore through Baltimore,*
> *In a baggage-car with fastened door;*
> *And left his wife alas! alack!*
> *To perish on the railroad track!*
> *Fight away for Dixie's land."* [5]

Gar listened to the words and hummed while Laurel sang. "I'll remember 'em," he said.

Wyeth said, "Don't you like Lincoln? I thought most colored people liked Lincoln." He didn't know why he said "colored people." He thought Gar might like that. He was embarrassed before this man and felt humble and slightly guilty of something.

Gar didn't change his expression. "I ain't got nothing much against Mist' Lincoln."

"There's talk that he is going to try to free the slaves," Wyeth looked away when he said it.

"It'll take more than him to free us. A little old piece of paper ain't going to free nobody. Besides, if the Yankees free us then what are we going to do? Will the white folks let us work?"

Laurel changed the subject. "Where is Mort?"

"He's about four or five miles up ahead. He's making tracks."

Wyeth touched up the mare and they waved a farewell to Gar. They wanted to check with Mort before the caravan stopped for a noon-day lunch. "You know," the Missourian said when they were out of Gar's sight, "that Wolof bothers me."

"How?"

"It's something I can't put my finger on. But every time he looks at me he seems to be asking me for a chance."

Laurel didn't say anything and Wyeth watched the road and was pensive. Eventually, the girl spoke. "The slaves are going to be free some day. The South will free them. Then what?"

"White men will still keep their feet on the necks of Negroes."

Laurel said, "Papa says that you can't keep a man down in a ditch without staying in the ditch with him."

Wyeth said, "My father used to say that as long as one man is a slave, then no man is free. I've never thought about such things much, but that Gar gets me. If he is ever free what will happen to him? He can't read. We won't let him work at what he'll want to do."

"Do you want to work with a Negro?" Laurel was watching him intently.

"No. I suppose not."

"Do you want to do business with a Negro? Buy clothes and such things from a Negro merchant? Borrow money from a Negro banker?"

"No. Of course not. But it won't have to go that far."

"Oh, yes it will if they are really going to have real freedom."

Wyeth shook his head. "It's too much for me. When I was a boy we used to buy butter and eggs from a Negro. What's the difference in buying butter and eggs and in buying—well, a steamboat? Buying is buying."

"It has got to be faced," Laurel said. "And men like you have got to face it."

Wyeth sighed and said, "I suppose so."

Laurel pushed her feet against the dashboard and stretched. "Mort *is* making tracks. It might take us an hour to catch him at this rate."

"Shall I drive faster?"

"No. This is killing weather on a horse. And on me, too." She put her head on the back of the seat and closed her eyes. Wyeth noticed that beads of perspiration were on her upper lip. Her hair was dusty and grime was forming on her palms. He liked her then more than at any time since they had met. She was sharing danger with him and wasn't complaining about the heat or the work, and was not eternally talking about herself. He had seen many Southern women who made loud promises and then complained because silk was no longer available. Laurel, however, was willing to work for the Cause; do man's work, and sweat. She was only as big as a minute, but to Wyeth she was becoming as important as a whole day, and life is timed by days.

He slowed the horse to a steady walk and Laurel's head fell lower and lower until it was on his shoulder and she was asleep. Wyeth drove on for a mile or so, his sharp eyes taking in everything.

The buggy reached a sprawling bend and Wyeth scouted the surrounding woods in a few glances. Then he closed his eyes quickly and opened them. The heavy silence oppressed him and a warning seemed to slip into his blood and pound against his brain. He didn't want to frighten Laurel, so he let her sleep, but held the horse to a crawl.

Then he saw it. Through the woods and around the bend. It was Mort's body dangling from a scrub oak. The little man's feet were only a few inches from the ground and his warped body was swaying slightly.

Wyeth took a deep breath and tried to check the pounding of his heart. He reined the mare to a stop and Laurel woke up. "What is it?" she asked.

"Yanks. Just around that bend."

She took the reins and he felt for his knife and pistol. "Let's cut through the woods," he whispered, "and maybe we can miss them."

Laurel looked at him. "Those Yankees didn't pass us, so they came from the other way. Mort is up there."

The scar showed on Wyeth's face again and his clefted chin was set. "Laurel. Mort is dead."

"Are you sure?" The blood left her face, but she didn't cry out. She clamped her lower lip and braced herself.

"I'm sure. They hanged him. I saw his body through those trees."

She touched the mare with the reins and they moved on. "We've got to face them. If we try to slip by and they catch us, then we'll be in trouble."

They drove around the bend and there by the side of the road not twenty yards from where Mort was hanging were five bushwhackers. One was a Northern soldier. Another wore the coat of a Federal cavalry officer. The others were in dirty denims. Laurel scarcely glanced at Mort's body, but kept her eyes on the guerrillas.

The leader, the one in the officer's coat, stepped to the middle of the road and stopped them. "Where to?" he said it rather politely.

"I'm going to Grand Gulf," Wyeth said. "My business is my own."

[73]

"Maybe," said the man, and three of his companions gathered around him. The fourth went to the tree and cut down Mort's body. He didn't want a lady to see the sight. "But maybe not. I might have to make it my business."

Laurel was looking straight ahead. Wyeth said, "It looks like you have made somebody else's business your business. Have you the authority to hang a man without trial?"

"He killed a man. He killed a man last night down near Natchez. We had him dead to right."

"Who was he?"

"Old man Kincaid. We've been after him a long time."

"Well, I suppose you know your business. It's none of ours."

"And if I were you," the man said, "I'd keep my mouth out of it. That man who was killed was shot out of a boat at two hundred yards. It took a real shot to do that and old Mort Kincaid had a good eye. The man was a darkey, but he had on a Federal uniform."

"Is that all the evidence you had?" Wyeth forced a smile, thinking the smile might convince them that he really wasn't interested.

"Nope. The man was killed by a snipper bullet and as soon as I saw it I knew it came from old Kincaid's snipper gun. He was the only man around here who had one. We got the gun."

"Well, it's too bad." Wyeth took the reins from Laurel's hand and her hand was cold. He pressed it. "May we go on?"

"Going together?" The man looked closely at Laurel.

"I am taking this gentleman as far as Port Gibson," she said calmly. "Then I am going on to Vicksburg. To visit a friend. Mrs. Nelle Simpson, just in case you want to check. I am Laurel Mac-Kenzie. Everybody in Natchez knows my father."

The man stepped back. "Yes'm. I recognized you. I'm sorry you saw him hanging there. It ain't a nice sight for a lady."

The men's horses pricked up their ears and their ears shot forward. Wyeth felt the blood grow sluggish in the pit of his stomach and Laurel was taut, for from down the road came Gar's voice. He was singing, *Sometimes I Feel Like a Motherless Child.*

The men fingered their rifles. The leader said to Wyeth, "Pull your horse over to the side of the road. If there is shooting, I don't want you to get hit."

Neither Wyeth nor Laurel dared look at Gar when the wagon

rounded the bend and stopped. Then Wyeth stole a glance toward the Wolof and saw that he was peering at Mort's body, stretched on the ground in the blazing sun. The Negro's expression of calm indifference didn't change.

"All right," the leader of the men said to Gar. "Where you going?"

"Old man Mort Kincaid." Gar said it slowly. "So you finally caught him. Did you find my gun?"

The Negro's cool nerve brought a gasp of admiration from Wyeth and he looked closely at Gar. The Wolof didn't betray any emotion. He just looked from one face to the other.

"Your gun?" The leader demanded.

"That's right, Mister. Mist' Kincaid took a snipper off'n me right after the wah started. I ain't saying where I got it. He took my knife, too. And a hoss. That's the hoss right over yonder hitched to that wagon."

"You've got no business with a rifle."

"Maybe not. Maybe so." Gar wrapped his reins around the iron bar that supported his wagon seat. "A heap of folks are doing things now they ain't got no business doing." He looked at the guerrilla captain, and the white man averted the gaze.

"Describe the gun. And the knife."

Gar gave every detail of the weapons. The bushwhacker shifted his weight nervously and glanced around at his men. "I was sort of aiming to keep that gun. Is it for sale?"

"It ain't for sale. 'Course, there ain't no way I can make you give it to me. I reckon you had a right to stop a white man on the high road and hang him. The Secesh in Natchez are going to be rightly put out, though. And the regular Yankee troops may have a heap of explaining to do. It ain't none of my business."

The guerrilla said, "Get your horse and tie him behind your wagon. I'm your friend. Now what do you know about this?"

"I ain't seen a thing." Gar took the weapons and went over and got one of Mort's horses, the best one. He stopped near the body. Wyeth heard Laurel's deep breathing and his own hands were trembling. "What are you going to do with this?" Gar looked down at the corpse, then led the horse to the rear of his wagon and tied him.

"We'll bury him," the bushwhacker said.

"It ain't none of my business," said Gar, "but he'd fit rightly nice in the river."

"That's a good idea. We'll sink his body."

Gar got back in his wagon. Wyeth saw his eyes then and they were cold, the coldness of impenetrable blackness. His lips were tight, too. The Negro nodded towards Laurel and Wyeth. "What about them?"

"They ain't talking." The guerrilla was relieved that the situation had eased so favorably. "I know the man. He was in Natchez yesterday. He likes cotton. And he ain't no Secesh. The lady is Wall MacKenzie's daughter. She's all right." He bowed to Laurel and motioned for them to be on their way.

Wyeth struck the mare with the ends of the reins. The horse shied and clamped her bit. Wyeth held her to a rapid walk. He didn't want the bushwhacker to think he was too anxious to be away. Gar gave his mules the reins and they followed the mare, lumbering along.

Laurel's first words were, "Poor Gar."

"He is crazy mad," Wyeth said. "I saw it in his eyes."

Laurel got out her handkerchief and wiped her face. Wyeth wondered if she were crying and was relieved when he saw that she was not. "Mort would want to be buried in the river. Gar knew that."

"There's no need of talking about it, Laurel."

"I know that, Wyeth. We knew that Mort wouldn't live long and he knew it, too." She put her handkerchief away. "It's going to break Papa's heart. Mort had his faults, but he was a friend."

"Why don't you cry?" he suggested. "It might make you feel better."

"I can't cry. Maybe it hasn't dawned on me yet. It was so quick, Wyeth." She didn't realize she was using his first name. "We were riding along and I fell asleep and when I woke up Mort was dead."

Wyeth looked back down the road. "We are safe now. Gar is waving for us to stop."

The wagon came alongside and Gar got out and took off his hat. "They've gone to the river. They'll camp around here som'rs and bushwhack and steal cotton." The cold light still was in his eyes. He reached under the wagon seat and got Mort's Whitworth Snipper rifle and handed it to Wyeth. "You take it. Maybe somebody on the *Arkansas* will need it."

Wyeth didn't argue, knowing the danger of the slave carrying a gun. It was against the Black Code for a slave to arm himself and the penalty was severe. "I'll look after it properly," Wyeth said. "But it's yours."

Gar didn't surrender the Bowie. From under the seat of his wagon he pulled a horsehide box and opened the box quickly as though he didn't want the white couple to see its contents. He put the knife in the box and then climbed back onto the seat. "There ain't noth-ing fit'n to say, Mis' Laurel. I know you were rightly fond of Mist' Mort. I ain't forgettin' them that killed him."

Laurel said, "We will stop for the night at the Oliver Place, Gar. Mr. Woodward and I will go on ahead and you keep your eyes on the other wagons. I'm pretty sure there are no more marauders be-tween here and Rodney." She nodded to Wyeth and he touched up the mare and they soon were out of sight of Gar.

"That Wolof is going to revenge Mort," Wyeth said.

"I suppose so. The regular United States officials would punish those bushwhackers if they knew the truth."

"Maybe. Maybe not. Those men acted high-handed, all right. They should have taken Mort to the proper authorities. You can bet your last dollar that if Confederate bushwhackers hear the story there will be the devil to pay. They'll string up two Yankee sympa-thizers."

"Perhaps it would be best for us to make a report."

Wyeth shook his head. "No, Laurel. Let Gar handle it."

They lapsed into silence and there was no sound except the soft noise of the mare's hooves digging into the road. They stopped once and rubbed the horse down, but didn't give her water and did not allow her to eat. Then they resumed their journey to Rodney,* a thriving town of four thousand. Two miles from Rodney was the Oliver Place and they were there before sundown.

The Oliver family, an old man, his wife, a consumptive daughter and an aunt, didn't question them, but escorted them to their rooms, and slaves fetched water. Wyeth bathed and shaved. Old

* Once an important river town, Rodney now is shown on few maps because it became a ghost town in 1876 when the Yazoo and Mississippi Valley Railroad was built, and missed the town. The river also has changed its course and the hamlet now is three miles inland.

man Oliver gave him a change of linen, and Wyeth and Laurel ate supper with the family. The death of Mort was not mentioned. Neither was their mission. Laurel was too tired to talk and Wyeth answered the few questions that the Olivers asked, questions about the well-being of Wall MacKenzie and Nate Frome.

After supper, Laurel retired. Wyeth was rather sorry. He wanted her company for awhile. He wanted to sit on the verandah and watch the river. Mr. Oliver gave him brandy and a cigar and they went to the gallery and watched the night close about the land, gripping it.

"Hottest summer I can remember," Mr. Oliver said. "Wells that have never gone dry before are now as dry as a powder house. The temperature hit 112 degrees in my fields today. Two men fell out."

"I have an idea this spell is going to break up in a wild storm," Wyeth said.

"That Negro Gar showed up a little while ago. He's sleeping in his wagon out near the barns. Wouldn't go to his cabin. What's eating him?"

"Search me," said Wyeth. "He's a funny one. Looks like a nightmare, doesn't he?"

"What's in that box he carries?"

"I haven't the slightest idea. Why?"

Mr. Oliver inhaled of his cigar and blew the smoke around his head to drive away the mosquitoes. "One of my bumboes offered to take care of it for him and got his hands on it. Gar knocked him down and stomped him."

"I reckon he just doesn't want anybody fooling with his box. Even a Negro is entitled to have a few private possessions." He got up and yawned. "I'm whipped down, Mr. Oliver. Will you excuse me?"

"Certainly, Mr. Woodward. I'm going in, too. The mosquitoes are getting bad. Just one thing. A string of barges is about two miles south of here. Making pretty good time, I hear. The river's so low that there isn't much channel."

"Moving right along, eh?"

"That's right." Mr. Oliver yawned, too. "Two tugs are handling them. Yankee tugs, but some men the Yanks hired in Natchez are running them. Mighty good men, too. They know how to make time. By running all night, I'd say they'd get to Grand Gulf late tomorrow."

"Thanks."

Wyeth began then to form an idea of Frome's Grand Gulf plan. They went inside and a slave lighted a candle and showed Wyeth up to his room. The young Missourian didn't waste a glance on the slave, but was thinking about Gar. Wyeth was incapable of worrying about the plight of a race, but an individual was another matter. He lay in bed, rolling and tossing and cursing the heat. Then he heard a tug whistle from the river, one long blast followed by three sharp ones. He wondered if it meant anything and got up and went to the window. The light of a lamp was streaming from out the window just below him. Then the light went out.

He heard footsteps on the stairway and cracked the door just a bit. Mr. Oliver and his consumptive daughter were walking down the hall. Wyeth said, "If I leave the door open then I'll get more air in my room."

"That's right," said Mr. Oliver and took an unlighted lamp from his daughter.

"Careful," she said. "It's hot, Papa."

"I heard the tug," Wyeth said.

"You can go to sleep now, Mr. Woodward." The daughter's drawn face was pallid in the shadows. "I heard you walking around." She smiled at him. "I hear very well. Sometimes, too well. Did you see my light go out?"

"Yes'm."

"I have a friend on one of the tugs. I was telling him that you and your party are here. Then I put out my lamp." She looked at him and Wyeth drew back. There was fever in her eyes. She seemed to read his thoughts and laughed almost hysterically. "Yes, before long my lamp will go out forever." She said it poignantly in the low dramatic tone that dying persons sometime affect. "I just hope I'll live long enough to see the *Arkansas* come by here, and to see every dirty Yankee in the world dead and in hell."

"Come on, daughter," Mr. Oliver said, and led her away.

Wyeth went back to bed and was nervous. He wanted to be away from this accursed land where men worked in caverns and a Wolof wore a pointed beard and guarded a strange box, where a dying woman flashed signals with a lamp and where the heat baked his brain and curled his spirit. The land was too moody, too mysterious, too sad. The river crawled by and there was no rush or snap to it. The moss was too heavy and the trees were too tall. He wanted to be back with Ves and Mr. Granville and Dolly. Then he began wondering where Laurel was sleeping and reasoned that she might be in the next room. Thinking of her, he was unable to sleep.

A horse neighed out near the barn and the echo of galloping hooves came to him. That took his mind away from Laurel and he went to sleep, steaming in his own sweat.

To the exhausted sailor, it seemed the night scarcely had begun before a slave came to his door and shook the knob gently, a signal that he was coming in. The man was shielding a candle with his hand and called softly to Wyeth, then put the candle on a table. The western sky still was black, but there were traces of gray to the east. Wyeth swung his feet out of bed and sat there, his head in his hands. He attempted a deep breath, but his nose was stopped up. Then he sneezed. Even in such heat, he was catching cold. His head hurt, too, and there was a vile taste in his mouth. A bit bilious, he reckoned.

He rinsed his mouth with salt water and for the first time in his life allowed a slave to help him bathe. The Negro had him stand in a tub and poured cold water on him, but the water closed his pores and Wyeth soon was as limp as a wet towel.

Laurel and Mr. Oliver were at breakfast, but the remainder of the household still was sleeping when Wyeth went to the dining room. The girl had been weeping and her eyes were red. Her face was pinched, too, and there was a suggestion of circles under her eyes. Wyeth nodded a greeting and accepted coffee. The punkah over the table was swinging back and forth, circulating air in the room, but the slave who operated it was sweating. He was sitting on a stool near the door, slowly pulling a cord that ran through a pulley in the ceiling and caused the punkah to fan the room.

"Everything is ready, Mr. Woodward," Mr. Oliver said. He raised a glass of whiskey and wished the Missourian good fortune. Wyeth thanked him. He had seen Mr. Granville drink so early in the morning, but thought of whiskey on an empty stomach made him cringe.

"I'll need luck," Wyeth said. "I'm going blindly into this thing."

"You are not blind, sir," Mr. Oliver cleared his throat. "There are a hundred eyes seeing for you. And, by the way, a messenger rode by here a little while ago. He came from somewhere up the road and was going to Natchez with a report to Nate Frome."

"Yes?"

"Uh huh. He said to give you a message from a friend of yours. The message is, 'Tell Woodward I'm dry and intend to take a drink to Dolly about sundown today.'"

Granville! Wyeth tried not to show his excitement. Laurel, however, felt his sudden elation and she, too, was elated just because he was. The limpness went out of Wyeth and he was alert again. "So the affair at Grand Gulf will be over by sundown," he said.

"Yes," said Mr. Oliver, then turned to Laurel. "If you are through with your breakfast, my dear, you might as well pack. You'd better be on the road by sunup."

Wyeth said, "I'll meet you out at the buggy, Miss MacKenzie."

"All right, Mr. Woodward. I won't be long."

The mare had been hitched to the buggy and over near the barn was Gar's wagon, ready to roll. The Wolof was waiting by the wagon. Mort's horse was tied to the rear axle. Wyeth examined the harness, pretending to know something about it. He had a feeling that Gar was laughing inside at him. So he said, "I don't know why I did that, Gar. I don't know much about horses."

"Yes suh," the Wolof said.

Wyeth patted Mort's horse, then looked searchingly at Gar. "No, I am not much for horses. But I do know this one is mighty hot."

"I used him to haul some wood for Mr. Oliver befo' you got up." Gar was stroking his beard and seemed to know that Wyeth knew he was lying.

"Very well." Wyeth saw traces of foam on the horse's back, proof that he had been saddled and ridden hard. "But, Gar, I want to warn you to be careful. If you kill white men, even Yanks, the folks down here won't stand for it. You know that."

"Yes suh."

"How many did you kill last night?"

"Just one, Mist' Woodward. Knifed him. I'll get the others. I've got lots of time."

The fact that the Negro told him the truth so readily was evidence of his faith in the white man.

"Where were they?"

"Camping down near where they hung Mist' Mort. The one that was wearing that Yankee coat was on guard. I cut his throat, then rode back here." The Wolof spoke simply and without emotion. It came to Wyeth then that the man expected aid from him if aid should be needed. It was a strange feeling, an uncomfortable feeling, a feeling of responsibility.

Wyeth glanced at the horse-hide box under the wagon seat. "You'd better give me that Bowie. If any questions are asked, let me answer them."

Gar threw a ragged blanket over the box, but reached to his side and got the Bowie and handed it to the sailor. Then he stood there, his long fingers running over his beard, his little black eyes piercing Wyeth's guard.

"If anything is said," Wyeth mumbled, "I killed that man last night. The Yanks will hang me anyway if they catch me, but the folks down here will be glad if I knifed the man who killed Mort."

Gar said, "Yes suh." But there was a sparkle in his eyes and Wyeth believed he had touched a spring in the man's spirit. The Negro no longer was fathomless to the white man. They had something in common and for a minute Wyeth was able to forget that Gar was black. He was a comrade then. The thought buoyed the Missourian.

Laurel joined them and they got underway, veering northeast toward Port Gibson. "Did you sleep well?" the girl opened the conversation.

"Just fair. And you?"

"All right, I guess." She looked back at the Oliver Place. "I feel sorry for the Olivers. Miss Oliver is dying and her mind is going." She took off her bonnet and shook her head, then ran her fingers through her brown hair. "You know, yesterday you called me Laurel. But this morning you went back to Miss MacKenzie."

Wyeth was in no mood to do any explaining or to carry his end of a casual conversation. He was worried about what faced him at Grand Gulf. Uncertainty is a cloak that smothers confidence. However, he didn't want the girl to know that he was nervous for she might think he was afraid. So he said, "If Mr. Oliver heard me call you by your first name he might misunderstand."

"Misunderstand what?"

"Oh, I don't know. Just misunderstand. I've only known you since day before yesterday."

"I don't mind if you call me by my first name," she said frankly. "I rather like it. But some other folks might think it's improper. So I tell you what let's do."

"What?"

"We can call each other by our first names when nobody else is around. That is, if you want to."

Then they both laughed. It seemed sort of silly. But it wasn't. It was important, and they knew it. The sun burst upon them and Wyeth's cold vanished. He felt somewhat gay, and tapped the mare. He switched his hat to a jaunty angle and they laughed again.

"Mr. Granville is somewhere around," he said. "Everything is going to be all right."

"You have a heap of faith in him, haven't you, Wyeth?"

"I reckon you can call it faith. He's a good man to have around when trouble is borning."

"You know that Sharon Weatherford is in love with him."

"I don't know anything of the sort," Wyeth snapped.

"Wait a minute, Mister. Don't bite my head off. Is it a sin for a woman to be in love?"

Wyeth slowed down the horse for a bend and peered into the woods, then gave the mare her head and let her swish around the curve, throwing dust. "I'm sorry, Laurel. And I might as well tell you. I'm worried about Mr. Granville and Sharon. She is a cousin of our best friend. She's barking up the wrong tree because Mr. Granville just doesn't marry his women. I might as well be frank."

"You were," she said and was not embarrassed. "But even if he loved her, he couldn't marry her and hold his head up."

"Why not?" he demanded.

Laurel sat erect and her little chin came up. Her gray eyes snapped. "Now, look here, Wyeth Woodward. Don't be on pins and needles with me. You know well enough that Sharon is a Cajan and that Cajans may have Negro blood in them."

"There's no proof of that."

"Sharon's aunt was sold into slavery. . . ."

"That doesn't mean a thing. In the slave system, any dark person might be seized and sold.[6] There are Moorish slaves down here." His face was white and the scar showed again.

Laurel's face was set. "Take a deep breath, Wyeth, and cool off. Don't jump down my throat. If I were a man and loved a Cajan I'd marry her and let the world go whistle up a stump."

"So would I," said Wyeth. "And so would Mr. Granville if he really loved a Cajan."

The sailor's thoughts floated away to Grand Gulf and he was irritated and fidgety. He simply did not feel up to more conversation and then it came to him that perhaps Laurel knew he was nervous and was talking to keep his mind off of his mission.

"Where is all of this going to lead us?" she said. "Have you read Dr. Nott and Dr. Morton?"

"I haven't had time for much reading. . . ."

"Dr. Morton is a Northerner and he and Dr. Nott say that man did not come from Adam and Eve. They argue for a plurality theory, that there are several distinct types of mankind. Other scientists say the Negro is the inferior race."

Wyeth said, "Maybe all of that is just an excuse for white men to think they are superior to Negroes. I know the Negro is inferior when it comes to money and education and all that. But take Gar, for example. He's smart. I know he's brave. And he knows more about some things than I do. Horses, for one. Now suppose instead of studying horses, he'd studied steamboats. Couldn't he be a good steamboat man?"

Laurel leaned toward him. "If I tell you something, you'll never tell on me?"

"Never."

"Charity is as black as midnight. She nursed me and she learned to read when I did. Just by watching me with that picture book I told you about. She learned the words by sight."

"It's against the law down here to teach a Negro to read," Wyeth said.

"I know it. But look, some folks say Negroes can't learn important things and then they have to pass laws to keep them from learning."

"You talk like an Abolitionist," Wyeth laughed and turned his face toward her. The circles were gone from beneath her eyes.

"I hate Abolitionists," she said. "They are hypocrites. Some of them live on profits from the slave trade. They take Negroes North and then forget them, and they starve. Why don't they clean up their own houses?"

Wyeth agreed and nodded his head slowly. "I don't like the things they say about us. We are not immoral scoundrels. I don't cuss out all Yankees just because some of them are rascals. Mr. Granville says the Abolitionists are beating the drums for Yankee politicians and businessmen who are determined to wreck the South and run the country. That's why I'm fighting. As much as I hate this war I am not going to let the Yanks come onto my land and steal it." The speech made him feel better.

Laurel looked away and rubbed her hands on her handkerchief. "I know all of that. But we are fighting for slavery and I have an idea that you and I don't believe in it."

"I believe in living, though. And we're fighting for our lives. We're fighting a revolution and the Declaration of Independence says revolution is our right. Abraham Lincoln said not so long ago that if folks get tired of a government they have the right to dismember it or overthrow it by revolution."

"Fiddle-de-de, but you can really talk when you get wound up." Laurel glanced around for familiar signs as the mare pricked up her ears. They were nearing Port Gibson. "You talk like a lawyer. You are a funny man. Sometimes you clamp your jaws and don't want to talk, but once you get started you talk a blue streak."

"I wish I was a lawyer. . . ."

"You!" She tilted her head and her laughter startled the horse. "Papa says lawyers are leeches and that they cause a lot of our troubles."

Wyeth bristled and his face reddened. "Some merchants are leeches, too."

At her direction he halted the horse under some shade and they waited until Gar's wagon came into sight. The other wagons were not far behind. The girl got out their lunch and Gar went over the ridge for a bucket of water. They refreshed themselves and rubbed down the animals. Then they drove into Port Gibson.[7] The town, shaded by huge trees and resting in the curve of Bayou Pierre, impressed the Missourian. The place was clean and contented, not too rich and not too poor. This was the kind of land that Wyeth liked; rolling land that tumbled down to clear streams, guarded by oaks and friendly pines that were willing to share the earth with other trees. They went to a livery stable and the owner, after a few pleasantries, fetched a saddled horse. No money passed hands for the hire of the mount. The owner handed the reins to Wyeth and then went away.

"You leave us here," Laurel said. "Grand Gulf is that way." She pointed toward the river.

Gar came up then and said, "I'm going with Mist' Woodward. I'll take Mist' Mort's hoss."

Wyeth started to protest, but Laurel said, "All right, Gar. We can handle your wagon."

The sailor swung onto his horse and was conscious that he didn't sit a good saddle. He looked down at Laurel and tipped his hat. "We will meet again."

"If God wills." She bit her lower lip to still her tongue.

Gar got his box from his wagon and mounted, holding the box under his arm. Wyeth asked Laurel to hand him the snipper rifle and he held it in the crook of his arm. Then without another word he headed his horse down the pike along the little railroad that connected Port Gibson with Grand Gulf. Gar was a few paces behind him.

Neither man spoke until they reached The Hermitage, home of General V. G. Humphreys, classmate of Robert E. Lee at West Point until he was expelled for participating in a Christmas riot. They stopped their horses near a creek and Wyeth handed the rifle and Bowie to Gar. The Negro put the knife in his box and balanced the rifle across his saddle. "If anybody says anything I'll tell them you are toting them for me," Wyeth said. "You have a right to defend yourself."

The Wolof didn't comment, and they rode on.

Grand Gulf was five miles from The Hermitage, and about a mile from their destination they stopped again and rubbed down the horses because they didn't want anyone to suspect that they had been riding so hard.

"You'd better watch yourself in Grand Gulf," Wyeth said. "I don't know what I'm getting into."

Gar said, "I'll be hanging around near the woods. I'll watch you."

He opened his box and took out his Bowie and put the knife at his side. Then he looked at Wyeth out of the corners of his eyes. "This box has been bothering you, ain't it?"

"Sort of." He didn't lie and neither was he patronizing.

"If I let you see it you won't tell anybody? And you won't laugh?"

"No. It's your business."

Gar put the box on the ground and opened it. Wyeth didn't know what he expected, and he almost laughed when he saw the jars of paint. The Wolof said, "I paint pitchers."

"That's good looking paint. Where did you get the money to buy it?"

"I made the paint. I made it out of clay and oil, and bark and roots. These here are my brushes." He held them up and Wyeth took one and examined it. He didn't know much about such things. The brushes were crude. One was a bit of sweet gum chewed at one end. Another was made from strands of a horse's mane glued to a stick. The Negro was watching his friend intently. "Sometimes I use my trigger finger as a brush. Just dip it in paint and spread it on."

"What do you paint?" Wyeth was impresed and felt humble, and didn't know why.

"Just pitchers. I've been painting on one since yestiddy." He reached into the box and got a smooth pine board and gave it to Wyeth.

The sailor frowned. The picture was a river and there was haze over the water. The river was blue. "What is it?"

"That's the Mississippi," Gar said. "I ain't done with it yet."

"The Mississippi is not blue."

"It oughta be blue, Mist' Woodward. It seems sort of blue to me just because it oughta be blue. A sort of a whispering blue."

Wyeth looked sharply at the Negro. "What is whispering blue?"

"Blue that whispers."

"What does it say?"

"Nothing much. It just whispers. It just sorta says that 'I'm a river and God made me, and I'm doing the best I can.' There is a whispering blue and a singing blue, and a blue that yells at you. Red yells at you, too. It plum' hollers at you. You don't know what I'm trying to say, do you?"

"I think I do," said Wyeth. "And I think this is a very pretty picture."

"No you don't, Mist' Woodward." The Negro was hurt. "You're just saying that."

"Well, maybe it's not pretty, but it does whisper to you."

"What does it say to you?"

"It says, 'I'm a river and I'm tired of just being the same old river every day, but that's what I'm here for.'"

Gar began stroking his beard again. "Some day I'm going to paint a pitcher of the river a'flooding. When she's cutting up. Because she's not always the same and when she gets tired she up and does something about it."

"We'd better be going," Wyeth said. Something in the Negro's tone bothered him.

"When I finish this pitcher I'll give it to you if'n you want it."

Wyeth thanked him and they cantered to the outskirts of Grand Gulf and then parted. Gar went into the woods and Wyeth rode up the cliff under which nestled the thriving little rivertown.* From the top of the cliff he could see the Warren County Courthouse at Vicksburg, twenty-five miles north. Grand Gulf, named for the eddies formed in the Mississippi by the current from the Big Black River, was among the most important commercial centers along the river. Its cotton was barged down the Big Black from as far away as Jackson. Cotton also was brought in over the railroad to Port Gibson, a line so rough that Joseph Jefferson, the actor, screamed in indignation when he played in Grand Gulf. A sandstone cliff jutted into the Mississippi just below the mouth of the Big Black and Wyeth took in the scene from the elevation.

He wiped the sweat from his eyes and they smarted when he stared at the river, shimmering in the dazzling heat. Then he saw the thing he feared; a sleek Union gunboat. By her lines he recognized her as the *Scioto*. Her starboard guns were in battery, scowling at the town. Wyeth gaped at the center gun. It was a 13-inch Dahlgren capable of hurling a 280-pound shot. The gun weighed 36,000 pounds and was the biggest gun on the river, although the United States was using 20-inch Rodman guns for siege work. The Rodmans weighed 100,000 pounds and threw 1,000 pounds of steel.

* Time, war and the river destroyed Grand Gulf. Today there's one store and a few houses left. The government has set up a Geodetic Survey Station on the cliff.

Farragut had ordered the *Scioto* to cover Grand Gulf while he went up to Vicksburg. They hadn't told Wyeth that back in Natchez and he was furious. Then he convinced himself that Frome didn't know it himself. Well, to take several barges of cotton from under the gunboat's nose was a task he didn't relish.

He looked down the river, his sharp eyes piercing the lather of haze, and he saw the barges creeping along, the tugs huffing and straining. They should reach Grand Gulf in an hour or so. The outside tug sounded its whistle and the tow swung to larboard. Wyeth saw then that the cotton bales were stacked so that there were tunnels between the bales. He was convinced then that he knew Frome's plan and was angry at himself for being frightened.

He took one more look at the gunboat, swallowed his heart that seemed to be in his throat, and entered the town, riding by huge stores stocked with fancy goods from New York and Liverpool. He saw a dozen grog shops in one block and stopped at one and got directions to the McGill House.

The boarding house was near the Big Black River and a Negro took Wyeth's horse. The Missourian took a deep breath and walked up the path to the house. At the side of the dwelling an old man was raking rubbish into a pile. He waited until Wyeth was near the steps and then approached him. The sailor introduced himself.

"Want lodging, huh?" The old man spat.

"That's right."

"I'll be right with you. Got to burn this rubbish." He walked to the pile and lighted it. Then he threw on some pine boughs and black smoke spiraled up. "Guess you think I'm crazy having a fire on such a hot day. But I wanted to get rid of that rubbish before the rain comes. And rain's a'coming. The weather's going to change because it's time for a new moon."

Wyeth wondered if the old man heard his sigh of relief. His confidence was returning. He knew that back near the cliff Gar was hiding and felt that the snipper rifle was covering the McGill House. And back there somewhere was Granville.

He gave the countersign and watched the smoke. It could be seen for a long ways.

Chapter Six

THE innkeeper led the way to the second story of the dwell ing, a gray house with tall shutters and high ceilings. The inn faced the Big Black and was only about one hundred and fifty yards from the wharves. The shutters were opened wide to admit any breeze that might come that way. There was nothing distinctive about the house except that eight windows and the doorway faced the river.

When they reached the second floor, the old man showed Wyeth to a room and then introduced himself as Rockland Bradford, a riverman. "Folks gen'ly call me Rock," he said. He had fought in the Texas War with Sam Dabney and in the Mexican War with Jefferson Davis and Keith Alexander. That was his only claim to fame and the subject of his conversation when people would listen to him.

He mentioned it casually to the Missourian and when Wyeth didn't show any interest the old man grumbled and began instruct ing him for the duties at hand. He called Wyeth to the window and nodded toward the Big Black. "The tugs will line the barges up along those wharves. The speculators will come up here to see you."

Rock's calm demeanor irked Wyeth. "And what will that gunboat be doing?"

"Sort of nervous, ain't you?"

"You're damn right." Wyeth took off his coat and threw it across

[90]

a chair. "You'd be, too, if one of those Dahlgrens were looking down your throat. If one shot is fired that gunboat will blow this town to hell and back."

"I reckon so." Rock watched the *Scioto* and then turned to Wyeth. "You'll go down to the barges with the men to look at the cotton. A man don't buy nothing sight unseen. That's all you got to do."

The sailor was so exasperated that he flopped on the bed and glared at Rock. "All I do is go aboard those barges like a kitten walking into a pack of hounds. Of course, it's not important, but I happen to be a Confederate gunner and out of uniform. I value my neck."

"Me, too," Rock said. "But when you get on the barges you're going to be surprised. Maybe I'll be surprised, too, because I don't know exactly what's up."

"Where will you be?"

"Right behind this window with a gun aimed at the man nearest your left hand."

That was better. "Don't miss." Wyeth sat on the side of the bed and took off his shoes and rubbed his feet. "What else?"

Rock went down stairs and returned with a leather satchel, dropped it on the floor and shoved it under the bed. "That's money."

Wyeth jerked the bag between his feet and opened it. "What the hell! There's not this much gold in Mississippi."

"T'ain't gold. Just looks like gold. It comes from up in Arkansas and we stamped it out and shined it up. The Yanks have been printing counterfeit Confederate money and passing it on us, so we aim to pay 'em back. We've used that same satchel and them same pieces over and over."

"Suppose they look at the money?"

"If you let 'em examine that bag then you're a bigger fool than I think you are. That's all. Want a drink?"

"No. Maybe some cold water if there's any cold water around here."

Rock walked to the door. "Rain's a'coming and things will cool off. Don't blame you for being a mite upset. But if one of them men make a move toward you we'll cut him down."

"Then the gunboat will open up." Wyeth went to the washstand, filled a bowl and scrubbed the dust from his face. "How would you like that?"

"Well, hell can't be no hotter than this." The old man closed the door.

Wyeth got out his pistol and checked it. Then he put his shoes back on and went to the window. He heard feet scraping in the next room and his door opened and two men grinned at him. Each had a rifle and one said, "We'll be working at the next window if you need us." Before he could speak they closed the door again and Wyeth breathed easier.

He stood by the window and his muscles tightened and that sluggish feeling came back to his stomach as he saw the barges creep by the *Scioto*, then wheel into the Big Black. He forced himself to look away, fearing that even at such a distance somebody on the gunboat might see him and be curious about his interest. He looked up and the smoke from the rubbish was wafting away. The smoke was a dirty gray now, and suddenly it was beaten earthward by a wind current.

Smoke beating downward meant rain and while the sailor was watching the smoke, a black cloud rolled up in the west. It came from nowhere. One minute the sky was clear, and then it was black. The Missourian had seen sudden tropical storms before and they always fascinated him. The sun dropped west of the clouds, between the black mass and the horizon. A gust of wind swept across the Mississippi, stirring it and rocking the *Scioto*. Sailors on the man-of-war began scurrying about spreading tarpaulins, covering the deck carronades and securing the guns. The wind whipped the American flag into action and it began snapping.

The people of the town poured out of grog shops and stores and hurried for their homes. Shutters were banged closed. The wind caught the rubbish pile and scattered it. In a minute or so the streets of the town virtually were deserted save for a few men who huddled under trees along the river waiting for the shower to come and go. The casual little groups were scattered, but Wyeth's sharp eyes picked up every detail and he saw rifles lashed to the branches of several trees.

He pursed his lips and his lips were dry. So was his throat and his heart was in his throat, jumping. If a fight started then Grand

Gulf could be blown apart by the huge Dahlgren. He wondered why the Confederates hadn't fortified the cliff. A battery up there would command the river and Farragut might have been stopped. He assumed, and quite rightly, that the Confederacy couldn't spare guns for Grand Gulf and that they had been taken by surprise when the Federals swept up the river from New Orleans. He wondered, too, why Farragut hadn't seized the town and garrisoned it. That was just another Yankee slip. Or so Wyeth thought.

The rain came in a deluge and a roar, a deep who-o-o-shhh sound. It blotted out everything for a minute and then it ceased abruptly. The big cloud broke up; then raced together again and hail came, walloping the land, flaying it. Branches were peeled from the trees and weeds and grass were beaten flat. The hail was gone as quickly as it came and the cloud disintegrated. The whole storm lasted only a few minutes and the earth was hot, steaming hot this time.

That was just a teaser. Nature was playing a game and cutting capers. Soon she must cease her fun-making and get down to business. A rain had to come. Nature owed a debt to the lower Mississippi and she always paid. The earth had a right to draw on the sky for succor from the heat. Men were suffering, but, more important, the fields were parching and the grass was in torment. Nature is good to grass. So a good rain was on its way. That knowledge lightened Wyeth's spirit. He actually began humming.

The barges eased alongside the wharf and from off the tugboat came four men. They looked around and approached two loiterers under a tree. The loiterers pointed toward the McGill House and Wyeth stepped back from the window, licking his parched lips. Sweat poured into the palms of his hands and he wiped them. And waited.

Rock showed the strangers to Wyeth's room and when they asked him if he were Mr. Woodward he nodded and they came in, and Rock closed the door. Alone with the men, Wyeth's fears vanished and he was calm again. He looked the men over carefully. Three were cotton speculators and the fourth was a Union officer who didn't mind dirtying his hands for a profit. The sight of the uniform angered the sailor and his face flushed. That caused his scar to show and one of the men laughed and said, "You've got a nasty one there, Mr. Woodward. Looks like a Bowie cut."

"I assume, gentlemen, that you're ready to do business."

"You bet," the spokesman of the crowd said. "My name is Wells. I'll do the talking for us. The cotton is right down there."

Wyeth said, "Your money is right here." He reached under the bed and dragged out the bag.

"Gold, of course?"

"Naturally, Mr. Wells."

A second man moved toward the bag and said, "Mind if I see it?"

Wyeth's face was burning again and the scar was vivid. The man drew back. Wells said, "No offense, Mr. Woodward. He's new. We heard about you in Natchez and your money's good." He turned to his companion. "Don't be a fool. Use your head. Mr. Woodward wants to stay in business and so do we."

"Thank you, Mr. Wells. *You* may examine the money if you care to." He offered the bag to the speculator. "I hope your cotton is just as good as my money. You can bet I'm going down to the barges and look at what I'm buying. I never have any trouble getting good cotton."

Wells forced a laugh. "I wouldn't offend you, sir, by counting the money until the deal is struck. Believe me, we want to be friends. Come on and look at the cotton and let's get this thing over with."

The Missourian reached for his hat. The Union officer opened the door. Wyeth brushed past him, swinging the bag. "How are you going to get the cotton away from here?" the officer asked.

"That's my business."

"We are going back on the tugs," the officer said. "You may be stuck up here with a fortune of cotton. There are Confederates about twenty miles east of here."

"Confederates do not bother me," Wyeth snapped. "I am not in uniform. I am a neutral and trade with both sides. But I hope, sir, that they never catch you. Or that your government never learns that you are speculating in cotton while your men are fighting."

The officer paled and Wells said, "Let's not argue, gentlemen."

The men walked out of the house and down to the river. Wyeth didn't glance back, but he felt the rifle sights were following him. As they approached the barges, the master of one of the tugs walked by, and then proceeded toward the Mississippi and the *Scioto*. "Where's he going?" Wyeth demanded.

Wells said, "Probably out to the *Scioto* to learn about the return trip. We hired him in Natchez. If it hadn't been for him we might have got here sooner."

"Yes?"

"He tied up late last night. Said fog was too thick. We laid over for an hour along a bank where mosquitoes were as big as horses."

The memory of the Oliver girl and her lamp came back to Wyeth and the spirit of the game made his nerves tingle.

They reached the first tug and along the deck was stacked a row of Plymouth rifles. Wyeth took in everything. The tugs were ready for trouble. The sailor glanced back at the McGill House, then toward the woods where Gar was. His eyes roamed down to the *Scioto*. Then he stepped aboard the first barge just as the second tug master came up.

"We've got to move up stream a bit, Mr. Wells," the riverman said. "We're blocking the wharf here and it's against the law for tugs to leave barges against the wharf."

Wyeth's blood seemed to freeze and his palms were wet again.

"That's all right if the *Scioto* is informed," Wells said.

"They know about it," the master replied indifferently. "My pardner went down there and told them and they just signaled for us to move up to that bend."

Wyeth leaned against a cotton bale and watched the tugs get under way, nursing the barges into a huddle and then nosing them up the Big Black. The sun was going down and that quick still twilight was almost upon them. He put the satchel at his feet and tried to appear nonchalant. Wells was gabbing and his associates were watching the river bank. Wells was saying, "We bought this cotton in Natchez. If the folks who sold it could have got tugs they might have come up here and got all the cream. But we tied up every tug man in town and got the boats from some military nabobs. Important men."

"Uh huh." Wyeth pulled his elbows close to his body, then released them. That relaxed him a bit. He was so tense that his temples pained him and he knew his scar was showing.

The tow crawled around a wooded bend and the *Scioto* was out of sight. So was the McGill House and Wyeth felt desperately alone. The tugs inched the barges along to the side of an abandoned, crumbling wharf and banked their fires. Steam hissed slowly from the safety valves and frogs, disturbed by the steam, began sounding protest. Shadows were racing across the Big Black, pursued by darkness.

"All right, Mr. Woodward," Wells said. "How does the cotton look to you? When you buy you can leave your barges right here as long as you want. Of course, we're not responsible for their safety."

Wyeth glanced around, playing for time. "The stuff on this barge looks pretty good. But I want to look at the other cotton."

He and the speculator turned to step from the barge to the wharf when the voice came from the other side of the barge. "Don't move a peg. And don't put up your hands."

Wells and his comrades froze, but Wyeth wheeled toward the sound and cried out, instinctively, "Pass out those Plymouths!" His own pistol was out.

Wells, so frightened that his words ran together, yelled, "We are attacked!"

A hatchet hurled from across the barge felled him. The Federal officer crouched behind a bale, his pistol in hand. A long knife thrown from underneath the wharf pinned his shoulder to the bale. The voice on the larboard side of the barge called out, "I told you not to move. Don't blink an eye!"

Wyeth saw the man's cap then, sticking an inch or so from behind a pile of bales. He saw the gray shirt and the Enfield rifle, sure signs of a Confederate, and while he stared the owner of the gun climbed to the top of the bale and approached them, his piece cocked. Then from out the narrow passageways between the bales on every barge poured Confederates; guerrillas, Marines and Regulars. Wyeth had an urge to whoop. However, he had presence of mind enough to restrain himself and kick the money bag into a crack. None of the other men uttered a word. The Federal officer pulled the knife from his shoulder and clamped his hand over the wound. Wells stirred, got to his hands and knees, and slowly to his feet.

The tugs began hissing loudly, drowning all other noises, and the frogs bellowed. The Confeds scrambled over the bales and popped out of a dozen holes. Most of them were grinning as they fanned out along the bank and on the barges. Quickly, noiselessly, they went to their posts. The *Scioto* was unaware that the tow was in

Confederate hands, less than a mile from the prow of the Union gunboat.

The efficiency of the coup so impressed Wyeth that he peered to the north, across the Big Black, expecting more soldiers from that quarter. His back was to the wharf when he heard the words, gay and careless, "That's all, gentlemen. You've been very kind."

The Missourian gulped and turned quickly just as Simeon St. Leger Granville crawled on his hands and knees from beneath the wharf. Wyeth almost laughed at the sight of the Englishman on his knees. Then Granville straightened. He had a bone handled revolver in his right hand and a cutlass in his left. He scowled at Wyeth, then at the others. "Stay just as you are and you will live to tell your grandchildren about this, you thieving bastards."

Wells leaned against a bale, his head hanging wearily. The Federal officer pointed to his wound and mumbled, "I'm hurt." The other speculators stood stock still. Wyeth watched Granville. The Englishman yanked a handful of cotton from a bale and began rubbing mud from his Wellington boots. Then he brushed his clothes and turned to a Marine at his elbow. "Tell the tugs to get underway. Slowly. Tell them to use dry wood. No pine, or fats. We want no smoke."

Wyeth surrendered his pistol when Granville asked for it. "Piracy is one way to win wars," the Missourian said.

"So it is," Granville said. "All of you get over there and hug those bales. Look sharply now. I don't want you to be seen."

Wells started to protest and Granville pushed him gently. Wyeth did protest and the Englishman grasped his shoulder, spun him around and shoved him against the bales. That was too much. The scar flashed down Wyeth's cheekbone. He swallowed his anger, however, when as saw the twinkle in Granville's eyes.

Without speaking, the Union officer pointed again to his wounded shoulder. Granville handed him some cotton. "Wipe it with this. You like cotton. You are not going to die."

Two of the guerrillas came up and retrieved the hatchet and knife and then sat on top of the bales. The tugs kicked off from the wharf and moved away gently. There was no smoke as they nudged the barges upstream, hugging the bank. The *Scioto*, swaying in the strong current of the Mississippi, was left to her peace. Grand Gulf disappeared from sight, too, as the prize slipped away, and darkness enveloped the land. The stars burst out and there was the shadow of a moon, a new moon. A bell sounded on the *Scioto* and the gunboat's lookout cupped his hands and cried that all was well, never suspecting that around the bend iron for the *Arkansas* was inching up the Big Black, safe from the Union guns. The *Scioto* changed her watch and the men grumbled at the monotony of war on the Mississippi.

The coup took less than ten minutes and not a shot was fired. Soon the barges were far enough up the Big Black to be assured safety from the gunboat which could not navigate in shallow water.

The reaction came to Wyeth then and he was weak and almost nauseated. Granville forbade any words until the tow of barges was about a mile up the Big Black and then he sent word to the masters of the tugs to lay to, and they put the barges along the right shore near a protecting bluff. They banked their fires, keeping an even head of steam in their tugs. A glow from the grates lighted the barges.

Wells, rubbing his bruised back where the hatchet had struck him, said to Granville, "I suppose it is out of order to ask an explanation?"

"It would be silly," Granville said. "We're taking this cotton, the barges and the tugs."

"And us?"

Granville ignored him. "And we are taking your money," he said to Wyeth and reached down and lifted the satchel, passing it to an orderly.

Wyeth said, "I have a permit from the Confederacy to buy cotton. May I ask who you are?"

"I am an officer of the Confederacy's Horse Marines."

"Your humor is very impressive," Wyeth said. "The Confederacy has no Horse Marines down here."

"And neither have you any permit. The Confederacy doesn't buy cotton. It grows it." He turned to the Northern officer. "How is the wound, Yank?"

"Not too bad. Am I a prisoner of war?"

"That is correct."

"Is there anything I can do?"

"You can blow your brains out. We will furnish the pistol.'

Granville's tone was grating, contemptuous. "These other men are speculators, scum, cowards and leeches. But you are a soldier who has disgraced his army."

The officer didn't wince. He held a wadding of cotton to his bleeding shoulder. "I have money. Mr. Woodward has a lot of money. . . ."

"So your name is Woodward?" Granville smiled at Wyeth. "We've heard about you. I am taking you to Jackson to check on that permit."

Wells said, "What about us?"

"Some of my men will see you to safety. We do not take civilians. That *would* be piracy. They will escort you over to the Natchez Trace. You can find your way from there."

"They'll shoot us," one of the other speculators said.

"These men do not waste lead on weasels." Granville motioned for an escort and six Confederate infantrymen came to him. "Take these three men with you. Free them tomorrow."

"In the swamps?" a sergeant asked.

"I don't give a damn. Just get them out of my sight."

The soldiers ordered the speculators off of the barge. Wells told the officer and Woodward goodby. He shrugged his shoulders and said, "It might have worked. The game was worth the candle." He bowed to Granville. "Tell me, sir, how much did you pay the captains of the tug boats?"

"Nothing," Granville said. "You paid them enough."

Wells actually smiled. "Are you going to sell the cotton, sir?"

Wyeth's tongue stuck to the roof of his mouth and he thought surely Granville would strike the man. But, instead, the Englishman twisted the ends of his mustache, then yanked off a handful of cotton and handed it to the speculator. "Eat it. You like the damn stuff so much, eat it. Chew it up."

Wells looked into Granville's eyes and took the cotton and began chewing it.

"As for you," Granville said to the other speculators, "reach for your own. Get a good handful."

The others began eating cotton, too. Granville leaned against a bale and looked Wyeth over casually. "Help yourself, Mr. Woodward."

Wyeth began spluttering protest. Granville snatched a handful of cotton and jammed it into his friend's mouth. "It is good for you."

The Confederate onlookers laughed and Wyeth was so furious that he almost choked. He chewed the cotton, however, and gulped some of it down.

"God's shirttail!" Granville guffawed. "You gentlemen do like cotton." He motioned to an orderly. The speculators were marched off, still chewing, and the darkness swallowed them and their escort.

The Englishman summoned another guard. "Take this Yankee officer to your camp and turn him over for imprisonment. Get him away from here. We are in a hurry. There are decent Yankees waiting to be killed."

Soon the officer was out of sight and Wyeth spat out all the cotton he hadn't swallowed. "Damn you, Mr. Granville. . . ."

"Shut up," Granville said.

"What have I done wrong? I did as I was told." Wyeth accepted his pistol from his friend.

"It would have tasted better with salt, eh, Wyeth?" Granville sat on a bale and laughed. "By God, you looked funny. Wait until Ves hears about that."

"I'll make you eat cotton one of these days if it's the last thing I do," Wyeth sat on the same bale, and they both laughed.

Granville slapped his boots with his open hands. "You are a hero, Wyeth. A modest, bloody hero. We have got iron enough to finish the *Arkansas*. And men to help build her and man her. Marines and swamp rats." He waved his hand at the Confeds sprawling on the bales. "There is part of our crew. A motley assortment, eh?"

"They'll do," said Wyeth.

"And now that that task has been done, may I have a drink, you pap-loving nurse-maid?"

"I'm going to have one, too." He was as happy as a child home from a trip to strange lands. He was always rather subdued around Granville, but now he felt closer to the Englishman than ever before. And he was confident, too. Granville gave him confidence. He did wish, however, that his friend wouldn't twirl his mustache. It was the gesture of a fop. But Granville loved his mustache and pointed beard even more than his distinguished sideburns and white-flecked hair, and almost as much as his bone-handled pistol, a heavy weapon built for heavy duty.

They went aft along the barges to the larboard tug, the power boat on the left side of the tow, which was not being towed at all, but pushed. On seeing Granville, the master of the seized tug broke out a bottle of whiskey from his medicine chest.

The whiskey excited the Englishman so much that he forgot his manners and neglected to present Wyeth to the captain. Only drink could make Granville forget such a thing. He reached for a tumbler and drank in gulps. The master eyed Wyeth and shook his head.

"You saw my family last night," the riverman said. "How was my sister?"

"Then your name is Oliver?" Wyeth offered his hand.

"Yes. Prentiss Oliver."

Granville put down his glass. "Excuse me, gentlemen. Mr. Woodward, Mr. Oliver. Prent Oliver, late of Captain Raphael Semmes' command. Wyeth Woodward, the best gunner's mate in the Confederate Navy." The Englishman's eyes were becoming watery and red, and his lips were forming into a snarl. Whiskey always did that to him. It made Wyeth unhappy to see the change in his friend. Under drink, Granville, usually precise, got haughty and loquacious. His tongue thickened quickly, and he was boastful and ill-tempered.

Wyeth accepted a drink from Prent Oliver and said, "Yes, I was at your house last night. Your sister is very sick."

The riverman took a small swallow of his drink and stared at the floor of his tug. Then he called his engineer, checked his steam pressure and gave orders for the tow to proceed up the Big Black to Rankinson's Ferry. He gave his engineer a drink, and returned his attention to Wyeth. "My sister is dying."

"She is a brave lady, and very lovely," Wyeth said.

Prent shook his head. "She is not lovely. And I doubt if you know just how brave she is."

Granville finished his first tumbler and filled another. "All women are lovely," he said. "In the dark."

Wyeth ignored him and addressed Oliver. "When did the Confeds board the tow? When you tied up last night?"

"That's right. They came aboard and hid among the bales. Mr. Granville and his men went to Grand Gulf late this afternoon and hid. Everything went off like clockwork."

"But you can never go back to Natchez so long as Yanks are there. They know you now."

"True enough. I am going to stay on the Big Black. I'd like to find Ralph Semmes and sail with him. But I have orders to stay here. Semmes soon will have his new ship, you know.[8] She was launched in the Mersey last April."

Granville began laughing. "The Yankees will raise hell about that ship. Already they are screaming that England is building her."

Wyeth stepped to the deck of the tug and looked around. The sky was overcast and a cool breeze was coming down the river from the northeast, a wet breeze. The Missourian drank in the air and went back to his comrades. "We are in for a rain."

"It's about time," Prent said.

"So you were with Semmes?"

"Yes. On the *Sumter*. I was her pilot down the river when she ran the blockade."

"What do we do now?" Wyeth asked.

"Drink!" Granville wagged his head. His hair was tousled. "Drink until it runs out of our ears. And then for the *Arkansas,* and Dolly. I'm going to shoot the lobe off of Farragut's ear when we come down the river."

"Which ear?" Wyeth asked.

"The left one."

Prent and Granville laughed, but Wyeth was solemn. He went to the medicine chest and counted the bottles of liquor. He knew that was silly, but worry drove him to it. If Granville were beginning a long spree then there was trouble ahead. Prent saw the sailor's anxiety and tried to take his mind off of the problem. "I don't know what we do next. Nate Frome never lets his right hand keep tab on his left. My orders are to tie up at Rankinson's Ferry."

The tow took the inside of a bend where the Big Black cut through Thompson's Bluff. The bluff was one of the series that ran from Natchez to Vicksburg, and once through the bluff, the party left the loess land to the west and entered the rolling wooded lands where farms took the place of big plantations.

Granville finished his bottle and got to his feet and tossed the empty bottle into the river. Then he put his hands above his head and yawned. "That takes care of that. I am just drunk enough for comfort. Wipe that frightened look from your face, Wyeth. That is my last drink until the *Arkansas* is finished."

"Until you shoot Farragut's lobe off?"

"Good God, no. I might miss."

The Missourian's relief showed on his face. Prent was relieved, too. He didn't want the responsibility of having a drunken Granville on his hands.

"I can tell you this much." Prent got up and locked his chest. "We leave these tugs at Rankinson's Ferry and pick up a paddle wheeler. The *Music*. These tugs can't work in the shallow water above the ferry."

The tow cut in close to the bank to take advantage of slack water and the cry from the bank startled the men. They ran on deck as a barge almost scraped the shore. They saw the horse before they saw the man. The rider judged the distance from land to barge, dug his heels into his horse and the animal leaped onto the barge. Granville reached for his pistol. However, it wasn't necessary for Confederate Marines pulled the man from his horse and half dragged him to Prent. Granville took one look at the man, then covered his face. "My God. The D.T.'s! I am having D.T.'s."

The newcomer glanced from Prent to Granville to Wyeth and said in a hurt tone, "You must have been aiming to leave me, Mist' Woodward?"

Wyeth had forgotten about Gar and was ashamed and told his friends who the man was.

Gar began stroking his beard. He had his box under his arm. "I seen you to the river, Mist' Woodward. Then I seen the tow leave. So I got on my hoss and followed. I knew the tow would shave the bank on this bend."

"If you had called to us we would have stopped," Wyeth said.

"I wasn't taking no chances."

A few raindrops splattered against the barges and the Confederates began whooping in delight. Most of the men ducked into the tunnels between the bales. Gar followed Wyeth inside the tug. The rain began gently and then came in torrents.

Prent motioned for Gar to sit on a bench, and asked Wyeth, "What are you going to do with him? He's armed. He has a Bowie in his belt and the boys took a rifle from him."

"They are my weapons," Wyeth said. "He brought them to me. He is going with me. Wall MacKenzie asked me to see that he gets to Vicksburg."

Granville cocked one eye and watched Wyeth. Then he looked Gar over carefully. The Negro returned the look and smiled. He had never smiled that way at Wyeth. It was a smile of tolerance, but not of understanding or fellowship. Wyeth felt the difference then and there. Gar expected something from him because he was a Southerner and the black man and the white man had the land in common, and the yellow rivers. Granville was a stranger. He didn't belong and couldn't belong to that mysterious fellowship of Southerners. Gar always would keep Granville at a distance. Granville might criticize him, but Wyeth could not. Granville might offend him and Gar would shrug it off, but if Wyeth did such a thing then the offense would leave a wound. The Negro expected nothing from Granville. Prent understood and smiled rather sadly when he went on deck to check the weather.

Granville looked at the Bowie at Gar's side, then over at Wyeth. "Your weapons, eh? And MacKenzie told you to take him to Vicksburg? You know, Wyeth, if you could drink as well as you can lie you would be a good companion."

Gar took out his knife and handed it to the Missourian. "You like him, don't you?" He looked from Wyeth to Granville. "He knows all about you."

"Sure I know him," Granville said. "Like a book."

The Wolof put his box behind the bench and his long fingers began tapping against his knees. "Mis' Laurel is at Rankinson's Ferry, Mist' Woodward. I know'd all along she was aiming for there to meet this tow. I didn't tell you because I figured you and me was fixing to get killed at Grand Gulf. Maybe."

The news was a tonic to Wyeth and it was on his tongue to ask when they would reach the ferry, but then he felt Granville's gaze and tried to hide his delight. The Englishman was a bit tipsy, but by no means drunk. The sparkle was returning to his eyes and he said, "Oh, yes. I heard about her. How was the journey to Port Gibson, Wyeth?"

"Quite pleasant," Wyeth said airily.

"Is she pretty?"

"Rather." His answer was blunt. "I have seen women who are more beautiful."

"I am anxious to meet her."

"You shall. But, Mr. Granville, I must warn you that Miss Mac-
Kenzie is different from most women. . . ."

"All women are the same. It's only that some are more so than
others."

"Damn it, man!" Wyeth's scar was blazing. "I get sick of your
stupid sarcasm. Miss MacKenzie is in my care. You can be a gentleman if you work at it, and I tell you I expect good conduct in her
presence."

Granville looked out at the rain, then at Gar, then over at Wyeth.
"Tell me," he looked back at Gar. "Has Mr. Woodward been so
touchy very long? Or just since he met Miss MacKenzie?"

The Wolof said, "Mist' Woodward is rightly fond of Mis' Laurel.
It sticks out like a wart."

"Shut up, Gar." The sailor silenced the Negro with a scowl. "Remember who you are and don't take liberties."

Gar retreated into his shell and was sullen. Granville wrapped his
hands around his right knee and pulled his knee up to him. Then
he stared at the ceiling of the steaming little room on the tug. "Yes,
indeed. I have wanted to meet Miss MacKenzie for a long time.
Several years. I've always wanted to know what kind of woman my
best friend would love."

Wyeth forced a laugh. Gar's mood passed when he heard the
laugh. Granville wagged his head and addressed the Wolof. "Yes,
my old friend and your new one is falling in love."

"I know it," Gar said. "So does Mis' Laurel."

"Go to bed, Gar," Wyeth snapped. "You can crawl into one of
those passageways and sleep."

The Negro picked up his box and started away. "What is in that
box?" Granville asked.

"Some things I'm keeping for Mist' Woodward." Gar was polite,
but his tone was firm. He told the white man goodnight and walked
into the rain.

Granville accepted the rebuke without anger, proof that he was
an Englishman and not a Southerner. "That is the ugliest man I
ever saw," Granville said. "How do you stand him around?"

"I like him."

"Now there's a Southerner for you." Granville shed his coat and
loosened his waistcoat and silk cravat. The tug's boiler, located aft,

made the room insufferably stuffy. "You won't tolerate some Ne-groes and yet you pick up a man who is a first cousin to an ape. Or a fish. It is a shame Charles Darwin didn't meet Gar."

"Who is Charles Darwin?"

"Just another Englishman. You will read about him someday, if you only take time to read." He wasn't aware that his words hurt his friend. A few days before Wyeth would have laughed, but now he was serious, and sensitive because he didn't know who Darwin was and he must be somebody important.

The wind shifted to the south and the rain began falling in gusts, sweeping across the barges. Wyeth and Granville were silent, each in his own mood. The rain made them moody, and lonely. Wyeth was thinking of Laurel. Granville was thinking of Dolly, wondering if Ves kept the big gun covered against such weather. Prent Oliver came back to his tug and reported that all was going well and that they should raise the ferry by dawn. He told the men he was going to catch forty winks and without further explanation he went to his chest and got his Bible. He sat near a lantern, thumbing the pages, then began reading to himself. Granville started to light a cheroot, but changed his mind and sat there staring at the floor and listening to the rain. Wyeth was still, too.

Prent finished a chapter and put the Book on his seachest and closed his eyes. When he opened them, Wyeth said, "Do you read the Bible every night?"

"Yes."

"My father used to do that. But I do not even own a Bible."

"Then take this one," Prent said. "I have another."

Granville lighted his cheroot then. Wyeth accepted the Bible, knowing that Prent wanted him to. The master excused himself and went forward. The Missourian didn't look at the Englishman, but began turning the pages of the Bible. "I wish I knew this Book."

His friend puffed his cigar and didn't reply. Wyeth let his eyes roam over the pages until the words arrested him and he read them to himself, his lips moving slowly. "The words of the wise are as goads, and as nails well fastened are the words of the masters of assemblies, which are given from one shepherd. And furthermore, my son, be admonished of making many books there is no end, and much study is a weariness of the flesh."

He closed the Book and he, too, began staring at the floor, then at the rain.

Granville said, "What did you read?"

"That 'the words of the wise are as goads.' "

"There is much knowledge in the world, Wyeth. But not much wisdom. What is wrong with you? Is something bothering you?"

The sailor said, "Oh, I don't know. There are so many things I don't understand. I don't understand why this and why that."

Granville knocked the ash from his cigar. Some of the ash fell on his boots and he brushed it off. He reached for the Bible and found what he wanted and read aloud, "to everything there is a season, and a time to every purpose under the heaven. . . ."

" 'A time to be born, and a time to die,' " Wyeth added. "I remember that."

"Everybody does, but few stop to think what the words really mean. 'A time to kill, and a time to heal; a time to mourn and a time to dance; a time to seek, and a time to lose.' Can you finish it?"

Wyeth went to the door of the tug. The bank of the Big Black was hidden by darkness and rain. The barges were groaning. From one of the passageways, snug against the weather, came the song of the Confederate Marines. The sailor looked over at his friend. "Sure, I can finish it. 'A time to keep silent, and a time to speak; a time to love, and a time to hate; a time for war, and a time for peace.' " He walked out of the room and into the rain and found his way forward. Then he sat there on a cotton bale and let the rain fall on him. He took off his hat and the rain felt good to his head.

He didn't hear Granville approaching, but was not surprised when his friend sat down beside him. "I thought I understood you, Wyeth. But now I'm not so sure."

"I wish I was a wise man," Wyeth said impulsively. "There are so many things I don't know."

"That is wisdom. Only the wise realize how little they know."

"I wish I knew law."

"Law is not hard to learn. But it's damn hard to respect." Granville turned up his coat collar. "You have a conscience and a conscience is a taskmaster. Miss MacKenzie has touched something in you. I hope it is love."

"I think it is, Mr. Granville."

"That Gar has touched something in you, too. I think I know what it is. That is why I think you are the finest man I ever knew. You are so damned decent."

It was the first time Granville ever had said such a thing to Wyeth and the Missourian was amazed. It simply never had entered his head that his friend liked him as much as he liked his friend. "I wish I knew as much as you, Mr. Granville." It was the only thing he could think of to say.

"And I wish I knew how we are going to finish the *Arkansas* and bring her out. I'm frightened."

"You!"

"Yes. And so are you. I have an idea we may not have long to live. Remember that when you see Miss MacKenzie. And don't let that conscience of yours prevent you from taking all that life offers."

"There's a thing on my mind," Wyeth said quickly. "How did Sharon Weatherford take your departure?"

"I will not discuss that. She is a beautiful woman. Too beautiful to be left alone. . . ."

"She is in love with you, Mr. Granville."

"That is just too damned bad."

"What if Ves finds out?"

Granville's cigar was cold. He jerked it from his mouth and threw it into the river. "So you want to know law, huh? You ask questions as a lawyer does. You expect to get four from two and two. I am sorry I ever met Sharon Weatherford. I hope I never see her again, but I know I will. Man always goes back to good wine. I will not explain my behavior to you or Ves or anyone else." He walked away seeking a dry spot.

Wyeth was very miserable. The prospect of a break between Mr. Granville and Ves made him miserable. The three men had been together so long and had shared so much. He hated Sharon Weatherford then.

The sky opened up and the rain came in torrents again. Prent woke up and took command. Wyeth heard him shouting orders and the barges were run along the bank and tied up. The pilots couldn't see in such weather and the river was tricky. It was a good time to catch some sleep and Wyeth ducked into the nearest passageway.

Then he heard the horse stamping on the first barge of the tow. His sharp eyes pierced the weather and he saw the horse leap from the barge to the bank. "It's that damn nigger," somebody shouted.

The darkness swallowed Gar and Wyeth wondered what kind of weapon he had. Wyeth had the Bowie. He walked over to the tug and got his Bible and put it under his coat. The words kept echoing in his mind—"A time to kill, and a time to heal." Then he found Granville and went to sleep near his friend. The rain beat a lullaby and the frogs and night things bellowed and buzzed their gratitude for the rain.

Chapter Seven

RANKINSON'S FERRY was the first crossing of the Big Black north of Thompson's Bluff and Grand Gulf, and was a haven for barges plying between the upper reaches of the tributary and the Mississippi. There was no town at the ferry, but nearby was the home of the widow Wright and W. Lumin. The ferry operator lived in a shack on the bluff and reported for work when a customer pounded an iron bell tied to a mayhaw tree. The bell was gone now; its iron had been rolled into plate for the *Arkansas.*

An acre of barges, tied just below the ferry, nudged and bowed to the whims of the stream. Most of the barges were loaded with produce, but two carried dismantled cannon, rifled 32 pounders and eight-inch naval guns. The *Music,* a shallow-bottom paddle wheeler with a low-pressure boiler, was tied in deep water. She was a crazy looking thing, an odd craft with a make-shift super-structure near her stern and a pilothouse forward. A tall gin, really a crane, was amidship. It was made of three pine trunks, braced at the bottom and drawn together at the top. A heavy rope ran over a spindle on the top and was looped over a steam winch on deck. Frenzied hands had converted the little river steamer into a workshop, a tender for any Confederate fighters that might get a chance to operate on the lower Mississippi.

The *Music's* armor was cotton bales and her armament was a

pivot howitzer on a casement carriage near the bow. The Confederacy's Battle Flag was flapping from her stern mast, popping in the early morning breeze.[9] In many ways, the *Music* was a sad looking craft, but saucy.

Pickets were on duty at the ferry, protecting their fellows who were sleeping on the bank and barges. The rain was gone, blown south, and the sun was struggling up, blazing angry because of the long climb. The earth was sweet-smelling and humming. Prent Oliver's tow of barges hugged the channel, parting the river in the final surge to the ferry. All aboard the tow were sleeping except Prent and his crew.

Blue jays darted and circled over the tugs, scolding and bluffing attack. Doves and thrush called from the fields and larks sailed the sky. A medley of trees lived in close communion along the banks, none lording it over the others; redbud and oak, bay and magnolia, dogwood and mayhaw. Pitch pine took the high ground and cypress took the low ground, and there was ample ground for all. The woods were warm with color and hummed as the land went about its business of living and dying.

Prent wheeled his tow toward a landing, then reached up and pulled his whistle cord, blowing one long blast. The noise awakened the men on his barges, including Wyeth and Granville.

The young Missourian woke up with a start, then remembered where he was and crawled out of the passageway. He studied the faces of the group at the ferry, but Laurel wasn't there. Gar was, however. He was slumped forward on Mort's horse, sound asleep in the saddle.

Granville joined his friend and they went to Prent's tug and had coffee and bacon and grits. Wyeth remembered Gar's box and got it, and he and the Englishman went on deck again while Prent jockeyed his barges for a landing.

"So she's not here yet," Granville said. "I don't see any girl in that crowd." He realized Wyeth was disappointed and changed the subject. "But I see that black ghost of yours." He pointed toward Gar. "Looks like he has been out all night. What the hell?"

"Don't ask me," said Wyeth. "Look at those guns on that barge. Thirty-two pounders. Rifled. Wonder what's up?"

Granville lit his first cigar of the morning and brushed his clothes. "I have an idea we may try to fortify Grand Gulf."

"How do they get those guns down here?" The sailor dipped his hand in the river and wet his face and hair.

"From Jackson. And they bring them there on trains." Granville twisted the ends of his mustache and combed his hair with his fingers, preening himself.

"But this river doesn't run by Jackson. . . ."

"No, you looney. But there is a railroad from Jackson to Vicksburg. And this river runs under the railroad up near Bovina Station. They bring supplies out from Jackson to Bovina and then transfer them to barges, and the barges come down here and on to Grand Gulf and the Mississippi. Is that clear?"

"Uh oh. Bad humor again, eh? Big head?"

"Not on one quart," the English gunner snorted. "Look at those trees, Wyeth. There is some fine timber there."

"That's a fact," the Missourian said, wondering where Laurel was. "A few of those trees would be enough for a house."

"House?" Granville inhaled of his cigar. "Huh, those cypress and oak are ideal for gun carriages and those pines for spars. There is some hickory on that hill. Best mortar bed timber in the world."

The barges ground to a landing and the two gunners stepped ashore, followed by the Marines, Regulars and guerrillas. The crowd at the ferry landing welcomed them with shouts. The tumult aroused Gar who dismounted and walked toward Wyeth.

"She'll be along t'reckly," the Negro said. "She spent the night at Mrs. Wright's. She's all right, Mist' Woodward. She busted out crying when I told her you made it."

"Here is your box, Gar. You left it on the tug."

"I know'd you look after it."

"How far did you have to ride last night?"

"Pretty far." The Negro used his foot to scrape dirt into a little pile, then kicked the pile down.

"What did you use?" Wyeth asked.

"My hands. And a pine knot."

"How many?"

"Just one, Mist' Woodward. I'll get around to the others. I ain't got nothing but time."

Wyeth tugged at his pants and adjusted his suspenders, then blinked up at the sun. The earth was still again and the sun was in command, priming for work. The heat wave was coming back from its short retreat before the rain. "We'll be here awhile," the sailor said. "Maybe you can sort of slip back yonder into the woods and get some rest."

Granville and Prent were standing by a tug watching the men haul the bales off the barges and line them along the bank. When Wyeth approached, Granville said, "Salute him," and nodded toward Prent. "He is now Lieutenant Commander Oliver of the Black River Fleet, C.S.N."

"Well, now," Wyeth said, drawing himself erect. "When did this happen?"

Prent didn't reply. His face was haggard and his jaw was squared. Granville said, "His orders from the Navy Department and Secretary Mallory were waiting here.[10] Now he can sport gold stripes and his pay is $2,550 a year. Confederate money, naturally. And his stripes will cost him about half a year's pay—if he can find any."

Still Prent didn't reply, and neither did he smile. He commanded a crew to start ripping into the bales where the iron was hidden. They stacked the iron at the river's edge.

"The Black River Fleet." Granville laughed merrily. "What a war. That is the Black River Fleet, Wyeth." He pointed to the *Music,* the stolen tugs and the barges.

The new commander apparently didn't hear him. He was staring at the cannon on the flatboats. His silence puzzled Wyeth, but Granville kept talking. "You know, Commander Oliver, I would like to have some of this cypress up on the Yazoo. It would make a fine carriage for my Dahlgren."

"You'll have cypress for your gun," Prent said gruffly. "The timber around here is good, but the best timber comes from over in Lebanon. You'll have some of that."

"How can we get it?" Wyeth asked. "Lebanon is fighting us. Do Keith Alexander and Hoab Dabney sell us timber?"

"Alexander does," Prent said. "He'll sell anything."

"Everytime I turn around I hear about that cove," Granville said. "What a rogue. A bravo, eh?"

Prent scowled and said, "You two should get along well. At 20 paces. Now, I have work to do. . . ."

"Begging the commander's pardon," Granville saluted properly, but there was a twinkle in his eyes. "Where are the cannon going?"

"That depends on you and the *Arkansas.* I have an idea we will try to fortify Grand Gulf. I am taking the tugs and the cannon back down to Thompson's Bluff and will wait there for further orders."

"And us?"

"The *Music* will take the iron up the river. Woodward, you will have charge of loading the iron back onto the barges. But the *Music's* master will take over once you get underway. Now assemble the men. I have something to say to them." He ran his hand across his face, flipped away the sweat, then stalked off.

The two gunners watched him. "Wonder what's eating him?" Wyeth said.

"I don't know. He's not the kind of man to act up because he has got his commission. He is worried. . . ."

"And mad. He's mad as hell about something." The Missourian dismissed it from his mind and walked to the top of the river bank. Then he cupped his hands and called the men from their work. "Line up down there along the river," he shouted. "Commander Prentiss Oliver will speak to you."

The men poured off the barges and left their tools. They showed no surprise, for, after a year of war, they were beyond surprising. Prent waited until they were in line and then addressed them. "I have been made commander of a new fleet, the Black River Fleet. . . ."

Somebody laughed. Prent smiled, too. "You men were recruited for the *Arkansas*, but I'll need most of you. Captain Brown will have to get men from Vicksburg." He turned around and looked at Wyeth and Granville. Then he took a deep breath. "I am leaving within ten minutes. All of you go with me except ten Marines and the guerrillas. I have no command over the bushwhackers. You go with the iron to the *Arkansas*. Mr. Woodward will take over until the *Music* gets underway. He used to steamboat on the Missouri and will know how to reload the iron. . . ."

"What's up, Prent?" somebody called.

"I don't know. See those cannon on those barges? They arrived last night. We are to take them to Thompson's Bluff."

Wyeth and Woodward exchanged glances. The crowd began whispering.

"Big doings a'coming, eh, Prent?" somebody shouted.

"Probably. How many men are here from the 6th Mississippi Regiment?"

"I'll count 'em, sir," a sergeant called. "But we ain't got many. We lost 71 per cent at Shiloh." [11]

"Very well. You get your men aboard the barges. The first ten Marines from the left over there will go to the *Arkansas*. The remainder get to my boats. That's all." He turned to Wyeth. "You are in command now, Mr. Woodward."

"Aye, ay, sir. But you are sort of stripping us. . . ."

"Can't be helped. There are no Yanks between here and the *Arkansas*. Ten Marines are sufficient for picket duty. The crew can attend to the loading and all that." He started away, then turned and offered his hand to the two gunners. "God bless you."

They watched him step down the bank toward his tug. "Just a minute, sir," Wyeth called and caught up with him. "We may not be seeing you again. Good luck to you, and my respects to your family, especially your sister."

"My sister is dead," Prent said. "So is my father. They burned our place last night." He turned on his toes and walked away.

Wyeth's throat went dry and the blood burned his face. He started to say something, some words of sympathy, but, instead, he, too, turned away. Granville was kicking at the grass on the bluff with his shiny boots. Then he stooped over and wiped his boots and watched the blood retreat from his friend's face. Neither spoke as Prent went aboard his tug, lined up his barges and disappeared down the river.

"Well?" Granville said. "You are in charge."

"Let's get busy."

"There is one thing we must do first." The Englishman called one of the guerrillas, a chieftain of the bushwhackers. "Prent Oliver's home was burned last night. His father and sister are dead. Do you know what a reprisal is?"

"Naw," the guerrilla said.

"It is an eye for an eye."

"And teeth for a tooth," Wyeth said. "Find out who did it and if they have homes, burn them. And kill four."

The guerrilla rounded up his clansmen and they waved their guns at Wyeth, then vanished in the woods.

"Is that war, Mr. Granville?"

"Yes, Wyeth. Civil war always leads to such things."

The two gunners took off their coats and Granville folded his neatly and left it on the bluff. Wyeth loosened his collar and rolled up his sleeves. They walked to the river's edge and the Missourian surveyed the job at hand, the task of getting the iron out of the bales and back onto barges. The men were watching him, uncertain of his leadership.

"All right, you buckoes," Wyeth called. "This won't take long. We'll work twenty minutes and rest five. Twenty and five. If a man falls out then drag him to the shade and prop up his head. Don't throw water on him. Don't any of you drink water until you're cool. . . ."

"That'll be next winter," somebody yelled.

Wyeth joined in the laughter. He went to the *Music* and had the pilot maneuver the craft alongside the barges. Then he used the winch and crane to swing the bales to the bank. He gave the men cotton hooks and they tore into the bales, salvaging every bit of iron. This was stacked in neat piles. The men worked twenty minutes and the *Music* sounded her whistle. They rested five minutes and returned to work. The sun climbed up the morning path and the heat became so intense that the iron blistered the fingers of the workers. There was no talking. The winch groaned and spun and the crane creaked. There was a thud when the bales were lowered and then the sound of cotton ripping, and the clanging of iron. A few men fainted.

Granville worked on the bank, supervising the sorting of the iron. His finery was wringing wet and sweat dripped from his beard. Wyeth was on the *Music*. But the work moved rapidly and the men were pleased. Wyeth Woodward knew his business. Midway of the job, he passed among the men, giving them precious salt from the *Music's* stores. The salt, worth $5 a pound, revived them and gave them strength. He made them rest after taking the salt and let them sponge their faces. Then he gave them sugar. Even Granville was impressed and by the time the sun reached the day's half-way mark, all the bales were off and most of the iron was stacked.

Then Wyeth went to Granville. "Laurel should be here any minute now. Take a horse and go down the road and meet her. You'll know her."

"Go yourself. She is your girl."

"I must stay here. But I don't want her to find us this way. Many of the men are just half dressed and as soon as we finish I am going to make them wash. So yell before you and Laurel get here."

"Very well, Admiral."

"And wear your coat, Mr. Granville. Fix your beard, too." It was the first time the sailor ever had given orders to the Englishman. Granville laughed and put on his coat and combed his hair and beard. Then he twisted his mustache which had been drooping. He got Mort's horse and rode toward the widow Wright's. Wyeth went back to work.

By noontime, the iron had been removed from the bank back onto two barges and the cotton was scattered along the bank. They set the cotton on fire as it was useless to the Confederacy. They ran two empty barges flush with the ferry road and then lined up the other barges. The *Music* took her position at the stern of the tow, fastened all the barges into one unit, and was ready.

"That's all, men," Wyeth called to the workers from the bow of the *Music*. "Now take a wash if you have cooled off a bit. Wash your socks, too. Here is soap." He threw them soap from the boat.

The men shouted and shucked off their clothes and went into the river. Wyeth sought Gar and found him in the woods. The Negro had his pine board and brushes and was painting. He knew why Wyeth hadn't used him with the unloading. Most of the white men would have objected to working with a Negro.

"We'll be going soon," Wyeth said.

"I'm ready." He put his picture and equipment back into his box. "Has Mis' Laurel got here yet?"

"No. Mr. Granville has gone for her."

The Wolof and the gunner's mate walked down to the ferry and waited. The men finished their baths, dried in the sun, and lay on the bank, resting and smoking. Wyeth made a roll call of his available man-power. He had ten Marines, 35 guerrillas and 15 river rats. The *Music* had enough coal aboard to reach Baldwin's Ferry, half way between Rankinson's Ferry and the Vicksburg & Jackson Railroad.

Meanwhile, Granville was almost to the widow Wright's home before he met Laurel. She was alone in her buggy and behind her were the wagons that had come from Natchez. Mrs. Wright was driving one of the wagons. Laurel reined her horse when she saw Granville and he doffed his hat and bowed, then presented himself as a courier from Wyeth.

Laurel began laughing and Granville was abashed. "What is funny?" he asked.

"You. I would have known you anywhere. You look as though you rode right out of a book."

"A good book?" He was smiling.

"An interesting book."

The Englishman looked at her sharply for he was puzzled. He was distrustful of clever women and wanted this woman to be different because of Wyeth. He made no attempt to shield his gaze and Laurel returned the stare. She was smaller than he had expected and much prettier, in a windblown sort of way. He had never approved of Wyeth's judgment of women and wasn't sure that he approved now. Granville liked tall full-bosomed women and Laurel simply did not fit his idea of beauty. And, yet, there was something about her that arrested his eyes and fascinated him.

"Do I pass muster, Mr. Granville?" Laurel asked.

"Yes." There was nothing else to say.

"Then you may ride in my buggy and tell me about Wyeth. Tie your horse to the rear axle. That lady in the second wagon is Mrs. Wright. She is going to Vicksburg with us."

"Chaperon?" Granville climbed into the buggy beside her.

"Yes. Now tell me everything that happened at Grand Gulf."

The English gunner told the story and exaggerated a bit about Wyeth's part of the coup. "And you should have seen him at the ferry this morning." Granville was very enthusiastic. "The pup is an organizer. He knows how to handle men. It is a shame he doesn't know women."

"Perhaps you can teach him." Laurel took off her bonnet and shook her hair free.

"Shall I?"

"No." She said it quickly and firmly. Then they both laughed and she passed the reins to him. "I hope you know more about horses than Wyeth does. We will be at the ferry in a few minutes."

Granville held the reins in his left hand expertly. "I know all about horses." It wasn't a boast. It was a fact and he stated it as such.

As they rode along, he frequently glanced over at her and her beauty began to grow on him. Her gray eyes were so calm and confident. Granville noticed every detail and realized that she was alluring; not tantalizing as Sharon was, but very feminine and very capable. And he was glad. Her trim ankles showed from beneath her hooped skirt and her bodice was tight around her small breasts. She knew he was looking at her and she looked straight ahead. Finally she said, "I have a tiny birthmark on my shoulder, Mr. Granville. Aside from that you've missed nothing."

The suave Englishman actually was flustered and tried to laugh off his embarrassment. "Yes, you pass muster. Wyeth has the best eyes of any man I ever saw. In the fur country he could spot animals half a mile away in a snowstorm."

"Could he spot a minx?"

"God's wisdom tooth! What a tongue. Are you trying to impress me by being blase?" Granville cocked his head to one side and laughed. "Let's understand each other, Miss MacKenzie. You're a chick. And I like you already. But even if I didn't you would never know it, for if Wyeth Woodward likes you then I am your friend."

Laurel blushed in spite of her efforts to be calm, and a smile chased the blush away. "I *was* trying to be smart. And I have been sufficiently rebuked. But I wanted you to like me so much."

Her frankness and girlishness disarmed him completely. Her whole demeanor flattered him and, yet, it made him feel old. She was talking to him as a girl talks to a middle aged man. He knew then that she was in love with Wyeth and that she wanted his friendship not for the pleasure it offered but for his influence on the young sailor.

They reached a bend that led down hill to the ferry. Granville stood up and shouted. Several cries answered him and when the mare trotted down the incline to the river Wyeth walked rapidly toward them and he and Laurel were looking at each other and smiling as though there were no other persons in the world. The sailor was so entranced that he stumbled over a root and almost fell. The Englishman shook his head knowingly at the clumsy antics of his usually agile friend. Wyeth offered his hand to the girl and she took it and he helped her from the buggy. They stood there a second and she took her hand from his, but not her eyes.

"Did you hear about the Olivers?" They were his first words.
"Yes."

"What happened?"

"I don't know exactly," she said. "The *Scioto* got suspicious and put a landing party ashore. There was a fight and Rock Bradford was wounded. He got away, though. One of the speculators must have got away, too, because he got word to the landing party. The news spread like wild fire and a bunch of bushwhackers rode down to the Olivers and did their meanness. The speculator was with them."

"Was his name Wells?" Wyeth demanded.

"Yes, that's his name. The Yankee sailors did not participate. And you are quite a hero. To the Yankees."

"What are you talking about?"

"Well, they are telling that you wanted to fight. They say you got so mad that your scar flashed like white lightning and that you demanded some guns to defend the cotton."

Granville got leisurely out of the buggy then. "Wyeth is quite an actor. But he was surprised and reacted very realistically."

The wagons arrived in a cloud of dust and Laurel presented the men to Mrs. Wright, a rawboned woman whose hair was done into a roll on the top of her head. Laurel explained that one of the drivers was stricken the night before and that the widow volunteered to take his place.

"That's only part of the story," Mrs. Wright said as she studied Wyeth. "This child was in a nervous fit half the night. I'm not sure who or what she was worrying about, but I reckoned I'd better stay with her. Wall MacKenzie is my friend."

"We are glad to have you." Wyeth helped her from the wagon and called a man to handle her baggage. He issued instructions quietly. Another man took Laurel's trunk. The Missourian assigned the ladies to quarters on the *Music* and they went aboard. The empty wagons were driven onto a barge and the animals were unharnessed and fed.

"Efficient devil, what?" Granville showed Laurel to her room.

"So it seems. Apparently he is efficient at many things."

"No, he is quite bashful about some things. He is a very proper young man. However, I will use my influence. . . ."

"And vast knowledge." Laurel took off her bonnet and put it on a chair and looked around the hot, stuffy little cabin. "I am afraid,

Mr. Granville, that you are a matchmaker or a meddlesome busy-body." She smiled when she said it.

"I will not meddle. I promise. But you two remind me of a couple of powder kegs. A spark is going to strike some day and then . . ." He shrugged his shoulders.

"But I've known him less than a week."

"That is probably on his mind, too."

"Yes, I know it." She moved her bonnet and sat in the chair. "Propriety is a pest, isn't it?"

"It is a safety valve, Miss MacKenzie."

"Oh, fiddlesticks. You may call me Laurel, too. Do you think I'm reckless?"

"Yes."

"And bold?"

"Yes."

"Oh, my goodness. Do you suppose he thinks I am?"

"No. He is incapable of reason so far as you are concerned."

Laurel folded her hands and sighed. "I can't hurry him. I've only known him . . ."

"You said that before." Granville walked to the door. "I will send water and coffee, if we have any coffee. Meanwhile, I understand you have some medicine in your trunk. If you will separate it we will be that much ahead."

"All right. But promise me you won't say a word to him about this. About how I feel. You might give him the wrong impression."

"I promise. It is a vow. But if he is too slow showing any spirit then let me know and I will prod him." Granville bowed and closed the door.

She changed into a skirt and jacket of imperial blue. The jacket was closed in front and had short sleeves that showed cambric under-sleeves. She got out her black lace gauntlets and a black hat with a rolling brim and put the finery on a chair. It was one of Laurel's prized ensembles and was purchased in New Orleans before the war. She wished she had a flower for her hair, a jasmine perhaps. Then she laughed to herself at her frivolity. She was not the type to wear a flower in her hair. She sat on the floor by her trunk and began sorting the medicine and humming a tune, "When This Cruel War Is Over."

The *Music* got underway, her paddle wheel churning the river into foam. Laurel went to her door and peeped out. The barges stretched ahead. The horses and wagons were on the first barge as far away from the living quarters as possible. Then came an empty barge, and then the flatboats carrying the iron. Most of the men were on the first barge and Wyeth was among them, giving orders. She saw him leave the first barge and cross to the second. Then he turned around and shouted to the men, "No drinking. And if you must gamble then stay up there to do it. Clean your guns. I'll keep you busy if I have to make you scrub down these scows."

Laurel saw him leap onto the *Music* and then swing up to the pilothouse. She wished he would look her way. She wanted to wave at him.

Then she saw Gar. He was back near the stern rake, just sitting there, a pine board in his hands.

Wyeth glanced down toward her cabin, but didn't see her. Then he summoned Granville and went to the texas, a narrow cabin on top of the skylight roof and near the pilothouse. The pilot's quarters were in the texas. The master of the *Music* was there and Wyeth turned command of the men over to him. "From here on," the Missouri sailor said, "you handle everything. Mr. Granville and I are at your service. There is no room in the texas for us."

"I'll make room," the pilot said. "I'll move some of my crew."

"Never mind. Mr. Granville and I will manage. We can sleep on one of the barges."

Granville started to protest, but changed his mind. It wouldn't be fair to Wyeth for him to put up a howl.

"There's only one thing," Wyeth said. "We must keep your men away from my men. My men are idle now and ready for a squabble. With your permission I will have them work around the tow. Anything to keep them busy."

"That's all right," the pilot said. "Just keep them out of the way. I aim to give this here boat her head and get on up the river. We should raise Hall's Ferry tonight and get to Baldwin's tomorrow. There ain't no Yanks this far up the river, that I know of. But you better post some of them Marines, just in case."

"Have you any quinine?" Granville spoke for the first time.

"A little bit."

"So have we. But we'll need it for the *Arkansas*. If I may presume, then I suggest you pass out some of the quinine to our men."

The master got the medicine from his chest and gave it to Wyeth. Granville peered into the chest and saw the whiskey. The pilot offered him a drink and Granville refused much to Wyeth's amazement. "Don't look so damned happy about it," Granville snorted. "I told you I would not take one until the *Arkansas* is finished."

The two gunners went forward and set the men about various chores. Laurel, realizing that Wyeth was busy, was quite put out and stayed in her cabin. She took off her jacket and skirt and lay down. Her hair got sticky with sweat and when Mrs. Wright dropped in she asked the widow to help her wash it. Mrs. Wright got rain water from the texas and castile and washed the girl's hair. She rolled it up, too.

"Does your father like him?" Mrs. Wright asked. She hadn't mentioned Wyeth to Laurel before.

"Papa barely knows him. But he will like him. Don't you think so?"

"He might as well. Who is he? What's his background?"

Laurel told her all she knew about Wyeth.

Mrs. Wright shook her head. "That ain't much to go on." She kept shaking her head. "So he's a gunner on the *Arkansas*. Don't fall too madly in love, Laurel. Ain't many men on the *Arkansas* going to live."

"He will," said Laurel calmly. She was irked with Mrs. Wright.

The *Music* sashayed on up the Big Black that afternoon, taking the inside of the bends. The master was pushing her as fast as possible without shaking her apart. But she was a sturdy boat and did her work without complaint. They tied up before dark and issued rations to Wyeth and his men, who went ashore and cooked. Mosquitoes poured out of the woods and Granville began cursing. He and Wyeth made the men take quinine.

Laurel ate with the pilot and after supper they got underway again and Wyeth came to the texas and saw the girl. She had put her blue jacket and skirt back on and had a bit of ribbon in her hair. They walked together on deck. There were many things each wanted to say, but they said little. Neither dared express the thoughts closest to the heart as each was afraid of the other's reaction.

"How do you like Mr. Granville?" he asked.

"All right." Her tone was flat. She didn't want to talk about Mr. Granville. "I like him all right. Very much, in fact. He is your friend."

"Are you comfortable in your quarters?"

"Everything is all right." She looked at the bank and watched the darkness settle. The shoreline was a wilderness of cypress and a jungle of vines and tangled trailers. The night animals began prowling and bull alligators thrashed through the muck. Frogs called and fireflies glowed in the swamps. Clouds of mosquitoes settled on the boat and barges, and the men up forward were miserable. They spread canvas over the wagons and sought refuge from the insects. Ants crawled from under the planking and aided the mosquitoes in their work of torment. A sticky mist formed just over the water.

"You'd better go to your cabin," Wyeth said. "This is terrible. Take some quinine."

She had anticipated a pleasant trip and was disappointed at everything. The night before she had dreamed of being in the moonlight with him, and now this—mosquitoes, ants and heat. There was a moon, all right, a glaring sliver that hung just over the swamps. But there was nothing romantic in the moon. It looked weary and dejected and seemed to hang there limply. She sighed her disappointment, bade him good night and retired.

Wyeth found a spot under one of the wagons and took off his shoes and shirt. Granville was there, rolling and tossing and slapping at mosquitoes. The *Music* kept plowing ahead, throwing sparks and swishing her wheel. The sound pleased Wyeth and reminded him of his boyhood on the Osage.

Granville mumbled in his sleep and the Marine pickets stamped around the barges, fighting mosquitoes. Wyeth slept fitfully and was half awake when he heard the master cry out, "Hello! the raft!"

The Missourian reached for his pistol and shook Granville. The Englishman, however, just grunted. "Get the hell up," Wyeth said. "We have sighted something."

"Just a raft." Granville tucked his head on his arm. "If you need me then hiss like a goose. Or whistle like a dido."

They came abeam the raft and Wyeth exclaimed, "Good God! Look at that, Mr. Granville."

The raft was loaded with cannon and was floating with the current. Two men worked its sweep and more than two score Confederates were standing among the guns waving at the tow.

"Prent will be glad to see that," Granville said. "The Yanks are in for a surprise." He folded his hands under his head and went back to sleep.

Wyeth, however, was wide awake. He slipped on his shoes, intending to do a quick inspection of the barges. Most of the men were sleeping, but a few called to him as he passed by. The Marine pickets greeted him with news that all was well and he went to the *Music*. As he passed by Laurel's cabin, he listened, hoping to hear her. But her cabin was quiet and he went to the stern. Gar was sitting there staring at the river as though he understood its dark secrets. The mosquitoes were not molesting him and he was oblivious to the heat. He glanced up at the sailor and got slowly to his feet. "Is ever'thing all right, Mist' Woodward?"

"Uh huh. Why aren't you asleep?"

"Been thinking. About this and that." He reached for his box and found the pine board. "I'm done with the pitcher. It's yours."

The creamy moonlight struck the picture and Wyeth tried to make it out while Gar watched him apprehensively. The river was there in the background, a winding curve of whispering blue. And there were trees along the bank, willow and oak. But in the foreground was one lonely tree, stark and ugly, and a twisted body was hanging from a limb. The Missourian shuddered. "Is that Mort hanging there?"

"Yes, suh. In a way. But I sort of mean it to be ever'body who gets hung. Do you like it?"

"I don't know," said Wyeth truthfully. He couldn't take his eyes from the crude painting, however. "I don't know much about pictures."

"Me neither. But pitchers make me feel funny inside."

"This one does me that way," Wyeth said. "It makes my stomach sort of jump and my chest fill up. It's very pretty in a way, and yet there is something ugly about it."

"Yes, suh. That's how things are. Pitchers say things to me just like writing does to you. You ain't going to tell on me?"

"No. But what is there to tell?"

"Folks would laugh at me. And it might get me in trouble. If it's against the law for me to learn how to read and write then it must be against the law for me to paint pitchers."

The sailor looked at the picture again and its strange beauty began growing on him. "It's crazy," he mumbled. "The whole thing is crazy."

"What's crazy, Mist' Woodward?"

"Everything. It's crazy to tell a man that he can't read or write. What is your last name, Gar?"

"I ain't got any. Mist' Taliaferro was my master and he's gone. I don't belong to nobody so I ain't got a name. Cep'n Gar."

"Gar Taliaferro." Wyeth shook his head. "No, that's too much." He looked at the picture. "Rivers. Gar Rivers. How is that? Your name is Gar Rivers."

"It don't make no difference. Ever'body calls me Gar. A last name don't mean nothing."

"It will some day. You should be free. When I can, I'll ask the legislature to free you. Have you got another pine board?"

Gar reached in his box and handed him one.

"And paint," Wyeth said enthusiastically. "Some thin paint."

The Negro handed him a jar. "That's been oiled down. It's thin as water."

The sailor took a sliver of wood, dipped it into the paint and wrote "Gar Rivers" on the board. "That's your name. Look at it and write it over and over."

The Wolof stared at the white man. "Go on," Wyeth was impatient. "Do as I say. You need a quill. By God, you're entitled to a name and you have the right to write it."

Gar produced a quill from his box. "I made it. I use it to draw lines on my pitchers."

Wyeth laughed at the absurdity of the situation. "It's all right for you to draw lines for a picture, but if you draw lines for letters then you're breaking the law. Of course, it's crazy. Now start copying your name. I'll be back in a minute."

He hurried forward and got the Bible that Prent had given him. He got a lantern, too, and returned to Gar. The Negro had copied his name several times on the board. It came easy to him because his fingers were so deft. "It's like painting a pitcher," Gar said happily. "My name is a pitcher and I just keep painting it."

"That's right," Wyeth said. "Now look. I can't teach you to write many things. But writing is not as important as reading. And reading isn't hard. Not if you know the words. Do you know anything about the Bible?"

"A heap of it. By heart."

The sailor opened the Book and began reading, "In the beginning God created the heaven and the earth."

"I know all of that, Mist' Woodward. I know all the first part by heart."

Wyeth pointed out the words to him and explained their meanings. "That word is 'heaven' and that one is 'earth'."

"Earth is plum' near as big as heaven, huh, Mist' Woodward?" Gar moved the lantern closer to the book.

It was sight reading and Gar learned the first line quickly because he already knew the words. Then he recited the second line and picked out the words and learned "form" and "darkness" and "face" and "deep" for, "the earth was without form, and void; and darkness was upon the face of the deep."

Wyeth felt good inside. It was a beginning. He left the Book with the Negro. "It's yours. They can't punish you for having a Bible and they can't punish me for giving you one. It is a good swap, Gar. A Bible for a picture. Keep practicing your name and read those words over and over so you'll know them wherever you see them."

"Yes, suh." He closed the Bible and put it in his box. "And I'm rightly obliged."

Wyeth went back to his barge and crawled under a wagon. He couldn't go back to sleep, however, and lay there listening to the night things. Granville rolled over and grunted and propped his head on one elbow. "Been reading the Bible? I saw you get it."

"Yes." Wyeth tried to hide the picture under his coat, but the Englishman spied it and held out his hand and the sailor handed it to him.

Granville sat up suddenly and held the picture in the moonlight. "Gar?"

"How did you know?"

"I put two and two together. Light that lantern." He studied the picture then put it aside and looked at Wyeth. There was compassion in his eyes. It was the first time Wyeth had ever seen his friend show such an emotion.

"Is the picture any good, Mr. Granville?"

"Yes. It is not great. But it is good, Wyeth. That blue is beautiful."

"It's whispering blue. Gar made it."

"Incredible." Granville put the picture under Wyeth's coat and propped his back against a wagon wheel and looked up at the moon. "If Gar were in France or even the Indies he could be somebody. He has talent. He is an artist, Wyeth. Any man who understands whispering blue is an artist. Yet, there he is. A slave without a master. With money at his disposal and facing a law that says he can not have money. He can make pictures, but he can not make words and pictures tell more than words."

Then Wyeth told him what he had done. "I'm going to teach him to read. I can do that much. I'd do as much for a parrot."

The Englishman looked at his friend a long time. "Did you ever hear of Santo Domingo?"

"Where the blacks revolted?"

"Yes. They stuck knives through white babies and held them aloft as banners."

Wyeth didn't reply. He propped his elbows on his knees and put his chin in his hands.

"And Jamaica." Granville said. "Great Britain emancipated her slaves in '39. Up to that time Negroes in Jamaica were among the most prosperous peasants in the world, but when they took over their own affairs Jamaica became a pesthole."

"White men have pestholes, too," Wyeth said softly.

"That's right. But have you ever thought that the Negro has lived in bondage in Africa for a thousand years? His God was a piece of wood. He never thought of a sail for his boat. He slept under trees but never thought to cut one down and build a house."

Wyeth said, "I wonder what would have happened if the white man had lived along the Congo and the Negro in Europe."

Granville smiled. "You will make a lawyer, all right. Dammit!"

"Understand," Wyeth said. "I do not hold with the Abolitionists. I loathe them. But I do think slavery must go. Do you think I'm a fool?"

"Yes. But thank God for fools like you. Don't worry about the Abolitionists. They are beating the tom-toms for Yankee industry. They are cold, calculating men who care nothing about the Negro as a man. They sit in cold studies and write ponderous themes on right and wrong. Then they go to cold beds and cold women. A pox on them. The South has many sins. But, by God, people live down here. They breathe and breed and fight and live. No, you will never be an Abolitionist. You are a Southerner who dares to think."

"I want to help Gar get his freedom. . . ."

"Of course, you do. Hand it to him on a platter. Give it to him as you would give him bread. Patronize him. No, Wyeth! Great God, no! Don't stuff freedom down a slave's throat. Give it to him in small doses and then he can digest it. . . ."

"But there's no such thing as degrees of freedom. . . ."

"Do not practice your arguments on me. I am no jury, no judge. Of course, there are degrees of freedom. Give the Negro economic and political freedom in one gulp and you will have chaos. Then all will suffer. Take it easy, man. Freedom is not a gift from man. It is a state to which man must aspire and a thing for which he must fight."

"Words. Those are just words."

Granville rolled up his coat into a pillow. "I know it. It is too much for me. I will help you with Gar. I will help any man who talks of whispering blue. Now, get some sleep."

Wyeth was smiling when he lay down again.

The heat forced Laurel to stay in her cabin the next day. She was suffering from a headache and dizzy spells, and Mrs. Wright put her to bed and dosed her with quinine. Wyeth made no effort to see her, knowing it would not be proper for a young man to visit a girl in her bedroom. Granville was admitted, however, because of his age and he told Laurel about Gar's picture and Wyeth's determination to teach the Wolof to read. Laurel was not surprised.

They reached Baldwin's Ferry about noon, coaled the little steamer, dropped an empty barge at the ferry and added a coal barge to the tow. They left the swampy lands and came about sundown to the valley near the Champion Hills. The river was getting shoaly. There was a breeze from the hills and the breeze blew away the clouds of mosquitoes. Everybody slept well that night except Gar, and he pored over the new words he had learned. The new moon was passing its quarter.

The Marines were the first to sight the Big Black bridge where the Vicksburg & Jackson Railroad crossed the river about twelve miles east of Vicksburg. The bridge was almost a mile long. The pickets called out, "Bridge ahead." The *Music* sounded her whistle in the muggy air of the dying night, crept almost under the bridge to a good landing, tied up and blew her steam.

They had reached the rendezvous, a spot selected by Captain Brown of the *Arkansas*.

The crew and passengers of the tow crowded on deck and cries of amazement and delight came from them, for in the grayness of dawn they saw lines of wagons waiting near the bridge; huge ox wagons and sturdy mule wagons. Men were bustling about and they shouted at the *Music* and some fired their guns in a salute of welcome.

The wagons were loaded with rolled iron from Tennessee, railroad iron from Georgia, bolts from Chattanooga, rope from Pensacola, food from North Alabama and medicine from Wilmington and Mobile. The supplies and iron had been gathered bit by bit all over the South and shipped by train to Jackson, thence out to the rendezvous.

As soon as the barges touched the bank, Granville and Wyeth leaped ashore and ran to a tent pitched near the bridge. At the entrance of the tent was Lieut. Henry K. Stevens, executive officer of the *Arkansas,* and second in command to Captain Brown. Stevens was beaming. The two gunners saluted and Granville said, "The iron from Natchez, sir. Iron and powder and men."

Stevens was so enthusiastic that he forgot his rank and offered coffee to the gunners. Then he shouted for his cooks to prepare mess for the *Music*.

"Take your ease," he told the gunners. "Thank God you made it. I was getting nervous."

"Why, sir?" Granville asked.

Stevens frowned and then he remembered. "Of course, you haven't heard. Bloody Ben Butler has sent General Thomas Williams' Brigade up the river. Three thousand men and a mess of guns on transports. They burned Grand Gulf yesterday."

"Prent! I mean Commander Oliver . . . " Wyeth was alarmed.

"He is still at Thompson's Bluff. He didn't lose a gun. I tell you, boys, the Yanks are shuttling men between New Orleans and Vicksburg like they intend to fight. They have a big camp across the river from Vicksburg. Ben Butler told Williams to destroy the town. Williams has Everett's battery, the 31st Massachusetts, the 7th Vermont and Magee's cavalry with him."

"The more, the merrier," Granville said. "Since we have got to fight the Union Navy we might as well include the Army, too."

Stevens said, "Butler has it all mapped out. The son of a bitch. He doesn't want Farragut to get any credit. He has instructed Williams to dig a canal just opposite Vicksburg and change the course of the river." [12]

Granville looked around at the supplies. "Much has happened since we left. How are things with the *Arkansas*, sir?"

Stevens said, "I left soon after you did. I went over to Canton and had six gun carriages made. Drew the plans from memory." He began laughing. "The man who took the contract had never seen a gun carriage. But they are beauties. See that lumber?" He pointed to a wagonload of prime hardwood. "The carriage for your Dahlgren will be made at Yazoo City. From that. I bought that lumber in Jackson and it came from Lebanon."

"How far are we from the *Arkansas* now?" Wyeth asked.

Stevens pointed northeast. The sun was coming up and he blinked when he pointed. "The *Arkansas* is about fifty miles that way. It'll be hell getting these wagons through the swamps, and the roads are pretty bad where there are any roads at all. You two are to report to General Van Dorn in Vicksburg. We'll load everything on the wagons and I'll head for Yazoo City and the *Arkansas*. Now let's get to work while it is a little bit cooler than hell."

Wyeth asked him to take Gar to the *Arkansas* and Stevens agreed willingly when he learned that the Negro was a good hand with mules and oxen.

The medicine that Laurel brought was loaded into a wagon and Wyeth instructed Gar to guard it. "Mr. Granville and I should be in Yazoo City before the wagons get there. But if we are not, then you look up Vespasian Gillivray. Tell him I sent you. Take the Bowie and snipper. I will explain to Lieutenant Stevens that you are taking them for me."

Laurel still was not feeling her best and Wyeth was rather worried, fearing malaria. He had her horse and buggy removed from the barge and suggested that she and Mrs. Wright leave immediately for Vicksburg. "Perhaps it will be better," he said, "for you to return to Natchez. After all, Vicksburg is under fire."

"Folderol," she said. "The Yanks are across the river from Vicksburg. They are walking the streets of Natchez. Besides, Papa told me to stay here until he sent for me. I will be at Mrs. Nelle Simpson's house. It's on Cherry street, near the courthouse."

Wyeth said, "I will call tomorrow afternoon."

Mrs. Wright took the reins and the buggy swished over the sandy road that ran parallel to the railroad.

On Stevens' instructions, Granville and Wyeth used the *Music's* crane and winch to swing the iron from the barges into the wagons. Dust and rust rose in clouds and the workers choked and their flesh cried out in agony against the labor, the heat and the insects. Eight oxen were hitched to each ox wagon and as fast as a wagon was loaded it was moved away and another was moved alongside the barges. Ten mules were hitched to each mule wagon and by mid-afternoon the wagon train was ready. The drivers gathered around Stevens and got their orders. The guerrillas and Marines were divided into armed parties and instructed as to picket duty and line of march. Cooks were chosen and stones were gathered for stoves as there were no rocks in the swamps between them and the *Arkansas*. Axes were lashed to the wagons. Guns were primed. Spades were taken aboard. Between them and the Yazoo River where the *Arkansas* was being built was nothing but wilderness, cut here and there by trails that served as roads. And swamps, muck and mire. . . .

Stevens got into the first wagon and the caravan moved off, creaking and groaning. Drovers walked beside the oxen, prodding them, and the beasts bellowed. The wagon train disappeared to the north and Wyeth and Granville suddenly felt lonely.

They walked down to the *Music* which had been headed downstream. There was a sinking feeling in their hearts. The pilot lined up the empty barges, waved goodby to them and moved back down the river for Thompson's Bluff. He blew for a bend and the echo came to Wyeth and Granville. The rendezvous was deserted. They went and sat on the railroad bridge, watching the river, and sat there until a train came. They flagged it and rolled into Vicksburg about dusk. A mile out of town they began passing entrenchments. From the river came the sound of Yankee cannon, for the might of the Union Navy was anchored out there, throwing shells into the city.

"Sounds natural," said Granville.

"They are wasting a heap of powder," Wyeth said.

"Wonder when they will realize that they can't take Vicksburg from the river." Granville cocked his ear as a mortar shell exploded.

"To hell with 'em," said Wyeth. "I'm going to find a nice soft bed."

They found one in a tavern near the river. From their window they could see Farragut's ships-of-the-line and Davis' ironclads, lighted by the flare of their own guns. Ellet's rams were out there, too, sniping, and Porter's mortar boats hurled 1,000-pound balls into the town. Just across the river, Thompson's brigade kept up a steady fire. The Confederates seldom bothered to reply. They were troubled more by the mosquitoes than by Yankee shells.

The blo-o-o-m, swiss-sssh, blo-o-om didn't even annoy Wyeth. He opened the window to their room and blew out the lamp. Granville was already asleep.

Chapter Eight

Every minute, day and night, at least one Union shell fell on the fortress of Vicksburg, the keystone of that political and military conglomeration that was being held together by the iron will and nimble brain of Jefferson Davis, and the steel of the South's armies. The authorities in Washington, desperate for a victory to offset the disasters in Virginia, conceived the fantastic plan of taking Vicksburg from the Mississippi River. Farragut knew it could not be done; General Ben Butler thought it could.[13] Farragut wanted to go from New Orleans, which he had captured, to Mobile. But Butler had his way, as he often did, and the United States Navy was commanded to lay siege to Vicksburg and subdue it.

A month or so before, a landing party from a rowboat could have taken the town. It was not defended then because the Confederacy never dreamed that New Orleans and Memphis would fall and leave the river virtually at the mercy of the Federals.

However, the minute the danger was realized, General Mansfield Lovell, commander of the South's forces along the lower Mississippi, instructed General Van Dorn to prepare Vicksburg for defense. In the meantime, General M. L. Smith rushed men and guns into the town before Farragut could push his fleet up from New Orleans. When Smith arrived he found Colonel J. L. Autry of Bragg's Tennessee Army on the ground and together they began fortifying the hills that commanded the Mississippi.

Accompanied by transports and 3,000 soldiers, the *Oneida* of Farragut's flotilla hove to in the Mississippi on May 18, and demanded surrender of the town. But Vicksburg was no Natchez, waiting to be plucked like a ripe grape. A few Confederate guns were in battery and a handful of soldiers were behind the parapets. General Smith told the Federals to "come and take us" and Mayor Lindsay of Vicksburg informed the *Oneida* that "neither the municipal authorities nor the citizens would ever consent to the surrender of the city." So the siege was on.*

Federal soldiers occupied the village of DeSoto on a jut of land just across the river in Louisiana. They set up their guns and began the attack. The *Oneida* hurled a few shells and then hied away down the river to report to Farragut that Vicksburg was going to fight.

General Smith combed the territory thereabouts and scraped together a makeshift army of 5,000 Regulars and Partisans. They were armed with shotguns and smoothbores and were entrenched along the bluff that protected the town. The Confederates had six batteries in place and were drilling cannoneers when Farragut's fleet of 35 vessels arrived from down river. Dave Porter's mortarboats, 19 of them, were anchored just below the town and began a bombardment. Farragut, aware that another Union fleet was coming down the river from Memphis, ran his ships by the Vicksburg batteries to rendezvous above the city with the Upper Mississippi Squadron. To his own surprise and the amazement of the Confederates, he ran the batteries without serious loss. He learned then that the batteries could hinder but never stop a fleet, but he also learned that Vicksburg was impervious to shells thrown by ships steaming up and down the river. He so reported to Washington and was told to keep trying.

Broadside after broadside of shot, shell and grape were belched into the town, but not a single Confederate gun was disabled. For days on days, Farragut's fleet and Porter's mortars pumped lead and steel at the fortress. Vicksburg, however, just shook herself and kept the Federals at a distance.

* Officially, the campaign for Vicksburg began on May 18, 1862, and ended July 4, 1863.

Davis's Upper River Squadron of ironclads and gunboats, and Ellet's fleet of rams joined Farragut's fleet north of the fortress and combined operations were begun.[14]

It was the greatest concentration of power ever assembled by the United States Navy. Major General Van Dorn assumed command of the defenses in June, 1862, and the siege settled down to give and take.[15]

Some citizens of Vicksburg fled to other towns, but most of the residents stayed at home and attended to their affairs. They dug cellars in their yards and caves in the bluffs and sought safety there when the bombardment got dangerously heavy. The Federal ships, about 60 in number, concentrated their fire on the casements and batteries along the river and apparently made no deliberate effort to destroy homes. The food situation in Vicksburg was strained but not acute. So long as the railroad to Jackson and the east was open the town would not starve. Food prices, however, were exorbitant and the poorer people already were eating mule meat and bread made of pea flour.

Wyeth and Granville woke up to the swishing and booming of the sunrise cannonading that the Yankees usually enjoyed before breakfast. The Missourian stepped to the window and looked out. Granville, however, rolled over for another snooze. A low smoke cloud hung over the river from Warrenton, six miles south of Vicksburg's courthouse, to Milliken's Bend, eight miles northwest.

"That smoke cloud," Wyeth said, "should help keep the sun off of the Yankees. You'd better get up, Mr. Granville. We've got a heap to do."

The Englishman crawled out of bed then and stood in the middle of the floor, stretching and yawning. They called the proprietor and had him send a Negro for their uniforms which they had left in Vicksburg before going to Natchez. They shaved and bathed and put on their dress uniforms of light grayish blue. The trousers had big black buttons and the jackets were slip-on affairs with wide flapping collars. Their caps were round and flat, decorated by bands of red ribbon and bows. Granville had a black silk kerchief, but Wyeth had none.

It was good to be back in uniform again. The Englishman stood before the mirror and trimmed his beard, then waxed his mustache. "And now," he said, "I can eat a horse."

"You probably will," Wyeth said. He wrapped their civilian clothes into a bundle and gave them to the proprietor for safe keeping. Granville cautioned the man to guard his Wellington boots and silken finery with his life. Then the Englishman did a strange thing. Without so much as glancing at Wyeth, he took out his watch and the chain with the tiny dragon and handed them to the proprietor. "Give me a receipt for these and keep them in your safe. If I am not back here within six months, send them to Miss Sharon Weatherford in Natchez."

Wyeth dared not question the Englishman about his personal business, and they went into breakfast and ordered fried chicken, hominy, hot rolls and Jorum, a black coffee brew named for Mark Jorum who, legend said, drank three gallons daily. The meal cost them $20, Confederate money. While the food was being prepared, Wyeth picked up a bill of fare from the table and began laughing. It was a mock menu written by some Confederate wag and contained:

SOUP:—Mule tail
BOILED:—Mule bacon, with poke greens, mule ham, canvassed.
ROAST:—Mule sirloin; mule rump, stuffed with rice; saddle of mule, a l'armee.
VEGETABLES:—Boiled rice; rice hard boiled; hard rice, any way.
ENTREES:—Mule head, stuffed a la Reb; mule hoof jerked, a la Yankee; mule ears, fricassed, a la getch; mule side, stewed new style, hair on; mule liver, hashed, a l'explosion.
SIDE DISHES:—Mule salad; mule hoof soused; mule brains, a l'omelette; mule kidneys, braised on ramrod; mule tripe, on half (Parrot) shell; mule tongue, cold, a la Bray.
JELLIES:—Mule foot (3-to-yard); mule bone, a la trench.
PASTRY:—Rice pudding, poke berry sauce; wood berry pie, a l'Iron-clad; china berry tarts.
DESSERT:—White-oak acorns; beech nuts, blackberry leaf tea, genuine Confederate coffee.
LIQUORS:—Mississippi water, vintage 1492, very superior, $3; lime-stone water, late importation, very fine $3.75; spring water, Vicksburg bottled, $4.
Meals at few hours. Gentlemen to wait upon themselves. Any inattention in service should be promptly reported at the office.

JEFF DAVIS & CO., Proprietors.

CARD: The proprietors are now prepared to accommodate all who may favor them with a call. Parties arriving by the river will find Grape, Cannister & Co.'s carriages at the landing, or any depot on the line of entrenchments. Buck, Ball & Co., take charge of all baggage. No effort will be spared to make the visit of all as interesting as possible.

Wyeth showed the menu to Granville and they both laughed until their food came. They ate in silence, enjoying every bite, for each was aware that they wouldn't have good food again for a long time, and maybe never. They ordered the best cigars in the house and smoked them slowly. The innkeeper gave each a plug of chewing tobacco which neither used. But they thanked him.

"Secesh Navy, huh?" the host was trying to be friendly.

"Swiss Navy," Granville said.

Wyeth appreciated the man's curiosity, however, and told him they were gunners of the Confederate Navy and under command of Captain William F. Lynch. That was the truth as Captain Lynch was in charge of Confederate naval operations in that district.[16] He was at Jackson, a long ways from open water. The Missourian didn't dare discuss the *Arkansas* with the innkeeper.

The Federal fire had become desultory. "The Yanks are at breakfast," the proprietor said. "The shooting will slack off now until late this afternoon when the sun gets in our boys' eyes. Then the Yanks will start kicking up a fuss again. If you aim to look 'em over, this is the best time. You can see everything from the roof."

He went to the roof with them and pointed out the sights. The artillery duel was in progress along a 14-mile front and Vicksburg, named for the Reverend Newitt Vick who settled there in 1814, was baking in the morning sun that seeped through the pall of smoke. The guide pointed south to Warrenton where a Confederate battery was being served. The Vicksburg entrenchments began there. From down Grand Gulf way, the bluffs rolled along the east bank of the Mississippi and began rising to a height of 200 feet at Warrenton. Vicksburg was on the bluff, a precipitous hill that formed a sheer wall at the river's edge and fell away in rolling knolls to the east, toward the Big Black River and Jackson. The bluff, called Walnut Hills, ran north a few miles to the Yazoo River and then, following the contour of that stream, veered east to Haynes Bluff and Yazoo City.

Swamps, bayous and old beds of the Mississippi were to the north between Vicksburg and the Yazoo. So the citadel was protected from the south by hills, from the north by swamps, rivers and hills, and from the west by the Mississippi and a bluff. The only way in or out was to the east over the Vicksburg & Jackson Railroad or along the pike that paralleled the line. The fortress resembled a box with the east end knocked out.

The Mississippi was a mile wide from the base of the Vicksburg bluff to the village of DeSoto, directly across in Louisiana. In normal times, a ferry ran from Vicksburg to DeSoto and there connected with the Shreveport & Vicksburg Railroad which had been completed only as far west as Monroe. The river swept down like a boa in the first movement of constriction. It came to Milliken's Bend, past the mouth of the Yazoo and then twisted north around Tuscumbia Bend. There it changed its mind again and headed south, crawling in front of Vicksburg. A toe of swampy land jutted into Tuscumbia Bend. This land was in Louisiana, a mile across the river from Vicksburg, and on it was General Williams' Federal brigade.

Most of Dave Porter's mortar fleet, armed tenders and three ships-of-the-line, the *Brooklyn*, the *Kennebec* and the *Katahdin*, were south of town, between Vicksburg and Warrenton. The combined fleets of Farragut, Davis and Ellet were anchored from Tuscumbia Bend to Milliken's Bend, north of town. Dozens of transports, hospital ships and tugs were with both squadrons and other army transports were moored to the Louisiana toe. These supplied Williams' men.

Wyeth said, "We've got to fight all those ships."

"It is going to be an interesting experiment." The Englishman flipped away his cigar and it fell on a dusty street. A Negro snatched it up. He lived in the slums along the river, a stinking district that rivaled Natchez-Under-the-Hill.

The sailors left the roof and went to the street and walked north to the headquarters of General Van Dorn. An orderly admitted them and they found Van Dorn in conference with Gen. S. H. Lockett, chief engineer of the Vicksburg defenses. Van Dorn eyed the pair critically and said, "Just a minute, men. Sit over there in the corner."

Granville was surprised at permission to sit in a general's presence, but Wyeth accepted it as a matter of course. Van Dorn dismissed Lockett, picked up a paper and told his aide to copy it. It was an order to him from Jefferson Davis placing the *Arkansas* at his disposal.

The order should have come from Secretary of Navy Mallory, if it had to come at all. But Davis, an army man, simply could not keep his fingers out of the business of his subordinates.

"I heard you were here," Van Dorn said. "I congratulate both of you. I want you to take some orders to Captain Brown." He called the *Arkansas'* commander captain although Brown had only a lieutenant's commission. Being in command of a ship, however, his title was captain, whereas his rank and pay were far down the scale.

"Aye, ay, sir," Granville said as he and Wyeth stood at attention.

"And tell your captain I will send him 200 volunteers from General Jeff Thompson's Missourians. They are soldiers and have never been on a gunboat. But that's the best I can do."

"The *Arkansas* is, or will be, a steam sloop, sir," Wyeth said.

Van Dorn smiled and gave the men their ease. The informality of the Southern services rankled Granville. He had heard men call their officers by their first names. He took his ease because Wyeth did, but, being a stickler for such things, asked the general to give them orders in writing.

Van Dorn looked at him sharply. "You are right. I will have the orders prepared. You men will have to wait a few minutes."

The gunners walked over to a window and watched Federal transports disgorge men on the toe of land across the river. Then Wyeth shielded his eyes. "Look, Mr. Granville, they are digging a ditch across that jut."

Van Dorn heard him and joined them. "You have good eyes, sailor. Yes, they are digging a ditch across that promontory. They are using about 3,000 Yanks and 1,000 Negroes for the work."

The ditch was slightly south of Vicksburg and ran directly across the toe that protruded into Tuscumbia Bend.

"They're wasting time," Wyeth said.

"Perhaps not," Granville said. "If they dig that canal down there then the river will flow from Milliken's Bend directly across that peninsular and join up again south of here. That will isolate Vicksburg because it won't even be on the Mississippi."

Van Dorn was watching the two men. He was riverborn as was Wyeth. The Missourian said, "Man doesn't tell the Mississippi what to do, Mr. Granville. Low water is coming and the Yanks are wasting time. God runs the Mississippi."

The general nodded his approval. "The Yanks are counting on God."

And so they were. At that minute Flag Officer Charles Henry Davis of the Federal Upper River Fleet was writing in his diary that the canal would be a success and he entered a plea for God to punish Vicksburg, a "Hesperian dragon," by isolating the fortress from the river.

Two Napoleon guns and an 8-inch Parrot opened up from across the river and the shells hissed into the Confederate entrenchments. A Rebel gun replied and a crackle of musketry followed. Then came a broadside from Farragut's *Hartford* and from Davis' *Benton*. Porter's mortars joined in the melee.

"They are changing watches," Van Dorn said. "They always fire a few broadsides when they change watches."

"Who is in command out there?" Granville asked.

"God knows," said Van Dorn. "It is more or less every man for himself."

The Union command was confused and petty jealousies were rampant. Farragut was in charge of one squadron and David D. Porter commanded the mortarboats. Dave Porter and Farragut got along, but to complicate matters further, Farragut and William D. Porter, Dave Porter's bickering brother, were brothers-in-law.[17] Bill Porter was on the *Essex* of Flag Officer Davis' Upper River Squadron. He hated Farragut as much as he hated Ben Butler, nominally in command of operations against Vicksburg.

But that was only half the trouble. Flag Officer Davis had the same rating as Farragut, but the Davis ironclads, built for inland waters, were under jurisdiction of the War Department while Farragut's fleet was under the Navy Department.

And just to top things off, there were two Ellets on the fleet of Union rams, Lieut. Col. Alfred W. Ellet and his nephew, Colonel Charles Rivers Ellet, 19, and called Little Boy Blue. Lieutenant Colonel Ellet was in command of the rams, yet he was ranked by his own nephew, son of the Union hero of the Battle of Memphis. The rams also were under the War Department.

Williams and his soldiers were under Ben Butler and Butler was at New Orleans, more than 400 miles away. So there it was, a 19-year-old boy ranking his own uncle and commander; Farragut trying to work with Davis, himself a Navy man under orders from the War Department. Bill Porter was under Davis, hence under the Army. His brother, Dave, felt slighted because he was rated by Davis and Farragut. And poor Williams was under command of an oaf who thought Vicksburg could be subdued by cutting a canal across a bit of marshy land. Small wonder Farragut was disgusted and wanted to forget the whole thing and sail against Mobile. But Lincoln had ordered him to take Vicksburg to counteract Lee's victories in Virginia.

When Granville realized the confusion that was sapping his enemies' unity, he shook his head and faced Van Dorn. "Begging the general's pardon, but the trouble with this war is that there are too damn many men named Davis and Porter."

Van Dorn ran his hand over his own beard and looked enviously at Granville's mustache. He was smiling. "You men had better sit down. It will be ten or fifteen minutes before your orders are ready."

Wyeth said, "I wonder, sir, if those Yanks don't know we are building the *Arkansas* just six hours away up the Yazoo and that we aim to come out and blast hell out of them?"

"They are certain to know it," Van Dorn said. "They have spies everywhere."

"Then why don't they try to get up the Yazoo and wreck the *Arkansas* before she is finished?"

"I don't know," the general said. "I have a feeling they must be thinking we never can finish the *Arkansas*. To them, the idea of building an ironclad in the wilderness is absurd. Even I won't believe it until I see the boat."

"Ship, sir," said Granville. "And you'll see her. She is about ready and is lying alongside a wharf at Yazoo City, just waiting for iron enough to finish her and men to man her."

The *Arkansas* was there, all right, a rusty hulk that looked like an ark on a raft, an ark with sloping sides and ten gun ports. In Richmond, they were giving odds of 100 to 1 that she would never fight, and in Memphis, where she was begun, the odds were 10 to 1 that she would never float and 50 to 1 that she never would fire a shell at the Yankees.

Almost a year before, on July 31, 1861, President Davis, in a special message to Congress asked for $160,000 to build two ironclads for defense of the Mississippi. The Confederate Congress approved the amount on August 24 and that same day Secretary Mallory contracted with John T. Shirley of Memphis to build the *Tennessee* and *Arkansas*.

Shirley hired Prime Emmerson of Memphis as construction boss and began the task by building two sawmills. Pine timber was cut a hundred miles away in a virgin forest and hauled in ox wagons to the mills. Five more sawmills, more than ten miles from Memphis, were leased to cut hardwood. The contractor purchased iron in lots of from ten to one hundred pounds and procured a shipment of T-shaped railroad rails from over in Arkansas. Bolts and spikes were rolled in Nashville and when they arrived Shirley built stocks at Fort Pickering, near Memphis, and began his hulls, using pine and oak.

He was unable to get skilled shipwrights, carpenters or mechanics. So he drew the plans himself from a general outline furnished by the Navy Department. Then he rounded up native labor and went to work.

A foundry on Adams street in Memphis was taken over and somehow, by the grace of God and gravity, two low pressure engines were made, each capable of 450 horsepower. Two propellers were pounded out by hand and the shafts were fitted. Memphis never had seen such a miracle and the populace gathered around and watched Shirley.

The two ships were contracted for delivery to the Confederate Navy for December, 1861, but by the date for delivery only the skeletons were in the stocks. Shirley soon was without money and no more was available from Congress. So he mortgaged his home and continued work.

It was then he decided to concentrate his efforts on the *Arkansas* and finish the *Tennessee* later. The *Arkansas'* hull was shaped from choice pine, braced by oak and reinforced by iron rails. An ark, a huge box with sloping sides, was amidship, planked with oak and bolted to the deck. Then the *Arkansas* was launched simply by knocking away the stocks. She slipped into the Mississippi and rode easily, her hull submerged and only the deck and ark above water.

Captain McBlair of the Confederate Navy was sent to take command of the new ship, but found only a clumsy looking hulk of wood and iron. The Federals had begun their invasion of Tennessee and were pounding down the Cumberland River, but Shirley and Prime Emmerson kept working, begging iron and raising money by devious means.

They got the two engines aboard and fitted the propellers. Then they built the gun deck and coal bunkers. The *Arkansas* looked like a fat goose with a long neck and a long tail. However, Shirley knew she was well made.

Her bow was sharp and her stem tapered to permit water to close rapidly behind her. She was thiry-five feet amidship, and in the center of her hull, where the ark was fastened, she was strengthened by oaken beams and iron. For nearly eighty feet along the middle of her hull she was almost flat-bottomed, but her stern and bow were keeled. The iron of her mail ran horizontally on the deck and ark, the top of the T outward, and bolted through the flanges.

Her beak was solid castiron, sixteen feet long, and covered ten feet of her bow. The prow was bolted through solid timber, eight inches thick. The bulwarks were made of oak.

Her construction was four months behind schedule and she was about half completed when the Union's Upper River Fleet silenced Fort Pillow and Island No. 10, opening the way to Memphis. McBlair telegraphed for orders and Richmond instructed him to float the *Tennessee* and *Arkansas* to New Orleans and finish them. But the *Tennessee* was still in her stocks. About then, Farragut captured New Orleans and the Union had pinched off the Mississippi at either end of the great river.

McBlair was disgusted, but Shirley had worked too long on the *Arkansas* to give up. He loaded iron and machinery on her deck and pointed out that she might be towed to the Yazoo River and completed. The idea was fantastic, but they tried it. Using light tugs, they maneuvered the hull of the *Arkansas* three hundred miles down the Mississippi to the mouth of the Yazoo, thence about two hundred miles up the Yazoo to Greenwood, Miss. The Yazoo was flooding and the day the *Arkansas* arrived a barge load of drilled iron, intended for her sides, sank and the current scattered the bolts and rails over the river's bottom.

Then the *Arkansas* began leaking and her engines and bunkers flooded. That was the last straw. Shirley hauled the engines on deck and dismantled them to dry. And there floundered the *Arkansas*, in a river in the heart of the State of Mississippi, helpless, forlorn and useless.

Memphis fell and in the battle that cost the South that city, Granville, Wyeth and Ves managed to save their Dahlgren from the *Jeff Thompson* before the *Queen of the West* rammed her into splinters. The three sailors got their beloved Dolly onto a raft and were floating her to Vicksburg when they heard that Lieut. Isaac N. Brown had taken command of the *Arkansas*.[18] They met him in Vicksburg and went with him and Lieutenant Stevens up to Greenwood and the *Arkansas*.

The sight that greeted them sickened Wyeth, for the Yazoo had broken through her levees and the ship was four miles from dry land.

Five carpenters, with two hammers between them, were piddling around on the deck and one blacksmith's forge was at work. The iron armor had been warped and ripped by the flood and dismantled guns, machinery and scrap iron littered the deck.

Brown closed his eyes and shook his head. Lieutenant Stevens whistled in amazement. Ves cursed and Granville laughed. Wyeth just stood there, staring at the wrecked hull. Then Brown went to work.

He sent Ves back to Memphis, through the Union lines, to recruit Confederate sailors who were hiding out since the battle. He gave Stevens a list of officers he wanted and sent him to Vicksburg. "The steamer *Capitol* is there," Brown said. "Get it if you have to steal it."

"Funds?" Stevens grinned.

Brown signed his name to a batch of blank papers. "Fill them out for notes," he said. "If necessary, sign Mr. Mallory's name. Or President Davis'. The Dahlgren that was salvaged from Memphis is in Vicksburg, too. Bring it back. And meet me at Yazoo City."

Stevens was chosen then as executive officer and headed for Vicksburg. That left Brown, Granville and Wyeth. They went into Greenwood and Brown stood on a street corner and began recruiting labor.

A crowd gathered around and he spoke to them, putting his cards on the table. "If you will help us," he said, "we will build the *Arkansas* and fight her. That I swear."

He got eighteen volunteers. Wyeth got four more by betting them that Granville could pick off an oak leaf with a pistol ball at fifty paces. When the Englishman did it the men bought drinks and Granville got three more volunteer workers by betting them he could down a tumbler of the hottest brandy without taking the glass from his lips.

The town of Greenwood furnished a bell boat, a relic equipped with a bell and hopper. The apparatus fitted over the top of the boiler and the steam blast from the boiler forced up the bell through the hopper and furnished power.

Several plantation owners sent slaves and then worked alongside them. The bell boat was provided with ropes and grappling hooks and Brown dragged the river bed, salvaging much of the iron. It was stacked on the *Arkansas'* deck. The temperature reached 100 degrees, the hottest weather in the memory of the planters. And that was late Spring. The preachers said God sent the heat wave to punish the cold-blooded Yankees. The Confederates also believed in God. Flag Officer Davis didn't have a monopoly on His services.

They strung lanterns around the *Arkansas* and worked at night and eventually got her on an even keel by shifting the iron and machinery. There was nothing else to be done at Greenwood so Brown thanked the natives and dismissed most of them, keeping fifteen of the best hands. They lashed the *Arkansas'* hull to the bell boat and crept 160 miles down the flooding Yazoo River to Yazoo City and tied up alongside a floating wharf.

Brown appealed to the Confederate Army and got 200 workers. He recruited more labor in Yazoo City and got 14 forges from neighboring plantations and set them up on the bank.

Ves arrived from Memphis with 10 Confederate seamen, and more were on the way. Stevens and two pilots brought the *Capitol* up from Vicksburg. The Dolly was aboard, slightly rusty. Granville and Ves used sand and lard to clean the gun.

The *Capitol* was tied alongside the *Arkansas* and a crane was rigged from tree trunks. Part of her power was diverted to drilling machinery, made on the forges.

Within a week, Brown had the two engines together again and

fitted below deck. The propellers were adjusted and the boilers fired. Her decks still were cluttered with iron and her smoke stack was a stove pipe when the *Arkansas* kicked off from the wharf and floated downstream. Brown operated the engines himself. He watched his steam pressure rise to 120 pounds, then threw the lever that controlled the gears. The engines sputtered and caught and the propellers turned. . . .

Brown was biting his lower lip. Granville was on deck. J. H. Shacklett, a Yazoo River pilot, was at the wheel and Wyeth was with him. Ves was feeding the starboard boiler. No man spoke as the *Arkansas* shook herself, raised her iron beak and got underway. Her captain called for a starboard rudder and she wheeled slowly. Then he called for a touch of the port rudder. She obeyed promptly.

"Full speed!" Brown intended to shout the order, but his voice cracked.

The engines began pounding and wheezing, rattling and trembling. The pilot turned her full against the channel and she worked up to four knots. He steered her into still water and she made six. Then they turned her around and headed back for the wharf.

"She works, gentlemen," Brown called. He had collected his composure and now was master of a homemade ship that could run.

Stevens, on the unfinished quarter deck, actually laughed. So did Ves, a bit hysterically. Granville put his hands on his hips and shook his head, wondering if he were drunk. Wyeth, so excited that he was shaking, forgot himself and sobbed. But Brown got on his knees there in the engine room and thanked God.

He ran his new command near the bank and tried to ease her off, but when the steam was cut she didn't obey her helm. He had tried to synchronize the stoppers on the two engines and, failing, then had equipped each engine with an automatic stopper. The starboard engine, however, always turned several more strokes after the port engine was still, and the ship kept circling. Well, that couldn't be helped. So Brown instructed the pilot to pitch his rudder and offset the pull. In that way, they lined her up again alongside her wharf.

The workmen were standing on the wharf, gaping. They simply didn't believe what they had seen.

The *Arkansas* was about one-third complete, but there she lay in the Yazoo, surrounded by the wilderness. She was 165 feet from the tip of her beak to her two propellers, thirty-five feet wide amidship and displaced twelve hundred tons. She drew fourteen feet of water.

That night the men celebrated and the next day half of the workmen were down with malaria and dysentary. Two men came down with smallpox and were isolated. Dr. H. W. M. Washington arrived with one little kit of medicine. Lieutenant Alphonso Barbot rode a mule the last ten miles to his ship. Lieutenant George Gift came in a skiff. He brought a slave and a guitar. Soon most of the officers were on hand and the work of plating the *Arkansas* and mounting her guns got underway. Every rail of iron had to have six holes drilled in it, and there wasn't enough iron. There were no gun carriages and no powder.

Vicksburg notified Brown that heavy grain powder was not available there, but sent him a load of shells. Brown got a supply of saltpetre from Tennessee. It was shipped by rail to Bovina Station, then brought by wagon to Yazoo City. He got sulphur from Louisiana and set a crew to burning charcoal. He would make his own powder. . . .

But he couldn't make iron. That was when he got in touch with Nate Frome in Natchez and the word went out—"iron for the *Arkansas.*"

A Sunday School class in Montgomery collected bars from old gates, plantation bells were melted—iron for the *Arkansas;* a Natchez whore got six pounds of brass and twelve pounds of iron from a Yankee sailor and gave it to Sharon Weatherford—iron for the *Arkansas*. Frome bought some from Keith Alexander. Iron bars, ladles, pots, wrought iron balconies, a boiler from a locomotive, iron rings—anything.

It was then that Brown sent Granville to Natchez and Wyeth followed a few days later. Stevens was sent to Canton.

Memphis children sneaked lumps of coal from the Federal barges and it was moved down by wagon and boat. Some Catholic sisters sent quinine and castor oil. The oil was used on the engines. A Meridian preacher went from house to house collecting iron boot jacks. . . .

An aide brought the orders to General Van Dorn, written on brown wallpaper in ink made of pokeberries and soot. He read them carefully, made a few corrections and handed them to Granville. "You two leave immediately," he said. "My orderly will furnish horses."

Wyeth's face reddened and the scar flashed from the cleft in his chin to the tip of his jawbone and his chestnut hair seemed to bristle. He started to protest, but caught Granville's glance. Van Dorn gasped when he saw the scar. "What is wrong, sailor?"

"Nothing, sir." Wyeth was struggling to control himself.

"That's a nasty scar. Cutlass?"

"Capstan." He saluted and turned on his heels.

Granville folded the orders and put them inside his jacket. Then he, too, saluted and started out. "Oh, Granville," Van Dorn called. "What do you use on your beard?"

"Ear wax on my mustache, sir, and gun grease on my beard." He didn't crack a smile. An orderly followed them out.

Wyeth was shaking in rage when they reached the street. "It's not fair, Mr. Granville. I am due a leave. And I told Laurel I'd call this afternoon."

"Come on," Granville said. "We had better be on our way. That is another trouble with wars. Men have to do as they are told."

The orderly walked between them. "The horses are around the corner. What's wrong, sailor?" He glanced over at Wyeth.

The Missourian didn't reply, but Granville told the soldier to mind his own business.

"No offense," the orderly said.

Wyeth put his hand on the soldier's arm. "Hey, let's ride by Cherry street and let me stop a minute. . . ."

"Sorry, bub. I have orders to get you jacks to Chickasaw Bayou. That's north of town a piece, t'other side of the hills. But I'll deliver a message for you when I get back."

"All right." Wyeth was exasperated and downcast. "Go to Mrs. Nelle Simpson's house and ask for Miss Laurel MacKenzie. Tell her I had to leave suddenly. She knows where I'm going. . . ."

"So do I," the soldier said. "God help you."

"And tell her," Wyeth said, "that I'll see her when I can. Tell her I won't have time to write letters but I'll take time to read them. And tell her that if she can, to wait here for me. I'll be back."

Granville looked away down the bluff. The orderly lowered his head. "I'll tell her, bub."

They mounted horses and rode north across Glass Bayou to the Walnut Hills and when they reached the top they rested their animals. Wyeth stared back at Vicksburg, thence out at the Union fleet. Suddenly he gripped Granville's arm. "Look! On that jut of land where they are building the canal. . . ."

"I can not see the land," Granville said.

"My God!" the soldier said. "Can you see that far? What's up?"

"Yankees and Negroes are scattering." He threw back his head and laughed. "The canal. It's caving in. And no wonder. I can see the layout from here. The fools were digging a ditch perpendicular to the direction of the current."

"But what has happened?" Granville snorted.

"The river has seeped in there and caved the whole shebang in. Good Lord! Even if they could finish it, it wouldn't work. The current hits the shore exactly opposite from each end of the ditch. The Mississippi never would in the world cut through that canal. The ninnies." He laughed again. Then he checked his laughter quickly.

"What now?" Granville asked.

"Hospital ships. They are lining up over there."

"About half of Williams' Yanks have malaria," the soldier said. "Poor devils. Well, let's move along."

A swamp steamer, a tiny paddle wheeler with a tea-kettle boiler, was waiting at Chickasaw Bayou and as soon as the gunners were aboard it began picking its way up the sluggish stream, dodging stumps and vines. Then it swung out of the bayou and into the Yazoo, wheeled right and started upstream.[19] At Snyder's Bluff they stopped for fuel, pine knots, and Wyeth and Granville had their first opportunity to talk with the master.

"What do you hear from the *Arkansas?*" Wyeth asked anxiously.

"She's coming along."

"Did Captain Brown ever fix those engines so they will stop at the same time?"

"Naw. Can't be done. Them twin screws stop on the center at the wrong time and they never stop together. The automatic stoppers just naturally won't keep time with each other. I'd hate to risk my neck in that thing."

"You won't have to," said Granville sarcastically.

They pushed on up to Haynes Bluff about half way to Yazoo

City. A raft was across the river there to block any Union ships that might venture up that way seeking the *Arkansas*. Downstream from the raft, their fires banked and their decks deserted, were three Confederate craft, the *Livingston, Polk* and *Van Dorn*.

Wyeth recognized the *Van Dorn* as she had fought at Memphis. "She got away," the master explained, "and hid out in a slough. She slipped down here the other day. Don't know how the Yanks missed her. The other two were at New Orleans and got up here ahead of the Yanks. Pinckney is in command."

"They don't look very shipshape," Granville said.

Inasmuch as the raft blocked the Yazoo above Haynes Bluff, the two gunners left the boat and got horses and drove them without mercy up the road to Yazoo City. They and the horses were exhausted when they reached the town shortly after dark. However, as they rode through Yazoo City, their hearts were light. Wyeth didn't think of Laurel then. She seemed far away. There was a glare from down along the river, the dull red glare of forges. A sound of hammering and the clanging of iron reached them and then, in the glare, they saw the *Arkansas,* riding her anchor alongside the wharf. The *Capitol* was lashed to the ironclad and her crane was huffing and her drilling machinery was shrieking. Lanterns were hanging from ropes around the two ships. The *Arkansas'* deck was armored, but her ark was bare, the rough oaken planks and beams showing dully in the light of the fires.

Wyeth and Granville spurred their horses and galloped down the levee to the river. They dismounted and ran toward the ship. Then they saw Ves. He was sitting there, his back propped against the Dahlgren, and was cutting fuzes with a pair of scissors.

"Ves!" Wyeth yelled and he and Granville hurried toward their friend.

The Cajan looked up and around, then scrambled to his feet, a broad grin on his face. He was a huge man, a head taller than Granville or Wyeth. He was wearing dirty duck trousers and his chest was bare and covered by mosquito welts. He had rubbed lard and turpentine on his skin. The lard was rancid and he stunk. Naturally dark complexioned, the sun had burned his skin almost black, as blackish-brown as wet horsehide. His hair was flaxen and fell to his shoulders and he was clean shaved, but his chest and shoulders were matted with yellow hair. He just grinned at his friends and his eyes danced. The whites of his eyes showed in startling contrast to his dark skin. The pupils were big and black, however, like black marbles in a cup of milk. His eyes were like Sharon Weatherford's.

Wyeth reached him first and they hugged each other and pounded each other's backs, mumbling friendly curses.

"And Sim! You drunken whore-hopping stud!" Ves grabbed Granville's hand. He didn't call the Englishman Mr. Granville. Not Ves. . . .

Simeon St. Leger Granville was grinning, too. "Ves, you stink!"

"Rotten lard." The Cajan rubbed his hands on his greasy chest. "You'll be stinking, too, before morning, if the mosquitoes don't tote you off. They are as big as colts. Just yesterday, me and Cap'n Brown were gabbing and I was telling him to put a hawser on about half a dozen of them things, tie 'em to the *Arkansas* and let 'em pull her."

"Where is Captain Brown?" Granville asked.

"Around and about," Ves rubbed some of the lard on Granville's cheek. "Man, man, that beard. Will the lice love that. They'll crawl in there and sing 'Give Me Three Grains of Corn, Mother' while the mosquitoes do the tenor, the bullfrogs the bass and the rats'll play Mr. Gift's guitar. . . ."

"Shut up, Ves." Granville rubbed off the lard, smelled his hands and made a wry face. "We must see the captain. We have orders. . . ."

"Aw, to hell with orders, Sim. Tell me about the trip. Did you get some? I ain't had a piece in so long I've forgot how to do it."

Wyeth's blood chilled. Granville, however, ignored the question and said, "We got some iron. Has Lieutenant Stevens arrived?"

"Naw. Bogged down, mor'n likely. Cap'n Brown is expecting you. He said hold you right here until he gets back. Now tell me about Natchez. Did you get drunk? Did you meet Sharon?"

Again Wyeth was tense. Granville said, casually, "Yes, I met her. She's fine, Ves. I'll tell you all about it later. Now, how is Dolly?"

The Cajan rubbed his big hands together. His fingers were so strong that he could put three fingers down as many rifle barrels and lift the guns from the ground. He led them over to the Dahlgren, resting on two logs, and jerked off the canvas covering. "There she is, Sim."

Wyeth walked the length of the gun, rubbing his hand from the knob to the lip. Then he felt the neck and fillet, the trunnions and the face. They were greasy and slick. Trust Ves to keep the gun clean.

Granville was examining the vent and firing apparatus. Then he looked closer at the base of the breech and almost exploded. "What the bloody hell is this?"

Ves patted his chest. "A little surprise. That's a nameplate. Pure D silver. Won it off'n a man in Yazoo City."

Wyeth joined Granville and they looked at the nameplate, then at each other. The plate was about four inches long and two inches wide and on it, in crude letters, was engraved "Dolly." It was fastened to the gun by four screws.

"How you like it?" Ves asked. "Bored them holes myself, then packed 'em with wood so the screws'd hold. I cut them letters, too. How you like it?"

"All right," said Wyeth weakly and without enthusiasm.

Granville was not so polite, however. "It is terrible. And it must come off. Get me a screwdriver. . . ."

"Aw, Sim. It's pretty."

"It comes off, I tell you." Granville was fuming. "Dolly is a personal name and I will not have it used that way. And, too, the engraving is atrocious."

He loosened the screws and removed the plate. The four holes stared up at him and he fumed. "Ves, I should kick your tail over your bloody head. . . ."

"Have to get on a stump to do that, Sim. Might as well put the plate back. Them holes are ugly."

"Just a minute," said Wyeth. "Why not turn the plate over and engrave something on that side. . . ."

"But what?" Granville demanded. " 'In Deo speramus,' in God we trust! God forbid."

Ves' low forehead wrinkled. "Why not put *Arkansas* on there?"

The Englishman ran his tongue over his lips and was thoughtful. "Has the State of Arkansas got a motto?"

"Sure," said Wyeth. "Wait a minute, let me think. 'Regnant Populi.' That's it."

"Hmmm," said Granville. " 'The people rule.' I don't like it."

"Me neither," said Ves rather sullenly. "Don't mean nothing."
As a Cajan he was not allowed to vote. "Maybe Mississippi's got a
good 'un. We'll be fighting this gun for her."

Granville looked at Wyeth. "You know it?"

"Uh huh. 'Virtute et Armis.' By Valour and Arms." [20]

Ves slapped his shoulder and mashed a mosquito. "Say, now.
That's more like it. Sounds good and rightly pretty."

"So it does," said Granville. "By Valour and Arms. But it has got
to be done right. Who can engrave it?"

"I can," said Ves. "Just get a good knife and scratch it on."

"Hell," said Granville. "You can't write ten words."

Wyeth suddenly remembered something. He looked around
quickly at the *Arkansas,* the forges and the cook tent. "Hey, Ves.
Have you seen a Negro around here who looks like a fish. His name
is Gar?"

"Naw. What's a nigger got to do with it?"

"I thought maybe he came on ahead of Mr. Stevens. He's with
him. He can engrave that plate. Mr. Granville, if you write the
words he can copy them, and make 'em even and pretty and curly."

"What will he use?"

"A Bowie knife," Wyeth said. "I'll bet you he can do it."

Chapter Nine

A FEW days after his return to the Yazoo it seemed to Wyeth that he had never been away, and Natchez and the Big Black, Mort and Prent became places and men to remember, and his memory exaggerated details about all of them. Everything about the trip reminded him of Laurel, however, and he found himself recalling certain little things that his mind enlarged and dwelt upon.

Often, fitting iron rails on the *Arkansas,* he wished it were possible for her to see all the way from Vicksburg. He wanted her to see him, stripped to the waist, working under the sun, sweating and suffering. She might think he was doing it for her, and he was, in a way; and that might impress her and draw out her sympathy. He didn't exactly want her sympathy, but he wanted it to be on tap, ready to overflow and comfort him. He tried to remember everything about her. At first, he remembered her freckles and her smile, then her hands and feet. She wasn't really as beautiful as he remembered her to be. As the days wore on, he found himself thinking of the curves of her breasts and he was ashamed of his thoughts. Sometimes, sleeping on the bare ground near Dolly, he dreamed strange chaotic things about her. That, too, made him ashamed, yet the only reason he welcomed the nights was because they might bring more dreams.

The first letter from her called him "Dear Wyeth" and she signed herself, "As ever, Laurel."

She sent him a blue kerchief, larger than Mr. Granville's black one. He wondered where she got the silk. He was sure it came from one of her dresses and that thrilled him.

Of course, he found time to write her. He told her about Ves and Dolly, but scarcely mentioned the *Arkansas* because, for some reason, he didn't want her to know that the ship was almost finished and that the time was nearing for her to go out.

He worried over how to sign his first letter. He wanted very much to say something tender and personal. However, he signed it "As ever." Then he looked at the words and, impulsively, wrote "always" in front of them. "Always as ever." Her next letter was signed "As ever—always, too."

Granville and Ves watched their friend suffer the pangs of his first real love and, in the way of men, had no sympathy for him, only curiosity. The three gunners worked on the *Arkansas* from sun-up until sundown and in the early evenings they usually sat around their dismantled gun and did chores on her, polishing, cleaning and bringing her to her prime. Just as Ves had predicted, lice had found Granville's beard and he rubbed turpentine on his face. His beard grew ragged and he, too, coated his body with rancid lard. Wyeth let his whiskers grow and the scar was visible because no hair grew there. The men seldom wore jackets and their skin was sore to the touch. Redbugs, fleas, and gnats ate them during the days and mosquitoes and ants ate them at night.

Half of the men in camp were down with malaria, but, somehow, the Missourian, the Englishman and the Cajan escaped the malady. They were sitting early one night by their Dahlgren, each working and thinking his own thoughts. Ves was whittling a staff for an eccentric handspike used to throw the eccentric axles of gun carriages in and out of gear. His handspike had an iron head with a hexagonal hole which fitted the extremities of the eccentric axle-tree.

Wyeth was adding coloring material to powder to be used as signals and to frighten the enemy. To produce red he used sulphate of strontia. The material came from Vicksburg and as he readied the preparations he stored them in small canvas bags. He used nitric of baryta for green, bicarbonate of soda for yellow, lampblack for rose, and powdered flint glass for white. Near him, where he could watch them, were several pots of tar which were being boiled down to pitch. Often he got up and stirred the fire under the pots.

Granville was making friction powder to fire the Dolly main charge. He used two parts chlorate of potassa to one part sulphuret of antimony. He stored his powder in tiny linen bags. Beside him, on a shingle, were several crane quills that he had cut and cleaned. These he would use in the Dahlgren's vent if his friction tube failed him. Granville had never been satisfied with his gun's vent as the heat of the inflamed gases in the gun enlarged the hole's diameter. So he had a vent-piece made of copper and forced it into the vent. That protected the tiny opening. Most gunners fired their pieces simply by filling the vents with fine powder and igniting it with slow matches. Granville, however, made his own friction apparatus by soldering a short copper tube to a long copper tube at right angles. The short upper tube was for friction powder and a rough jagged wire loop ran into the tube. The long tube was filled with priming powder and inserted into the vent of the Dahlgren. To fire his gun, the Englishman tied a lanyard to the wire loop and jerked it violently. The friction generated sufficient heat to ignite the powder in the short tube and that set off the priming powder in the long tube. The priming powder in turn ignited the main charge in the chamber of the gun. However, the friction tube often was unreliable so Granville got quills to be inserted in the vent to insure the proper flow of priming powder in an emergency.

The work bored them and often they glanced at one another, hoping somebody would say something. Each had heard the other's stories and jokes and there was nothing to say. So they sat there doing their tasks and slapping at mosquitoes. Eventually Ves picked up a tiny clod and tossed it at Granville, attracting his attention. Then he pointed at Wyeth. The Missourian was staring into the night, his mind obviously far away.

"Tell me, Sim," Ves said, "what does she really look like? I can't go by what Wyeth says. Is she half as pretty as he makes out like?"

"Prettier," Granville said.

Wyeth ignored them.

"Got any bubbies?" Ves was very serious. "I'm a sap-sucker for bubbies."

Wyeth felt his blood rising and then he smiled. Ves was the only man who could say such a thing. Coarse, friendly and faithful, the Cajan was forgiven by his comrades simply because they expected nothing from him.

Granville, aware that the conversation was indelicate, tried to brush it off for Wyeth's sake. "She is a very lady-like person. How is the eccentric handspike coming along, Ves?"

The Cajan held up the piece. "It'll do. Is this here girl of Wyeth's a yummy?"

"What the hell is a yummy?" Wyeth demanded.

"You know, yum yum. A big piece of pie is a yummy. Haven't you ever seen girls you just wanted to eat? They're yummies."

"I've never had that desire," Wyeth said.

"You will. You'll want to bite her some day. Then she'll squeal like a colt. . . ."

"Oh, for God's sake, shut up." Granville shook his head at Ves, warning him. "Don't you ever think about anything except women?"

"Not unless I have to." Then it came to him that Wyeth didn't like his talk so he got up and walked by his friend and rubbed his big hand in the Missourian's hair. "I didn't mean nothing. She must be a fine lady."

A whistle sounded up the river and the men looked that way, then at one another. Without speaking, they stopped their work and ran to the water's edge. Work on the *Arkansas* ceased and every man peered up the river, watching a ship that was churning downstream, showing two green lanterns on her bow. Granville recognized the boat first and shouted, *"Star of the West!* [21] There she comes, boys."

The men began yelling, for the ship had coffee aboard and the seamen that Ves had recruited in Memphis.

"She finally got out," Ves said. "She was way back up the Tallahatchie."

"She came out on high water," Wyeth said. "Captain Brown will be tickled pink."

"We are getting quite a little fleet," Granville said.

And so they were, for five craft had joined the *Arkansas* since she was towed down from upriver. First there was the *Capitol,* the workship, then the *Era No. 2,* a little steamer that had slipped out of the Yalobusha River, also a tributary of the Yazoo. The *Era* had been lurking near Grenada where Captain Brown's family was refugeeing. Then there were two armed tugs, rubbing their noses against the *Arkansas.* And now the *Star of the West.*

The new arrival moored about 100 yards upstream and in the glow of the *Arkansas'* lanterns, the three gunners saw Captain

Brown go aboard the *Star* and welcome her master. The seamen were marched off and the supplies were unloaded. Wyeth, Granville and Ves went back to their work, grateful for the interruption.

They talked about the *Star* for the next hour and then became silent. They didn't see Captain Brown until he was almost upon them. They scrambled to their feet and Granville and Wyeth saluted. Ves said, "Howdy, Cap'n."

Brown's face was lined and there were signs of fever in his eyes. The lower part of his face was covered by a heavy black beard and he looked like Robert E. Lee looked twenty years before. He commented on the men's work and then said, "Woodward, come with me."

Wyeth followed him into the night, walking beside him, in step.

"Do you know what was in those orders you brought me from Vicksburg?" Brown asked.

"Yes, sir."

"Have you told the men that my command now is under jurisdiction of the War Department, or that General Van Dorn is going to send me two hundred Missouri soldiers?" They were walking along the bank down stream from the *Arkansas,* heading for the powder works.

"No, sir."

"Good. I want the Missourians to be a surprise. Their arrival will cheer the men." They reached the spot where the charcoal for the powder was being pulverized and Brown and Wyeth stopped to watch the work.

Brown was using carbon, saltpetre and sulphur for his coarse powder. The pulverized saltpetre came from Tennessee and they made their own charcoal by burning hemp and willow. The charcoal and sulphur were pulverized in barrels, partly filled with zinc balls and rolled on the ground until the ingredients became a powder.

Then the sulphur, charcoal and saltpetre were mixed in barrels made of leather stretched over wooden frames. The mass was worked for two hours and pressed into millcakes, then granulated by hand and pounded into powder. To grade the powder and make it uniform, the Confederates worked it through three sieves and glazed it by putting it in a barrel and revolving it ten times per minute. Each grain was 0.31 inch in diameter, the proper size for cannon powder. It was glazed and dried until the grains were smooth, angular and irregular, but without sharp corners. Each grain was very hard and Captain Brown dipped his hand into a keg of the finished product and let it pour between his fingers, feeling it. He smiled for the first time since he and Wyeth began their tour. "It is all right, Woodward. The powder is all right."

They walked on down the river while Brown inspected everything, the medical supplies, the food and the sanitary facilities. They were on their way back to the *Arkansas* when Brown said, "I brought you along to talk to you. You know rivers. How does this one look?"

"She's got a full head right now, Captain. But the crest of that flood is passing and soon we will get low water. Can the *Arkansas* work in low water?"

"That's the point," the master said, shaking his head slowly. He looked up at the sky, at the stars that seemed limp in the heat. "The *Arkansas* draws fourteen feet. We'll go aground if we let low water catch us."

"Then we're about ready to go out?"

"We're not ready. But we'll have to go out soon."

"Lieutenant Stevens hasn't arrived yet, sir. We haven't mounted a single gun or drilled our crew. . . ."

"And the *Arkansas* is a long ways from being finished. We'll have to work harder. Five weeks. That's all the time I gave myself." He stopped and Wyeth stood beside him. "Sometimes, Woodward, it is wise for a commander to get opinions from his men. Have you wondered why the Yankees haven't tried to come up here?"

"Yes, sir. I don't understand it. They must know that we're up to something."

"There are only two men in the Yankee fleet who worry me. Farragut and Ellet. I'm afraid of a trap. Farragut is not a man to waste time. And Ellet is a scrapper."

"A. W. Ellet, sir?"

"Good heavens, no. I'm not worried about him. It's that boy, Colonel Charles Ellet."

"Little Boy Blue?" Wyeth was surprised. "He's only a shaver. Just 19."

"He'll fight. When you came up the river you saw the Pinckney ships down at Haynes Bluff on the other side of the raft?"

"Yes, sir."

"Just between us, Woodward, how did they look?"

"Rusty, sir. The *Livingston* and *Polk* were moored to the bank and the *Van Dorn* was moored to the *Livingston*. Commander Pinckney is taking a chance. If the Yanks should dash up the Yazoo they would have him in a corner. But they'd have trouble getting up here. They would have to blow that raft that blocks the river. . . ."

"But if they sunk Commander Pinckney's ships what would keep them from blowing the raft? And if they got through, the *Arkansas* would be at their mercy. We haven't got a gun ready."

"Yes, sir."

Brown picked up a stick and threw it into the Yazoo. "You are a sensible man, Woodward. I'm going to send you to Commander Pinckney. You see, I can't give him orders. But I can suggest. Do you mind lying?"

"Not a bit, sir."

"Then go to him. Tell him that when you were in Vicksburg you heard about some Yankee ships in the mouth of the Yazoo and that they might be getting ready to come up and look things over. Tell him my suggestion is that he keep up steam, point his ships downstream and be ready to fight. We can't afford to lose those ships. Be diplomatic. If I send an officer, Pinckney will think I am applying pressure. He's a very sensitive man."

"When do I leave?"

"Within an hour. Take the *Era No. 2*. And before you ask me the answer is no. You can't take Granville or Gillivray. I need them here."

Wyeth borrowed Ves' snipper rifle for the trip and chose ten seamen who had survived the Battles of Memphis. He got a full crew for the *Era No. 2* and worked the pressure to the limit, using spoiled bacon fat to hasten the pressure. He confided in Granville and Ves and they refused to answer the many questions asked along the wharf. Wyeth went to the pilot house and took over the wheel and made the little boat cut didoes on the way down the Yazoo, running in the light of the moon and showing green and yellow lanterns. The *Arkansas* resembled a rusty skeleton in the glow of the workmen's lights as she fell behind him. The Yazoo, heavy with flood waters that sweetened the land, coiled and returned on itself in great swollen loops. Wyeth took the inside of the bends. He forgot about the war and his spirit was exuberant. This was as it was years before when he was a steamboat man on the Osage. He wished Laurel could see him now. . . .

Captain Brown was standing by his tent when the *Era* disappeared down the river. He went inside, took a bit of quinine and water and then sent for Granville. They walked together along the upstream bank to a long lean-to which was the cannon factory. Guns of many sizes were resting on logs and gunsmiths were working over them, taking pieces from this and that one and adding them to others. They, too, worked by lantern light and scarcely noticed their commander. They simply were too tired to be smart.

The guns included three eight-inch Columbiads, one old fifteen-inch Dahlgren that weighed 42,000 pounds and a nine-inch Dahlgren, similar to Dolly. Parts from the big Dahlgren were being fitted onto the small one.

The assortment also included two eight-inch sixty-four-pounders, rifled, two rifled 32s, four carronades, six dismantled Parrots and odds and ends from three Napoleons. The guns had been collected from Texas to South Carolina.

Rammers, chocks, pouches and other implements were stacked neatly at one end of the lean-to and men were working on various other paraphernalia for cannoneers, including tompions, sponges, vent-covers, elevating bars, rollers, and handspikes.

"How do they look, Granville?" Brown asked. "Do you think we can get ten good guns out of the bunch?"

"We need only nine, sir. Our Dolly is ready when she gets a carriage."

"I expect Lieutenant Stevens tomorrow. He is bringing cypress and we can begin your carriage immediately." Brown led the way out of the factory. "You will draw your own plans."

"Yes, sir." Granville, in the British fashion, walked a step behind his superior officer. "A casement carriage on an iron chassis. The carriage will weigh 1,120 pounds and the chassis a ton."

They went down and sat on the bank and as far down the river as they could see there were lights, lights for the *Arkansas*. Without apology, Captain Brown stretched on the ground and put his hands under his head. He looked up at the stars, then over at Granville who was sitting upright. "Falmouth, Granville?"

"Yes, sir. For a while." He, too, looked up at the stars. He was surprised to hear Brown mention the naval station at which he had trained as a boy. The Englishman didn't resent the questions, knowing his captain wasn't prying. "I was at Plymouth, too. I left Her Majesty's Navy because the Admiralty did not approve of my drinking habits."

"How is the drinking now?"

"Very slow, sir."

Brown put his hand on the ground and pushed himself up. Then he ran his hand over his beard and scratched, for lice are no respecters of rank. "I need a quartermaster, Granville. And if we get out of here alive there will be another promotion in Vicksburg."

Granville looked down at his feet and then away. "The Confederate Articles of War give me the right of refusal."

"I reckoned you had read the Articles. And I figured you would refuse. May I ask why?" Brown was smiling. "Is it because of Woodward and Gillivray?"

"Partly, sir. We have been together a long time."

"I can promote Woodward. Gillivray is not officer material." Brown said it slowly as though he disliked saying it. He knew it was not necessary for him to explain further or to go into the fact that Ves, as a Cajan, was barred from promotion by an unwritten rule. He was the only Cajan in the service and, although nothing had been said about it, there always was a possibility that some men might refuse to serve with him, and the certainty that many men would refuse to serve under him.

Granville said, "I am aware that Ves is not officer material. So with the Captain's permission I will stay where I am. I do not want to leave my gun and do not want the responsibility of a commission. It does not become an officer to get drunk, and two hours after you give me leave in Vicksburg I will be drunk."

Brown stood up and put his hands in the small of his back and stretched. He went to his headquarters and gave Granville the list of officers to be posted. "I'd hoped you would be among them," the captain said.

Granville studied the list and read the names aloud:

"Executive Officer, First Lieutenant Henry K. Stevens; Lieutenants, John Grimball, A. D. Wharton, Charles W. Read, Alphonso Barbot, George W. Gift; Surgeon, H. W. M. Washington; Assistant Surgeon, Charles M. Morfit; Assistant Paymaster, Richard Taylor; First Assistant Engineer, George W. City; Second Assistant Engineer, E. Covert; Third Assistant Engineers, William H. Jackson, E. H. Brown, James T. Doland, John S. Dunny, James S. Gettis; Acting Masters, Samuel Milliken, J. L. Phillips; Midshipmen, Richard H. Bacot, T. S. Wilson, H. Canas, Dabney M. Scales, Clarence W. Tyler; Master's Mate, J. A. Wilson; Pilots, J. H. Shacklett, William Gilmore, James Brady and John Hodges."

Brown was almost asleep on his feet. "Your Dahlgren will be the center gun of the port broadside. Lieutenant Barbot will be in command of the port battery."

Granville said, "I like the port."

"Good. And just one more thing. When Jeff Thompson's Missourians arrive I want you to start training them to work the guns." Then he laughed, the first time Granville ever had heard him laugh. "Most of Thompson's men are Irish."

"We should get along fine," the Englishman said and took his leave. He went back to Ves and told him as much of the conversation as he wanted the Cajan to know.

"So Mr. Stevens gets here tomorrow and Wyeth's nigger will be with him?" Ves didn't like the idea of a Negro taking up their time. He was boiling some turnips over one of the pitch fires. The Cajan and his two friends had their own mess to avoid any complications.

"I assume Gar is still with the party," Granville said. He got paper and a quill and began blocking out the words *By Valour and Arms*.

Ves peered over his shoulder and moved the lantern closer. "Yes, sir, that's rightly pretty. If that nigger don't do a good job I'll stomp him. You know, Sim, if I'd thought about it I'd have held out for another saying for the nameplate. 'Touch not the cat bot a glove.' That's a beaut."

Granville almost dropped the quill. "God's hindleg! Where did you hear that?"

"I've heard it all my life," Ves said casually. "Maw said it's an old saying in our family. It means don't touch the cat without a glove."

The motto of the Clan Gillibhreac, the proud Mac Gillivray Clan in Inverness-shire. The Englishman knew that Vespasian Gillivray's name possibly came from the famous line, but it simply never had occurred to him that the best blood of Scotland was in his friend. He was staring at the huge Cajan. Ves stirred the turnips. "There's another saying among my folks—'Loch moy!' I don't know what it means."

That was the rallying cry of the Gillibhreac, a clan that traced its line back to 1263. Granville put the quill away. "It means gentle lake," he said. Suddenly he was thinking of Sharon, a descendant of the clan and yet beyond the pale in the South because her blood lines were mixed. Her Indian blood was royal and her Scotch blood was high caste. He wondered again if there was any Negro blood in her and knew he would never know for she didn't know and nobody was certain. Then it came to him that if she did have Negro blood it might be Moorish, possibly a strain from the rulers of Carthage or the conquerors of Spain.

Ves said, "The ponds down where we live are gentle. I didn't know you knew all about them things. There's a heap of stuff among my folks that we don't know nothing about. Here's another saying, 'Tha mi deonach a chall ma chuireas tu mo dhruim ri balla.' "

The Englishman picked up his quill and resumed his work. "That is pure Gaelic, Ves. Many, many years ago your family said that when it was challenged. It means, 'I am content to lose if you are able to put my back to the wall.' "

"So that's it. I reckon the old folks just forgot what it means. You oughta come down and see us when the war's over. There's a heap of stuff you might like. We've got a skirt that a man wore. It's made out of plaid. Sharon has it now."

"It is probably part of your family's tartan," Granville said. He was finishing up the lettering.

The Cajan took a sharp stick and tested the turnips. Then he sat down by Granville. "I haven't asked you much about Sharon, Sim. You two hit it off all right, huh?"

Granville's flesh tightened. "Why, yes. She's a very fine lady. I haven't heard from her. . . ."

"Course not. It wouldn't be proper for her to write you unless you wrote first."

"Naturally." Granville didn't look up. He wanted to forget Sharon, knowing that was best.

"She don't write so good. She never got to school. I'm glad you and her hit it off. Meeting a good fellow like you did her a mite of good. I fret about Sharon."

Granville finished his task and put it aside. "How are the turnips?"

"About done."

The sun was clawing its way up the eastern rim when the *Era No. 2* came to a landing on the upper side of the raft that the Confederates had moored from shore to shore to block the Yazoo at Haynes Bluff. Wyeth instructed his seamen carefully and marched them down to Commander Pinckney's camp which was on the bank near the *Livingston,* his flagship. The Missourian was surprised that a sea-faring man established his headquarters ashore. The three Confederate ships were squatting in the Yazoo. There wasn't a pound of steam on the *Van Dorn,* and the *Livingston* and *Polk* didn't have enough pressure up to sound a whistle.

Wyeth reported to Pinckney that he had heard about Yankee gunboats in the mouth of the Yazoo and then delivered Brown's suggestion that the ships be made ready to fight. Pinckney ignored the report. He was quite polite and thanked the gunner and told him to inform Lieutenant Brown that he had the situation under control.

The Missourian was stunned. "I have been in Vicksburg, sir. I tell you the Yankees won't sleep forever. Colonel Ellet is just rash enough to run up this river and knock hell out of your ships."

Still Pinckney was polite. "I can handle Little Boy Blue."

"But, sir, you can't fight without steam, and your ships are headed upstream. A battery on the bluffs can control this river. I will help you install them. . . ."

"It is quite obvious that discipline on the *Arkansas* is rather lax," Pinckney said casually. "You're dismissed."

Wyeth turned away. He was so angry that he knew if he stayed there longer he might talk himself into a court martial. He snapped his seamen into line and marched them up the bluff. They scarcely had reached the summit when one of the sailors shouted, then pointed downstream. And from around the bend came two Federal rams, the *Lancaster* and the *Monarch.* Their decks were swarming with sharpshooters from General Williams' Brigade. A commander's flag was flying from the *Lancaster,* a signal that Colonel Charles Rivers Ellet, Little Boy Blue, was aboard.

Wyeth's heart almost stopped beating and his mouth went dry. The alarm was sounded aboard the *Livingston* and the rolling of a beat to quarters sounded from the helpless ship. Wyeth saw Pinckney run aboard and onto the quarter-deck. The commander sized up the situation quickly and then ordered most of his men ashore. Men began deserting the two other ships. . . .

The Missourian was dumbfounded. He threw his little company into skirmish line and they opened fire. Pinckney's men formed a line along the bank and began shooting, but there wasn't a shot fired from the three Confederate ships. Then suddenly a yellow flame shot up from the *Livingston.* Wyeth cursed frantically. "I ought to shoot him! Goddammit! He's burning his own ships without fighting. He was trapped like a rat!" The gunner began crying in sheer anger.

The Federal rams bore in like terriers after moles, pouring rifle fire into the *Livingston.*

Pinckney ran from the *Livingston* to the *Polk* and in a few minutes both ships were enveloped in flames. The fire spread to the *Van Dorn.* Three explosions thundered and echoed against the bluff. Wyeth and his men just stood there staring at the debacle. Wyeth still was crying and cursing.

Pinckney deployed his men to the raft to defend it. The rams hove to, however, fired a triumphant volley at the sinking ships and turned around. The Confederate battleflags slipped beneath the Yazoo and it was all over in a few minutes. Ellet had dared venture up the river with two ships and his daring brought its reward. Pinckney and his men were safe, but there wasn't a Confederate ship left between Haynes Bluff and the Mississippi, and the raft was the only barrier between the Yankees and the *Arkansas.*

Pinckney's behavior sickened Wyeth although he knew it was good policy to scuttle the ships rather than run the risk of having them captured. And they couldn't have fought. The rams could have battered them into submission and with the captured ships and his own two rams Ellet might have destroyed the raft and proceeded up to the *Arkansas,* which was unmanned and ungunned.

Wyeth firmly expected Ellet to attempt to blow the raft and poke on up the river, and was amazed when the rams scooted down the Yazoo to rejoin the Mississippi fleets. He gave his men the double quick and they hurried back to the *Era,* whipped her around and plowed back up the river. He was sorely afraid and heartsick. Bucking the flood channel, it took the *Era* 20 hours to reach her base. . . .

Wyeth began sounding his whistle before he reached the *Arkansas* and Captain Brown was at the landing. Tears came to the sailor's eyes as he made his report. His captain chewed his lower lip and turned away. "It just made you sick," Wyeth said. "Three good ships burned without firing a shot."

"The mistake was not in burning his ships. The mistake was in not being ready to fight. You will probably be called to testify at a board of inquiry."

"Why do you reckon Colonel Ellet didn't blast his way through that raft and come on up here after us? The Yanks are bound to know that we're up to something."

Brown began smiling. "The enemy is timid and a timid man will believe anything. We have seen to it that some wild tales have been circulated about the *Arkansas.* She is two hundred and fifty feet long, a monster with twenty guns. I have a feeling that Colonel Ellet went back for help and that he will be coming up the river again before long."

"Are we going to wait for him?"

"No, Woodward. We are going out to meet him, his rams and Farragut's ships and Davis' ironclads and Williams' artillery."

"You forgot Porter's mortars."

"So I did."

Wyeth went back to the *Era's* pilothouse and dismissed his crew and turned the boat over to a regular pilot. Then he walked slowly down the bank where he thought he would find Granville, Ves and Dolly. His friends were not with the gun, however, and he went to the powder works. They were not there. He heard hammering and shouts from beyond the powder works and hurried in that direction. First he saw the oxen and mules and then the wagons. A huge piece of canvas was stretched over a clearing and under the covering Lieutenant Stevens was working a crew, shaping carriages.

Granville was supervising one job and Ves was lugging iron. The Cajan saw Wyeth and yelled a greeting. "They got here yesterday," Ves shouted. "We are building a carriage for Dolly."

Quickly, Wyeth looked around, but Gar wasn't in sight.

Granville nodded to his friend and heard the story of Haynes Bluff.

"Now that's a hell of a note," Ves said.

Wyeth started to speak. Granville anticipated his question and said, "He is over there tending to the mules."

"Oh, yes," Ves said. "Your nigger got here with Mr. Stevens. What a funny looking bumbo he is. An alligator gar must have climbed right out of the river and got in bed with his maw."

The Missourian sauntered over to the mule pen and there was Gar sitting on a stump, engraving *By Valour and Arms* on the silver plate. He was using his Bowie and copying Granville's letters carefully. He jumped up when he saw Wyeth and bowed politely. Relief and joy showed in his eyes. "We made it, Mist' Woodward. We bogged down a heap and lost one wagon. I have your snipper and here's the Bowie. And I've learned just about ever' word on the first page of the Bible."

"I'm glad to see you, Gar." That feeling of responsibility came back to Wyeth and his conscience began prodding his determination.

"Some of them words were rightly hard. I put marks by 'em and Mist' Granville told me about 'em last night."

Wyeth stood over him and watched him resume his work. Then he said, "When you get through with that I want you to paint me a picture."

"The *Arkansas?*"

"That's right. How did you guess?"

The Wolof handled the big blade as though it were a penknife. "Mist' Granville asked the same thing. I'll do it. What you want me to do with it?"

"See that it gets to Miss Laurel."

Gar finished one word and brushed his hand across the name plate. "I can't go with the *Arkansas*, huh, Mist' Woodward?"

"No."

"Maybe they need a cook. . . ."

"The cook must be a member of the crew and Negroes are not allowed to fight for the Confederacy. When you finish that job take it to Mr. Granville."

Wyeth walked away. He was moody again and thoughtful, and

was silent when he reported to Granville at the carriage works. Ves was mouthing about the heat and the Englishman was shaping the two cheeks of the Dahlgren's carriage. Each cheek was made of cypress, cut to a triangular shape, reinforced by boiler plate and stiffened by ribs. The ribs were trough-beams bolted to the inner sides of the cheek.

A half-circle was cut in the top of each cheek and trunnion plates were placed in the depressions. Each cheek was propped upright and the pieces were spaced at the proper distance and then bolted into a carriage by fastening iron transoms from one cheek to the other. Next an eccentric axle and two iron wheels were added. Each wheel had holes for handspikes.

Granville worked harder than he had ever worked before and wouldn't stop to eat the baked sweet potatoes that Ves brought him. Wyth refused food, too

But Ves ate and when he wiped his mouth on the cotton kerchief that protected his neck he looked over at the Missourian. "What do you aim to do with that nigger?"

"I don't know," said Wyeth without looking up. He was helping Granville adjust the transoms between the two cheeks.

"Want me to run him off?"

"No. Leave him alone."

"That nigger can read a little bit. Sim was showing him how last night. Readin' ain't good for niggers."

Neither Granville nor Wyeth answered him. Ves picked up a handful of the potatoes. "He's got to eat."

The Englishman and the Missourian exchanged glances. They had forgot about food and quarters for the Negro.

Ves cupped his hands and shouted for Gar and when the Wolof appeared the Cajan handed him the potatoes. "Here, eat 'em. I'll fix you a place to sleep down near us."

Gar began munching the potatoes. Gar understood Ves. The Cajan was feeding him. The Cajan would see that he had a place to sleep. Gar and Ves were friends then, the mysterious friendship between some Southerners and some Negroes, a kinship born of necessity, an affinity that baffles reason.

Ves watched the Negro finish his meal. "Boy, you are the ugliest man I ever saw. Are you sure no gar-fish ever messed around your maw's bed?"

The Wolof was not offended as that was what he expected from Ves. But he didn't smile. He merely said, "I don't know, Mist' Ves. I don't remember."

Then Ves began laughing and Gar laughed, too, and ambled off, back to tend his mules and finish the name plate.

The Cajan glowered at his comrades. "You look after his mind, but I have to look after his belly. That's how it always is with niggers. Folks want to learn 'em stuff and then forget that they have to eat." He walked away, mumbling to himself.

Granville shook his head in bewilderment. "Wyeth, if you had said such things to Gar he never would have forgiven you."

"You, either."

"I suppose not. He worships you, rather from afar. I think he respects me and accepts me because I am your friend. Yet he loves Ves."

"Uh huh. I know. So you helped him with his words?"

"Naturally. But I am making him do something in return for my help. The engraving for one thing. And I am going to have him teach me some of his songs. He must pay for knowledge. He must work for it."

"He learns fast, doesn't he?" Wyeth said it proudly.

"So so. But knowledge after the fact is easy. Don't forget that."

The days began melting one into the other and to the *Arkansas* crew and workers there was no beginning and no ending of each day, for the afternoons ran into the nights and the nights into the mornings. The sick list began to grow and some men deserted. The sun gave the company no mercy and Captain Brown drove them until tears actually showed in his eyes when he gave orders. Men toppled at their jobs and were dragged to the shade, then carried to the sick bay. The heat soared to 110 degrees during the day and the metal of the ship was hot to the touch.

The Yazoo was falling fast and Brown took soundings. He had 20 feet at his mooring. That was sufficient, but downstream at Satartia Bar, which they must pass, the river was down to eighteen feet. Brown showed his first sign of nervousness when he got the news. He sent to Haynes Bluff for information as to how long it would take to cut through the raft and the engineers said two weeks. Debris and drift had piled against the raft. Brown tried not to show the fear that was gnawing at his spirit. He couldn't wait two weeks. The Yazoo was down to nineteen feet at the *Arkansas'* berth. He confided his fears to Lieutenants Grimball, Gift and Read. They went down and sounded at Satartia Bar, thence to the raft. They reported that the raft could be broken in a few hours by blasting its mooring at the right bank and allowing the channel to clear the debris. Brown breathed easier and called for the last ounce of his men's energy.

The carriages were finished and hoisted aboard. Granville saw to it that his carriage fit properly on the iron chassis, a movable railway along which the carriage moved to and from battery.

Then they went to the Dolly and with aid of a gin, a tripod of pine poles, they got the big gun under a sling cart. The cart simply was two big wheels, an axle-tree, a tongue and a sling. It took twenty men to get the Dahlgren slung under the cart and Gar used twelve oxen to haul the cart to the water's edge. The *Capitol's* crane lifted the cannon, then lowered it through the top of the ark, onto the carriage, the gun's trunnions fitting into the trunnion beds of the carriage.

The Dolly was the first gun aboard, and the first one tested. Ves and Granville sponged her barrel, then rammed 13 pounds of coarse powder down her maw. The powder was in a linen bag. Linen burns quickly and completely and never leaves a glowing ash that might explode the next charge prematurely. Granville asked for a seventy-pound shell and that was rammed in. Then, at a nod from the Englishman, his two friends seized handspikes, inserted them into the eccentric maneuvering wheels which were underneath the carriage and slightly in front of the trunnions. The wheels were in gear and the men moved the gun forward along the chassis and into battery. The muzzle was poking out of the port.

"So far, so good," Granville said. Sweat was pouring from his face and Ves and Wyeth were breathing deeply.

Captain Brown came aboard the gundeck and stood aft. Granville motioned to the stern of the chassis and Ves and Wyeth got another handspike and rolled the gun on its traverse circle, moving the piece horizontally. Granville shook his head when the gun moved one foot each way and then was blocked by the port. He looked over at Brown and the Captain said, "Yes, I know. It can't be helped. To fire we will have to come alongside. Try your elevation."

The Missourian stepped to the elevating screw, which was worked by a geared nut. The nut was revolved by a bevelled spurwheel, attached to one end of a shaft at right angles to the cheek of the carriage. The other end of the shaft projected from the right side of the carriage and was equipped with a handle with four branches. Wyeth seized a branch in both hands, applied all of his strength and turned the handle to the right. That forced the gun's breech upward and the muzzle downward. The Dolly was aimed into the water.

Granville apparently was satisfied. He simply said, "Gear."

Wyeth and Ves got gear wrenches, fastened them over two nuts on the wheels, heaved, and threw the wheels out of gear. The Dolly's carriage slipped onto the iron rail of the chassis.

"Touch her, Granville," Brown said calmly.

The Englishman yanked the lanyard and his friction tube set off the blast. The shell plowed into the river. The Dolly dipped her nose as all cannons do when the gas escapes. Then she lurched into recoil, sliding along the rail. The friction and the incline checked her backward plunge before she reached the hurters, pieces of iron riveted to the top of the rail to prevent her sliding off of her chassis.

The smoke filled the gundeck and when the cloud passed away Brown was smiling. So was Ves. A cheer sounded from the *Capitol* and from the men working topside on the *Arkansas*. The ship's first shot had been fired. Granville was solemn, however. He motioned to Wyeth and Ves, and they threw the wheels back into gear and rolled the gun into battery.

The Englishman leaned over and patted his gun. Then Wyeth smiled, too. Granville turned smartly and said, "This gun is ready, Captain Brown."

The other guns were brought aboard, ten in all. Two eight-inch Columbiads were put in casement at the two bowports. The starboard Columbiad was under command of Lieutenant Grimball, and the port bowgun was given over to Lieutenant Gift. Midshipman Dabney Scales of Memphis, was attached to Grimball's gun and Midshipman John Wilson of Baltimore was assigned to Gift.

Dolly was the center gun of the port broadside and Lieutenant

Barbot accepted command of the three guns on that side of the ship, the nine-inch Dahlgren, one six-inch rifled gun and one thirty-two-pounder, smooth bore.

A similar battery was on the starboard line and Lieutenant Wharton of Nashville was in charge.

Lieutenant Read, a Mississippian, had the two stern guns, six-inch rifled pieces.

Each gun was fired once and Brown nodded approval.

The crew began working on pulleys and slings, fixed near the ports and used to lift the heavy shells to the mouths of the guns. Then powder and projectiles were taken aboard; shells and shot for Farragut's wooden ships, solid shells and fuzed shells for the ironclads, and grape and cannister for all.

The Yazoo had dropped to sixteen feet at Satartia Bar. . . .

Realizing he never would have time to finish his ship, Brown began patching it. The quarter and stern were given a thin coating of boiler iron. An iron shield was fastened to the front of the ark and the wheel was behind the shield. The pilothouse was two feet above the shield and exposed. Brown got a little boiler iron around the pilothouse, but that was all. He had his choice. He could have protected the pilothouse and his own quarterdeck by closing the bow and stern ports and bolting iron all the way up each end of the ark. But he needed the guns more than safety, so he left his deck exposed.

The crew's quarters were forward and below the waterline. Most of the men slung their hammocks on the gundeck which they called the slaughterhouse. Their mess was forward, too, a cubby hole of a room that was so hot the men preferred to mess in the slaughterhouse. The officers' wardroom was amidship, next to the powder room, but their mess was near a tiny galley, built aft.

It was Ves who said, "You know, in this ship you would have to swing a cat up and down by its tail, you couldn't swing it sideways."

Wyeth said, "You'd never skin a cat aboard without getting fur in your mouth. We're so packed in that I figure the first morning we sail I'll put my shoes on Mr. Granville's feet."

"The first day we sail you won't have time to get your shoes on," Granville said.

They were loading coal and the Yazoo was down to fifteen feet at the Bar when Captain William F. Lynch, Commander in those waters, rode over from Jackson on a tour of inspection. He took one look at the *Arkansas* and turned white. Then he wrote out a dispatch to the Navy Department and sent it by messenger back to Jackson and the telegraph wire. The message said:

"The *Arkansas* is very inferior to the *Merrimac* in every particular. The iron with which she is covered is worn and indifferent, taken from railroad tracks, and is poorly secured to the vessel, boiler iron on stern and counter; her smokestack is sheet iron."

And she was a patchwork quilt affair, scraps of iron bolted to plates; wrought iron laced over holes. Her engines wheezed when they turned and rattled when they got up steam.

Captain Lynch was aghast when he saw that the fire front of the boilers were not lined and that every time a shovel full of coal was put on the whole mass of iron about the boilers became red hot.

"Do you intend to fight in this thing?" he demanded of Captain Brown.

"Yes."

"It will be a slaughter pen."

"The men call it a slaughterhouse."

"The Yanks have sixty ships waiting. . . ."

Brown said, "They won't have to wait long. As soon as the Missourians arrive, I'm getting underway."

In Lynch's presence he sent for Lieutenant Stevens and instructed him to ride to Vicksburg and inform General Van Dorn that the river was falling so fast that the *Arkansas* must make a run for it.

From Lynch, Brown learned that Commander Pinckney was in Vicksburg trying to explain his losses at Haynes Bluff. Brown told his superior, "I suggested to Commander Lynch that he get ready to fight. The Yanks caught him flat-footed."

"He was waiting for me to take command of all the naval forces in Western waters," Lynch said. "That is the reason he did not assent to your program. I will conduct an inquiry in Vicksburg."

Captain Brown sent for Wyeth and asked him to make a deposition concerning the affair. Lynch said, "I can take testimony in Vicksburg."

Brown didn't reply and Wyeth felt sorry for his commander, seeing his drawn look, and the sadness in his eyes. "It's like this, Captain Lynch," the gunner said. "Captain Brown doesn't want to say so in front of me, but if you want my testimony, you'd better take it now. I may never see Vicksburg."

"Very well," Lynch said and Wyeth made a written report to him.

Captain Lynch took the report and told Captain Brown goodby. His horse was waiting on the bank, and Wyeth saw the captain to the topside of the *Arkansas* and said, "We'll be going down in a day or so. There's plenty of room, sir."

But Lynch went to Vicksburg by land.

Brown upbraided Wyeth for suggesting that his superior go with them. "It wasn't proper, Woodward. However, you have done good work. I personally am in debt to you. Is there anything I can do for you before we sail?"

"Yes, sir. I was going to ask you. Have you seen that Negro who has been following me around?"

"Yes."

Wyeth told Gar's story. "He has no master. I want to write the legislature to free him and to give him that money that Wall Mac-Kenzie is taking care of. A note from you would have influence with the legislature."

"You can count on me."

The Missourian worked for two hours preparing his petition for Gar's freedom. It was his first legal paper and it was short and simple. He stated Gar Rivers' case without wasting words and sent the petition and Brown's recommendation to Jackson. Then he breathed easier, feeling that he had done a good thing.

The last of the coal was brought aboard late that afternoon and Granville and his friends built racks for their rammer and sponger. They oiled the chassis and elevating screw and ran the gun in and out of battery, unlimbering her. Then they sent for Gar and fastened the nameplate onto the gun.

"This should call for a drink," Granville said.

"The *Arkansas* is not finished," Wyeth protested.

"She will never be finished," Granville felt his beard and mustache and scowled. The lard had dried on his chest and face.

"I'm going to finish her in my pitcher," Gar said.

Wyeth nodded. "Good. And make her look like she's painted gray."

Actually the *Arkansas* was a dull red for her iron was rusty and no paint was available.

The Dolly's crew slept aboard that night and woke up when they heard Lieutenant Stevens' horse arrive. He had ridden all day and most of the night, wearing out four mounts. A light appeared in Captain Brown's quarters and his first officer handed him a message from General Van Dorn. It said:

"The enemy has thirty-seven vessels in sight of my headquarters and many more up the river. Proceed at once. Take your vessel through the raft at Haynes Bluff, then sink the *Star of the West* in the opening of the obstruction. Then proceed out of the Yazoo and into the Mississippi and meet the enemy. Our shore batteries will try to cover you. God bless you."

Captain Brown folded the orders and put them away. "The Missourians?" he asked anxiously.

"They will arrive about daybreak," Stevens said. "Sixty men."

"Lord help us. I asked for two hundred."

"There were two hundred, but malaria hit them. The sixty men are in command of Captain Harris and Captain McDonald. Ragged, sir, and green."

Brown sent for Granville. "The Missourians will arrive soon. Begin training them the minute they get here."

"Aye ay, sir. Within a week or ten days I'll have them acquainted with the guns."

"You have twelve hours, Granville. We get underway late this afternoon."

Granville stared at Stevens and Stevens stared at Brown. The captain said, "Turn in. Daylight is almost here."

Two seamen who had been planning desertion for several days saw Stevens go to his berth and heard Captain Brown call his chief engineer. The deserters slipped off the ship and headed for Farragut and the Federal fleet with the message, "The *Arkansas* is coming." The Yanks should pay them well.

The eastern sky turned a dirty gray and then burst into red. It was Sunday, July 13th, 1862.

Chapter Ten

GRANVILLE groaned when he saw the sixty Missourians trudge aboard the *Arkansas*. Several of them stumbled on the gangplank and one almost fell into the river. Their mouths and eyes were opened wide in curiosity and amazement as their captains, Harris and McDonald, assembled them on the gundeck and presented them to Brown.

They were gaunt and ragged, and so land-locked that they didn't know the difference between a trunnion and a transom. Granville, always the good sailor, stared at their hands and feet and felt better, for they were capable men. Their feet were big and their hands were rough. Captain Brown inspected them and told them they were going out and get a bellyful of killing Yanks.

"That's how come we're here," one of them said.

His captain scowled at him, but the other Missourians laughed. Brown laughed, too.

The soldiers didn't salute their new commander. The believed in more shooting and less saluting and as Brown passed along their ranks several of them offered their hands, and he shook them. Captain Harris tried to make his men look smart. It was a waste of time. The captain shrugged his shoulders and turned his men over to the Navy. Then he presented Brown with the Battle Flag of the Confederacy, sent by General Van Dorn. The commander handed the flag to Midshipman Scales and the Memphis boy went to the *Arkansas'* bow, hoisted the flag on a hickory pole and saluted it smartly. The sailors cheered, but the Missouri soldiers ignored the ceremony and began prying around the gundeck, asking questions.

Granville took them in hand and tried to restore order. The soldiers paid him scant heed and he lost his temper and began cursing them. Wyeth tried his hand and told them he was a Missourian. They grinned at him and poked among the guns.

"I'm from up along the Osage," Wyeth said.

"We are from around the Ozarks," one soldier replied.

It was Ves who got them in hand. He climbed to the breech of the Dolly, waved his fists and roared, "Keep still, you goddam Missouri Pukes!" *

The Missourians stopped abruptly and faced him. It was good to hear their nickname again. The milling ended and they crowded around the Cajan. "This man," Ves pointed a long finger at Granville, "is the best gunner in the world and he aims to learn you a few things. I'll be right beside him and the first man who gets smart will have me on his back. . . ."

"How you mean?" One of the soldiers stepped close to Ves and looked at his mahogany-colored skin.

"Like this." Ves leaped from the gun, kicked the soldier in the belly and knocked him down.

Nobody moved. The soldier got to his feet, shook his head to clear it and said, "I catch on."

Granville assembled the men around the Dolly and explained the parts. He avoided technicalities and gave them only the fundamentals of gunnery. Their jobs were to run the guns into battery after the recoil, and to sponge, ram and load. The men were willing, but clumsy. Ves stood on one side of the Dolly with thirty men and Wyeth took the other side. Granville gave the orders.

"Sponge!"

Wyeth and the Cajan showed them how to dip the sponge in a bucket of water and clean the barrel.

"Load!"

The simple pulley system was demonstrated. A shell was rolled onto a sling. One man heaved on the pulley rope and another swung

* This inelegant nickname was given Missouri pioneers because they often drank impure surface water and became ill.

the shell to the mouth of the Dolly. Another rammed in a powder charge and then the shell was shoved in.

"Heave!"

The men grabbed handspikes and rolled the gun into battery. Then the eccentric wheel was thrown out of gear, then into gear, then out—over and over. Every man went through the routine. It was killing labor and between lessons the Missourians sat on the hot gundeck and panted.

All morning they worked, doing the same thing time and again, learning every gun. Food was served while they worked and Granville allowed each man to drink only one cup of water. By midafternoon of that scorching Sunday, the Missourians' hands were bleeding masses of flesh, rope-burned. Several had mashed fingers and hanging nails. They were sullen and snarling. But they kept working, for their pride was up.

The Englishman gave them their ease and propped against his gun and looked them over. "Now I understand why England has never subdued the Irish."

The Missourians began grinning.

By four P.M. when the sun was rolling its heat onto the gundeck, the last of the supplies were brought aboard the *Arkansas*. Tourniquets were served out to division officers by the surgeons and the tubs were filled with drinking water.

The ship's company numbered two hundred, including the Missourians. The crew was made up of rivermen recruited along the Yazoo and from the remnants of the Confederate force that had fought at Memphis. The Missourians never were listed as members of the crew as they objected to being called deckhands. They were soldiers assigned to help get the *Arkansas* from Yazoo City to Vicksburg.

Fire buckets were put in place, cutlasses and pistols were passed out and strapped on. Rifles were loaded and bayonets were fixed. Spare breechings for the guns were put into place and the magazines and shell rooms, forward and aft, were inspected. Fire tubs for heating shot were lashed to the gundeck.

At five P.M., Lieutenant Stevens gave the men thirty minutes shore leave and Wyeth ran down the gangplank and found Gar. The Negro was working on the picture of the *Arkansas*. He scarcely looked up and when he did he was very solemn, and then he went back to his work.

"Where are you going?" Wyeth asked.

"Vicksburg. I aim to ride Mist' Mort's hoss. I'll see you there. I'll take this pitcher to Mis' Laurel."

"Thank you, Gar. And goodby."

"God bless you, Mist' Woodward. Here's the snipper."

Wyeth hesitated a second and was embarrassed. So was Gar. Then Wyeth offered his hand and the Wolof shook it. He handed the Missourian the snipper gun and they parted.

Back on board the *Arkansas* Wyeth, Granville and Ves stored their gear and assembled on the gundeck. Coffee made of acorns was served in tin cups. Captain Brown went to his quarterdeck and beside him was Chief Pilot Hodges and J. H. Shacklett, the Yazoo pilot, and Lieutenant Stevens.

Brown nodded to his executive officer and Stevens cupped his hands and shouted, "Cast off."

Seamen from the *Capitol* disengaged the hawsers and they were hauled aboard the gunboat. The propellers began turning at half speed and the *Arkansas* moved upstream, wheeled to the left and headed down the Yazoo. The *Capitol* sounded her whistle and the workmen lined the bank and cheered. Six weeks before, to the day, the *Arkansas* had been a rusty hulk away up the river at Greenwood. Wyeth's heart was pounding and Ves was leaning out of a port and waving his huge hands at the crowd. Granville was working on the Dolly's sight and friction tube.

The *Era No. 2* and the *Star of the West* fell in behind the gunboat. Wyeth went topside and looked back. Gar was sitting on his horse. Then the shipyard faded behind a bend and Yazoo City disappeared from sight. . . .

Stevens came to the gundeck and took a piece of slate and marked a line on the trunnions of every gun. "Don't elevate your pieces above those lines," he said. "You will have plenty of time for broadsides only. Wait until we come alongside. You can't miss. We're heading for sixty ships, more or less."

Granville glanced up from his gun. Ves watched the Missourians and they seemed unconcerned. Wyeth leaned against the Dolly and stared out of the port, listening to the wheezing of the engines and the rattle of the shafts. The *Arkansas,* the ship that couldn't be built, was going to her rendezvous.

Riding the falling crest of the Yazoo, she looked like a small sea-going vessel, cut to the water's edge at both ends and leaving a big box amidships. The box was the ark and had straight sides, a foot thick. Over each side was one layer of railroad iron. The ends of the box were closed by timber, one foot square and planked across by six-inch strips of oak. The strips were covered by one course of railroad iron laid up and down at an angle of thirty-five degrees. The ends would deflect any missiles that might strike at short range but were no protection against a plunging fire. The ark was flat on top and covered with oaken planks and half-inch iron. The smoke stack, a chubby, fat, rusty thing of heavy iron came through the top of the ark and just forward of the stack was a blister, a shield, in which was located the quarterdeck and the pilothouse. This shield had a thin coating of iron.

The *Arkansas'* deck was flush with the river and her iron beak was under water. The ark seemed to rise right out of the Yazoo. There was no worry about the sides of the box as the iron was good, but any mortar shell could pierce the craft from the top which had only a skin of iron and oak. She was a dull rusty red and her ports looked like windows.

On Brown's orders, most of the gundeck crew was allowed topside and aft of the smokestack and there they lolled while the vessel plowed down the Yazoo. Night brought a breeze and the men went to the galley and got their supper and came back on deck and ate it. Running lights were fixed and the *Era* and *Star* came as close to the *Arkansas'* stern as safety permitted. Pilot Shacklett, seeking slack water to conserve coal, heeled his ship to the inside of a bend and ran into a tangle of overhead branches. The alarm was sounded and Midshipman Scales snatched a rope and climbed into the trees. He pulled back the branches and they grazed the smokestack, but did no damage. Shacklett wheeled back for the channel and stayed there until they reached Satartia Bar. Soundings were taken and the *Arkansas* crept over the Bar with only four inches to spare.

One shift of the engine room crew came topside and reported that the heat in the boiler room, far below the water line, had reached 130 degrees. The fire boxes were red hot. . . .

Shacklett suggested they tie up and try to insulate the fire boxes, but Brown said, "Hold her as she is."

Most of the men were sleeping when the ship rounded the last bend north of Haynes Bluff and Wyeth woke up when the lookout called, "Raft dead ahead."

Signals were flashed to the *Era* and *Star* and they turned for shore. The beat to quarters was sounded and the men staggered to their feet and went to their posts. It was past midnight. Axes were issued and the *Arkansas* anchored near the right end of the raft while a crew went ashore and began hacking away at the obstruction. Dawn was breaking when the men abandoned their work and powder charges were placed on the raft. The explosions scattered debris and mud, but the raft held. Captain Brown called for a broadside from the bow guns and shots were poured into the raft.

It gave way then, slowly at first. The river caught the disengaged end of the raft and swung it downstream and there the barrier lodged again. Pilot Hodges surveyed the opening, steadied his rudder and the *Arkansas* crept through. She was below the raft and there was nothing more between her and the Mississippi, and nothing between her and Vicksburg except the strongest fleet of American history.

Brown changed his plan and called for the *Star of the West* to remain above the raft. He had orders to sink her in the opening, but substituted the smaller *Era*. The little boat was run into the hole and her bow was fastened to the shore. The force of the channel turned her across the opening and she was made fast. A crew chopped holes in her bottom and she settled. So the barrier was there again; the *Arkansas* below it and the *Star* above it. Brown sent orders for the *Star* to go back up the river. He had a feeling that some day she might be needed up there and he knew she could give him no protection in the Mississippi, for she was wooden and weak. He stood in the shield, his head above the sides, and waved goodby to the *Star*. The *Arkansas* got under way again, crept under the lee at Haynes Bluff and the men were given an hour's rest.

That was Monday, July 14th.

Wyeth and his two comrades used their hour to cleanse themselves and shave. They removed their filthy clothing and threw it overboard. Then they dived into the warm water of the Yazoo and scrubbed themselves. Several other sailors were doing the same thing and the soldiers poked fun at them.

Granville clipped his mustache and shaped it properly. Wyeth was glad to be clean shaven again. Even under his beard, Ves' skin was very dark. The Englishman put on white ducks and an open jacket. Wyeth and Ves left their chests bare and wore only duck trousers. They were barefoot. The Missourian tied his kerchief, the one Laurel had sent, around his head to check the flow of sweat.

Deckhands began sprinkling sand on the gundeck, and on the ladders to the topside and below to the sick bay. "What is that for?" one of the soldiers asked.

Granville twisted his waxed mustache. Wyeth felt the kerchief and was thinking of Laurel. Ves cocked his left eye at the soldiers and said, "That's to keep us from slipping when your brains and guts are blown out."

The soldier aimed for a port and spat. "Is that a fact? Well, Bub, we needn't worry about slipping on your brains."

Captain Brown came down from his quarterdeck for another inspection of the gundeck. He called for more sand. A coal fire was smoldering in the sand of the hot shot tub and the master told the attendant to ease up on the heat. A shot can be heated red in half an hour. "We'll have time to heat shots after we sight the Yanks." He examined the hot shot wads made of hay, rope and clay and used to prevent the red hot metal from touching the powder while the guns were being loaded.

Ves sidled up to Brown and said, "Hey, Cap'n, if we get down there and change our mind can we come back up here?"

The skipper laughed at the irrepressible Cajan. "No, we can't turn around. Our stern is not protected except by boiler iron and a good man can throw a rock through it. Once underway we'll have to keep going."

"Do you aim to cut through Old River?" Ves asked. Granville was shocked. He couldn't accustom himself to hearing enlisted men chat with officers.

"That's right," Brown said. "We're going down the Yazoo to Old River and then through Old River to the Mississippi. However, I expect to flush the Yanks an hour or so away from here. Surely they're scouting the Yazoo."

The Yazoo had two mouths into the Mississippi, the regular channel and a secondary channel that flowed through an old bed of the Mississippi. Many years before when the lower valley was shaken by earthquakes, and the stars fell, the big river abandoned the old bed and cut a new course. The old bed was called Old River and still was navigable during high water. Old River really was a lake caused by a cut-off from the Mississippi. The Yazoo entered the lake at the north curve and, mingling with the wide expanse of the lake for ten miles, broke through a narrow strip of land and into the Mississippi, twelve miles north of Vicksburg. The mouth of Old River was three miles south of the regular mouth of the Yazoo which entered the Mississippi between Milliken's Bend and Tuscumbia Bend.

"When do you expect to be in Vicksburg, Cap'n?" a soldier asked.

"Don't be so friendly with your superiors," Ves snapped.

Brown winked at the Cajan. The master was unsteady on his feet and fever and fatigue showed on his face and in his eyes. He rested against a gun carriage and wiped his face. "We'll be there six hours after we leave here. I hope." He straightened himself and, with visible effort, went back topside. He looked down at the men, reached for his speaking tube, rang the engine room bell and shouted, "Cast off."

The *Arkansas* moved away from Haynes Bluff, picked up speed and waddled down the river. The crew had every reason to expect the enemy to appear around the next bend and the men fingered their small arms and stood at attention beside the big guns. The Missourians kept spitting on their bayonets and polishing them. Ves and Wyeth put their snipper rifles in a rack by the Dolly and stood close to Granville. The Englishman was tampering with his friction tube, roughing the wire that ignited the powder. Wyeth was so tense that his nerves actually pained him and he had difficulty swallowing the saliva that flooded his mouth. His head seemed to be splitting as the blood pounded his brain, and his scar was a hard streak from the cleft in his chin to the top of his cheekbone.

The *Arkansas* was taking all the steam the two boilers could muster and the pilot was swishing her inside the bends, hugging slack water. She was within sight of Drumgould's Bluff and John Snyder's Mill when Stevens saw the bar stretching out from the bank and covered by a few feet of water. The Yazoo had thrown out the bar the night before. The pilot gave his boat a hard rudder. Stevens put his hands over his head to protect it and Brown closed his eyes and prayed. The 1200-ton ironclad turned on her stern, nipped the end of the bar and then went fast aground.

The impact threw many men sprawling and toppled one of the big guns from its carriage.

Wyeth began cursing. His emotions were released by the accident and the tears ran down his cheeks and onto his bare chest. The Missouri soldiers scrambled to the ports, their rifles cocked. Ves cursed, too. "It ain't Yanks. It's a sand bar. The rivers down here heave 'em up in a few hours and you never know when you're going to bump one."

Granville checked his Dolly to be sure no damage was done. Then he sighed. "This will hold us for a long time. Our luck is running out."

Brown was the calmest man aboard and called for reverse propellers and straight rudder. The *Arkansas* began trembling as the engines pounded and the propellers spun. The heavy craft was settling on the bar and digging a trough. To lighten the ship, every seaman except the engine room crew was sent ashore. Granville and his two comrades stayed aboard, however, rigged a gin and worked the disabled gun back onto its carriage. And while they worked the *Arkansas* was trying to kick herself off of the bar.

It looked hopeless and Wyeth was frightened, for if the Yankees caught them there it would soon be all over. He reported to the quarterdeck and explained to Captain Brown that often he had worked steamers off of bars back on the Osage, and then he outlined his plan. The chief pilot said it might work and Brown gave his consent for the effort.

Three big ropes were wound together and the hawser was made fast to the stern of the ship. Then a piece of greased tin was tacked to a cypress butt about twenty yards upstream and the hawser was slipped around the tree. Its loose end was brought back to the ship and wound around a steam winch in the engine room. Brown called for full speed reverse. The winch began grinding, tightening the hawser and the *Arkansas* pulled herself off of the bar.

Nobody cheered. The ship was back in deep water, but the men were silent. Luck seemed against them and, being backwoodsmen, they were superstitious. The *Arkansas* lost six hours on the bar and was scarcely underway again before the powder room crew reported that steam had seeped into the magazines and dampened the powder, making it useless.

Stevens hurled his cap to the floor. The pilots threw up their hands. Brown picked out a sluice that indented the left bank and ran his ship to a mooring. When the crew heard what had happened they were so disgusted that they began squabbling among themselves, and the Missouri soldiers expressed contempt for the whole undertaking.

Brown came to the top of the ladder of the gundeck and looked his men over. His lips were white and parched and peeling, and his eyes were hollow. "If I hear another word of grumbling I will throw you in irons. I am going to take this ship to Vicksburg."

He almost collapsed and Stevens caught him. The men were ashamed and Ves looked around at them. "The Captain is dying on his feet. I'll kill the next man who squawks." He turned and faced the quarterdeck and called out, "What you want us to do, Cap'n?"

All the powder on the *Arkansas* was taken ashore and spread on canvas. The men held the ends of the canvas and shook it, spreading the powder thin and exposing it to the blistering sun. It took six hours more to dry the powder and darkness caught them before it was loaded aboard again.

The moon was full and the men worked by its light, afraid to use lanterns so close to the powder. By midnight the last of the dry grains was stored back into the kegs and the kegs were aboard ship. Fourteen men had collapsed during the work and were sent to the sick bay. Three of them were delirious and one died from cramps after drinking too much water.

July 14th passed with the *Arkansas* moored in the sluice. The night was hideous with the screams of catamounts from the swamp and the whine of mosquitoes. The men slung their hammocks topside and tried to sleep, but sleep was impossible. . . .

Meanwhile, down in the Mississippi not far away, a skiff crept alongside the *U.S.S. Essex*, Bill Porter's gunboat of Davis' squadron. A lookout hailed, and two men in the skiff, deserters from Captain Brown's command, shouted, "The *Arkansas* is coming!"

The word was passed from ship to ship and some men laughed. It was a ruse, a Rebel trick. Nobody could build an ironclad in the wilderness. The deserters were taken to the *Hartford*, Farragut's flagship, and reported their story. Farrugut, Davis, Porter and Lieutenant Colonel A. W. Ellet heard the report. Colonel Charles Rivers Ellet was downstream with the mortarboats. The deserters told the truth and Farragut just looked at them. He was tired and sleepy and disgusted. His ships were lined along the east bank of Tuscumbia Bend, within shot of Vicksburg. None of his ships had up enough steam to turn their wheels.

A strange thing happened to Farragut. He ignored the warning. Inertia had him in a vise and the divided command had him confused. There is no other explanation for his behavior. Maybe he didn't believe the deserters. Maybe a thousand things, but he did nothing. It was Charles Henry Davis, the sanctimonious commander of the Upper River Squadron, who insisted that something be done. "I don't believe the Rebels have such a ship either, but we musn't underestimate them. . . ."

"Do you think one ship will face this fleet?" an officer asked.

"The Rebels will try anything," Davis said.

It was agreed that a squadron would be sent on an exploring expedition up the Yazoo "to procure correct information concerning the obstructions and defenses of the river, and ascertain if possible the whereabouts of the *Arkansas*."

Captain Henry Walke of the ironclad *Carondelet* was summoned and was told to head up the Yazoo at daybreak. He was to take with him the gunboat *Tyler,* commanded by Lieutenant William Gwin, and the much-used *Queen of the West*. Lieutenant James Hunter had command of the *Queen,* the same ship that did the Confederates so much damage at Memphis, the one that sunk the *Jeff Thompson* on which Wyeth, Granville, Ves and Dolly had served.

The three Federal ships got up steam, raised their anchors and stood for Old River. The Union fleet went back to sleep. Walke's squadron hove to in Old River about 2 A.M.

That was July 15th.

Wyeth was sleeping aft of the smokestack and it seemed to him that he had just dozed off when a lookout called the bells. It was three A.M. Wyeth got up to move his hammock to a cooler spot. Granville stirred and propped on one elbow and nudged Ves. Soon most of the men were squirming.

The mess call sounded and the men, rubbing sleep from their eyes, stumbled below and drank coffee and ate bacon and cold bread. It was pitch dark when the men went to their posts, strapping on their cutlasses and priming their small arms. A dog over at Snyder's Mill, near where they were moored, bayed and one of the Irishmen of the Missouri Company shuddered. The *Arkansas* crawled out of the sluice and sped downstream, her running lights glowing yellow and green and her two propellers churning away. The sky turned gray, then yellow, then red. Captain Brown entered in his log: "Underway at three A.M., July 15, 1862. Dawn at 4:27. Windage favorable. God help us."

He went to the gundeck for another looksee and the men gathered about him. Maybe their luck had changed, for the engines were humming and the ship was parting the Yazoo and piling foam behind.

Wyeth said, "Good morning, Captain. It is going to be a scorcher."

Brown said, "Vicksburg is about three hours away. In that direction." He pointed to the southwest. "Spirit level the big guns and use no elevation. Blast them. That's all we can do."

Back in his cockpit on the quarterdeck, he called his officers around him and said, "Gentlemen, in seeking the combat as we now do, we must win or perish. Should I fall, whoever succeeds to the command will do so with the resolution to go through the enemy's fleet, or go to the bottom. Should they carry us by boarding, the *Arkansas* must be blown up, on no account must she fall into the hands of the enemy. Go to your guns!"

All the men, except Brown and Stevens, stripped off their shirts. Brown was standing in the shield, scanning the horizon with his glass. Below on the gundeck, Ves began humming. Granville hummed, too; one of the songs Gar had taught him. Wyeth was sweating huge beads of sweat, yet his skin was cold.

A white crane lifted itself from the river, circled the ship, and flew away. Some of the Irishmen crossed themselves. Ves said, "That's good luck. A white crane means good luck."

The cry came down from the quarterdeck. "Smoke dead ahead! About a mile away."

The men stiffened. The *Arkansas* veered into Old River, leaving the Yazoo. Granville nodded to Wyeth and the young Missourian loaded the Dolly with a seventy-pound solid shot. The gun was run into battery and Granville tested his sight, flicked a bit of grime from the instrument, and waited.

Another cry came from the quarterdeck. "Three ships dead ahead!"

Captain Brown wrote in his log: "Sighted enemy in Old River, 6:09. Three ships, *Carondelet, Queen of the West, Tyler.*"

The men on the gundeck could not see the enemy as the bowports were too small for wide vision. Granville kept calming the crew around the Dolly. He watched them closely and they watched him. There was no sound except the pounding of the engines.

One Irishman broke under the suspense and stuck his head out of a starboard port. A deep hollow *bllooom* sounded, then a shrieking whistle and a rifle bolt thudded against the *Arkansas*. It was the first shot. The bolt splattered against the iron ark and a piece of metal severed the Irishman's head. His head rolled down the side of the ark and his body crumpled on the gundeck.

The soldiers stared at the corpse. Stevens, realizing the mangled body might demoralize the men, sprang forward and seized the dead man's feet. He looked at the nearest soldier and said, "Grab his shoulders and throw him overboard."

"Oh, my God," the soldier said. "I can't do that. He's my brother."

Stevens dropped the man's feet and stared at the soldier, gulping in surprise. Ves, however, lifted the body in both hands and threw it out of the nearest port. Then he scraped sand over the blood.

Lieutenant Gift was peering down his bowgun when the enemy came into view of the men on the gundeck. Shells and rifle balls were pounding the bow and hissing into the water. "There they are," Gift shouted. "I can see them now. The *Carondelet* is in the center. The *Tyler* is to her port and the *Queen* is on her starboard." He held up his hands to his gunner's mate. "Steady. Hold it!"

Ves shouted with joy when he heard that the *Queen* was facing them. He had a score to settle. . . .

The Federals came head on, throwing iron, and there was no reply from the *Arkansas*. She kept plowing ahead, keeping her beak aimed for the squadron. Gift waited until the enemy was so close that he recognized Gwin on the *Tyler*. "All right!" The *Tyler* swept directly in front of Gift's gun and his mate yanked the lanyard. An eight-inch shell with a five-second fuze plowed into the *Tyler*, exploded on her deck and hurled guns and debris into the air. Eight men were killed, including the *Tyler's* pilot. The other bowgun opened up. Brown heeled the *Arkansas* to starboard, showing his port broadside. Granville touched the Dolly and sent seventy pounds of iron into the *Carondelet*.

"Hot shot," Granville said.

Ves and Wyeth snatched up the tongs, ran to the fire tub, seized a red hot ball and hurried back to Dolly. The gun was sponged and wadded with hay and rope. Then the hot shot was rammed in.

"Gear . . . Heave." Granville lined her up and threw the hot shot into the hole that his first shell had opened. Screams of pain and dismay came from the *Carondelet*.

Black smoke and yellow fumes filled the *Arkansas'* gundeck and the noise beat against the men's eardrums. The steady *bllooom* of the big guns, the clattering of small arms—the thud of shells against the ark . . . the shriek of the cannon recoiling on friction, and the constant commands of the gunners . . . "ram! load! gear! heave! . . ."

Wyeth was relaxed. The first shot relaxed him and he went about his duties automatically. He was crying and was not aware that he was crying.

The *Queen of the West* tried to circle the *Arkansas* and get in position to ram her. The Federal ship beat to the starboard and a broadside from the Rebel rocked her. The *Queen*, exposed and battered, turned on her heels and fled.

Then the *Tyler* bore in, seeking an opening. Another broadside from the port battery swept her decks, felled ten men and riddled her boilers. The *Tyler* staggered and fourteen shots were poured into her in less than a minute. Bleeding, limping and almost helpless, the *Tyler* stood down Old River at all speed and deserted the fight, leaving the *Carondelet* to battle it out alone.

Walke had thirteen guns on the *Carondelet* and jockeyed for a broadside. The *Arkansas* kept her on her nose, however. The Yankee wheeled her head with a sharp starboard rudder and circled, seeking the *Arkansas'* vulnerable stern. Brown tried to stop his engines, to reverse them, but the automatic stoppers failed and the starboard engine kept churning forward. The Rebel turned in a huge circle and the *Carondelet* let fly a broadside.

Two shells ripped through the shield and Chief Pilot John

Hodges fell, his chest blown away. Brown reached for the wheel and another shot tore the spokes from his hands, grazed his temple and he staggered. A one hundred-pound shell chewed through the shield and Brown went down, bleeding from a dozen cuts and unconscious from concussion. His body toppled through the hatchway to the gundeck. Pilot Shacklett grabbed the wheel and was shot down by a Minié ball. The wheel spun out of control and the *Arkansas* was reeling when Jim Brady, a Mississippi River pilot, grabbed the wheel and brought the ship under control.

Stevens lifted Brown and the chief surgeon was running to his side as the commander opened his eyes and got to his feet. He staggered back to his quarterdeck. . . .

The men began cheering him and he lifted his speaking tube and called, "All steam! We will ram her."

The surgeon dressed his wounds there in full view of the *Carondelet* and gave him a drink of brandy. Brown brought his ship back to midstream of Old River and kept the *Carondelet* on his bow. One! Two! Both bowguns thundered. Brown wheeled his ship to starboard. One! Two! Three! The port broadside roared. Then he heeled over and his starboard guns pounded the Yankee.

It was too much. Twenty shots were thrown into the *Carondelet* as she turned and darted for shallow water. The *Arkansas* tried to ram, then began shaking and hissing.

A report from the engine room showed that steam was down to sixty pounds. The *Arkansas*' smokestack was riddled and the funnels couldn't suck in oxygen to keep the fires at their peak. The fire boxes were white hot and the temperature in the engine room was up to 150 degrees. The men worked in five-minute shifts.

It was impossible to ram with so little power. Brown shouted, "Prepare to board her."

Ves and Wyeth reached for their snippers. Granville pulled his pistol with his right hand and took a cutlass in his left. The *Carondelet* swept into shallow water and Pilot Brady dared not follow, knowing he would go aground.

"Rake her!" Brown shouted. "We will pass her on the port."

Granville stepped back to the Dolly's breech. "Chains and canister," he said.

The big Dahlgren was stuffed with ten pounds of powder and fifty pounds of chain and bits of metal. The *Carondelet* was almost on her side as the *Arkansas* moved by her. Granville gave her the charge and the chains chewed into the ship, scattering men and guns. Ves and Wyeth were firing their snippers out of the port and every gun on the lee of the *Arkansas* opened up.

The *Carondelet* fired one more shot. It whistled through a port and cleaned out one gun crew. Three men literally were torn apart. The concussion pitched Wyeth against the Dolly and his head was laid open. Ves was thrown against the carriage and the left side of his mouth caved in. The end of the upper jawbone was broken off and as Ves looked around wildly a piece of bone and four teeth slipped out of his mouth. Granville wasn't scratched.

As they came alongside the *Carondelet,* no gun spoke from the Yankee. "She has struck!" Brown called.

Four broadside guns of the Federal gunboat were run out, but they were silent. The *Arkansas* covered her and waited. There was not a sign of life aboard the enemy. Brady touched his wheel and the *Arkansas* sheered off, back to midstream.

"His colors are down," Lieutenant Gift shouted. "He is showing white flags."

Granville didn't see the surrender and was ready for another blast, but Brown forbade it. The *Carondelet* fell behind and a lookout called that she was out of the fight.

Old River was cleared. The smoke rose from the gundeck and Brown entered in his log: "We have defeated three of the enemy. The *Tyler* and the *Queen of the West* fled. The *Carondelet* struck. 7:10 A.M."

Blood from his wounds dripped onto the log, and then he closed the book and went to the gundeck. Eight of his men were dead and ten of the deck crew were wounded. Half of his engine room crew was unconscious from heat and exhaustion.

Dr. Washington, the chief surgeon, examined Ves and ordered him to the sick bay. The Cajan refused to go. There was no pain in his jaw and he knew it would be some time before the agony really set in. The blow had made his jaw numb. Wyeth's injury was ugly, but not serious. The skin over his left ear was lacerated and his hair was bloody and matted.

The *Arkansas* cut her speed and inspection was held. All the big guns were intact although their crews were decimated. Her stack was like a sieve and Stevens counted 225 Minié ball holes in it. The connections between the furnaces and stack (called breechings) were shot away and there virtually was no draught to the fires. Steam was down to twenty pounds. The engine room was so hot that Stevens' skin peeled when he entered it.

They patched the breechings as best they could and worked the pressure back up to seventy pounds by burning spoiled pork—a shovelful of pork and a shovelful of coal. Quickly but without haste, the men brought the ship back to fighting trim. The guns were shotted and pulled in from battery. Pistols and rifles were cleaned. Coffee was issued and the men stood to. Brown called for full speed and the *Arkansas* worked up to six knots in the still muddy waters of Old River, standing for the Mississippi.

Brown trained his glass to the west where Old River narrowed into a channel and poured into the Mississippi. He saw the *Queen of the West* and the *Tyler* reach the big river and knew that the alarm was spread. Surely the Federals had heard the shots, anyway. The *Queen* and *Tyler* were thirty minutes ahead of the *Arkansas*.

Brown didn't know, and had no way of knowing, that the crew of the *Queen* and *Tyler* began shouting, *"Arkansas! Arkansas!"* when they reached the fleet. The *Tyler* ran under protection of the *Essex*.

Farragut was dumbfounded. He moved as a man in a dream. Perhaps the heat had slowed his hot Southern blood. Perhaps his mind was wandering. There is no accounting for some things. Farragut's fleet was caught with little steam up. However, he had sails. His crew began stacking coal into the furnaces. Davis' gunboats gulped coal and got up steam, then crawled to the west side of the river. Farragut's ships were on the east side and seven rams were waiting beside his men-of-war. Armed tugs and tenders darted about like water-bugs, taking position.

The *Arkansas* churned out of Old River into the Mississippi and swung downstream. Every man saw the fleet then, a forest of spars and acres of ships. Nobody troubled to count them. More than two hundred cannon on the ships and hundreds of rifles pointed at the Rebel. Along the shore, many more guns and four thousand muskets covered her.

"Great God!" Ves said it out of the side of his mouth, the right side, for his left side was a gaping hole.

[194]

Brown entered in his log: "Sighted main fleet 8:10 A.M." Deliberately, he put his quill away, and his glass. He called to Lieutenant Stevens, "Make fast your ports."

The iron doors of the gunports were clanged shut and the men were locked in the gundeck. They couldn't see out. Only Brown and his staff on the bridge had vision. The captain, aware that the strain soon would be almost unbearable, called out to the men the things he saw. "They are lining up. Ships-of-the-line on the left and gunboats on the right. The *Benton* is maneuvering to midstream at the end of the line. To block us! Depress your guns. You can't miss."

The crew was silent.

Pilot Jim Brady gripped his wheel and said, "Course?"

Brown said, "Shave that line of men-of-war, Jim, so the rams will not have time to gain headway. Then dead ahead. Right down the middle. We'll run the gauntlet." He turned to his mess boy who had fetched him water. "Well, son, did you know there were that many Yankees in the world?"

"There's a heap of them." The boy was trembling. The sun was high up its route and the sky was blue and cloudless. There they lay, just waiting. The *Hartford, Richmond, Iroquois, Oneida, Wissahickon, Scioto, Kineo, Winona* and *Pinola* of Farragut's fleet; the *Essex, Tyler, Queen of the West, Louisville, Cincinnati, Lancaster, Benton, Sumter, Champion, Dickey, Great Western,* and a score or so more of the Upper River Fleet. Then there were the sixteen mortars of Porter's fleet, protected by the *Brooklyn, Kennebec, Katahdin,* and attended by the *Octoroon, Westfield, Clifton, Jackson, Harriet Lane,* and the *Owasco.*

Brown called out the names and even Granville held his breath as he heard the strength they were facing. Wyeth wiped powder from his eyes and stared at the Englishman. Ves ran his tongue over his injured mouth and grimaced. The pain was beginning. The gundeck was dark, for the port doors barred all sunlight. And the deck was so hot that the men burned their feet and kept moving around. The breechings had broken down again and flames from the furnaces licked the iron floor of the ark. The temperature reached 140 degrees.

From his quarterdeck, Brown called, "Hold your fire until we start our run. We're going right down the middle."

A feeble shout arose, then died in the throats of the men. Wyeth's head was throbbing and there was a bloody lump over his left ear. Ves was drooling blood. Granville asked for brandy for his friends and the surgeons sent an extra portion for the Englishman. He handed his drink to Wyeth who took half, then passed the cup to Ves.

The gundeck was strangely quiet. Moans came from the sick bay, but the men at the guns moved about in the shadows of the barred deck, glancing at the closed ports beyond which was daylight and the Mississippi. The *Arkansas* dipped her bow and made for the center of the river. The current caught her and she began picking up speed. . . .

Some Federal gunner fingered his piece nervously and yanked a lanyard on the *Hartford*. A sheet of yellow flashed across the river and a solid shot struck the *Arkansas'* bow. The ship recoiled under the impact, then her beak bit into the river and she slipped on down, holding her fire.

The single shot was the signal for a salvo and two hundred guns roared from ships and shore. One shot crashed through the sheet iron covering and exploded under the rear gun of the starboard broadside. The gun toppled from its carriage and fell across a seaman. He shrieked, then the shriek trailed into a gurgle. The other men drew back and covered their faces, for the heavy gun was across his stomach and the sight was sickening. A surgeon severed all flesh above and below the gun, hacked through the bones and lifted the body in two parts. Ves cringed and began babbling. Wyeth vomited and Granville turned away.

Another seaman went stark mad when he saw the operation. He grabbed a smoldering greased rope that was used as a slow match and began running around the deck. The men tried to hold him, but he jerked away and waved his match over the powder sacks. Granville picked up his revolver from beside the Dolly and shot the man. Ves lugged the body to the end of the gundeck and covered it with powder sacks.

The *Arkansas* was within four hundred yards of the first ship of the gauntlet. Shells began raking her bow. She took the bone in her iron beak and bore in, shaking herself. Her iron creaked and rattled. Six thousand pounds of metal struck her in one salvo. She reeled on her haunches. Her flag was cut from the hickory pole and Midshipman Scales crawled onto the exposed deck that was being swept by a hurricane of shot and shell, bent on the colors again, knotted the halyards and hoisted the flag. The next volley ripped the banner to shreds.

The clatter of musket shot sounded like hail against the *Arkansas* and every ten seconds a ton of shells pounded her.

From the quarterdeck came the command, "Hold your fire."

A quartermaster named Eaton was passing shells from the forward shellroom and superintending the powder boys. He talked as he worked. "Nine-inch shell, five-second fuze. Here you are, my lad, with your rifle shell. What's the matter with you gunners? Can't you move that piece?" He sprang from his place and threw his weight on a handspike and the gun moved. "What are you doing here, mate? Wounded? Where? Aw, hell! Go back to your gun or I'll murder you. Here's your nine-inch shell. Mind, shipmate. The ladder is bloody. Don't slip."

It was too much to expect of men, standing there, barred in and unable to see the enemy—absorbing hot iron and unable to fight back. Some broke and began screaming. Ves knocked one down and that silenced the others. Stevens walked among them, erect and inspiring. Caged in the iron ark, they felt the ship tremble as every kind of shell and explosion known to man pounded the *Arkansas*. And they just waited.

On the bridge, Brown judged his distance. The bluffs of Vicksburg were over there in the blue haze. He couldn't see the town, however, as a cloud of black smoke hung over the river and the explosions lighted up the clouds as a battery firing at midnight. It resembled a lightning storm that precedes a tornado.

His messboy was standing beside him one second, and then the next he was down, bleeding from musket fire. Brown called a surgeon. The boy began praying, "God help me, God help me. . . ." The captain and the surgeon lifted him and the boy recognized Brown. "I'm all right. I'll make it. So help me, God. I'll make it. But, Captain, I'll never love another country again. So help me, God. So help me, God. And God damn Yankees."

Brown said, "You shouldn't talk that way, son. You need God now."

"Do you reckon He heard me?" the boy asked anxiously. "Reckon He did? I didn't mean it. Honest, God, I didn't mean it."

The surgeon took him away.

Brown saw his gunners itching for action and shouted, "Hold it. Hold it."

It was a steady chant and the men took it up, "Hold it, hold it, hold it. . . ."

The thudding of the shells was a bass for the chant and the whistle of the balls was the alto. Each shot had a distinct *blloom,* then a grinding thud. The rifle fire ran together, a steady whine and shriek as the small shot ricocheted.

"Hold it, hold it. . . ." Brown fingered his own pistol. "Hold, hold . . . *now!*"

The port gates were jerked open and the guns were slammed out. The men began shouting as the sunlight entered the ark. Some screamed in excitement. Others soiled their clothes. Sweat and urine left brown stains on their trousers and the odor of bloody flesh, powder and offal seeped through the ship.

The *Arkansas* was only fifty yards from the first Federal ship, the *Hartford,* flagship of Farragut's squadron. The Yankees were holding a perfect line, the ships pointing into the river from both sides so they could swing right and left and work broadside. It was a gorge of ships, a dead-end gorge, for at the far end of the gauntlet the *Benton* was midstream, blocking the exit to Vicksburg.

An Irishman of Gift's battery put his eye to the gun and peered out. Seeing the immense force assembled there he mumbled, "Holy Mother, have mercy on us; we'll never get through there!"

Lieutenant Read at the stern battery shouted, "If you see the *Kineo,* she is mine. She will have a No. 6 on her stack. She killed my commander at New Orleans."

The *Arkansas* plowed into the smoke cloud and a gust of wind caught the cloud and vision was cleared. The *Kineo* was the first to break the line and seek battle at close quarters. The men-of-war hung back, hugging the bank, and the rams hugged their big sisters. The little *Kineo,* however, came out like a gamecock and passed directly in front of the *Arkansas,* throwing everything she had at the Rebel.

Gift saw the No. 6 and called to Read. The officer snatched a primer lanyard and walked to Gift's bowgun. He touched her off, a charge of grape that swept the *Kineo.* It was the first shot from the *Arkansas* against the main fleet. The *Kineo* snarled and wheeled to fight back.

With a sharp touch of his helm, Pilot Brady laid the *Arkansas'* portside to the *Kineo*. Granville drew his sight and handed his lanyard to Read. The Dolly lurched and hurled a bolt through and through the Yankee and men began diving from the *Kineo's* deck. She limped away, firing as she went.

Those two shots opened the *Arkansas'* counterattack, the run of the gauntlet. Brown began firing his pistol, picking his shots, for his ship was shaving the bows of Farragut's men-of-war.

No one ever knew and none ever agreed exactly what happened during the next few minutes. The smoke was so thick on the gundeck that Granville couldn't see the end of his gun. They just loaded and fired. The Dolly lurched and spat, roaring a crescendo. Her breech got hot and her vent melted. Granville used his crane feathers to get ignition into his gun. One man was singing a hymn and many shouted prayers.

The *Arkansas* rocked to port under a starboard salvo, then to starboard under a port salvo. She was staggering like a drunken thing, foam in her teeth and flames and iron streaming from her pores.

The *Hartford* fell behind, still firing. The *Lancaster*, a ram, rumbled out for a blow at the Rebel. Gift gave her a five-second shell from his bowgun. It struck the *Lancaster's* mud-drum, emptying the hot steam and water into the barricaded engine room. The crew and a company of sharpshooters came pouring up the scuttles, ripping off their shirts and leaping overboard. The *Arkansas* closed over some of them, struggling in the river.

Another ram came out and sought the *Arkansas'* stern. Read drove him back with his two stern-chasers, firing both of them simultaneously.

The shots were like sledge-hammers against the *Arkansas*. Captain Brown was knocked from his bridge again and his glass was broken in his hands.

Midshipman Tyler went down. They were passing the center of the gorge and a heavy shot struck abreast of the bowgun. The concussion knocked down a seaman who was taking a shot from the rack. The man rubbed his hip and said, "They won't strike twice in the same place." Another shell entered the breach, cut the man in two and bedded itself on the inside of a bulwark. There it exploded and sixteen men were chewed to bits. Granville's beard was singed. Ves was hurled across the deck. Wyeth gripped the Dolly and a patch of hair at the base of his head was blown off by the concussion. Two guns were wrecked and Quartermaster Curtis was the only man left at the aft gun of the starboard battery. That gun was still on its carriage and six Missouri volunteers, shouting curses and prayers, took it over and worked it as best they could.

Fire began lapping along the deck. The fire division formed and extinguished the blaze.

No one knew exactly where they were, for the river was a maze of Federal ships, darting out to fire, then swinging alongside the *Arkansas*, pounding her.

The *Tyler* dared poke her nose out and Granville gave her a burst. Then the *Sumter* got a broadside. They passed the ships, two by two. The *Louisville* and *Cincinnati* turned in the river and tried to follow the *Arkansas*. Read dispersed them.

The engine room crew was exhausted and the men were dragged to the gundeck which was almost as hot as the furnace room. Grimball recruited enough men to man the boilers. The smokestack was like a nutmeg-grater, peppered through and through. The cast-iron ram was broken and a hawse-pipe was demolished. The four life boats were shot away and dragging.

Mangled bodies were spread about the deck and rivulets of blood flowed away from them. The live men slipped in the blood and stumbled over the bodies. Brains, hair, legs and arms were scattered about and in the sick bay sixty men were suffering the agonies of wounds and heat.

The iron on the *Arkansas* was becoming loose under the pounding. Granville heard it rattling, and kept serving his gun. The *Champion* fell behind, then the *Dickey* and *Great Western*. Gift saw the *Benton* dead ahead, the last of the line north of Vicksburg. His throat was so dry that he couldn't shout. He just pointed at her. His gun spoke. Brady heeled the *Arkansas* and gave Granville a shot. The *Benton* dashed for the shore.

Two more gunboats fell in behind. Then the shore batteries of Vicksburg opened up, driving the Federals back.

They were through the gorge and under protection of Vicksburg's biggest guns.

The Federals retreated up the river and the *Arkansas* steamed out of the smoke and flame, around Tuscumbia Bend. Brown shouted the news. He saw the courthouse in Vicksburg and the Confederate flag flying there. "We're through! We made it."

A few of the men tried to cheer, a croaking cheer that hurt their swollen lips. Ves wavered, then collapsed. Granville touched his moustache and the burnt hairs crumbled in his hand. Wyeth put his arms on Dolly and his head on his arms. The hot metal burned his flesh. He rested for a second and then he and Granville lifted Ves and began wiping blood from his mouth.

A drink of water revived the Cajan and he tried to grin. The effort was too much. He sat there by the gun, his head hanging on his chest. Wyeth pulled himself to the gunport and looked out. Sunshine was dancing on the river. And there was Vicksburg, fifteen minutes away. He thought of Laurel then. Maybe she was in the crowd that was lining the bluff, and waving.

Brown knelt on his quarterdeck and prayed. Then he entered in his log: "Ran through the enemy's fleet. Arrived under protection of Vicksburg at 8:47 A.M."

Chapter Eleven

A DEADENING weariness, a lethargy, overcame the crew as the *Arkansas* idled her propellers and began drifting under the upper batteries of the fortress. The engines still were pounding away, hissing and rattling and the ship trembled with vibrations. The bearings of the starboard shaft were so loose that the rod clanged every time it turned.

The coal bunkers were almost empty and three guns were disabled. Half of the crew was dead, wounded or in the sick bay. And below Vicksburg, within range of any mooring, was the Lower Fleet, Porter's sixteen mortarboats and the protecting men-of-war and tenders.

The men of the *Arkansas*, however, paid no attention to the Lower Fleet. Already, their run had changed from a nightmare into a dream. They simply were unable to comprehend the magnitude of their triumph and were interested only in getting ashore and to sleep.

Wyeth leaned as far out of his gunport as possible and studied the crowd on the bluff. His usually sharp eyes were dimmed, blood-red and heavy. He knew the crowd was cheering but he couldn't hear them because of the noise of the engines. There was a multitude on the bluff, waving flags.

"Is she there?" Granville walked to the port and looked out.

"I can't make out anybody," Wyeth said. "But I'll bet she's there."

He removed the kerchief she had sent him and tied it to the end of his snipper, and put the rifle into the barrel of the Dolly. A breeze caught the piece of silk and it fluttered alongside the ship. If she was there she should see it and know that he was all right.

Captain Brown finished his log and came down among his men. "Load your guns," he said. "The fight has just started."

The upper batteries of Vicksburg were thundering away at the Upper Fleet, keeping it at a distance. The *Arkansas* was moving with the channel and the Warren County Courthouse was plainly visible in the center of town.

Dr. Washington, limping from an injury to his leg, asked the commander if he planned to tie up. The men watched Brown, waiting for the answer. "Not yet," the captain said. "We will drop down to the coal depot."

"I must get the wounded ashore," Dr. Washington said.

"We will take them ashore down there. We must have coal."

The men groaned. Ten bodies still were on the gundeck and fifteen crewmen, slightly wounded, were sticking to their posts. There were almost one hundred wounded and sick men below. The *Arkansas* was able to muster only forty-two wholly ablebodied men.

There was a panicky commotion among General Williams' Federals opposite Vicksburg as the ironclad slipped on down the channel. Williams began burning his supplies, spiking his guns and loading his men aboard transports. Many of the men were running into the woods and hiding. Transports were only half filled and men were clinging to the sides as the ships ran away, down the river to the protection of the Lower Fleet.

The Rebels began laughing. Ves laughed in spite of his pain. "They're afraid of us. They are lighting a shuck away from here. We couldn't whip a skiff now."

And so it was. Before the *Arkansas* reached Vicksburg the land opposite the city was free of Federals. Without firing a shot in that direction, the ship had disrupted all the plans of General Ben Butler.

Below the town, Porter's fleet waited for the transports and then fled too. The men of the *Arkansas* looked on in amazement. A Federal mortarboat was stuck and her crew burned it. Utter confusion and panic seemed to grip the Lower Fleet and fifteen mortarboats, three men-of-war, a half-dozen tenders and a score of transports, tugs and other craft ran away. They dropped down the river, keeping an eye on the *Arkansas*.

Vicksburg's lower batteries began shelling the Lower Fleet, driving them farther. It was fantastic, unbelievable. One crippled ship with forty-two able-bodied men at her guns had chased away an army and a fleet. One ship was wrecking a whole campaign.

The *Arkansas* came opposite of Vicksburg and the big guns of the fortress saluted her. Brown's glass was gone and he couldn't make out the figures along the bluff, but he called down to his men, "Everybody in town is out. They're yelling and jumping up and down." He didn't have a flag to dip, so he pointed his pistol into the air and answered the thunderous salute by firing one shot.

They dropped down below town to the coal depot and tied up alongside a coal barge. The Lower Fleet lost some of its timidity and came back to its mooring, and began throwing mortarshells at the Rebel. The *Arkansas* ignored the firing, leaving the Federals to the attention of the lower batteries.

The wounded were removed and the dead were taken ashore. Dr. Washington patched up Ves' jaw and left him on board, telling the Cajan, "You'll be all right. But you'll never whistle again."

"How 'bout roastin' ears?" Ves asked. "Can I eat 'em?"

"Not out of that side of your mouth."

Stevens was the first whole man ashore. He stepped onto the coal barge and began recruiting labor from the men who were standing there, gaping at the *Arkansas*. Thirty river rats volunteered to help with the coaling.

The engines were cut and stillness settled over the ship. From Vicksburg, almost a mile north of the coal depot, came the echo of shouts and the men looked at one another and shrugged their shoulders. The town was hysterical with joy. There was whiskey and excitement back in the town, but the *Arkansas* still had work to do.

Stevens organized his men. Gift and Read were put in charge of the guns. Granville and Ves were assigned to them and they began mounting the disabled pieces.

Grimball was told to clean ship. He had three helpers and they scrubbed up the blood and removed fragments of men and machinery. Much of the blood had dried in the terrific heat and the stains could not be removed. They didn't scrub the decks, waiting until after the coaling.

Brown went below and worked with the engineers. The starboard engine was virtually useless. The rock-shaft's crank pin, called the wrist on river boats, was broken in two. The engineers were disconsolate and troubled. Brown instructed them to remove the pin and that made the starboard engine completely useless.

"We will use the port engine," the commander said. "The pilot will pitch his helm to offset the pull. It's the best we can do until we get a new crank pin."

Stevens took charge of the coaling crew and Wyeth worked with him. They lugged the fuel aboard in hampers and dumped it into the bunkers and the black dust settled over the ship, mingling with the rust on the sides of the *Arkansas*.

Wyeth noticed it first and pointed out to Stevens that the *Arkansas* had turned the same color as the bluffs, a rusty brown.

"Well, I'll declare," Stevens said. "You're right. If I were across the river I couldn't see this ship against the bluff. That coal dust and the rust make it look just like this loess land."

They were about half through coaling when Porter's Lower Fleet crept up the west side of the river, the far side, and began a steady fire. Brown went to his deck and was puzzled. Most of the shots were off their mark although the *Westfield's* one hundred-pounder rifle gun sent several shells hard by and kicked up spray.

"It is beyond me," Brown said. "We're in full view and they haven't touched us. The enemy can shoot better than that."

Stevens pointed out the color of the *Arkansas* and Brown began smiling. "That's it. Of course, that's it. They can't make us out clearly. From where they are this ship looks like a part of the bluff. Thank God we didn't have any paint."

Brown sent for Wyeth and thanked him for his discovery. The young Missourian stayed on the quarterdeck for a few minutes, drinking in the breeze and looking around at the shambles. He never knew why he looked up at the bluff, and when he did he pointed, then croaked a cry of joy and began waving his arms.

A buggy was moving along the bluff and Laurel was standing in it, jumping up and down and shouting, "Wyeth, Wyeth." She wasn't watching the horse and the animal was picking his way along the bank.

Brown saw her and then noticed Wyeth. The fever seemed to go out of his eyes. "You're covered with coal dust, Woodward."

Wyeth didn't hear him. He was waving so frantically that the exercise loosened some of the dust from his body and hair, and the sweat ran down and streaked his chest.

Stevens tugged Brown's sleeve and winked. The commander said, "Woodward. *Woodward!* Look lively, man! come out of that brown study. You may go ashore for ten minutes. . . ."

He didn't finish the sentence. Wyeth leaped down the hatch and was running across the gundeck, seeking his shirt. It was below in the crew's quarters. Stevens stood at the hatch and jerked off his jacket and threw it to the gunner.

Granville began brushing coal dust from his friend's trousers and Ves looked around for a pair of shoes. He found some that didn't match and Wyeth put them on. They were much too large and he clomped back topside, ran along the crown of the ark, down a ladder to the main deck and onto the coal barge.

He heard Laurel calling to him. "Look out, look out. You'll fall."

He stumbled off of the barge and onto land and began running up the bluff. She jumped out of her buggy and stood there a second, and then ran to him.

His first impulse was to bow and take her hand. But without realizing what he was doing he opened his arms and she ran into them and began crying. She reached up and found his face through her tears and began kissing him.

Wyeth held her so closely that he felt her heart pounding. Then he caught his breath and his sanity returned, and he was flustered. He glanced back at the *Arkansas* and his shipmates were smiling at him. Ves and Granville were at the Dolly's gunport and Ves removed the kerchief and the snipper.

"They saw us," Wyeth said. "They saw me kiss you." Those were his first words.

"I don't care," she said.

He swung her into his arms and took her behind the buggy and over the crest of the bluff. A mimosa tree was there and he put her down under it and pulled her to him again. They didn't speak for minutes and she seemed to melt into him.

"I've got you all dirty," he said and noticed for the first time that coal dust was on her face and dress.

"I don't care." She said it again, and got as close to him as she could.

"I've got to go back aboard in ten minutes. . . ."

"That is time enough to tell me." The coal dust was on her eyelashes and over her freckles. But none was on her lips and they were red and trembling.

"I love you," he said. "Is that what you wanted me to say?"

"Yes." She sat down under the tree and pulled him beside her. "Say it again."

"I love you."

"How much?" She kissed his ear and made a wry face when the dust got on her lips.

He kissed the dust away. "More than anything."

She began sobbing then and was ashamed of her tears and tried to explain them. "I've been so frightened, Wyeth. I saw the battle. It was terrible. I was on the bluff and saw the kerchief. I got in my buggy and came down here. If you hadn't got off of that ship I was going right out there and get on it."

"Is everything all right?"

"Yes." Quickly she gave him the news. Frome and Wall MacKenzie still were at Natchez, apparently above suspicion. "Oh, yes. Gar. . . ."

"What about him?"

"He's free. General Van Dorn got a message for you from the legislature this morning. They've set him free."

"Where is he?"

"He got here yesterday and was on the bluff until he saw the kerchief and knew that you were all right. Then he left. He said you would understand. He rode south, down toward where Mort was killed."

Wyeth looked out toward the river and then back at her. "He'll be back. Kiss me again, Doll. I must return to the ship."

She kissed him, holding his face in her hands, "What did you call me?"

He blinked his eyes. "Oh! Doll? It just slipped out. You sort of remind me of a doll, I reckon."

"I like the name. I like everything you do and everything you say, because I love you so much. I knew I was going to fall in love with you. I knew it all the time."

"If you hadn't I would have made you. That night on the *Music* I wanted so badly to tell you how I felt. . . ."

"Why didn't you? I was waiting to hear it."

"But I'd only known you a few days." He got up and pulled her to his side and they began walking to the top of the bluff. "I was afraid you might be offended. . . ."

"Fiddlesticks. I was dying for you to kiss me. When will I see you again?"

They reached the buggy and Wyeth kissed her lips, then her forehead, then her neck, and her lips again. "I don't know. I don't know what Captain Brown has up his sleeve."

"I will be at Mrs. Simpson's house. Come there as soon as you can, my darling."

He walked down the bluff and she got in the buggy and waited until he was aboard ship and then she turned her horse and started back to Vicksburg.

Wyeth was blushing when he got back to the gundeck. He expected his shipmates to tease him. They did not, however. Granville merely said, "It had to happen." Ves said, "You should have washed your face. That's no way to treat a lady, getting coal dust on her."

The young Missourian was so light-hearted as he returned to his duties that he tried to lift two hampers of coal. He thought he could lift the world, that he could swing it free and hold it on his shoulder. The battle of the morning, less than an hour before, seemed years behind him. He actually tried to whistle, a thing he never could do.

The *Arkansas* was coaled by noon and every man fell to for the job of scrubbing decks. Ves polished the nameplate on the Dolly and every time he noticed Wyeth stepping around like a schoolboy he grinned, either at Granville or to himself. Finally he could stand it no longer and said to Wyeth, "When do you aim to get married?"

"Don't be a loon," Wyeth said. "I've only known her for a little while. Hell, Ves, you can't marry a girl when you first meet her."

"From the way you two jumped together up there on the bluff it might be a good idea to get married."

"That's my business. It's not right to get married in the middle of war. Besides, I've got to talk to her father."

Ves said, "If old man MacKenzie had seen what I saw he'd do the talking. . . ."

"Leave him alone," Granville said. "Wyeth is right. This is no time to get married. His head is still swimming and he doesn't know if he is going or coming. Wait until he comes down from the clouds."

"Some things just won't wait," Ves said. "And a man and a woman are among them. It's mighty hot weather to be falling in love, though." He rubbed his tongue over his injury and felt his jaw. "I aim to do me some love-making as soon as I get leave. I don't care how hot it is."

"What about your face?" Wyeth asked.

"What the hell has my face got to do with it. I don't make love with my face. How about you, Sim? Vicksburg is full of girls."

Granville shrugged off the invitation and Wyeth turned away. He didn't want to hear about harlots so soon after leaving Laurel's arms.

Porter's Lower Fleet kept inching up on the *Arkansas*, blasting away with no effect. Captain Brown cast off his bow and the *Arkansas'* beak swung toward midstream. He called down to the gundeck, "Give them a duster, Granville."

The Dolly spat a solid shot down toward the Lower Fleet and Brown cast off his stern and the *Arkansas* got under way, running on one engine. The Lower Fleet, fearing an attack, fell back down the river and watched the Rebel from afar as a pack of wolves watches a bear.

Brown had no intention of fighting Porter. The Lower Fleet was completely demoralized, but the *Arkansas* was in no shape for battle. So he headed his craft upstream and came to anchor directly under the middle batteries of the fort, at the base of a road that led down from the city hall to the river. A crowd of civilians still was milling about the bluff, shouting, back-thumping, and getting drunk.

As soon as the *Arkansas* was made fast, General Van Dorn walked down to the gangplank and stepped gingerly aboard. With him was Major General John C. Breckinridge of Kentucky, who as vice president under President Buchanan was the youngest vice president in the history of United States. Although his own state had not seceded, he had cast his lot with the South.

There was no bos'n's pipe aboard the *Arkansas* so Stevens fired a stern chaser to welcome the visitors onto the ship. They went immediately to the quarterdeck where Captain Brown received them and made his formal report.

The *Arkansas* had fired 97 shots from the big guns. (Seventy-three of these struck Union ships, killed 42 and wounded 69. The count did not include the missing.) Half of her complement of 200 were dead, wounded, injured or sick.

"We drove one ironclad ashore, disabled a ram, forced the enemy to burn a mortarboat, and damaged several other ships," Brown reported.

"It was magnificent," Van Dorn said. "You also forced Williams' Brigade to forsake their positions across the river and burn their supplies and skedaddle."

"As soon as I repair the ship I will strike the Lower Fleet," Brown said.

They talked for several minutes and then the two generals took their leave. Meanwhile, in the Confederate capital, the Congress was passing resolutions of thanks to Brown and his command, and Mr. Secretary Mallory was preparing Brown's promotion from Lieutenant to Commander.

Farragut announced "with deep mortification" the day's events to the Federal Navy Department and added, "the continued existence of the *Arkansas* so near us is exercising a pernicious influence upon the confidence of our crew, and even upon the commanders of our boats." Farragut called a conference aboard his flagship and pointed out that the *Arkansas* could smash the Lower River Fleet of mortarboats, wooden tenders and wooden men-of-war and then steam down to New Orleans. One ship had upset completely the Federal plans and Farragut was the first to admit it. There was but one thing to do; Farragut's fleet must get between the *Arkansas* and New Orleans. That meant passing the Vicksburg batteries again.

No sooner had Generals Van Dorn and Breckinridge left the *Arkansas* than Brown began pushing repairs on his starboard engine. It was then that his Missourians left the ship. They had volunteered to help get the *Arkansas* to Vicksburg, and had done their duty. They were soldiers, not sailors. Their captains lined them up and explained to Brown they must report back to their command.

There was nothing Brown could do. He thanked them and his

crew gave them a cheer, then watched them trudge off of the boat. Of the 60 who joined the *Arkansas* in Yazoo City, 29 were able to walk away.

A heavy silence enveloped the ship when they were gone and Brown gathered his tiny crew around him, including deck men, firemen, mess boys, officers and doctors. "Well, boys, here we are. Twenty men will go to the engine room, and the remainder will work the guns. If God is willing, we're going to attack this afternoon."

But God apparently was not willing. It was impossible to get the starboard engine working again and sundown found the *Arkansas* moored close to the bank.

The first suggestion that another battle was beginning came from the upper batteries which suddenly began firing to the northwest. Brown called Wyeth to the bridge and asked for a report. The commander still didn't have a glass and fever had dimmed his eyes.

The Missourian shielded his eyes against the setting sun and surveyed the river. "They are coming down, sir. I see the *Hartford*, the *Richmond* and many others. The *Hartford* is leading. . . ."

"Farragut is desperate," Brown said. "He has got to get south of us and he is bringing his squadron by. They will attack us on the way down." He stuck his head through the hatch and shouted, "Prepare for action! Here they come again. Use a spirit level on your guns and fire dead ahead." He turned back to Wyeth. "What else do you see?"

"Every one of Farragut's men-of-war is coming. He has the ram *Sumter* with him. The Upper River Fleet has moved into position to draw the fire of the upper batteries, to give Farragut a chance to slip by. . . ."

"Yes?"

Wyeth was very calm. After the morning's battle, the prospect of another battle did not bother him. He forgot about Laurel. He forgot everything except that the Yanks were coming again. "The *Louisville* and *Cincinnati* are coming part of the way. The main fleet is in Tuscumbia Bend now and soon will round this way and come right to us. It is beautiful, sir, if I may say so."

"You may say so, Woodward. Go to your gun and we will see how long it will remain beautiful."

And beautiful it was; beautiful, desperate and tragic. The sun was to Farragut's back and the *Arkansas* seemed to melt into the bluff, to be a part of the land.

As they left Tuscumbia Bend, the Federals swung down before the main batteries of Vicksburg and opened up. The *Richmond* moved ahead of the *Hartford*. Then came the whole fleet of Farragut's squadron. They were out to mob the *Arkansas,* to gang up and blast her into rubbish.

The Dolly was the first to speak. Granville waited until the *Richmond* loomed through the port. The sun was setting and shadows were on the river, but the sun gave him light and outlined the ship. He hurled a hot shot into the *Richmond,* breaking a steam pipe and wrecking a bulkhead. Commander James Alden of the *Richmond* tried to reply, but his gunners couldn't see the *Arkansas.* So the crew crowded on coal and the *Richmond* dashed by, taking nine shots from the fortress and three from the *Arkansas'* broadside.

Then came the *Hartford* standing close to the bank, determined to locate the *Arkansas* in the fading twilight. The Federals almost brushed the Rebel. The two ships were so close that Wyeth heard a Yankee gunner yell, "I can't see her. She looks just like the bluff. I can't make her out."

Granville was reckless for one of the few times in his life. Ves and Wyeth rammed an 80-pounder with a three-second fuze into the Dolly and Granville set off the charge. The concussion was terrific and yellow flames poured out of the gun's mouth. The shell did not explode, but ripped away the *Hartford's* starboard foretopsail sheet and bitts on the berthdeck.

The flash from the Dolly was a target and the *Hartford* let go a broadside. Charles Gilmore, a pilot, was mangled and Jim Brady was knocked overboard. An eleven-inch shot pierced the *Arkansas* a few inches above the waterline, passed through the engine room, cut two men in two and wounded six others.

The sick bay was wrecked and the dispensary was shattered. The precious medicines were thrown into the engine room.

One shot passed entirely through a bulkhead and lodged between the woodwork and the armor, bulging the armor into the shape of a huge red blister.

The *Arkansas* was leaking badly. Stevens and four men patched the leak with mattresses.

The great men-of-war with their towering spars came sweeping by in a single line, roaring out broadside after broadside. The *Arkansas* spat back and often the Federals were so close that the crew of the Rebel heard the groans of the wounded and dying. From the bluffs, every waterfront battery of the fortress was firing as rapidly as possible and the air was alive with shells, and the sky was red and yellow from explosions, and black with smoke.

The first ship got by at 6:45 P.M. and at 7:20 the squadron was below Vicksburg where it joined with Porter's mortarfleet and took up position, licking the wounds of the day. Never again was Farragut to appear above Vicksburg.

Above the fortress, the Upper River Fleet lurked and waited. Below the town, the Lower Fleet began repairing its damage. The commanders snarled and offered alibis. Even Farragut lost his temper. The mortification was so intense that charges of stupidity and cowardice were made among the Federals. One Southern ship, built in the wilderness, had challenged, confused and divided four Federal fleets and a brigade of soldiers. Two hundred men had defeated several thousand.

Vicksburg went to sleep that night with a light head and a gay heart.

Laurel went to the roof of Mrs. Simpson's house and looked down at the *Arkansas,* hoping Wyeth could get leave. She waited for two hours and then retired and lay awake thinking of him.

Aboard the victorious Rebel, the men were too exhausted to enjoy their triumph. They sent another burial party ashore and then went topside and ate their supper and watched the night close in, praying that it would bring a breeze or rain.

The land batteries still were spitting at the divided fleets and answers came back, hot shot and star shells and Greek fire. The sky was red and the moon was not visible through the pall of smoke.

Ves was lying down on the top of the ark. He didn't even blink when the shells passed over. Granville was below, working on the Dolly and Wyeth was staring up toward the town.

Captain Brown held a lantern as he walked onto the gundeck and found Granville alone. "Quite a day, Granville."

"Yes, sir. Quite a day."

"The enemy is in confusion. We whipped them."

"Aye, ay, sir. They are in a predicament. If the Upper Fleet tries to join the Lower Fleet we can go north and retake Memphis."

Brown nodded. "And if Farragut tries to come up this way again, we can go south and take New Orleans, or at least wreck every enemy ship between here and the gulf."

"They know that, sir. So half the fleet will stay up the river and half will stay downstream."

"And we will take them one at a time, bit by bit. We will nibble and bite, Granville, until they are forced to flee."

"And then what, sir? If I may ask?"

Brown put his lantern on the Dolly and sat on the deck, resting against the carriage. "The day Farragut leaves we will fortify Grand Gulf and Port Hudson. Commander Oliver is ready. That is the program. We will drive Farragut as far south as Baton Rouge and by fortifying Port Hudson we will control the mouth of the Red River, and the Red cuts up throught the heart of Louisiana."

Granville was smiling. Now he saw the pattern of the campaign, the Confederate strategy. "It is a fine plan, sir."

"It is great. President Davis must have credit for most of this. He understands the importance of Vicksburg. The Virginia crowd does not and never will, but this war will be won or lost right here. As long as we hold Vicksburg we are safe. And we can hold Vicksburg as long as we control the Red River, the Big Black River and the land between here and Jackson."

Granville thanked him for his information, still puzzling over the friendship that Confederate officers had for their men. "We can supply Vicksburg from the Red River Valley forever. Is that it?"

"Precisely. Port Hudson is the key. As long as we can get supplies from Louisiana down the Red River, and from Mississippi down the Big Black, and from Jackson over the railroad, we are as snug as a bug in a rug. The Yankees will beat out their brains trying to take us." He got up and took his lantern and motioned for the Englishman to follow him to the quarterdeck. There he got a bottle of brandy, poured out a drink and handed it to the gunner.

"The day's work is done?" Granville asked.

"And the night's work, too. They won't bother us again for awhile. You may go ashore for the night. You and Gillivray. Woodward must stay aboard. I gave him a brief leave this morning. Let him think about that tonight, and tomorrow I will give him liberty."

Granville downed the drink and smacked his lips. "Noble men bore me, Captain Brown. However, I will be glad to stay aboard and let Wyeth go ashore."

"No. Woodward will stand watch tonight. He needs to do a heap of thinking. I saw what happened on the bluff. He will enjoy being alone on watch and reliving those minutes. He will have a thirty-six-hour leave when you and Gillivray return. I can't spare all of you. Don't tell Woodward about the long leave. I want to surprise him."

"You're very kind." Granville stepped to the hatch. "May I go now?"

"Yes. I hope you can walk aboard for breakfast. If you can't I will come and get you."

"I never eat breakfast when I drink. Are you going ashore? You're a sick man."

Brown opened his log and began writing. Then he looked up. "Noble men bore you. Heroics bore me. So don't misunderstand me when I say that I'm not going to leave this ship until I either am taken off or until Farragut is driven south of Baton Rouge and Davis' fleet is forced far back up the river. Goodnight, Granville."

Wyeth was not surprised or too disappointed when Granville reported the news. He said, "I saw her today. I can think about it tonight. And I'll bet the captain will let me see her tomorrow. Please, Mr. Granville, before you get drunk go by Mrs. Simpson's and tell her that I'm all right. And take Ves. I want him to know her."

The Cajan ran his hand over his swollen mouth and looked up into the smoke, up at the bursting shells of the night bombardment. "You know, Wyeth, that's the nicest thing that anybody ever did for me. I want to meet her."

"Then what are you going to do?"

"Two guesses."

"One is enough," Wyeth said and walked to the ladder with them. "While you two are ashore sinning I will work on the gun."

"Good." Granville swung over the side. "We have got to line that vent again. And clean her out. She is all stuffed up."

They stepped ashore and walked up the bluff. Granville was singing one of the songs Gar had taught him:

"With a beard that was filthy and red,
  His mouth with tobacco bespread,
Abe Lincoln sat in the gay White House,
  A-wishing that he was dead.
Then, in a voice not very strong,
  He slowly whined the Despot's song:
    Lie! lie! lie!
I've lied like the very deuce!
  As long as lies were of use;
    Drink! drink! drink!
Til my head feels very queer!
    Drink! drink! drink!
Til I get rid of all fear!
Brandy, and whiskey, and gin,
  Sherry, and champagne, and pop,
I tipple, I guzzle, I suck 'em all in,
  'Til down dead-drunk I drop."

A new day had spent its youth and was beginning its middle hours when Wyeth heard Granville and Ves coming down the bluff, back to the ship. They were shouting and singing and the Missourian went to the gangplank and waited for them. The Englishman was drunk and the Cajan was supporting him, and behind them was a line of twelve river-rats, gawking at the *Arkansas* and stinking of cheap whiskey.

Granville waved at Wyeth and then at the line. "They wanted to fight Yankees. So I fetched them down with me. We need men and they are hardy. Straighten up, you!" He shook one of the new men. "Report to Lieutenant Stevens. He will sign you on."

Wyeth got on one side of Granville and helped Ves lug him to his quarters. The Englishman's eyes were glazed and his mouth was curled into a snarl. "We saw her, Wyeth. She's fine. Pretty as a daisy. . . ."

"Thank you, Mr. Granville." He jerked off his friend's shoes.

"Now let's have a drink. Ves! Let's have one."

"Not me," the Cajan said. "I'm hungry. I've had enough."

Granville reached under his jacket and pulled out a bottle, tilted it and drank until he was forced by time to take a breath and remove the bottle from his lips. "Got three more bottles," he said.

"Going to hide them One down Dolly's throat. They will never find it there. One right here with my gear. Now get me a string and I will show you a trick. Learned it in the British Navy." He measured the string, tied one end around a bottle, lowered it overboard into the river and fastened the other end to the *Arkansas*.

Ves looked at Wyeth, shook his head and shrugged his shoulders.

Stevens, to warn the men of his approach, was singing as he walked toward the crew's quarters and Ves jerked Granville upright and massaged his face quickly. The Englishman was weaving, but on his feet, when the executive officer confronted him. "We can use those men, Granville. Your watch is next up."

"Aye, ay, sir."

"Did you bring any liquor aboard?"

"No, sir."

"Very well. There's no punishment against lying in this navy, but it's hell if you get caught. Commander Brown is a hard master if he has to be."

"Aye, ay, sir." Granville was smirking. "We skinned them yesterday, eh, sir?"

"And we must skin them again. There is black coffee in the galley. I warn you, Granville. Get sober! And you, Gillivray. You are on watch. Woodward, you have a thirty-six-hour leave, beginning in one hour." The second in command walked away and Ves and Wyeth followed him.

As they left Granville, he was singing:

> *"Hail! Texan Bombastes! You must be a stunner!*
> *Some powder-begotten fierce son-of-a-gunner!*
> *What sights you have seen! O wonderful story!*
> *Eclipsing all records of old Roman glory!*
> *But there's a wee dit-of-bifference betwixt me and you,*
> *To tell the plain truth; you lie, knave—you do.*
> *Why, what are you doing, O fierce Texas Ranger*
> *Who sleeps on volcanoes and breakfasts on danger?*
> *You hide in your forts and sulk in your garrisons,*
> *Indulge in self-complacent, boasting comparisons."*

Stevens laughed in spite of himself. Ves called back to his comrade. "Avast there, Sim. That's a Yankee song."

"I know it," Granville roared. "But it's funny. It is as funny as some of ours. Take care of yourself, Wyeth."

The Missourian and the Cajan went to the gundeck where Ves must stand watch. Stevens glanced at them. "Don't look so damn worried. I'm not going to ask you if he brought liquor aboard. I know his habits. His reputation is known from India to Hull. But for God's sake get him sober."

"It can't be done," Ves said. "He's on a spree. It'll last a week, maybe a month."

"Like hell it will." He walked toward the bridge, then turned. "Woodward, I have some new ducks if you want to wear 'em. And some good socks."

"Thank you, Mr. Stevens. My jacket is clean. May I borrow your razor? Mine is missing."

"I'll send the things to you. Good luck."

They waited until Stevens was out of sight, then Ves sighed, "He drank all night. What do you reckon the cap'n will do when he can't stand his watch?"

"I don't know. How is your jaw?"

"Sore. But it'll heal. A busted bone like that can't be set. It'll knot together in a few days." Ves began inspecting the deck, pretending to ignore Wyeth. Then he began grinning. "Go ahead and ask me. Go ahead."

"What?"

"Don't be a ninny. Sure, I met her. She had retired when we got to Mrs. Simpson's, but she got up. No, Sim hadn't had a drink up 'til then. She's the kind of lady I knew you'd pick, Wyeth."

"Then you like her?"

"Uh huh. And she's daffy about you. Go be getting ready. Your liberty starts soon."

"Maybe I'd better stay here and watch out for Mr. Granville. I can take his watch," Wyeth said.

"I'll try to cover him up. You go on."

The young Missourian was walking across the gundeck when Brown and Stevens came down. The commander looked fresher after a night's sleep, but fever still showed in the lines of his face. "Good morning, men." He nodded to Wyeth and Ves. Then he walked over to the Dolly, rammed his arm into the gun's mouth and

[218]

pulled out the bottle. "Sailors never change," he said. "Especially gunners. I used to hide a bottle in my gun when I worked the deck. Hmmm." He winked at Stevens. "Wonder who put it there?"

Ves and Wyeth held their breath. Stevens said, "I don't know, sir. I haven't the slightest idea."

"Well, well. No harm done." Brown walked to the side of the ship and peered out of a port. Then he got a hook, leaned out, caught the string and hauled the second bottle aboard. "Makes me homesick for the deck, Stevens. Good brandy. We didn't have good brandy when we used to hide our stuff overboard. We had only rum. Called it Kill Devil." He tucked the bottles under his arm. "Fetch Granville."

"He is off duty, sir," Wyeth said quickly. "He is not due on watch until . . ."

"Stevens, fetch him," Brown said.

The Englishman was very erect when he reported and was holding himself together by sheer physical and mental power. He saluted smartly. The master looked him over carefully, then said casually, "Put him in the brig, Mr. Stevens. No irons, just the brig."

Granville backed away, protesting. "Just a minute, sir. It is not against the articles for a man to drink off duty. . . ."

"You are right, Granville," Brown said. "But you are not wearing your kerchief in the presence of your superiors. That calls for punishment, a hitch in the brig. If you are in the brig, I can't expect you to stand your watch and then won't have to punish you for being drunk on duty. I assume you have another bottle. Take it to the brig with you. Drink it slowly. You won't get any more. Be sober by morning. We fight tomorrow and if you are drinking I'll take you off your gun. That I swear. Take him away, Mr. Stevens."

The Englishman was too surprised to protest further, and was led away. Brown finished inspecting the gundeck. "Shipshape, all right. You put in a good night, Woodward. Don't you two worry about your mate. He'll be all right. Enjoy yourself, Woodward. My compliments to the young lady."

"Thank you, sir. And by the way, Captain Brown, the legislature has freed that Negro. . . ."

"Now what will you do with him?"

"I don't know."

Granville was singing in the brig, ribald songs and ditties, and Wyeth was on topside, shaving in the sunlight. Ves was hard by, standing his watch and peering up and down the river. The Federal fleets still were throwing shells, trying to locate the *Arkansas* and below, Brown and his engineers were working on the starboard engine.

Ves came over and sat down and watched Wyeth shave. The Cajan was frowning. "Say, Wyeth, I want to know the truth about something."

A premonition gripped the Missourian and he nicked his skin with the razor, for he suddenly was nervous. "Sure, shoot."

"Was Sim at Sharon's house when you got to Natchez?"

Wyeth didn't dare look toward the Cajan. "Uh huh," he said slowly, straining to be casual. "He got there a few minutes before I did."

"Where did he stay while he was in Natchez?"

"Where does he usually stay when he's drunk? What's eating you, Ves?"

"Last night he went out of his head and began mumbling about wine from the Valley of Sharon. Just the way he said it. . . ."

"That was the password. That's all."

The huge Cajan looked away across the river, then up at the bursting shells. "No, that's not all, Wyeth. He's the kind of man Sharon would go crazy over. I know it. Sharon is Cajan and Sim is from a different sort, but I know that when my cousin falls in love she will go whole-hog. Sim ain't like you, Wyeth. And Sharon ain't like Miss Laurel. My brain tells me that Sim wouldn't mess around my cousin. But I ain't so sure. . . ."

"Aw, for God's sake, Ves. Don't talk that way."

"I hope I'm wrong," Ves said. "But I got a feeling. I hope Sim wouldn't do nothing like that to me, that is mess around with one of our women unless he aims to marry her and do it right. I'd have to kill him, you know."

Wyeth was cold inside, but sweat was pouring from his face. "You are talking like a fool." He finished shaving and rubbed his face. "How do I look?"

"Fine. Spic and span. And I won't say nothing else about Sim and Sharon. But I just got a feeling. . . ."

"Forget it." He slipped on his jacket and knotted his kerchief.

Then he combed his hair and it crinkled. He wet it and combed it again. It curled. Ves saw him to the ladder and waved as he stepped ashore and walked up the bluff toward Mrs. Simpson's house.

Laurel was waiting in her buggy just over the bluff. She moved over in the seat and he climbed beside her, glanced around, then kissed her quickly. "How did you know to be here?" He picked up the reins and headed the horse toward the Jackson pike.

"Mr. Granville and Ves told me you would get leave this morning. I'm half in love with Ves, by the way. Are they all right?"

"Sure. Shall we go to Mrs. Simpson's?"

"Not yet, darling. On out this road." She blushed when she said it and Wyeth laughed at her, slipped his arm around her waist and hugged her.

They drove slowly and came at last to a quiet place, a shady place, and got out and sat under a tree. Laurel smoothed her dress and reached up and pulled his face down to hers.

"Listen, Doll," he said after several minutes. "What will your father think about this?"

"Oh, he'll make out like he's upset because it happened so quick."

"I'll call on him as soon as I can. . . ."

"And ask for my hand? You'll have to now, you know. After what happened yesterday. Right in plain view of everybody." She rubbed her nose against his and patted his cheek.

"That's what I wanted to talk to you about. I want you to marry me as soon as the war is over. . . ."

"How long will it last?" she asked quickly.

"Maybe a year longer. We are winning everywhere and the Yanks soon will sue for peace."

"Then what?"

"Oh, I suppose we'll fuss and fume around and then go back into the Union and take up where we left off. But they won't bother us anymore."

"I'm not talking about politics. I'm talking about us. What will we do?"

Wyeth leaned against the tree and watched heat waves dance along the pike. The Confederate and Federal batteries were rumbling in the distance and black puffs floated in the sky. "Laurel, I haven't a thing to offer you. Yet . . ."

"Oh yes you have. You have yourself. And we have each other. That's all it takes to start; a man and a woman in love."

"I've made plans. . . ."

"So have I. I want a white house. Not too big. Just a nice size. And a wide porch and a second story gallery."

"I am not going back to the fur country. Or back to steamboating. I am going to read law, Doll. And practice." He watched her reaction and was disappointed. "Why, aren't you surprised?"

"No. Not a bit."

"Huh! Doesn't anything surprise you?"

"Not any more."

"Well, this will," he said. "When we get married we are going to move to a new land. . . ."

"Texas?"

"Maybe. But I like Mississippi, except Natchez. I'd like to see Lebanon. I remember Sam Dabney talking to my father about it. I might go there after the war if Hoab Dabney were not fighting for the Union."

"He won't be fighting long. The Confederates have sent an army to wipe him out and put a stop to his rebellion against the South. They will hang him and Keith Alexander. . . ."

"If they catch them," Wyeth said.

"And I am sort of sorry. Somehow I like Mr. Dabney and his little republic. It stands for something, Wyeth. There he is, defying the whole South because he believes certain things. And you know what?"

"What?"

"I hear that Morna Dabney is in love with Keith Alexander. I know he loves her and now I hear that she loves him. It would be so nice if they got married. Even if Mr. Alexander is nameless."

"What do I care about Morna Dabney and Keith Alexander? We have our problems. . . ."

"But they are so romantic, darling. And I'll tell you who else is romantic."

"I know. You needn't say it." He picked up a pine cone and hurled it away.

"How did you know what I was going to say?" She snuggled close to him and rubbed her head against his chest.

"You were going to say Sharon and Mr. Granville."

"That's right. I don't want to pry. I hate prying women. But does Ves know about it?"

"That's prying, Laurel."

"It's not. It's just normal curiosity."

"No, Ves doesn't know. But he suspects something. Everything will be all right, though. Mr. Granville won't see her again and it'll pass away."

Laurel got up and brushed pine needles from her dress and fluffed her hair, then wiped perspiration from her face. "You darling. You trustful darling. No wonder I adore you, Wyeth. No wonder Mr. Granville and Ves love you. . . ."

"What are you driving at?" He got up, too.

"It's like Mr. Granville said. You are incapable of a mean thought. Of course, Mr. Granville and Sharon will see each other again. When a man has known a woman like her, he always goes back."

"Laurel! That sounds . . ."

"I know it does. And it is. But face facts, my love. A lawyer must. It is you I am thinking about. I don't want you to be hurt. Mr. Granville can no more leave that woman alone than he can leave drink. And she won't let him. They are in each other's blood. I saw it last night when he asked me if I had heard from her."

"Was Ves there when he asked?"

"Yes. He heard it, too. Mr. Granville tried to be casual. He wasn't. Now let's go back to town. Mrs. Simpson is expecting you for dinner."

Mrs. Simpson was impressed by the sailor and insisted that he remain for supper and for the night. She was wise enough to leave him and Laurel to themselves and they sat in the cool of the living room that afternoon and made plans. After supper, they sat on the verandah and watched the fireworks. The bombardment was raging down along the river, but Vicksburg went about its business as though no war was being fought. General Van Dorn was at a ball. . . .

In a good bed for the first time in many nights, Wyeth slept until 9 o'clock the next morning and might have slept on if Laurel hadn't knocked at his door. When he answered the rap, she peeped around the door, kissed him quickly, then said, "A friend of yours is here. He will be up in a minute."

It was Gar. He came into Wyeth's room and stood on one foot, then the other while the sailor dressed. "How many?" Wyeth asked.

"One, Mist' Woodward. I found him near Grand Gulf. I drowned him. That was mighty fine fightin' yesterday on the *Arkansas*."

"She's a good ship." Wyeth was combing his hair.

"I gave that pitcher to Mis' Laurel."

"She told me. Miss Laurel and I are going to be married some day and we will put that picture in our house. The first one you gave me—well, I intend to put it in my office when I start my law career." He said it nonchalantly, expecting Gar to show surprise. But the Negro wasn't surprised either.

That annoyed Wyeth. It seemed that nobody was surprised that he planned to read law. He finished his toilet and said, "Sit down, Gar."

The Wolof hesitated. Never before had he been asked to sit in a white man's presence. However, he sat on the edge of a chair and watched his friend.

"Miss Laurel told you about your freedom?"

"Yes, suh. I reckoned it'd come along when you ask the folks at Jackson to do it." He smiled, and he wasn't so ugly when he smiled. It was a gentle smile, a smile of infinite patience and understanding. "You'll make a good lawyer, Mist' Woodward. You going to be an honest lawyer, and help folks. Po' folks."

Wyeth cleared his throat and tried to be professional. "Now that you are free, what are your plans?"

"I ain't got none. Jes' keep on like I was, I reckon. The readin' is coming along pretty good. Mis' Laurel helped me with the kinks, and I can write my name without copying it. As soon as we win this war, I aim to let you learn me some figures."

"You are a free man of property and responsibility now."

"Yes, suh. But it don't make no difference. I can't spend the money 'cause there ain't nothing to buy. I may be free, Mist' Woodward, but I'm still black. And this is a white man's country. It always will be, I reckon."

"Gar." Wyeth sat on the edge of the bed. "You've got talent. But you haven't got a chance down here. Not now. Maybe later, but maybe not. This *is* a white man's country and it always will be. Why don't you go to the West Indies or France? You could be somebody there. Jamaica. Santo Domingo."

"Way off there?" The Wolof shook his head. "You forgetting,

Mist' Woodward. I was born here. This is my home and I aim to stay here. I ain't going to run off nowhere."

Wyeth was impatient. He had anticipated such an answer and had no argument. "Very well. It's your life."

"You know, suh. Some day the white folks are going to let the black folks learn to read and write. Maybe I can help 'em. Like you helped me."

A lump came to the sailor's throat and he looked away. "All right, Gar. Good luck. I have things to do."

"I'll be around, Mist' Woodward. I ain't never going to be far away from you. Never. When you holler, I'll be around. I know I'm going to need you and maybe you going to need me." He squared his shoulders and went to the door. "When you get back to fighting, don't fret about Mis' Laurel. I'll be nigh."

Wyeth and Laurel spent every available minute together that day and she left him at sundown on the bluff that shadowed his ship. When he got out of the buggy she didn't look back and neither did he.

Granville was on the gundeck, reaming the Dolly's vent. He was sober and smiled sheepishly at Wyeth. Ves said, "Married yet?"

"Not yet. But I had the best time I've ever had. She will marry me. Next year, more than likely. Soon as things settle down. How's the ship?"

The starboard engine was patched and the iron beak had been repaired. A new flag floated from the bow and fifty men, mostly river trash, had been recruited. The *Arkansas* was humming with activity and the Missourian scarcely had got back into his deck clothes before she moved from her mooring and stood for downstream and the Lower Fleet.

But there was no fight. The Federal tenders hauled the mortar-boats out of danger and the men-of-war used steam and sail to avoid the Rebel. The *Arkansas* chased the entire Lower Fleet four miles, then gave up and cruised upstream, scattering the Upper Fleet. For the first night in almost two months, Vicksburg was spared a bombardment. The Yanks disappeared from before the city and sought safety miles away. Until midnight, the *Arkansas* cruised the Mississippi, looking for trouble.

"They are completely demoralized," Granville said.

And so they were. Separated and jittery, the Federal fleets hadn't had time to plan a campaign. So they avoided combat, knowing the *Arkansas* couldn't cruise forever up and down the river. That was the night the weird tales started about the *Arkansas*. A Federal tug up north of Memphis saw the shadow of an unidentified barge, burned the tug, took to the woods and began spreading word that the dreaded Rebel was on the prowl. That same night the *Arkansas* was reported off Cairo, Ill., and as far down as Baton Rouge.

Farragut and Davis did their best to check the rumors, but two days after her first fight the *Arkansas* became a phantom in the frightened imagination of the Northerners, a ghost ship, three hundred feet long, that was lurking behind every bend. Federal traffic on the lower Mississippi came to a standstill. Sailors simply refused to venture out at night. The Confederates contributed to the hoax and dropped hints here and there that the *Arkansas* was heading for St. Louis, Pittsburg, New Orleans. Actually, she never was thirty minutes away from Vicksburg.

The Navy Department in Washington was in a dither and even the Virginia clique of the Confederate Navy Department raised their eye-brows. Petty jealousies were as rampant in the Confederacy as in the Union, and the seaboard crowd would not admit that the *Arkansas,* built by Western barbarians, and Mississippi was the West, could be mentioned in the same breath with the *Virginia.* Their minds were bounded by Tidewater on the east and the mountains on the west, and they never saw over the mountains. It simply never occurred to the seaboard that the Western barbarians were settling the war a thousand miles from Richmond and Washington.

A Federal mailship was captured near the Yazoo and Vicksburg laughed over the reports going north about the *Arkansas,* for the seized letters and dispatches contained fantastic reports.

For four days, the Rebel wheeled from one fleet to the other, inviting a fight. The Federals were sulking, however, and the *Arkansas* chased them around almost at will. The Upper Fleet expected the Lower Fleet to attack, and vice versa. The commanders were squabbling, each blaming the other. No man had control over combined actions. Farragut fumed in helplessness. His wooden men-of-war didn't have a chance against the Confederate ironclad. Neither did Porter's mortarboats. Farragut had no authority to order Davis' ironclads to battle, and Davis was not foolish enough to send his ironclads into a fight without ram support, and the rams were waiting for support from the Lower Fleet.

The first siege of Vicksburg was settling into a fiasco. General Williams' soldiers were useless without naval support, so they stayed on transports and died like flies from malaria.

But malaria played no favorites and began striking down the *Arkansas'* crew until only thirty men were left to man her. They included Wyeth, Ves and Granville. There were not enough men left to keep up steam and Brown began sending frantic telegrams to Richmond. President Davis begged the governor of Mississippi to help raise a crew, and the Confederacy began recruiting men from Mobile, Pensacola and every city that had idle seamen. Most of the seamen wanted berths on blockade runners and raiders. The pay was better. The Confederate conscription law did not cover the South's Navy.

Meanwhile, the *Arkansas* virtually was helpless, thirty men facing the Federal fleets. The Yanks surmised that something was keeping the Rebel at her mooring and ventured back to within rifle range of the ship and resumed the bombardment.

Dr. Washington was forced by illness and injury to give up his post and a new senior surgeon came over from Clinton, Miss. He was delighted with the ship until the Yankees started their routine shelling. Then the doctor stood on the companion-ladder, watched smoke rise from the mortarboats and ducked as the shells whizzed over. One shell exploded just over the bridge and another rocked the ship. Brown didn't look up, but the doctor put his hands over his ears and moaned, "Oh! Louisa! Louisa and the babes!"

Louisa became a byword among the *Arkansas'* crew—Oh! Louisa! Louisa and the babes!

The Federals bombardment became so regular that fish, killed by concussion, floated by the *Arkansas*. "By God," Ves protested. "Look at that. Them upper river Yanks are killing fish for the lower river Yanks. Oh! Louisa!"

A sunset bombardment drove the crew to their guns, suggesting an attack was coming. However, the Federals were as far away as their guns' range permitted, just pumping shells. One shell whammed against the portside and tiny missiles scattered through the opening, clattering on deck. The Confederates stared in amazement as marbles rolled down among the guns. The Federals were using marbles as grape, trying to find little holes in the *Arkansas'* armor. Ves and Wyeth gathered more than one hundred marbles from the gun deck, white-alleys, taws, agates and jugs. Then they sat there on deck and played marbles. Oh! Louisa and the babes!

It was midnight of July 21 when Brown sent for Wyeth. He had need of the young man's sharp eyes. Wyeth rubbed away the sleep and looked up and down the river. Every Federal ship had up steam.

"Farragut, Dave Porter, Davis and Ellet had a conference aboard the *Benton* last night," Brown said. "They have hatched something."

"We haven't got enough men to fight, sir," Wyeth said.

"You are mistaken, Woodward. We haven't got enough men to run away. Our condition is such that we can't retreat if we wanted to. So if they want a fracas, they know where we are. To your gun, Woodward, and tell the drummer to sound beat to quarters."

The roll of the drum came from aft, and the men tumbled from their hammocks. The drummer put aside his drum and reported to the powder room. The *Arkansas* was pointed upstream, her iron beak toward the north and against the current.

"What the hell is up?" Ves asked.

"The Yanks want to play marbles," Wyeth said.

"Oh! Louisa!" Granville tested his friction tube. "A man can't get any sleep in this war."

They didn't have long to wait. It was four A.M. and the sky was barely opening to admit the sun's reveille for that day, July 22, when the entire Upper Fleet of ironclads and rams steamed into Tuscumbia Bend and engaged the upper batteries. The Lower Fleet crept up and drew the fire of the lower batteries.

Brown came down from his bridge and helped load every big gun, and passed out small arms and cutlasses. His eyes were bright with fever and his face was flushed. His skin was so dry that it looked parched. He sent three engineers below, barely enough to keep up steam. Twenty-seven men, including officers, were available for deck duty. . . .

"Mr. Stevens," Brown said to his executive officer. "If I go, you are in command. Don't surrender this ship. If they board her, blow her up."

"They won't board us, cap'n," Ves shouted.

"Do you think thirty men can hold off a fleet? They'll sweep down on us like locusts."

"What do you think we'll be doing all that time?" Ves asked. "Reading a book?"

"You might try praying." Brown put his hands on the ladder that led to his deck. Then he glanced back and smiled. "Oh! Louisa!"

The fire of the Federals stopped suddenly and as•the smoke lifted and rolled away, the *Essex,* a bulldog of an ironclad, was seen bearing down on the *Arkansas,* charging like a mad bull, snorting and roaring.

"Bill Porter's ship," Brown said to Stevens. "He looks angry. I knew Bill in the old Navy. He's stubborn and hard-headed, but he'll fight, Mr. Stevens. Dust him off, if you please."

The *Arkansas'* two bowguns barked and the *Essex* jerked up her square nose, then came on, her big guns blazing. A shell found the forward port of the Rebel and careened along the deck, killing seven and wounding six; almost half the crew.

"Make every shot tell," Brown shouted.

Officers and men began running from gun to gun, loading and firing. Granville touched off the Dolly, then leaped to the next port gun while Ves and two engineroom men loaded the Dahlgren and shoved her back into battery.

Wyeth was working one of Gift's bow Columbiads as the lieutenant had a ball in his leg and was hopping about, working as a deckhand. Gift was the first to see the *Queen of the West,* luffing down from the Upper Fleet, her prow out of water and her nose swarming with sharpshooters.

He called a warning to his commander and Brown immediately divined the Federal strategy. "Mr. Stevens! Stand ready to cast off the bowlines. Bill Porter intends to strike our larboard with his *Essex* and shove us onto the bank. Then the *Queen* will attack and try to ram us to bits."

That was Porter's plan, all right. He veered toward midstream, then cut sharply and aimed his ship's stubby bow for the *Arkansas'* port side. The Dolly raked his deck. Granville actually laughed and Wyeth began laughing, too. He had cried during the first battle, but now he was laughing, a wild high laugh. He didn't know he was laughing.

The Englishman glanced his way and caught his breath. The scar on Wyeth's cheek was shining white through streaks of powder and his chestnut hair was standing on end, blood-matted.

"Are you hurt, Wyeth?"

"No. This blood got on me when that shell bashed in those poor devils." He laughed again.

"Well, now. I must say, Wyeth, that you look and sound like an Indian. But do you see what I see?"

"Uh huh. The *Essex* has a broad flat bow. Our beak is sharp. . . ."

He didn't finish the sentence. "Cast off the bowlines!" Brown's command echoed into the morning.

The *Arkansas'* bow swung free. The current caught her nose and turned it directly toward the nose of the *Essex*. A cry of dismay came from the Federal and Bill Porter's voice was heard clearly. "Port rudder! Hard! Hard over!"

The Yankee came up sharply, wheeled and grazed the Rebel's beak. A full blow would have cut the *Essex* from bow to stern.

"Good steamboating," Wyeth muttered and fired into the iron-clad.

The *Essex's* charge was so powerful that, despite reverse propellers, she piled her nose onto the bank.

It was a daring thing to do, a brave thing. It wasn't Bill Porter's fault that Brown outmaneuvered him. But there the Yankee was, hard aground and within ten feet of the *Arkansas,* right under the main batteries of Vicksburg. The land guns didn't fire, however, for fear of hitting the *Arkansas.*

"Prepare to repel boarders!" Brown commanded and began firing his pistol into the *Essex's* ports.

"Shall we board her?" Grimball yelled.

"No. The *Queen* is coming. We must be ready for her. If they will send some soldiers down from the bluff they can capture the *Essex.*"

Bill Porter knew that. He lined his sharpshooters on deck, yelled for steam and kept his propellers churning in reverse, trying to back off of the bank.

Gift got a big gun loaded and almost blew the *Essex* out of the river. The Rebel crew lined up along the *Arkansas'* rail, yelling and shooting.

The Federals took one look at them and screamed, "Wild men!" Then some of them dived into the river.

And wild men they were. Wyeth was at the rail, picking his shots. He kept shouting, "Oh! Louisa!" His snipper was hot and he often grabbed the barrel and swung his weapon as a club, trying to reach the Yankees. Granville was firing his pistol methodically. Blood was dripping from his mustache and his nose was bleeding from concussion. Ves was leaning against the iron ark, raking the *Essex's* deck with his snipper. He was yelling, "Louisa and the babes!" The two ships were so close that the Yanks saw Wyeth's scar. Ves spat at one of them and Granville leaned forward and slashed a rifleman with his cutlass.

The *Arkansas* swung around then, her bow downstream and her stern to the *Essex*. Read gave the Yankee a blast from his sternchasers and the explosion helped rock the *Essex* free from the bank. Bill Porter kept fighting back, trying to get a boarding party organized. Then four shore batteries opened from above and a company of Confederates ran down the bluff to board the *Essex*. Porter knew the battle was lost. His engineers choked off the safety valves, gave the *Essex* all the steam she could handle and the propellers clawed the river, dragging the ironclad from the bank.

Porter headed downstream then. He was licked. His ship was leaking and he had to heel to starboard to keep a port waterline hole above the river. He was fuming and cursing Farragut, his own brother-in-law, for not supporting him. On the way down, the *Essex* was rocked time and again by the shore batteries.

The handful of men still on the *Arkansas* stacked their small arms and went back to the big guns and were ready when the *Queen of the West,* making 15 miles an hour, spun on her stern, then cut in to ram the Rebel's starboard. A broadside slowed her down and she staggered and plunged ahead.

The *Arkansas'* big guns soon were empty and inboard. The *Queen's* side-wheels were throwing foam. Her bow was plated and her sides were protected by wooden and iron beams and cotton bales. Lieut. Col. A. W. Ellet was in command. His nephew, Little Boy Blue, was back with Davis.

Frantically, the Rebels tried to reload their cannon. Wyeth's laughter died in his throat and his throat was dry, as dry as the hot shot he rammed into the Dolly.

The *Queen* took everything the *Arkansas* hurled and kept coming in, her ram poised for the kill. The Dolly's hot shot set fire to the cotton bales. Federal sharpshooters stood there in the flames and fired at their enemies while their clothes burned and their skin peeled.

Brown waited until he was able to see the ripples from the *Queen's* bow, then he put his rudder over hard, threw his starboard engine into reverse and his port engine forward. The strain was tremendous. The *Arkansas* groaned, then turned on her stern, her long iron beak facing the *Queen*.

It had worked again. The *Queen* pulled up sharp to avoid the deadly beak, wavered and tried to stop. The *Arkansas'* prow bit into her side. The blow reeled the Rebel and she wobbled from side to side. The *Queen,* however, began taking water and was out of control for a minute. Her bow piled onto the bank, astern the *Arkansas*. Read began puncturing her with his big rifles. The Dolly's vent was blown again and Granville was firing her with a compressor lever.

Again soldiers ran down from the bluff to board the enemy, but the *Queen,* taking a merciless fire from a dozen batteries, reversed her huge paddle wheels and backed off. She was riddled and steam was hissing from her sides. Her decks were shambled as she limped away, rather proudly, back upstream to Davis' fleet.

"Louisa! Oh! Louisa!" Brown called down from his deck. "That's all, boys."

Somebody laughed. But there were no cheers from the victors. Victory had become a habit. They had met the Federal fleet three times in pitched battles and had won.

"Muster your men," Brown told Stevens.

Seventeen men answered roll call.

"Start cleaning ship," Brown said. "We'll have replacements in a day or so. A full crew. And then, men, we'll be away for New Orleans. Then for Mobile."

That brought a cheer. Brown issued whiskey and winked at Granville when the gunner declined a drink. "I'll take mine later, sir," said Simeon St. Leger Granville. "That won't wet my tongue."

Crowds began swarming along the bluffs and cheering the *Arkansas* again. Wyeth went topside and saw Laurel in the crowd and waved at her. Gar was there, too. Awnings were spread on the gunboat and breakfast was served, hot bacon and good coffee. The sun was high, but clouds were banking to the east. A breeze was rippling the Battle Flag on the ship's bow. It was popping. . . .

Wyeth said, "A rain is coming. Feel that breeze?" He looked up at the sky, then up the bluff at Laurel. She threw him a kiss.

"It's going to set in for a long rainy spell," Ves said. He glanced up and down the river. "Wonder why the Yanks don't start shooting again. I ain't heard a gun since we whipped the *Essex* and *Queen*."

"Hey!" Wyeth shielded his eyes. "The Yanks are leaving. Under full steam. All the transports with Williams' men are way downstream, making time. The mortar fleet and tenders are right behind them, and Farragut is making tracks, too."

"How 'bout the Upper Fleet?" Ves asked.

"Can't make them out," Wyeth replied. "But it looks like they are moving. Sure, they are. Oh! Louisa. I can see the *Carondelet!* So she's back in service. And the *Benton*. The *Queen*. The whole shebang. They are standing up-river."

Rumors began flying among the crew and they stared at one another. Captain Brown left his bridge and stepped ashore for the first time since the *Arkansas* fought her first battle. Ves whispered to Granville, "He said he wasn't going ashore until the Yanks gave up."

"The Yanks won't give up," Granville said. "Maybe they are falling back now. But they'll come again. And again and again."

"Why the war is almost over," Ves said.

"No, Ves. It has just started. And you, Wyeth, don't wait until this war is over before you marry Laurel. That will be too long."

All that day rumors spread like wildfire and the men didn't know what to believe. The Federal fleets had disappeared. Two cooks came aboard that afternoon and by nightfall a crew of 104 sailors from Mobile and Pensacola reported and signed on. They brought news from the outside; good news. The Confederacy was living her brief hour of glory.

Supper was cooking in the galley, fresh beef and good bread, when Brown came back from Van Dorn's headquarters. He scarcely could walk and his skin was yellow and tight from fever. He leaned against the Dolly and called his men around him. He tried to speak, swallowed and tried again. His voice was low and husky.

"Men," he said, almost in a whisper. "The siege of Vicksburg is lifted."

The men gaped at him, then at one another. "The hell you say," Ves grunted.

"Yes, Gillivray. The hell I say. Louisa and the babes are safe."

Nobody laughed. Brown put his hands to his head and pressed his temples. "Farragut and his men-of-war and Porter's mortar fleet have sailed. Maybe for New Orleans. Williams' brigade is with them. Davis' ironclads and Ellet's rams are standing for Memphis. We have cleared the middle river of our enemies."

Granville whistled under his breath. Wyeth's eyes filled and his mind went up the bluff to Laurel. Ves suddenly was thinking about the swamp country, his home. Granville was thirsty.

The captain cleared his throat. "We are off the beaten path out here and the world may never hear what you have done. And if it hears, it won't believe. I scarcely believe it myself. You built a ship out of scrap-iron. Built her in the wilderness. You defeated four fleets and an army. There will be prayers on my deck after supper. I hope some of you join me there. God bless you."

Still the men didn't cheer. They couldn't take it in. Without orders, they began cleaning ship, loading the guns and repairing damage. Wyeth went to the bridge and found his captain in prayer. The Missourian bowed his head until Brown looked up. "Yes, Woodward?"

"May I have leave, sir?"

"Tomorrow, Woodward. She can wait that long."

"Sir, if I am with you a year from now, will you marry us?"

"Yes. Here on my quarter-deck, son."

"Do you think the war will last another year?"

"Yes. They'll be back, Woodward. Would you give up now if you were in their shoes?"

"Of course not, sir."

"They are the same sort of folks we are. They'll be back."

But for the time being Vicksburg was free of Federals. The strongest fleet ever assembled by the United States, a combination with more power than the British, French and Spanish fleets at Trafalgar, had been baffled by one ship, a home-made hulk of rusty iron.

There was nothing else for the Federals to do but give up the campaign. Farragut had been right all along. Vicksburg couldn't be taken from the river. An army was needed, a big army. Farragut's communications were too thin and his line of supply was too long. He had to give up. His wooden ships and his mortars couldn't face the *Arkansas* and two battles had proved that Davis' ironclads were no match for the Rebel.

The river was falling, too, and there was danger that Farragut's ships-of-the-line might be trapped. So he swallowed his pride and fled. The mortarboats had to follow him and with the Lower Fleet gone, the Upper Fleet had to fall back. The house of cards fell down. The *Arkansas* simply knocked down a few cards, and they all fell.

To the casual observer, it seemed that the whole Union was falling apart in that summer of 1862. England was debating recognition of the Confederate States of America. France had her fingers in Mexico and the Monroe Doctrine was ignored. In all the world, the United States seemed not to have a friend among the powers. That was when a Russian fleet steamed into New York with a message of good will from the czar.[22]

The North's heart beat warmly for Russia then and the Yankees waved their fists at England and France. They were ready to fight the world, if need be.

The Confederacy was riding high, sitting in the big chair. In Virginia, Lee was cutting his enemies to ribbons. Bragg was on the move in Tennessee. Blockade runners were making faces at Yankee skippers and Confederate ships were raiding the seas. . . .

Halleck was in command of the Federal armies and was floundering. The blustery Pope was facing disgrace and the vain-glorious McClellan was check-mated. Grant's army was bogged down and Sherman was chewing his nails in Memphis. And over in Lebanon, Hoab Dabney's backyard rebellion against the South was being pinched to bits by a besieging army.

Farragut reported back to New Orleans. The *Essex* put in at Baton Rouge and his men told strange tales about the *Arkansas,* and about a man who laughed and cried when he fought, who had a long scar that showed white. And about two other wild men, one with a trim mustache and another with yellow hair. . . .

The mere mention of the *Arkansas* struck terror as far north as Cincinnati and the Federal Navy Department ordered more ironclads from Jim Eads and his assembly lines. Somebody had to be the goat for the fiasco at Vicksburg. Farragut was too powerful to be ridiculed. So they picked on poor Charles Henry Davis of the Upper River Fleet. His *Carondelet* and *Essex* were the only ships that really challenged the Rebel, and yet he was blamed. The real blame, however, was in Washington, at the White House and the Navy Department. Lincoln had ordered the siege over protest of Farragut and other fighters. Let the blame be where it belongs. . . .

Prent Oliver took his little Black River Fleet into the Mississippi, fortified Grand Gulf, north of Natchez, and Port Hudson, south of Natchez. The plan was executed perfectly. Port Hudson controlled the mouth of the Red River, and the Red, at some seasons, was navigable as far west as Shreveport, La., almost to Texas. Federal ships had to pass the Port Hudson batteries to get to the Red, and Confederate supplies were pouring out of the Red, thence north to Vicksburg.

The Yanks left Natchez, too, and soon there was not a Federal gun between the mouth of the Yazoo and Baton Rouge. The heart of the lower valley was back in Confederate hands. No wonder Granville got drunk again. So did Ves. And Wyeth, too.

Chapter Twelve

T HE rain began gently. Clouds rolled up in black loaves and bluffed a storm, then flattened into thick gray blankets and released the water that nature had been hoarding for months.

In the beginning, the rain fell straight down, beating the river's face into dirty pocks. Vicksburg sang. The people came out of their houses and stores and stood in the rain, smiling. The Yankees were gone, and the heat was gone, and the rain had come, slipping in like an army bent on raising the siege of Inferno.

The rain was in no hurry to spend its strength, for it expected to take over from the heat and rule the land for a long time.

The dust was settled quickly and from Warrenton and the lower batteries to Walnut Hills and the upper batteries the defenders of the fortress covered their guns and lay on the ground, soaking in the rain and enjoying its cool touch. The guns were silent for the first time since May. The rain cooled the guns, too, and little waterfalls poured from the lips and breeches of the pieces.

The crew of the *Arkansas* gathered on the deck, under the awning, and rested and talked and laughed as sailors do; swapping stories and exaggerating their experiences. Often the men laughed out loud at nothing in particular. Such was the effect of rain.

Ves began telling some wild stories about the deluges that fell in the swamp country and Granville told stories of the monsoons of

India and of England's dreary rains. Wyeth had an overwhelming urge to be with Laurel. It would be good to sit on the porch with her and watch the rain, and say nothing.

A recruit from Pensacola, half Spanish, began singing a ribald ditty. Nobody joined in and the singer broke off his song in embarrassment. The gentle rain did not go with ribald songs. Granville, remembering one of Gar's songs, began singing it:

> *"We'll meet old Abe with armies brave,*
> *And whip the lying scoundrel knave.*
> *Look away, look away, look away to Richmond town;*
> *As he pleads for terms and whiskey,*
> *We'll give him hell to the tune of Dixie."*

The words trailed off. The song was not appropriate in the peace and contentment of the day. It just didn't fit. Somebody started an old spiritual, "Jesus Goin' To Make Up My Dying Bed." They all sang that, all except Granville who didn't know the words. Then, without comment, most of the men filed forward to the bridge and joined Captain Brown in prayer. The Confederates were long on prayer. They were short of everything else, but prayer was free and plentiful.

A south breeze came and the rain began slanting and swishing. The *Arkansas'* ports were closed and the guns were covered. The rain found cracks in her armor, however, and seeped through, forming rivulets on the gundeck. Coal dust and rust were washed away.

Captain Brown held a conference with Mr. City, the chief engineer, and it was decided the engines should be overhauled. The work was begun late that afternoon and Brown was supervising removal of the troublesome starboard wrist, the king pin of the engine, when he collapsed.

He sank to the deck and his eyes rolled. Mr. City picked him up and called for help. His temperature was 103 and the surgeon ordered him ashore. The men gathered around in small knots. The master reached the gangplank and turned his face up and let the rain cool his skin. The malaria had splotched his eyes and colored his skin a parched yellow. His lips were masses of blisters. The master looked back at his ship and his crew and said to the men, "I will be back and lead you away from here. In my absence, Mr. Stevens will be in command. Follow him and don't ever surrender the *Arkansas*."

They took him first to the Marine Hospital in Vicksburg and then sent him upstate to Grenada to be with his family.

A pall settled over the *Arkansas* and melancholia gripped the crew. The rain became melancholy, too, and swished a sad song against the iron of the ship, beating out a hollow note. Night came and the ship's lanterns swung in the south wind, throwing yellow streaks across the river.

Stevens kept his men busy. He worked his new men in the engine room and let his old men putter around the gundeck, dressing up the batteries. Granville lined the Dolly's vent. Wyeth cleaned her insides and Ves polished the nameplate.

Wyeth had a watch that night and stood it up near the bow, watching the river to the north. The rain was falling in sheets and he walked over to starboard, propped on the rail and stared up the bluff.

He saw the lantern up there and recognized Gar walking down toward the ship. The Wolof stood on the bank and called softly to his friend. "She's right up yonder, Mist' Woodward. You can't see her in this rain and she can't see you. But she just wanted you to know that she is nigh."

"Has she got an umbrella?" Wyeth asked.

"No, suh. She's just sitting there in her buggy. She says she likes the rain. If you'll go to the bow and stand under that lantern maybe she can see you. I'll tell her you're there and I'll wave my light three times and you'll know where she is."

He walked back up the bluff and Wyeth stood under the bow-light. Then he saw Gar's lantern and knew that Laurel was right up there about 200 yards. His heart began pounding. He wanted to call out to her and might have, but Stevens came up to inspect the watch. He noticed Wyeth staring toward the town and said, "Yanks?"

"No, sir."

"She will get wet."

Wyeth felt his face redden. "How did you know she was up there?"

"Your face, man. Nobody could look that way unless he were looking toward his sweetheart or an angel."

"I suppose you think it's silly. . . ."

"No. It's not silly. I wish I could let you go up there and see her, but you can't break your watch. However, you have leave tomorrow."

Wyeth watched the light fade and knew that Laurel was going away. He walked the deck in the rain, making plans and counting the hours until daybreak.

By morning, puddles were standing in Vicksburg's streets and the town was drenched, and the rain showed no promise of a letup. Wyeth was off ship immediately after breakfast and ran up the bluff. Gar was waiting in Laurel's buggy.

"She didn't know if you could get away," the Negro said. "She told me to come here and wait, just in case."

Laurel met him on the porch of the Simpson house and took his hand, leading him to the library. There she kissed him and was close to him when Mrs. Simpson knocked discreetly and entered.

She looked at the couple. "My home is your home, Mr. Woodward. Come here whenever you can." She squeezed Laurel's shoulder. "I must go marketing. I do my own buying now."

"Your slaves?" Wyeth was just being polite.

"We had only two. One is with my husband in Tennessee. The other doesn't know how to buy. He is wholly unreliable."

"Has he given you any trouble?"

"Law! no. No one around here has had any trouble with slaves. A few Yankee agents have tried to stir up trouble, but the slaves are loyal to us."

That was something else that puzzled Wyeth. Here and there particularly in the Natchez district, Negroes were getting restless and were inclined to insubordination and desertion. With the masters away at war, the plantations were at the mercy of Negroes. By and large, however, instead of rebelling, the slaves remained docile and took orders from women who had no way of enforcing discipline. Loyalty of some slaves was heroic and many actually took over the tasks of running the plantations and producing for the armies that fought to keep them in bondage.

Isolated cases of insubordination and violence reached the ears of authorities and harsh punishment was administered, but most slaves did not raise a finger against the South. Wyeth knew, as did every Southerner, that the slaves could have cracked the Confederacy wide open simply by threatening rebellion. If word had spread that their homes were endangered by rebellious Negroes, the Confederacy's soldiers would have left the battle line and gone home to save their families.[23] Lincoln knew that, too, and that's why, even then, he was waiting only for a Union victory before issuing the Emancipation Proclamation, hoping to arouse the Negroes.

Wyeth realized that the Negroes held the fate of the South in their hands and he wondered why they didn't strike for their freedom. Such a thing never bothered the simple mind of Vespasian Gillivray. Had he been asked why, he would have said, "The niggers know we trust 'em. Hell, they ain't going to knife us in the back. That wouldn't be right."

But it baffled Wyeth's orderly mind. He knew that the argument of some Southerners that the Negro didn't want freedom was absurd.

"It is beyond me," said Wyeth, looking for an argument. "I know the slaves want freedom, yet they are passing up the best opportunity that any slaves ever had. Imagine the white slaves of Greece or Rome missing a chance like this. If I were a slave, I'd fight. With a stick. . . ."

"But you are not a slave and you have many generations of freedom behind you." Mrs. Simpson bristled and her voice was cool. Typical of her position midway between the merchant class and the planter class, she thought as did most Southerners whose slaves were members of the household. "My husband is a judge, you know. I hazard the suggestion, Mr. Woodward, that you have been heeding the prattlings of reformers who have one eye on heaven and the other on their purses. The Negro was enslaved by his own people. He never heard of freedom until the white man set the example. To be worthy of freedom, one must accept certain responsibilities. The Negro will not accept them. . . ."

"How can he, ma'am?" Wyeth asked.

She brushed aside the question. "To you, freedom is a religion. It is the white man's heritage because he made it his heritage. To the Negro, freedom means an economic barbecue, a fish-fry. The bumbo belongs to an inferior race. Slavery is the natural state for the average black man. He is the white man's burden."

"Now, wait a minute, Mrs. Simpson. I knew you were coming to that." Wyeth fumbled with his collar. "If he is a burden, then why not get him off of our shoulders? Have you ever heard of anybody carrying a burden voluntarily unless that burden is valuable? A crusader will carry a burden because he is a crusader, but we are not crusaders. Your slaves possibly are burdens to you. However, you are forced to tote them because a few men are making money by having their profitable slaves tote them. . . ."

Mrs. Simpson gasped. "Mr. Woodward! That's Abolition talk."

Laurel was nervous and tugged at Wyeth's sleeve. However, the sailor was wound up and ready for controversy. "It is common sense, ma'm," he said and forgot Laurel for a second. "Some planters down here have hundreds of slaves, I understand. You have two. They are a burden to you, but you dare not free them because you think they can't shift for themselves and because your position demands that you own a slave or so. Yes, the Negro is a burden to you and me because we have been trapped by the system. We have to tote them, but they are toting the few big planters. Therefore, we are carrying the planters and that makes us slaves. Why not shake the Negro off of our backs and let him walk on his own feet?"

"He would starve, or be a menace to us. We'd have to support him anyway."

"I can't agree, Mrs. Simpson. The white man and the black man have got to work double-team down here. Oh, I know, the black horse will get less oats than the white horse for a long time and will get more blows. . . ."

"Mr. Woodward!" Mrs. Simpson drew herself erect. "Are you willing to work alongside a Negro?"

Laurel was wringing her hands. Wyeth was erect, too. "Yes, Mrs. Simpson. So long as the South is the load we've got to pull, I'll work alongside anybody or anything. Madam, I'll team up with the devil if he will help me win this war and help me save the South. I mean help me save it not only from the craw-thumping Yankees, but also from Southerners who have turned us into the most caste-ridden people this side of India, men who have put Quitman and Yancey and Rhett at the head of the table where Thomas Jefferson and Madison belong, those folks who confuse culture with caste, who are turning this garden into a patch of weeds while they stroll in a rose garden, unable to see the weeds through the beautiful blooms that they bought, but never produced." Wyeth caught his breath and was surprised at himself. He glanced over at Laurel, then at Mrs. Simpson, who was smiling.

"Bravo, Mr. Woodward. Laurel said you wanted to be a lawyer.

You will. But you will always be the one who brings in the minority report. You'll lose ten cases while you are winning one. You'll be called a turn-coat, a renegade and a fool. No man who loves the South as you do can ever be a renegade. Those who will call you a turn-coat never fought on the *Arkansas*. Maybe I am the fool. I think you are. But let's be friends. This land is ours. Let's beat the Yankees first, then you and I can feud in peace."

Wyeth bowed. "Thank you, ma'am."

"Whew." Laurel sat down and was limp. "For a minute there, I was worried."

Mrs. Simpson took Wyeth's arm. "When you are as old as I am, Laurel, you will know that Southerners always fight among themselves, but cling to one another when there is a common enemy. Now, you two make yourselves at home."

Laurel jumped up. "Let us do your marketing."

"Yes," said Wyeth. "It is raining hard. We like rain."

"Very well." Mrs. Simpson's eyes twinkled. "You had best learn marketing, Laurel. It looks as though the knowledge soon will be needed."

The sailor and the girl got umbrellas and went out to her buggy. They were laughing as they walked across the lawn.

Mrs. Simpson stood in the doorway and watched them, then went to her desk and wrote her husband and Wall MacKenzie that Laurel was in love and said, "As usual, she is showing good judgment and good taste."

Wyeth and Laurel cuddled under the same umbrella and rode through the rain, ignoring the stares of people. They went first to the courthouse and studied the price lists posted there by the Confederacy.

The document, printed on wallpaper, announced:

"All persons within this district are hereby required to take Confederate notes as currency at par in all business transactions. The following tariff of prices is hereby established throughout this district for the articles specified."

The ceiling price of flour was $8 a hundred pounds. Bacon and beef were cheap and chickens sold for $2.40 a dozen. Hay was $1.50 a hundred pounds. Most commodities were down as food and goods were pouring into Vicksburg. However, the price of salt was fixed at $15 a pound and quinine at $10 an ounce.

The medicines were adulterated and some European firms were getting rich by running a mixture of quinine and talc through the blockade. Jefferson Davis had appealed for an international conference to fix agreements that only pure medicines could be sold in time of war or peace.

Some citizens of Vicksburg were violating the price ceilings and were hoarding. Laurel, however, wrote down the ceilings on the things she wanted, potatoes, turkey, corn meal and butter, and paid no more than the regulations specified. Some merchants refused to take Confederate money and their stores were padlocked. Others were fined for charging illegal prices.

Already, in various cases, the price-ceiling plan was failing because some of the people demanded special favors. Some of those with money offered exorbitant prices for goods and many merchants were able to absorb the fines and still make a profit. The legal machinery for enforcing the rules was breaking down. General Van Dorn, realizing that inflation could do for Vicksburg what the Union hadn't been able to do, had clamped the city under martial law.

Most of the people accepted martial law as a necessity, but others began howling, contending their constitutional rights were being violated.

President Davis, as much a stickler for Confederate constitutional law as he had been for Federal law, overrode Van Dorn and put the town back under civil authorities. President Lincoln was suspending the writ of habeas corpus in the North, but Davis felt the military did not have legal grounds for controlling the civilian population.

So the law of supply and demand was allowed its natural course in Vicksburg and inflation began. The demand was great and the supply was small. The authorities were able to control the price of many things, including pork, poultry, corn and other commodities produced thereabouts. Salt and silk, however, were the first to break the barrier, and once the barrier was breached, the flood set in.

Laurel stuck rigidly by the rules and Wyeth was pleased. She bought only what she needed and they returned to the Simpson house and had dinner. Mrs. Simpson took a nap after the heavy midday meal and Wyeth and Laurel had the afternoon to themselves.

The rain had settled to a steady drizzle and they sat in the living room discussing what they would do when the war was over. The sailor returned to his watch that night and was promised another leave within a week.

The days piled one on the other and July passed. Reports from Grenada were that Captain Brown still was very ill and that it might be a month before he could rejoin his command. Repairs were completed on the *Arkansas* although Stevens still was not satisfied with performance of the engines. The starboard machinery kept breaking down on trials and replacements were not available.

There was rain every day and the lowlands were flooded. The South was flexing her muscles, for the gamecock had met the eagle in a hundred places and turned him back. Lee's Army of Northern Virginia was ready for Second Manassas and Maryland. Bragg was ready to move into Kentucky and strike for the Ohio where Morgan's raiders were spreading terror. Van Dorn looked south toward Baton Rouge and determined to drive the Federals out of Louisiana's capital and possibly attempt the relief of New Orleans.

The Confederacy had the initiative for the first time. At Baton Rouge, General Williams' men, their ranks thinned by the Vicksburg campaign, took up positions and awaited the Rebel blow that they knew was coming.

Van Dorn, confident that Vicksburg was safe for the time being, split his army in contemptuous affrontery to Yankee power. Many of his men were sent to Bragg. Others were taken from the fortifications of Vicksburg and moved a hundred miles north into a skirmish line, facing Grant who was mulling in a brown study. Van Dorn gave General Breckinridge five thousand men and told him to take Baton Rouge. The army moved out of Vicksburg while bands played and people huddled in the rain, cheering the departing Confederates.

Van Dorn went part of the way with Breckinridge and promised the Kentuckian that he would send the *Arkansas* down to take care of the Federal ships that protected the Yankee flank at Baton Rouge. No one on the *Arkansas* knew of the promise then and none suspected that Van Dorn, a soldier, ever dreamed of trying to plan naval strategy. Such behavior, the Army encroaching on the Navy, was a daily occurrence among the Yanks, but the Confederates expected better judgment from their leaders. They seemed to forget that Jefferson Davis was an army man and that army men often think ships can be handled as regiments.

Breckinridge went to Jackson, then led his army south with the promise that the *Arkansas* would come to his support. Meanwhile, on the ship, Stevens drilled his crew and waited for the return of Captain Brown. Every man on the *Arkansas* thought they eventually would go leisurely down the river, destroying Federal ships, then cut Ben Butler's supply lines to New Orleans and force the Yanks to evacuate that city. Then for Mobile, and maybe Pensacola. . . .

Wall MacKenzie arrived in Vicksburg with a boatload of powder, percussion caps, medicines and woolen goods. Much of the stuff had come from France to Mexico, thence to Texas. Frome's organization had gathered it from abroad and at home and had got it eventually to Shreveport. There Wall picked it up on a river boat, moved it down the Red to the Mississippi, thence up to Vicksburg. It was the first load to come all the way over the western route that the South was fighting to keep open.

The little Scotchman came to Vicksburg ostensibly to deliver the cargo to General Van Dorn. The delivery, however, was a job that any member of the organization could have done. Wall's real reason for visiting the fortress was to see Laurel and decide for himself the status of the affair between her and Wyeth.

His daughter was not surprised when he arrived at Mrs. Simpson's house. She told him frankly that she was in love with the Missourian.

"It didn't take you long," Wall said. "You must know what you want."

"It wouldn't have taken me this long, Papa. But Wyeth is sort of shy."

Wall smiled and rubbed her hair, then kissed her forehead. "The young man might have got in touch with me. That's the usual procedure."

"He couldn't," Laurel said quickly. "He has been on duty. He refused to write because he wanted to talk to you. Now don't you go scaring him, Papa."

Wall promised, then went to Van Dorn and got a pass to visit the *Arkansas*. Granville saw him approaching the ship and told

Ves. Wyeth was below, standing watch in the engine room, relieving an engine man who was working on a shaft.

"So that's him." Ves watched the little Scotchman waddle aboard. "Reckon he's after Wyeth?"

"Yes." Granville twisted his mustache and straightened his jacket.

"Shall I chunk him overboard?"

"Good God, no. Let me handle this."

The Englishman went topside and met Wall and took him to Stevens. The commander was polite and told Granville to show Mr. MacKenzie over the ship. "I assume you came aboard just to see the ship?" Stevens said and winked at Granville.

"That's right," Wall snapped.

"Our men are very busy," Stevens said. "Granville has a few minutes. Our best man, a young gunner from Missouri, is on watch. Otherwise I would leave you to his care."

Wall turned his eyes from Granville to Stevens, then walked to the end of the bridge and spat into the Mississippi. "Gentlemen, if all of our men were as smart as you two we could end this war before breakfast. Lead on, Mr. Granville. I can't wait to see the ship."

The Englishman took him first to the gundeck and began explaining the Dolly. "She is our gun," Granville said. "Wyeth Woodward and this big Cajan and myself work her. We will send for Mr. Woodward in a few minutes. You remember him."

"Yes." Wall began grinning.

"He is a humdinger," Ves said. "Steady, honest. Ain't scared of nothing. His watch is up pretty soon and I'll go fetch him. I know he's hossin' to meet you. I heard him say that he is rightly fond of you. . . ."

Ves was overdoing it, so Granville broke in. "Did you ever see a Dahlgren before? Notice that she is made of cast iron, cooled from the exterior. Admiral Dahlgren invented this type of gun."

Wall said, "That's very interesting."

Ves thought then that Granville was overplaying his hand. "You should have seen us whip the Yanks, Mr. MacKenzie. This fellow Woodward was all over the place. I'll bet he killed fifty Yanks, don't you Sim?"

"Just a minute," Wall said. "I came to see Mr. Woodward. I

don't know beans about ships and don't care. Mr. Woodward is a close friend of mine and I came to pay my respects. I will be up on the top of this damn boat. Please tell him to wait upon me there." The little Scotchman walked away.

Ves and Granville exchanged looks and the minute that Wall was out of sight they both ran down to the engine room and told Wyeth that he had a caller. Ves took over his watch and Wyeth started topside.

"You'd better clean up," Granville said. "It's old man Mac-Kenzie."

"Oh, my God." Wyeth swallowed. "Did he act mad?"

"Sor'n hell," Ves said. "Mad as a wet hen."

"What do you reckon I ought to say?" Wyeth looked frantically from one to the other.

"Throw him overboard," Ves said.

"Don't be worried," Granville reassured his friend. "We sounded him out. Everything is going to be all right."

Wyeth washed up and put on his best uniform and walked boldly topside, swinging along toward Wall MacKenzie. He offered his hand when he saw the Scotchman and stopped trembling when the little man grasped it and shook it warmly.

They sat under the awning and talked about everything except the one thing that was important to both of them. Wyeth answered questions about the battle and tried to be modest, thinking that would impress MacKenzie. Then their discussion switched from Vicksburg to Lebanon and Wall reported that Hoab Dabney's republic was being strangled by the Confederates and was cut off from the outside world. The situation in Natchez was so confusing that Wall didn't understand it.

"Most of the Yankees are gone," he said. "But a few still are around buying cotton. There is sort of an armed truce down home. The Yanks live at the homes of Unionists. The Confederates come and go as they please, and never bother the Yanks." [24]

"What a mess."

"It's worse than that. If we raided the homes and took the Yanks, then the Federals might send up ships and blow up some of our fine homes. So Natchez winks at the Yanks and Confederates and goes about her business. The town is not of any strategic importance, so I reckon it's all right."

About the only fight that had rocked Natchez concerned the wealthy Surget family. Frank Surget was the richest man in Natchez and their home, called Clifton, was a showplace. When the war started, Surget transferred his money to Europe and it was assumed that he was a good Union man. He was told by the United States government to take an oath of allegiance to the Union and refused, explaining that he had cotton under control of the Confederacy and that it would be destroyed if he took the oath. He was warned that the Federal government would ruin him if he defied the Union and he said, "There are two things you can't make me do. You can't make me take the oath of allegiance and you can't break me. I will match the United States dollar for dollar."

Mr. Surget tried to play both ends against the middle. He gave a dinner for Union officers in Natchez. As luck would have it, however, he overlooked an army engineer and soon Surget was informed that the Yankees intended to build a fort exactly where the Surget mansion stood. The Surgets crated their art treasures and sailed for France. Surget died on the voyage and his wife never returned to America. The slighted Northerner had his revenge, for the Surget mansion was blown to bits and an excavation was dug for a fort. There was no more need for a Federal fort in Natchez than in Maine.

Wyeth smiled wryly when he heard the story. He had respect for Hoab Dabney who was fighting the Confederacy over in Lebanon, but he held such Southerners as the Surgets in contempt. Dabney loved the Union for what it was and for what it might be, and was an Abolitionist. The Surgets were compromisers.

The conversation between the two men dribbled off and they looked out at the rain and then at each other. Wyeth's face, usually red when he was under an emotional strain, now was white. "Mr. MacKenzie, I've been wanting to see you. It's about Laurel."

Wall said, "What would you do if I said no?"

Wyeth was taken aback. He had expected to get slowly to the point. However, he parried the blunt question. "What would you have done if your father-in-law had refused to give you his daughter's hand?"

" 'Ygod! Sounds like a lawyer." Wall rolled his eyes upward. "God forbid. But anyway, young man, I would have married my wife anyway and would have told her father to go to hell."

"Very well, sir." Wyeth was looking straight ahead. "I love your daughter as much as you loved his daughter."

The little Scotchman walked over to the Missourian and offered his hand. "It's damn nonsense for a young man to be expected to come spluttering around a girl's father. It's a silly custom. She loves you and you love her and that makes me a prospective grandfather."

Wyeth laughed nervously in sheer relief. "I will be good to her." It was a silly thing to say and he realized it, and blushed.

"Don't be upset. That's exactly what I said. They always say the same thing. Now let's get down to business. When do you expect to get married?"

"Next year, sir. I think the war will be over by then."

"You're crazy. The war will just be starting by then. But I'm glad you're going to wait a year. That will give both of you time to collect your wits."

"I don't know what I can say, sir."

"Then don't say anything, Wyeth. You suit Laurel and that suits me. How long will your ship be here?"

"Until Captain Brown gets back. Maybe two or three weeks more."

"Good. I will leave Laurel here for two weeks. You two might as well enjoy each other's company. When you sail I will come back up here and get her."

Wyeth tried to thank him, but Wall waved aside his thanks. "One more thing. So you got Gar his freedom?"

"Do you think I made a mistake?"

"I don't know. I still have his money and will keep it until he asks for it. Tell him to be a little careful. Yankee sympathizers down around Natchez are wondering about some bodies that have been found. They know that Gar and Mort Kincaid were friends. Just tell him to be careful, but to keep up the good work."

Wyeth walked with him to the gangplank and they shook hands again. "I get another leave tomorrow," the Missourian said.

"I will tell Laurel. I won't be here. So God bless both of you."

The little Scotchman stepped off the gangplank into the rain, pulled up his coat collar and walked up the bluff. Wyeth watched him out of sight and then hurried to tell the good news to Granville and Ves. They paid no attention to the aide who came aboard and went to Stevens and asked him to wait immediately upon General Van Dorn.

The commander of the *Arkansas* accompanied the aide up to Van Dorn's headquarters and was flabbergasted when the army leader instructed him to leave immediately for Baton Rouge and support Breckinridge.

Through illness and misfortune, the Confederate force had lost half of its men before Breckinridge reached Baton Rouge, but the assault had been launched against General Williams' Army. General Williams, one of the ablest men in the Union Army despite the association of Ben Butler, was killed and the transport that was taking his body to New Orleans had been sunk. The Confederates had invested Baton Rouge and Butler, safe in New Orleans, was in a frenzy and accused the Seventh Regiment of Vermont Volunteers of unsoldierly conduct. New England was up in arms against Butler, but Baton Rouge still was in Union hands.

The Rebels were in some of the fortifications and were assaulting the town daily. But they needed naval support because Bill Porter's *Essex* and a flotilla of gunboats were offshore harassing the Confederate advance. Farragut's fleet had gone to the Union Naval Station at Pensacola for repairs.

Van Dorn explained the picture to Stevens. "You must take the *Arkansas* down at once. We can't take Baton Rouge as long as the enemy has ships there."

Stevens just stared at the general. He finally found his voice and said, "Good God, General Van Dorn, the *Arkansas* is not ready for such a trip. Besides, what about Captain Brown?"

"We can't wait for him to get well."

"May I send him a message?" Stevens was desperate.

"Of course. However, Lieutenant Stevens, may I point out that the *Arkansas* is under command of the War Department and that I represent that department. We must have the *Arkansas*."

There was no need to argue. The telegraph lines still were up between Vicksburg and Grenada and Stevens wired Brown for instructions. Brown wired back that the *Arkansas* must not be moved until he was on the bridge. He explained that he had arranged for a special train to take him to Vicksburg. He didn't tell that his fever was at 102 degrees and that he must be taken aboard the train on a cot.

Van Dorn shook his head when he read the message. "It will take him a day or so to get here. We can't wait that long. I have taken the liberty of notifying Captain Lynch of this controversy and he instructs you to take the *Arkansas* out immediately."

"May I see the orders?" Stevens asked stiffly.

The general showed him a message from Lynch. Still Stevens protested. Lynch was at Jackson and didn't know the condition of the *Arkansas*.

Van Dorn listened patiently, then said, "Captain Lynch is the senior naval officer in this district. I must ask you to obey his orders and mine."

Stevens wet his lips and swallowed the words on his tongue. "Aye, ay, sir. We will leave within the hour. Please be so kind as to wire Captain Brown in Jackson to join us in Baton Rouge. The captain's train can reach Jackson tomorrow." He saluted the general, turned on his heels and walked out into the rain, thence to his ship. He was so angry that he stammered when he told his second in command to cast off.

The crew of the *Arkansas* assumed they were going on a trial run to test the engines, and the ship was passing Warrenton before the men got suspicious. They knew by the pounding of the engines that the *Arkansas* was crowding on all steam. Then an engine room man came to the gundeck and reported that something was up, as the ship was being pushed beyond her capacity.

Rumors began spreading among the deck sailors and the Vicksburg fortifications were falling behind in the rain and twilight when Stevens assembled his men and told them that they were going to Baton Rouge.

When he heard the gasp from his crew, Stevens turned away.

"Will Captain Brown meet us there?" Ves asked. He was the only man who dared ask such a question.

"If he gets there and if we get there," Stevens said sadly. "I didn't want to do this, men. But apparently it is necessary. General Breckinridge has driven the enemy into the shadow of the Yankee flotilla. If we can whip the *Essex*, then the army can take Baton Rouge."

Wyeth, fearing that Stevens might think the men didn't want to follow him, said, "That shouldn't be hard. You can whip them, sir. We're with you."

The men cheered. There was no spirit in the cheer, however. It was a polite cheer, an attempt to convince Stevens that they trusted him. It wasn't a matter of trusting their commander. It was a matter of taking a crippled ship into battle.

Stevens thanked them for their confidence. "Breckinridge's strategy is based on our arrival. That's all there is to it. We must get there as quickly as possible and drive off the Union flotilla."

The *Arkansas'* engines were rattling. Baton Rouge was three hundred miles away and the ship was shaking violently in protest against running full speed. The temporary lining of a firebox burned out before they reached Sargent's Point and Palmyra Bend. Mr. City, the chief engineer, patched it up and they sped on. They were running at night into rain and high wind. The men put pineknots in wire baskets, fired the wood, then suspended the blazing mass out of the ports. The pilot steered by the fires. The wind was from the south and the *Arkansas* trembled as she bit into the wind, splitting the channel and ripping out her iron insides under the strain.

The men off watch turned in. Wyeth slung his hammock on the gundeck. "I won't get my leave tomorrow," he said to Granville. "Surely, Mr. Stevens will give it to me as soon as we get back. I wish I could have got a message to Laurel."

The rain beat against the sides of the ship and she was throwing sparks. Granville listened to the groaning of the engines and shook his head. Ves took off his shoes and hurled them across the deck. "They are tearing her guts out."

The river rolled over the ship's long beak and she pitched in the wind, plowing by Killykrany Plantation and New Carthage. Then past Hurricane Island and around Hurricane Bend where Jefferson Davis spent his boyhood with his brother Joe. The *Arkansas* took the inside of Big Black Bend, at Turner's Point, flanked Hard Times Bend and tied up at the Louisiana village of Hard Times while Mr. City patched another firebox.

They rounded Coffee's Point at dawn and hurried by Grand Gulf, passing under the batteries that Prent Oliver had installed. The big guns covered the river and Wyeth fired a signal at Stevens' command. There was an answer from Grand Gulf. The town was not visible through the rain and Wyeth found himself thinking of Prent. Then he remembered Rock Bradford and wondered whatever happened to the old man.

Captain Brown reached Jackson four hours after the *Arkansas* left Vicksburg. There he begged use of a locomotive and one baggage car from the Confederate Army. They put mail bags in the baggage car and Brown lay on them while the engine rolled away for Baton Rouge. Brown, half delirious, kept saying over and over, "Oh, Lord, let me get there before they take my ship into battle. Save my ship, God."

Chapter Thirteen

W YETH, using a cape of canvas to keep off the rain, was on duty at the bow, peering into the river for driftwood and bars, when the *Arkansas* beat over to the right side of the Mississippi toward Bonjourand Landing, then veered sharply across the stream for Bruinsburg.

The behavior of the ship warned him that something was amiss. Stevens was fuming in impotent rage when they tied up and Chief Engineer City was brought out of the engine room, unconscious. An attack of rheumatic fever had felled him at his post. A landing party took him ashore and Stevens summoned Wyeth and Granville to the engine room.

"We have lost Mr. City," Stevens said. "You two men know ships. How do those engines look to you?"

Granville threw up his hands. "I know nothing about such engines. Wyeth is a steamboat man."

The Missourian examined the machinery and was glum when he reported to his commander. "These are short-stroke engines and I'm not acquainted with them. But I know this, sir. They are falling apart."

The landing party returned, bringing word that Breckinridge was waiting for the *Arkansas* before making his final thrust at Baton Rouge. Civilians in Bruinsburg knew all about it. The Army, however, hadn't seen fit to take the Navy into its confidence. Stevens, usually placid and seldom given to profanity, began cursing. "Everybody knows what is going on but us."

Wyeth said, "Under ordinary circumstances, we should turn back. I'd say our chances of reaching Baton Rouge are about fifty-fifty."

"The circumstances are not ordinary," Stevens snapped. He stomped up the ladder to his bridge and sent for the second engineer, a young army lieutenant who had joined the ship a few days before.

The engineer explained that he had never worked with a screw vessel or short-stroke engines until he boarded the *Arkansas*. "However, sir, I watched Mr. City at every opportunity. I will do my best."

They shoved off again and the engines began purring. The young lieutenant was so delighted that he beamed, and even whistled a jig tune. Stevens was smiling, too, and the crew perked up. Only Wyeth was worried and said to Granville, "I never saw it fail. Steamboat engines always act their best just before they collapse."

The *Arkansas* picked up so much speed that her heavy beak came out of the water and she took a bone in her teeth. Everything was going just right. She obeyed her helm perfectly. The fireboxes were glowing and the engines were sucking air and throwing out smoke when the ship wheeled by St. Joseph and raised Rodney to the larboard.

The ruins of the Oliver home were visible through the rain and Wyeth pointed them out to Ves and Granville. Across the river was Waterproof, and Stevens, in a gay mood, sounded his whistle to the crowd that had gathered along the Louisiana levee, waiting for a glimpse of the *Arkansas*. Ves waved at the people. Granville was scowling. "If the public knows we are coming down, then so do the Yanks."

"I'm not worrying about the Yanks," Wyeth said. "It's those engines. They're running too good. That engineer thinks they're perfect and he's pushing them too fast."

The ship raced by Rabbit Harbor and Gun Ridge and then, poking up into the rain clouds that were hugging the earth, was the spire of St. Mary's, and Natchez. Wyeth took Ves topside and pointed out the sights. Granville was there, too, staring at Natchez-Under-the-Hill. Ves asked, "Can you see the house where Sharon lives?"

Granville didn't reply, but Wyeth said, "No. It's raining too hard. But the house is right over yonder under the bluff."

"And your girl? Where does she live?"

"Back in the town. Back yonder not far from that church steeple."

The three men watched Natchez fall behind and the ship was beating down the Louisiana side when the starboard engine began coughing and then stopped. Stevens was puzzled and the young engineer was baffled. It was Wyeth who found the trouble. The wrist of the shaft had, under constant friction, developed a groove. There was nothing to do but get a new wrist. Angered at the engineer's ignorance, Wyeth went ashore to a plantation and got a coupling pin from an ox wagon, filed it to shape, and substituted it for the wrist.

Stevens called a council of war and the officers and crew assembled on the gundeck. Lieutenant Gift and Midshipman Bacot were sent ashore for information and came back with news that Breckinridge was going to attack again at daybreak. The Federal flotilla was the only thing between the Confederates and victory and the flotilla consisted of Bill Porter's *Essex*, two wooden gunboats and some armed transports.

"We will reach Baton Rouge early tomorrow," Stevens said. "That is, if we reach it at all. Our engineer says he thinks the engines can make it. What say you?"

The men looked from one to the other. The prospect of fighting the flotilla with faulty engines frightened them, but they said nothing.

"If we turn back the South will think that we have done our best," Stevens said. "But we will know that we have not. So we will go on. We will attack the *Essex* first. We will try to ram her and then get below the gunboats and transports and cut off their retreat."

He instructed the men to see to their small arms and they stood for Bayou Sara. The sunset was not visible through the rain and darkness caught them creeping under the batteries of Port Hudson. The *Arkansas* fired a signal and hove to.

Rain was coming in sheets and a lookout screamed a warning at the approach of another ship. Stevens blew his whistle and Wyeth ran to the gundeck. He recognized the *Music*. She still had her crane and the structure loomed in the darkness. A red lantern was dancing on the top of the rig. The *Music*, under skillful handling, eased alongside and Prent Oliver leaped aboard the *Arkansas,* greeted his old friends, then went to Stevens.

Wyeth and Granville used the opportunity to study the *Music.* Her pilothouse had a sheeting of boiler iron and cotton bales were stacked along her decks. Her only weapon was a bowgun, a howitzer mounted on a heavy barbette carriage.

At Stevens' suggestion, Wyeth joined him and Prent in the *Arkansas'* engine room and Prent looked the engines over. Then he shook his head. "I'd hate to go into battle on such power. You may make it to Baton Rouge, but that starboard engine is ready to fall apart."

"We must go on," Stevens said.

"I will follow you in the *Music.* Maybe I can help." He clapped Wyeth on the back as he went out, and waved to Granville as he stepped from the *Arkansas* back onto his own ship. The big Rebel got under way again and Stevens posted a skeleton watch and sent every other man to the hammocks.

Wyeth couldn't sleep and lay awake listening to the rain and longing for Laurel. Granville was awake, too, but Ves was snoring. The engines of the *Arkansas* were allowed to idle and she began floating with the current. They were nearing Baton Rouge and Stevens wanted to fight by daylight, and was in no hurry to reach the Louisiana capital before dawn. Wyeth heard the big guns in the distance and closed his eyes. The *Essex* was pounding the Confederate skirmishers. The *Arkansas* was rocking gently, floating to her battle station.

They rounded Prophet Island, then came about and waited for the dawn. There was a crackle of musketry to the south. Breckinridge's skirmishers were inching forward, pinning the Federals to the river. Stevens, red-eyed and worried, was exposed on the quarterdeck, peering into the rain and darkness and watching the flashes from the *Essex,* anchored just off Baton Rouge, a few miles downstream.

It was three A.M., August 5th, when the commander called for beat to quarters and the drummer rolled the alarm. The crew was mustered and poured out of their hammocks as bees pour from a hive. There was no excitement among them now, for battle had become their natural way of life. Divisions were inspected and the big guns were shotted and run into battery. Granville put a seventy-pound solid shot in the Dolly.

The men huddled around their guns, talking about everything except the war. Granville told Wyeth to stand by. "This rain hampers my vision," he said. "I need your eyes." He put his kerchief over the lower part of his face to protect his mustache and beard from fire.

The *Arkansas'* engines began turning slowly, for dawn was breaking, gray and dreary. The rain settled to a slow drizzle and dripped in through the open gunports. Prent Oliver moved his *Music* alongside and Wyeth saw the coal barge lashed to the little Black River workship. "My God," he muttered, "are we going to coal now?"

Stevens heard him and replied, "No. Of course not. Commander Oliver got the coal last night just in case we need it after the fight."

Prent, a shadow in the grayness, called over to Stevens, "We will drop this barge into a slough over along the east bank, then fall in behind you to protect your rear."

Wyeth noticed then that the barge was armed, a bow howitzer on a barbette carriage. He laughed nervously. "We are arming skiffs."

The *Music* pulled away and disappeared into the rain.

Every man of the *Arkansas'* company was staring out of the ports when Baton Rouge came into view, a cluster of buildings on the east bank along a straight reach of the river. There was the tower of the state capitol, poking up toward the low clouds. The *Essex* was just offshore, hurling broadsides into the Confederates, and below the *Essex* were the *Kineo* and *Katahdin*. Lieutenant Read smiled when he saw the *Kineo*. "There's my old friend again," he said.

The besieged Federals were lined along the river, their backs to the stream and the Confederates were closing in, taking fearful punishment from the ships. The situation was crystal clear. Only the three Federal ships were keeping the Confederates back, preventing them from driving the Yanks into the river.

"All right, men," Stevens called down. "We'll make first for the *Essex*. Put your faith in God and the *Arkansas*." He held his speaking tube to his lips, rang for the engine room and asked for half-speed.

The propellers began churning again. The *Arkansas* shook and the engines, idle most of the night, began throbbing, then rattling. The men looked around, then at one another. "Full speed," Stevens commanded.

The men cheered feebly.

The *Arkansas* lurched ahead, her beak aimed for the *Essex*, less than a mile away. The Yanks saw the Rebel then, and the *Essex* turned to meet the new challenge. The *Kineo* and *Katahdin* moved up beside the *Essex*, presenting a solid front. The Confederate soldiers near the bank began cheering and the Federal soldiers, almost in the river, began looking for a route of escape. There was none. Breckinridge's army was to the north, south and east. The river was to their west. If the Union flotilla were driven off, then Williams' army was trapped.

Pilot Brady, old Jim Brady, was the first to notice that the *Arkansas* wasn't behaving properly. He glanced over at Stevens. "She steers hard, sir."

"Keep her dead ahead," Stevens said.

The ship's starboard engine began shaking dangerously and a cry of rage and helplessness came up from the engine room. There was a clattering, then a hissing and a grinding of broken iron. The starboard engine coughed and was dead. Brady tried to bring up his ship to meet her helm, but the port propeller kept turning and the *Arkansas* went hard aground, scraping some cypress knees on the east bank.

Then there she lay, hissing and panting, within gun range of the *Essex*.

Granville threw down his primer lanyard and yanked off his kerchief. Ves began cursing. Wyeth watched the *Essex*.

"Now what?" Stevens was trying to appear calm.

"The starboard wrist again," the engineer said. "It's busted, sir."

Stevens raised his head above the shield of the bridge and studied the *Essex* through the rain. "Bill Porter can carry us now. But he is not moving."

"Of course not," said Brady. "If he leaves now to attack us, Breckinridge will shove the Yankee infantry plum' into the Mississippi."

Stevens was so angry and so disgusted that he didn't reply. His luck had run out. He wondered if he ever had any luck, for the *Arkansas* had been in trouble almost every minute since he assumed command. He looked down at the gundeck and into the eyes of his men. Then he turned away, muttering, "I'm sorry for the men. They are ready to fight and the ship isn't."

The men milled around the deck, grumbling and cursing the jinx that had settled on their ship. The echoes of firing from Baton Rouge increased. "They are counting on us down there," Wyeth said. "And here we are stuck in the mud with a broken engine."

Ves said, "Quit your bellyaching. Mr. Stevens is rightly down in the mouth and this is the time he needs us." The Cajan shouted up to his commander, "Oh, Louisa! Louisa and the babes."

Stevens swallowed the lump that formed in his throat. "God bless you, Ves."

The other men quit their grumbling and gathered around the hatch, waiting for orders. Stevens came down, surveyed the situation, then said, "There is much to be done."

Granville appreciated the man then. It is not difficult to be a good commander of a winning combination. But the great commander is the one who fights fate and the enemy, and keeps fighting when he is losing. Lieutenant Stevens squared his shoulders.[25] "I'm hexed, boys. But surely our luck will change. First, we've got to lighten ship and get afloat again. Then we'll have to make a new wrist. I doubt if Porter will leave the battle and come after us. But if he does we must be ready."

"Why do you think he won't come and take this ship?" Gift asked.

"Because if he leaves his anchorage, Breckinridge will smash the Yankee infantry. Remember, Porter's ship is under control of the War Department and he won't dare forsake the army even to capture us."

He set the men to ripping iron from the *Arkansas'* deck, and throwing it overboard to lighten the ship. The starboard guns were kept in battery, covering the *Essex* just in case she tried to move upstream. A blacksmith forge was improvised on the gundeck and four smiths were found among the crew. Stevens put them to work forging another wrist. Rain often blew across the deck, sending white smoke from the forge.

Prent Oliver brought his *Music* and the coal barge alongside, and went into conference with Stevens. Then they called Wyeth, Granville and Ves to the bridge. In simple words that gave no ground for argument, the commander told the gunners that their Dolly must be removed from the *Arkansas*.

To his amazement the men were not surprised. Granville said, "It is the thing to do. With our gun off of the port the *Arkansas* will float again."

"Will your Dahlgren fit that barbette carriage on the barge?" Stevens asked.

"I will investigate," Granville said and left them.

The fight at Baton Rouge increased in fury and Wyeth stood on the bridge, staring downstream. He saw yellow flashes from the Yankee gunboats and knew that every shot was ripping into the Confederates. Porter couldn't even spare a few shots for the *Arkansas*. Wyeth imagined that Bill Porter was fuming, and he was. There was his enemy, the Rebel that had bested him twice, lying helpless within range and he couldn't throw a shell in that direction, knowing that if he turned his guns from Breckinridge's Army the Seceshers would rush the trapped Federals and overwhelm them. So there was nothing for Porter to do but keep beating back the Confeds.

Granville returned and reported that the Dolly might fit the howitzer barbette. "It is risky," he said. "But it is worth trying."

"Very well," Stevens said. "We will put your Dahlgren on the barge and then anchor the barge in that sluice down yonder. You will be between us and the *Essex*. If Porter makes a move this way you can beat him off."

Prent Oliver used the crane on the *Music* to lift the howitzer from the barge and swing it aboard the workship. Then they ripped a hole in the top of the ark of the big Rebel. Rain poured onto the gundeck through the opening. The *Arkansas'* anchor chain was rigged to the *Music's* crane and the Dolly was made secure. Then they hoisted the gun off of its carriage, through the hole and swung it aboard the barge. The Dolly's trunnions fitted the barbette carriage all right, but the barge went down by the head and almost floundered under the weight.

Granville shook his head and whispered to Wyeth, "She won't stand much firing. She will rip that carriage to bits."

The Dolly looked like a long cigar on a tiny box.

The barge was towed downstream, then maneuvered into a sluice. The Dolly was pointing toward the *Essex* and Granville loaded his gun quickly and was ready if Bill Porter came up that way. Ves and Wyeth tried to run the gun back and forth on the barbette, a wooden carriage on four wheels. They were able to move it all right, but the carriage creaked under the strain.

Granville went back aboard the *Arkansas* and got canvas and put a covering over his gun. The hole in the ark of the big ship was patched and Stevens eased steam into his good port engine and rocked the *Arkansas*. Then, lightened by removal of the Dolly and iron platings, the ship freed herself and floated, swinging around in the eddy. They fastened her to some cypress stumps and kept working on the wrist.

It was midafternoon before Granville got his Dolly in battery and primed and then he and his comrades ate a plate of cold beans and lay down on the barge, almost exhausted.

The *Essex* didn't threaten that day and Stevens sighed in relief when night came and the rain turned into a downpour, cutting visibility to fifty yards. He kept his smiths working in relays and sent his other men to their hammocks. All that night, salvo after salvo thundered from the Federol flotilla, checking every attempt the Confederates made to rush the Yankee soldiers, clinging desperately to their last foothold along the river bank.

It was two A.M., August 6th, when the smiths finished the new wrist and the engineer fitted it into the starboard engine. They let a little steam into the engine and the machinery began turning slowly. Stevens prayed silently.

"It works, sir," the engineer said. "The starboard engine is ready."

"We will attack at dawn," Stevens said.

He sent for Wyeth and Granville who were sleeping on the barge and offered them coffee when they reported. The Englishman looked like a drowned man. His mustache and beard were dripping water and his eyes were blood red. Wyeth was so tired that he leaned against a wing of the bridge and fell asleep standing up.

"We will move out as soon as there's light," Stevens said. "We will go into deep water. The *Music* will then bring the barge alongside and we will put your Dolly back aboard."

The firing down at Baton Rouge slackened. The Confederates were digging in, waiting for the *Arkansas* to drive off the flotilla.

Wyeth took coffee back to Ves and the three men huddled on the barge, watching for the dawn. It came forlornly, a patch of gray that lighted the clouds to the east. Neither of the three spoke when smoke began pouring from the *Arkansas'* stack. The boilers of the big Rebel were fired until steam reached one hundred and thirty pounds of pressure.

Wyeth counted the minutes, then said, "She should have enough steam by now. She'll be moving off in a minute."

"Can you see the *Essex?*" Granville asked.

"No. Not through this rain. And Porter can't see the *Arkansas*. We'll be on top of him before he knows it."

Prent Oliver brought his *Music* down to the barge. He cautioned his howitzer crew to be ready with their gun and then boarded the barge and stood by the Dolly. "Just as soon as the *Arkansas* is in the channel we'll take this barge out and put your gun back where she belongs."

"She's moving." Wyeth watched the Rebel ironclad back out. They didn't hear the crew's cheer, for the rain was drumming against the barge. "She's underway, all right."

It was then that nature deserted them. The rain beat a wild tattoo and ceased abruptly. Prent Oliver swore and Wyeth stared up at the sky and began sobbing, "Why?" he begged. "Why now, oh Lord?"

The sun broke through and the men on the barge turned their eyes toward the *Essex*. Smoke was rolling from the stack of the Federal ironclad and she began pulling away from her position, turned in the channel and pointed her nose toward the Rebel. The *Kineo* and the *Katahdin* kept raking the Confederate soldiers, pinning them to the trenches they had dug during the night.

"I knew Bill Porter wouldn't wait forever," Prent said. He signalled to his *Music* and the howitzer threw a shell toward the *Essex*. It fell short, and the *Essex* kept creeping up.

Then the bowgun of the *Arkansas* roared. The *Essex* checked herself and began floating back.

"My God," Wyeth said. "It may be starting. Mr. Stevens may have to fight without us. . . ."

He never finished his sentence. Ves grabbed his arm and pointed toward the *Arkansas*. The big ship wheeled in a circle, rocked wildly for a second, then began limping toward the bank. The *Essex* crowded on all power and moved up for battle.

Granville calculated his range quickly, yanked his friction lanyard and the Dolly thundered. The big gun bucked under the force, recoiled and leaped out of the trunnion bed. It fell beside the barbette carriage, crushing the chassis.

Wyeth pounded the carriage with his fists and roared curses. Ves just stared at the gun and Granville leaned over it, examining it for injuries. The Dolly apparently was not damaged. It had leaped the little carriage and had fallen on the barge, dismounted and useless. The shot, however, had grazed the *Essex* and Bill Porter put about quickly and dropped downstream beyond range.

The *Arkansas,* trembling like a leaf in the wind, touched her nose to the bank not twenty yards from the barge. Gift was at the bow. He was cursing, too, and looking up into the sun.

"What now?" Prent Oliver called.

"A shaft," Gift yelled, a catch in his voice. "The port shaft. It broke in two."

And the port was the reliable engine.

The *Essex,* suspecting something was amiss, began easing cautiously back upstream. She threw one shot. It struck near the *Arkansas'* stern and the Rebel answered with a starboard gun. Then Stevens came on deck and called for Prent and the three gunners to come aboard.

Silently, their hearts so heavy that their chests felt like lead, the four men left the barge and joined the ship's company on the gundeck. Stevens was pale, but his voice was firm and calm. "We are helpless," he said. "Porter can pound us at will and then capture us. If he takes this ship he can go back to Vicksburg. What happened to your Dahlgren, Granville?"

"She jumped her carriage."

"I was afraid of that. Help the other men load the guns."

The men went from one gun to the other shotting them and running them into battery. The task completed, Granville saluted the quarterdeck and called, "Aye, ay, sir."

Midshipman Scales went to the bow and made sure that the Battle Flag was secure to the mast.

Wyeth kept eyeing the *Essex*. The Yankee cut for the west bank, feeling her way. She was timid and approached the *Arkansas* as a hunter approaches a wild boar. She threw another shot and it missed. "They are nervous," Wyeth said. "They don't know what to think."

Stevens adjusted his cap, walked down from his bridge and saluted the empty quarterdeck. He was thinking of Brown. Then he said. "Abandon ship."

He said it slowly, sadly.

The men filed off. Lieutenant Gift led the way. He didn't look back, but took his men onto the bank, thence to the sluice where the barge was. He put them into skirmish line.

Ves and Wyeth got their snipper rifles and Granville got his cutlass and they followed Lieutenant Barbot ashore. They, too, went into skirmish line. The three comrades were on the barge, crouching behind the dismantled Dolly.

Read, Grimball and Wharton brought their divisions to the bank, and soon the ship's company was at battle stations on and around the barge. Prent was on his *Music,* standing by the howitzer. The *Essex* was crawling up the west side, keeping one eye on the *Arkansas.*

Stevens watched the last of his crew ashore. Then he went to the powder magazine and filled buckets and placed them along the gundeck. He got his ship's log and put it under his jacket. Next he went below and started the starboard engine. The shattered shaft of the port engine lay across the starboard shaft. Steam was hissing from the machinery.

Stevens took a deep breath, eased the starboard engine into gear, backed the *Arkansas* from the bank and cut his engine. A shot from the *Essex* whined overhead and he ignored it. He got handfuls of fine priming powder and lined it from the magazine to the gundeck. Then he fastened a rope to the lever that controlled the starboard engine. Quickly, but without excitement, he laid a tarred rope alongside the line of powder.

Then Lieutenant Stevens, to whom fortune was never kind, lit the rope and it began smoldering and burning toward the powder. He counted up to sixty and yanked the other rope. The starboard engine caught, wheezed and began churning the propeller.

Stevens ran topside to the bow, poised a second, then dived. He swam to shore just as the *Arkansas* backed into the river. The channel caught her, turned her downstream and she headed for the *Essex.* The Federal backed away frantically.

A lookout on the *Essex* pointed a trembling finger at the big Rebel. "I can't see a soul aboard, but here she comes."

Bill Porter called for a broadside. The *Arkansas* took the salvo, then dipped her beak into the river and bore down, her flag flying and the sun dancing on her rusty red sides.

The *Essex'* lookout was so frightened that he scarcely could speak. It wasn't the *Arkansas* that scared him. It was the fact that the ship seemed to be under control of unseen hands. "My God," the lookout whispered. "I tell you that ship is empty. But look at her. She's a ghost ship, sir. We can't fight ghosts."

The *Arkansas'* crew, lying as still as stones on the barge, watched their ship into midstream. Stevens crawled close to Wyeth and lay there trembling, although the sun was shining.

A shadow passed across the sky and black clouds, herded by wind, ran together and melted into a big cloud. The superstitious sailors of the crew watched the heavens, trying to keep one eye on the cloud and the other on their ship. A finger of lightning sizzled up to the west and thunder echoed, a grumbling, rumbling echo; far away.

A bowgun of the *Arkansas* went off, belching a yellow flame and throwing a solid shot toward the *Essex*. Then a starboard gun roared. It was difficult to tell the guns from the thunder. "The heat," Stevens whispered. "The heat is firing the guns."

A gust of rain swept across the river as a wisp of smoke escaped from the gundeck and curled above the *Arkansas*. That's all many of the men ever saw. One wisp of smoke. Wyeth's keen eyes, however, made her out clearly even in the rain. She was rolling from side to side, plowing ahead. A puff of white smoke bellowed out of a bowport as the priming powder went off. Then there was a hollow rumble that sounded like wind in a cavern, and it rolled for a second and then exploded into a mountain of metal and flame, hurling twelve hundred tons of iron up and out.

Wyeth bowed his head. And when he looked up again it was all over. There was not a trace of the ship. It had disintegrated, vanished completely. Bits of metal kept falling on the river and forming ripples. The bits came down with the rain. . . .

Even Bill Porter was awed.

Ves was the first to find his voice. "She just went away. Like a cloud after a thunder storm."

Granville said, "The hull went straight down. The decks were blown into tiny bits and ground to pieces."

Wyeth said nothing. He stared up at the sky and the rain felt good on his face.

Stevens dried his hands on his undershirt, opened his log and entered:

"I, Lieutenant Henry K. Stevens, Confederate States Navy, destroyed my command, the steamsloop *Arkansas,* by setting fire to her magazine at 9:12 A.M., August 6, 1862. The ship went down without a trace just off the first point north of Baton Rouge." He closed the log and put it away, then licked his lips and wiped sweat from his face. He was sweating in spite of the rain. "She lived less than a month," he said. "Poor Brown."

"She was a great ship, sir," Wyeth said. "A magnificent ship. She raised a siege and killed more Yankees than were lost at the battle for New Orleans. She went down because she couldn't fight any more and couldn't bring a gun to bear. No Yankee foot ever touched her."

"I wish there was something left of her," Stevens said. "Something we could give Captain Brown."

"My Dolly is still here," Granville said. "She will fight again."

"And there's a picture," Wyeth said. "A friend of mine painted it and I will give it to Captain Brown."

The rain drove them to cover under canvas of the barge and the men huddled there, wet and hungry. A few cursed the rain and then were thankful for it as the *Essex* steamed by. They heard her although she couldn't be seen through the downpour, and couldn't see them. The *Music* hugged the sluice and every man fingered his gun, fearful that Porter might land a party and seek them. They talked in whispers and the *Essex* moved beyond hearing and the throb of her engines died away. There was no sound then except the splashing of rain on the river, the heavy breathing of the men and the faraway echo of thunder that joined the rumble of guns at Baton Rouge.

"We're safe for awhile," Stevens said. "They'll never find us in this rain." However, for safety's sake, he sent the *Music* downstream to watch for Porter.

The cannonading at Baton Rouge increased as the *Essex* went back to anchorage before the town and resumed her pounding of the Confederate lines. General Breckinridge, having seen the destruction of the *Arkansas,* knew his fight was hopeless, and called for retreat. The Confederates abandoned their trenches and fell back. The Federals were too exhausted to follow. They had saved the capital for themselves and had given the Union her first victory in many weeks. Porter went ashore and wired a message to General Ben Butler that the *Arkansas* was destroyed.

Night found the desolate Confederate sailors bunched on the barge, lying in puddles that formed on deck. Granville took most of the available canvas and threw it over the Dolly. The men made shelters of pine branches on the deck and sought comfort there, not daring to show a light.

"Try to get some sleep, men," Stevens said. "We will make plans tomorrow."

"Sleep," a sailor mumbled. "What the hell does he think we are? Fish or tadpoles?"

"He thinks you're sailors," Wyeth said. "But he could be wrong."

"That's right, bub. He's been wrong before."

Captain Brown reached Breckinridge's headquarters that night and heard the story. The army man didn't dare criticize Stevens, but suggested vaguely that if the *Arkansas* had arrived in time he could have won Baton Rouge. Brown fastened his feverish eyes on Breckinridge. "General, only a fool would have sent my ship on such a mission. I'm in no mood for discussion. My ship it gone and my men are up the river somewhere. Maybe in a swamp. I'm going to them."

"You're mad," Breckinridge said.

"I will find them," Brown murmured.

On his orders, a stretcher was slung between two mules, bony, sickly mules that were no good for the army, and he was put on the stretcher. A guard of ten soldiers led the mules away, moving northward. The men carried medicine and food, and several carried pine torches that spluttered in the rain.

They stopped first at a burned plantation where a group of Negroes explained that their master was dead and that they were alone. Brown asked directions. The Negroes looked at his drawn face and were afraid. One, with more courage than his fellows, leaned over the stretcher and told Brown, "That boat blew up right out yonder in the river. Ever'body on her musta been killed."

The party moved on. Brown nudged one of the men and whispered hoarsely, "Call out. Call out 'Oh, Louisa!' "

Ves heard them first. He thought he was dreaming and then aroused his comrades, shaking them excitedly. The men grabbed their guns. "Louisa and the babes!" Stevens shouted. "Who is it?"

"Commander Isaac N. Brown, Confederate States Navy, reporting to his command."

Stevens lifted his face in prayer and the rain beat upon it, mingling with his tears. He heard his men moving and whispering. "Captain Brown is back," he said. "Let's get a fire started."

The *Arkansas*' crew, forlorn and bedraggled, was pitiful in a defiant sort of way as Captain Brown was lifted from his stretcher and lowered to the deck of the barge, under a lean-to. They crowded around him, sobbing without shame. Ves leaned over and stroked his face. Wyeth touched his hand and Granville, usually aloof, took part of the canvas from the Dolly and spread it over his commander.

Stevens knelt by Brown and embraced him. "Scuttled, sir," he sobbed. "Scuttled like a pirate. I should have fought. . . ."

"Nonsense, Stevens." Brown used his hands and forced himself to a sitting position. "Never confuse heroics and heroism. Porter would have captured the *Arkansas* and used her against us. She is gone, and so is yesterday. When sadness is sleeping, never arouse it."

A fire was kindled on the barge and hot food was prepared. The men's spirits rose and they began singing and shouting in the night, trying to cheer their leader.

It was a strange sight, men huddling in the rain, singing chanteys. A few lanterns were rigged on the barge and danced crazily in the rain. The noise attracted the slaves from the nearby plantation and they hid in the cypress and watched the Confederates, then fled, believing they were ghosts, spirits from the *Arkansas*. They had seen the ship explode, yet there was her crew, haggard, wet and riotous.

The frightened Negroes started the myth of the *Arkansas*, spreading tales that her crew of ghosts was haunting the riverbank. The stories reached the Federals at Baton Rouge and some of them shuddered and began whispering strange tales, too.

Why, the stories went, the *Arkansas* fought to the last, yet there was no man aboard. Who steered the big Rebel to midchannel and wheeled her to face the *Essex?* Who aimed the guns and fired them? And the *Arkansas* didn't blow up, she vanished into thin air just as a cloud passed over. . . .

She wasn't down at all, one story went. The Confederates had blown up a decoy. The *Arkansas* had passed the *Essex* in the rain and was standing for New Orleans. No, she was heading for Cincinnati, St. Louis! She had rounded the Mississippi passes and was in the Gulf. . . .

Brown was dead. Why, he died in Grenada. But he had been seen, a ghost on a big bed between two snow-white horses. He was back on the *Arkansas,* standing on his bridge, exposed to rain and shot. And below his bridge, on the boarding deck, was the ghost of a young man who wept and laughed when he fought, a man with a white scar that blazed like lightning. There was a bearded man beside him, and a huge man with yellow hair. . . .

That thunder in the swamps was the *Arkansas!* The hissing of rain was her steam! Those sighs in the canebrakes were her men!

Oh Louisa. Louisa and the babes.

Ben Butler heard the tales and notified Washington that a ship of his department had sunk the Rebel and that there was nothing to worry about.[26] Butler had to take a little credit. Porter didn't know if one of his shells had set off the explosion or not. He assumed so, and he claimed the honors for the *Arkansas'* death. Then he and Butler began quarreling over the glory. Bill Porter didn't have long to live, so it really didn't matter.

The men on the barge never suspected that they were becoming legends. Their bellies were full and their commander was back. Brown seemed to get better that night and was able to sit up and josh with his men.

Finally, he sent them to quarters and dispatched a messenger down to the *Music,* asking Prent Oliver to bring his ship up to the sluice. Then Brown and all the officers went into conference. It was dawn when the council broke up, and Brown, stronger than he had been in weeks, walked alone across to the barge and watched the men eat breakfast.

"What we aim to do now?" Ves asked. "Get a skiff and fight 'em with slingshots?"

"Why, we're going to start all over," Brown said.

"Another *Arkansas?*" Wyeth asked.

"Of course," Brown said. "You never thought otherwise, did you?" He pulled up a stool and sat with his men. "We're going back to Vicksburg on the *Music*. . . ."

"My Dolly?" Granville demanded.

"We will tow the barge, Granville," Brown said and laughed. "We won't leave your gun. She is the first of our new battery. We will go to Yazoo City and begin another ship."

The men looked from one to the other. They were not fooled. They knew how hard it was to build the *Arkansas,* and her sister would be much harder to build. But they said nothing.

Ves asked, "When?"

"Right away," Brown said. "Maybe we can convert the *Star of the West* into an ironclad. Remember her? She's around Yazoo City. Maybe we can use her engines and build another ship around them. She was in ferry service in New York and her engines are good. Maybe we can get two or three ships and have a flotilla. . . ."

The men were smiling again. "Sure," said one, "We'll do it, Cap'n. We'll do it for Louisa and the babes."

"Iron?" Granville looked over at Brown.

The commander rubbed his hands across his withered face. "Now that's the hitch. That's what I want to talk to you about. Woodward, you or Granville will have to go to Natchez."

Wyeth started to speak. He wanted very much to go back to Vicksburg where Laurel was, but Natchez was the one place he didn't want Granville to go. Sharon was in Natchez, Laurel could come there and he could see her at her own home. It was on his lips to volunteer when Granville said, "I'll go, Captain Brown. I know my way around there."

He tried to make his words sound casual. They did to Brown. Granville didn't look at Wyeth and was conscious of Ves' stare. The Cajan said, "What the hell, Sim? Wyeth is the man for that work." His tone was cold.

"I'm the one," said Granville. Then he leaned close to Ves. "Shut your mouth, you big baboon. Laurel is at Vicksburg, not Natchez. So I'm going."

"That's goddamned noble of you," Ves said sullenly.

[272]

Wyeth didn't utter a word. His tongue was cleaving to the roof of his mouth and his mouth was dry. He wondered then if Granville were thinking of Sharon or whiskey, and reasoned correctly that his friend was thinking of both, and the knowledge hurt him.

Brown said, "Very well, Granville. You leave at once. If we take you to Natchez on the *Music* somebody will get suspicious. So leave from here. Go to Frome and tell him I need iron for another *Arkansas*. Join us at Yazoo City or Vicksburg."

The Englishman tried to be gay and nonchalant. His heart was jumping, however, and his blood was racing. Sharon and whiskey. Brown caught his eye and said, "Must I warn you?"

"No, sir," Granville said.

Still he didn't look up at Ves or Wyeth. He borrowed clothes from a deckhand on the *Music* and put his pistol under his belt. Then he shook hands with his two comrades and tried to stare them down. Wyeth said, "Good luck, Mr. Granville. We will take care of your gun."

"Uh huh," Ves said. "We'll look after Dolly. You look after yourself. And, Sim, if you happen to see my cousin . . ." he said it slowly, "give her my love."

Granville stepped off of the barge into the rain, turned and waved, then disappeared to the east toward the road to Natchez. Wyeth glanced at Ves, and walked away. He went over and helped lash the barge to the *Music*. He covered the Dolly, then sat on it while rain trickled down his face and under his jacket. Prent Oliver and Brown went to the *Music's* pilothouse and the ship kicked off and moved upstream, pushing the barge.

The big Cajan came and sat down on the Dolly by Wyeth and tapped his foot against the deck. He put his finger in his mouth and felt the wound he had suffered in the Vicksburg fight. The flesh still was sensitive although the bone had knitted. There were no upper teeth on the left side of his mouth, however. He removed his finger and looked over at his friend. "Well?"

"Well what?" Wyeth snapped. "We are off for Vicksburg and I'm glad. Dammit, I'm glad. Now I can see Laurel and forget about all this."

"She could have met you in Natchez."

"Maybe. Maybe not."

Ves got up and looked down at the Missourian. "Wyeth, look at me. Sim wouldn't do that to me, now would he? He wouldn't go messing around Sharon unless he aimed to be fair and square."

"Of course not," said Wyeth, and the words sounded hollow.

"But he was so anxious," Ves mumbled. "He was just so damn anxious."

"Oh, for God's sake, Ves. Shut up. If you're suspicious of him then take it up with him. Quit mouthing around. He was the man to go. He's smart. . . ."

"He sure the hell is. And so are you. I'll never mention it again, Wyeth. I won't bother you no more about it. I ain't going to think about it. I like Sim as much as you do. But we both know he's a heller. And you make me sick. Mr. Granville this, and Mr. Granville that. You got just as much sense as him. More in some ways. On the other hand, you ain't so damn bright all the time. Sometimes you act like a little boy. Dammit, Wyeth, quit worshiping Sim. He's just like us."

Wyeth got to his feet and walked away. He didn't want to talk about it any more.

Bucking the channel, it took the *Music* several days to reach Grand Gulf and there they learned that Van Dorn had left Vicksburg, leading most of his army into North Mississippi, for a campaign to recapture Corinth. General Martin Smith was left in command at Vicksburg with six thousand men. General W. N. R. Beale had 5,500 at Port Hudson and those were the only important Confederate forces along the east bank of the Mississippi.

General John McClernand, another of the North's political soldiers, had got leave from Grant's Army and gone to Washington to see his old friend, Abraham Lincoln. He impressed upon the president the importance of taking Vicksburg and asked for an independent command. He got it. Grant was not even notified. . . .

When Brown heard the news at Grand Gulf he was amazed. Grant and Sherman were the only generals the Confederates feared in the valley, and Washington apparently had sidetracked both of them for a politician.

"They'll never learn," Stevens said.

"Yes they will," Brown said. "Someday they'll learn. But now Vicksburg won't be hard to hold. The Yanks are so busy fighting among themselves that they're helping us." He began making plans, mulling them in his mind.

The *Music* and the barge reached Vicksburg late one afternoon. Half of the batteries were not manned, but there was a feeling of suppressed excitement about the town. Wyeth got an hour's leave and ran up the bluff and to Mrs. Simpson's house.

Laurel wasn't there.

"I thought you had heard," Mrs. Simpson said. "She is in Natchez. Soon after you left, General Van Dorn ordered every civilian to leave Vicksburg unless they could show cause why they should stay here."

Wyeth stared at her, then looked out at the rain, thence down the bluff to the *Music*. "We passed right by Natchez, too," he said. "It looks like my luck is running out." He dared not let Mrs. Simpson see his face, or the hurt in his eyes. "I'll write her and tell her that I am all right."

"She knows that, Wyeth. General Breckinridge's dispatch from Baton Rouge was published. She knows you're alive. She started to appeal personally to General Van Dorn for permission to stay. But she had no excuse except that she was waiting for her betrothed. The Yankees are coming again, you know. This was no place for her."

Chapter Fourteen

W YETH was bitter and moody for several days and then his good humor and optimism returned. A visit from Gar helped his spirit and a letter from Laurel enlivened it.

Laurel had seen Granville. That was all she said about him, that she had seen him with Frome. She didn't mention Sharon. And she didn't whine because she had missed Wyeth in Vicksburg. Her letter was cheerful and gay.

Gar met Wyeth near the gangplank of the *Music,* which was being coaled for a trip up the Yazoo, and when the Wolof heard that his friend was returning to Yazoo City he said, "I'll be there, too, Mist' Woodward. I ain't got but one more man to get and then I'll meet you at Yazoo City and help you build your new boat."

"How is the reading?" Wyeth asked.

"Fair to middlin'. Miz Simpson is giving me a lift ever' now and then on the hard words. She makes out like she don't want to do it and then does it. White folks are funny."

"We will probably be at Yazoo City a long time and I can help you. But first, I want you to go to Natchez and take a letter to Miss Laurel. She will give you that picture of the *Arkansas.* I'm going to give it to Captain Brown, Gar. I hope you don't mind."

"I know how you feel. I don't mind a bit. I'll get on down to Natchez. Maybe I'll find my man down there som'rs."

The crew of the *Arkansas* stayed in Vicksburg only long enough to catch up with lost sleep. Brown went to the Marine Hospital and was on his feet again within a week. He attributed his recovery to quinine and rest. His men, however, attributed it to determination.

The Dolly was taken aboard the *Music* and the little ship left Vicksburg and moved up to Haynes Bluff where the raft still blocked the Yazoo. Lieutenant Stevens and a party that included Ves went up to the Tallahatchie River where the *Star of the West* was being used as a supply ship for Van Dorn's men who were preparing for the assault on Corinth. Stevens brought the *Star* down the Tallahatchie into the Yazoo, thence down to the raft.

The Dolly was moved from the *Music,* around the raft and onto the *Star.* Prent Oliver turned his *Music* around then and headed back for Grand Gulf and the Big Black River. Brown took command of the *Star* and went to Yazoo City.

The shipyard and powder works were still intact although the yard was flooded and rain water was standing in the cannon foundry. The *Capitol,* their old workship was far up the Coldwater River, another tributary of the Yazoo that veered northwest almost to the Mississippi.

Another party was sent up to the *Capitol* and while they were away Brown and his men moved the cannon foundry to dry ground and threw a small levee on the flank of the shipyard, protecting it from high water. There was no indication of a letup in the weather and if rain were falling along the tributaries as steadily as it was falling at Yazoo City then there was danger of high water all along the Yazoo.

Two hundred slaves were recruited from nearby plantations and Brown began scouting the territory for lumber. He made contracts with two saw mills in Yazoo City and two more over in Canton, agreeing to haul the lumber from Canton to Yazoo City in ox wagons.

Wyeth was so busy that he almost forgot about Granville until a letter from Laurel told him that the Englishman had gone to Mobile, seeking iron. She knew how Wyeth's mind worked and told him that Granville "looked fine and was fine" when he left. Then she said, "Tell Ves that I saw his cousin. She is fine, too."

Gar came back from Natchez and was rather disgruntled because the last man of the group that hanged Mort apparently had gone to

New Orleans. "I couldn't go after him," the Wolof said. "I got that pitcher from Mis' Laurel and reckoned you wanted it. I'll get the man later."

Wyeth took the picture to Brown and really was glad when the commander declined the gift. The sailor didn't want to part with it, but felt better for having made the gesture. Gar was glad, too. Wyeth hesitated to ask the Negro if he had seen Granville. Gar seemed to read his mind and told him, "I saw Mist' Granville down there."

"Is that so?" Wyeth wanted to appear uninterested. "How was he?"

The Wolof caught the look in his friend's eyes. "Mist' Woodward, you ain't no actor. Yes, suh, Mist' Granville had been drunk'n a blind goat. He was under the hill. I helped Mis' Weatherford get him on his feet."

Wyeth was silent and Gar understood the silence. "You can count on me, Mist' Woodward. I ain't saying nothing. I know Mist' Ves would be killing mad. I know Mis' Weatherford is rightly fond of Mist' Granville."

"All right, Gar. Just keep your mouth shut."

In the days that followed, the Negro worked as a free man in a Yazoo City sawmill, cutting lumber for Captain Brown. His pay was $1 a day, which was more than Wyeth earned as a Confederate gunner. There wasn't much time for the Missourian to help his friend with his reading, for when the mill wasn't running Gar helped Ves run trot lines in the Yazoo, catching channel catfish for the crew. The three men, Wyeth, Ves and Gar, often hunted in the swamps and brought in fresh meat, deer and bear, coons and squirrels, and, occasionally, a wild beef or a wild hog.

August surrendered to September and Summer to Autumn before Brown was able to get shipwrights and begin the keel for the new *Arkansas*. She was to be one hundred and fifty feet long. Brown wrote to the Navy Department, requesting permission to use the *Star's* engines in his new ship and was stunned when permission was refused. The Navy Department suggested he use the *Star* instead of building a new ironclad. Brown prepared a detailed explanation, pointing out that the *Star of the West* was not capable of carrying armor or armament strong enough to challenge the Union ironclads. He even suggested that he be allowed to put the *Star's* engines in his new ship and put the *Capitol's* engines in the *Star*. His report and request were pigeonholed somewhere along the line.

But he kept working.

The Battle of Antietam and Lee's rebuff in Maryland was known to most of the world before the news seeped into the wilderness where Brown and his men were laboring day and night, fighting the rain, the mosquitoes, malaria and red tape. Then came the news they had expected. Farragut was on the move again. Farragut knew the South and knew how to hit where it hurt. He got shallow draft boats and sent them up the bayous from Florida to Louisiana, destroying salt works. Some of the wise men at Washington laughed at him. The ridiculous idea of a fleet commander wasting his time destroying salt! Farragut, however, knew that salt and quinine were two things the Confederacy had to have and two things they couldn't get.

Mississippi reacted quickly to the salt problem. A state salt department was organized to supply the families of soldiers. The people began distilling brines from marshes and from the soil around smokehouses. A substitute of ashes and lye was tried. The salt famine soon became acute, however, and the rich began paying fantastic prices for it. That broke all the barriers and inflation took hold. The price of slaves soared to $3,000 for an eighteen year old man. . . .

The government of Mississippi, threatened by mutiny in certain sections due to the salt shortage, appealed to the other states for help. Only Louisiana responded and sent some of its precious store into Mississippi. Yes, Farragut knew what he was doing. The weakness of the Confederacy's civil structure was apparent to him. States Rights? Then each state had the right to starve and had no call on the other states for help. Virginia had some salt. Georgia had some salt. In those days, early in the war, several states had salt. But there was no law to force them to share with Mississippi, and Mississippi had Vicksburg, and Vicksburg was the keystone of the Southern military arc.

Brown was unable to get even a pound of salt from Vicksburg. He remembered a salt lick in North Mississippi and sent a party up there. Civilians, however, beat him to the lick and excavated every foot of the ground around the deposit.

Then came the news that the United States Navy Department

finally had aroused itself from its stupor and fixed commands in the west. Farragut was given a free hand with the Gulf Squadron, stationed at Pensacola, and Dave Porter was given authority to reorganize the Mississippi River Middle Fleets into one unit. He took over Davis' ironclads and demanded use of the Ellet rams. The War Department hesitated to turn its ships over to the Navy and Porter trained a battery of guns on the Union rams and told them that if they moved from anchorage he would blow them to bits. And he meant it. Of course it was rather irregular, the Navy declaring war on the Army. But it worked. The rams were given to Porter and for the first time all Union ships on the Mississippi had one commander.

Immediately, Dave Porter established his base at Cairo and demanded enough power to patrol every mile of the Mississippi from Cairo to Vicksburg. Ironclads began pouring in from the Eads' assembly lines—the *Lafayette, Chillicothe, Choctaw, Tuscumbia* and the powerful *Indianola*. They all were of improved design and had wheels that worked independently, allowing them to maneuver in tiny places.

He was given permission to buy four light draft boats. He bought seventeen, paying for them with sight drafts, then plated the steamers with light armor and called them tinclads. Soon he had a real fleet at Cairo; five new ironclads, twelve rams, seven gunboats, three timberclads and seventeen tinclads.

Porter's command was the middle Mississippi basin. He had open river from Cairo to the mouth of the Yazoo where the Vicksburg fortress began. The Confederates were in command from Vicksburg to Port Hudson, but from that fortress to New Orleans the Union Navy was not opposed except by guerrillas who sniped from along the banks. The Navy's job was to open the river from Vicksburg to Port Hudson and to cooperate with the Army in attacking the two citadels.

As soon as Brown heard of the developments, he sent Wyeth and Ves and their Dolly to Haynes Bluff and they put the Dolly in battery near the raft. Work ceased on the ship at Yazoo City and the Confederates began making torpedoes.

The first torpedo was made of a five gallon demijohn. Brown filled it with powder, attached an artillery friction tube to it and strung a wire across the river. The jug was tied to the middle of the wire and submerged.

Ves didn't understand how the thing worked and Wyeth explained that if the wire were disturbed it would ignite the friction tube which would set off the powder in the demijohn.

Brown made fifty torpedoes and sowed the lower Yazoo with them. He got directions from the Torpedo Bureau at Richmond and the Naval Submarine Battery Service and made spar torpedoes, suspending torpedoes from underwater spars attached to the banks and to the raft.[27]

Ves and Wyeth were left at Haynes Bluff to tend the Dolly, and Brown took most of his men back to work on the new *Arkansas.* The keel was in the stocks when they got word that Bragg's advance into Kentucky had been checked at Perryville and that Van Dorn had been defeated before Corinth. The tide was turning again, and from Virginia to Mississippi the Confederates went on the defensive.

"Now they'll really strike for Vicksburg," Wyeth told Ves. "I wish Mr. Granville would come on back."

Brown, unable to get engines for his new ship, kept his men busy building fortifications at Haynes Bluff. He got in touch with Frome and learned that two short-stroke engines might be obtained in Mobile. Frome reached Granville in Alabama, around Selma, and sent him back to Mobile. The wooden keel of the new ship was ready and no more could be done until iron was obtained. So Brown put his shipwrights to laying three more keels, one for the *Republic,* one for the *Mobile* and one for an unnamed vessel. There was plenty of lumber and Brown had the time and men to lay keels, hoping that some day he might turn them into fighting ships.

The Union Navy got the jump on the Army in reorganization and was itching to reopen the campaign against Vicksburg. Then Grant began bestirring himself up in North Mississippi, sizing up Vicksburg from afar. He watched Van Dorn shatter his lance against the Union lines around Corinth, and began mulling his own problem, conscious that he still was under the cloud of Shiloh. He couldn't afford to make a mistake. The road from First Manassas to Vicksburg and back to Second Manassas was strewn with the wreckage of Union hopes and the reputation of Union generals—McDowell, Fremont, McClellan, Pope—

The South had a winning combination in Virginia and a seemingly impregnable fortress in Vicksburg. The Union had a winning pair in the west and didn't know it; the stubby Grant, who was so shy that he wouldn't undress in front of his own aides, and the tireless Sherman.

Sometimes Wyeth, thinking on the course of events, almost was sorry for the Yankee soldiers who died because of confusion of Union leadership. The Washington authorities thought they had their fingers on the people's pulse and believed the United States would not stand for a blood-letting even to save the principle of Unionism. As usual, the people were away up the road, calling for the politicians to catch up with them.

Grant was hurt that Lincoln had allowed John McClernand to form an independent army. It was a slap at Grant and the timid little man who loved horses so much didn't know how to handle the politicians in Washington. Perhaps no other soldier in the world would have taken such an insult from his own commander-in-chief, for Lincoln, frantic for a victory, picked McClernand from Grant's own army, from under his nose, and told him to take Vicksburg.

Then Grant began scheming, a thing he never did well. He knew that if McClernand won at Vicksburg then his own goose was cooked. Grant wasn't ready to have a go at the Mississippi fortress, but he couldn't allow McClernand to beat him to the prize. He met with Sherman and they mapped their strategy, hoping to block McClernand and beat the South at the same time.

The War Department, following the lead of the Navy, began reorganizing in the west and played into Grant's hands. The Union Army of the Mississippi was abolished. Rosecrans superceded Buell and was given command of the Army of the Cumberland to work in middle Tennessee. That suited Grant just fine, for he was left alone along the Mississippi, save for McClernand. Washington even agreed to send Grant new levies raised during the summer through Lincoln's call for 300,000 volunteers. The North hadn't begun to draft manpower in 1862.

General Butler was removed from New Orleans and General Banks, who had been treated so badly by Stonewall Jackson in Virginia, was sent to the lower Mississippi with orders to march on Port Hudson, subdue it and attack Vicksburg from the south.

Grant gave Sherman thirty thousand men and told him to take them down the Mississippi from Memphis and strike at Vicksburg from the north along the Yazoo. Grant planned to march south west, scatter the Confederates around Grenada, then take Jackson and push into Vicksburg. Sherman, if he hurried, should reach Vicksburg ahead of McClernand, lay his siege and then Grant would crack the nut from the east. It was beautiful strategy—On paper.

When the Union moved, the Confederacy moved to checkmate. Van Dorn was given a cavalry command in North Mississippi and General John C. Pemberton, Pennsylvania born, was selected personally by Jefferson Davis to defend Vicksburg. Pemberton went to Jackson to raise an army and stop Grant in North Mississippi, then wheel to the west and beat Sherman, and McClernand, too, if he would fight. Beale was left in charge of the Port Hudson garrison and Martin Smith of the reduced Vicksburg garrison.

The Confederate forces in Mississippi had been drained for the campaign in the east and Jefferson Davis came down to his home state and appealed for soldiers. Military wisdom suggested he call his Arkansas Army into Vicksburg, but there were political complications that could not be overlooked.

It was Jefferson Davis who raised an army for Vicksburg. He cajoled and threatened and by sheer force of will scraped recruits from the Deep South. The South's conscription law was dropped to include mere boys and was raised to include old men. An army was gathered, however, and Pemberton had something to work with.

Davis thought of bringing Stonewall Jackson to the west, or Longstreet. But Joe Johnston was the senior officer and Davis assigned him to command all Confederate troops between the Alleghanies and the Mississippi, including Bragg's Army and Pemberton's Army.

So Pemberton was cast against Grant, Sherman and Banks, Bragg against Rosecrans, Johnston against the field, and Isaac N. Brown, with one Dahlgren gun, fifty homemade torpedoes and no worthy ships, against Porter and Farragut.

Brown, simply by refusing to admit defeat, managed to get eight cannon from Columbus, Ga., and put them in battery at Haynes Bluff alongside the Dolly. He reasoned that the Yazoo was blocked from the south, or Vicksburg gateway, but the river still was open to the north and if Grant got to Grenada he could send troops down the Yalabusha into the Yazoo, thence down to the shipyard. It was necessary to block the Yazoo to the north, too.

It was Brown, aided by Stevens, who envisioned a fort up near Greenwood and it was he who built the first entrenchment at Fort Pemberton. He dug a hole along the bank of the Yazoo, braced it with cotton bales and timber and mounted an old brass cannon. The fort was south of the mouths of the Coldwater, Tallahatchie and Yalabusha rivers and any Yankee craft that came down, seeking entrance to the Yazoo through its tributaries, must pass his fort.

General Pemberton quickly realized the importance of the fort and took it over, manning it with a strong garrison and ample cannon.

When that was done, Brown went back to Yazoo City and resumed work on his ships. October lived its appointed time and November brought a welcome nip to the air. And the rains stopped. It was then that Granville returned.

Wyeth was so happy to see his friend that he forgot the reports of the Englishman's behavior in Natchez. But Ves was cool. He tried not to be. He pumped Granville's hand and pounded his back and tried to be as friendly as ever, but something was missing. Granville knew it and Wyeth knew it and after the three men exchanged greetings they looked at one another and there was an embarrassing silence.

They were at Haynes Bluff and Granville came that way en route to report to Brown. He looked his Dahlgren over carefully and was told why the gun was in battery near the raft. He looked older; much older. His eyes were tired and heavy and some of the spring was gone from his step. Ves forced himself to ask about the trip.

"I went as far as Wilmington, North Carolina," Granville said. "We will get some iron all right. Frome will see to that. But an engine—" he shrugged his shoulders.

"We need two," Wyeth said. "We can't make engines."

"It seems we may have to. Those people over on the seaboard will not send us engines. They want them for their own ships. They don't think much of us over there."

"What the hell?" Ves demanded. "We're all in the same war, ain't we?"

Granville looked at him, seeking the friendly twinkle of the Cajan's eyes. But the twinkle was not there. So Granville looked away. "They think this is just a side show to their war. To them, this is the wilderness and nothing we do is of much importance to them. Frome is after engines and perhaps he will get some. All we can do is wait."

"Tell us about Natchez," Ves said softly. "Did you see Wyeth's girl?"

Then Granville was ashamed. His shame showed on his face. He twisted his mustache and looked from Ves to Wyeth. "There is a thing I must say. And you two must believe me. I thought Laurel was in Vicksburg. That I swear. Had I known she was in Natchez I would have insisted on Wyeth going there." He said it simply and seemed to feel better for having said it.

"I know that, Mr. Granville," Wyeth said. "You don't have to explain."

"Did you happen to run into Sharon?" Ves asked.

The Englishman was ready for that. "Why, of course, you ninny. You do not think I would go to Natchez without calling on your cousin, do you? Yes, I saw her. She is doing splendidly. . . ."

"So is Mr. MacKenzie and all the others, eh, Mr. Granville?" Wyeth broke in smoothly, changing the subject.

"Yes. Now what has happened here?"

They told him and he nodded slowly while they talked. So the Yankees were coming again. "I knew they were up to something," he said. "They have abandoned Baton Rouge, you know. They are regrouping and will throw all their strength at us the next time."

"Are you worried about it?" Wyeth asked.

"Not particularly. Another siege will delay the new *Arkansas*. But they will not get Vicksburg."

The Cajan and the Missourian went with Granville up to Yazoo City and he made his report to Brown. Then the three comrades got instructions to stay at Haynes Bluff with their Dolly. They made the trip back to the Bluff in a skiff as there was no ship available. It was a pleasant trip and, moving down the Yazoo, it seemed like old times to them, like the days they had spent up in the Dakota country. The moonlight made them mellow and the bonds of their friendship tightened again although there still was a vague feeling of uncertainty between Ves and Granville. They both felt it and they both did their best to overcome it.

They didn't talk of the war, but of the fur country and the streams they had traveled and of the things they had seen. Granville happened to say, "I saw some great country on my trip. I cut across the upper part of the Valley of Lebanon. That is the kind of country I like."

Ves was smoking a cigar and leaning back in the skiff while Wyeth rowed. "You didn't happen to bump into old man Dabney over there, did you?"

"No. I wonder what happened to him?"

"He's fighting," Wyeth said casually.

Granville looked quickly from one to the other and frowned. "Fighting?"

"Sure," said Wyeth. "The last we heard an army of Confederates had him under siege."

The Englishman puckered his lips and whistled. "My God! Perhaps they were right over along Tidewater. We *are* out in the wilderness. Why, man, Hoab Dabney has been smashed."

"You're crazy." Wyeth almost dropped the oars and the ashes from Ves' cigar fell on his jacket front.

"It is true. Weeks ago. The Confederates wiped out Hoab Dabney's republic. They hanged one of his sons and burned his capital."

"The old man?" Wyeth said. "Old man Dabney?"

"He got away. So did one of his sons. And that Keith Alexander got away, too." He began smiling.

"What's funny? What's funny about Keith Alexander?" Wyeth took up the oars again. He was rather sorry about Lebanon. Hoab Dabney and his little country had fought the South and yet Wyeth felt sorry for them. They had tried so hard, so few against so many.

"I was just thinking how we never hear anything out here." Granville took the oars to give Wyeth a rest. "The Battle of Lebanon is all you hear in Mobile. That and about Alexander. One of Dabney's daughters is in love with him and they say in Mobile that she is going to marry him."

"Her name is Morna," Wyeth said. "And Alexander is a bastard. I don't believe a Dabney will marry a bastard."

"They will bet you in Mobile that Alexander marries her. She is quite a lady I hear."

"She's a bitch," Ves said. "Always in heat. A bitch if there ever was one."

"I am sorry I missed her," Granville said.

"Laurel told me a few things about her," Wyeth said. "She must be a humdinger. Pretty as hell. . . ."

"She's hell all right," Ves said. "But that Keith Alexander will handle her."

They were silent then and Ves took the oars. Granville lit a cigar and sat in the bow of the little boat. The river and the moonlight made him think of Sharon. And Ves seemed to sense that he was thinking of her. There was a hurt in the Cajan's eyes and the hurt passed and anger took its place.

At Haynes Bluff, the days passed slowly and a monotony overcame the men. There was nothing to do except keep the Dolly ready and watch the lower Yazoo. Two wagonloads of iron reached Yazoo City from Frome and Brown bolted it to the deck of the partly finished *Arkansas*. It was just enough iron to cover a few feet of the bow. Brown kept his workmen busy, however. They sawed wood and did all they could, waiting for iron and praying for engines.

Gar got permission to go to Haynes Bluff and stand watch with his friends and help them hunt and fish for food for the Yazoo City crew. Wyeth and Granville were glad to have him as his presence gave them an opportunity to break the routine. They taught him and watched him paint and Granville learned new songs.

It was Ves, however, who really was happy to have Gar there. The Cajan felt alone, as though Granville and Wyeth were growing away from him and the Negro gave him comfort and understanding. Gar, without asking a question, realized the situation and longed to say something to the Cajan. White folks are funny. He said it over and over to himself. His sympathy was with Ves. He wasn't surprised at all that morning when Ves came down to the river bank where he was painting and sat down, staring at the Yazoo and at the blue haze. A touch of winter was upon the land and the air was clean.

Ves felt in his pocket for a cigar and offered it to Gar. The Negro declined the smoke and Ves lit it. Then he looked over at the Wolof and started to say something. No words came, however, so Gar said, "Mist' Ves, don't make no mistake."

"You think I am?" The big man was seeking help. He knew something about the Negro that Granville would never know and that Wyeth would never understand. He knew the strange deep wisdom of the Wolof.

"How long have you three men been together?"

"A long time."

"You been through heaps, huh, Mist' Ves?"

"Heaps. But I can't take this. I just can't have it, Gar. You know that."

"Don't make no mistake."

Ves peered down the river, then ran his tongue around the roof of his mouth. His wound had healed completely. He turned on Gar and his soft eyes narrowed. "I want the truth, Gar."

"Yes, suh."

"When you were in Natchez did you hear anything about Sim and my cousin?"

"Yes, suh. I went down under the hill and helped Mis' Sharon get him sober."

"He was at her house wasn't he?"

"That's right. I'm going to tell you the truth, Mist' Ves. The truth might save trouble. Mist' Woodward told me to keep my mouth shut. But that ain't right. You and Mist' Granville are heading for trouble and one of you will get killed. So I'm going to tell you the truth. Mis' Sharon is plum' batty about him."

"I know that."

"But you don't know that he is rightly fond of her. You don't know that. You don't know it and she don't know it because he don't know it."

"But you do." Ves never took his eyes from Gar.

"I do."

"Maybe so. But he won't do it right. Hell, Gar, he can't do it right. We're Cajans. Folks like Sim don't marry my kind of folks. He has taken up with my cousin. I've been thinking and thinking about it. And I don't know what to do."

"Don't do nothing. I'm black and you're Cajan. I know how you feel. So don't make no mistake."

"What must I do?"

Gar went back up the slope to the camp and returned with his box, from which he got the Bible that Wyeth had given him. He turned the pages slowly and, finding what he sought, started to hand the book to Ves. He remembered, however, that the Cajan couldn't read, so he swallowed and began reading himself, stumbling on some of the words:

"And Cain talked with Abel his brother: and it came to pass, when they were in the field, that Cain rose up against Abel his brother, and slew him.

"And the Lord said unto Cain, 'Where is Abel thy brother?' And he said, 'I know not: am I my brother's keeper?'

"And he said,

" 'What hast thou done? the voice of thy brother's blood crieth unto me from the ground. And now art thou cursed from the earth, which hath opened her mouth to receive thy brother's blood from thy hand. When thou tillest the ground, it shall not henceforth yield unto thee her strength; a fugitive and a vagabond shalt thou be in the earth.' "

The words trailed off and Ves didn't look up for a minute and when he did his eyes were wet and there were tears on his long lashes. "You read good," he said. "I'm rightly proud of you."

"Them words tell you what I mean. Look at it this way, Mist' Ves. Ain't nothing hurt about you except your pride. Your cousin ain't moaning. She loves him. It's him I feel sorry for. He's all tangled up in his own rope."

"I ain't making no promises. I'm just thinking."

Gar put the Bible back in his box. "White folks are funny. They put up a heap of fences to keep folks like you and me from getting over into their pasture and then along comes a white man and climbs the fence and gets bogged down in our pasture. Mist' Granville is hurting. He's eating his heart out. He don't know what to do, either."

"Maybe you're right. Get your Bible and read some more to me. I ain't never told nobody before, but I like reading. Sharon can read a little bit."

The Negro read and the two men sat there until the sun seemed to drop into the Mississippi and the earth was cold. Ves said, "Sometimes, Gar, I wish I was black. Or that I knew I was all white. I don't know what I am."

"You are a rightly good man. That's what you are. I reckon, Mist' Ves, taking it coming and going, I like you better than any man I know of. Mist' Woodward is my friend and he's done a heap for me. Mist' Granville is my friend. But I feel that if the Judgment Day came tomorrow I could count on you."

They sat there until the big swamp mosquitoes, unworried by the winter, came out and drove them up to the camp. Ves was so pensive, so wrapped up in his own worries that he neglected to put canvas under his blankets. He spread his blankets on the earth and lay down. Soon he was coughing and was not aware that he was coughing until Granville heard him and said, "Where did you get that cough?"

"Oh, I don't know, Sim. A touch of swamp fever, I reckon. I've had it before."

Granville got quinine for him and made him get up. Then the Englishman spread canvas on the ground and rearranged the blankets. Ves went back to bed and to sleep. Granville waited until his friend was breathing heavily, then felt his temples. There was a trace of fever, but the quinine should take care of that. He didn't tell Wyeth. There was no need to bother him. He sat by the Cajan until midnight and the fever went away.

The Englishman went back to his own blankets and was staring up at the top of the tent, listening to the sentries among the guns, when he heard the horse approaching. The rider was challenged and Granville heard a sentry say, "Great God! Go on! Captain Brown is at Yazoo City."

Without being told, Granville knew that the Yankees had come again. He aroused Wyeth and the two men stumbled into the darkness and went to their Dolly.

"Where's Ves?" Wyeth asked.

"Let him sleep. If we need him, we can get him."

Brown was at Haynes Bluff before dawn and inspected the guns. Then he told his men that Admiral Porter was sending the ironclad *Cairo* and the tinclads *Marmora* and *Signal* up the Yazoo to reconnoiter.

"It means that Sherman is somewhere around," Brown said. "It means they intend to attack Vicksburg from the Yazoo side."

Porter's three ships never reached Haynes Bluff, however. The tinclads, light draft boats, pushed up the river dredging for torpedoes. They removed many, but the heavy *Cairo* caught one near her starboard bow and sank in a few minutes.[28] It was a new type of torpedo that Brown had rigged, a demijohn of powder controlled by an electric contraption on the bank.

With the *Cairo* down, the tinclads fled the Yazoo without ever reaching range of the Dolly.

Then came Sherman. He brought thirty thousand men a few miles up the Yazoo on transports and landed them near Walnut Hills, six miles north of Vicksburg. His plan was to attack from the Yazoo side and pinch off the fortress while Grant was bringing his big army down from Holly Springs in North Mississippi.

Stephen D. Lee marched one brigade from the Vicksburg garrison and entrenched it in the Walnut Hills that controlled Chickasaw Bayou. Sherman ordered the assault, saying callously that it would take five thousand men to capture Vicksburg and "they might as well be lost here."

The result was tragic. Time and again Sherman threw his men against the hills and the Confederate brigade cut them to shreds. Sherman simply couldn't believe that a mere brigade could hold off his thirty thousand. But they did. In desperation Sherman chose to attack at the strongest point of the Confederate line, a triangle whose apex pointed at Chickasaw Bayou. His men were slaughtered. He tried to throw up a pontoon bridge and get across the swamps. His men, withering under the fire of sharpshooters, worked all one night and the next morning were dismayed to discover they had been building the bridge in the wrong direction.

That broke the back of the assault and Sherman withdrew to his transports and back to the Mississippi, waiting for Grant to attack.

Grant was moving toward Vicksburg from the northeast and was meeting little opposition. That should have warned him. He was in a brown study again. He piled up supplies at Holly Springs and moved down toward Grenada. Then the Confederates caught him out on a limb and sawed off the limb. Forrest struck in Tennessee and destroyed the railroad that fed Grant, and Van Dorn swooped down on Holly Springs and destroyed his base. Mrs. Grant was at Holly Springs, planning to spend Christmas with her husband. The Confederates captured her, too, and then released her with many apologies.[29]

Sherman got word of the fiasco and abandoned his campaign. And so was lifted the second siege of Vicksburg. Grant was cut off from his supplies and his army straggled back to Tennessee. Washington was horrified at the news and Grant was heartbroken. Sherman was in disgrace as his army retreated back up the river. McClernand superseded him.

Grant sent word for Sherman to meet him in Memphis. The sad

little man had learned something. Never again would he under-estimate the Confederates. Never again would he try to outwit them. They must be outfought, overwhelmed. And he learned something else; the most important thing he ever learned. His army could live off the land because Southerners would not destroy their homes and farms; they would not scorch their earth.

The Dolly did not fire a shot at Sherman's men as the assault was made down the river from Haynes Bluff. However, a few days after Sherman's retreat Porter sent eight ships up the Yazoo to test the strength of Haynes Bluff.

Under Brown's orders, Wyeth went down the river and spotted the range. He notified Granville and the big Dolly pounded the Federals without taking a shot in return. The Dolly outranged them and battered the *Benton,* flagship of the expedition, for two hours. The *Benton's* commander was killed and Porter called off the attack. Again Vicksburg was free and defiant.

"They'll come again," Brown said. "But not this way. The next time they will come from the north and try to get down the Yazoo."

He sent most of his men back to Yazoo City to work on the ships, but left Wyeth, Granville and Ves with their gun. The three sailors were disgusted because they had missed most of the fighting. The Cajan's fever had not returned. Granville saw to that and kept him dosed with quinine. The medicine, however, was just about gone, and there was no salt at all.

Then came news that Lee had crushed Burnside at Fredericks-burg, in Virginia. The tide had turned again in favor of the South. The year of 1862 went out in a blaze of glory for the Confederacy, and in a pall for the Union. Off Sabine Pass in Texas, a fistful of Rebels lured five Federal ships into the mouth of Sabine River, and carried them in what Farragut called a most "pusillanimous sur-render." But that was not all. Off Texas, the U.S.S. *Hatteras* saw a strange ship and challenged. The reply came, "We are the Confed-erate man-of-war *Alabama!*"

The *Hatteras* went down.

So the Confederate Navy had her dreaded man-of-war on the high seas. And there were more to come. Why, the Yankees were whipped. Vicksburg and Fredericksburg! The *Arkansas* and the *Alabama!* Oh Louisa. . . .

President Lincoln issued his Emancipation Proclamation, hoping the slaves would rebel and do what his soldiers couldn't do. The South laughed at his *tour de force,* a military document frothed with political icing and high sounding phrases. It didn't abolish slavery. It made no provision for the freedom of slaves in Southern territory that was loyal to the Union. It was a weapon, a political and military club that the North tried to use as a bludgeon. Then Lincoln, haunted by his mistakes, rose to the full stature of his greatness. No longer was he a politician trying to appease. He warned his country to tighten its belt and get ready for a deluge of blood. Some of his followers said the United States would not stand it. Lincoln knew better.

The South knew, too. "They'll come back," Brown kept saying. "Now they'll fight."

Grant brushed the fog from his brain and reached for his hammer to pound his way.

"Take Vicksburg," Lincoln told Grant. "I will back you."

"Hold Vicksburg," Davis said.

And down in New Orleans, where the occupying Federals also were glum at the beginning of 1863, Keith Alexander married Morna Dabney from the Valley of Lebanon. General Banks attended the wedding on orders from Washington to be attentive to Alexander. Most of the Union's officers down there went to the church where old Sam Dabney's granddaughter pledged herself to Keith Alexander, the Black Knight of Vengeance, illegitimate son of a Confederate bigwig, a poet of sorts, a flamboyant bravo who slept with his pistols until he took a bride.

Morna Dabney wore white satin and lace at her wedding. Then she put on green because Alexander liked green. There was a ball at the St. Charles Hotel and every Yankee who was anybody was invited. No Southerners were asked and many spat at Sam Dabney's granddaughter and her husband when they rode down St. Charles Street to the old hotel.

A Mr. Wells was at the ball, the same Mr. Wells who lost his cotton to Wyeth and Granville at the coup of Grand Gulf. He knew Alexander. The men were at the bar drinking brandy flips and congratulating Alexander when Wells offered a toast. Keith Alexander acknowledged the tribute and then laughingly asked what had happened at Grand Gulf.

Wells told him the story and Alexander frowned.

"Who is this Woodward?" he asked. "I know every cotton buyer between St. Louis and New Orleans and I never heard of him. And the man with the mustache? You say he wore Wellington boots and and carried a cutlass?"

"Mr. Woodward is a brave man," Wells said. "He wanted to fight. A funny thing. He's got a scar on his face that gets white when he gets mad. When those Rebs jumped us, this Woodward told our men to pass out the Plymouths. But we didn't have time."

"Plymouths?" Alexander glanced toward the ballroom where a Northern officer was dancing with Morna. "Are you sure he said Plymouths?"

"Sure I'm sure. That man with the mustache popped out, waving a cutlass and a pistol and this Woodward yelled, 'Pass out the Plymouths!' He wanted to fight I tell you."

"And the *Arkansas* came down a few weeks later." Alexander began smiling and looked around at the Federal officers. "Gentlemen, I'm glad I'm a Southerner. A renegade, perhaps, but a Southerner. Somebody has made fools of you. And now if you will excuse me."

"Tell us what happened in Lebanon," Wells said.

"You wouldn't understand," Alexander snapped. "There was a war in Lebanon, not a ball. Men got killed. The Confederates wiped us out."

"Is Hoab Dabney safe?"

"Yes. He hid in the woods until the Confederates left and went over to Vicksburg to kick Billy Sherman. Then Mr. Dabney and his wife and their son went back to the Valley. I brought his daughter here."

He brushed by the men and found General Banks and they talked for a long time until Morna, tiring of Yankees, found her husband and they went to their suite. There he told her Wells' story and said, "We are going to Natchez. I think I know where they got iron for the *Arkansas*."

"Is it safe for us to go there?" Morna asked.

"Yes. Natchez is neutral more or less. And, darling, learn something right now that our Northern friends seem to have forgotten. A Plymouth rifle is a naval piece." Keith began laughing. "If a stranger with a scar suddenly yelled to you, 'Pass out the Plymouths!' what would you think?"

"A navy man, of course."

[294]

"They think he is a cotton speculator." Keith removed his cravat. "And the man who led the attack carried a cutlass. Sailors carry cutlasses. I do not get the connection between the cotton and the iron, but the bearded man and the man with the scar were working together."

Morna took down her hair and let it fall about her shoulders. General Banks had put a maid at her disposal, but she didn't want a maid on this night. Her hair was a deep red, so red that it shone in the light of the candles on her dressing table. The light danced in her blue-green eyes and she turned and smiled at her husband and went to her trunk and got a lettuce green gown. Then, feeling his eyes upon her, she teased him and began prattling about Natchez. "I wonder if the bearded man's mustache is as graceful as yours," she said. "It's romantic, Keith. A bearded man and a man with a scar." Her smile passed quickly as she remembered something and she was angry at herself for not remembering it sooner. "I'm beginning to see, my sweet." She went back to her dressing table and brushed her hair. "Those wild stories we heard about the *Arkansas*. About a man with a flashing scar who laughed and cried when he fought, and a bearded man, and a man with yellow hair."

"You're the most charming woman in the world," he said gayly. "Your body is perfect and your mind is almost so."

"When do we go to Natchez?"

"Tomorrow. I want to see Nathan Frome. I have a feeling that some of the iron on the *Arkansas* was iron that I sold."

Morna put down her brush. Being alone with Keith was no new experience. But she was thrilled. She always was. "Frome? My grandfather had a friend named Benjamin Frome."

"Nathan Frome is Benjamin Frome's son. He is the only man I know, besides myself, who is smart enough to have conceived such a plan. He and a little Scotchman named MacKenzie. But they don't get along." Alexander sat on the side of the bed and stared at his wife. "Or do they?" He repeated it slowly. "Or do they get along?" Then he began laughing again and motioned for her to come to him.

She went gladly.

Chapter Fifteen

KEITH ALEXANDER was a rake, a man of few principles who let his two dueling pistols, Alpha and Omega, answer any questions that crossed his bitter vanity or touched his ruthless pride.

There were a thousand stories about the man, about his duels and the women he had loved. Actually, he had fought eighteen duels and really loved only one woman, his wife. He wrote maudlin poetry and played the harpsichord rather well, having studied the instrument in France where he roamed after being expelled from West Point for dueling.

He was a bastard. Few men knew that one of the leaders of the Confederacy was his father, and Alexander hated his father and the South he represented.

A sensitive, melancholic egotist, Keith Alexander fought the Confederacy from within. He wanted money and power to offset the shame of his birth and he picked the Union as the winner and was determined to be on the winning side. He held most Yankees in contempt and took from them all they offered and then reviled them. He remembered Sam Dabney, too. And he loved Hoab Dabney as only a lonely frustrated man can love an older man he respects.

Women said his hair was as black as a raven's wing. It was. He had curved lashes that shadowed the blueness of his eyes and made them look black. His mustache was a trim thing and when he slept he fastened a bit of silk around his upper lip to keep his mustache curled.

In many ways he resembled Simeon St. Leger Granville. They were about the same age and the same size. Alexander had spent years winning Morna Dabney and now that he had her he was happy for the first time in his life. And they had plans. He would squeeze wealth from Federals and Confederates and give her all the things she wanted, and she wanted everything. Already he had amassed quite a fortune by trading with both sides. There was a price on his head when he was fighting in Lebanon, supporting Hoab Dabney in his backyard rebellion. But now that Lebanon had fallen, he was safe to go to Natchez and continue his personal feud with the South.

He knew he was safe in Natchez. That's why he wasn't worried that morning when a groomsman hitched two white horses to a carriage, an imported carriage that Morna had selected. She was wearing a green habit when she got into the carriage and watched him hand a silver dollar to the groomsman and then sit beside her and touch up the horses. Morna was the best dressed Southern woman in New Orleans. Keith smoked imported Cuban cigars.

And so they started for Natchez, he to solve a problem for the Union and to trade in cotton, and she to enjoy the gaiety of a town that laughed while the rest of the South wept. Officially, Alexander was an agent for the Union Army, commissioned to buy supplies. He was not a spy for he had never fought as a Union soldier. The Lebanon Army had considered itself independent of the United States as well as of the Confederacy.

Alexander was a Southern copperhead and was safe from civil law because the South didn't dare make a test case of the issue then even if the man could be arrested and indicted. And the military had no authority because Jefferson Davis himself had refused flatly to let his army interfere with civil law and States Rights.

Hence, Keith Alexander had no worries about taking himself and his bride to Natchez where Union and Confederate officers, soldiers and sympathizers drew the caste and social lines sharply, but seldom the business lines.

Morna took four trunks to Natchez and they rented a mansion on the outskirts of town. The house had belonged to a Southern soldier and had been confiscated. Natchez, accustomed to many things, was shocked at the audacity of Alexander, a nameless renegade who presumed to bring his wife into society. Many of the old families shunned them, but others were forced to receive them because the planters wanted to do business with Alexander. Having compromised once, some of the Natchez families had to compromise again and accept the Alexanders. The situation amused Keith and Morna. In their hearts they hated the compromisers and really admired those in Natchez who dared ignore them, those Southerners who held fast and defied the power of the United States and all the men who were capitalizing on the Union's might.

Wall MacKenzie was the first to cross Keith Alexander, a thing that few men dared to do. Keith went to MacKenzie's store ostensibly to discuss cotton, but really to size up the little Scotchman. Wall refused Keith's hand and told him, "I'll have no truck with you, 'ygod. I'll have no truck with you, Alexander. I sell cotton, but not to you."

"You are a reckless man," Keith said.

"I am an honest man. And it will serve you naught to swagger in here and offer your friendship. I'm not afraid of your damn popguns. Stay away from me. And tell your wife to stay away from my daughter."

Keith just looked at the little man. And suddenly he was sad. For a minute, he wished to have the friendship of men like MacKenzie. He dismissed the idea, however, and said, "Well, I'll be damned." Then he turned and walked out and went to Frome's store where he was received politely. He told Frome that Wall had insulted him.

"Wall is a fool," Frome said. He never took his eyes from Alexander.

"Perhaps." Keith offered Frome a cigar.

"I've never heard of a man living to boast that he has insulted you," Frome said. "What can I do for you?"

"I just dropped by to pay my respects."

"I've never known you to be respectful before." Frome lit the cigar and puffed it slowly. "I'm a business man, Keith. I will not offend you as Wall has done. I do not like Wall, but he will fight. I hope there will be no trouble. . . ."

"Nonsense. I wouldn't challenge the man. He might shoot me."

"That's right. He might. I will not ask you why you're here, but let's understand each other. There's money to be made. . . ."

"Iron?"

"Yes. Iron."

Keith was surprised at the merchant's frankness. His eyes narrowed and he studied the Jew. Frome matched his look and Keith smiled. "You and I may have trouble, Nate."

"That is regrettable. But you know where I am. I do not mind you coming here and brow-beating some slobbering Yanks and some money-mad Southerners. But I'm offended, Keith. I'm hurt that you think you can talk to General Banks in New Orleans one night, head for Natchez the next day and trick me. You have offended my intelligence."

Keith tried not to show his surprise. "So you want iron?"

"All I can get."

"Confederate money?"

"United States money. And I'm the man you're looking for, Keith. I will save you that much trouble. All you have to do is prove that I furnished iron for the *Arkansas*."

Keith flipped away his cigar and leaned against the counter. "It must be a great organization, Nate. No wonder the Yanks haven't been able to catch you. I will. I have no iron. Are you going to tell Wall MacKenzie why I'm here?"

"Wall and I never have occasion to talk." Frome threw away his cigar, too. "He and I do not get along."

Keith smoothed his broadcloth coat and adjusted his silk cravat. "Yes, it's a great organization. All right, Nate, the game is on. Don't make a mistake."

"And don't you make one, Keith. I use my brains instead of guns, but there are guns hereabouts."

"And cutlasses," Keith smiled.

Frome said, "You are having dinner with the Youngbloods to-night. Or so I hear. Give them my regards."

"My God," Keith said. "You *do* know everything. I don't like Youngblood any more than you, but his wine is good."

They were referring to Captain Youngblood, a Union officer who had found a haven in Natchez while he lined his purse and the purses of some of his superiors by cotton speculating.

Alexander got to the door of Frome's store and turned. "I've got quinine, Nate. . . ."

"Did you adulterate it?" Frome snapped and anger showed on his face for the first time.

"Yes. But it's still quinine. I can get salt, too."

"What is the deal?"

"Who is Wyeth Woodward? And who is the bearded man?"

Frome didn't hesitate. "Woodward said he was a cotton speculator from Missouri. A lot of them showed up. You never heard of him because you were cut off over in Lebanon while he was here."

"Where is he now?"

"I don't know. Probably out making some money while you are here trying to outsmart me by playing the role of one of Pinkerton's nincompoops."

Keith ignored the sarcasm. "And the bearded man?"

"Which one? Who hasn't got a beard?"

"You know who I mean. The man who worked with Woodward at Grand Gulf. Don't take me as a fool. You sold cotton to Wells and then this Woodward and his associate got the cotton. . . ."

"I wasn't at Grand Gulf. I sold the cotton. Yes. And I got the money. It's none of my concern if Wells lost his shirt. I've told you the truth. So bring the quinine here."

Keith's annoyance primed his temper. He controlled his anger, however, and was determined not to let Frome realize that he was angry for that would be a show of weakness. "And the salt? How badly do you need it?"

"Let's have the deal, Keith. Quit mouthing and being dramatic. We mean business."

"When I leave how will you get word to Wall MacKenzie that I am after both of you?"

"I will walk right up to his store and tell him what you have said. I will tell half the folks around here that the brilliant Mr. Alexander thinks Wall MacKenzie and Nathan Frome are working together for the Confederacy. So when you see the people laughing you will know they're laughing at you. Now bring the salt here."

Alexander was baffled. And Frome knew he was baffled. The truth often baffles honest men and always baffles those who seldom deal with truth. Frome's nonchalance and his willingness to involve himself puzzled Keith. He had expected to set a trap for Frome and had a vague feeling that a trap was being set for him. As he walked away he realized that Frome hadn't admitted a thing, that he had involved nobody, and that he had won quinine and salt.

For one of the few times in his life, Keith Alexander was flabbergasted. He crossed the street and watched Frome walk toward MacKenzie's store and the blood mounted to his face when Frome waved at him. He stood there until Wall and Frome appeared together on the sidewalk and he heard the little Scotchman shout, "You can go to hell, too. I'll have no truck with any Jew or with Keith Alexander. Keep the hell out of my store."

That evening at dinner, even Captain Youngblood baited Alexander for thinking that Frome and MacKenzie worked together. "They hate each other," Youngblood said. "The story of your visit to Frome is all over town, Mr. Alexander. Everybody knows Frome buys iron and salt. Sure, he sells them to the Confederates. You have done the same thing. We know the Rebels have an organization working out of Natchez. But MacKenzie and Frome. . . ." He smiled at Morna, then at her husband. "You are barking up the wrong tree."

That same night Laurel wrote Wyeth that Alexander was in Natchez to buy cotton. She didn't report his real mission, for she didn't know it. Wall spared her that anxiety.

When Wyeth told the news to his friends, Ves said, "Why, that son of a bitch. What's he doing at Natchez?"

"Buying cotton," Wyeth said.

Granville didn't comment. He was frowning slightly and his mind began working in that orderly routine that it always followed when he was sober.

"Why don't the Confeds grab him now and hang him?" Ves asked.

"On what charge?" Granville said.

Ves pondered the question. "That's right. He ain't no spy, is he? Ever'body knows where he stands. A spy has to spy on military doings and he's just buying cotton. Can't we hang him because he's a Southerner fighting against us?"

"Let Wyeth explain it," Granville said. "He has the legal brain. But don't forget, Ves, that General Thomas is a Southerner fighting us. So are Farragut, Fremont and Scott. Lincoln, too, if you go by a man's birth."

"Alexander is beyond us as long as he stays outside our lines,"

Wyeth said. "If we punish him for rebelling against us then the Union can punish us for rebelling against them. He's no spy. He is a citizen of the conquered republic of Lebanon, doing business in Natchez. He has figured all that out."

"Then let's go down there and kill him," Ves said. "Sim is a pistol man. Maybe he can trick Alexander into a duel."

Granville laughed. "I might lose, you know. Besides, I would be dismissed from the service if I challenged. Dueling is against our Articles of War."

"Hell, I'll kill him. I'll waylay the bastard."

"Forget it, Ves." Wyeth was impatient. Another fear had beset him and he wanted to think it out. "If we tried to kill every copperhead, scalawag and cotton buyer we'd never have time for the Yanks. We're sailors, not assassins."

But Ves would not be silenced. "It's damn funny to me that a big man like Alexander would go to Natchez just to buy cotton. He must have a dozen buyers. What's he doing in the field?"

Granville glanced at Wyeth and the young Missourian paled, then the blood rushed to his face. "Ves is on the right track, Wyeth," Granville said. "We might as well face it. This Alexander is not in Natchez on a cotton hunt."

"I'm sure of it, too," Wyeth said. "I'm thinking the same thing you are. He's after the organization. He's after Frome."

"I know we've got to kill him now," Ves said.

They ignored him. Granville walked over to his Dolly and examined the priming. Wyeth followed him, leaving Ves alone near their tent. Neither Granville nor Wyeth looked at the other and the Englishman was the first to speak. "And after Frome is Wall MacKenzie. And Laurel. She helped, too. What do you think?"

"I can't think where Laurel is concerned. Sharon also may be in danger. What do you think?"

Then Granville looked at him and his alarm showed in his eyes. He was nervous and Wyeth was surprised, knowing that he was nervous for Sharon's safety. It wasn't like Granville to worry about a woman. "Perhaps Ves is right," the Englishman said. "Perhaps I should kill that man."

Wyeth toyed with the friction tube on the Dolly. Granville wasn't thinking clearly and he wondered why. He wanted to think that the reason was Sharon, but the idea seemed absurd. "Something has dulled your wits, Mr. Granville. If we kill Alexander it will be an admission that he is on the right track. We must leave this to Frome."

"You are willing to risk Laurel's life to him?"

"I am. There's nothing else to do. I'm going to send Gar down there to find out what's going on. Meanwhile, we must trust Frome."

Granville walked away down to the river and Wyeth went back to Ves. "I have a letter to write," the Missourian said. "Find Gar and tell him to come here, will you, Ves? And you know, I just thought of something. You'd better watch Mr. Granville. I've got a feeling that he's sort of in love with your cousin." Wyeth was smiling.

"How come you say that?" Ves' eyes narrowed.

"Because he's worried about her."

"Is that a fact, Wyeth?" There was a longing in Ves' voice, a hope. "You wouldn't lie to me? Reckon old Sim really likes her like a man is supposed to like a lady?"

"I think so."

"So does Gar." Ves' joy and relief were apparent. "Maybe you two are right. God, I hope so."

There was a pallor on the Cajan's brown face as it had been touch and go with the swamp fever, his name for malaria. However, his step was light when he walked toward the woods behind the hills, seeking Gar. The Wolof reported to the tent and Wyeth told him what he feared in Natchez. He gave Gar a letter for Laurel and bade him goodby. The Negro had his Bowie. . . .

The days at Haynes Bluff became humdrum, and each day was like the other. So when Captain Brown came down to the raft on the *Star of the West* the men were glad, for his presence always meant a break in the monotony. Work on the ships at Yazoo City had stopped for lack of iron. And Brown was worried. He was disgusted, too. The three comrades were aware of his disgust when they reported to him aboard the *Star*.

"The Yanks are back." Brown said it without concern. That seemed to be of secondary consideration to him. "Grant has taken the bull by the horns. He has sidetracked McClernand and has brought all of his army down the Mississippi. Sherman is with him. They are over on the Louisiana side. We are in for another fight."

"I'm rather glad, sir," Wyeth said. "I'm tired of sitting around waiting for 'em."

"I have bad news for you men." Brown stroked his beard and frowned. "The army is taking over the fortifications here at Haynes Bluff. . . ."

"My Dolly?" Granville gasped. "They are not taking her?"

"No. We'll put her on the *Star of the West*."

The sighs of the three men caused Brown to laugh, the first time he had laughed in weeks. "We'll get your gun aboard and send the *Star* back to Yazoo City. I want you men to go to Vicksburg with me. A shipment of quinine, salt and other things has arrived from Frome."

It took two days to move the Dahlgren from the bluff and get her in battery on the *Star of the West*, and then the little steamer hied back up the river and Brown and his three gunners went to Vicksburg. Leaving the wilderness for the bustling town was like stepping into a new world and the three comrades were aghast at the activity in Vicksburg.

Pemberton had anticipated Grant's maneuver and was bringing his army into the fortifications. More than thirty thousand Confederates were entrenched from Walnut Hills around the bluffs and down to Warrenton. It was a glorious sight. Supplies were pouring in over the Jackson Railroad and S. H. Lockett, Confederate chief of engineers, had turned the series of irregular hills, bluffs and ridges into a complex, but efficient network of defenses. Grant's army was encamped across from Milliken's Bend, out of range of the Confederate guns. Porter's fleet of ironclads, mortarboats, tinclads and rams, was nearby and kept lobbing shells into the fortress, a nuisance that seldom drew a return fire from the defenders.

Wyeth was the first of his group to notice that the Federals again were attempting to cut a canal across the toe directly opposite from Vicksburg. He nudged Granville and smiled at Brown who was accompanying them on a sight-seeing tour of the defenses. "They're trying that old trick again, eh? They think they can isolate us."

"Yes," said Brown. "I don't know why Grant is wasting his time on a canal. Our gunners have paid no attention to the diggers. Every now and then they fire over there just to scatter them, but Vicksburg will never fall without an assault from the east. Grant has got to get around behind us."

The sun was dropping beyond the river, scattering the winter haze, and white puffs arose from the guns of Porter's ships. Most of the land around Vicksburg was dry and brown, scarred and ugly. Occasional clusters of evergreens showed in the swamps and gave life to the bleak, dreary landside. Ves was scratching his head and his long yellow hair rustled in the chilled wind that swept down the river. "I know I ain't got no sense," he said. "But if Bully Boy Grant has got to get south of us then why don't he just march his men down the Louisiana side?" Then he was embarrassed, realizing Brown was smiling at him. "Oh, my God. I see it now. Even if he did march down that way the Mississippi River would still be between us and him."

"Exactly, Ves," Brown said. "You have hit the nail on the head. Grant is in a pickle. His transports and army are north of us. He can get his army below us simply by marching down the Louisiana side. But then how will he get his army across the river?"

"Why can't his ships run by the Vicksburg batteries?" Ves asked. "Farragut did it."

"They can run by the batteries. But then what? Where can Grant cross the river? Baton Rouge? Then he'd have to subdue Port Hudson before he could march north toward us. Cross at Natchez? Pemberton could move his army down there and fight Grant in the hills. There is only one way."

The three comrades were watching him. "Up the Valley of the Big Black?" Granville said.

"That's the ticket. But to get up the Big Black Valley and in behind us, Grant will have to silence our guns at Grand Gulf which control the Big Black. Then he will have to cut himself loose from his base of supplies, leave the fleet and strike out for the Jackson Railroad."

"He's in a hell of a mess, ain't he?" Ves said.

They all laughed and Brown said. "It will take me several days to get ready to return to Yazoo City. The army demands part of the quinine and we have many details to settle. You men can enjoy yourselves. Stay out of trouble."

Granville got drunk that night. Ves went woman-hunting and Wyeth went to Mrs. Simpson's house. She had a little salt and some fresh meat and he ate his first good meal in weeks. After supper, they went to her second story gallery and watched the fireworks. Porter was bombarding the town again, and across the river, on the toe of land that poked into Tuscumbia Bend, a string of lights flickered in the darkness. The Federals were hard at work on their canal.

The canal was near the ditch that General Williams had tried to dig the year before. It looked like a good idea to those who did not know the Mississippi. Williams could have told them better, but Williams was dead. Ben Butler knew better, too, but Butler had been removed from the valley. Farragut knew better, and so did Bill Porter and C. H. Davis. But they were gone. A new army and new commanders were before Vicksburg and they must learn all over again. Thaws already had set in north of Memphis and rain was falling in the Ohio Valley. High water was coming. . . .

Grant had several tricks up his sleeve. He kept his engineers and several thousand Negroes working on the canal and then sent part of his army west into Louisiana where a series of lakes, bayous and marshes formed a chain between the Mississippi and the Red River. Grant tried to dredge the bayous and marshes, hoping to move his transports from north of Vicksburg, across Louisiana and into the Red River. Then he could bring them down the Red and be south of the fortress. It was a detour of four hundred miles, the Lake Providence route, and the effort failed before it scarcely was underway. High water came early to the Louisiana bayous and every time the Federals dredged a passage, the water rushed in, piling debris along the route. Grant gave up the Lake Providence attempt and went back to his camp near Milliken's Bend and stared toward Vicksburg, wondering how he ever would get south and east of the town.

Then a freshet came down the Mississippi and flooded the canal before it was finished and the canal was abandoned, once and for all. Grant was baffled, and, in desperation, took a lesson from Farragut and began draining off his enemies' resources. Farragut had destroyed salt; Grant began destroying Vicksburg's labor supply.

He waved the Emancipation Proclamation at Negroes, opened his ranks to them and offered good wages for workmen. Many Negroes walked off from the plantations and "jined Mist' Linkum." Perhaps Grant didn't realize it, but he had struck Vicksburg at its most vulnerable point. Negroes were needed to build defenses and to grow food and the Confederates raged in impotent fury as the slaves went over to Grant's command. And soon Mississippi had more men in the Union Army than in the Confederate Army. Her enrollment in the South's forces totaled more than her white population between the ages of eighteen and forty-five. There were seventy thousand white men in the state really eligible for military duty and yet seventy-eight thousand were in Confederate uniforms. But seventy-nine thousand Mississippi Negroes and 545 white men had joined the United States Army.

Grant was nibbling at Vicksburg, weakening it, draining its blood. And he had Lincoln behind him. For the first time since the war began, a Union Army was on its own, unhampered by political leeches. The United States was so worried about the Virginia campaigns that Grant's western army was forgotten, much to his delight. He had all the men he needed and more were coming, for Lincoln had won his fight for conscription.

Lincoln had learned the hard way that he could not compromise at home or outmaneuver the Confederacy by political sleight of hand. He grew in knowledge and determination and soon was standing head and shoulders above any man, North or South. His own Congress called him a dictator and a tyrant, questioned his humanitarianism and challenged his doctrines. He laid his case before the people and the people upheld him, and he upheld Grant.

The South was the first to realize that the immensity of Lincoln's patient wisdom was bearing fruit. The enemy always is the first to appreciate the greatness of the other side's leaders. Aware that time was working for the Union, the Confederacy tried to discredit Lincoln at home and abroad and succeeded in many cases, but never with the workers and fighters of the North. Then they tried to discredit Grant and failed again because Lincoln was behind Grant. Jefferson Davis knew and Pemberton knew that after two years of floundering the United States at last had found a winning combination; Lincoln and Grant. And Grant had Sherman. . . .

Wyeth was at Mrs. Simpson's the morning the canal was washed away and he went down to the river to see the excitement. Bells began ringing in the town and soon half the population was standing along the bluffs and on rooftops watching the river destroy men who had tried to rule a river that will not be ruled. The Confederates refrained from firing toward the canal where many Federals were trapped. And there was no cheering. The river gnawed at the canal's banks and then swept in, piling up logs and machines and ripping away trees and levees. There was something sad about it. Grant had worked as hard as Williams had worked, and it was all over in an hour or so.

The people, Confederates and Federals, were so engrossed with the drama on the promontory that few gave any heed to the steamer *Vicksburg* which came up the river and to a landing under the Rebel batteries. She had come from the Red River trade and Brown went aboard as soon as she tied up. He was glum when he left the steamer after a conference with her master. Wyeth knew he had bad news and the three gunners were waiting on the bluff and Brown walked up, looked back at the *Vicksburg* and shook his head. Across the river, the Yankees were rescuing the last of their men from the canal.

"Did she bring us any iron?" Wyeth asked and nodded toward the steamer.

"No," Brown said. "She brought some powder and food. But no iron." He looked sharply at Wyeth. "The master saw that Negro friend of yours in Natchez. He told the captain to tell you that Mort can rest well now. Do you know what he's talking about?"

"Yes, sir."

"And he said tell you that he's going to stay in Natchez in case Laurel MacKenzie needs him. He said tell you not to worry."

"Thank you."

Brown sat down on the bluff and pulled his gray cape around his chest, for a chilly wind had sprung up. He was pensive and the men eyed him, wondering what was on his mind. Then he looked up. "Yes, you've been sick. It shows in your eyes."

"Ailing," the Cajan said. "I'll be all right."

"Do you men know that Keith Alexander is in Natchez?"

The gunners nodded and their commander stood up, shaking his head in disgust. "That's why the *Vicksburg* didn't bring us any iron. Alexander is watching Frome like a hawk. The trouble with an organization like Frome's is that only one man knows all the ins and outs and if you check that man then the organization can't function."

"Is Frome in trouble?" Granville asked.

"Any man is in trouble with that butcher Alexander on his coattail. Frome dares not move for fear he will expose some of his men. His work is at a standstill. Alexander has neutralized the organization just by blocking its leader." Brown looked down at the ground and then away toward the river. "I'm beginning to think we never will finish the new *Arkansas*."

A blast of eight guns from the upper batteries interrupted his thoughts. A salvo from Porter's fleet replied. Wyeth shielded his eyes from the sun and stared toward the northwest, toward Tuscumbia Bend. "What is it?" Granville asked.

"I don't know," Wyeth said slowly, a note of bewilderment in his tone. "The Yanks are up to something."

Greasy black smoke was pouring from every ship of the fleet, even the transports and tugs. "They're going som'rs," Ves said.

"They're moving," Wyeth said. "But this way."

"That smoke is a screen," Brown muttered. "They're trying to hide something. Keep a sharp lookout, Woodward."

Most of the ships moved down into Tuscumbia Bend, came to anchor and began shelling the town. The river was almost hidden by the smoke. Then the powerful *Indianola* pulled away from the fleet and headed for the middle battery, firing as she moved.

"The *Indianola,* sir," Wyeth said. "It looks like she's going to try to run by the batteries and get below us."

"That's rather reckless," Brown said. "For one ship, even an iron-clad, to run these batteries is a reckless gesture. Courageous perhaps, but reckless. What else, Woodward?"

There was no reply from Wyeth. His commander turned on him. "Woodward! What else? *Woodward!*"

Wyeth seemed to be transfixed. His mouth was open and the scar was flaming. "The *Queen of the West!* The *Indianola* was a blind! The *Queen* was right behind, hiding in the smoke. And now she has cut out and is coming by."

Brown gasped and Granville swore. Silence hung over the fortress for a minute and the smoke lifted. Then they all saw the *Queen,* racing down the channel directly under the noses of every river gun of Vicksburg. Her flag was whipping and her two side wheels were throwing foam.

It was magnificent. One little ship against a fortress. Two rows of cotton bales extended from her guards to her upper deck and more cotton bales were around her powerhouse. To protect her from plunging shot, a layer of cotton bales was secured on her gundeck. Her two stacks were belching smoke and she was burning fat meat and coal.

She was directly opposite Vicksburg and all the guns along the bluff were holding their fire, lining her up. The *Queen* was shooting, however, throwing everything she had at the Confederates. And she had a bowpiece, a thirty-two-pounder Parrot on her main deck, a twenty-pounder Parrot and three brass howitzers on her gundeck. Six guns against the might of Vicksburg.

"My God," Brown said reverently. "There's only one man in the Union ram fleet who would try that run."

"Little Boy Blue," said Granville.

"That's right," Brown said. "Colonel Charles Rivers Ellet. He's just nineteen and I doubt if he'll live to be twenty."

The cannoneers of Vicksburg waited until the *Queen* was under the main battery, and then from Walnut Hills to Warrenton the order to fire was passed along and more than one hundred guns opened up on the little ship. Vicksburg's hills actually trembled. Windows in the courthouse were broken by concussion and a blanket of smoke covered the river.

Wyeth felt Ves grabbing at his sleeve and looked back toward the river. The *Queen* was visible through the smoke, still plunging ahead, her guns blazing. She wheeled and headed in for the steamer *Vicksburg*. The cotton bales near her starboard wheel were on fire and her stacks were riddled. But she still was alive and floating, and fighting. She had taken the concentrated fire of Vicksburg and now was veering to sweep toward the bank and attack the Confederate steamer. She was so close to the big guns of the middle batteries that her sharpshooters were able to pick off the Confederate cannoneers.

Ves and Wyeth ran to the water's edge and began firing their snippers at the *Queen*. Granville fired his pistol. A regiment of infantry rushed out of the trenches and sprinkled her with musket shot and the big guns kept hammering the little Yankee challenger.

The *Queen* was a wooden ram, a tiny, powerful boat; stocky, awkward and ugly. By all the laws of gunfire, she should be in bits, yet there she was bearing down on the *Vicksburg*. Her commander was outside his pilothouse, calmly directing the action.

The *Vicksburg*, riddled by shots from the *Queen*, managed to shift just in time and the ram's bow missed her head-on, but caught her obliquely and staved in some of her deck planks. The blow forced the *Vicksburg* high into the mud and the *Queen* showered her with hot shot and incendiaries.

Then Ellet, disdaining the Confederate fire, reversed his ship and backed out.

Another blast greeted him, and his ship again was enveloped in smoke. He reached midchannel, wheeled downstream and plunged into the fire of the lower batteries. God only knows how he made it, but he did. The *Queen* scrambled out of range below town and tied up on the Louisiana side. Her decks were on fire and one casemated gun was shattered. She had twelve big holes in her and hundreds of smaller ones. Colonel Ellet put his crew to extinguishing the flames and patching the holes.

The *Queen* was safe before Vicksburg realized exactly what had happened. And then the people cheered. Many civilians had seen the fight and they stood on their roofs and cheered the courage of Little Boy Blue. The cannoneers were angry at themselves and then they cheered, too. There was nothing else to do.

Brown was pale and Wyeth's eyes were popping. The Englishman was the first to speak. He glanced at Brown and said, "Sir, it seems you must share your laurel wreath with Little Boy Blue."

"I must give it to him," Brown said. "The *Arkansas* did no better."

"He caught us squatting," Ves said.

"But he caught us," Brown replied. "It was the bravest thing I ever saw."

"Why do you reckon he did it?" Wyeth asked. "Just to get the *Vicksburg?*"

"I doubt that." Brown began stroking his beard. "No, I'm sure it wasn't that. I have a feeling that Colonel Ellet is heading for the Red River. He will never try to run by Port Hudson and join Farragut down below. It's bound to be the Red River that he's heading for. To raid our commerce."

Granville jerked his head quickly toward Wyeth and they traded glances. "God's pompadour!" the Englishman said. "Are we thinking the same thing?"

Wyeth was so excited that his face reddened and his scar showed again. "We must be." He intended to address Brown properly but in his agitation he grabbed his commander's arm and began shaking it. "There are our engines! The *Queen,* sir. We can put her engines in the new *Arkansas.* . . ."

"You've lost your mind, Woodward. . . ."

"Like hell he has," Ves broke in. "I get it, too. If the *Queen* is going up the Red then she's got to come back some day. There ain't no Yankee base up that river. So we go after her. . . ."

"You all are crazy," Brown said. "We haven't got a ship to send after her. Besides, you men are in my command and I have no jurisdiction in Louisiana waters. That's another department."

"How come we can't slip off and you know nothing about it?" Ves asked.

Granville said, "We can get up the Red some way. It is worth the try, sir."

"Give us a chance," Wyeth begged. "The *Queen* is what we need. She used to be a freight boat in the St. Louis, Cincinnati and New Orleans trade. She's fast and strong. Her hull has been strengthened by oak timbers and her machinery is protected by a bulwark of solid wood about two feet thick. She's almost as strong as an iron-clad. . . ."

"Yes, I know." Brown was smiling.

"And her engines are the best. Built for paddle wheels, but we can change them." Wyeth was pleading. "We can put her engines in the new *Arkansas* and put the *Capitol's* engines in her. . . ."

"What are you talking about?" Brown demanded. "You three men have been mouthing about something ever since the *Queen* passed. What is it?"

"Nothing, sir," Granville said quickly. He had caught the look in his superior's eyes. "We were just asking you for a leave. About twenty-one days."

"Well now," Brown said. "You've earned a leave."

Wyeth and Ves ran up the bluff to get their gear. Brown turned away and Granville fell in step with him. "I know the regulations, sir. If anything is said about three of your men being in another department, then we will take the blame. Ves has a girl in Alexandria and what's wrong with three sailors using their leave to call on a girl? Of course, if we happen to encounter the enemy. . . ."

"You're supposed to fight the enemy wherever you meet him," Brown said. He offered his hand to Granville and the Englishman was shocked; a commander shaking hands with a deck gunner! "Be careful, Granville. I will take care of your Dahlgren while you are gone."

The *Queen* left her anchorage below the city shortly after noon and four miles below town she encountered the Confederate steamer *Natalie*, took off her Rebel crew and sank the cargo boat. Then

Ellet paroled the Confederates, set them ashore and fixed his course for the Red River.

The Federal raider, for that is what the *Queen of the West* had become, hardly was out of sight before the three gunners had mapped their plan of action. They couldn't get horses to follow the *Queen* and, of course, no ship was available. But they got a skiff. Ves bartered for it from a riverman and put his snipper and some blankets aboard, then rowed the craft to a landing near the disabled *Vicksburg.* Wyeth joined him. He had the snipper that had belonged to Mort and a side of meat. Granville brought a bit of quinine and some corn meal.

They cast off in midafternoon with Ves at the oars. He rowed to midstream, felt the channel catch his skiff, and his oars bite into the river. Grand Gulf was about forty miles away, river distance. Maybe Prent Oliver was there. And the *Music.*

Chapter Sixteen

P<small>ALMYRA</small> I<small>SLAND</small> looked like a huge dead log in the foggy moonlight and Wyeth, on the lookout in the bow of the skiff, motioned for Granville to row for the inside bend and take the island from the lee. His only idea was to save time, but Ves often thought the Missourian had a sixth sense, for their boat scarcely was down the inside channel before they met the *Grand Duke of the Inland Sea*, tied up at Palmyra Island and ready for a run to Bruinsburg.

The *Grand Duke* was a logging boat, an old scow with a wobbly paddle wheel and a patched boiler. Her master, lugging a shotgun, challenged the sailors and Wyeth identified himself and his comrades and they made the skiff secure to the boat.

"Have you seen the *Queen of the West?*" he shouted up to the captain.

"Lord, yes. She took the outside of the bend and missed us. Passed here yestiddy afternoon like a bat out'n hell. She's nigh to Red River by now."

The three gunners climbed aboard the *Grand Duke* and persuaded the master to get underway at once. He gave the men coffee and cornbread and let them sleep in his quarters while he worked the pilothouse, steering his old boat through the darkness by the feel of the channel.

The sun came up, misty and timid, before the *Grand Duke* reached Grand Gulf and put the sailors ashore.

The *Music* was nowhere in sight. Wyeth saw a little steamer, the *D. A. Elliott,* lurking under the guns that poked out from the bluff and he led his comrades to the boat and demanded to see the master. The *Elliott* was armed with one bowgun, a ten-inch Parrot.

"I'm the master," said the first man they met, an old man who limped when he walked. "And you are rightly high and mighty."

Wyeth frowned at the man, then his face beamed. "Rock Bradford. I didn't know you. You've changed." The Missourian offered his hand.

"Yankee bullets will change anybody," Rock said. "Looking for Prent, eh? He's up the Big Black a piece."

"The *Queen*. . . ."

"I know. She came by here last night, so close in that she tickled the beards of our cannoneers. She's heading for the Red."

"How do you know?" Granville asked.

"Common sense," Rock growled. "She's going raiding and we ain't got no boat that can say howdy-do to the *Queen* except the *Webb,* and she's way up at Shreveport." [30]

"We sure could use the *Queen,*" Wyeth said, watching Rock intently. "Her engines would just fit the new *Arkansas.*"

The old riverman fumbled in his pocket until he found his tobacco and he took a bite. "I'm way ahead of you. But what are we going to use to catch her?"

"Sense," Wyeth said. "Once she gets up the Red she'll have to come back some day. We'll waylay her."

"With slingshots?" Rock snorted. "That's crazy. Looks like I'll have to do some thinking for you boys. Old Jim Garocy is piloting the *Queen*. . . ."

"What has that got to do with it?" Granville demanded impatiently.

"Leave him alone, Sim," Ves said.

"Yes," Wyeth suggested. "Leave him alone. Jim Garocy may have a lot to do with it, eh, Rock?"

"Maybe." The old man spat. "I've known Jim, egg and bird, since he first sounded a channel. He knows the lower Red fair to middling. But he can't pilot up around Alexandria. Don't know the stream."

"Yankee sympathizer?" Wyeth asked.

"Now that is a silly question?" Granville was still impatient.

"If he isn't for the enemy why would he be piloting the *Queen?*"

Wyeth frowned at Granville. Rock scratched his dirty beard. "You don't know much about the Mississippi and the way some folks work around here." His tone was friendly, for he was amused at Granville's ignorance. "I can't rightly say that old Jim is for us or against us. He never talked much. Maybe he'll help us. But then again maybe he's gone whole-hog for the Yanks. No telling. But if the *Queen* is aiming to raid way up the Red she'll have to have another pilot. I'm the best Red River pilot there is." He looked around at the men. "That is, I used to be before I went to Texas. I fought out there with Sam Dabney. . . ."

"We know all about that," Wyeth said patiently. "Do you think you can get on the *Queen* as pilot?"

"Maybe." The old man was exasperating. "I've got a cousin who is a tophand Red River pilot, too. George Wood is his name. First cousin. He's on the *Era No. 5.*"

Even Ves was annoyed. "Aw, for God's sakes. Let's get going. Let's find Prent Oliver and get the *Music* and go after Little Boy Blue."

"Commander Oliver ain't going to let you take the *Music,*" Rock said. "She's his flagship and he ain't got no business in Louisiana waters."

"Then what is your idea?" Wyeth asked.

"Take it easy," Rock said. "Come on up to my texas and have some coffee. This here boat is mine."

Granville and Ves started to protest, but caught the look in Wyeth's eyes and followed him to the texas of the *D. A. Elliott.* Rock poured coffee and addressed the Missourian as one riverman to another. "Use your head, Woodward. Little Boy Blue is after shipping. Now up the Red a piece is Gordon's Landing. The Confeds have a battery there. Every steamer along the lower Red will run for the landing to seek protection. Sooner or later the *Queen* will head for the landing to gobble up those boats. . . ."

"I see it," Ves said. "Then the *Webb* comes down and gets the *Queen.*"

Rock's annoyance was apparent. "Your friends ain't rightly bright, Woodward. Ellet is going to duck the *Webb.* He can outrun her and he ain't going to get caught up the Red and let the *Webb* corner him. Besides, the *Webb* is a Louisiana boat. If she takes the *Queen* you'll never get your engines."

"I see all of that," Granville said respectfully. "We have got to seize the *Queen* and claim her as a prize."

"Now you're talking," Rock said. "Let me and Woodward run this thing."

"That suits us," Ves said.

"Then what's holding us?" Rock said and went ashore and got clearance papers for Alexandria. When he came back aboard there was a sour grin on his face. "Prent won't be back for days so we'll have to get going without seeing him. The *Queen* captured the *De Soto* last night with twenty thousand bushels of coal."

They made the mouth of the Red River the next night and came to a landing and no sooner had they tied up than a swarm of Confederate guerrillas came aboard. They had been firing on the *Queen* most of the afternoon. The Federal raider had captured another Confederate, the *Berwick Bay*, near the mouth of the Red and, after burning her, had proceeded up the river.

Rock and Wyeth chose twenty-five of the guerrillas as sharp-shooters and signed them on, and then the *Elliott,* running without lights, nosed up the Red on the trail of the *Queen* and her tender. They stopped at every plantation landing and got news. The *Queen* was raiding right through the heart of enemy country, dashing to landings and destroying all supplies, and when she encountered boats she overwhelmed them, paroled the crews and burned the craft. Her landing parties had destroyed every telegraph wire leading to Alexandria and Shreveport. The *Webb* was at Shreveport, unaware that the *Queen* was down river spreading destruction. Horsemen were dispatched to Alexandria and Shreveport with pleas for help, but meanwhile the *Queen* went about her business, methodically cutting the Confederate communications to shreds.

The *Elliott* reached the mouth of the Atchafalaya less than four hours after the Queen had passed that way. The raider had been fired on from the Atchafalaya as Confederate guerrillas were operating in that vicinity. Rock went ashore for news and was panting when he returned. "The *Queen* has gone down the Atchafalaya. They captured the *Era No. 5* about an hour ago. God loves us." Quickly he signaled for full speed and passed the tributary's mouth, getting his boat between the *Queen* and Gordon's Landing.

"Now what?" Wyeth asked. "Aren't you going to try to get aboard the *Queen* as pilot?"

"T'ain't necessary." Rock was jubilant. "Ellet put a prize crew on the *Era* and has her in tow because she is loaded with corn. He paroled every man on the *Era* except one. . . ."

"Your cousin?" Wyeth was beginning to understand.

"That's right. He took George Wood prisoner to do his piloting in the place of Jim Garocy. He put Jim on the *De Soto*. George has the *Queen* by her helm. And he'll trap Little Boy Blue. The Yanks may have a pistol at his head, but old George'll think of something. Let's go to Gordon's Landing. Little Boy Blue has made his first mistake."

And so he had. Things had moved too well for Charles Rivers Ellet and he was over-confident. He had run by Vicksburg and had destroyed Confederate shipping and supplies as far down the Mississippi as Port Hudson, and as far up the Red as the mouth of the Atchafalaya. He should have turned back then, but he had word of Confederate supplies down the tributary and of several steamers at Gordon's Landing. Surely he could get to the landing and take the ships, then retreat before the *Webb* could come down from Shreveport. So he went down the Atchafalaya, burning supplies at every landing. Partisans fired on him and in retaliation Ellet destroyed every house, barn and sugar mill between the mouth of the Atchafalaya and Semmesport. He captured a wagon train and destroyed seventy barrels of beef, nineteen pouches of mail and a wagon of salt. George Wood, working at the point of a pistol, piloted the *Queen* on the Atchafalaya raid and then brought her back to the Red. The *De Soto* and the *Era* were in the *Queen's* wake.

Back at the mouth of the Atchafalaya, Little Boy Blue learned from Union sympathizers that the *Elliott* had passed, heading for Gordon's Landing and the security of the Confederate battery there.

"Is the *Elliott* armed?" Ellet asked his informers.

"No," he was told. "She has cotton aboard." They hadn't seen the Parrot gun or the three sailors who were manning her behind the bales.

George Wood smiled when he heard the *D. A. Elliott* was thereabouts.

Ellet called a conference in his pilothouse, and his officers agreed that they should attempt to silence the battery at Gordon's Landing and carry the Confederate ships at anchor there. Three newspaper correspondents, assigned to cover the raid, attended the conference.

They were Finley Anderson of the *New York Herald,* Mr. Bodman of the *Chicago Tribune,* and Joseph McCullagh of the *Cincinnati Commercial.* They had been with Ellet since he left Vicksburg and their stories of the raid were thrilling the North. They, too, agreed that Gordon's Landing should be the next goal.

Little Boy Blue gave the order to George Wood and the Confederate prisoner wheeled the *Queen* to larboard and headed her up the Red. Ellet rang slow bell and the raider moved cautiously. It began raining then, a slow, teasing rain that threatened any minute to turn into a storm. Gordon's Landing was eighty miles from the mouth of the Red and sixty miles from the mouth of the Atchafalaya. Vicksburg and Porter's fleet were more than a hundred miles away. Ellet was alone. Only a brave man or a fool would undertake to go further up the Red. And Little Boy Blue wasn't a fool.

Back at Vicksburg, Porter was worried. He hadn't heard from Ellet for several days. So he sent orders to Captain George Brown of the ironclad *Indianola* to run by the Vicksburg batteries and go to the mouth of the Red, and there give aid to Ellet if he still was afloat.

The *Indianola* slipped by the Confederate fortress and reached the Red River the same day that the *Queen* left the Atchafalaya for Gordon's Landing.

A storm, blowing away the winter of 1863, was raging when the *Elliott* arrived at Gordon's Landing, dipped her flag to the army garrison there and cut for the opposite bank instead of joining the frightened steamers that were hovering under protection of the landing's battery. Rock backed his boat into a sluice and his crew, including the three gunners, went ashore and began cutting reeds, canes and branches.

They covered the *Elliott* with camouflage and from a few hundred feet away the little steamer looked like a part of the shore. The cotton bales were moved from around the Parrot gun and branches were piled about the piece. Then the men took their ease and waited while the storm mounted in fury, bringing a bombardment of thunder and a deluge of warm rain.

Ellet brought his *Queen* and the two escorts slowly up the Red until Gordon's Landing was raised and then Ellet ordered his ship cleared for action. Every gun on the *Queen* was loaded with solid shot and the sharpshooters were massed near the bow. The *Queen* gave no heed to the covey of merchant ships cringing behind the Confederate guns. Little Boy Blue knew that if he silenced the guns he could pick the cargo ships like ripe berries. His lookout studied the opposite bank and reported nothing over there except a sluice and a canebrake.

The Federal commander instructed the *De Soto* and the *Era* to anchor downstream out of range and then he gave slow bell and the *Queen* moved to the attack. Ellet fired the first shot, seeking the range. The battery at Gordon's Landing answered and the duel was on. It was five P.M. Ellet, cautioning George Wood that disobedience meant death, told the pilot to take the outside of a bend and approach the battery from an angle. The Confederate prisoner gripped his wheel and nodded.

Across the river, Wyeth's sharp eyes watched the *Queen* creep in, her guns barking as she sought an opening. Rock was watching Wyeth from the pilothouse and Granville was watching him from the Parrot. Then Wyeth motioned to the Englishman and a hot shot was slipped into the cannon. The *Queen* was less than a quarter of a mile away.

Rock reached for his bell. His hand was trembling. Wyeth gave the signal and Rock sounded slow bell forward and then full speed forward. The crew of the *Elliott* began ripping the cane from around the Parrot and Granville lined her up. The *Elliott* leaped from the sluice and headed for the *Queen*.

"Oh Louisa!" Ves shouted.

Granville laid his first hot shot into the *Queen's* gundeck and the cotton bales began blazing. Then he put another into the pilothouse.

The *Queen* turned to meet the new challenge and exposed her starboard to the land battery and took a fearful pounding. Ellet was dumbfounded. "We're trapped!" he shouted. "The Rebs have an armed ship up there. Let's get out of here."

The *Elliott* was bearing down and George Wood, recognizing the steamer, cut the *Queen* inside the bend and into the eddies.

"Turn her around," Ellet commanded.

"I am," George Wood said. "I want to get out of here, too."

Little Boy Blue didn't know the Red River. His ship was at the mercy of her pilot. George Wood leaned over and opened a window of the pilothouse explaining that he needed more visibility. He took one glance at the guard holding the pistol and then wheeled his helm hard over. The sandbar wasn't visible, but the pilot knew it was there. The *Queen's* nose was piled high on the bar and the blow threw every man off balance except Wood. He fouled the rudder by spinning his wheel too hard and then he jumped through the open window onto the texas, thence overboard.

Ellet was the first to recover from the surprise. The *Queen* was hard aground and helpless and the *Elliott* was pouring hot shots into the raider from one side and the land battery was pounding her from the other.

Two steampipes were severed and the engine room crew fled their posts and many of them dived into the river and were drowned. Smoke and steam filled the pilothouse and Ellet stuffed a woolen rag in his mouth to prevent suffocation. He was the last man out of the pilothouse and herded his men on the roof of the hurricane deck. "Abandon ship," he said calmly.

The three newspaper men shoved cotton bales into the river, then jumped in and clung to them. Twenty-two men refused to leave the *Queen* in spite of Ellet's orders.

"Surrender her," the men demanded.

"I'll not do it," Ellet said. "Get off and we will blow her up."

The *Elliott* was less than two hundred feet away, throwing shells so fast that the Federals thought the Parrot was a battery.

Ellet made one more effort to persuade his men to jump and when they refused again he jerked off his coat, dived into the Red and climbed aboard a cotton bale, trusting it to float him downstream to the *De Soto* or *Era*. Lightning was playing around the *Queen* when he last saw her and she was burning despite the rain.

He didn't see his men run up the white flag and didn't see the *Elliott* come alongside. Wyeth was the first Confederate aboard the prize. He snatched the Battle Flag from the *Elliott* and jumped onto the *Queen* just as the Rebel's bow scraped the raider's larboard. Ves and Granville were right behind him, covering the Union sailors. Wyeth ran down the white flag and ran up the Battle Flag, then shouted, "We claim this prize of war for the Confederate States Navy, Department of Mississippi."

"Louisa and the babes!" Ves shouted.

Rock put his crew and the guerrillas to extinguishing the blaze on the *Queen* and Wyeth began patching the steam pipes. The repair work was progressing rapidly when the army commander from Gordon's Landing came to the *Queen* and was informed that the ship was a prize for the Navy.

The commander didn't know what to make of that. He didn't understand such things. "Maybe you're right," he said. "We'll have to leave that up to General Richard Taylor, Commander of the Western District of Louisiana. He's up at Alexandria."

"We'll leave it to a court of inquiry," Granville said.

They didn't argue the question then as there was too much to be done. The prisoners were put aboard the *Elliott* and a line was run from that steamer to the *Queen*. George Wood came back aboard and after accepting congratulations took over the *Queen's* wheel and she was rocked and tugged off of the bar and into safe water.

Even a casual examination convinced Wyeth and Rock that she couldn't be repaired there so it was agreed to move her up to Alexandria.

Meanwhile, Colonel Ellet and the survivors of the disaster reached the *De Soto,* and Jim Garocy, the taciturn pilot, stood for downstream while the shocked Federals went to the boiler room to get dry. The *Era* followed the *De Soto*. Ellet's only concern was to get to the Mississippi.

Darkness had come and the storm was increasing. Then from the shores came the crackle of rifle fire as guerrillas opened up on the *De Soto* and *Era*. Ellet tried to remain calm and succeeded by his sheer force of will. The other survivors, wet, bedraggled and frightened, were numb. Some of them wanted to surrender to the guerrillas. Ellet threatened to shoot the first man who surrendered. They had no guns and no food. The storm cut their vision and there they were, a handful of men, moving through the heart of enemy territory, trusting to a pilot whose loyalty was not known.

At the first big bend, the *De Soto* ran aground. Jim Garocy apologized and blamed the storm. He got the boat afloat again only after some guerrillas had sprinkled her with rifle fire.

Three miles further downstream she unshipped her rudder. Again Garocy was sorry.

"What's up?" Ellet demanded. "Are you trying to delay our escape so the *Webb* can come down?"

"I'm sorry," the pilot said. "It's a bad night, sir."

Ellet put him under arrest. The *De Soto* was unmanageable, rudderless. Ellet rigged a sweep and tried to keep the *De Soto* under-way. She drifted for fifteen miles, sometimes head on and at other times stern on, swinging in the channel. There was nothing to do but scuttle her and Ellet ordered his men to the *Era* and blew up the tender.

The only food on the *Era* was dry corn and Ellet posted guards over it and refused it to his men. He tried to explain. "We've got to get out of here. There is not enough coal on this boat to make a fast run to the Mississippi. Even then we will have to get up to Vicks-burg or down to New Orleans. The corn is fuel."

The coal gave out before morning and Ellet began feeding corn to the ship's fires. He had no pilot he could trust, so he took the helm himself and tried to feel his way through strange waters. He ran his ship aground at Union Point and Federal sympathizers there told him that the *Webb* was coming.

Still he would not give up. It took three hours to float the *Era* and she was making only channel speed. Her men were hungry and panicky. Little Boy Blue strapped his pistol to his waist and stood at the wheel. He was wearing only a pair of drenched trousers and was barefoot.

In desperation, he tied up and sought cordwood for his boilers. He instructed his carpenter to rig a spar and sail and then they got underway again. The wood was waterlogged and wouldn't burn. Still he wouldn't surrender or abandon his boat.

They passed Ellis' cliffs, and, through the rain, the lookout saw black smoke soaring above the cypress and around a bend. It might be anything. It was coal smoke. Ellet armed his men with sticks. He gave the wheel over to his carpenter with instructions to hold her as she was and went to the bow of the *Era*. Calmly he addressed his crew. "If that's a Rebel we will board her. Fight for arms. I will not surrender." He took out his pistol and waited until his ship rounded the bend. And there was the *Indianola,* her Union flag wet and heavy. Her guns were in battery and she was waiting for the *Webb*.

Ellet couldn't speak. His crew began cheering and the *Era* settled beside the *Indianola*. The little band was fed and clothed. They hadn't eaten for thirty-six hours and were almost naked. Ellet explained to Captain George Brown of the *Indianola* what had hap-pened and urged him to put about and return to Porter's fleet.

George Brown ignored him. He thought his *Indianola* could

handle the *Webb* and any other boat that got in his way. His ship
was 174 feet long, with a fifty-foot beam. Her sides of oak were
thirty-two inches thick and covered with three-inch iron plates. The
Indianola's decks also were plated and her coal bunkers were seven
feet thick alongside her boilers. She had seven engines, two side-
wheels and two propellers. Her power was tremendous when she
used her paddle wheels and her propellers. She had all the latest
gadgets, an engine to work her capstans, another to supply water
and work the bilge and five pumps. She had five boilers and an elab-
orate system of communication between the pilothouse and every
part of the ship. The armament included two eleven-inch Dahlgrens
and two nine-inch Columbiads.

Small wonder Captain George Brown was confident. He gave Ellet
enough coal to run the *Era* back up the river to Porter's fleet. "Run
the Vicksburg batteries at night," George Brown told Little Boy
Blue. "And tell Admiral Porter that I will fight the *Webb* if they
dare send her after me."

"They'll dare," Ellet said, and went back to the *Era* and began the
long trip upstream.

Little Boy Blue was miserable. Already horsemen had reached
Grant's and Porter's base near Vicksburg with news of his defeat.
The praise of the North turned to bitter denunciation. He had lost
the *Queen of the West*. None remembered then what he had accomplished. None seemed to realize that single-handed he had disrupted
Confederate communications along the Red River, and that the one
wagon of salt he had destroyed was worth loss of the *Queen*. Little
Boy Blue was in disgrace. A nineteen-year-old boy had risen to the
pinnacle of fame over night and the next day was in the mire of
censure. He had done what no Federal ever had done, but they
forgot that. He had lost his ship, and so was he judged.

Wyeth brought the captured *Queen of the West* to a landing at
Alexandria alongside the *Webb* which had come down from Shreveport on word that the Federals were raiding the lower valley. An
army repair crew was sent aboard the prize and Granville watched
them with misgivings. Then came Captain James McCloskey with

orders from the Department of Louisiana to take command of the prize. McCloskey was an army man.

Granville filed a formal protest with McCloskey and Ves stormed in indignation. Wyeth began preparing his plea for the Board of Inquiry that he assumed would sit for settlement of the claims for the raider. McCloskey was polite and explained that he didn't understand the procedure. "All I know," he said, "is that General Taylor told me to take over."

"This boat is ours," Wyeth said.

"Perhaps your claim is just," McCloskey said. "That will have to be decided later."

None of the gunners left the *Queen* even for a minute while she was being repaired. McCloskey was happy to have them aboard because they were experts with naval armament. "But I don't understand," he said. "You three men were on leave and were coming to Alexandria. You are here now, so why not enjoy your leave?"

"We are staying on this boat," Ves said. "We took her and we aim to have her."

The case was submitted to General Taylor and he passed it along to Richmond. His position was that the *Queen* was the army's prize because she was captured in his district. The case was pending when word reached Alexandria that Ellet and his *Era* had rejoined Porter, but that the *Indianola* was down near the mouth of the Red, itching for a battle.

So the case of the prize was left in abeyance as there was fighting to be done. Major J. L. Brent was sent to Alexandria to fit an expedition against the *Indianola* and he took supreme command of the *Webb* and the *Queen*. He put two guns on the little steamer *Dr. Batey,* equipped the *Grand Era* as a tender and got his four craft ready to tackle the *Indianola.*

The three gunners from the Mississippi Department, still refusing to leave the *Queen,* were assigned to battle stations aboard the prize. Rock Bradford and George Wood were instructed to take the *Elliott* and the prisoners to Shreveport. They bade Wyeth and his friends goodby and watched the little squadron drop downstream, seeking the *Indianola.*

Captain George Brown moved his ironclad up the Red. It never entered his head, apparently, that the Rebels had repaired the

Queen or that they were able to outfit a flotilla at Alexandria. He was ready for the *Webb,* but when he saw four ships bearing down he turned and headed for the Mississippi. Just why an ironclad should run from four wooden boats was a mystery that only George Brown understood. Ellet would have fought. And Isaac N. Brown would have welcomed the chance to match an ironclad against the *Webb* and the *Queen* and the two other little steamers. But not George Brown. He reached the Mississippi and began picking up cotton. He seemed to forget that the *Queen* and the *Webb* were faster boats. . . .

At Acklin's Landing, the *Indianola* was forty-eight hours ahead of the Confederates, and at Natchez was only twenty-five hours ahead. The Confederates knew they could overhaul the *Indianola* at any time and decided to fight at night. They reached Grand Gulf at sunset on February 25th, making two miles upstream to the *Indianola's* one.

They shielded their lights and watched the moon. A veil of clouds moved across the sky and the Confederates crept up to Palmyra Island.

The *Indianola* was inching along, her lights blazing, and she was in the short channel, the narrow way between the island and the bank. She not only had run into a hole, but had pulled the hole in after her.

"There she is," Wyeth called and Ves rammed a solid shot into the gun. "Oh Louisa!"

It was 9:40 P.M. and Granville touched off the gun. The *Indianola* was so surprised that she swung to, and lay motionless. Then she doused her lights. The *Queen* hurled a salvo and darted for the flank, came about and aimed her bow for the ironclad. Then the *Webb* opened from the other side and churned in. The *Indianola* fired one round just as the *Queen* rammed her. Granville laid a solid shot into the *Indianola's* pilothouse and the *Queen* backed off. Then the *Webb* ripped in, ramming her beak into the helpless Federal and raking her with cannister. The *Queen* rammed again, reversed and gave the *Webb* another chance.

Suddenly the *Indianola* came to life and began firing. Her two eleven-inch Dahlgrens spat at the *Webb* as the *Queen* surged in for the third time. The Yanks brought two guns to bear on the *Queen,* but Granville silenced one and the other exploded. Then the *Webb* and the *Queen* put their noses to the ironclad and began grinding her to bits. Plates were ripped from the Federal and she was listing to her port. The two Rebels backed off for another go, and the *Indianola,* free for a minute, managed to raise a little speed and ran down the river. The *Dr. Batey* and the *Grand Era* hove into sight and then Captain George Brown struck his colors and surrendered his ship, lock, stock and barrel. The ironclad was leaking badly but still was afloat. It was all over in less than an hour and the Confederates, for the first time since the Battle of Memphis, had a real flotilla on the river, the *Indianola,* the *Queen of the West,* the *Webb* and half a dozen armed steamers.

Louisa and the babes! The *Arkansas* was avenged. And there in the *Queen* were two engines for the new *Arkansas.*

The *Dr. Batey* was sent to Vicksburg for workers to repair the *Indianola,* and the battered prize was towed to the bank. Stocks were built around her and it was reckoned that her repairs would take at least a month. Her guns were dismounted and her engines were taken apart to be overhauled. The *Queen* needed a few repairs, too, and Wyeth begged Major Brent, Commander of the flotilla, to let him take her up to Vicksburg, knowing that if he got the ship that far then engines for the new *Arkansas* would be assured. "You have the *Indianola,*" he said. "Let us take our prize to our base."

"We need the *Queen* as a work ship for the *Indianola,*" Brent said. "Besides, Richmond hasn't decided who gets the *Queen.* Wait until we get the ironclad in shape to fight and then we will see what we can see."

"Perhaps the major will relinquish his claim to the *Queen,*" Wyeth said hopefully.

"Perhaps," Major Brent said.

Porter, biting his mustache at his base north of Vicksburg, was fit to be tied when he heard that the *Indianola* has been captured. He thought the raids on the Red River had been a failure. He had sent down two of his best ships and the Confederates had taken both of them. Why weren't they scuttled? Porter raged and in his disgust wrote the Navy Department: "This has been the most humiliating affair that has occurred during the Rebellion and it almost disheartens me. I had a right to expect that the commanders of the *Queen* and the *Indianola,* carrying twelve guns and having passed all the batteries at Vicksburg and Grand Gulf, could manage to take such an old steamer as the *Webb*, or else have the wisdom and patriotism to destroy their vessels, even if they had to go with them."

It was a severe indictment, an unworthy charge against Little Boy Blue. But Porter was angry. The Confederates had outwitted him at every turn and he was weary of being outwitted. He sent off the message to Washington and sat on his flagship, mulling and fuming. Then there came to him one of those inspirations that set him apart from the run-of-the-mill men who were running the United States Navy. He sent for several Missourians and Kentuckians in his command and told them, "Take a week's leave. Go ashore and drop stories here and there about our new monitor."

"What new monitor, sir?"

"She is coming down," Porter said. "She is three hundred feet long and mounts twenty guns. We're going to send her by Vicksburg and watch the Rebels jump."

So the tale was planted. A monster was coming down the river. The Yankees boasted about her in sutlers' headquarters and in the bars as far north as Memphis. The Negroes took up the story and enlarged it and it reached the Confederates at Vicksburg, then at Grand Gulf and Natchez. The repair crew on the *Indianola* heard the tale and was alarmed. Major Brent, frantic with fear that the monitor might catch the *Indianola* disarmed, drove his men night and day. A monster was coming and the *Indianola* must be ready to fight.

Granville was skeptical at first. So was Wyeth. But Ves believed the fantastic report. "Three hundred feet," Granville mused, "and twenty guns. If there is such a ship and she gets by Vicksburg she can blow the *Indianola* and the *Queen* out of the river. But it may be a trick."

"Yes," Wyeth said. "It may be. But we'd better have the *Indianola* ready to fight, or at least to run. She's a dead duck as she is."

Porter, aware that the Confederates were jittery, got a huge old flatboat, equipped it with two wooden towers and armed it with twenty Quaker guns, pine logs that poked from portholes. The "monitor's" funnel was a pile of pork barrels and the pilothouse was an old privy. He waited for a dark night when the moon was hidden by clouds and then he towed his dummy around Tuscumbia

Bend and cut it adrift in the channel. The "monitor," a deadly looking thing in the darkness, began moving by the fortress. The lookout spotted it and shouted, "The monitor!"

Every river gun in Vicksburg opened on the enemy, riddling the dummy. But the flatboat and the privy moved by, wallowing in the channel, unmanned, unarmed—a hoax.

The moon came out and the shadows made the dummy look longer than it was, and by the time it floated past the Warrenton batteries the Confederates were sure that the most powerful ironclad in existence had run their guns and was heading for Red River.

Word of the approach spread like the wind down the Mississippi and the Rebels working on the disabled *Indianola* labored desperately to get the prize out of the stocks and into the channel, intending to tow her to safety. The big ship had settled in the mud near the bank just enough to block any rescue attempts. So there was only one thing to do. The "monitor" was approaching Palmyra Island, moving in the darkness, hugging the channel.

A conference was called aboard the *Queen of the West* and all agreed that the *Indianola* must be destroyed. Even Granville was convinced then. "There is nothing in the world to prevent the monitor from capturing the *Indianola*," he said. "We haven't got a gun in place."

Wyeth said, "Maybe we can hold it off with the *Queen* until we get the *Indianola* afloat and down river. . . ."

"No," said the other Confederates. "We'd lose the *Queen*, too. The *Indianola* is doomed. Let's save the *Queen*."

"I'm not so sure," Wyeth protested. "I can't understand how such a big ship got by Vicksburg. Let's wait until daylight. . . ."

"That will be too late," one of the Confederate officers said and Granville agreed. "That monitor will be on top of us in an hour or so. We can't defend the *Indianola* and we mustn't let the Yanks recapture her."

"I suppose you're right," Wyeth said.

The Missourian helped his comrades and the other Confederates lay powder from the *Indianola's* magazines to the top deck. They piled rich pine knots on the deck. The "monitor" was seen then, moving slowly north of the island, swaying as though preparing for an attack. For the only time in his life, Wyeth's keen sight failed him. He studied the craft in the moonlight. "She's a whopper, all right," he said slowly. "And her commander has nerve. He's running without lights. He's creeping up on us."

At a nod from the superior officer on deck, Wyeth threw a torch among the pine knots and the men scrambled over board and onto the *Queen*. Flames leaped from the *Indianola* and the *Queen* backed away, turned downstream and crowded on all speed to escape the "monitor" in case it tried pursuit.

The flames reached the *Indianola's* powder and the ship was blown apart. "Anyway," Ves said. "The Yanks can't use her either. Wonder why that monitor doesn't open fire?"

"We are out of range," Granville said, "and there's no need to waste shot on the *Indianola*."

The *Queen* reached Grand Gulf at dawn and crept under the guns there, safe from the flatboat with the privy pilothouse. All morning they waited, hoping the "monitor" would appear within range of the Grand Gulf batteries. Then it was decided to slip back upstream and take a looksee at the monster. The *Indianola* still was burning, and on the northern tip of Palmyra Island, awash and dilapidated, was the flatboat, rocking gently in the bright morning sun.

Granville was the first to realize what had happened, and he actually laughed. He laughed to relieve the strain. "There is the monitor, gentlemen. Porter tricked us."

"My God and Louisa," Ves said. "A dummy!"

Wyeth was too shocked to speak.

The *Queen* went alongside the flatboat and again Granville laughed, for on the privy was a huge sign: "Deluded Rebels, cave in."

No one said anything for several minutes, but just looked from one to the other, then at the dummy, then down the river at the skeleton of the *Indianola*. Finally Ves said, "I wonder how this will be explained to the Department. We destroyed the best prize of the war to save her from a privy."

Wyeth really was sick, so sick that he walked away to suffer alone. Granville accepted it philosophically; the fortunes of war. Of course, he, too, was chagrined. His first thought was that people would laugh at him. Already he could hear the men at Yazoo City and Vicksburg teasing him. The Privy Navy, they would say. Granville was thinking of his pride. He had fought around the world and yet here in the wilderness a damn Yankee admiral had made a fool of him. Wyeth was thinking about the loss of a good ship, and the fate of the *Queen*.

He hesitated to mention the *Queen* to Major Brent, but there was nothing else to do. Their leave was running out and he and Granville and Ves were expected back at Yazoo City. So he approached Major Brent and said, "The *Queen*, sir. May we take her to Vicksburg?"

"Of course not," Brent said. "She goes back to Louisiana. To the Army. Now that the *Indianola* is destroyed we must have something to show for all this trouble."

"But, Major . . ."

"No buts about it, Woodward. Richmond is deciding the case. If you care to return with me and await a decision, then all right. But the *Queen* is leaving for the Red River. Immediately."

Wyeth kept his temper and so did Granville, but Ves began cursing. His two comrades got the Cajan ashore before he talked himself into trouble. Major Brent told them he would take them as far up the river as Warrenton, but they declined the invitation. Brent explained that perhaps Richmond would award the *Queen* to the Navy and that he gladly would return the boat. "Meanwhile," he said, "she will be with us at Alexandria."

The three gunners did not wave farewell to the *Queen* and her crew. They sat on the bank and watched the prize, their prize, move into midstream and hie away for the Red. "We'll never see her again," Ves said. "Once the army gets its hands on anything, that ends it." [31]

Disheartened and disgusted, they waited there most of the day until a north-bound steamer came up the river. It was their old friend the *Grand Duke of the Inland Sea* and they signaled her and got passage to Vicksburg. They tarried in the fortress only long enough to hear jibes about the Privy Navy and then pushed on to Yazoo City. Work there was at a standstill and they found Isaac N. Brown on the *Star of the West*.

Wyeth went to Brown and Granville went to his Dolly. The big gun was in tiptop shape, but the commander was spiritless and moody. "I know," he told Wyeth. "I know all about it."

"It is possible, sir, that Richmond will give us the *Queen* after all."

"No," Brown said. "The Navy Department has decided that the army gets the prize." He looked at his three gunners, then to the yard where the new *Arkansas* was resting in her stocks, an unfinished thing, ugly and helpless. "Thank you, boys," the commander said. "Thank you for trying."

Granville and Wyeth were too upset to reply, but Ves said, "That's all right, Cap'n. We'll finish the damn boat. Frome will get more iron to us and we'll get engines."

Brown's eyes were hollow and he turned them on the men. "The Yanks have come again. This time they are coming down Yazoo Pass." [32]

"Where in the world is that?" Granville asked.

Yazoo Pass was more than two hundred miles north of the mouth of the Yazoo River and Vicksburg. In years gone by, there was a waterway from the Mississippi River through a string of lakes and bayous into the upper Yazoo River. But the Pass had been closed by levees, and cypress and underbrush choked the bayous and lakes. It was Porter who suggested cutting the levees at Yazoo Pass and allowing the Mississippi to flood the old waterway. Then, perhaps, gunboats and transports could work their way through the Pass, eventually into the Yazoo, thence down to Vicksburg's backdoor. The levees were blown in February. An army under General Ross followed a flotilla under Commander Watson Smith into the flooded bayous. . . .

"So they're coming from way up there?" Ves said. "If they ever get into the Yazoo, then our shipyard will go. And they can flank Vicksburg."

"That's right," Brown said.

"What are we doing to stop them?" Wyeth asked.

"Nothing," Brown smiled. "Nothing at all. You should see what they're undertaking. Their boats are making less than a mile a day. They have to dredge and cut timber almost every inch of the way. Grant is still trying tricks and he'll never take Vicksburg by tricks."

"How far have they progressed?" Granville said.

"They have reached the Coldwater. Half of the men are sick and Watson Smith is having a fit. I've known him a long time. He is not emotionally fitted for such work. They'll be in the Tallahatchie in about two weeks."

"Then the Yazoo. . . ." Ves was alarmed.

"Yes, then the Yazoo," Brown said and he still was smiling. "But there is Fort Pemberton. They will have to get by the fort. So we will just sit tight at Fort Pemberton and let them come to us."

"We?" Wyeth said.

"I am taking the *Star of the West* up to the fort. We will need the Dahlgren and two of you men to work her."

"Two?" Granville frowned. "We all work together, sir."

"One of you must go to Natchez. I haven't heard from Frome in weeks."

Ves started to speak, then turned to Granville and watched the Englishman. Wyeth, thinking of Laurel, watched Granville, too. The Englishman smiled at the Missourian and he, too, was silent.

"Which one will go?" Brown said. "It must be Granville or Woodward as you two men know the situation down there."

Ves' eyes had narrowed to pinpoints and they burned into Granville. Wyeth opened his mouth to volunteer, and then he swallowed his words, waiting for Granville to say something. The Englishman twisted his mustache and knew what they were thinking. Sharon and whiskey. But Laurel was in Natchez this time, so he said calmly, "I prefer to go with my Dolly. With my gun and Ves."

The Cajan looked away. Wyeth stared at Granville and the man smiled at him.

"Then you for Natchez, Woodward?" Brown said.

"Yes, sir. And thank you, sir. Miss MacKenzie is there. . . ."

"And Keith Alexander," Brown said. "Stay out of his way. I mean it. Don't let him provoke you. Don't even see him if you can avoid it. If any iron is around Natchez, get it. And God bless you." He gave his hand to Wyeth, then went to the pilothouse of the *Star of the West*.

Granville and Ves went ashore with Wyeth. The Cajan was very happy, not because his friend was going away even to see his sweetheart, but because Granville had behaved as he had.

They helped Wyeth pack his gear and between the two of them they managed to outfit him and make him rather presentable. Then Granville suggested he stop in Vicksburg to get the Wellington boots that were left there the year before. "And my gray trousers,"

Granville said. "And my silk waistcoat and beaver hat. Take them, Wyeth. Dress your best for Laurel. Mrs. Simpson can cut the clothes to fit you."

"I'll do it," Wyeth said. "All but the boots. They won't fit."

"My watch is there, too," Granville said. "Take it. And the chain that the French government gave me. . . ."

"No. The watch and the boots stay in Vicksburg. I'll be dressed up enough without them."

"Give our best to Laurel and old man MacKenzie," Ves said, still not mentioning Sharon in consideration of Granville's feelings. "And Gar. Tell him hello for me."

Granville closed Wyeth's seabag. "You'll see Sharon?" He tried to appear unconcerned and felt Ves looking at him again.

"Of course. Any message?"

"Tell her I am sober," Granville said. "And that I don't like it."

"Tell her we are winning the war fast," Ves said, "and if the Yanks give out of privies we'll end this thing by summer. Take care of yourself, Wyeth."

"Stay away from that Alexander," Granville said sternly. "He is a pistol man."

Ves said, "Don't do nothing reckless unless you send for us."

The Cajan embraced the Missourian and Granville offered his hand. Then they looked at each other and Wyeth wanted to thank him, but the Englishman just shook his head and smiled. The two gunners went back aboard the *Star of the West* and she kicked off and moved up the Yazoo for Fort Pemberton. Ves and Granville were standing by the Dolly when the boat disappeared around a bend.

Wyeth slung his bag over his shoulder and went into Yazoo City to get a ride to Vicksburg. He felt very alone, and then he thought of Laurel and his head and heart were light. His steps, too.

Chapter Seventeen

W YETH felt like a Natchez nabob, a planter's son just back from a season in Charleston or New Orleans. Granville's expensive trousers fit him perfectly, thanks to Mrs. Simpson's skillful needle. And he had silk next to his skin, a new experience. His beaver hat was at a jaunty angle and he felt reckless and gay, even devilish. Spring was in his blood.

But he was riding a mule, a bony mule that had given its strength to the artillery. It was the only mount available in Vicksburg. The young Missourian didn't dare enter Natchez on a mule and was thinking what he must do as his mount, too broken to jog, walked down the almost abandoned Natchez Trace, which was only two wagon ruts with weeds between. Commerce generally used the Port Gibson road, but Wyeth had taken the Trace because it was seldom used.

He had eaten well that morning and he felt clean inside and out. A river breeze rustled his waistcoat and the land was bursting with life; redbuds and red birds, blue haze and blue jays. This was the South he loved. The South of Spring and yellow rivers and the sheer strength of things predestined to grow. Nature was drunk with her own beauty and the earth was a conglomeration of sounds and colors and smells. Even the river, forgetting its age and dignity, tried to be coltish, like and old man teasing, arousing himself to cut a wingbuck.

The sailor kept trying to think what to do with his mule, but his thoughts always eventually came back to Laurel. And he was ashamed of his thoughts, for Wyeth Woodward was something of a prudish man, a conventional creature with a binding conscience that dominated his behavior and attempted to rule his emotions. A conscience is a terrible thing, a sadistic thing, in the Spring.

He reached a bluff north of Natchez, not far to the east from the subterranean workshop of Frome's organization, and dismounted. Then he looked the mule over carefully, making sure there were no identification marks on the animal. He gripped the mule's bridle and led it down the bluff and into some woods. Then he removed the bridle and the gunny sack that had served as a saddle and buried them. He slapped the animal on the flank and it walked away. Straggling mules were not common, but neither were they rare. Maybe some starving farmer would find the mule and claim it.

Then Wyeth walked back up the bluff and stood by the Trace, hoping a wagon might come that way. He waited for an hour and began walking toward Natchez. He didn't mind the walk. He rather liked it. The earth was spongy and good to his feet and the jasmines were in bloom. There were mockingbirds to echo his whistle and larks and doves to pretend fear when he passed.

The spire of St. Mary's Cathedral was visible to the south when Wyeth stopped under an oak and wiped his face with the big kerchief Laurel had given him. He opened his coat and let the breeze cool him and was ready to move on when he heard the approaching horses. He knew by their sound that they were good horses and he peered up the Trace until they came into view; two spanking white horses pulling a carriage. Wyeth hadn't seen such good horses since the war began. He studied them at a distance and then looked up at the driver, an erect Negro in a tall hat. Wyeth gulped and almost shouted. The driver was Gar. Then he saw the other occupant of the carriage, a woman in a green dress. She was wearing a plumed hat and her parasol was silk.

The carriage swept by him and Gar cut his eyes toward Wyeth and then looked straight ahead. The woman looked at him, too. She frowned slightly, a tiny frown that wrinkled her nose. She actually turned around and stared back at him, then leaned forward and nudged Gar with her parasol. The Wolof checked his team and the woman called back to Wyeth. "Sir! Are you in trouble, sir?"

Wyeth walked to the carriage and bowed. "My horse was stolen last night. A good animal. A Tennessee Walking Horse." He looked up at the woman and there was a catch in his chest where his breath should have been. Surely, she was the most beautiful woman he ever had seen, and he stared at her green eyes and red hair. He wasn't aware that he was staring.

"I am going to Natchez," the woman said. "This is rather unusual, but you are obviously a gentleman."

"Thank you." Wyeth bowed again. "I'm Wyeth Woodward. I'm in the cotton business."

When he looked at her again she was staring at him. "I am Mrs. Keith Alexander. You may share my carriage."

Gar looked back then and Wyeth's foot slipped as he stepped into the carriage. His mouth was dry one second and wet the next. So this was Morna Dabney. He was glad he was wearing such good clothes. She moved to one side of the carriage and he took his seat, not daring to look at her, for he felt that his face was red and that his scar was showing. "I have heard of your husband," he said.

"Most men have," Morna said. "Are you going to Natchez?" She nodded to Gar and the team pranced off.

"Yes, m'am. I buy cotton."

"You said that before." She was smiling at him and Wyeth's muscles tightened when he looked at her.

"Perhaps I will meet your husband. Maybe we can do business." He adjusted his hat and glanced at his shoes and was sorry that they were dusty. He tried not to look her way, but his eyes would not obey his mind. He looked slyly at her cape that was thrown back exposing her arms, and her arms were bare. Her dress was cut low and the curves of her breasts shocked him and he tried to look away, but couldn't.

She knew he was looking at her and she was glad, for Morna enjoyed the stares of men. And this was a personable young man. So she looked closely at him and smiled. She wanted to ask about the bearded man and the man with yellow hair. "Yes," she still was smiling. "You probably will meet my husband if you're in the cotton business. However, he is not in Natchez now."

Wyeth's wit was somewhat dulled by the experience of riding in Keith Alexander's carriage and by his wife, but it was not so dulled that he allowed his curiosity to entrap him. He didn't ask about her husband. Instead, he spoke of casual things and watched the back of Gar's head. Finally, he said, "You have a good driver."

"He knows horses. We were fortunate to find him in such trying times. He is not a slave."

"No?"

"Of course not." She pulled her cape around her shoulders and then opened it again. "Mr. Alexander does not own slaves. Surely you knew that. My father is Hoab Dabney. He is an Abolitionist."

Wyeth looked at her neck and ears, pretending to be looking into her eyes. "I forgot, Mrs. Alexander. I have been away. You cannot expect a man's mind to be at its best in your presence."

Morna was pleased. It was flattering to hear a young man pay her pretty compliments. She was 24, almost a year younger than Wyeth, but she felt older. Being married to a man the age of Keith made her wonder if young men ever again would say pretty things to her. "Your tongue is nimble, Mr. Woodward."

"And never offensive, I pray." He smiled then and Morna felt very young once more.

"I like it," she said boldly. "Are you acquainted in Natchez?"

"I have been there."

"Are you married?"

"No, m'am."

"Perhaps you know some ladies in Natchez?"

Wyeth didn't fumble. He was sure of himself now. So he was not evasive. "I hope to meet some. If I have time. I used to know a young lady from Natchez. . . ."

"Who?" Morna asked quickly.

"A Miss MacKenzie. A Miss Laurel MacKenzie."

He noticed Morna's lips tightening. He didn't know that the MacKenzies were among the people in Natchez who had shunned the Alexanders and that Laurel had given Morna an open insult by refusing to attend a musicale in her honor. "Where did you know her?" Morna asked brusquely, dropping her poise.

"St. Louis. I'm from Missouri and she was in school there. Do you know her?"

"Slightly. She is a rather attractive girl. A chick, but attractive. She has freckles. They are Secesh, you know."

Wyeth sensed the antagonism then. "No, I thought they were neutral. Her father is a merchant, isn't he?"

"Yes. He tries to be neutral. But in his heart he's a Confederate."

"I don't mind," Wyeth laughed. "I buy cotton. I'm not interested in a man's opinions."

She looked at him a long time then, and said slowly, "You sound like my husband. Perhaps you will call at our place. When my husband returns."

Wyeth removed his hat and felt her looking at his chestnut hair. "Your husband knows about me, Mrs. Alexander. I am the man who lost a heap of cotton to some guerrillas. The chances are your husband told you about it, and that you know who I am. . . ."

"Sir!"

Wyeth smiled and looked up at the sunny sky, then over at her. "You are more attractive when you pretend surprise. I always heard that Keith Alexander married the most beautiful woman in Mississippi. But your curiosity belies you intelligence. Yes, you know who I am. A cotton speculator. Being a Missourian, I am exempt from Confederate military duty. And if the Union attempts to draft me. I will buy a substitute. I am a business man, not a soldier."

Morna tilted her head and laughed. It was a merry laugh of genuine amusement. "Yes, I know who you are. I heard about your experience at Grand Gulf. What happened after that?"

"Nothing much," Wyeth shrugged his shoulders. "I was taken to Jackson and released with apologies. I had a permit from the Confederacy to deal in cotton."

She started to ask then about his captor, the bearded man, but feared too much curiosity might warn him. So she closed the subject and they sat in silence until the carriage reached Natchez. Wyeth was not conscious of the stares as they rode down Franklin Street. Morna was, however. And she held her chin high. "Where may I drop you?" she asked.

"At the hotel. And I'm grateful, Mrs. Alexander. I trust I will see you again."

The crowd outside the hotel gawked when he stepped down from the carriage and bade her good day. Gar clucked up the horses and they switched away. Around the corner, Morna glanced back, then leaned toward her driver and said, "Gar, go to Mr. Alexander and tell him that Wyeth Woodward is here."

"Yes, m'am," Gar said slowly. "I'll leave just as soon as I get you home."

Morna settled back in the carriage and was smiling to herself. Keith would be proud of her. So Wyeth Woodward was reckless enough to come to Natchez. And he was such a young man. Handsome, too. He had complimented her so prettily and that convinced her that she still was attractive to young men. It was exciting to be the wife of Keith Alexander. But Keith was away, and Natchez was dull. Morna didn't mind playing with matches as long as she didn't strike them. Those MacKenzies knew him, too. That haughty chick of a Laurel probably would receive him that very night and fawn on him. La, fiddlesticks! What did she know of men? Morna poked Gar with her parasol. "I've changed my mind. Don't go for Mr. Alexander. He will be home when he thinks it wise to come home."

Wyeth didn't glance toward the carriage as it whirled away, but went into the hotel and registered. The clerk he had met previously was not there. He didn't know anyone in the hotel. A dozen eyes followed him when he left the desk and walked outside, thence up Franklin Street. He wanted first to see Laurel. However, he didn't know exactly where her house was. So he headed for Wall MacKenzie's store, walking briskly. It was his intention just to peep in Frome's store, not a suspicious peep, but a naturally curious one. Frome's store was boarded up.

Without realizing it, Wyeth quickened his steps and swung into MacKenzie's store, ready to present himself as a customer and a stranger. It wasn't necessary. There wasn't a customer in the store and Wall looked up from his books, then stepped quickly toward the sailor, his hand outstretched. The little Scotchman was pallid, his face was worn and his eyes looked haunted.

"Laurel." Wyeth said and gripped the man's hand. "How is Laurel? And what happened to Mr. Frome? Gar. . . ."

"One at a time," Wall said and led him back to his office. "Laurel is fine, and will be better when she sees you. Nate is gone."

"Is he in trouble?"

"Maybe not. He left town. The organization it just about dead." Wall reached out and patted Wyeth's arm. " 'yGod. It's good to see you, boy."

"Where is Mr. Frome?"

Wall sat down and motioned for Wyeth to be seated. "We didn't dare write. That Keith Alexander is a bloodhound. Nate is in Lebanon, seeking sanctuary from Hoab Dabney. Alexander is over there, too, trying to get his father-in-law not to give sanctuary to Nate or to any other Confederate. It's a long story."

"Did Mr. Frome run away from Alexander?"

"Nate Frome doesn't run," Wall snapped. "He left to save us. That damn Alexander stayed right on top of him and was getting powerful close to the truth. The truth would involve too many people. Nate's business was ruined. Alexander saw to it that none of the Yankee sympathizers did any business with him, and the Confederate folks haven't got any money. Nate couldn't get goods. He reckoned if he left Alexander might leave the rest of us alone." The old man sighed.

"Go on," Wyeth said, and his scar was blazing.

"So Nate left. His pa and Hoab Dabney's pa were friends, so Hoab let him in. Dabney is rebuilding Lebanon and Nate has a little business at New Hebron. That's Hoab's town. Alexander went over there then to try to talk Hoab out of letting Secesh folks settle in Lebanon. The last I heard was that Dabney said Lebanon is sanctuary for any man, black or white, Secesh or Yankee, who wants to go there and quit fighting."

Wyeth rubbed the back of his hand and stared at the floor. Then he looked up at Wall. "So Mr. Frome left to save you. And Laurel."

"And a hundred other folks."

"Did it work?"

"No." Wall moved his chair closer to Wyeth just because he wanted to be closer to the young man. "Alexander ain't giving up. He's after me now. Oh, I'm in no danger. He hasn't pulled a gun. He's just ruining my business. I haven't had a customer in a week."

"We'll talk about that later, Mr. MacKenzie. And about iron, and the organization. I'm going to stay here until I get some iron for Captain Brown. Now what about Gar?" He told the little Scotchman about the ride in and was surprised when Wall frowned.

"You'll be seeing Gar. Alexander needed a man and Gar got the job. I'm sorry you rode with that woman. It'll be all over town."

"My hands are clean." Wyeth got up. "How do I get to your house?"

He listened closely to the directions and left Wall and began walking up Franklin and out to the MacKenzie place, a modest frame house that sat back from the pike, snug among the trees. Wistaria was in bloom and the trees were heavy with Spanish Moss.

The gravel crunched under Wyeth's feet as he hurried up the walk, hoping every second that Laurel would open the door and run out to meet him. He rattled the door knocker and waited. Then he saw Laurel walking down the hall to the door. She apparently was not surprised when she saw him. He stepped inside quickly, glanced around to be sure they were alone, then moved toward her, to take her in his arms.

But Laurel stood still. Her chin was trembling. He put his hands on her shoulders and she eased into his embrace and began sobbing. "Why did you do it?" she said. "Why did you ride with her?"

Wyeth slipped his hand under her chin and tilted her face. "What nonsense is this?"

She buried her face in his chest. "I heard about it. I heard about it before you got out of her carriage." She attempted to stifle her sobs. "Every old busybody around here is gossiping already." She tried to be angry then, but as he stepped away she clung to him.

Instead of attempting to explain, Wyeth followed a wiser course. He looked hurt and contrite. "Oh, that. I didn't know who she was, Doll. I haven't seen you for months and this is the welcome I get."

Laurel snuggled close to him again and took his arms and put them around her. But he didn't hug her. "I risk my neck to see you, and this is the reception I get," he said. "You know I love you and yet you don't trust me."

"Hush," she said. "Don't say another word. I'm sorry. I didn't mean a thing."

The sailor walked over to a chair and sat down and she stood before him. "Come here and sit by me," he said tenderly.

She tried to sit in his lap, but her hoops interfered so she took his hand and led him to a sofa and then sat beside him, and kissed him and stroked his face. Wyeth was rather proud of himself. Then he felt her body stiffen and she looked up at him. "With honors! Of course, with honors."

"And now what?"

"You will be a lawyer." She was smiling. "I had my mind made up to be angry and before I knew it I was apologizing to you. You are smart, my love."

"You are suspicious, Doll. Now, enough of this. Tell me about yourself. Everything you've done."

She kept her head on his shoulder as she talked and he stroked her hair and listened to every word while his eyes roamed around the room, a rather bare room.

Soon she realized what he was doing and said, "We have sold many of our things. If the house looks bare it is because we had to get rid of so much."

"Then your father's business is in such a bad condition?"

"Yes," she said. "We even sold some of our things to the Yankees. At triple prices. I thought Papa told you."

"He didn't tell me how bad it was." Wyeth walked into the adjoining room which had been the library and which now was almost wholly bare.

"Did Papa tell you that Gar offered him that money?" Laurel asked and took his arm when they went into the dining room.

"No." His voice was low and he was sad, then angry. The Mac-Kenzie house indeed was bare. Piece after piece of furniture had been sold in an attempt to keep Wall in business, and only a few pieces were left. That made him angry. But he was helpless, and knew he was helpless. Only the Yankees and the Yankee sympathizers had money, and they had boycotted Wall. Keith Alexander knew there was more than one way to skin a cat. He had wrecked the organization all right, without firing a shot.

Wyeth led Laurel back to the sofa and they talked until noon. He told her all about Ves and Granville and was describing the fight for the *Queen of the West* when Laurel said, "Do you think she is pretty?"

The man looked at her quickly and frowned. "You were not listening to me."

"Yes I was. I really was."

"Then why did you start thinking about Morna Alexander?"

"How did you know I was thinking about her?"

"Oh, for heaven's sake, Laurel." Wyeth really was annoyed. "Quit being a child. I rode into Natchez with Mrs. Alexander. I didn't know who she was. But even if I had known I probably would have done as I did. Yes, she's pretty. She's beautiful. I hate her. I hate her because she is Keith Alexander's wife."

His tone was so stern that Laurel changed the subject abruptly and began telling him about Sharon. They talked on into the afternoon, draining every drop of pleasure from the visit, and then he got up and announced that he was going under the hill to see Sharon.

Laurel got his hat and made him put it on and looked at him. "I didn't tell you how nice you look," she said. "I was trying to be mad. But you really are handsome."

"These are Mr. Granville's clothes."

"When the war's over and we're married I want you to dress like that."

Wyeth put the hat at an angle and squared his shoulders. They both laughed then and he kissed her. "I will be back tonight," he said. "No, not for supper. The folks around here will be watching me and I cannot involve you and your father. I will have to be cautious."

"But even if they know you are a Confederate they can't arrest you," she said. "The Yankees do not control Natchez. This place is neutral and you have as much right here as Keith Alexander. The Confederates do not molest him."

"That is all well and good. But I intend to get iron, Doll. I'm going to stay here until I get enough iron to finish the new *Arkansas*. And I don't want you and your father mixed up in it."

She wanted to walk down the path with him, but he kissed her goodby in the hallway and told her not to see him to the door. Then he stepped outside and walked away, trying to appear casual as though he had dropped into the MacKenzie home only to pay his respects to a friend of school days.

Most of the natives of Natchez were taking their afternoon naps when he walked down Broadway to Silver Street thence down to Natchez-Under-the-Hill. The day had grown warm and he took off his hat and wiped the band, pulling his sticky clothes from his body, then stepped nonchalantly to the unpainted house where Sharon lived.

The same mulatto girl opened the door and he followed her to the taproom. The room was empty. Sharon was upstairs enjoying her nap. He sent the mulatto for her and waited in the taproom until the Cajan woman appeared.

Sharon hadn't changed unless she had grown more beautiful. Her yellow hair was done in a loose roll and her coal-black eyes looked at Wyeth and then she swept across the room, her hands outstretched. He took her hands and there were tears in her eyes when she lowered her head and presented her cheek for a kiss.

"He is all right," Wyeth said. "He and Ves both are all right."

"You read my mind," she said. She was wearing black silk, the same dress she had on the first time Wyeth saw her. It was worn around the collar and around the sleeves. "You're very handsome," she said. "I didn't know you were so handsome." She sent the mulatto girl for coffee, and they were alone. She asked the purpose of the mission.

And she was calm and thoughtful while the sailor explained to her that he had to have iron, and that he intended to get iron and store it in the cavern until he could arrange to get it to Yazoo City.

Sharon poured coffee for them, then crossed her long legs. It wasn't a ladylike gesture, but she didn't mind. "Have you heard that Farragut is blockading the mouth of the Red River?"

"How many ships?" Wyeth demanded.

"Two. The *Hartford* and *Albatross*. They ran by Port Hudson day before yesterday. I just heard about it."

Wyeth's heart sank and he pressed her for details. If Farragut were at the mouth of Red River, then Vicksburg really was under siege again. And Farragut was there all right.

General Banks, attempting to silence Port Hudson from the south, had notified Washington that he could not capture the fort unless the Red were blockaded, and Grant knew he never could capture Vicksburg until the Union controlled the Red. So Farragut was instructed to bring a fleet up from New Orleans, run by Port Hudson and then close the mouth of the Red. He started out with eight ships and only two of them got by the Confederate batteries. The Federals took a deadly pounding from the Confederates and five of the ships were forced to float back downstream. One, the *Mississippi,* was battered to bits when she went aground.[33]

Farragut assumed he had been defeated, and it was a tactical defeat for the Union Navy. However, it was a strategic victory, for his two ships were between Port Hudson and Vicksburg and the Confederates had no vessel powerful enough to match them. So the Mississippi was again cut off.

Wyeth ran his hand over his chin as he heard the story and then he closed his eyes and sighed. Sharon was watching him. He smiled at her when he opened his eyes. "That's why we need the new *Arkansas*," he said. "If we can finish her, we can bring her down here and drive Farragut away and reopen the Red."

"I will help," she said.

"I didn't want to ask you."

"There is some iron in the cavern." She refilled their coffee cups. "It has been there since Mr. Frome left. We will get more. Now, tell me about Laurel, and then about Morna Alexander."

"You, too," Wyeth said. "I never heard of such a rumpus. She gave me a ride in her carriage. What's wrong in that?"

"She knows who you are," Sharon said.

"I told her."

"She knows more than you told her. She started to send for her husband and then changed her mind. I wonder why?"

"You are talking riddles." Wyeth's surprise was so genuine that Sharon put her hand on his and knew he was speaking the truth.

"She is a dangerous woman, Wyeth. She hates Laurel, by the way. You don't understand a woman's hate."

"I don't understand any of this. . . ."

"I hope you never do. Passion is an illness with that woman. And her vanity is an illness, too. She likes you. . . ."

"Nonsense. She doesn't know me."

"That's why she didn't send for her husband. In that rotten heart of hers she is wondering if she is attractive to young men like you. It's not that she doesn't love her husband. That's not the point. She is bored here and she, well . . . she would like to convince herself that she can take you from Laurel MacKenzie."

Wyeth laughed and shook his head. "That is the silliest thing I ever heard. Where do you get such ideas?"

"I'm a woman," Sharon said slowly. "And I also am in love." She got up and smoothed her dress. "Come with me."

They went to a backroom of the house and Sharon unlocked the door and opened it and Wyeth went in. Gar was waiting there.

For some reason that he didn't understand, the Missourian was not surprised. He was no longer surprised at anything. Somehow he had known that Gar would be on hand when he needed him. He offered his hand to the Wolof and the Negro took it, and was grave. Then he smiled slowly and the smile did not lessen his dignity.

"How is the reading?" Wyeth asked. He was so glad to see Gar that he actually was embarrassed, fearing his delight would manifest itself.

"It's gettin' better all the time," Gar said. "I nearly fell out of that carriage this morning when I saw you."

"How do you get along with the Alexanders?"

"All right. You told me to look after Mis' Laurel and her pa. The only man what can hurt 'em is Mist' Alexander, so I took a job with him. I got my eye on him."

"Is he good to you?"

"Yes, suh. He pays me $1 a day and that's more than most white folks get." The Negro glanced at Sharon, then back at Wyeth. "Most of the Yankees around here don't like for him to pay me so much. Even some of the Abolitionists say he is spoiling me. They want to free slaves, but they don't want to pay wages."

Sharon was leaning against the doorway. "I'll leave you two alone. You have much to talk about. Wyeth, you will stay here. I have a room and this is where many cotton speculators stay." She turned and went away.

Wyeth found a seat on a bench over near the window and Gar sat on an empty keg. The Missourian was silent and looked out of the window at the shadows that the afternoon sun was casting. The river was out there, too; placid and all-powerful. Gar didn't interrupt his thoughts and finally Wyeth said, "I'm after iron."

"I reckoned you was."

"When will Alexander be back?"

"It'll be some time. He went over to see Mist' Hoab Dabney and then he aims to go to New Orleans." The Wolof looked his friend full in the eyes. "Miz Alexander told me to go tell him that you're here. She may know a heap more than you think she knows."

"Why didn't you go?"

"She changed her mind."

"Why?"

The Negro looked away from Wyeth and down at the floor. Only then did Wyeth begin to think seriously that perhaps Morna Alexander was interested in him. And he wondered why. He bit his lower lip and when he realized that Gar was watching him the blood rushed to his face and his scar showed. In his embarrassment he said, "Am I that handsome?"

"No, suh. It ain't a question of being handsome. Some women are just like hunters. They all the time want the buck that they can't get."

Wyeth changed the subject quickly and Gar told him much about the general situation. His knowledge was amazing. He collected information from both sides and from other Negroes and he knew what was going on from Virginia to Texas. Wall MacKenzie, of course, had refused Gar's offer of money, but on the little Scotchman's advice the Wolof had invested some of his funds in several teams and in four wagons. Then he had leased the teams and wagons to Captain Youngblood, commander of the Yankee forces that stayed just outside the town and often in the town, if no Confederate soldiers were around. Sometimes, Confederates raided in Natchez, seeking the Yankee soldiers. But the Union sympathizers always warned the Yankees of impending raids and they either escaped into Louisiana or hid in the homes of the Natchez appeasers.

"What kind of man is Youngblood?" Wyeth asked.

"Just so-so. He hates Mist' Alexander because Mist' Alexander treats him like dirt. But his wife likes Mist' Alexander. So do most of the women folks around here. That is, the folks who are for the North. The old dyed-in-the-wool Secesh won't have nothing to do with the Alexanders, and Mis' Laurel treated Miz Alexander like trash."

"How much iron is in the cavern?"

"About four wagonloads. When Mist' Frome left the folks quit collecting iron. Things just went to pot. There's some iron down near Woodville. The Yanks tore up a railroad track down there and we can get the iron."

"Any more?" Wyeth asked.

"A little bit here and yonder. Just the other day I saw an old boiler in a gully back of where the Alexanders live. It's rusty, but it's still good. I'll show it to you."

"Later," Wyeth said. "Have you heard from Mr. Granville? And Ves?"

"They are on the *Star of the West* up near Fort Pemberton and the Yankees still are cutting their way through the Yazoo Pass. Dying like flies, too."

Wyeth got up from the bench and walked to the window. It was stuffy in the room and he was sweating. "Gar," he said, "I am not as smart a man as Mr. Frome, but I'm going to try to get the organization to working again. I don't want to bring Mr. MacKenzie into it."

"You can't keep him out. And you'll never get it back where it was. Mist' Frome was the organization. But we can get enough men to collect some iron. We can store it in the cavern."

"That's what I'm thinking. Once we get it, I won't have much trouble getting it hauled up the river. There are no Yankee ships between here and Vicksburg and we should be able to move our iron without much trouble. The big job is getting it, and fooling Keith Alexander. Maybe we can get it done before he gets back."

"Maybe."

"Can you meet me here about dark tonight?"

"Yes, suh."

"Then be here. And now is there anything more I should know?"

Gar ran his hand over his ugly face. "Just one more thing. Watch out for Miz Alexander."

"I'm in love with Miss Laurel. You know that."

"Yes, suh. I know it and Mis' Laurel knows it. And Miz Alexander is going to find it out. That's what I mean, suh. She's aiming to sport around just because she's that way."

"I am flattered," Wyeth said and laughed. He was trying to be sarcastic, but he really was flattered. The idea of Morna Alexander having any interest in him really pleased him. Any man the age of Wyeth would be flattered by attention from such a woman.

Gar put on his cap and looked down at his dusty shoes. "Mist' Woodward, if you stay here then sooner or later you and Mist' Alexander are going to have trouble. If he tries to kill you because you are doing your duty then I'll kill him. But if there's a mess about his woman and he tries to kill you about that, then I ain't in it."

Wyeth's anger sharpened his tongue and his face was flaming when he turned on the Negro. "You're forgetting yourself. And I don't like it, Gar. Not a damn bit."

Gar just looked at him, however. And then there were tears in the Negro's eyes. "I couldn't stand it, Mist' Woodward, if you got all mixed up in a woman mess. I just couldn't stand it."

"There's been too much talk about Mrs. Alexander. I've seen the woman once and all of you are making something out of nothing. I came here to get iron. To hell with the Alexanders."

"Louisa," Gar said softly. "Louisa and the babes."

Wyeth ate early supper at Sharon's house and noticed that most of the other guests were cotton speculators, Northern and Southern. Some of them tried to question him, but he was surly and secretive and they left him alone. At the first sign of darkness, he went back to Laurel's house and visited with her and her father until the blackness of a Southern spring night blanketed the land, then he returned to Natchez-Under-the-Hill where Gar was waiting.

The Wolof had a buggy and they rode out to the cabin where Mort Kincaid had lived, and there they hid the buggy and went down to the river. Gar found a skiff covered with dry branches. The boat was fast in the mud and partly filled with water. They baled it, then pushed it into the stream and rowed up to the mouth of the cavern.

Willows still hid the cavern's opening, but they were dry and a brownish-green in contrast to the luxurious greenness of other vegetation thereabouts. In the darkness, this fact was not discernible to Gar, and Wyeth was so excited that his usually sharp eyes failed to take in the difference between the dead willows, stuck rootless into the mud, and the live trees that flourished along the bank. He parted the willows and Gar rowed the boat into the canal. Then the Missourian lit a torch and they went to the abandoned workshop.

The floor of the shop was muddy, for the river had risen that Spring and flooded the canal. The cavern was empty and dank, and was filled with the echoes of their whispers.

Near the canal were several small piles of assorted iron, the last work of Nathan Frome before he fled to sanctuary in Lebanon. Wyeth examined the iron. "It'll do," he said softly and his words bounced back from the recess. "Anything will do. Get some men who will help you stack this iron closer to the canal. We will assemble all we can here, then get a boat and haul it to Yazoo City."

They left the cavern and were glad to be away as it was a depressing place. Again they passed through the dead willows and onto the river. Back at Kincaid's cabin Wyeth said, "Where do the Alexanders live?"

Gar said, "I'll show you." He took up the reins and they headed for Natchez.

"Just tell me the way after we get in town. I don't want you to be seen with me. I'm renting this buggy. How far behind the Alexander house is that old boiler you told me about?"

"About half a mile. It's in a gully. You can't miss it."

The Wolof got out of the buggy when they reached the outskirts of town and Wyeth drove on alone, out to Linden Road where moss hung in extravagant carelessness from giant oaks that lined the pike. The moon was out, and the stars, too. The land lay creamy and green and rich, puffed with the pregnancy of the season. The night stirred the young sailor and made him yearn for Laurel, and for peace and fellowship. It was a night of peace, if nature is ever at peace.

Two miles out the Linden Road he reached the mansion that the Alexanders had rented, a sprawling house with silver door knobs. The place was ablaze with lights, for Morna was entertaining the Youngbloods at dinner. Wyeth kept watching the house as he rode by and his mind went away from Laurel and to the Alexanders, and he loathed them and the Youngbloods and all their ilk. They were feasting at a time of fast. At that minute, Captain Youngblood was eating capon while Grant's soldiers died in the Yazoo Pass. And Morna was drinking wine from a paper-thin glass while other Southern women were starving.

About a mile beyond the house, Wyeth drove his horse into the woods and tied him, then circled behind the Alexander place until he found the gully. He passed by a summer cottage almost hidden behind wistaria and then stepped cautiously to the edge of the gully, scouted his surroundings, and walked down into the deep, wide ravine, for that's what the gully was. His eyes were accustomed to the night, and he moved silently down the draw until he found the iron boiler, a saw-mill boiler, rusty and partly covered by muck. He wondered how it had got there, and assumed that a mill once had been nearby and that the boiler was the only remnant of the industry.

It was a good hunk of iron, all right; enough iron to cover a part of the new *Arkansas*' deck. He sat on the boiler and made his plans. First, they would have to dig the dirt from around the iron. That could be done at night, and noiselessly. Then they would have to rig a gin and get the boiler aboard a wagon. That could be done some night when Morna Alexander was away, and when she was away most of her servants would be away, too.

Wyeth kicked the boiler and was pleased. It was a beginning. It wasn't much, but it was something. He wondered why Frome had overlooked that iron. Maybe the boiler had been covered completely by muck until the last rain. That didn't bother him then. He was too pleased to worry about things that he didn't understand. He stood up and stretched, and then walked to the rim of the gully and faced the Alexander house. Most of the lights were out, evidence that the guests were gone. He sat there on the edge of the ravine and waited until the house was wholly dark. He was reluctant to leave the spot, for the charm of the land and the night was upon him. He wondered if Laurel were asleep and if he would be guilty of bold behavior if he stopped by to see her before he went back to Natchez-Under-the-Hill. He just wanted to see her for a minute, long enough to kiss her goodnight.

He began walking back toward the road, hugging the rim of the gully and was passing the summer house when the voice said, "Mr. Woodward."

He thought the voice came from under a sycamore tree near the cottage and he wheeled and faced that way. The flesh seemed to creep up his back and his heart was in his throat, choking him.

"Here I am, Mr. Woodward." The voice was low and musical. "In the summer house."

Wyeth's first impulse was to flee, but he turned and walked slowly toward the cottage and saw what he knew he would see. Morna was there, almost hidden by the wistaria. He saw that she was alone and some of his fear vanished and his mind began working again, slowly at first, then rapidly. He took off his hat and stood there in the moonlight, feeling very foolish, and disgusted with himself.

"You are trespassing, you know." Morna was smiling at him and was leaning against a white column that helped support the cottage. She had a shawl around her shoulders.

"I didn't know it was your property." His voice was strained and he stepped into the cottage and bowed. "I thought you were a spirit. I never expected to see a lady out here alone at this time of night."

"I often come out here. I sleep better after a walk. And this place is good for my soul. It's very quiet, and very beautiful." She looked up at him and there was a mischievous twinkle in her green eyes. "Am I presumptuous to wonder why you are on our property at such an hour?"

Wyeth started to smile, knowing that a smile might be the best answer to her question. Her question had left her open to an embarrassing answer, for it was foolish to question a man's business along the road at night. However, instead of using such an alibi, Wyeth elected to tell just enough of the truth to spare himself. "You're not presumptuous, Mrs. Alexander. I came out here to examine that old boiler down in the gully."

She looked at him closely. "Are you in the iron business, Mr. Woodward?"

"I am in any business that is legal. I'm leaving town tomorrow for a day or so and this was the best opportunity to have a look at that boiler. I'd planned to drop by your house in a few days and ask who owned it. By then, I thought perhaps your husband would be home and that he might sell it to me. If it's on his property, of course."

"My husband will be glad to see you, I am sure."

"That makes me feel important. Why should your husband, the fabulous Keith Alexander, want to see a cotton speculator?" There was a hint of sarcasm in his voice.

"I didn't say he *wanted* to see you," Morna said quickly. "I said he'd be glad to see you. There is a difference, sir."

"I have no idea why he should be glad to see me."

"Fiddlesticks, Mr. Woodward. Let's quit toying with words. You know my husband is interested in the details of that affair at Grand Gulf. And since you figured in it, he'll be glad to talk to you. That's all."

Wyeth was relieved. He had assumed that was all the Alexanders knew about him, and he didn't mind anyone knowing that. So that was why Morna had started to send Gar for her husband, to give him a chance to get information about the Grand Gulf coup, "I'll be glad to tell him all I know," Wyeth said. "Perhaps he and I can get together on some business transactions around here."

Morna loosened the shawl from around her shoulders and sat on a bench. "My husband will not be home for weeks. You are a very straight-forward young man. Do you want the iron for the Confederates? They're the only ones desperate enough to use old boiler iron."

Wyeth leaned against one of the pillars, a fluted column that would have been out of place anywhere else in the world. "One of my agents tells me he can get a fancy price for iron. That is all I know. If it is going to the Rebels then it is no concern of mine.

Your husband has sold to both sides and he will understand what I mean."

"My husband does not sell to both sides now. He is a Unionist."

"And I am a neutral." Wyeth looked at her, and she looked away.

Then she got up and walked over to a wistaria bloom that was hanging down like a huge cluster of blue grapes. She walked slowly and Wyeth got the impression that she wanted him to see her walk. It was a tantalizing walk. He had heard that Morna could walk right into the desires of any man. He found himself unwillingly comparing her walk to Laurel's, and, being the type he was, he preferred the simple grace of his sweetheart to the languid, suggestive movement of this woman. There was something about her walk that revolted him, and yet it thrilled him.

He was staring at her and she turned and caught his stare. He blushed, but she did not. "I must ask you," she said, "how you knew that iron was here."

The directness of her question caught him off guard and, playing for time to think, he said, "Perhaps, m'am, that is a secret of my business."

"Wall MacKenzie told you." The challenge was abrupt. Her voice was low when she said it and there was a note of triumph in her words. "He told you. I know it, and that is proof that he is working for the Confederacy." Her enthusiasm loosened her tongue and Wyeth let her talk. "My husband will drive Wall MacKenzie away as he did Nathan Frome."

"Good Lord! does MacKenzie know about this iron?"

"You know he does."

Wyeth was frowning. His heart was light, but he was trying to appear perturbed for effect. "Then he will try to get it. MacKenzie needs the business. The only thing wrong with your premise, Mrs. Alexander, is that if MacKenzie knew about the iron he would not share the profits with me or anybody. He is almost bankrupt."

Morna pulled her shawl tighter around her shoulders and stepped closer to Wyeth. There was an odor of jasmine about her and she was near enough for him to notice the excitement in her eyes. "If he didn't tell you, then who did?"

"Nobody. I saw that boiler when I was out this way last year. I kept it to myself, knowing that some day the Rebels would pay any amount for iron." He said it glibly.

Morna turned her back on him and walked over to a bench and when she looked at him again, she was smiling. "I never thought of that." Her voice and demeanor were calm.

Wyeth was blithely ignorant that he was trapped. Keith Alexander had planted the boiler only a few months before, hoping Nathan Frome would take the bait and give Alexander the evidence he needed, but Frome had ignored the lure. It was on her tongue then to challenge him as a Partisan, a Confederate sailor who was out of uniform. But if she told him, he could escape, and she didn't want him to go away. She told herself that she would inform her husband that the man with the scar was in Natchez. She would send word to Keith tomorrow. But this was tonight. She was watching him intently, "You're a bold man, Mr. Woodward. You and my husband are rather alike." But they were not. They were nothing alike.

"Your words suggest that I am in danger."

"Any man who sells iron to the Confederacy is in danger."

Wyeth was enjoying himself. "Nonsense. That is not my danger. The danger is that I dare to look at the wife of Keith Alexander." His own words surprised him. And he was shocked at himself. He didn't mean for them to sound as they sounded, and yet they sounded nice, recklessly romantic.

The words pleased Morna. She looked up at the moon and then at him. "And you dare?"

"I dare." Again Wyeth was surprised at himself. It didn't sound like the Missouri sailor. It sounded more like Simeon St. Leger Granville.

"What am I going to do with you, sir?" Morna said. "I should report to Captain Youngblood that you are seeking iron. Why do I hesitate?"

"I don't know."

Morna lowered her eyes then. "I am afraid you do know."

"Go ahead and report me, Mrs. Alexander. I will tell Captain Youngblood or any other suckling Yankee that I will buy iron and sell it where and when I choose. And I will tell the same thing to any Confederate. The military has no authority in Natchez."

Morna stood up and was near him. There was nothing about him that thrilled her as Keith did. To her, he was a boy, an interesting youth with chestnut hair. But he was young, and she was young. Keith would have taken her in his arms then. It wouldn't have mattered whether they were married or not. And it wouldn't have mattered to him whose wife she was. But this boy just stood there, smiling at her.

"I have nothing to report," she said. "It is none of my business how you make your living." Yes, tomorrow she would send word to her husband that Wyeth was there.

He never knew why he did it, but he took her arm. "I'll see you home," he said softly and her flesh was pleasing to his touch.

Morna was silent. They were walking toward the house and the touch of his hand on her arm was warm. She tried to keep in her mind that this man was her husband's enemy. But the thoughts wouldn't stay. The enjoyment of the minute drove out all thoughts except those that sharpened the joy of walking in the moonlight with a young man who fascinated her. It was she who broke the silence. "You must go away tomorrow?"

"Yes. To Port Gibson." The lie came easily.

"Have you a horse? I can let you use one of ours."

"That is kind. But I have one. I rented it."

"I always ride out the Trace every morning," she said. "Perhaps we will meet again as we did this morning."

"I hope so," he said, and he suddenly was thrilled and was very conscious of her presence.

Morna paused and he removed his hand from her arm. "Have you seen Miss MacKenzie?"

"Yes. For a minute. I dropped by to see her father, too. It looks like his business is ruined. He is very happy that Frome is gone, and I have an idea he doesn't like me." Wyeth didn't want to mention Laurel while he was close to Morna. Something hurt him and he had a feeling he was doing wrong.

"Why should he dislike you?"

"Perhaps because I told him that a beautiful lady brought me into Natchez in her carriage."

"Oh, that." She took his arm and they walked closer to the house. "Of course, he wouldn't like you if he thought you liked us."

"Us? I do not know your husband."

"Your words flatter me, and I should be angry. But I am not."

They paused near the servants' cabins at the back of the house and she said, "You mustn't come any closer. Somebody might see you."

[356]

"Then goodnight."

"Goodnight."

He wouldn't have reached for her hand, but she offered it and he took it. Then she smiled at him again and turned and walked away, and he watched her in the moonlight.

Wyeth felt giddy and was almost entranced. That woman liked him. He knew she did. And he was pleased with himself. He meant no wrong-doing, but he was flattered by the knowledge that he, Wyeth Woodward, a rather prosaic young man, was attractive to the amazing wife of the famous Keith Alexander. Of course, he was foolish. Men are foolish. It had nothing to do with love or Laurel. Being a man, he was able to think of two women, and to love one and want another.

Chapter Eighteen

Sharon awakened Wyeth the next morning with news that the Federal advance through the Yazoo Pass had been repulsed disastrously. She was holding a letter from Granville in her hand when she told him and her hand was trembling. Her black eyes were softer, if possible, and she kept blinking them as though to prevent tears from coming.

"Are they all right?" Wyeth demanded and was wide awake in an instant. He was not embarrassed for the woman to be in his room. He simply never thought about it one way or another, but sat up in bed, pulling the covers around his shoulders.

"They are all right," Sharon said. "They beat the daylights out of the Yankees."

"Then why are you so nervous?"

"I'm not nervous." She sat on the foot of the bed and then, realizing that that was not exactly proper, got up quickly. "Get dressed and I will be back in a minute." She put her letter away and left him.

Wyeth didn't take time to shave. He dressed hurriedly and was combing his hair when Sharon returned. The slave girl was with her, fetching a tray. The information that the enemy had been stopped on its thrust through the swampy waterways of northwest Mississippi didn't surprise Wyeth. He ate his breakfast and watched

Sharon between sips of coffee, still wondering what caused her visible agitation. "All right," he said and pushed the tray away. "Now tell me all about it."

She was smiling to protect her pride and backed into the problem at hand. "I was going up to see Laurel. She likes to read my letters from Mr. Granville because they usually have a lot to say about you."

Then Wyeth remembered that Sharon scarcely could read. He didn't dare volunteer to read the letter as that might have offended her. He didn't know what to say at first, and then he said, "What was the maneuver?"

That gave her an excuse and she laughed. "I don't understand such things. Here, you read the letter. Out loud. I want to learn about maneuvers and such."

Wyeth felt her stare when he read the first words—"My lovely Sharon." How like Granville.

The sailor looked up and smiled and the Cajan's eyes no longer were blinking, but were wide, and filled with wonderment and hope.

The Federal army, on transports and convoyed by the ironclads *Chillicothe* and *DeKalb* and six tinclads had, after hellish hardships, hacked and inched its way through the Pass and into the upper tributaries of the Yazoo. And then, with triumph in view, they had started downstream for Yazoo City and Vicksburg's back door only to run head first into the blazing guns of Fort Pemberton. The *Chillicothe* was battered almost to bits. "Ves and I," Granville wrote, "kept Dolly hot and laid four solid shots into the *Chillicothe*. She was leaking at every seam."

The tinclads were of no use. Under Brown's orders, Granville and Ves removed the Dahlgren to a raft and the *Star of the West* was sunk across the Tallahatchie River, blocking it, and cutting off the Yankees' retreat up that stream to the northeast. There was nothing for the Federals to do but go back the way they had come. They couldn't go south because of the fort, and they couldn't go northeast because of the *Star*. So they had to turn around and head back through the green slimy hell of the Pass.

"In a way," Granville wrote, "I felt sorry for them. No soldiers ever deserved a better fate. They had almost completed one of the most amazing maneuvers in history. But they were poorly led."

Their naval commander, Watson Smith, went horribly insane

during the midnight council at which it was decided to retire back through the swamps.

The northern door to Vicksburg was safe and Granville and Ves and Dolly had returned to Yazoo City.

"It was a glorious victory," Granville wrote. "I only wish Wyeth had been with us. And I only wish I was with him, for then I could see you. . . ."

Wyeth looked up again, a question in his eyes.

"Go on," she said softly. "Keep reading."

Wyeth swallowed and continued. "As soon as I can, I will see you. I do not know when that will be, but I count the days and as each passes I say to my self that I am a day nearer to my lovely Sharon."

The Missourian folded the letter and handed it to her. "It must have been a good fight," he said.

"He wants to see me, doesn't he?"

"So it seems."

"You read it all?"

"Of course."

She picked up the tray and started out. Then he said, "Why did you ask me that?"

"I wanted to be sure about something. I can't read very much, Wyeth, and I wanted to be sure I didn't miss anything. But if it had been in there I could have read it. Any woman can read the word 'love.' It's just not in there."

Wyeth, too, had missed the word. "He said the same thing."

"All he said could have been told to me simply by saying he loves me." Sharon got to the door. "He has never told me that. But he will. He is bound to love me some because I love him so much."

Wyeth watched her close the door and sat there for a few minutes. He wanted to be with Laurel then and tell her what Granville had never told Sharon. Morna Alexander was nowhere in his thoughts and there was no desire or memory to bring her to his mind. He went out into the Spring sunshine and hitched his horse and rode out north of town, circling by the MacKenzie place, just hoping for a glimpse of Laurel. He didn't dare stop at her house at that hour of the morning. It was too early for a casual friend to drop by and he didn't want Natchez to suspect his feelings for the girl.

The MacKenzie house was still and she was nowhere in sight, so he continued out the Cemetery Road to Mort's cabin. There he hid his horse and stood on the bluff, watching the river. A cautious man, he didn't dare approach the cavern from the river side in broad daylight as there were too many travelers on the river. So he walked along the bluff until he came to the top of the punch bowl. The descent into the cavern would not be difficult, but the ascent would be a chore. However, there was nothing else to do. So he took off his coat, folded it under a tree and covered it with leaves. He hid his hat, too. Then he started down the steep side of the bowl, clinging to saplings and bushes as he went down. Often he slipped and cursed himself for wearing Granville's best trousers. He was more afraid of tearing them than of ripping his own skin.

Eventually he came to the roof that Frome had built over the workshop and knew it was the roof by the hollow sound of his footsteps. The roof was hidden perfectly under dirt and small trees and grass. He was walking across the roof, seeking an entrance into the workshop when he heard Gar.

"You sounded like a herd of cattle," Gar said. The Wolof was armed.

"This was the best way," Wyeth said. "If I had come by the river somebody might have seen me."

"This is a good way to get shot," Gar said. "We were in the shop and heard you clomping about up here."

"Then there is a way in from here?"

The Wolof just looked at him. "How do you think I got up here? There's a way out, so there must be a way in, Mist' Woodward."

It struck the sailor then that his friend was either in a bad humor or sullen. He followed Gar and the Wolof led him across the roof to the far side of the bowl, thence down the side to a small opening into the workshop. The iron had been stacked and a group of Confederate workers, white and black, were standing around looking at him.

"We came here last night and got the iron ready," Gar said. "These folks will stay here until night comes again and they can get out by the river."

Wyeth looked toward the opening to the river, then down at the iron and told Gar to follow him. They went to the back of the shop and sat down. "You can trust all those folks?"

"Yes, suh."

"There's no need for them to come back until we have more iron.

[361]

You and I can get the iron in here, so there's no need of anyone else coming here until we say so."

Gar began stroking his beard. "What's on your mind, Mist' Woodward?"

"I'm going to put torpedoes around the mouth of this cavern. Out there where the canal empties into the river. I'm not going to take any chances on anybody getting in here to our iron."

"That's a good idea. We'll tell our folks to stay away and anybody else will get hurt. Can you make the torpedoes?"

"Yes." He began scraping dirt from his shoes. "I almost ruined Mr. Granville's pants coming down the side of this cavern. And now I've got to go back up. I didn't expect to find anybody here."

"We've been here most all night."

"I saw that boiler. I think I can get it." That was the first time Wyeth had thought of Morna that morning. "I thought you would be working for the Alexanders today."

The Wolof propped his chin on his hands and stared at the canal. "Miz Alexander sent me word that she wouldn't need me today. Every morning when it's pretty I've been driving her out the Trace. I don't know why she didn't want me today. I just reckoned maybe she aimed to drive herself and didn't want nobody along." He looked over at Wyeth.

Only then did the Missourian remember that he had told Morna he would be on the Port Gibson road that day. He didn't want to see her, and yet the thought that perhaps she wanted to see him pleased his vanity. He wondered if she were scheming for a tryst with him, and that thought flattered him more than it thrilled him. He started once to tell Gar about the meeting the night before with Morna, but, on second thought, he reasoned it was none of the Negro's business. Besides, he had a feeling that Gar knew about the meeting. Perhaps that was Wyeth's conscience bringing a feeling of guilt, a feeling that his friend knew that he had enjoyed the few minutes with another man's wife. He got rebellious within himself although no charge had been made and he kept defending himself to himself.

He set the time and place for another meeting with Gar and then left him and began climbing the side of the cavern, pausing often for breath as it was hard work. He found his hat and coat and carried them in his hand and walked back to Mort's cabin and his

Morna looked at him closely. The blood was in her cheeks. "How charming," she said slowly. "What a naive way of telling me you want to see me. But let's not complicate matters. The situation is complicated enough. I told you last night that I always walk down to the summer house before retiring. I will be there tonight, Wyeth."

And before he could reply she touched her horse and was away. Wyeth's face was very red and his scar was showing. He wanted to see Laurel that night and didn't know how he could arrange to see both of them. But he could always see Laurel. She was his and she was what he wanted. His thinking simply was not clear. No man's is when there are two women. So he reasoned he could see Laurel for a few minutes, and then Morna, and then come back to Laurel.

His heart told him one thing and his desires told him another as he rode into town and out toward the MacKenzie place. He didn't care if he was seen. He didn't care about anything then. He wanted only to see Laurel. He felt soiled, and wanted to be cleansed. His conscience drove him.

Wall MacKenzie answered his knock and Wyeth was surprised to find him at home. "Is anything wrong?" Wyeth asked.

"Not much. There's no business at my store. We were wondering where you were. Laurel is sort of ailing."

"How bad?" he asked quickly.

"Nothing much. Just a headache. She'll be glad to see you, son. Wait here while I give her a chance to make herself presentable."

Wyeth began condemning himself because he had been talking to another woman while Laurel was ill. He waited downstairs until Wall returned and went with him to Laurel's room. She was sitting in bed and held out her arms and he went to her while Wall turned his face. Then the little Scotchman said, "I'll be downstairs. I want to talk to you, Wyeth. You were sort of crazy to come here in the daylight, but since you're here there's nothing we can do about it."

Laurel was wearing a pink bed jacket and he sat in a chair by her bed and held her hand. "I rode by here this morning, hoping to see you."

"I stayed in bed. I wanted to be all right by tonight. You'll be back tonight?"

"Of course," he said. "You know I will." At that minute he was determined not to see Morna that night, or possibly ever again.

They talked about the things that lovers always talk about, themselves and their plans. Laurel asked him all that he had done and, of course, he didn't mention Morna. They talked until dinner time and Wall called him downstairs for food. He kissed Laurel and sat on the bed beside her and held her.

He and Wall ate dinner in the kitchen and Wall asked, "Have you heard the news?"

"About Fort Pemberton? Yes, I've heard it."

"Not only that, but about Porter and Sherman." Wall poured coffee.

"No. What now?"

The Federals were making another stab at Vicksburg, using a fleet under Porter and an army under Sherman. The plan was to enter the lower Yazoo, around its mouth, then cut a channel through the network of bayous and creeks at the center of the Yazoo ovoid. If the gunboats and transports could get through they could by-pass Haynes Bluff and the batteries there, flank Yazoo City and get into the Yazoo River up south of Fort Pemberton, and be between the fort and Vicksburg. And once in the Yazoo behind Haynes Bluff, the Federals would be at Vicksburg's backdoor. So they were trying again, ten thousand soldiers, several tinclads and five ironclads.

Wyeth wasn't surprised. He wasn't surprised at any attempt the Yankees made to get past Haynes Bluff. "I wonder," he said, "why Mr. Granville didn't tell me this."

Wall said, "Have you heard from Granville?"

"Not exactly. But Sharon did. This morning." Then he told Wall all the news that Granville had written.

"Your English friend didn't know about Porter's and Sherman's expedition when he wrote that letter. They started the day the expedition through the Pass failed. They are trying first to get up Steele's Bayou and then around to the Yazoo."

"It will be another failure," Wyeth said. "Vicksburg cannot be flanked from that side." His coffee cup was almost to his mouth and then he put it down without drinking. "Mr. Granville and Ves are coming down the Yazoo. I see it now. That's why they put the Dolly on a raft. To bring her down and meet Porter and Sherman." He wished he was with them.

They finished the meal and went out on the front porch and sat in rocking chairs and smoked. The morning glory vines on the porch hid their chairs from passers-by on the road. Wyeth reassured himself from Wall that Laurel was not seriously ill. "Just upset," Wall said. "She'll be all right in a day or so. Your presence is a remedy. Now that you're here, I hope you can stay with her for an hour or so."

"Oh, I will. And I'll stay for supper and until she gets sleepy." Wall shook his head. "I wouldn't do that, son. Some of the neighbors will be dropping by later this afternoon. The word has got around by now that she's ailing and she'll have a heap of company. It won't do any good for the folks to see you here. Not too much."

Wyeth understood and didn't argue. Above all, he wanted to spare Laurel any involvement with his mission. However, he was unhappy about it, for he didn't trust himself away from her. "I know you're right," he said. "I'll go up and visit with her for awhile and then leave. I have much to do." Then he told Wall about his plans for mining the mouth of the cavern.

The little Scotchman nodded approval. "It's a good way to protect the iron. Let me know if you need me."

"You stay away from that cavern. People are watching you." Wyeth flipped away his cigar and went into the house and up to Laurel's room. He got a book and read to her until she was tired of the printed words and wanted to hear his own. So he pulled his chair close to her bed and held her hand and talked. She had no fever and her face was bright. He explained to her that he should not stay at the house too long and should avoid meeting her visitors and, being sensible, she agreed. So he took his leave, promising to return the next day or night if possible. Wall walked with him to the front porch.

Just to be on the safe side, Wyeth stopped at a tavern in town and, after a drink, mentioned to the tavern keeper that he had been out to old man MacKenzie's house to try to arrange some business. "The old man is in a bad way," Wyeth said. "I thought I might manage to buy a little cotton from him, but he's just about broke."

"Is the old man staying home these days?" the tavern keeper asked. "He ain't doing enough business to keep his store open."

"He's at home today. Somebody out there is sick. His wife or his daughter, I think."

"His daughter. He ain't got no wife."

Wyeth knew the story would spread and that his explanation was plausible if anyone had seen him go to the MacKenzie house or leave it. So he went down under the hill to Sharon's place and to his room. Sharon visited him there and he told her his plans for the torpedoes. She got four empty demijohns from her bar and Wyeth began making friction tubes, using scraps from her storeroom. As he worked, his mind kept jumping from Laurel to Morna and he tried not to think of Morna and kept saying to himself that he was not going out there that night.

He finished the friction tubes by dark and then Gar came and Wyeth sent him for powder. Together they loaded the torpedoes and drove back out to the cavern, approaching it from the river side. The sailor rigged the torpedoes so they would explode if the willows in the center were parted enough to admit a skiff.

Gar watched him finish the task, then said, "How are we going to get in?"

"Around the ends of the willows," Wyeth said. "I'll show you." He rowed their skiff to the right of the opening and slowly parted the willows there. Then they entered the canal. Coming out, Wyeth rowed close to the left bank of the opening. The torpedoes were submerged almost in dead center of the opening and the wires were tied to the middle willows. "A stranger will naturally head for the middle," Wyeth said. "You and I are the only ones who know how to get in and out, and live to tell about it. So you be damn sure that none of our friends come here without one of us."

"They won't come." Gar took the oars. "Even when Mr. Frome was here there was a rule that none of the folks was to come in here without a guide. Mort was the main guide."

On the way back to Natchez, Wyeth was silent and Gar reflected his mood and was silent, too. The moon was out, creamy and friendly, and the Mississippi was yawning in the lazy Spring weather.

"Want me to take you to Mis' Sharon's?" Gar asked after they had passed the first blinking lights of the town.

"Uh huh."

"Sort of tired, eh, Mist' Woodward? I'll bet you'll hit the covers this night."

Wyeth didn't look at his friend and had a feeling that Gar was watching him. "Maybe," he said.

"How is Mis' Laurel?"

"All right." Wyeth said it testily. "She's just a mite upset. Nothing to bother about. I'd go over there, but she's got a houseful of company."

Gar nodded as though he understood and when they got to Sharon's house Wyeth gave him a dollar, a United States dollar, just to be on the safe side. The Wolof was in business and there was nothing suspicious about a Negro livery stable owner driving a cotton speculator around as long as he got paid. Gar pocketed the money and said loudly enough for any eavesdropping ears to hear, "Let me know, cap'n, if you need me again."

Wyeth waited on Sharon's porch until Gar drove back up the hill, and then he went to the stable behind the house and hitched his rented horse to the buggy. He knew very well what he was going to do and wouldn't allow himself to think about it too much, and surely not sensibly. Most men would have laughed at their conscience. Granville would have brushed his conscience aside if it had presumed to question his wants. But not Wyeth. He loved one woman and by his rigid code of behavior it was wrong even to think of another. Actually, his conscience was prodded by fear, not so much a feeling of guilt, but a dread that Laurel might discover his guilt. The male simply is not a monogamic animal in spite of the efforts of the female to make him one.

There was laughter and lights in Sharon's taproom when he drove away up Silver Street and into Natchez. The town was crowded with revelers, Southerners who had hitched their wagons to the Yankee star, and Northerners to whom the war was a boom. And there were Negroes, too; drunk and bewildered. Many had left the plantations and come to town to enjoy the Emancipation. They thought it was something to eat, either a feast or a religion that would bring heaven to earth. Few of them worked. Some didn't want to work, others didn't know how to do anything except grow cotton, and still others loafed because there was no plan for them. None of the white people, Northerners or Southerners, mixed with them and the Negroes dared not walk on the same sidewalk with the whites. Wyeth was rather amused and completely disgusted to notice that the Northerners treated the Negroes in cold contempt while the Southerners merely ignored them. But no Confederates were on the streets. They were at home, burning firewood for light and allowing hatred and a desire for revenge to saturate their blood and warp their judgment.

Only one light was showing in the Alexander home and Wyeth wondered if the light came from Morna's bedroom. Perhaps she wouldn't be at the summer house. He touched up his horse and hurried by the mansion, then down the road to the spot where he intended to conceal his rig. Again his conscience bothered him and he was angry with himself. After all, he was a free man. He wasn't married. He cursed his conscience, reviling it as a nagging old woman. It was all a waste of time. Wyeth knew he was going to the summer house, and that's all there was to that.

He turned his horse off the road and looped the reins around the buggy whip, then fastened the horse to a bush. He removed his hat and let the moonlight play in his hair, then ran his fingers through his hair. That was a touch of vanity that was not like Wyeth at all. Glancing up and down the road, he walked quickly across the pike and onto the Alexander property. Then he made a bee-line for the summer house.

She was there all right. Of course, she was there. Wyeth wished the air were damp, for his hair always curled in damp air. And he wanted her to see his curly hair. He was thinking about his hair and his cleft as he walked closer to the cottage and to the figure that was standing there, dressed in organdy. Morna's back was to him and she was fingering a wistaria bloom. A wiser man might have laughed at the obvious affectation. Organdy and moonlight and wistaria. But Wyeth thought she was beautiful. She heard him coming and yet she didn't turn and face him until he stepped under the roof.

Morna was very pleased with herself. This was the way she always had wanted a lover to come to her. Keith Alexander would have tilted his head and laughed. Morna had always wanted so much to be a part of moonlight and wistaria. It was a long-wanted idyl to have a handsome young man come to her for a moonlit tryst.

"I heard your horse," she said and let her hand linger on the wistaria for a second and then she sat down.

Wyeth was entranced. "How did you know it was my horse?" Even at such a time he was practical.

"Oh, does that matter?" Morna was impatient. The man was asking silly questions already.

The young Missourian leaned against one of the columns and drank in her voluptuous beauty, drinking it in huge gulps that intoxicated him and made his head spin. "You know," he said rashly, "I wanted to get here before you. So I could be waiting for you. It is better for me to wait for you than for you to wait for me."

Morna lifted her eyes to him slowly, another gesture that would have brought laughter from her husband. "What a sweet thing to say."

"May I sit by you?"

"If you wish."

Wyeth sat on the bench beside her and didn't know what to say or what to do. He looked down at his hands and crossed his legs and put his hands over his knee. He wanted to say something and, daring not say what was on his mind, he looked away. "It's a beautiful night, isn't it?"

"Yes."

"You know," he said, "I'll be glad when your husband gets back. I still want that iron."

Morna was stunned. She stared at him and then was angry at him and at herself. "Iron! you can have the iron. Take it whenever you want it. Did you come here to talk about iron?" Her words poured out. "Or about my husband? Is this a time to mention my husband?"

Wyeth Woodward never knew why he did the thing he did. He turned for a second and looked at her and then he put out his arms and pulled her to him and kissed her neck and then her mouth while he cupped his hand under her breast. Morna gasped and her lips suddenly were hot. She hadn't expected this; not so soon. In her mind there was an idea that she could toy with this man for a long time and anticipate his love without actually feeling it. She was frightened, afraid of herself. She pulled her lips from his and put her hand on his chest and pushed him away.

"That's what I came for," he said hoarsely. "That and more."

"My God!" Morna forgot her role, the role of organdy and wistaria. His caress brought her back from that lotus land of romance, back to the realities of the situation. "You'd better go, Wyeth."

"So soon?" He reached for her again and she backed away.

"Now. And don't come back for several days. Until I send for you. I'll be on the Trace and you can find me there. But not for days, please."

"Have I offended you?" He didn't know what to do. "Have I rushed matters? I just met you yesterday. . . ."

"That has nothing to do with it. Yesterday or a year ago." She reached the side of the bench and found her shawl and put it over her shoulders.

"Then I didn't offend you?"

"No. But you surprised me. And I enjoyed it. That's what I mean." She stepped close to him and was trembling when he put his arms around her waist and pulled her so close that her body went limp in his arms. "Kiss me just once, and then go. I am a fool. I thought I could enjoy the wine without getting drunk. I can't do it, Wyeth. I thought you were a boy, a rather interesting boy. Now I know better. I fit into your embrace and I don't want to, and yet I do want to."

He removed one arm from around her and felt for her breast again. And again she pushed him away. "Goodnight. Goodnight, Wyeth. The wine was good and I want to think about it before I let it make me drunk. And it will. If I see you again like this I know what will happen. Please leave first."

"I will not leave," he said slowly.

"Then I must." She reached out her hand and touched his, then began walking away toward her house.

"Wait a minute, Morna. I will see you to your house."

"No. I had better go alone."

He watched her until she was swallowed by the night and then, his senses still reeling, he walked slowly back to where he had left his horse. But his horse wasn't there. Frantically, Wyeth glanced around the woods, then stooped over and examined the bush to which the animal had been tied. He realized immediately what had happened. The horse had jerked free. Wyeth cursed himself for the fool he was. He had never learned about horses, and had been so excited at the prospects of seeing Morna that he hadn't fastened the beast securely. He stepped to the road and looked around and then began walking toward Natchez.

He was passing the Alexander house when he saw the group of men up the road and heard them talking, and then he saw his horse and buggy. His first impulse was to cut through the woods and avoid them, but that would have complicated further an already complicated situation so he walked up to them and said, "Good evening. That's my horse."

There were several Negroes in the group and two white men, one an officer of the United States Army.

The men looked at him, expecting an explanation. Wyeth stepped to his buggy. "I rented this rig from a Negro in Natchez. I tied the horse in the woods down yonder and he obviously jerked free and headed back for his stable."

"Obviously," the officer said. "These Negroes found him walking back toward town and this gentleman and I happened to pass along. I am Captain Youngblood of the United States Army. This," he bowed toward his companion, "is Mr. Caleb Whitsitt. You are Wyeth Woodward, I think."

"That is correct." Wyeth offered his hand. Youngblood was about as he expected him to be, and he had heard of Whitsitt, a florid Natchez planter who sympathized with the Union because it was profitable.

"I've been wanting to talk to you," Youngblood said. "You're in the cotton business. . . ."

"That's right." Wyeth was anxious to be away.

"And I know you're a loyal man."

"Loyal to myself, sir. I am a neutral. Come to see me sometime, Captain. You, too, Mr. Whitsitt."

The planter was nodding as though his head were on a spring. Youngblood said, "I will." He was very affable as he had cotton to sell. "And I'm glad we recovered your horse. It's a long walk to town."

Wyeth got in the buggy and lifted the reins. "And I'm grateful. Goodnight, gentlemen."

"Did you find any cotton down there in the woods?" Youngblood was an oaf, a course lout. He meant the question in good faith and was trying to make humor of the situation. He assumed Wyeth had gone into the woods for wholly personal reasons, but was the kind to attempt a joke even about such matters.

The Missourian's nerves were on edge. Instead of laughing at the question as he should have, he was angry. "That, sir, is none of your damn business." He slapped his horse with the reins and rode off.

Whitsitt laughed and Youngblood grinned. "Touchy rascal, isn't he?" the officer said.

One of the Negroes began laughing, too, and Youngblood turned on the Negro and snarled, "What are you laughing at?"

"Just laughing," the Negro said. "I seen that hoss hitched down yonder across from the gully. Ain't no cotton down there and there wasn't no man round and about."

Youngblood and Whitsitt looked up the road at the disappearing buggy, then down the road, and the captain frowned. At that minute he happened to look over at the Alexander house just as the candle went out in Morna's room. He was a suspicious man, and a man who couldn't keep his mouth shut.

Whitsitt, mostly to make a jest, leaned over and whispered to Youngblood, "You don't suppose Alexander's wife was out looking for cotton, too, do you?"

"I don't know what to think," Youngblood said grimly. "Woodward rode into town with Morna Alexander yesterday."

"Well, that young buck may be writing his death warrant."

"It might be worth it." Youngblood laughed again.

It was after midnight when Wyeth returned to Sharon's place, stabled the horse and walked into the house. He was in a vile humor and, knowing that he could not sleep, he went to the taproom and ordered brandy. There were several speculators in the room and Sharon greeted him as she would any other customer. Wyeth scarcely nodded to her and sat alone in a corner, staring at his glass and then outside at the night.

One of the speculators, anxious to be on good terms with such an important man as Wyeth apparently was, called over to him the offer of a drink, but the gunner shook his head.

"I saw you this morning," the stranger said. "I would have taken you over to the Port Gibson road. Do you know who that lady was you were talking to?"

Wyeth felt the hair at the back of his neck stiffen and cold water seemed to spout from his veins and against his heart. He felt Sharon's glance and knew that his face was red and that his scar was visible. "Of course, I know her," he snapped. It would have been fatal to lie. "I met the lady yesterday. I understand she rides out that way every morning and that's why I figured she knew directions." He was talking too much, explaining too much.

The speculators thought no more about it then, but Wyeth was uncomfortable. To conceal his embarrassment, he ordered another drink, a thoughtless insult to the man who had offered to treat him.

The offended speculator began mumbling to his comrades. "Just because he operates on a big scale and knows Keith Alexander's wife is no reason for him to be so damned high and mighty."

Wyeth didn't hear him, but Sharon did.

"Alexander's wife gave him a ride into town yesterday," another man whispered.

"Maybe they are old friends," said another.

"They must be."

"They're about the same age. . . ."

"He's a slick one. . . ."

Wyeth gave no heed to the whisperings. The brandy had warmed him and he began thinking about Laurel and wondering if Sharon had heard how she was. He left his table and passed close to the Cajan on his way out. "Have you heard from her?" he asked softly.

"Which one?" Sharon asked and turned away from him.

The Missourian stalked up to his room, disgusted with himself and indignant at everybody else. He kicked off his shoes and went over to a window and looked out, just watching the Mississippi. He was standing there when Sharon knocked lightly and then entered. Wyeth reached for his shoes.

"Never mind," she said. "Be comfortable." She sat in the only chair in the room, a big rocker, and folded her hands in her lap and looked at him. "Wyeth, a lot of lives may depend on you and your behavior. What have you been doing?"

He resented the question and said so. "There's too much talk about it. I happened to see Mrs. Alexander on the road yesterday and again this morning. What's wrong in that?"

"Nothing. And I won't pry." Sharon unfolded her hands and rubbed her eyes. "Laurel is better. I know you were not by there tonight. . . ."

"Wall told me not to call. She had company. She understands."

"And last night? You left her house early last night. I must know where you go and what you do. My life depends on it." She crossed her long legs and stretched. "If you blunder I might have to pay for it. And you haven't been yourself. What's wrong?"

"Nothing is wrong," he said and sat on the bed. "I've been busy. Gar and I put torpedoes at the mouth of the cavern. . . ."

"Gar was back here before 9 o'clock."

"And last night I went out past the Alexander place to look at an old boiler. I think I can salvage it. . . ."

"Leave that boiler alone!" Her eyes were wide then. "Who told you about it?"

"Gar."

Sharon jumped to her feet and walked nervously to the window, then back to her chair. Wyeth sensed that something important was wrong and watched her closely, his heart in his mouth.

"That's the trouble," she said in exasperation. "We miss Nate Frome. No organization. Our left hand doesn't know what our right hand is doing. . . ."

"What about that boiler?"

"It's a trap. Keith Alexander planted it there. But Gar didn't know that and I never thought to tell you. *Wyeth!* what's the matter with you. . . ."

The Missourian was as pale as the mist that had begun rising from the river. His mouth was open and sweat stood on his lips. He looked frantically at Sharon and his nerves began creeping up and down his backbone. He had never been so frightened in battle, and because he was panicky he told the truth, seeking strength from the truth. "I saw Mrs. Alexander last night." He said it slowly and felt better for having said it.

"I supposed as much," Sharon said. "Now what else?"

Wyeth licked his lips and was glad to have her there, glad for someone to share his confidence and misery. "She came up on me when I was looking at that boiler. I didn't make any bones about wanting it. I don't care who thinks I buy and sell anything to anybody. . . ."

"There's no harm in that as long as you pose as a neutral." Her voice was low and she felt sorry for him, sensing that something was gnawing at his spirit.

"She asked me how I knew the boiler was there and I said the first thing that popped into my mind." Wyeth looked up at her, then back at the floor. He really wasn't worried so much about himself, but only about Laurel and Sharon, Wall and Gar, and the others. "I told her that I saw the damn boiler last year when I was here. She knows I was lying." His eyes followed a crack in the floor and to the wall. Then he looked toward the window, then the door

He looked everywhere except at Sharon and eventually his curiosity pulled his eyes toward her and she was just staring at him. "She knows more about me than I think," he said. "I'm sure of that. Maybe she even knows that I'm a Confederate gunner." Again he lowered his eyes. "But that doesn't mean she knows about the others, Laurel and you and the others. I can go back to my gun and leave matters as they are."

Still Sharon didn't speak and Wyeth walked nervously over to the window and back to the bed. "Naturally," he said, "I couldn't tell Captain Brown all the truth. I couldn't admit that a woman messed me up. I just couldn't tell him that there is no iron for our ship because I made a fool out of myself with a woman. I just couldn't tell him that. But he'd find it out."

He ran his hand over his eyes and shook his head. He wished Sharon would say something and his own misery drove him to volubility. "And Laurel will hear about it." The Confederate gunner who laughed and cried when he fought, the man with the scar whose boldness was almost legendary was like a little boy again, a boy caught snitching jam. "What am I going to do, Sharon?" he asked pleadingly.

"Quit talking," she said. "That's the best beginning. Just shut up and quit feeling sorry for yourself. You're not the first man who made a fool of himself. Now look at me. Did you touch that woman?"

Wyeth's face was livid. "I kissed her."

"Is that all?" Sharon was very calm and deliberate and was rocking slowly in the chair.

"My God, yes."

Sharon smiled in spite of herself and turned her face away.

"You don't believe me, do you?" he said.

"Yes." She tried not to smile. "Yes, I believe you. You've got no business in this kind of work. You're not sly and you're not a schemer. It's hard to believe that just one kiss made Morna Alexander as crazy as she apparently is. You fooled me, Wyeth. I never pictured you as a lover. . . ."

"This is no time for jesting," he growled. "And she's not crazy. I am."

"So is she. She's crazy about you. If she knows who you are, she hasn't told a soul. Not even her own husband. Her silence is evidence of her own guilt." She put her hands on the arms of the rocker and stood up. The candlelight danced in her yellow hair and the shadows made her olive skin seem darker. "Of course, Keith Alexander will try to kill you if he hears. But he also will teach her a lesson. . . ."

"Alexander is not my worry," Wyeth said quickly.

"Not now. You're thinking of Laurel. And yourself. No man enjoys being a fool and being caught at it. Just sit still for a minute and let me think." She walked over to the window and watched the river and then she went back to her chair and sat down and smoothed her dress. "The whole trouble is that you had a free hand. You were trying to get iron through an organization that really didn't exist. But it does now."

Wyeth scarcely heard her. His mind was on his problem. The realization that Morna was so infatuated with him that she was, in a way, protecting him came as a shock, and, although his vanity was flattered, his judgment had control of his vanity. He hoped he never saw her again. He wanted only to get iron and get back to the war, and fight, and then come back to Laurel.

"It's the only thing to do," Sharon was saying. "Wall MacKenzie can't do it because they are watching him too closely. Will you take orders from me?"

"What? What are you saying?"

"I am going to take up where Nate Frome left off. The Yankees think I'm as loyal as Abraham Lincoln. They should. I've fed enough Yankee sailors and speculators."

"You're crazy. A woman. . . ."

Sharon began rocking again. "What has that got to do with it? Somebody's got to do it."

"I wish Mr. Granville had come in my place. . . ."

"I don't," she said quickly. "That woman might have become attached to him and," she smiled to herself, "he wouldn't have let her off as lightly as you did. And then, Mr. Wyeth Woodward, I might have forgotten that I'm a lady. But that's beside the point. Will you do as I say?"

"Yes. I'll do anything."

Sharon left him and went downstairs and returned with a drink of brandy. "Most of my guests have retired. Drink this. You'll need it. You're going to Woodville."

"Tonight?"

"Right now. Go to the hotel there and wait until you hear from me. There's iron in Woodville. . . ."

"You want to get rid of me. Isn't that it?"

"That's it. I want you out of town. I will be in touch with you in a few days. The password is—" she looked up at the ceiling—"it is 'All men are fools.' And the countersign is 'Amen.'"

Even Wyeth smiled. "Are you serious?"

"Not about the password. It really will be 'It has been a long night' or 'It is or was or will be a long night.'"

"Countersign?" He reached for his shoes.

"It will be 'Oh, it just seemed long.'"

He drank the brandy and washed his face. "I'll do anything you say, Sharon. But what about Laurel? Should I tell her anything about Morna. . . ."

"Mrs. Alexander! Never call her Morna. And don't tell Laurel a thing. She would go to that woman and slap her face and we can't have that."

"She wouldn't do that," Wyeth said, shaking his head slowly. "Not Laurel. She's not that kind. She would break our engagement and hate me. . . ."

"Fiddlesticks! she'd claw that hussy's hair out. If she thought any woman was endangering her happiness she would fight. And she wouldn't hate you. She couldn't. She'd be hurt, then angry, but she would hate Morna Alexander and not you."

"I'm afraid she's going to hear about it," Wyeth said feebly. "I'm just afraid there might be gossip. Those speculators will tell about seeing me this morning. Laurel was mad just because I rode into town with Mrs. Alexander. . . ."

"Of course, she's going to hear. I'm going to tell her. But I'll tell her a lie and because she loves you she'll believe my lie. Now, get started." She put her hand on his shoulder and kissed his cheek. "Mr. Granville often said you are a good man, but about some things you're still a boy."

She opened the door for him and stayed in the room until she heard his horse clatter down the lane beside the house and up toward Silver Street and the hill. She went to the mirror and fluffed her hair. "He was like putty," she said to herself. "He didn't argue with me. Simeon," she faced the window as though she were talking to him, "you're right. He's honest and good, but he's not the smartest man in the world." She put cold water on her eyes and went to her own room and sent for her slave girl, instructing her to fetch Gar.

The Wolof met her in the storeroom at the back of the house and he spoke first, saying, "Where's Mist' Woodward?"

"I sent him on a mission. Why? What have you heard?"

Gar didn't answer. "I just want to see him, m'am."

"What have you heard, Gar? How much do you know about him and Mrs. Alexander?"

"He's aiming for a mess. His buggy was down by that gully on the Alexander place tonight. You know how colored folks talk."

Sharon straightened and put her hand at the small of her back to rest herself. "I know about that. He was down there looking at that old boiler."

"That's what I reckoned." The Wolof had caught her cue. "But Cap'n Youngblood and Mist' Whitsitt knows he was there and they're talking and hinting that maybe she was there, too."

"I'm glad you told me. Don't worry about Mr. Woodward. And now, I want you to be here about ten o'clock in the morning with your best carriage. If you can't come, then send me a driver. I am going to see Mrs. Alexander."

The Negro stroked his beard slowly. "It seems to me, Mis' Sharon, that somebody around here is taking hold again. I'm glad it's you. I'll trust you as much as I did Mist' Frome."

"Thank you, Gar. Mr. Woodward left for Woodville a few minutes ago. When you go home tonight it will be all right to drop the word here and there that he was out looking at that boiler and that Mrs. Alexander surprised him. The quickest way to kill a lie is to tell a better one. I don't care what you tell but remember that Mr. Woodward is away on a cotton buying trip and that you know he's in love with Miss Laurel. You can tell that all you want. Tell it over and over."

"Yes, m'am. But mightn't that get Mis' Laurel in trouble if the folks find out that her sweetheart is Secesh? And if them Alexanders know half as much as I reckon they know then they have got Mist' Woodward tagged as Confederate. If they ain't, they will have him tagged as Secesh when Mist' Alexander gets back and gets on the scent."

"Mrs. Alexander knows that Mr. Woodward is more than just a speculator. I have a feeling she even knows he is working for the South. But she hasn't told anyone."

"Yes, m'am. I'm thinking that you and me know why she ain't said nothing. But someday she's going to have to blab. She can't fool her husband. If they think Mist' Woodward is courting Mis' Laurel, then she'll be mixed up in it. And her pa . . ."

"Not at all. Miss MacKenzie doesn't love Mr. Woodward." Sharon was watching Gar closely. "You understand that, of course. He began courting her in Missouri and she sort of accepted his attentions until he made the war an excuse for making money. He saw her for a minute the day he got here and has been trying to see her ever since, but she will have nothing to do with him because he's a speculator and getting rich out of other people's misery. Mr. MacKenzie even threatened to run him out of town if he didn't quit pestering his daughter. You know all of that, don't you?"

Gar was smiling. "I recollects it now."

"Then be here tomorrow. I'm going in style to see Mrs. Alexander."

"I'll be here or I'll send a driver if I'm busy at the Alexander place." He stepped to the door and put on his cap. "I was just thinking." He glanced up at the moon. "Mist' Woodward is just about now leaving. You know he's bound to have stopped by Mis' Laurel's."

"Of course he did. Goodnight."

At this minute, Wyeth was at the backdoor of the MacKenzie place, having left his rig about a half a mile away. Wall answered his knock and when he learned the Missourian was going to Woodville he went up stairs and woke up Laurel and gave her a few minutes to make herself ready to see her sweetheart.

Wyeth stayed only a minute and they didn't talk, but he sat on the side of the bed and held her close to him. Her slight spell of illness had passed. "I'll be back before long," he said. Then he called Wall and told both of them that Sharon was taking Frome's place. "She's smart," he said. "I don't mind taking orders from her."

"Well, I'll be damned," Wall said. "That's a good idea. She's the one to do it. Now we're getting somewhere."

"She is endangering her life," Laurel said. "If the Yankees ever get control here and they find out the truth, there'll be some hangings."

"The Yankee army is a long ways from here and the few Yanks who are here can't do anything but threaten and talk. They won't catch Sharon."

The moon was waning when Wyeth got back to his buggy and headed his horse down the old King's Highway, down the sunken road to Woodville.

Almost three hundred miles away, at LaGrange, Tennessee, Colonel B. H. Grierson of the United States Cavalry, opened a dispatch from General Grant and assembled his staff. He cautioned them to secrecy and read his orders. He was to raid from Tennessee through the heart of Mississippi, destroy everything in his path and lay waste to the land that was supplying Vicksburg. And then he was to proceed to Natchez, put the town under Federal military law and await Grant's blow against Vicksburg itself. He must start his raid within three weeks.

The United States was laying a noose from Milliken's Bend up through North Mississippi, thence down and around through Port Hudson, and Grant was ready to tighten it and strangle the Confederacy, choke its windpipe and break its back at the same time.

Wyeth had never heard of Grierson. To him, riding by the old oaks of the sunken road along the river, it seemed that the war was far away. "It has been a long night." He repeated the password to himself and his horse heard it and perked up his ears and began trotting down the old King's Road over which the Spaniards once carried their tobacco and indigo and Cross.

Chapter Nineteen

SHARON was wide awake a few minutes after she opened her eyes and stretched luxuriously in her long bed. She lay there for awhile, watching the April sun stream into her room and then she got up and closed the shutters. It already was warm, but not extremely hot, for April is a pleasant month in Mississippi.

The Cajan bathed herself and was before her mirror when the mulatto slave brought breakfast and, at her mistress' orders, went to a pine chest near the foot of the bed and got out Sharon's best visiting dress. The garment was worn around the hem and the muslin undersleeves of the jacket were soiled. The two women examined the dress, a cinnamon colored Chalais that smelled of sachet. The slave took the jacket away to clean the muslin and Sharon began working on the hem. She sewed between sips of coffee and soon the dress was ready, and she put it on, meeting the approval of the mulatto.

The skirt was a bias piece of silk, cut out in large vandykes. The points turned upward and were surrounded by rows of black velvet. The jacket was trimmed with three rows of velvet and had rather long sleeves and muslin undersleeves. The bonnet was of white silk, undertrimmed with flowers and loops of ribbons.

Gar's best carriage was at the house by ten o'clock and the Wolof himself was on the box. Sharon let him wait a few minutes as was proper and went to her taproom ostensibly to give orders to her slave, but really to see and be seen by some of the speculators there.

Several loiterers complimented her on her appearance and Sharon affected a boredom, then said, "Only important business could get me out on a morning like this."

"Business?" one of the speculators asked. "I thought running this rooming house and taproom was your business."

"I'm going up to look at some of the furniture in the MacKenzie place," Sharon said. "I need some things and I understand the old man needs money."

And so with that story planted where it would spread, the Cajan took her parasol and went out to the carriage. Gar didn't look at her until they were almost up the hill and out of sight and hearing of anyone else. Then the Wolof looked over his shoulder and smiled and took the liberty of telling her that she looked as fresh as a daisy.

"I'm glad you could come," Sharon said. "I was afraid your work at the Alexander place might keep you."

"I ain't working there for awhile, Mis' Sharon. Miz Alexander likes to do her own driving and she said she wouldn't need me until her husband gets back. I reckon she figured there wasn't no use of paying me when she didn't need me." The Wolof smiled again. "They've got lots of money, but she don't waste it."

"Drive slowly," Sharon said. "I want to think. Head first to the MacKenzie place."

She sat back in her carriage and a hundred ideas danced in her head and when she examined the one she liked best she began twirling her parasol and tapping her right foot. So Morna Alexander didn't need Gar. That convinced her that Morna had no intention of sending word to Keith that Wyeth Woodward was in Natchez. They were almost to the MacKenzie place when Sharon leaned forward and said, "Gar, I want another driver. You are going for Keith Alexander."

The Wolof almost dropped his whip.

"That's right," Sharon said. "He is in New Orleans or Lebanon. . . ."

"Lebanon," Gar said. "He wasn't aiming to go to New Orleans for awhile."

"Then go to Lebanon. And tell Mr. Alexander that I sent you. Tell him that a cotton speculator named Wyeth Woodward is here and that I have a feeling he may be a Confederate. Understand?"

"I heard you, and maybe I understand, but I ain't sure."

Sharon twirled her parasol again. "Good. It is best for no one to understand my ideas except me. That's the way Mr. Frome worked. Mr. Alexander will ask you about his wife. Use your head. All you know is that Miss Sharon Weatherford who runs a rooming house under the hill gave you $25 to go to Lebanon and tell him that Wyeth Woodward was here. And I hired you because you have the fastest horse."

Gar nodded his acceptance of the instructions. "I'll get another driver for you while you're in Mist' MacKenzie's house, and I'll be on my way to Lebanon by the time you come out."

Sharon walked up the front path to the MacKenzie place and as Wall had gone to his store, Laurel answered the door. The younger woman was surprised that the Cajan would call in broad daylight, but Sharon reassured her and they went into the parlor. Laurel was as chipper as ever and her appearance convinced Sharon that the snowball of gossip about Wyeth and Morna hadn't begun rolling yet.

"It's good to see you up again," Sharon said and took a chair.

"It's good to be up." Laurel pulled a chair close to Sharon and sat down, too. "And now I'm worried about you. It's dangerous for you to try to take up where Mr. Frome left off. . . ."

"So Wyeth came by here?" Sharon was smiling.

"Of course. You didn't expect him to leave without seeing me, did you?"

"He wouldn't have anyway." The Cajan laid her parasol on the floor near her chair and took off her bonnet and her yellow hair was in a loose roll and hung low at the back of her neck. "Did he mention Morna Alexander?"

"Why, no," Laurel said quickly. "Why should he?" Her tone was sharp and there was a suggestion of belligerence in her eyes. They were a cold gray for a second, and then they warmed again as they looked at the Cajan.

Sharon was rocking slowly and Laurel began rocking, too. Her feet scarcely touched the floor and she looked very small there before the tall woman. "He is a good Southerner," Sharon said slowly. "He will take orders even from a woman if he can help the Cause."

"Of course he's a good Southerner," Laurel snapped and quit rocking abruptly. "What did you mean about Morna Alexander?

Wyeth rode into town with her, but he didn't know who she was until after he was in her carriage. What are you getting at, Sharon?"

Sharon quit rocking also. "That woman has taken quite a fancy to your betrothed."

"Folderol! that woman would take a fancy to any man. Especially while her husband is away." Laurel tossed her head as though she was dismissing the whole thing. Then she looked closely at the Cajan and her lips suddenly were narrow and white. "Has she been after Wyeth?"

Sharon nodded.

"I hope her husband finds it out. He'll—he'll *beat* her. And I hope he does." Laurel jumped up from her chair and stood before Sharon. "And if she doesn't look out, I'll beat her." The freckles were visible then and the skin on her cheeks was tight and red with anger. "I mean it! She had better leave Wyeth alone. . . ."

"Sit down, Laurel. Sit down and listen to me." Sharon took a deep breath. "I have done a thing that might upset you and I want to explain the situation before you hear stories from other sources. I told Wyeth to see that woman. . . ."

"Did he see her again after he was in her carriage?"

"I'm coming to that. But you must listen for a minute. I am taking over Nate Frome's work and I'm going to do it as he did. I will give orders and I will not discuss certain matters with anyone. If I have to sacrifice any one man for the good of the whole I will not hesitate. . . ."

"Wyeth is in danger!" Again Laurel jumped up. "You mean him when you say you'll sacrifice any man. Would you sacrifice Simeon Granville? Or Ves? Tell me that. . . ."

"I'll sacrifice *any* man or any woman to get iron for the new *Arkansas*." Sharon reached for her parasol and stood up. "I'll be going. If you won't hear me, then I might as well go."

Laurel grasped her arm. "Sit down. I'm sorry. I'll listen. I won't say a word until you're through. And I won't pry. I know that whatever you're doing is for the best."

Sharon patted her hand and sat down again and motioned for her to sit down, too. "Now understand," Sharon began. "Wyeth wanted to tell you this, but I forbade it. I'll do the talking for the organization. The night after Wyeth arrived here he went out to the Alexander place to look for a piece of iron that he heard was out there. That woman saw him and got to questioning him."

Laurel couldn't keep her tongue still. "How much did she learn?"

"I don't know." Sharon sighed. "Your sweetheart is not a crafty man. Thank heavens." Then Sharon told her the whole story up to that point. "And so, you see, that iron was a trap and that woman is almost bound to know that Wyeth is working for the Confederacy."

"Yes." There was not a trace of alarm in Laurel'. tone. "And then what?"

"He went to the cavern yesterday morning and she met him on the road coming back. No, there's no reason to believe she knows about the cavern, but there is reason to believe that she met him because she wanted to see him."

Laurel looked down at the floor and then up at Sharon. "And she didn't send word to her husband that Wyeth was here?"

"No. And do you know why?"

"Naturally." She swallowed the bitter words on her tongue. "She wants some attention from him."

"That's it. Wyeth told me about the meeting on the road and wanted to tell you, but I thought otherwise. I sent him back to the Alexander place last night. So you can blame me."

"If nothing wrong has been done then there's no blame."

"You're a sensible woman, Laurel. I wanted Wyeth to try to find out just how much that woman knows. So I sent him out there and they met again. She revealed nothing. I wouldn't have told you this because what you don't know will never hurt you, but Wyeth lost his horse near the Alexander place and Captain Youngblood and Mr. Whitsitt found it and know that he was out that way. They've started talking. . . ."

"I am not interested in gossip."

"Regardless of what you hear, don't be a fool. Remember, I sent Wyeth there and he was doing his duty."

"That doesn't bother me, Sharon." Laurel's jaw was set. "I'm not worried about Morna Alexander and my sweetheart." Her chin went up. "She has no weapon that I haven't got, and I have one that she hasn't got because Wyeth loves me. So all of that is not important. But when Keith Alexander gets back . . ."

"He'll hear the gossip."

"And he will try to kill Wyeth." Laurel put her hands on the arms of her chair and her knuckles were white.

"Yes. He may challenge him," Sharon said. "And that mustn't happen. No man, except maybe Mr. Granville, can face Keith Alexander in a duel. My first task is to get iron for Captain Brown and my second task is to keep Wyeth and Keith Alexander from meeting."

"But *she* is responsible." Laurel relaxed in her chair and the chair seemed to swallow her. "What will he do to her?"

"Her husband worships her and will believe anything she says. Now, don't be alarmed until there's more cause for alarm. Let me handle this. You will hear a dozen tales about your sweetheart and that woman. Some of your own friends will carry the tales. You know Natchez. Gossip is the life blood of this place."

"I will not tolerate a scandal about Wyeth. . . ."

"You will take orders. His life and your father's life and your own life depend on all of us working together. My life, too. And the South. So you'll take orders, Laurel, or I'll wash my hands of the whole thing."

"I'll take orders," Laurel said softly.

"You don't love Wyeth Woodward. . . ."

Laurel laughed in spite of her tension.

Sharon laughed, too. "No, you don't love him. You have spurned him. He loves you. Lord, yes. He began courting you in Missouri and you liked him a bit then. But now . . ." Sharon shrugged her shoulders. "Why, he's a cotton speculator and a MacKenzie couldn't love a coward who makes money when there's fighting to be done. So that woman is second fiddle. She's tried to get what you cast away."

"And you expect me to tell such a lie?"

"Yes."

"But Sharon, when my lips say I don't love him, my heart and eyes will be saying otherwise. . . ."

"Fools listen to lips. Do you understand what you are to do?"

Laurel didn't hesitate. "I understand and yet I don't. I'll do as you say but I don't know what for. Only one thing, keep that woman out of my path. I'll forget myself. I just know I will."

"There's no reason for you to meet. If you pass her on the street ignore her as any lady should ignore such a woman." Sharon sighed again and got her parasol and stood up. Then she stooped and kissed Laurel's forehead. "I knew you had sense and courage. I knew we could depend on you. I will be in touch with Wyeth soon and will send your love. Much of this he doesn't know and he mustn't know it. Men are very silly about their honor."

They walked together to the door. "Just one more thing," Laurel said. "How much to tell Papa?"

"I will get word to him. We're back under Nate Frome's rules. Just don't talk unless you say what you're told to say."

"My word is binding. That is, unless my sweetheart is cornered. If he is, I will go to him and stay with him and everything else can go to the devil."

"If he's cornered, then everything *will* go to the devil." She stepped onto the porch. "No, don't go to the steps with me. I came by here to try to buy furniture from a merchant family that is in financial plight. I am a loyal Union woman, Miss MacKenzie."

"You are a darling," Laurel said and watched her walk down the path and to her waiting carriage. Then she went back into the parlor and sat in a chair and rocked furiously, trying to calm herself.

Sharon looked far more important and confident than she felt as her carriage wheeled out Linden Road toward the Alexander home. She had no idea what to expect and was trying to prepare herself for any emergency. The driver turned his team up the winding way to the mansion and at Sharon's order asked a gardener if that were the Alexander place. In a way, the Cajan was relieved to learn that Morna was not at home.

"She is out riding," the gardener said. "She should be home soon."

"Then I will call later," Sharon said and instructed her driver to go on down Linden and keep his horses at a walk. It was the first time she had had an opportunity for a morning ride since the war began and she tried to enjoy it. But she was nervous and her emotions were tense.

She rode for almost an hour and then returned to the Alexander house. Because of her station, her first impulse was to go to a side door. Negroes went to the back door and equals to the front and Sharon wondered if it would be proper for her to seek entrance from the side. Such thinking made her angry at herself and she stepped to the front door and tapped the knocker. Never before had she called at a mansion, but she was a Weatherford, a descendant of the Clan Mac Gillivray. True, she was a Cajan, a tavern keeper, but she refused to bow her neck to anyone.

The servant who answered the knock looked at her closely and took her name and asked her to wait. That was an offense, for it was bad manners not to ask a visitor inside. Sharon tossed her head in haughty displeasure and waited on the porch. She heard Morna reviling the servant and didn't know that she was in a bad humor because she had missed Wyeth on the Trace that morning. She had rather hoped that the Missourian would dare to be there. Morna opened the door herself and said cordially, "Miss Weatherford, my apologies for my servant's stupidity. She should have asked you in."

Sharon was taken aback at the reception. Morna, dressed in green, looked cool and confident, and Sharon admitted to herself that she was beautiful, and poised.

"I trust I am not presumptuous, Mrs. Alexander." Sharon bowed and was surprised when Morna offered her hand.

"If you're who I think you are, you're welcome here," Morna said and opened the door and invited her guest into the music room.

Sharon accepted a chair and sat quite straight and proper. "I am Sharon Weatherford." Then she lowered her eyes. "I am owner of a rooming house under the hill. A loyal Unionist, you understand, but I have to earn my own livelihood."

Morna sent a servant for coffee. "If I remember correctly, Miss Weatherford, you are a descendant of Billy Weatherford, the Creek warrior who was called the Red Eagle."

"He was my kinsman."

"And he and my grandfather were friends." Morna worshipped the memory of Sam Dabney and it mattered not to her if Sharon were a Cajan and tavern keeper. Let Natchez titter. There was no snobbery in Morna.

"Yes, they were friends," Sharon said.

"Then I'm honored that you called. I have heard about you and wondered why you did not come to see us. I would have gone to see you. . . ."

"It was my place to call first. However, I didn't want to be bold."

"Fiddlesticks!"

Sharon took a deep breath. Morna's friendliness had almost disarmed her. "You're very kind. However, this is not exactly a social visit. I need to talk to you or your husband or some Unionist I can trust."

"Oh, the war again." Morna served the coffee herself and put hers aside to cool. "I'm tired of war. I had hoped you came to see me to talk about Billy Weatherford and my grandfather and the things that we have in common—Lebanon and the swamp country where you were reared." She looked away out at the trees and flowers of the bloated Natchez country. "I'm rather homesick. Aren't you?"

"Sort of."

"Do you remember my grandfather?"

"Yes. He was a great man. I sat on his knee once when I was a very little girl. I visited your home once, but you were away."

"You'll come back to see me, won't you? I don't like Natchez, and the people here are not my sort."

Sharon liked her then. She, too, wanted to forget the war and talk about home. She finished her coffee and put the cup aside. "Mrs. Alexander . . ."

"Why don't you call me Morna? Nobody here calls me Morna. You call me Morna and I'll call you Sharon. I'm tired of being formal and you are homefolks."

"All right," Sharon said softly and hated her mission. "All right, Morna. There is a roomer at my house. A young man named Wyeth Woodward." She looked at her hostess quickly.

Morna did not betray any surprise although she was surprised. "Mr. Woodward? I know Mr. Woodward. What about him?"

"I suspect him of Confederate sympathy," Sharon said.

"He is a cotton speculator, isn't he? And a very charming young man. But what has this to do with me?"

Sharon was baffled by her reaction. There wasn't a flicker of an eyelash to suggest any guilt on Morna's part. "I don't trust Captain Youngblood," Sharon said. "That's why I came here."

"Let's get to the point, Sharon." Morna's tone was somewhat brittle then. "I have seen Mr. Woodward a time or so. Why do you suspect him and why do you come to me with your suspicions?"

Sharon didn't like being on the defensive. "The man lives at my house and naturally I see and hear things. He has acted rather strangely. I know he figured in that mess at Grand Gulf and that your husband is interested in what actually happened there. That's why I took the liberty of sending word to Mr. Alexander that he is here."

"You did what?" Morna's eyes opened widely and Sharon noticed then just how green they were.

"I hired a Negro to go to your husband and tell him that Wyeth Woodward is on the scene again." Sharon smoothed her dress and looked into her empty coffee cup. She was trying to be indifferent. "I got suspicious the first night he was in town and I drove out here to talk to you. But you apparently were not at home and I didn't want to talk to your servants at that hour. I was here last night, too, but your house was dark." She was watching the other woman and saw that Morna's knuckles were white.

"When did you send a messenger to Mr. Alexander?"

"This morning. I was afraid Mr. Woodward might leave. I hope I didn't do wrong."

Morna didn't reply immediately and Sharon was confident that her mind was seeking a solution to her problem. And again Morna surprised her. "You did exactly right, Sharon. If you think there is something about that man that my husband should know, then you did right. I'm sorry I was not at home when you came. But that's not important. To be truthful, I wondered about Mr. Woodward, too. One of my servants saw him prying around an old iron boiler down yonder in that gully. . . ."

"And I know he talked about iron at my place. I think he's after iron and when speculators buy iron it usually means a tie-up with the Rebels."

Morna was composed again and sent for more coffee. "I had half a notion to notify my husband that Mr. Woodward was here. But I wasn't sure that his visit meant anything. My husband is too busy to be bothered with every wild rumor. I didn't want to send him on a wild goose chase."

"I hope I haven't. But if I'm right and that man is Secesh then I will feel that I have done my country a service." Sharon watched Morna refill the cups. "And I understand that Mr. Alexander pays well for information."

"He does," Morna said and there was a trace of disgust in her words. "He'll pay you. You know that my husband drove Nathan

Frome out of town and that he is after a group that has been helping the South. I suspect Wall MacKenzie, too. Have you noticed anything unusual about Mr. Woodward and Mr. MacKenzie?"

The Cajan forced a smirk to her face and she giggled. A giggle simply did not fit Sharon and Morna looked at her sharply. "Mr. Woodward wishes there was an association between him and Mr. MacKenzie," Sharon said.

"I don't understand. . . ."

"Haven't you heard?"

"Heard what?" Morna leaned back in her chair and tried to appear relaxed, but she was tense.

"Why, Mr. Woodward is in love with Laurel MacKenzie."

"That's preposterous," Morna said quickly and without giving thought to her words. "That homely little chick could not interest any man." Then she realized that she was on dangerous ground and sought to correct the impression. "I gave Mr. Woodward a lift into town after his horse was lost and he told me that he scarcely knew Laurel MacKenzie. Mr. Woodward may be working for the South and may even be a spy, but he's a gentleman. He wouldn't waste his time on that little upstart."

Again Sharon smirked. "You're mistaken about that. He has tried for years to win her hand. His interest began when she was in school in Missouri. . . ."

"Nonsense!" Morna was visibly agitated.

"It is true. It is common gossip. And Laurel MacKenzie will have nothing to do with him. She cast him aside like an old shoe."

Morna was white then. The mere thought that she was playing second fiddle to the girl infuriated her. She forgot her composure and stood up, facing Sharon. "How well do *you* know Mr. Woodward?" She regretted saying it the minute the words were out and yet she was so angry and mortified that her brain had no control over her tongue. "He lives at your house and you live under the hill."

Sharon stood, too, and her black eyes were cold. "I do not know Mr. Woodward as well as you do."

For a second, Morna entertained the idea of slapping the Cajan. But she suddenly was afraid, not knowing how much Sharon knew. However, she decided to brave it out and looked her visitor over from head to foot. "If ever again you have occasion to call here, then go to the back door."

Sharon actually laughed and was pleased. She had managed to keep her wits while Morna was losing hers. She felt that she had met a test and had triumphed. "I won't be back, madam. You might try your wiles on Captain Youngblood now. He found Mr. Woodward's horse out here last night. . . ."

"Get out," Morna said hoarsely. "Get out, you slut! And if Captain Youngblood mentions my name then my husband will kill him. And Wyeth Woodward and any other man who talks about his betters."

"Good day, Mrs. Alexander." Sharon moved to the door. "I mean Morna. You had better begin thinking. Your husband will wonder why you didn't send for him. . . ."

"You came here to get money. . . ."

"I came here to do my duty." Sharon was on the porch. "I even might have warned you that your name is being connected with a Rebel. But you insulted me."

Morna followed her to the porch and her voice was shrill. "It is impossible to insult such a woman as you." She gripped the back of a porch chair. "You've got nigger blood in you. I know why all those men stay at your house. . . ."

Sharon could afford to laugh and she enjoyed it. "At least, if I wanted men they would come to me. I wouldn't have to chase them and I wouldn't have to take what a girl like Laurel MacKenzie threw away." She was at the steps.

"I will report all of this to my husband and he will run you out of town. . . ."

"Stop screaming." Sharon tossed her head and stepped to her carriage. "You had better be thinking up a story to fool your husband. I won't talk. I'm in business and I don't want my name mixed up in this thing. You're safe as far as I'm concerned. Mr. Woodward should return in a few days. . . ."

"Where is he?"

"I don't know. He didn't confide in me." She put her foot on the carriage step. "He left late last night and was a little drunk. He said that when he came back he would see the most wonderful woman in the world."

"The idiot. . . ."

"Oh, he wasn't referring to you. He had Laurel MacKenzie on his mind. But her father has threatened to shoot him if he hangs around there any more." Sharon entered the carriage and opened her parasol, then nodded to her driver.

Morna hurried into her house and ordered a servant to find Gar. He had the fastest horse in town, that is, the fastest one available for hire. He could get her message to Keith before Sharon's messenger got to Lebanon. She had to be the first to tell Keith that Wyeth Woodward was back.

Her servant, however, shook her head. "Gar ain't nowhere around. You told him you wouldn't need him until Mist' Alexander got back. The lady who just left hired him to ride over to Lebanon on business for her."

Sharon got out of her morning dress as soon as she got home and put on something more comfortable. She wished that Granville had seen her with Morna, for she was proud of her behavior. She had muddied the water so thoroughly that she alone could see through it. She went down to her taproom to be seen by the speculators there, and then retired to her own room and sent for a courier she could trust.

The messenger was given the password and told to go to Wyeth with instructions to buy and store all the iron available in Woodville. She knew that once duty-bound Wyeth got on the trail of iron nothing could pull him away. "Tell him," she instructed the courier, "that regardless of what he hears he must stay down there until he gets orders from me. Tell him to buy railroad iron first and haul it to the river. We will get it here and hide it in the cavern."

Then she took up her work at her rooming house as though nothing had happened. That night she sent for Wall MacKenzie, met him by the river and told him all she wanted him to know. "Keith Alexander will be watching you," she said. "He will never dream that a woman is running the organization. You must act aloof from the whole thing and if I need you, I will use you."

"Very well," the little Scotchman said. "I'll start muttering a few threats against Wyeth tomorrow."

"Don't overdo it. The snowball has started rolling downhill and all we have to do is duck behind the trees and watch it roll. When it hits bottom it will fly into a thousand parts. Maybe there will be some iron in the snowball and we can pick it up in the confusion."

Wall scratched his head and grunted. "Only a woman could create such confusion and then see daylight. Wyeth told a saloon keeper that he scarcely knew me. Didn't even know I'm a widower. Now you tell that he's in love with my daughter and that we hate him. It's too much for me."

Sharon said, "It's very simple. The best way to kill a lie is to tell a bigger one and then keep lying until the other side doesn't know what to believe."

"Of course, Sharon, you know that Alexander will start shooting."

"Who?"

"Those who are talking about his wife."

"Youngblood and Whitsitt? Let him shoot. . . ."

"And maybe Wyeth."

Sharon was preparing to leave. "Wyeth can shoot, too. But it won't be necessary. Alexander won't go to Woodville. The Confederates are in control there and he won't walk into a Confederate camp. I know what I'm doing, Wall. Believe me." She went home then and had no trouble falling asleep. Her mind was made up and was at ease. It was about one hundred and forty miles to Lebanon and she knew Gar would ride all night. . . .

Over at Captain Youngblood's house, a courier rapped gently until he awakened the officer and then handed him a dispatch. Youngblood read it slowly and dismissed the man, and then read the orders again. Colonel Grierson and his Union cavalry would leave Tennessee on April 17th and Youngblood was to be ready to receive them in Natchez. He was to assemble every soldier available and work with the Union sympathizers and be ready to seize Natchez and prevent any demonstration against Grierson. Grant was almost ready to tighten the noose.

Captain Youngblood burned the message and scattered the ashes. Then he went back to bed and told his wife the visitor was a soldier seeking information. That satisfied her, for her mind was not on war, but on the gossip that had Natchez tittering and gasping. "And to think," Mrs. Youngblood said, "that Morna Alexander could accept attention from another man so soon after her marriage. Is this Mr. Woodward such a handsome man?"

"Aw, go to sleep," the captain said.

Keith Alexander, riding a showy white horse, arrived in Natchez four days later. There were silver trappings on his saddle and his pearl gray hat was at an angle, and his pearl-handled pistols were slightly forward of his hips. He was wearing a black coat and gray trousers. He left Gar on the outskirts of town with instructions to report for work the next morning, and then rode through downtown Natchez, tipping his hat to the ladies and waving nonchalantly to the men who stared at him in awe and fear, and some in contempt.

The dust scarcely had settled behind his horse before the word spread that he was back. Captain Youngblood and Whitsitt looked at each other and smiled. The Union women of the town tittered and their men put the backs of their hands over their mouths and repeated coarse jests about Morna. The Confederate folks lifted their chins a bit higher and said nothing, although their eyes showed their disgust with the whole thing. Gar went to his stable and rubbed his horse down, then reported to Sharon. His faded denim jacket covered the Bowie knife at his side.

Out Linden, Keith galloped, a confident, conceited man who knew only that Wyeth Woodward, the man with the scar, was thereabouts and that Sharon Weatherford had sent for him.

He halted his horse by the veranda of his house and jumped onto the porch and hurried inside, calling for Morna. Recklessly and jubilantly, he flung his hat on a table, removed his pistols and ran up the stairs, two at a time. She appeared at the head of the stairs and opened her arms to him and he swung her off of her feet. At that moment she forgot that there was such a man alive as Wyeth Woodward; forgot that there was another man in the world beside this one.

Keith kissed her roughly and she laughed and he cradled her in his arms and took her to their room. He was laughing, too. "Now don't smother me with questions," he said. "Your father and mother are fine. The whole family is all right. We will go into that later. . . ."

"Much later," she said and put her arms tightly around his neck. "I'm so glad you are home. I wanted to send for you, but Gar was the only man I could trust and that Cajan woman hired him right out from under my nose. . . ."

"Then you expected me?" Keith was surprised.

"Didn't Gar tell you? Wyeth Woodward has been here." Morna blinked rapidly, for she, too, was surprised.

"I know that. But how did you know it?"

Morna laughed to give herself time to think. "That Gar! the perfect servant. I fetched Mr. Woodward into Natchez." She smiled proudly. "I thought you'd be surprised. Yes, I brought him into town in my carriage and Gar was driving. . . ."

"He didn't tell me that." Keith was puzzled and annoyed.

"Of course not. A good servant never tattles the mistress' business to the master. Then he didn't tell you that your wife forgot about you the minute you were out of sight and accepted attention from a handsome young man. . . ."

"What the blazes are you talking about?"

"Wyeth Woodward, my love. I was seen with him. You know Natchez."

Keith looked at her quickly and his blood began racing. "I didn't run up those steps to hear gossip. Mr. Woodward and the war can wait until later."

"Much later," she repeated and moved close to him, confident of her power. She had faith in her weapons and was proud of her charms. And, too, she loved her husband and knew that he loved her.

They had their supper in a little alcove just off their bedroom. Morna was wearing a negligee of green silk and Keith's dressing gown was black silk. He was at peace with the world and was content to sit there by her and smoke a cigar. It was good to be home. "And," he was saying to her, "your father intends to let Frome live in Lebanon." He shrugged his shoulders. "Anyway, as long as he is there he can't do any harm. The war is over for Nathan Frome. I didn't catch him, but I pulled his claws." He stretched out his legs and put his arms above his head and sighed.

Morna got up and poured more coffee and he watched her. They drank their coffee slowly and often she leaned over and teased him. They had had the afternoon together, but the night was before them. Wyeth Woodward was unimportant and Keith just happened to say, "So you lured the young man into town, this Mr. Woodward. The Union has no call on your charms, you know."

"He is a very attractive gentleman," she said and swished her negligee and rolled her eyes in mock fascination. "And I think that Weatherford woman sort of likes him. Is she a *bad* woman, Keith?"

"*Bad* woman?" He put his hand to his forehead and groaned. "You mean a whore? Has Natchez done that to you? I hate the expression 'bad woman.' "

"Yes, that's what I mean." Morna peered into her cup, then sipped her coffee and it was cold.

Keith knocked the ashes from his cigar into a saucer and the evening breeze stirred the ashes, blowing some of them onto his dressing robe. He brushed away the ashes, leaving a grayish smudge. "I don't know the woman, but I've never heard that charge against her. So far as I know she just runs a rooming house under the hill. Of course, under the hill means whoredom to lots of folks, particularly to the pots that revile the kettles."

"She is very beautiful. . . ."

"Have you been under the hill, my dear?" His laughter was deep. "I don't mind you giving Mr. Woodward a ride in your carriage, but going under the hill . . . tut, tut. No wonder some of the old hens around here are cackling about you."

"She came out here, Keith." Morna was tapping her foot against the floor. "She came out to tell me she suspected Mr. Woodward and to report that she had sent Gar for you. I think she expects money."

"Without doubt. I must see her soon. . . ."

"Tonight?"

"Well, now. Perhaps not tonight. But I certainly must look up Mr. Woodward tonight. He might fly the coop."

"He's not in town right now. But he'll be back in a few days. So Miss Weatherford told me."

"Good. I was not anxious to leave you on my first night home." He moved his ash-tray away from the window. "However, I must call on the Cajan woman tomorrow. After all, she spotted Woodward and I will pay her well."

"I spotted him first, I tell you. It seems that you are not impressed that I am the one who recognized him first. He even told me his name. But I would have known him anyway. By his scar."

"Then you should step forward and claim the reward. . . ."

"I intend to," she said and when he laughed she added, "I wish I could blush. And I wish I could keep my mind clear when you're with me. You haven't heard my story. . . ."

"It'll keep."

"But I tell you, my name is being prattled from tongue to ear all over Natchez. You won't take it seriously."

"Should I?" he asked and slipped his arm around her waist. "I know the women here are envious of you and that if you so much as lift an eye-brow they will gossip."

"Oh, fie on the women! But the men . . ."

"What men?" His arm tightened around her, then he relaxed it and withdrew it and looked at her.

Morna accepted the look without wavering, and returned it. "I'm not sure, but I think Captain Youngblood and that old fat-necked Mr. Whitsitt started it." She knew it was possible that she was signing their death warrants and she didn't hesitate. "They and some Negroes found Mr. Woodward's horse near here one night and the next thing I knew the story was out that he had been visiting me."

Keith removed the cigar from his mouth and put it in his coffee cup and it sizzled for a second. There was a tiny frown between his eyes. "Let's have the whole story," he said slowly. "I'd hoped it could wait until later, but let's have it. From beginning to end."

"So at last you're interested?" She pinched his chin, then kissed him where she had pinched.

"Let's have the story, Morna." He said it again and his words were as brittle as thin ice, but she was not alarmed.

She told him what she wanted him to believe and, of course, he believed her. She didn't tell the story as though she had rehearsed it and she knew he believed her. Keith Alexander thought he understood his wife and was under no illusions. So he thought. He knew that in years to come it might take all of his domineering power to keep her for himself. It never occurred to him, however, that she could even glance covetously at another man so soon after marrying him. Such was his conceit. He interrupted her only a few times, once to ask why she didn't send for him that morning she first met Wyeth.

Morna was ready for that. "I realize now that I should have," she said. "And I started to. Then I got to thinking that maybe he was heading for Port Hudson or somewhere and I wanted to watch him for a day or so. I didn't want to call you here to find that he had moved on."

Keith nodded slowly. "You did right. Go on."

"Besides," she said, "I was a dunce. Maybe I was excited. I let Gar off. No need of paying him if he wasn't working. And when I was sure the time had come to send for you, he had been hired by that Cajan woman for the same mission. I didn't trust Captain Youngblood or anyone else, so I just sat tight and waited for your arrival."

"I see. Now, tell me, after you saw Woodward the first time did he go to Wall MacKenzie?"

"Yes. But maybe it's not what you think. He knew that MacKenzie girl in Missouri and I gathered that he was calling on the old man to pay his respects." Morna's mouth tightened. "One story is that he's in love with Laurel MacKenzie and that she has spurned him. But I don't believe it. . . ."

Keith's eyes twinkled. He rather admired Laurel. "Why not?"

"It's fantastic. Mr. Woodward is a gentleman. I must say that. He wouldn't waste a look on that little bundle of baggage. . . ."

"Now, now. You never forgive, do you? All that girl ever has done to you is ignore you. She and her kind always will, my dear. Remember that we may beat them into the ground, but they will never give up and they will always hate us. So don't let your own hate warp your judgment. Let's get back to the story. And you saw Woodward out here that night? Looking at the boiler?"

"Yes. And I tripped him, too. He walked right into the trap you set for Nathan Frome."

Keith ran his hand over his chin and frowned again. "And the next morning?"

"As I told you, I was riding on the Trace and ran into him. He wanted to know the way to Port Gibson. . . ."

"But he didn't go to Port Gibson?"

"He couldn't have," she said. "His horse was found out near here that night. . . ."

"We'll get to that later." Keith got up and took off his dressing gown and slippers and reached for his boots. "Did he visit Wall MacKenzie again?"

"What have the MacKenzies got to do with it?" she asked sharply.

"Everything." He said it with obvious impatience and then smiled at her and patted her arm to soothe any hurt his attitude might have caused. "You see, darling, I'm sure Wall MacKenzie was Frome's right hand. After Frome left, MacKenzie probably dropped the organization like a hot rock because I was closing in. It is the Confederate Navy that needs iron and when no more iron was forthcoming I have an idea that Captain Isaac N. Brown sent one of his bright young men down to revive the organization. I think that bright young man is Wyeth Woodward. So I am trying to establish a connection between Woodward and MacKenzie."

Morna folded his dressing gown and put it across the foot of their bed. "So far as I know there is no connection. Unless you care to believe that silly story about him being in love with Laurel Mac-Kenzie. . . ."

"Oh, for God's sake! I'm not interested in romance. Let's get back to the story. Then the last time you saw Woodward was that morning on the Trace. And some men saw you talking to him?"

"Yes." She sat on the bed and watched him adjust his cravat. "I was driving along the Trace and he came down the Trace. In a buggy. He spoke properly and asked me the direction to the Port Gibson road. I wasn't sure myself and was trying to figure it out when some men rode by. He asked them and they told him."

Keith looked down at his boots and flicked off a bit of dust. "Woodward knows the way to Port Gibson." He looked up quickly at his wife. "Now back to the first time you met him. On the Trace. The morning he said he had lost his horse. How far was that from where you met him the second time?"

Morna hadn't thought of that. "Why, it was in the same vicinity."

"There's no cotton out there. Or anything else." He put his pistols around his waist and slipped on his coat. "No one lives around there since old man Kincaid was hanged." He sat on the bed beside her and took her hands. "You've done fine, my love. Now, about Youngblood and Whitsitt. Take your time. But be careful, Morna. Don't accuse any man falsely. If this is a lot of woman talk, then we must stare it down. But I won't tolerate men discussing my wife. What makes you attribute the slander to Youngblood and Whitsitt?"

"They found the horse."

"Maybe the Negroes are responsible."

"No, Keith. Negroes don't put hidden meanings behind everything. That's the way of white folks, not Negroes."

He clamped his lower lip between his teeth and then his slow sardonic smile came to his lips. "Perhaps Youngblood and Whitsitt just happened to tell their wives that they found Woodward's horse out near here and the women jumped at conclusions. You had been seen with him twice."

"Maybe that's it," she said. "All I know is that I was getting ready to retire and heard voices up the road. I didn't pay any attention to them. The next morning I heard that Mr. Woodward's horse was found on the road, that he had left his buggy in the woods down near the gully and his horse had jerked free and headed for town. And the next thing I knew it was all over town that he was with me. In the woods, Keith."

He arose from the bed and that bitter smile was playing around his lips and that contemptuous coldness was in his eyes, the first time Morna had seen the look since the Battle of Lebanon. "I am calling on Youngblood and Whitsitt," he said.

Morna opened the door for him and stood there, then moved close to him and put her head on his chest. "You'll be careful, won't you? Mr. Whitsitt is an important man. . . ."

"Whitsitt is a lout. I wouldn't do him the honor of challenging him. If necessary, I will slap his face and run him out of town. But Youngblood is another matter."

"Don't let him provoke you into a duel, Keith. I might be wrong, but I've felt for some time that Captain Youngblood would like to embarrass you. Maybe he is hitting at you through me."

"I think I have underestimated Youngblood." Keith cupped her chin in his hand and kissed her. "He is afraid of me and, therefore, he hates me. And I haven't been exactly polite to the cove. . . ."

"He is jealous of your influence in Washington. . . ."

"Exactly. But if I should make the mistake of challenging an officer of the United States Army then I wouldn't have any influence in Washington. As an officer, he could decline the challenge with honor. So he has the advantage of me. I'm not a suspicious man, Morna. But perhaps Youngblood is after my scalp and is using you to get it. I won't challenge him. And I won't kill him. We'll see what we can see." He kissed her again and she walked with him to the front door.

"I'll stay up until you return," she whispered. "And hurry."

"I will." He laughed then. "You know, Morna. You are sizzling powder. Every time you open those green eyes you'll cause trouble. I knew that when I married you. I think I told you that I'd have to spend the rest of my days killing men because of you. But I didn't expect to start so soon."

He put on his hat, moved it to the side of his head and went to the stable and saddled his horse, not caring to call a stableman. He headed first for the Whitsitt place which was between his house and town. Keith didn't know much about Whitsitt and had never wasted time to know him. He did know about Whitsitt's business, however, and that he had borrowed heavily from a New Orleans and British factor and had used the money to buy land confiscated from Confederates. He was a rich man, but he wanted more. He had pledged cotton for the money and planned to buy or seize the cotton at that fall's harvest. His own land didn't yield enough to cover his debt, but it wasn't difficult to get cotton if a man were friendly to the Youngbloods. Keith had a sour taste in his mouth as he thought of Whitsitt.

The planter was not at home. He was over in Louisiana buying confiscated property.

Youngblood wasn't at home, either. His wife was, however, and she answered his knock as she never had learned enough to allow servants to do such things. Keith bowed elaborately to her and she gasped, then tittered and was excited and nervous. "My husband is not here," she said and curtsied. "Won't you come in? Unless, perhaps, you are afraid the neighbors will talk." She tittered again.

"We will give them something to talk about," Keith said and followed her into the house.

She looked over her shoulder at him and Keith read a dozen meanings in her look. She was flustered and pleased, and sympathetic. Mrs. Youngblood naturally had sympathy for Keith. He had been home only a few hours and a husband doesn't leave his wife for a minute, particularly a wife such as Morna, so soon after his arrival unless there is cause. And Mrs. Youngblood understood the cause. Poor Mr. Alexander. That was in her look. Had his mind not been so intent on other matters, he might have laughed at her. The idea came to him then that this was the opportunity to learn just how much talking Captain Youngblood had done.

He sat on the edge of a chair in her living room and looked miserable and hurt and baffled. Sympathy, and a bit of yearning, was evident in every gesture of Mrs. Youngblood. She bustled to the kitchen for coffee and poured cream into his portion. Keith preferred his coffee black, but Mrs. Youngblood was trying so hard to be polite that he accepted the creamy drink.

"I am sorry my husband is not here," she said.

"I'm not." He looked at her over the rim of his cup.

Much to his surprise she didn't giggle, but looked him squarely in the eyes and said invitingly, "Captain Youngblood is often away these days."

"Government business, I presume?"

"I suppose so. He never tells me anything. Strange men come here at all hours of the day and night." She leaned forward in her chair and whispered, "Something is brewing. Do you know what it is?"

Keith scowled. He didn't like for anything to be afoot without being a part of it. "No, I know nothing about it. Perhaps it concerns the military. After all, your husband is an important military man and I am only a civilian."

Mrs. Youngblood folded her hands and sighed. "It's all too much for poor little me. And how is that beautiful and lovely wife of yours?"

He cringed within himself and wondered if he could stand it much longer. Then he assumed a woe-begone expression and looked at the floor. "She is all right," he said slowly. He looked up at her quickly. "You know, Mrs. Youngblood . . ."

"Yes?" she said eagerly.

He looked away as though he couldn't face her. "No," he said dramatically. "I have no right to bring my troubles to another."

Mrs. Youngblood pulled her chair closer to him and took his coffee cup and put it on the table. She sat down again and leaned toward him and for a second Keith actually feared she was going to take his hands to comfort him. "You can trust me. I understand."

"I must talk to somebody."

"Of course. And my heart is big and my shoulders are broad." Her shoulders were not the only broad things about her. "I understand men. I've always understood men more than I understand women."

"I'm glad of that," Keith said and reached out and patted her hand. "I'm baffled. Tell me the truth, dear lady, have you heard any talk about my wife?"

She lowered her eyes. "I don't gossip, sir."

"I realize that. And I am ungracious to think of bringing my woes to you. I got home only a few hours ago." His head sunk to his chest.

"There, there," she said in a dulcet tone. "You mustn't be too harsh or too quick to judge your wife. She is young and headstrong."

"I want to be just." There was an unctuous quality in Keith's tone that disgusted him with himself. "I am older than Mrs. Alexander. Much older. But there are things no gentleman can tolerate."

"Don't jump at conclusions, I beg of you. That's what I told my husband. . . ."

Keith's muscles tightened.

"Those were my very words," she said. "The night he told me about it and I said to him, 'Don't jump at conclusions.'"

"That's why I want your understanding and advice," he said. "I trust my wife."

"What have you heard?"

"That a Mr. Woodward called on my wife while I was away." He put his hands on his knees and watched her.

"I was sure that was what you had in mind. But don't jump at conclusions. I saw them together myself. With my own eyes. He was in her carriage. There's nothing wrong in that, I hope."

"No. But his horse was found near my house at night."

Mrs. Youngblood glanced away and there was a glint in her eye. What a fool Morna Alexander was to pay any attention to another man when she had this one. "Yes, his horse was found near your house. Captain Youngblood found it. And Mr. Whitsitt. I don't trust Mr. Whitsitt." She lowered her voice. "He is a lecherous old busybody." She raised her voice a trifle. "I don't know Mr. Woodward, but don't jump at conclusions. Just because your wife's bedroom light happened to go out a few minutes after Mr. Woodward was seen nearby is not proof that they were together. That's what I told Captain Youngblood."

So the Captain was responsible for the story. Keith was so angry for a second that he almost dropped his pose. He caught himself, however, and stood up and took Mrs. Youngblood's hands. "You have been very kind."

"It is easy to be kind to you."

"You tempt me and flatter me." He bowed.

She tittered then. "I hope I've been of service."

"You have. I was upset. But I won't jump at conclusions. I was a fool even to allow an ugly suspicion to cross my mind. I have not behaved very gallantly toward my own wife. Thank you for defending her against the stupidity of her husband."

That was not what Mrs. Youngblood expected and she was very disappointed. She wanted to reopen the conversation and increase any suspicion he might have, but he had closed the subject. He walked to the door and she followed him.

"I don't know when my husband will be home," she whispered.

"It must be important business. Only important business could keep a man away from such a charming lady. Goodnight, Mrs. Youngblood. And thank you so much."

He went out to his horse and that bitter smile was back on his lips. He really was baffled. There was no way he could force an officer of the Army into a duel and he couldn't kill the man without giving him a chance. He was determined, however, to shut the man's mouth and punish him. His pride was hurt and Keith could not stand for his pride to be bruised. Still, he gave no credence to the story, but put it down as a lie spread by Youngblood, a scandal that grew out of a chain of coincidences. His hands were cold when he lifted the reins, but his hands were steady. There was a fury in his heart, an open-eyed fury that, instead of exciting him, rather calmed him and made him cautious and deliberate and crafty. The instinct for killing was a part of his being and there was no mercy in his makeup, and no pity. Death was the only payment for a debt against his honor.

He scarcely gave a thought to Whitsitt. That oaf could be brushed away or smashed as an annoying fly is brushed away. Keith had no desire to kill him. But Youngblood . . .

The street lights of Natchez glowed a dirty yellow as he rode through town and was conscious of the stares of men. He knew they were staring at him. And he knew what they were thinking. They were laughing at him. At him—Keith Alexander. He had never been laughed at before. They were saying he couldn't hold his own wife, that he, the Black Knight of Vengeance, had married a tart and couldn't manage her. Youngblood was responsible. Youngblood and his filthy lying tongue. His hatred blazed for a minute and then the blaze subsided into a smoldering ash and he knew it never would go out until he had revenged his name and the name of his wife.

He was in no hurry, as haste might be folly. He had days to think and weeks to act. He turned his horse toward Silver Street and went under the hill and to Sharon's house. Without knocking, he opened the front door and went in, glanced around and then walked briskly to the taproom.

Sharon looked up when he entered. A handful of speculators looked up, too, and the expressions froze on their faces. Keith scarcely noticed Sharon, but walked across the room and stood before her, erect and haughty. "Are you Sharon Weatherford?"

She just looked at him and her chin went up and the pupils of her eyes became pinpoints. "I am *Miss* Weatherford."

"I am Keith Alexander. I want to talk to you."

Sharon continued to look at him, a contemptuous smile on her lips. Then she turned her back to him and put a glass on the bar.

"I said, Madam, that I want to talk to you."

Sharon turned on him and her voice was frigid. "Take off your hat in my house, and keep it off in my presence."

Keith recoiled as though she had slapped him and for the first time he really saw her. He looked into her eyes and his smile was as bitter as hers. Then he removed his hat and bowed. "My apologies, Miss Weatherford. I'm sorry."

And he was. He admired her instinctively. He admired her pride and her haughty demeanor. She, too, was sensitive and ruthless. "May I have a few words with you at your convenience?"

"Sit down, Mr. Alexander. I will be with you after I attend to matters of more pressing importance."

She served her guests and let him cool his heels. It was a new experience for Keith Alexander.

Chapter Twenty

T HE mulatto slave girl lit the candles in the upstairs sitting room and Sharon invited Keith up there and asked him his pleasure. He wanted brandy and she took coffee. He crossed his legs and sat for a minute, moving his right foot up and down and watching her serve the refreshments. Then she sat down across from him, a rhythm of grace. She smoothed her dress and sat quite properly, poised and dignified.

"And now, sir, what is your mission?" She moved slightly forward in her chair and smiled at him.

"Where is Mr. Woodward?" his voice was genteel and polite as he was using his best manners and was ashamed that he ever had used less in this woman's presence.

Sharon sipped her coffee and frowned at the taste. The brew was a mixture of acorns and coffee. "I do not know. I did my duty in sending word to you that he was hereabouts. Is it my task to find him now?"

The sarcasm amused Keith. "He will be back here?"

"I assume so. He hasn't given up his room and if he is what I think he is he most surely will come back."

"What do you think he is?"

"An intelligent and brave man, Mr. Alexander. A rarity in these times." She took another drink of coffee and pushed the cup and saucer aside. "And a Southerner who is risking his neck for the South. That's what I think he is. I think he is the head of the organization that Nathan Frome started and then lost to your persistence."

Keith looked at his empty brandy glass, then put it aside. "What is the basis for your thoughts?"

"Common sense. And a woman's intuition."

"Why did you send for me?"

Sharon laughed. "I am a loyal Union woman, sir."

"You expect to be paid for your service?" Keith was smiling.

"Naturally. You are paid for your service to the Union."

Keith uncrossed his legs, glanced at his boots and then up at her. "What do you consider fair payment? Five hundred dollars?"

"That is a good retainer, Mr. Alexander. That is a fair price for sending for you. My future services will be worth $1500."

"You are an expensive assistant."

"It is an expensive war." She reached for his brandy glass and put it in her coffee cup, unconsciously stacking the dishes as a woman will. "I'm very busy downstairs."

Keith cocked his head to one side and laughed. She was delightful and he almost told her so. "Oh, I will pay the money. I will send it down tomorrow by my groomsman, Gar Rivers. You can trust him. Now tell me, where is Mr. Woodward?"

"I really am not sure. I heard him mention Baton Rouge and Woodville. Baton Rouge is the more likely. There is more iron there than in Woodville."

Keith rubbed his chin and then stroked his mustache, a gesture that reminded her of Granville. "That is reasonable," he said. "And what is his connection with Wall MacKenzie?"

"Not what you think. . . ."

"How do you know what I think?" Keith reached for a cigar and asked her leave to smoke.

Sharon got one of the candles and held it while he lit the Havana. "You think Wall MacKenzie took up where Nathan Frome left off. I know Wall. He is a rabid Southerner, but he has not involved himself with the Confederacy. Had he assumed charge of the organization it would not have been necessary for the Confederacy to send Mr. Woodward here for iron."

"But there is some connection," Keith insisted.

Sharon smiled at him and her smile warmed him and when she

looked away the candlelight danced in her black eyes. "Love, sir. Love is the connection. Mr. Woodward is in love with Laurel Mac-Kenzie."

"That is to his credit. She is a spirited young lady. Oh, I know that Mrs. Alexander doesn't like her. There is a personal feud between them. Miss Laurel snubbed my wife. I'm sorry she did that, but it is a matter for the ladies to settle." He was smiling again.

Sharon said, "That doesn't concern me. As a loyal Unionist . . ."

"Oh, come now, Miss Weatherford. Your loyalty is profitable."

"So is yours, sir," Sharon snapped.

Their eyes met and Keith clamped his teeth on the end of his cigar and let his gaze roam around the room. "You are a Southerner, too," he said softly.

"And so are you. You buy and I sell. You love the South and hate the Confederacy. I love the South and hate nothing, but I want to be on the winning side. And I need money."

"You think I need you."

"You do, sir. You have been baying up the wrong tree. Wall MacKenzie is not the man you want. Wyeth Woodward is the key to the puzzle."

Keith removed his cigar and looked at the ash. "Miss Laurel has given him no encouragement?" Keith didn't like to gossip about such a personal thing as another man's love affair.

"Lord, no. She has refused to see him and Wall has threatened him."

"What are the objections to him?"

Sharon shook her head slowly. "Now, I know you need me. You need my brain. And ears." She put her hands behind her head and looked up at the ceiling. "Their objection is that he is a speculator, a man who thinks more of his purse than of his honor. . . ."

"That's what I'm getting at," Keith said eagerly. "But he's not a speculator. He is a Confederate. And the MacKenzies are Southern sympathizers. One word from him would eliminate the barrier between him and Miss Laurel."

He was getting dangerously close to the truth and Sharon's heart began beating rapidly. She appeared calm, however, and said slowly, "I have only my opinion and intuition to go on. But in this business one learns a lot. I told you he is an intelligent and brave man. The fact that the MacKenzies shun him convinces me they do not know his mission and that eliminates them from any connection with the organization. And he hasn't told them because he loves Laurel so much that he doesn't want to involve her father." She sighed and folded her hands in her lap. "We have some very gallant enemies, Mr. Alexander."

The way she said it suggested to Keith that she was impressed by Wyeth and that reminded him that his own wife had spoken of the Missourian's gentlemanly traits. That brought back to his mind the slander against Morna and he scowled. He was convinced that Wyeth was the leader he wanted, but he had no intention of lessening his pressure against Wall.

Sharon, seeing his scowl, thought she knew what he was thinking. And she was right, but was too tactful to mention it. Instead, she said, "As soon as Mr. Woodward returns I will let you know."

"Do you think I intend to sit here and wait for him to come back? No, indeed. I am going to find him."

"The Confederates are in force at Woodville. . . ."

"I know that. I will avoid Woodville and go around to Baton Rouge. The Federals are in control there. Woodward is a desperate man to risk capture in Baton Rouge."

"I'm not sure he's there," Sharon said. "He may be in Woodville. I know he went south. . . ."

"Baton Rouge is the place to seek him." Keith got up and stood before her. She stared up at him and watched the color drain from his face. "You hear much down here, don't you, Miss Weatherford?"

"More than I care to reveal." She stood and her eyes never left his.

"You are in my employ?"

"Until I have earned the $1500."

Keith's gaze wandered for a second and then he snapped his eyes back and they burned into hers. "I am at a loss for words."

"You needn't be," she said.

"Good. Then is there anything else I should know?" His feet were wide apart and his head was to one side.

"You already know it. Don't be a fool. Youngblood is jealous of you and will do anything to destroy you. Even to involving your wife in a scandal, hoping that you will challenge him."

"You have met my wife?" Keith's voice was low and filled with feeling.

"Yes. I went to your house."

"And you have heard the gossip?"

"Naturally. Youngblood has seen to it that everybody has heard it. You're a man, Mr. Alexander, and sensitive of your honor. Surely you are not fool enough to believe the stories of Mrs. Alexander's indiscretions. The stories are lies. Your wife's behavior has been above reproach. . . ."

"I need no assurance on that matter," he said quickly. "But I can't understand Youngblood. Have you noticed anything strange about him lately?"

Sharon sat on the arm of a chair and crossed her legs and dangled her right foot. "Only that he has been receiving many visitors. Some in uniform. The Federals are taking a sudden interest in Natchez. . . ."

"Yes?"

"Now, I ask you. If by some chance the Federals seized this town who would be selected to run it?"

"I would." Keith was sure of that, reasoning the United States would prefer sympathetic civilian rule in Natchez to harsh military rule.

Sharon was shooting in the dark. "But if you were discredited then who would take over?"

Keith pursed his lips. "Probably Whitsitt if they insisted on a civilian, or Youngblood if the military continued control after seizing the town." He hadn't given such a thing a thought, but the thought was planted in his mind and already was growing. He stood very erect for a second, then bowed. "Miss Weatherford, I am glad you are my ally. You could be a dangerous adversary."

She offered him her hand and he shook it warmly and Sharon breathed easier. She had deceived the fabulous Keith Alexander. Perhaps if he hadn't been so concerned about the slander against his wife—perhaps he had so much on his mind that he wasn't thinking as clearly as usual. Perhaps a hundred things, but the fact remained that a lowly Cajan had outwitted the lordly Alexander. She saw him to the door and then went back to her room and drank brandy to soothe her nerves. Again, she wished Granville had seen her. Her triumph gave her new energy and she dispatched a rider to Grand Gulf with instructions to Prent Oliver and Rock Bradford. She assumed rightly that Prent, under command of the Navy, could not leave Grand Gulf, but surely she could count on Rock and his

D. A. Elliott. So she told them to get a steamer and two barges down to the landing nearest Woodville and be ready to haul iron up to the hiding place. Next, she sent word to Wyeth to be at the landing with his iron and to come back to the cavern with the cargo. Then she undressed and blew out the candles and lay in bed, listening to the night. Keith Alexander, she knew, was not one to delay his trip to Baton Rouge and while he was there they could be getting their iron to safety.

Meanwhile, Keith rode slowly back up the hill and to Gar's stable where the Wolof slept. He woke up the Negro and told him to be at his house at the crack of dawn with his most comfortable carriage.

"I am going to Baton Rouge," Keith said. "I want you to drive me so I can rest during the trip." And without waiting for a reply he wheeled his horse and galloped away. Gar was stroking his beard when the white man left and there was the trace of a smile on his lips.

Keith intended to go home, but, passing the Whitsitt house, he saw lights and impulsively turned into the lane and rode up to the porch. He pounded sharply on the door and when a surprised slave informed him that the master was in bed, Keith brushed by the servant and headed for Whitsitt's library. "Tell your master to wait upon me. *Now*."

"He just got back and is mighty tired. . . ." the Negro said.

"Tell him Keith Alexander is waiting."

The slave hurried away and Keith was standing facing the door when Whitsitt, wearing his nightgown stuffed into his trousers, waddled into the room, a greeting on his lips but a look of apprehension in his eyes. "Why, Mr. Alexander. This is an unexpected pleasure."

Keith ignored the outstretched hand and looked at the planter coldly and then slapped his face with the back of his hand.

Whitsitt stepped back against the wall and put up his hands to defend himself. His lips were trembling and his eyes were darting from one corner of the room to the other. Keith dropped his hands to his sides and waited.

"I won't accept," Whitsitt said hoarsely. "I don't have to."

"Don't worry, you fat bastard. I won't kill you. That slap was to teach you never to talk about your betters."

Whitsitt pulled himself erect and some of the fear left his eyes.

[414]

"You can't hold me responsible for your wife's behavior. And you will answer to Youngblood for your attack on me."

Keith unbuttoned his coat slowly and watched Whitsitt stare at the pistols, then he said, "Leave Captain Youngblood out of this. He is an officer and a gentleman. He is above slandering the name of his friend's wife."

The planter's jowls began shaking and he smirked. "Youngblood is my friend. And he represents the Union here. You think you do, but just wait."

Keith hadn't dignified the home or the man enough to remove his hat and so he pushed it gently to the left side of his head. "I was just telling some men that you will be leaving Natchez, Mr. Whitsitt. Two weeks. I give you two weeks. And don't return while I am here or I will step on you as I do on all worms."

Whitsitt started to speak, but Keith shoved him aside and walked out of the house. He felt better. On his way home he actually recited poetry aloud, not the maudlin verses that he used to write to flatter women, but line after line of Shakespeare's sonnets. He knew his own power and felt it. Soon he would wind up his business in Natchez, smash the organization once and for all and revenge his honor at the same time. And then for Washington to claim his just dues. A new day was coming, and it would bring a new structure and he would be on the ground floor. A light was burning in Morna's room, and that thrilled him.

Gar reported for the journey in the still of the morning just before dawn. One of his best horses was between the shafts of his light buggy and a spare horse was tied to the rear axle. The Wolof assumed Keith would want speed on the trip. There was a pillow and a quilt on the seat for the white man.

Keith was in his office, a small room off the library and he called Gar to his presence and gave him the $2000 in gold to deliver immediately to Sharon. And while the Wolof made the trip back into town, Keith wrote a letter to Whitsitt's factor in New Orleans. He didn't mince words. Whitsitt, he explained, would not be able to buy cotton and speculate, hence could not meet his obligations to the factor. The man had overspread himself.

He sealed the letter. He was one of the few men in Natchez who had envelopes, and put it in his inside coat pocket. He was in a gay mood and went into the library for his first cup of coffee. Morna joined him there and he expressed his pleasure that she had got up so early to see him off. "You really should not have done it," he said.

Morna kissed his forehead and rubbed her nose playfully against his. "You knew I would." She, too, was in a happy mood, relieved that Sharon had not revealed the truth to her husband. She attributed the Cajan's behavior to a desire to associate herself with the winning side, the wealthy element. Morna was too intelligent to reopen events of the night before and was content to leave well enough alone. Her curiosity was burning as to any romance between Wyeth and Laurel, but she kept her opinions to herself. Morna's practice was never to tamper with a watch that was running on time and she was convinced that Keith had the situation under control, and that she had Keith under control.

The extra horse was not with Gar when he returned, for Sharon had instructed him not to race to Baton Rouge and back. He explained to Keith that the other horse had developed a limp. "I ain't got no more fast horses except the one we're driving," Gar said. "But we'll make good time."

Morna walked to the buggy with her husband and fluffed the pillow and made him comfortable. "If you find Mr. Woodward," she said, "are you going to bring him back to Natchez?"

"I'm no police officer," Keith laughed. "I can't arrest the man. My only mission is to keep the Confederates from getting iron. So I will turn the young man over to the proper authorities. If he is a spy, they will hang him. If he is a civilian agent he will be imprisoned."

The prospect of Wyeth being imprisoned or hanged disturbed Morna, but not much. Her first thought was of Laurel and she was pleased that Laurel might be denied something she wanted. Wyeth was no longer in her mind, for now that Keith was back there was no other man in the world who interested her. She stepped back to the porch and waved goodby as Gar drove his buggy out to the road and headed southeast. Keith ordered him to take the long way around, circle Woodville and Port Hudson and so avoid the Confederates there, pick his way through back roads and approach Baton Rouge from the east. The sun and birds were out when they rode away. . . .

Sharon put away the $2000 that Keith had sent, unconsciously balancing its weight against tons of iron. Maybe she could buy iron in Mobile. Maybe she could extend the organization to Mobile and keep a flow of essentials, medicines, salt and iron, moving from Mobile to the Mississippi Valley. All that day she was light-hearted and proud of herself and kept wishing that Granville, by a psychic trick, could look down from the Yazoo and see her and understand her strength and appreciate her triumph.

That night she went to her front porch and leaned against a post, watching the river. It crept by, broad and yellow, and there was no moon as the clouds hung low, threatening rain. She stayed there for more than an hour and then she saw the signal, a dim yellow light that flashed up at the sweeping bend. It flashed once and then went out and she counted ten and it flashed again. The smokestacks of the steamer silhouetted against the Louisiana side of the river. The boat's paddle wheel was still and she was drifting by. Directly opposite from the landing, the light flickered for a third time and Sharon counted one, two, three . . . eight, nine, ten. Then there was a light again. Sharon stepped to her door and opened it and light streamed out. She counted three and closed the door. Steam and smoke began rising from the boat and the paddle wheel turned slowly. Sharon wanted to wave and shout. Instead she closed her eyes and thanked God. Old Rock Bradford was bringing his *D. A. Elliott* down to meet Wyeth and fetch iron . . . iron for a new *Arkansas*.

She slept that night with her pillow in her arms and dreamed of Simeon St. Leger Granville and when she woke up she laughed at her girlishness.

Rock Bradford, following instructions to the letter, eased his steamboat and two barges into a sluice near Stump's Landing, the terminal of an old abandoned road that connected Woodville to the Mississippi River.

Wyeth was waiting there. He stood on the bank and grinned at the old riverman while the *D. A. Elliott* was made secure, and then the Missourian jumped aboard and embraced Rock, pounding his back until the skipper protested and pushed him away. They hadn't seen each other since the capture of the *Queen of the West* and Rock wanted to talk. Wyeth, however, waved his hand toward the bank and said, "I've got some iron stacked out there. Let's get it aboard."

"You're to go back with me."

"To Vicksburg?" Wyeth asked eagerly.

"Later. But first we go to the cavern and hide this iron until another batch is brought in."

They went ashore and examined the iron and Rock called his crew and they began loading, stacking the iron in the middle of the barges and surrounding it by cotton bales. "You didn't stop at Natchez?" Wyeth asked. He assumed the old man hadn't, but wanted to be sure.

Rock mouthed his disapproval of such a silly question. "Only a jackass in love would ask such a thing. Of course, I ain't been in Natchez. I've been at Grand Gulf with Prent." Then his faded blue eyes twinkled. "But your girl's all right. I know that. And Sharon, too. A mite bossy, but all right. She's running things to who laid a chunk."

Wyeth and the old man lugged a piece of railroad iron aboard and the gunner wiped his face and stretched. "I want to get back to the shooting. They need me to help run Porter and Sherman out of those swamps."

Rock grinned out of the side of his mouth. "They are doing pretty good without you."

"You don't happen to know where Mr. Granville and Ves and the Dolly are, do you?"

"Somewhere along Steele's Bayou just north of Vicksburg. Killing Yanks. Last I heard, Porter and Sherman were making about half a mile a day through those swamps and still trying to cut in behind Vicksburg. Our boys were picking them off like fleas. The Yanks are barking up the wrong tree again."

And so they were. The Steele's Bayou campaign already had failed. The Confederates had allowed Porter's gunboats and transports and Sherman's army to inch forward through the swamps until their communications were stretched into a slimy trail from the bogs to the river. Then they had begun pinching the Federals, and Sherman and Porter were in a trap. The ships took a frightful beating and the Union soldiers were at the mercy of sharpshooters. After days of bewildering frustration, the Federals managed to escape by backing their ships out of the swamps. The whole thing was a miserable failure, a loss of men and time. Grant, Sherman and Porter had tried every northern approach to Vicksburg and had been defeated five times, first at Chickasaw Bayou, then at Holly Springs, and next on the Lake Providence route; then at the Yazoo Pass and now at Steele's Bayou.

Rock and Wyeth didn't know it, but the second siege of Vicksburg was over and after a year the Federals were as far from taking the town as ever.

It took two days to load the barges and Rock, running only at night, moved his tow back up the river to the cavern and dispatched a messenger to inform Sharon of their arrival. They anchored at the mouth of the canal and Wyeth removed the torpedoes, and the barges were eased into the canal, thence into the cavern. Sentries were posted and it was far past midnight when Sharon arrived.

Wyeth helped her from the skiff and squeezed her hand. Sharon smiled at him and said, "She's all right." Then she gripped Rock's hand and glanced about at the crew and the iron. "Leave that iron on the barges and leave the barges right here in the cavern. I've spotted some more iron at Port Gibson and it's being floated down. When it arrives, you will have your load. . . ."

"And then for Vicksburg?" Wyeth asked.

Sharon nodded. "The *D. A. Elliott* will take it up. But get the steamer out of here. Tonight."

"This is the safest place to hide until the other iron gets down," Rock said. "Why not leave my boat right where she is?"

"Get it out," Sharon ordered. "Take it around the bend and hide it in a sluice. Keep your fires low and stay there until you get word from me." She wanted, above all, to keep Wyeth away from Natchez and also to protect the steamer. On the river, the *D. A. Elliott* had a chance to escape if detected.

"Yes, m'am," Rock said and began grinning. Taking orders from a woman was a new experience to him and he didn't mind it a bit. "Anything else, your majesty?"

"As soon as you get the *D. A. Elliott* out then lay the torpedoes again."

"Rock can handle the steamboat," Wyeth said. "I'll see you back to Natchez."

"You will not!" Her tone was stern and immediately she repented and called the young Missourian away from the group. "Laurel doesn't know you're here," she said. "If you try to see her you will jeopardize her safety and the iron, too."

"Very well, Sharon. You know best. I did want to see her before I go back to Vicksburg."

"I will try to arrange it. But she must come to you. You stay out of Natchez. Keith Alexander returned a few days ago. . . ."

"What's that to me?"

"Just your life, you fool." Sharon was annoyed because he apparently didn't appreciate the danger. "Your life and Laurel's and mine. . . ."

Wyeth looked down at the ground. "Does Alexander know that I saw his wife?"

"He knows only what I want him to know and what his wife dared tell him. He blames Youngblood and Whitsitt for the story that his wife accepted your attentions. He thinks it's a lie. So does Laurel. So far, so good."

"Does Laurel think I'm afraid of Alexander?" Wyeth demanded.

Sharon stamped her foot. "That's a man for you. There's a man's stupid vanity. Because Laurel loves you she believes you're invincible. And I know you're not afraid of Alexander. You haven't got sense enough to be. . . ."

"Now, wait a minute," Wyeth protested. "Just because I made a fool of myself once is no reason for such ridicule. . . ."

"We won't argue. You agreed to take orders from me and I'm holding you to the agreement." Again she was sorry that her tongue had lashed him and she reached out and squeezed his arm. "There's no question about your courage or your intelligence. You just don't know women. Our duty is to get iron and we're getting it. Now go back to your boat."

"Gar is all right?" There were many questions he wanted to ask her. He wanted a dozen details about Laurel and asked about Gar to prolong the possibility of a conversation.

"Everything is all right. I told you that." She began walking back to the group and Wyeth fell in step with her. He and Rock helped her into the boat and one of the *D. A. Elliott's* crew rowed her away, out of the canal and onto the river.

Rock and Wyeth looked at each other for a second and the old man shook his head slowly. "Now, there's a woman."

Wyeth didn't reply. They made the barges fast to the bank, then unlashed them from the steamboat and backed the *D. A. Elliott* out of the canal and cavern. Rock took her upstream about a hundred yards and Wyeth went back to the mouth of the canal, set the torpedoes again, and dawn found them in a sluice around the big bend just north of Natchez.

A lull settled over Natchez and extended as far south as Port Hudson where General Banks was throwing men and steel against the Confederate ramparts without visible results, and as far north as Milliken's Bend where Grant gazed south and east at the green bluffs of Vicksburg where spring had turned the river and the hills into a fairyland. He didn't take time to mourn for the thousands he had lost since he had pitted his wits and power against Pemberton and those sharp bluffs over yonder. The Union thought he had failed again. But he would make one more attempt. It never entered his head to do otherwise. The fleet, battered and torn, was up at Cairo undergoing repairs, and his men were resting in the lazy April days. Occasionally a big gun boomed from Vicksburg. The second siege petered out into long sunny days of inactivity.

Sharon selected a cotton speculator whose loyalty to the Union was beyond question and posted him to watch the river at night while she pretended to keep a sharp lookout during the day. He was to warn her at the first sign of any craft and she asked him to do the task as a favor to her. The man was so flattered that he asked no questions.

Mr. Whitsitt left town after confiding to a few men that Keith Alexander was trying to break him. His New Orleans factor called for his money or for cotton to satisfy the loan, and Whitsitt tried to buy cotton on credit. None of the speculators dared trust him, for such was the power of Keith Alexander in the cotton world. The speculators shunned Whitsitt and even Youngblood couldn't help him, so the planter went to New Orleans to beg leniency from his factor. Every cotton man in Natchez knew that he would never be back. Youngblood held the military reins in Natchez, but Keith Alexander controlled the cotton.

The harsh quick vengeance of Keith rather thrilled Sharon. In so many ways he reminded her of Granville that she admired him when she should have hated him. Morna wasn't worthy of the love of such a man. Often she found herself comparing him and Granville and the Englishman always came off best in the comparisons, but, nevertheless, she liked Keith Alexander.

When a week went by without any word from him or Gar, she began to get nervous. The town was filling with strange men and the lull was so intense that Sharon felt it was preceding a storm. She assumed correctly that the strangers had some connection with Youngblood and was alarmed lest he really anticipated seizing Natchez. She talked to Wall MacKenzie about it and the old Scotchman assured her that her alarm was groundless, pointing out that the Federals could gain nothing by seizing Natchez so long as Grant was stymied at Vicksburg, and Banks at Port Hudson.

Sharon had more faith in her intuition than in Wall's knowledge of military things and made up her mind that in the next day or so she would instruct Rock and Wyeth to pick up the iron in the cavern and get it away without waiting for the load from Port Gibson. Maybe, she reasoned, the Port Gibson iron could be intercepted up at Grand Gulf by the *D. A. Elliott.*

Having determined her course, she felt better and enjoyed her first good night's sleep in a week and woke up refreshed and very early. She was on her way to her kitchen for a snack when she saw Gar at her back door. His face was drawn and he was reeling from sheer exhaustion. Sharon let him in and helped him to a chair.

"We got back about two hours ago," Gar said. "That white man ain't human. We rode day and night and I'm whipped to a frazzle."

"Where is he?"

"Out at his place. I would have got here sooner but I had to look after my hoss. He's plum' near dead."

Sharon got a drink of her best brandy for the Wolof and told him to go into the storeroom and sleep. She hurried back upstairs and rearranged her hair, then went to her taproom and waited. When she saw Keith Alexander riding up, she marveled at his strength. He was freshly shaved and his clothes were immaculate, but there was a scowl on his face and a suggestion of impatience in the way he sat his saddle.

She walked to the porch to meet him and when he dismounted she turned to the cotton speculator on lookout duty and dismissed him. Keith looked at the man, then quickly at her, and stalked into the house and to the upstairs sitting room. Sharon got brandy and followed him. "So you didn't find him," she said and put the bottle beside him.

"How do you know that?" His eyes were hard.

"Because he wasn't in Baton Rouge." She sat down and smoothed her dress and her words were calm although her heart was beating wildly. "I told you I wasn't sure where he was. He must have been in Woodville."

"And why?"

"Because he bought iron there a few days ago. That much I know. But no boat has passed here, so the iron must still be at Woodville. I've had a lookout posted all the time. The man on the porch was watching for me."

Keith reached for a cigar and started to light it. Then remembering himself, he asked her permission. "I can think better when I smoke," he said.

"I rather enjoy seeing a man smoke a good cigar," she said and her smile was so warm and friendly that Keith felt better.

He puffed his smoke in silence and walked to the window several times. "There's nothing I can do but wait for that damned Woodward to return here. He'll have to come this way. He will just have to." He looked quickly at her. "Won't he?"

"That's my opinion. He will have to bring his iron up the river. And if I know him, he will stop here."

"To try to see Miss MacKenzie?"

"Exactly. He will come here to my house and I will notify you."

Keith got up again and they shook hands warmly. "Good," he said. "We will just sit tight and wait." He got to the door and turned and smiled at her. "How is my friend, Captain Youngblood?"

"Very busy. Natchez is overflowing with strangers and I think they have been sent here to help Youngblood stage a coup and seize the town."

"Hardly that," Keith said. "Not yet, anyway. Natchez is no good to the Union unless Grant heads this way. Then its only importance would be to forestall a Confederate seizure."

"I don't understand all of that, but something is in the wind."

"If Grant moves this way, the Confederates could use Natchez as a fort. Its only use to the Union would be to prevent the Rebels from fortifying along here. But don't worry about that." His conceit came out then. "I am very close to General Banks. I saw him in

Baton Rouge and if any plan were afoot to seize Natchez he would have told me."

Again Keith Alexander had guessed wrong. Banks knew nothing of the plan. It was Grant's plan and Grant didn't trust Banks. Colonel Grierson was almost ready to begin his raid and Banks was as much in the dark as Alexander was.

His assurance comforted Sharon, but her mind was still disturbed. "Then what is Youngblood up to?"

"I think it is a big cotton steal," Keith said. "I think those men are being sent to him to scour the countryside for cotton. That's one reason Whitsitt and Youngblood were so friendly."

She walked down the stairs with him. "I assume you know that Mr. Whitsitt is no longer with us."

"Yes, I know." He hesitated on the front steps and took her hand again. "You have done well, Miss Weatherford."

She allowed him to hold her hand a second longer than decorum permitted, then withdrew it slowly. He thanked God that she didn't lower her eyes. Instead she faced him frankly and said, "Thank you. Thank you, Keith Alexander."

"You are a rare combination, Sharon Weatherford. Intelligence, charm and beauty seldom are found in the same person." He swung into his saddle and lifted his hat, then galloped up Silver Street to the brink of the hill. Natchez was not fully awake yet.

Sharon went back to her room and looked at herself and laughed. "See," she said as though Granville were there. "See, Sim. Even the great Keith Alexander thinks I am charming. And you, my love, treat me like dirt." She didn't allow herself to muse too long, however. The day was still and close and Sharon, with faith in her intuition, was jumpy. She would wait one more day for the iron to arrive from Port Gibson. If it hadn't arrived by the morrow, she would order Rock and Wyeth to pick up the barges from the cavern and get away before the storm struck. And she knew a storm was coming. She started to wake up Gar and tell him to follow Keith. The Wolof was sleeping so peacefully and was so tired, however, that she let him sleep. One more day would not make any difference. The storm was over the horizon and she could wait until it got closer.

Keith checked his horse on the rim of the hill and drank in the early morning air. He glanced back down toward Sharon's house and there was a stirring within him. The woman fascinated him.

He wondered what might have happened had he met her before he met Morna and, without realizing what he was doing, he began comparing her to Morna. She wasn't as beautiful as his wife or as voluptuous, but there was something comforting about Sharon. And, yet, in the comparison, Morna won every test. That was simply because Keith loved his wife so much.

Thinking of Morna, he was of a mind to go home to her and take her riding through Natchez so the people could see them and know that he trusted his wife. However, there was a thing he first must do to appease his curiosity. So he touched his heels to his horse's flanks, turned down Broadway Street and galloped out toward the Trace.

The coincidence of Wyeth being near the same spot both times he met Morna puzzled Keith. Reaching the Trace, he slowed his horse to a walk and studied the woods. It was high ground and offered no concealment. The trees were small and there were no swamps. He turned off the Trace and headed for the river and came to the deserted cabin where Mort Kincaid had lived. The land was still and brooding and the only sounds were the cawings of crows, the scolding of jays and the blithe melodies of mocking birds. Keith unfastened his coat so he could reach his pistols if necessary and dismounted and walked to the cabin.

Roaches scurried through the shack when he entered and there was a damp odor of decay about the place. He found no evidence that anyone had been there since Kincaid's death, then went out to the well and got a drink of water and watered his horse, and stood there gazing at the river and at the caverns that pockmarked the bluff. Those holes in the ground always had intrigued him and he walked down to the Devil's Punch Bowl and peered into its maw. He wondered if there were any truth to the legend that river pirates had used the Bowl as a rendezvous. If they had then the river must have swept in closer in those days than it now did in order to provide a connection between the river and the cavern.

With no purpose in mind other than to look at the freaks of nature, he walked toward the river and reached the gaping crater nearest the water. The exercise brought sweat and he sat on the rim of the hole and watched the river, the blue haze and the cranes rising from the swamps across in Louisiana. It was very peaceful there and Keith was glad he had come. He liked to be alone. He looked down into the yawning depression and tried to guess its depth. Then he picked up a heavy pine knot and tossed it into the crater and listened to it crash through the branches of the trees down there.

A hollow thud rolled back up and Keith was surprised. He thought all the caverns along the bluff were so deep that no man, on the rims, could hear any sound from the bottoms. The floors of the caverns, he knew, were soft earth and soft earth does not throw an echo. Again he peered over the rim. He couldn't see the bottom and a blast of chilly damp air came up.

He started to shout down into the crater and listen for the echo and then the truth dawned on him. That pine knot had not struck the soft spongy bottom of the cavern, but had struck wood, and that thud was a booming bass. Quickly he hurled another knot and listened for the sound. It came back and Keith almost laughed out loud. He jerked off his coat and pushed his trouser legs into his boots and swung over the rim and began a slow descent into the recess. He clung to the trees as he went down and reached the roof of the workshop. His footsteps made a hollow sound on the roof and he found the knots and realized that in striking the roof they had given off the sound of a heavy object striking a drum. Keith took out his pistols and checked them, then put one back at his belt and kept one in his left hand. He began scraping away the shallow coat of soil on the roof and found the boards that stretched across the cavern.

The sunlight scarcely filtered down through the trees and the shadows were so heavy that it was hard to believe twilight had not come. Keith stamped on the roof, then ran to the side of the crater and hid behind a tree.

When no one appeared, he walked cautiously around the edge of the roof until he found an opening and swung down and into the workshop. It was so dark there that he was blinded for a minute and he pushed himself against the side of the wall and waited. Both pistols were out and although his hands were steady, his heart was in his mouth. His spine was tingling and a clammy sweat rolled down from his face onto his neck.

He saw the canal first and then the barges. Slowly his eyes became accustomed to the darkness and, convinced the workshop was deserted, he walked to the barges and stood there staring at the iron. Then he put his pistols away and sat down and laughed. So this was it; this was Nate Frome's secret and the rendezvous for his organization. From here had come iron for the *Arkansas,* and that iron on the barges was for a new *Arkansas.*

There was no way for him to tell how long the iron had been there but he knew that sooner or later the Confederates would come for it, that Wyeth Woodward would come. At first, the bits of cotton along the bank of the canal puzzled him and he wandered around the workshop until he found the cotton hooks and the press the Confederates had used to reshape the bales after stuffing them with iron.

Keith visualized exactly how the Confederates had worked and his admiration for Frome increased, and for the first time he deigned to consider Wyeth as an enemy worthy of his talents. So they had hidden iron in cotton. He even understood the Grand Gulf coup.

Why they should leave their precious iron unguarded worried him. Surely, Woodward was too intelligent to blunder so crudely. Keith stepped aboard one of the barges and sat there thinking. Still puzzled, he began walking along the canal's left bank until he reached the mouth of the waterway and the willows that hid the opening from the river. He looked around for a skiff and was disappointed as he wanted to row out of the canal onto the river. He even thought of swimming out through the willows, but inasmuch as he couldn't carry his pistols with him he gave up the idea and climbed back to the roof and began the torturous ascent to the rim.

There he rested for a few minutes and then put on his coat and walked down to the river and along the bank until he found a skiff. It was covered by branches and he noticed closely how each branch was laid and then removed the covering and got into the boat. He put his pistols on a plank near at hand and, using an oar as a pole, he pushed the boat upstream, hugging the bank.

Gazing intently to the right where he knew the canal connected with the river, he was almost opposite the entrance to the workshop and would have passed it but for the dead willows. In the daylight the contrast between the dry willows and the live trees along the river was apparent. Keith wondered immediately how Wyeth had overlooked such a thing. That made him extra cautious and he rowed his skiff almost to the willows, then stopped. It was too simple, he thought. Woodward wasn't fool enough to leave his iron there for any prying stranger to find. It must be protected. Keith stared closely at the willows and then rowed to the bank and cut a long cane and moved it through the water between the willows.

The cane touched lightly the wires that connected the torpedoes and Keith jerked the pole away. Again he laughed, and got back into the boat and felt between the willows until he found the wires. Then he raised one of the demijohns and looked at it. Confederate torpedoes. They were the guards. Woodward was a sailor and it was natural for him to protect his iron with torpedoes.

Keith lowered the torpedo back into place and made sure there was no evidence that it had been disturbed. He still was pondering the mystery of the dead willows as he moved the skiff back to its hiding place and covered it just as he had found it. The bluff was steep and he walked slowly back to Kincaid's cabin. They must work only at night, he was thinking. That was the only solution and at night the dead willows looked no different than the live trees. He satisfied himself he had the answer and then began making plans to trap the Confederates when they came for the iron.

He would need help. That's when he thought of Youngblood, and thinking of Youngblood he forgot about Wyeth and that cold, bitter hatred began gnawing at his spirit, and his yearning for revenge overwhelmed his desire to catch Woodward. He could take care of Wyeth. That chore could wait. With Sharon helping him there was no chance for Woodward to come that way without him knowing it.

It was Youngblood who had tried to taint his honor and who had dared to spread scandal about Morna. Youngblood was the man he wanted. Keith's lips tightened and he sat on the porch of Kincaid's cabin and kicked the ground and let his plan of action crystallize in his mind. Youngblood thought he was safe behind his epaulets, and he was safe from Alpha and Omega, Keith's two pistols that always heretofore had paid his debts of honor. He couldn't challenge an officer and remain in good standing at Washington. And if he killed Youngblood, it would be counted as murder.

The more he thought about it, the more his cold fury bit into his heart and then that sardonic smile came back, and he was relaxed, for his mind was made up.

The sun had passed its zenith and was scampering down the long afternoon when Keith got up from the porch and took one last look around the cabin. Satisfied that no one had seen him, he patted his horse and mounted and, holding the animal to a walk, went back to

Natchez where he presented himself at the home of Captain Youngblood.

Mrs. Youngblood greeted him warmly and then ushered him into the office where the Federal commander attended to his affairs and to any other business that profited him. As angry as Keith was, he had his nerves under control.

Youngblood didn't do Keith the honor of rising to meet him, but turned his head slightly, nodded toward a chair and said arrogantly, "I've been expecting you, Alexander. I do not approve of the way you treated Mr. Whitsitt."

Keith moved his chair so he could face the man and said unctuously, "Perhaps I should have consulted the captain. . . ."

"Major," Youngblood said. "I've been promoted to my majority. Were you a military man you might recognize my insignia." He frowned and crossed his arms. "Yes, you should have consulted me about Mr. Whitsitt. I have been thinking of writing Washington about you."

The man's pomposity almost brought a smile to Keith's lips, but he controlled his desire to ridicule the lout and said meekly, "Major, there has been some talk. . . ."

"Damn the talk, Alexander. If you can't handle your family affairs then it is no concern of mine. The army is above such matters, but I feel it is my duty to inform you that you should open your eyes to certain matters of extreme delicacy; matters that concern you and your wife."

Keith just looked at him and waited.

Youngblood unfolded his arms and rested his hands on his chair. "Washington has never defined your authority to me, but as a major of the army I naturally represent my government here. . . ."

"Naturally," said Keith. "I am only a civilian sent here to handle Nathan Frome and his organization."

"That's what I'm getting at. Frome has escaped you and the organization has fallen apart of its own weakness. I've been thinking of so informing Washington. Perhaps your talents can be of better use elsewhere."

Keith looked away and did not try to hide a smile then. "There is much cotton around here, eh, Major Youngblood?"

The veins stood out in Youngblood's face. "What are you insinuating. . . ."

"I'm not insinuating," Keith said calmly. "If I leave Natchez you can accumulate a fortune in cotton. The speculators will look to you if I am gone. Calm yourself, sir. We understand each other. I have no intention of leaving here."

The major folded his arms again. "And if I write Washington that you have allowed your honor to be darkened by a scandal that touches your wife?"

Had Youngblood really known Alexander he would have recognized his bitter smile as evidence of his fury. Keith measured him from head to foot. "You won't write Washington. Iron is still going to the Confederacy from Natchez and if I leave they will hold you responsible. The organization is functioning again."

The surprised major scrambled to his feet. "Who is leading it?"

"I am not sure." Keith arose, too, and felt Youngblood looking at his pistols.

"You are bluffing, Alexander."

"And you bluff easily. But I am telling the truth and am reporting to you because you are an army man. I have found the rendezvous of the organization."

Youngblood sat down again and Keith told him about the cavern, pretending he had stumbled onto the secret by spotting the dead willows from the river. He didn't mention the torpedoes. He knew Youngblood. The type is always the same.

After listening patiently to the story, the major said, "What are your plans?"

"I will watch the place from across the river. They will go there some night and we can catch them redhanded." Keith reached for a cigar and didn't offer one to the officer. "Frankly, the only reason I reported to you is because I will need men."

Youngblood ran his finger across his lips and a crafty look was in his eyes. "What night do you expect them?"

"I haven't the slightest idea," Keith said. "Most any night now. The Confederates need the iron desperately and I'm of the opinion they will attempt to move it within the next few nights."

Youngblood put his hands on the arms of his chair and pushed himself up, and was beaming. "You did well in coming to me. We will catch them. Do you need any lookouts?"

"No. I will take up my post tonight and will watch 'til dawn and every night hereafter until they come. Then I will get word to you and you will meet me at the mouth of the cavern with a company of soldiers." He stretched lazily and flicked away the ash from his cigar.

"An excellent idea," Youngblood said slowly and his mind was not on his words. "And what are your immediate plans?" His tone was casual, too casual.

"Right now I'm going home and have dinner. Later this afternoon I'm going over into Louisiana to look at some cotton. I will be on duty at dark." He buttoned his coat and put on his hat, an impolite thing to do in the presence of a major.

But Youngblood didn't notice. He was thinking rapidly. What a fool Alexander was. Already he could see his report to the War Department explaining how he, beyond his line of duty, had trapped Confederate iron smugglers while Alexander dawdled. He could be a colonel, maybe a brigadier, if he played his cards wisely. It would be simple to take a company and hide in the cavern and wait for the Rebels while Alexander was across the river on lookout duty. He was so pleased with himself that he offered his hand to Keith.

"No hard feelings, Alexander," he said. "We will forget about Whitsitt."

Keith looked down at the outstretched hand, then removed his cigar and put it in Youngblood's hand. "Good day, Major."

The officer hurled the cigar out of the window. "What the hell?" he blazed and his face got puffy and red.

Keith tilted his hat to the side of his head. "Just to satisfy my curiosity, Youngblood, tell me if there's any chance that you have enough courage to resign from the army long enough for me to kill you. It will only take a minute. Write out your resignation, remove your coat and that's all there is to it."

Youngblood was too surprised to speak.

Keith opened the door. "You might kill me, you know. And then you would be famous."

"You're crazy!" Youngblood spluttered.

"There was no harm in asking. I assumed you wouldn't do it, you cotton pimping son of a bitch. When the war is over I will kill you anyway if I can get within pistol range." He laughed in Youngblood's face, stepped out of the door and bowed to Mrs. Youngblood who was waiting in the hall. Then he pinched her cheek playfully and patted her backside. Mrs. Youngblood giggled and Keith looked back at her husband and laughed again.

He wished he had time to go down and tell Sharon about his discovery. He just wanted her to know and to share his triumph. He had no idea of telling her about the torpedoes, but only about the cavern. He must tell no one about the torpedoes. Not even Morna. Some day Morna might forget herself and let it slip that he knew about them. And, too, as much as he loved his wife, he didn't dare give her a weapon that she could ever use against him. Keith Alexander never fully trusted any man or any woman.

Tomorrow he would tell Sharon that it was he who found the cavern and instruct her to double her vigilance for Woodward. As he rode out to his place, he was so light-hearted that he began whistling and, reaching home, he ran into the house calling for Morna and swung her into his arms.

When he put her down, he kissed the tip of her chin and she teased him about his exuberance. "You behave like a boy in love," she said.

"I am in love." He removed his pistols and pulled her to him again and told her about the cavern. "I had to tell Youngblood as I will need his help."

"But to call on him, Keith, after he told all of those slanderous lies about me? How did you keep your temper?"

Keith looked into the dining room and nodded to a servant his indication that he was ready to dine, and then turned to Morna. "I will settle my score with Youngblood in my own way, sweet. The war won't last forever and he won't always have the protection of his uniform. I can wait."

Morna had eaten her midday meal, but sat at the table with him while he ate. She wanted to ask about Wyeth but restrained the impulse. She was thinking of him even in Keith's presence and, in a way, was sorry that he was being trapped. But not very sorry. After all, he apparently had made no further effort to see her since that night at the summer house. It wasn't that she particularly desired his attentions now that Keith was home, but she wanted him to want her.

She watched her husband enjoy his food, a crab gumbo and beaten biscuits. "I hate to think of you staying up all night to watch that cavern," she said. "I like you home at nights."

"It won't be long. I will have to be away from you this afternoon, too. So don't expect me back until tomorrow."

"You have been away a lot lately."

He put his napkin by his plate and walked to her chair and leaned over and kissed her hair. "I must go over into Louisiana this afternoon and look at some cotton. And I will go from there directly to a spot opposite the cavern and take up my vigil. Things are coming to a head, Morna. I will break the organization and then we will leave here."

Morna sighed and walked into the living room with him and watched him fasten on his pistols. "I'll be glad to leave. I hate this place. Where will we go?"

"Washington. I will have a debt to collect from the Union and I will want interest. Then New York perhaps."

That pleased her and she handed him his hat and kissed him longingly, before he mounted his horse. She stood on the porch and waved when he turned down Linden, heading for Natchez.

Morna had no intention of remaining at home alone on such a lovely day. There were many new faces in Natchez and she wanted to ride through the streets and see the sights. So she dressed in a cool afternoon frock and ordered the light buggy, taking the reins herself.

She reached Natchez soon after Keith was aboard the ferry for Louisiana, and rode down Franklin Street, rather enjoying the stares of the populace, especially the men. She held her chin high when she passed Youngblood's house. A group of men were waiting on the officer's porch and some of them tipped their hats to her and some bowed. She didn't return the greetings. With no purpose in mind other than to enjoy the air and scenery, she turned her horse toward the Trace. It was her favorite riding place. The afternoon was in its prime and she had time to ride several miles and get back before dark. . . .

Youngblood joined the men on his porch and one of them told him that Morna had just passed. He shrugged his shoulders, and led the company down to the river and aboard a tug. He was impressed by his own importance and gave orders in a loud voice, but didn't condescend to tell his men his plan. The tug moved up the river and Youngblood braced himself near the bow and watched the shore until they reached the bluff where the cavern was.

On the major's orders, the pilot cut the boat to slow speed and Youngblood spotted the dead willows. "Men," he turned to his company. "Those willows hide the opening to the rendezvous of the Rebel iron smugglers. There is a canal behind those willows and we are going in."

He waved his signal to the pilot and the tug turned in mid-stream and its nose was aimed for the center of the willows. Youngblood was crouching at the bow when the boat parted the willows.

They never knew what happened, for none lived to report the incident. The tug tripped the wire and the first torpedo went off directly under the bow. Youngblood's neck and back were broken by the blast and with him died the orders to seize Natchez and be ready to meet Colonel Grierson and his raiders. Then the other torpedoes exploded and the river heaved and there were sodden bl-l-oooms. The tug disappeared and debris and mud were hurled half-way across the Mississippi. There was a yellow flame and then a black ball of smoke rolled out of the cavern's mouth. Tons of earth slipped down the bluff, choking the mouth and blocking the cavern forever.

The echo rolled along the Mississippi and Sharon and Laurel heard it. Natchez held its breath and men looked at one another in frightened apprehension and then ran to the river. Keith Alexander heard it and smiled. Morna heard it, too, and turned her horse and rode furiously back down the Trace.

Around the bend from the cavern, Wyeth was playing dominoes with Rock aboard the *D. A. Elliott* and waiting for orders from Sharon when the hollow echo spread up the river, pounding against the shores. For a split second, neither man spoke and then Wyeth jumped to his feet. "Torpedoes! Those were my torpedoes!'

"Sounded like it," Rock said, cocking his head to one side. "Somebody must have tried to get in."

Wyeth was racing for the pilot house and was screaming for steam. The engine room crew ran to stations and began throwing rotten pork and pine knots onto the fire. Rock reached the pilot house soon after Wyeth and put his hand on the young man's arm. "What do you aim to do?" He asked it so calmly that Wyeth wanted to shake him.

"Alexander must have found the cavern. Anyway, something has gone wrong and anything is liable to happen. I'm going to Laurel."

"I reckoned you had that in mind. But, son, you ain't going in this boat." The old man stepped to the wheel and faced the Missourian."

"I need this boat, Rock. . . ."

"So does the South. I'm rightly sorry, Wyeth, but I ain't exposing the *D. A. Elliott*. Sharon told us to stay here and if we lose this boat we ain't got many more."

Wyeth realized the old man was right. "You don't think I'm going to stay here, do you?"

"No. You ought to but you won't, and I reckon I can't blame you. I'll take you down the river a piece and then across to the Mississippi side. But I ain't going to Natchez."

He glanced at his steam gauge. He had enough power to back the *D. A. Elliott* out of the sluice into mid-channel. Then he swung downstream and cut over as close to the bank as possible to avoid being seen. Wyeth was at his side. His scar was flaming and his knuckles were white. They approached the spot where the cavern's mouth had been and Rock whistled softly. Youngblood's body was floating in the eddies and rubbing against the bank. Wyeth counted eighteen bodies in the vicinity and none of them was Keith.

"Alexander would never have been with Youngblood," Wyeth whispered. The presence of death made him whisper. "I don't believe he would."

"Anyway," Rock said, "there is one pas'l of Yanks that'll never draw a bead on us." His boat ground against the bank and he handed a pistol to Wyeth. "Watch your step, son. Tell Sharon I will be back up in the sluice."

The gunner leaped ashore and scrambled up the bluff. He was winded when he reached the top and paused for a minute to catch his breath. Then he began running toward the Trace. That was his only chance to flag a wagon or some conveyance heading for Natchez.

Reaching the Trace, he looked around frantically for some sign of a traveler and, disappointed, he began jogging down the road toward town. He didn't hear Morna's horse on the sandy pike until she called out, "Wyeth! Wyeth Woodward! What has happened?"

He jumped to the side of the road and was fumbling for his pistol when he recognized her. His first thought was that here was an opportunity to get to Laurel quickly. He was determined to share that buggy with Morna. Sweat was pouring from his face and his throat hurt, and was dry. He swallowed and stepped to the buggy. "I don't know what happened," he said. "I heard an explosion."

"So did I." She looked down at him and all the emotions she had enjoyed that night at the summerhouse came back to her in a flood of ecstasy.

This woman wasn't worried. Wyeth saw that and interpreted it as evidence that Keith Alexander was safe. He tried desperately to be calm and put his foot on the step of the buggy. "May I ride into town with you?"

Morna moved over. "Did you lose your horse again?" Her tone was friendly and warm.

Wyeth smiled at her, forcing the smile to his lips. He was anxious to be off. "Not this time. I was across the river looking for cotton and came over in a skiff. I thought at first a steamboat had blown up. But it didn't sound like a steamboat. It was more like gunpowder."

She lifted the reins and slapped her horse. "My husband is in Louisana looking at cotton. You two didn't happen to meet, did you?" The horse swung into a rapid gait.

Wyeth braced his feet against the bottom of the dashboard. "No, I still have not met Mr. Alexander. I didn't know he was back. I've been away, you know."

Morna didn't reply immediately. She was very conscious of his nearness and wondered if it could be possible that he was hurrying to Natchez to see Laurel. The thought disturbed her. "No, I didn't know you had been away. I wondered what had happened?" she lowered her voice. Her green eyes were softer than Wyeth ever had seen them before. She moved her shoulders back, accentuating the curves of her breast. "I came out here the day after I saw you last. I thought maybe you were angry."

"You know better than that." He didn't want to talk. He wanted to hurry up the horse, but, more than that, he didn't dare give Morna any reason for suspicions or anger.

"What else was I to think, Wyeth? One night you showed at least some interest in me. And then you left without so much as a goodby."

Her honeyed words annoyed him. He was in no mood to answer a lot of questions. And yet, he must be careful. He decided then to flatter her, hoping to avoid too many questions. "I didn't trust myself with you," he said, knowing that would please her. "I was afraid that I might dare love the wife of Keith Alexander."

He heard her gasp and she tightened the reins and slowed the horse to a walk. "My husband is away now." She looked at him boldly. "He won't be back until tomorrow."

Wyeth was too human not to be thrilled at the invitation although he had no intention whatsoever of accepting it. However, he slipped his arm around her shoulders and held her tight and kissed her ear. "Summerhouse?" he whispered.

"No. Come to my house. It will be safe."

A feeling of revulsion swept over Wyeth. Her flesh was softer than Laurel's. He noticed that and removed his arm quickly. "I forgot it was broad daylight."

"So did I," she said. "You had better get out here on the outskirts of town. It wouldn't be wise for us to be seen together."

Wyeth agreed and as he stepped down from the buggy she said, "Come early. Immediately after dark."

"I will." He lifted his hat and she smiled suggestively at him, touched up her horse and moved away. She wondered then why she had done such a thing. Something within her rebelled and she was ashamed, just a bit. She was inviting trouble for herself and murmured, "I'm a fool, but I can't help it." She really wanted to see what Wyeth would do and have the pleasure of watching him answer her beckon, and run to her as men had always done.

Parties of horsemen were forming in Natchez to determine the cause of the explosion and the results. Crowds were gathering on every corner and most of the excited populace assumed a steamboat had blown up somewhere around the bend. The Northern sympathizers milled and fumed, expecting Major Youngblood to appear and assume command. They were hopelessly disorganized. In the crisis, the civil authorities awakened from their lethargy and took over. The sheriff called a posse and, because the incident demanded a unity of purpose, the Southern sympathizers met the crisis. Misery and travail had molded them into a unit. The populace was calmed and assured that no army was marching on Natchez and that a steamboat probably had blown up beyond sight of the town. Wall MacKenzie, knowing the truth, helped spread the story.

In the excitement, no one paid any attention to Wyeth as he ran and walked through town and out to the MacKenzie house. He took cover behind a board fence at the rear of the house and, convinced he was not being watched, slipped into the back yard, thence to the back porch. Laurel was at the back door and she cried out in delight and ran into his arms, sobbing and laughing.

"I knew you would come," she said, moving her mouth from his lips to his ear. He still was holding her tightly, but she pulled her head back and looked at him and began wiping sweat from his face. "Sharon told me you were up the river. I knew you were not hurt. I just knew it."

Wyeth, hearing footsteps, released her and looked up, and Sharon was walking down the hall from the front door where she had been waiting. She was walking in long strides. "Who did it?" she cried before she reached him.

"Youngblood." Wyeth's right arm remained around Laurel.

"Dead?"

"Blown right through the pearly gates." There was a trace of triumph in his voice. "He and his whole party. But Alexander wasn't with them."

"He is in Louisiana." Sharon looked down at Laurel and then at Wyeth and there was something sad about her smile. She leaned against the wall and shook her head to clear her brain. "I knew you would come here." Her eyes darkened and she was frowning. "It was a silly thing to do. I told you to wait for orders from me."

Wyeth ignored her, but tightened his arm around Laurel and took Sharon's arm in his other hand and escorted both of them to the living room. There he arranged chairs and when the Cajan was seated he said, "Sometimes, Sharon, your tongue is ahead of your brain. Of course, I headed for here the minute I heard the explosion. My behavior does not call for an explanation." He went over and sat by Laurel and she slipped her hand into his.

"Don't mind her too much," Laurel said. "She is thinking of safety. I am thinking of love." She glanced over at Sharon. "I can take care of myself."

The Cajan pulled another chair before her and propped her feet in it. She was very tired. She didn't even bother to apologize for her posture. "Arguments are no good now." She closed her eyes and then ran the tips of her long fingers along her forehead. "I came here when I heard the racket. I suppose you realize, Wyeth, that the explosion also blew my work to kingdom come."

He hadn't really thought seriously about that. She was so capable that, in the back of his mind, he had assumed that she was beyond defeat, that she would do something.

When he didn't reply, she opened her eyes and fixed them on him. "The explosion also probably blew the new *Arkansas* to bits. We will never get iron now."

"Oh, we'll do something," said Wyeth in masculine optimism. He didn't want to think about such things. He was with Laurel and the war could wait. Captain Brown would do something.

Sharon was too weary and too disgusted with things in general to pursue that line of conversation any further. She was not thinking so much of the Confederacy, but of Granville. She had wanted to succeed for him, to show him her ability. She knew how hopeless things were now and there was no need to harp on them. So she got up and put her hand on Wyeth's shoulder. "You go back to Vicksburg tonight. Gar will have a horse waiting."

The Missourian nodded. He still was not downcast. Iron would come. They had got it before and would get it again. "I suppose," he said, "I made a mistake in planting those torpedoes."

"Those torpedoes saved your life," Laurel said quickly. "But for them the Yanks would have trapped you."

Wyeth knew she was right.

Sharon brushed a kiss against Laurel's cheek and began walking toward the door. Wyeth went with her. "We all made mistakes," she said generously. "Luck was against us. Anyway, get out of town as soon as it is dark. When Keith Alexander gets back I intend to have a message waiting for him that you have been in town. I want to stay in his confidence." She opened the door slowly and her eyes were brimming with tears. She hated herself for weeping. "Don't you dare tell him you saw me crying. Don't you dare. Just tell him I did the best I knew how."

"I'll tell him everything," Wyeth said. "Everything."

"Go back to Laurel." She turned her cheek to him and he kissed it, closed the door when she went out, then hurried back up the hall to his betrothed. The sun was suspended over the Mississippi, waiting to retreat behind the west bank when the day had spent its allotted hours.

Cicadas were singing in the sycamores at the Alexander place and the long shadows of twilight brought cool relief to the sultry April day. Morna was alone. She had sent all the servants to their quarters behind the house and was waiting in the living room, watching the darkness chase the shadows across the lawn. A few candles were burning and time and again she walked to a mirror and fluffed her hair and straightened the neck of her dress. She didn't allow herself to think of the predicament she might be creating. The excitement and anticipation of seeing Wyeth again smothered her judgment. Maybe she would laugh at him. She tried to make herself believe she would. She even tried to deceive herself, telling her conscience that she had asked him there to trap him and hold him for Keith. Her conscience laughed at her and she knew that when he stepped close to her she would not move away, and that when he held her she would compare his embrace to her husband's and find it pleasing. The night moved in, shepherding the twilight before it, brushing the last gray shadows up from the lawn.

Morna listened to hoofbeats pounding down the road and her heart rose slowly to her throat. A horse and rider went by and she was angry at Wyeth, for he should have been on the horse just because she wanted it that way. She was annoyed at herself because she had walked toward the door to meet him.

So she sat down again and was determined not to meet him, not even to answer his first knock. That should show him that she wasn't as anxious for the tryst as he probably thought she was.

She heard another horse galloping down the pike and told herself that she just knew that wasn't he, hoping in that way to prepare herself against another disappointment. But when she heard the horse coming up the drive she got up quickly and went to the door and cracked it and was waiting.

Her husband swung from his horse onto the porch and Morna felt perspiration rise in the palms of her hands and the doorknob she was holding felt clammy and cold.

She looked so beautiful there in the doorway with the candlelight behind her that Keith didn't notice how pale she was and when he hugged her and felt that she was trembling he laughed at her. "You shouldn't have worried about me. Youngblood tried to steal a march on me and went to the cavern. We needn't worry about him any more. A matter of torpedoes, my dear."

"I couldn't help worrying about you when I heard that noise." Her voice was shrill and she glanced out toward the road. The echo of her own words pounded her eardrums and her mind was leaping frantically from one possibility to another. Keith took off his hat and coat and pistols, and she began lighting more candles, trusting that they would reveal to Wyeth the fact that her husband was home. If he came in anyway, she knew what she would do; she would betray him. She would curtsy to Wyeth and turn to her husband and say, "Mr. Alexander, may I present Mr. Woodward." Then she would smile triumphantly at Keith and say, "Here is the man with the scar, my love." Keith would be too surprised to question her then even if he dared think of questioning her in the presence of a stranger. And he would be busy with Wyeth and that would give her time to perfect a story. Oh, she would do something. She would save herself from any suspicion regardless of what she had to do to Wyeth.

Keith closed the door and put his arms above his head and stretched. Her nervousness flattered him. "I told you I would be in Louisiana," he said.

"That made it worse." She sat on a divan, her hearing attuned to every sound. "I didn't expect you until tomorrow and I couldn't have stood the suspense all night."

He sat by her and turned her face to his and stroked her hair and shoulders. "We soon can close that chapter. As soon as I heard the explosion I hurried back. I wanted to see how Wall MacKenzie was reacting to the emergency."

"And did you see him?"

Keith crossed his legs and examined his imported handmade boots. "No. I went by the house." Then he began smiling. "Laurel MacKenzie was there. . . ."

"You didn't dare speak to her." Morna's lips tightened.

"No. Even had I anything to say to her I wouldn't have disturbed her." Again he smiled. "She didn't see me and I'm glad, for she was with a young man and was telling him goodby. A very fond goodby."

He felt Morna stiffen and glanced at her in surprise. It came to him then. He leaped to his feet and reached for his pistols without realizing what he was doing. "Woodward!" He looked over at her. "That was Wyeth Woodward."

Fury and hatred and jealousy rose up in Morna and pounded against her brain. So he had gone to Laurel when he could have been with her. He had chosen that chick instead of her—Morna Alexander. She had been scorned and degraded. Laurel MacKenzie was laughing at her. Sharon Weatherford was laughing at her and Wyeth Woodward had dared let her expose her heart and then had turned his back and walked into the arms of the woman she hated.

She scarcely noticed Keith and was not aware of what he was doing or what he was saying. She was looking at him, but she didn't see him, for her mind was away from that room. There were red spots before her eyes and her brain was reeling; such was her fury.

"It's too late to catch him now." Keith's words seemed to come from far away. Then he actually laughed and his mirth galled Morna. "There he was about thirty feet from me," Keith said. "Beside his horse. It was dark and I never dreamed it was he. Now, I'm sure it was. . . ."

"Of course it was Wyeth Woodward." Morna squirmed about on the divan, then flounced to one end of the seat where she pounded a pillow with her fist. "And he was with that little hussy." Her laughter was a brittle cackle. "Sweet and gentle, is she? Harmless. She surely pulled the wool over your eyes. Why, I'll bet he has been hiding in her house while you and that Cajan woman looked for him. Hiding in her bedroom. In her bed. . . ."

"Why are you so sure it was Woodward?" Keith was frowning slightly as his wife's behavior puzzled him.

"I *know* it was." Morna stood and was shaking in anger and mortification. She would revenge her pride. Her eyes were wide as she fixed them on her husband and she was filled by a maddening urge to make Wyeth pay for slighting her. "I know it was he because he came here first."

That lie primed her tongue and her words poured out, first to Keith and then to the walls as she paced the floor and gave release to her fury in a torrent of abuse. "He came here. Tonight. Before he went to her." She paused at one end of the room and kicked a table leg, scarring it forever. "That's why he went to her. Because I drove him away. The sneaking lecherous fool. . . ."

Keith tiptoed to the divan and sat on its edge and watched her. His left eyebrow was raised slightly and that sardonic smile dominated his face.

"He came right to that side door." Morna nodded toward the door. "I thought it was you until he called to me. I started to ask him in and send for you and then I divined his intentions and I was afraid. So I sent him away. You know what he wanted, don't you?" Morna walked to the divan and stood directly in front of her husband. "He wanted me. He didn't want that girl. He went to her because I scorned him."

Keith watched her walk to the end of the room and back, then said, "Why didn't you tell me this when I got home?"

Tears formed pools in Morna's eyes and it was easy for her to weep for her mortification released the tears. "Because I was afraid you wouldn't believe me. Once, before we were married, you said I was too beautiful and too desirable to trust. I was afraid of what you might believe. I thought you might believe what the Youngbloods and the others believe. I didn't know what to do, Keith."

Deliberately he crossed his feet and entwined his fingers and stared at their tips. "Youngblood told the truth, didn't he? Woodward was out here that night?"

"Yes." Her voice was a hoarse whisper. "He was here. He tried to get in. He laughed at you, Keith. He said that you are old and that he is young. . . ."

"Youngblood was telling the truth." Keith's face turned an ashy gray and his eyes were dull. He suddenly was very tired and was filled with shame and remorse. He had sent Youngblood to his death. He had done a cowardly thing. He had killed before, but always on the field of honor or in battle. This time, however, he had sent a man into the hereafter without giving the man a chance.

Morna was staring at him, trying to read his thoughts, struggling to learn what impression her story had left. She wanted him to jump up and go after Wyeth and kill him and then punish the Mac-Kenzies, degrade them and drive them away. She noticed then just how old Keith looked. There were lines in his face and his mustache, usually so trim, drooped at the ends and the sparkle was gone from his eyes. "Youngblood," she hissed. "You think of him at a time like this. He didn't tell the truth. He spread tales about me and left the wrong impression. To hear him tell it, I wanted Wyeth Woodward to call on me."

She expected Keith to question her and was ready with a hundred answers. He just sat there, however, gazing at the floor. She couldn't

stand silence, for silence condemned her. "Now I suppose you realize that the MacKenzies are as guilty as all get-out. They have
tricked you."

"I am not interested in the MacKenzies," Keith said slowly. "That
explosion smashed the organization to bits. I am interested only in
Wyeth Woodward." He looked up quickly when he heard a rear
door open, and snatched one of his pistols and went to the back of
the house. Morna resumed her pacing.

She heard her husband say, "Oh, hello, Gar. I didn't know who
you were."

"I didn't know you were back," Gar said. "Mis' Sharon told me
to be here when you got back and tell you that Mist' Woodward got
in late today and left in a hurry."

"Which way did he go?"

"North."

"He's going to Vicksburg," Keith said. "He is going back to fight.
Thank you, Gar. Tell Miss Sharon that I'm leaving town. I, too,
am going to fight. And I'm going to find Wyeth Woodward if I
have to kill every man in the Confederate Navy to get to him."

Morna heard the door close and hurried across the floor and was
sitting on the divan when Keith reentered the room. "I am going
away, Morna," he said and sat by her.

"I heard what you said to Gar. Are you going into the army?"

"Yes." The dullness passed from his eyes and the sparkle was
back. The lines seemed to vanish and he looked young again. He
was going to fight. He had enough of intrigue and lies. He wanted
the clean, brutal conflict of battle where he could meet his enemy
with ball and powder.

"They will make you an officer, of course." Morna moved close
to him.

"That's not important. I am going to General Banks and resign
my task here. The Union no longer needs me in that capacity. I
will tell General Banks that Major Youngblood died in the line
of duty and ask Banks to send me to the Vicksburg front as a
trooper in the Scouts."

"You will be a colonel at least," she said.

Keith ignored her and seemed to be talking aloud to his conscience. "I have plotted for the Union and now I will kill for her.
Banks will send a man to take Youngblood's place. I would go

straight to Grant, but I don't know Grant and he might give me desk duty." He folded his hands behind his head and closed his eyes, smiling again, that slow bitter smile of a man who knows that life is a sham.

Morna put her head on his shoulder. "You will find Wyeth Woodward?"

"I will find him."

A surge of elation warmed Morna and she snuggled close to him. "When are you leaving?"

"Tonight, Morna."

"But you are tired, my love. And I haven't seen you much lately. There is no need to leave right now, is there?" She began stroking his neck and her breasts were hard and she pushed them against him.

Keith looked over at her and his eyes became narrow and there was a flush on his face. "You are a remarkable woman, Morna. Surely, nowhere in the world is there another just like you."

She accepted it as a compliment and stood up, then reached down and took his hand and led him toward the stairs. He watched every movement of her body as they walked up to their bedroom, and he still was smiling. Yes, life was a sham, and it offered just so much and Keith Alexander was a realist, or thought he was. When the cup was full he drank. Life had never given him the things he wanted; a name and peace and goodwill. He was a bastard and life had snarled at him and he had always snarled back. So when life offered him a brimming cup he took it and drank it all. It always had been that way and he knew now that it always would.

Morna opened the door to their room. Candles were burning and Keith looked at them and then at her and said nothing. She assumed the look had the meaning it always had had before, for she was untying the ribbons of her dress. She removed the garment slowly, watching him intently. Then she kicked off her shoes and teased him with her bare toes.

"Do you remember the first time?" she asked and waited for him to come to her.

"Yes," he said. "I always will."

The night wind swayed the curtains and rustled the young green leaves of the Chinaberry tree just outside their windows. The stars seemed to come into the room and to dance in an abandoned frenzy of brilliance and the bed was a cloud that moved into the sky and away through space. And then the stars went out of the room and back to their appointed places, and Morna was at peace with the world. She put her head on her husband's shoulder and her breathing was a purr.

Keith lay there for almost an hour, staring into the night. Then, slowly, he removed his arm from around her and got up. He thought she was sleeping and stood over her for a minute, watching the moonlight on her face. Then he picked up his boots and his clothes and tiptoed out of the room.

Morna was smiling. So was Keith. Her smile was one of triumph and contentment. His was bitter and sad.

Chapter Twenty-One

WYETH, approaching Vicksburg along the river road, was stunned by the complacency and confidence of the town. Some of the Confederate leaders actually believed that Grant, rebuffed at every turn, was giving up the campaign as a hopeless undertaking.

The South had every reason to be proud, but no reason to be confident. General Joseph E. Johnston, old Joe who never got along with Jefferson Davis, had been given supreme command of the Army of Mississippi, and Pemberton was his field commander in charge of the defense of Vicksburg. Old Joe, mending from wounds, was in Chattanooga, half way to the seaboard from the river.

Pemberton was at Jackson, trying to figure out just what the Federals might try next. He was groping in the darkness of ignorance, for most of his cavalry had been taken from him and given to Bragg up in Tennessee. The cavalry was his eyes and having no cavalry, the Pennsylvanian was blind.

He had 61,000 men present for duty, of whom 48,000 were fit to fight, had they all had weapons. His force was spread from the Tennessee line to Port Hudson, Louisiana, 48,000 poorly equipped men to defend two hundred miles of bluffs and swamps. And no cavalry. Pemberton's first command of about 22,000 effectives occupied the main Vicksburg position, extending from Haynes Bluff on the Yazoo to Grand Gulf on the Mississippi.

Against these men, spread as thin as the watered molasses they ate, Grant had 130,000 soldiers at his disposal, of whom 50,000 were grouped northwest of town, rested and ready. Porter's fleet, overhauled and brought to peak, was around the big bend from Vicksburg; the greatest concentration of iron ships and naval fire power in the history of the world.

Wyeth had an inkling of all that and no wonder he was flabbergasted to find Vicksburg sunning itself in the calm April day and boasting how the Yanks had been whipped in every battle and swearing death and destruction to Grant if he dared attack again. The Missourian had no difficulty in getting through the lines until he reached the lower batteries at Warrenton and there a picket took him to a brigade commander.

The gunner identified himself and the commander said, "Privy Navy, eh?"

It was the first time Wyeth had heard the expression in several weeks and he was glad to hear it again.

"Your battery is at Fort Hill," the commander said. "The Upper Water Battery. And watch out that somebody doesn't steal your horse. Horse meat is highly prized around here."

The army and the civilians of Vicksburg already knew the feeling of hunger and nobody ever had quite enough. With the Mississippi and the Red River cut off by Union ships, Pemberton had to depend on one little railroad and a few highways for supplies. He was trying to provision Vicksburg, but the railroad to Jackson was falling apart and the highways often were impassable. The blockade had its fingers around the South's throat and Mississippi was the first to suffer convulsions.

Wyeth rode slowly through town, watching the river to his left. Two Confederate steamers were in port, but their boilers were cold and commerce was at a standstill. The hulk of the *U.S.S. Lancaster* lay on the far side of the river and Wyeth smiled at the sight. Northwest, in Tuscumbia Bend, a few Federal gunboats and mortarboats were lobbing shells into the town. Occasionally the Confederates replied, but not often as powder and ball were scarce. Then came a hollow roar from the water battery and Wyeth checked his horse and listened to the echo. That sounded like the Dolly. He crossed Glass Bayou, galloped by the Harwood-Gaines House and to the base of Fort Hill, a ridge to the north of town and along the southern edge of Mint Spring Bayou.

The Fort Hill redoubt, sometimes called the Upper Battery and sometimes called the Water Battery, commanded the mouth of Mint Spring Bayou, the upper reaches of Tuscumbia Bend, and the City Road that ran to Yazoo City. Fort Hill was one of the keys of the Vicksburg fortress as it controlled the northernmost approaches to the city both by water and land.

Reaching the redoubt, Wyeth rode by the cannon of the battery. He spotted one twenty-four pounder, two six pounders and a three-inch rifled gun. He also recognized the cannoneers as volunteers of the 14th Mississippi Light Artillery Battalion and the First Tennessee Heavy Artillery Company. The artillerymen stared at him and his horse, most intently at his horse, as he passed their guns. He didn't see the Dolly and turned to one of the soldiers and said, "That shot I just heard. It sounded like a Dahlgren. . . ."

"Oh, that." The cannoneer laughed. "It came from the Privy Navy. Just the other side of this ridge, bub."

Wyeth dismounted and, leading his horse, picked his way over the hill and there was the Dolly and Granville and Ves. Wyeth began crying, and choked up when he tried to yell. Granville was tampering with the friction tube of his beloved gun and didn't see him. Ves was sprawling on the ground, his eyes shielded by his arm. The Dolly was as neat and trim as ever and the silver nameplate caught the reflection of the sun.

The Missourian stood there a second looking at his friends. Granville's face was almost hidden behind a ragged beard and he was barefoot. His chest was bare and his only garment was a dirty pair of duck trousers, held up by a piece of rope. He was wearing his watch, however, and the chain that France had given him, the chain with the ebony dragon.

Ves looked like a scarecrow stretched on the ground. His shirt was held together by thorns and a strip of canvas served as suspenders to support his filthy trousers. He had on Granville's Wellington boots and his bare toes stuck out where he had cut away the leather to make the boots fit his feet. Wyeth, looking at them, suddenly hated all Yankees, blaming them for his friends' misery. Then he found his voice and cried out, "Mr. Granville! Ves!"

The Englishman turned around and was grinning when Wyeth ran to him. Ves scrambled to his feet and embraced the Missourian and then looked at the horse. "Fat," the Cajan said. "By God, a fat horse. Oh, Louisa."

Wyeth's tongue clung to the roof of his mouth and a feeling of nausea came over him as he looked closely at Ves. The big man's eyes were hollow and there was a greenish pallor around his eyes. Most of his teeth were gone and his cheeks were sunken. His hands were a sickly yellow, and bony.

"We've been expecting you," Granville said. "We heard about the cavern blowing up. Is everybody all right?" He looked down at Wyeth's trousers, his trousers, and shook his head. The trousers were of no further use to Granville. Besides, Wyeth would have to have them as no more were available.

"Everybody is all right," Wyeth said and continued to look at Ves. "I didn't get any iron. Where is Captain Brown?"

"Yazoo City," Granville said. "Still piddling with the *Arkansas*. He told us to stop you here. Make out a report and send it to him."

Wyeth took off his coat and laid it across the gun. Then he began rolling up his sleeves. "But why here?"

Ves laughed, a haunting laugh that revealed his shrivelled gums. "This is as good a place as any." He still was eyeing the horse. "I ain't doing so good, Wyeth, and I'm rightly glad you're back with us. I'm ailing bad and have lost most of my teeth. They just fall out. But, hell, I don't need 'em. We ain't got nothing much to eat."

Granville then explained that after checking the Federals up at Fort Pemberton, the Dolly had been floated down the Yazoo to Steele's Bayou and had helped chase Sherman and Porter away. It was too good a gun to take back to Yazoo City when Vicksburg was desperately in need of cannon. So at the army's request, Captain Brown had ordered Granville and Ves to add their Dolly to the Water Battery.

"Who are our officers?" Wyeth asked.

Granville said, "We are pretty much on our own. Officially, we are attached to the 14th Mississippi Light Artillery Battalion with Captain J. H. Yates in command. We are a part of Company B, commanded by Lieut. W. J. Shelton."

Ves walked over and felt the fat belly of Wyeth's horse. He and most of the other Confederates had been living on bread made of pea flour and acorns for days. "There ain't no use of fooling ourselves," he said. "There ain't going to be another *Arkansas*. The Cap'n gets a little iron now and then and slaps it on the ship, but we are still a long ways from taw. That's why he sent us here. There's something to shoot at here and there ain't no use of letting the Dolly get rusty at Yazoo City when there are Yanks to be killed around here." He sat down and rested his head against the carriage of the Dahlgren.

It was a barbette carriage, high enough for the gun to poke over the parapet. The big piece recoiled on heavy iron wheels and an eccentric roller.

"You're not shooting much," Wyeth said.

"Saving up," Ves said and jerked his thumb toward Tuscumbia Bend where Porter's fleet was at anchor. "Them yellow-hammers ain't going to mess around out there forever."

Wyeth stared at the Union ships that had slipped down from the main fleet to throw a few shots. Most of them were protected by cotton bales and some were covered by branches, a perfect disguise. "Does Captain Brown know that I failed in Natchez?" he still was watching the Union flotilla.

"You didn't fail," Granville said. "You never had a chance. Captain Brown knew you couldn't get iron. I couldn't, so how could you? He sent you down on a long chance. Luck was against you, that's all. Now tell us about everybody."

He told about Laurel and Wall and Gar in a few words and even told about meeting Morna, but most of his story was devoted to Sharon. When he talked about Sharon, Granville resumed his work on the friction tube and tried to leave the impression that he wasn't interested in hearing about her. However, Wyeth noticed that he didn't miss a word. Ves noticed it, too.

"She's right bright, huh, Wyeth?" the Cajan said.

"She's more than that. She fooled Keith Alexander completely and with one bit of luck she would have had iron. Now you tell me what happened. Was there much excitement at Fort Pemberton?"

Granville just grunted, but Ves began grinning. "We whipped 'em to a frazzle. They came inching through the Pass and then busted into the river, slap-dab up against the fort. Me and Sim laid the Dolly on 'em and knocked 'em sky-winding crooked. Scattered Yanks and ships all through them swamps. . . ."

"One of their commanders went stark mad," Granville said. "The enemy has made many blunders, but that was the worst."

"Then we high-tailed down the Yazoo and waited in Steele's Bayou until Sherman and Porter got in," Ves said. "I felt downright sorry for the Yanks. We captured a pas'l of 'em and they ain't bad fellows, the blue-bellied bastards. They had a lot of gumption. They cut a channel through them swamps a tree at a time. They rigged saws and cut right under the water and used their ironclads to push down some trees. And all they got for it was a dose of our lead. This is a hell of a war."

"They will try again," Granville said. "That Grant is a goat and he will keep butting away until something gives."

The sun was getting hot and Wyeth took off his shirt and offered it to Granville. The Englishman refused to take it. "Keep it. My skin is tough and you'll need that shirt to keep off mosquitoes."

Ves said, "Sim made me take his boots. They come up high enough to give my legs some protection from mosquitoes. You never saw such mosquitoes. But they ain't so bad. It's the ants. And the gnats and flies. Don't know what they eat around here, cep'n us. Reckon, Wyeth, them generals and folks over in Virginia know that a war is going on out here?"

The Cajan was expressing the sentiment of most of the Confederates in the West. The best of everything was going to the Army of Northern Virginia. The South's best was virtually nothing, but what was available was being given to Lee. He had the good generals and the pick of the draft and supplies.

"Quit mouthing," Granville said.

"Mouthing, hell," Ves snorted. "You know it's true. Just the other day you said that our Dolly really was defending Richmond and that nobody up there seemed to get the idea. And look at them generals—Jackson, Stuart, Longstreet, them Hill boys and God knows who else. They got so many good generals that they are falling over each other."

Wyeth didn't like such talk as there was a trace of defeatism in the words. "Pemberton is a good man. . . ."

"Hell, yes. But they ain't giving him nothing. They expect us to whip the biggest Yankee Army in the field with pine knots and slingshots. We ain't got no cavalry worth spittin' at. And look at that Bragg. He's got Forrest and Van Dorn and Wheeler. There

[452]

ain't a man in Virginia who can hold a candle to Forrest, but instead of giving him to us they keep him with Bragg. The nabobs won't listen to him. They don't like him because he can't write long reports and I hear tell that he eats with his knife."

Granville finished filing the tube and sat down by Ves. "There's no need of deceiving ourselves. The Seaboard does not realize the importance of Vicksburg. Richmond may be the London of the Confederacy, but Vicksburg is the Hastings. And if this goes, everything will go."

The horse was munching grass when a detachment from the supply department arrived and led the animal away. Ves shook his head. "They'll use him in the artillery until he is skin and bones and then somebody will get his meat. Maybe we'll get a hoof." His toothless grin was infectious. "Me and Sim got a hoof last week and I made a good soup, huh, Sim?"

"Some of the boys down by the Harwood-Gaines House have rations," Wyeth said. "I saw the food as I was coming this way."

Ves and Granville exchanged glances, then scrambled to their feet. "Give me that shirt," Granville said and winked at Wyeth. He put the shirt under his arm. Ves felt in his gear for a tin plate and the three walked over the hill. Wyeth was grinning for the first time since his arrival.

They went down to the Harwood-Gaines House, passing unit after unit of men who greeted them with boisterous shouts. The Confederates were hungry and almost naked, but, being Southerners, they were volatile and carefree. "The Privy Navy," some shouted at the three sailors and others called that familiar cry of all Confederates—"Hey, bub, where's your mule?"

All along the road groups were playing cards or singing. The Confeds were inveterate gamblers. They had no money and didn't need any, for there was nothing to buy. Their pay averaged nine dollars a month, Confederate money, and was worth about ninety cents in barter. So they gambled for clothes and bits of food, and sang while they gambled. They put on minstrel shows and read their Bibles and listened to long-winded preachers. But mostly they sang and their favorite was:

"We are sons of old Aunt Dinah,
And we go where we've amind to

And we stay where we're inclined to,
And we don't care a damn cent."

Near the Harwood-Gaines House, a rambling, comfortable structure, the 61st Tennessee was encamped and their fires were burning cheerfully. They had food, mule meat and corn bread. Some of the men were playing town ball, a game in which two bases were used, and a pitcher, a catcher, five fielders and a batter. The game was an outgrowth of Indian ball. The bat was a pine stick and the ball was made of twine wrapped around a hickory nut. Ves glanced around until he spotted a group playing Fox and Geese, a game that resembled checkers. He nodded toward the group and Granville approached the Tennesseans, waving the shirt before him.

Ves hung back and affected an air of modesty as becomes a champion and Wyeth was at Granville's side.

"See that man," Wyeth pointed to Ves.

"Privy Navy," one of the soldiers said contemptuously. "Uh, huh, we see him. Ain't the Navy feeding regular?" He was looking at the shirt that Granville spread on the ground.

"He's the best lice-man in the Confederate Navy," Wyeth said, "and that shirt says he's better than any Johnny."

The soldiers laughed. "Talk is cheap," one of the men said and stood up, running his hand over his coarse black beard. "I'm a lice-man. You looking for a race?"

Ves came up then and stuck his face close to the soldier. "If you ain't scared. That shirt against a hunk of mule meat that I can out-lice you."

"It's a go," the Tennessean said. His comrades gathered around and the men examined the shirt and put a piece of raw meat on the ground by it.

Ves and the soldier faced each other. A counter was chosen and he examined the contestants. "Chose your field," he instructed.

The soldier said, "Beard."

"Here," said Ves and rubbed his hand over the hairs of his chest.

The counter, who served as judge, took Ves' tin plate and marked it. Then he took a plate from the soldier. He stood between the two men, holding the plates close to them. "Get set," he said. "We play it up to twenty."

"That's satisfactory," said Granville. He patted Ves's back and

Wyeth instructed the Cajan carefully, cautioning him to take his time and make sure that he wasted no motions.

Ves folded his hands on his chest and his opponent clasped his hands under his beard. The counter said, "One—"

The two men began searching for lice. Ves used both hands to pull the hideous little things from his chest and as fast as he caught one he put it in the plate. The soldier used both hands, too, but Ves had more experience and a more fruitful field. By the time the counter reached twenty, the Cajan had nine lice in his plate and the soldier had only six.

Granville and Wyeth began boasting, but Ves was modest. He took his plate from the counter and pointed at one of the lice. "Ol' Charlie," Ves said and turned the louse over with his finger. "Ain't used ol' Charlie since he beat the Georgia champeen. Good ol' Charlie."

Wyeth picked up the mule meat, but left the shirt on the ground. Ves accepted the meat and walked over to a fire and seared it, burning off the hairs. The Tennesseans followed him and their champion challenged again. "Some corn meal against the shirt that my Rose can outrun your Charlie."

Ves nodded acceptance and took his louse in his left hand, holding his tin plate in his right. The Tennessean did likewise and while the soldiers gathered around their comrade offering words of encouragement, the Cajan slipped his plate through the flames, warming it.

The judge had the men face each other again and issued instructions. "The contestants must be placed in the center of the plates and the first louse to reach the edge wins."

Then he gave the signal and Ves put old Charlie in the middle of the warm plate. The heat drove Charlie over the edge before Rose got underway. "Good ol' Charlie," Ves said and put him back on his chest. Then he picked up a bag of corn meal and the Privy Navy bowed away, leaving the 61st Tennessee growling at their champion.

Wyeth cooked the mule in a camp kettle and Ves made hoecake. They ate their fill that night and the Cajan, exhausted from the events of the day, stretched a piece of canvas on the ground and turned in before the moon came up, warm and yellow and friendly. Mosquitoes swarmed from along the soggy banks of Mint Spring

Bayou, and the night things began prowling and crying. Wyeth borrowed pen and pokeberry ink from an officer of the artillery unit, sat by a fire and began his report to Captain Brown.

He had forgotten the date. Days no longer meant anything to him. He asked Granville the date and the Englishman looked at his watch and said, "Eleven o'clock."

Wyeth laughed. "I asked for the date, not the time."

Granville's mind was in Natchez, but Wyeth's laugh brought it back and he began counting, then said, "April 15th. And it's 1863 just in case you've forgotten the year."

The Missourian glanced up at the moon, then at the river. "Good Lord, the war's been going on for two years. Do you think it is about over?"

"No. It's just beginning." Granville took his own canvas bedding and stretched it over the Dolly to protect it from the night air. He lay on the bare ground and stared up at the sky. "Yes, it's just beginning. I had hopes once that we could win in two years. Now I'm wondering if we can win at all."

The Confederacy was cracking at its base. It never had a firm foundation, for it was built on the *status quo* and offered no hope of a better future to the multitude that was fighting its war. The South was struggling to expel invaders, but then what? The North already was thinking of tomorrow and the South was thinking of yesterday, and yesterday never wins wars. The people needed a promise and the *status quo* offered no promise. So, to the South, the war had become a matter of killing Yankees and starving. Those Southerners who had ridden out as crusaders now began asking why, and there no longer was a crusade; only the deadening realization that if they won they would be right back where they were.

The states were squabbling among themselves and the united front was crumbling at home. Planters began thinking only of themselves and small farmers took up the cry of "a rich man's war and a poor man's fight," and hid provisions from Confederate purchasers. Speculation, inflation and extortion swept the land and Confederate bonds went begging. The people grumbled about taxes and criticized their leaders, whispered lies about Jefferson Davis and began defeating themselves.

The United States was almost as badly shaken, but there was one big difference. The United States could stand the strain because, in a vague way, it offered a better tomorrow. The struggle had begun as a mystery to the Northern masses, but was growing into a crusade for them.

Wyeth knew all of that and Granville knew it better than his friend. The Englishman seemed to read the Missourian's mind and said, "Remember one thing, the United States can afford blunders. We can't."

Ves began groaning in his sleep and Wyeth brushed mosquitoes from the Cajan's face. "Why isn't he in a hospital, Mr. Granville?"

"Because he can walk," Granville snorted. "As long as they are on their feet, they can fight. Just the other day one of the men had his leg shot off and thought he might get his discharge. They put him to driving an ambulance team."

"Ves has got to have quinine and attention. When did he begin to get so much worse?"

"Up at Fort Pemberton," Granville said and leaned over the Cajan and put a square of dirty netting over his face. "It is the same old malaria, and there is no way to arrest it without quinine."

"We've got to get him into a hospital."

Granville walked to the end of his gun and jerked the covering over the mouth. "There is no room," he growled. "And if there were, Ves would not try to get in. They might refuse him, you know."

"Like hell they would," Wyeth said bitterly. "I don't care if he's Cajan or Negro, they wouldn't refuse a man who has fought as Ves has. You don't understand the South, Mr. Granville."

The Englishman looked away toward the river, then up at the clear sky. "Who does?" he said softly.

Wyeth followed his gaze. The river was sulking and was moody and whispered to itself as it crawled along, a swishing whisper. It was so big and so strange. The two men gazed at it in awed silence. The Mississippi makes men silent. Sometimes, in its presence, a word is as out of place as in a cathedral. The Mississippi is a cathedral. The stars are candles and the jasmine perfume is incense.

For many minutes, the men sat there, enjoying the spell that the river casts. Then Wyeth looked up and around. "Say, I haven't heard a Yankee shell in two or three hours."

"Neither have I," Granville said.

The heavy brooding silence frightened Wyeth. Nothing is as

awesome as silence on a battlefield. He looked back at the town, sleeping the drugged sleep of the doomed. Then he studied Tus-cumbia Bend. "There are no ships there, Mr. Granville. They have gone."

"Probably upstream to coal."

"I don't like it. I don't like it, Mr. Granville."

"Let's go to sleep, Wyeth. It's after midnight."

Wyeth slipped off his boots and tied them together, then fastened them to his arm just in case prowlers came that way, some of the shoeless men who were desperate enough to kill for a pair of boots.

Up at La Grange, Tennessee, Colonel Grierson called in the officers of his 6th Illinois Cavalry and two other regiments and told them that the hour had come. It was 1 A.M., April 16th. "We go south," Grierson said. "Then west and into Natchez. Our men there will be expecting us and will have the place ready for us to ride in and drive a wedge between Vicksburg and Port Hudson. Burn as you go. Burn everything. Kill every chicken, every pig. Trample down the corn, rip down the fences. The only way we can beat these people is to burn them out and starve them. . . ."

"Sir," one officer said. "Do I understand you to mean that we must lay waste to the land to starve civilians?"

"Burn everything," Grierson said sadly. "If the people at home suffer enough then the soldiers will crack."

And so began Grant's master plan. Grierson's raid was the first move. His men rode due south, toward Ripley and Pontotoc, Mis-sissippi, following the highways just west of the Mobile and Ohio Railroad. Burn everything. Trample the corn. War is murder and there are no rules for murder. There in the West a new pattern for war was resurrected, the pattern of Scipio at Carthage, of Atilla. Sherman was to watch and learn. Burn everything. Trample the corn.

Ves seemed to be stronger when he woke up just as the sun peered over the Walnut Hills, driving the mosquitoes away. He was the first of the three to wake up and he rolled over and touched Wyeth. "I dreamed that you went away again," he told the Missourian. "And I touched you to be sure I wasn't dreaming."

He felt better because Wyeth was there and because the three were together again. Granville went to the well at the Harwood-

Gaines House and fetched water and Wyeth fixed a breakfast, insisting that Ves enjoy some leisure. He scraped together some wormy oatmeal and pea flour. Then using all that was left of the mule meat, he made it into a burgoo. He and Granville stood over Ves and made him eat two portions of the food.

Commissary soldiers, too old or too cripped to fight, brought three days rations to Fort Hill and the Privy Navy took their pea flour, goat meat and corn meal and cached it down by Mint Spring Bayou. Wyeth made Ves bathe in the stream and then began delousing him, picking off the vermin. All but old Charlie. "Leave him be," Ves insisted. "The whole thing is silly. I'll be covered by tomorrow again. So will you. Sim ain't got many. They don't like him."

"These are American lice," Wyeth said. "They avoid Englishmen."

"They are saving me for dessert," Granville said.

The Dolly was uncovered and Granville lined her up. But there was nothing to shoot at on the river and Ves began wondering why the Federals had withdrawn from Tuscumbia Bend. Granville said, "Build up the fire and start on the hot shots." They laid out their powder, too, and stacked grape behind the parapet. All along the Confederate river front, cannoneers were watching the river and they were restless. Their officers were restless, too, and tried to give the impression that they were not worried.

Wyeth spent the afternoon writing letters, the first to Laurel. He told her of Ves' illness and begged her to get quinine to him. "I don't know how this can be done," he wrote, "but you can find a way. Do not tell Sharon that her cousin is ailing. Just tell her we all need quinine and she will help you get it."

Then he wrote Sharon and told her how Granville hung on to every word he reported about her. He took the letters to headquarters and a rider picked them up before dark.

Ves was standing on the parapet watching the river when Wyeth returned to his station and took up his lookout. The fire was kept burning and all down the bluff, fires were burning and shots were being heated. Twilight brought song. The fireflies came out. Then the moon came up, at first quarter. Granville, an old campaigner, looked at the moon and shook his head. It didn't give much light, and the river was dark. Down in Vicksburg, a company of soldiers was giving a burlesque, "Pocahontas, or Ye Gentle Savage." A Texan played the role of the Indian maiden.

At his comrades' insistence, Ves turned in early and Granville and Wyeth sat on the parapet and smoked. Neither was sleepy. Wyeth couldn't keep his eyes off the river and a vague feeling of uneasiness was upon him. He saw the scout boats go out from the landing, little skiffs that patrolled the river every night. He heard the men shouting to one another.

A musket flashed at the tip of the land that flanked Tuscumbia Bend and Wyeth jumped. It was the first shot he had heard all day. He looked over at Granville and the Englishman got up and walked to the breech of his gun, arousing Ves as he passed him.

"They are coming," Granville said calmly. It was ten P.M.

Wyeth tumbled from the parapet. "How do you know?"

"I just know." Granville looked at the moon again and watched it slip behind some clouds. He felt for the sight on the Dolly.

Ves and Wyeth stood by him. "I can smell 'em," Ves whispered. "They're coming all right."

"Give her a solid shot," Granville said. "Thirteen pounds of powder and a solid shot."

They extracted a load of grape from the Dolly and rammed in the solid shot.

There was a long cry, a wavering "O-o-o-ho-o-o" from one of the patrol boats, followed by a crackle of rifle fire, from pickets over near the bend. Wyeth saw the first ship then and tried to shout, but his tongue seemed to collapse and fall to the bottom of his mouth and he gurgled and pointed his finger. The *U.S.S. Benton,* Porter's flagship, hove into Tuscumbia Bend, throwing black greasy smoke. Behind her, in single file, came the bulk of the Union fleet, creeping along in the darkness. They showed no lights and their wheels were still as they let the channel bring them down noiselessly.

Granville cursed the darkness and tried to lay his gun on the *Benton.* She had coal barges lashed to her sides.

"They're coming! The fleet is coming down! About a million of 'em!" Scouts shouted the alarm. Patrol boats scuttled for shore.

The *Benton* was flush in the bend and Granville muttered, "I am going to take a chance. It is a long range." He leaned over his gun and wiped a drop of moisture from the sight. Then he held up two of his fingers, forming a V, and framing the *Benton* between his fingers. He jerked the lanyard and the Dolly roared and lurched. Wyeth scrambled to the parapet. The shot fell short, throwing spray against the *Benton*.

"Hot shot," Granville said.

Ves and Wyeth grabbed a cradle and ran to the fire and fetched the ball. They shoved thirteen more pounds of powder down the gun, then a wadding of clay, and rammed in the hot shot. Granville was lining her up again when the 14th Mississippi Light Artillery began serving their guns. Then every gun on Fort Hill spoke, a trembling, howling salvo that crushed the coal barges and left the *Benton* exposed.

The heavy damp night air caught the smoke from the cannon and pushed it down and the flagship was hidden from the gunners. "Oh, for a moon," Granville said. "I am blind. Can you see, Wyeth?"

"Nothing but smoke," the Missourian said.

Ves began cursing. "And they've been telling us that ol' Bully Boy Grant ain't got no sense. Goddamit, look at the night he picked. Quarter moon and wet air. . . ."

"A sailor picked this night," Granville said. "Probably Porter."

The smoke lifted a bit and Wyeth began jumping up and down in excitement. "Great God Almighty! Look yonder."

The Union fleet, aware that the element of surprise was gone, began churning the river, plowing around the bend and racing by the fortress. The *Benton* was out front. Then came the *Lafayette*, with the *General Price* lashed to her starboard. The *Louisville*, *Mound City*, *Pittsburgh* and *Corondolet* followed in orderly array, like goslins following their mother. Coal barges protected each ironclad. The ships were burning damp fuel and the smoke lay on the river like a blanket of tar. Directly behind the ironclads, their wheels biting into the Mississippi, came three transports, the *Forest Queen*, *Silver Wave*, and *Henry Clay*. They were protected by cotton bales. The *Tuscumbia* brought up the rear of the file. Every ship had a barge in tow, loaded with 10,000 bushels of coal.

"Louisa," Ves said. "Louisa and the babes! Get the barges, Sim. If they get below here without coal, they'll be stuck."

"But I cannot see," Granville said and fired a hot shot.

Every gun along the river lurched into action and the sky turned into a canopy of red and yellow. The ships began firing, training their guns first on Fort Hill and then sweeping the waterfront as they wheeled by.

An order to cease firing was shouted from gun to gun, from Vicksburg to Fort Hill and the Privy Navy crouched behind the parapet, wondering why such an order was issued.

At Vicksburg Landing, three skiffs of soldiers moved into the Mississippi, picking their way through the Union fleet. One of the little boats went down under musket fire, but two got across to the village of De Soto. The soldiers set fire to the hamlet, then took to the swamps in a hail of bullets from sharpshooters. Yellow flames roared along the waterfront across the river as the village burned and Granville leaped back to his gun. The order to resume firing came and half a dozen guns from Fort Hill raked the *Henry Clay*. The transport caught fire and was abandoned and those flames aided the gunners until a downwind caught the smoke and pressed it against the river. Wyeth began laughing and crying. Ves was gasping for air, and was coughing as fumes from a hundred guns spread along the bluff, clinging to the redoubts.

Orders then were given to fire every building along the waterfront on the Vicksburg side, and the fleet was silhouetted between flames from De Soto and Vicksburg. For ten minutes the Confederates had vision and began blowing the coal barges out of the river and smashing grape into the ironclads.

The river began surging as though lashed by a storm. The shells cut waves and screamed as they ricocheted across the water, skimming the river and churning it into yellow foam. Vicksburg trembled. The bluffs, shaking under the recoil of the guns, quivered and crumbled. There were few shouts, for this was a battle of artillery, and cannoneers seldom shout. There were no Rebel yells. Leave that to the infantry. Let them yell when they charged. This was drudgery. . . .

"Hot shot—easy! Heave. Hard, now. Grape! Damn that smoke. Heave. . . ."

From Fort Hill to Warrenton the commands were the same and the guns bucked and roared. Louisa and the babes!

The tumult drove thousands of rats from the bogs along the river and they scurried up the bluffs, squeaking in fright. The

Confederates killed hundreds of them with clubs. Hunger knows no delicacy.

The bluffs trembled so violently that ants and worms poured out of the earth, and the din of the guns frightened the wild things, driving deer and foxes out of the swamps and into the blinding glare of the fortress. Thousands of bats and swallows circled over the town, shrieking in frenzy, and many were stunned by concussion and fell to earth. The river was swarming with fish, floating bellyup, and the Mississippi reluctantly gave up the bodies of sailors it had been holding for weeks.

Civilians hid their children in the woods east of town and went to the waterfront and began collecting dead fish, taking their chances with death. The courthouse stood out starkly against the flaming sky. Wyeth was able to count the windows and saw them shatter, one by one. Many of the Confederate guns were firing in unison and the fury rolled along the bluffs as a ball of thunder rolls during a summer storm. The sound crashed against the bluffs at Warrenton and scattered echoes.

Ves was unable to stand the strain and collapsed while lugging a bag of powder to the Dolly. Wyeth pulled him under the parapet and stretched him out. Granville came down from his gun and helped Wyeth load it, and together they tried to serve it. Neither had anything to say. Powder was caked around Wyeth's eyes and the tears streaked the powder. His trousers were wet with sweat and urine, for his bladder had flushed in the excitement.

It took the *Benton* thirty minutes to travel from Tuscumbia Bend to Warrenton. Once she was turned around by a salvo against her bow. Then she veered, firing her eighteen guns, and waddled off down the river. One by one the ironclads passed, taking every bit of iron the Confederates hurled. Most of the shots went wild because smoke concealed the targets. Those that did strike damaged the ships but did not disable them.

Midnight passed and still the fleet floated by, a steady stream of men-of-war. The Dolly was firing only once every fifteen minutes, for it took Wyeth and Granville that long to prepare their gun. They begged for help from the 14th Mississippi Artillery and got two men.

At two A.M., the last of the ships passed Warrenton and into the safety zone down below. There was one last clap of thunder from the Lower Battery and then Vicksburg was still.

The silence suddenly was so heavy that the men could feel the stillness. Flames were licking along the waterfront and the *Henry Clay* was burning. But the guns were quiet for the first time in four hours. Ves sat up and Wyeth doused him with water. Then the Missourian sat down by the Cajan and rested his head on his hands. His ears were ringing and his head was pounding. Granville felt his gun until it was cool and then examined it for cracks. Finding none, he patted the Dolly and stepped down and sat by his friends.

"What happened?" Ves asked.

"Just a bit of hell," Wyeth said. "The Yanks brought God knows how many ships by. I don't know why. Grant's Army wasn't aboard."

Porter had run the batteries with loss only of the *Henry Clay* and some barges. Twelve of the sailors had been wounded, and the Confederate casualties were so light that a report was never made.

More than half of the Union fleet was below town, between the guns of Vicksburg and the guns of Grand Gulf. But why? The Confederates were mystified. It had been proved time and again that ironclads could run the batteries, so what was the purpose of this? Grant's Army still was at Milliken's Bend. However, the chubby, sensitive little man with the cigar knew why. They had called him a drunkard and a dunderhead; this man who loved horses, who had received from his wife a dowry of slaves, and whose real name was Hiram Grant.

He was at New Carthage, Louisiana, just down the river from Vicksburg when the fleet made its run. Then he got his army under way. He divided his forces, a thing no Northern general had dared attempt before. Lee had done it and won, but Lee was Lee. Grant was long on pounding and short on strategy. That's what they said. But now Grant was fighting with his head and not with his brawn.

He completely outmaneuvered an army that couldn't be out-maneuvered. He outwitted Confederates who didn't know what it was to be outwitted.

He had no supplies, the South said. Then live off the land. He couldn't move an army through the Louisiana bogs. Then build roads and bridges. Washington and the War Department had only a vague idea what he was doing. They had almost forgot about Grant. Poor old Joe Hooker was massing more than 180,000 men

[464]

near Chancellorsville to crush Lee's 57,000. The newspapers virtually ignored Grant and he was left alone. He thanked God for that. Joe Hooker had the spotlight, Fighting Joe and his German Bounty Boys, mercenaries who were not called mercenaries and who had boasted that they would teach Americans how to fight.

Grant was out of his brown study now. His bottle of rye and his brandy were forgotten. He scattered his army as a queen bee scatters her workers after the swarm. There was a diversion in Arkansas, and the South wondered. A part of Sherman's Corps was ordered to feint up the Yazoo and make a demonstration against Haynes Bluff. Pemberton, never too brilliant and now in a daze, assumed the Federals would strike his right flank and made ready. Already, however, Grant's engineers, perhaps the cream of both armies, were laying out corduroy roads from Milliken's Bend around through Louisiana to New Carthage. As fast as the road was constructed, Grant moved the bulk of his army down, circling Vicksburg from across the river.

The Confederates never quite understood what was happening. Grant was going away from Vicksburg. Pemberton rushed from Jackson to Vicksburg and collected his wits. He threw out enough men from the fortress to handle Sherman in the Yazoo Basin, then reinforced the garrison at Grand Gulf. He called on Joe Johnston for more men, and didn't get them, and then he began begging for cavalry, for eyes to keep him posted.

But they gave him no cavalry. The invincible Forrest was in Tennessee, smashing Yankees and cursing Bragg, his own commander. Van Dorn and Wheeler were there, too, but the vertebrae of the Confederacy had no cavalry. There was cavalry for every battle in Virginia. There were cavalrymen to wear gaudy sashes and listen to banjoes. There were horses and men and sabres for Bragg, but whoever heard of Vicksburg? A village on a loess bluff, over in the wilderness. Who ever heard of Hastings until it was too late?

Pemberton, worried but not alarmed, scraped together a meager cavalry under Wirt Adams, and Adams might have scouted Grant and learned his intentions, but then one regiment of Grierson's raiders moved down to Columbus, Mississippi, and on to Okolona and Tupelo, wrecking the railroads. Grierson himself struck for the Vicksburg and Meridian Railroad at Newton. He was coming down the heart of Mississippi, snipping the capillaries that supplied the arteries of Vicksburg. There was only one thing to do—stop Grierson. So Wirt Adams' cavalry pulled out from the Vicksburg area and began chasing Grierson.

Grant had earned a drink. He didn't take it.

Wyeth and his two comrades knew that part of the Yankee army was marching down the Louisiana side, but they were busy with Sherman's men who were feinting up the Yazoo. Some of the Federals even tried to land near the mouth of Mint Spring Bayou, almost under the nose of the Dolly on Fort Hill.

To save their dwindling supply of grape, the three sailors loaded their big gun with pebbles and bits of chain. One blast from the Dahlgren scattered the Northerners, and the Confederates began picking them off with small arms.

The Federals' thrust at Mint Spring Bayou accomplished its purpose, however, in that it tied down a brigade of Rebels on Fort Hill while another Union force pushed on up the Yazoo and laid siege to Haynes Bluff, the gateway to Yazoo City.

Granville understood the magnitude of the Federal strategy and was not surprised when Captain Isaac N. Brown appeared on Fort Hill that morning and informed them that Yazoo City was doomed. Ves was too ill and too miserable to take in the news, and Wyeth simply didn't understand how the situation could have changed so quickly.

However, the army had ordered the evacuation of Yazoo City because Pemberton needed to shorten his lines. Brown had dispersed his men, sending some of the officers to Louisiana and the others to Mobile.

"We can stop them here and then go back to Yazoo City and finish the ship," Wyeth said.

Brown began shaking his head and then said calmly, "I burned the *Arkansas.*"

Ves sat on the ground near the Dolly and stared at his yellow hands. Wyeth looked away toward the river and Granville began rubbing his gun with a greasy cloth. Brown couldn't look at his men while he talked. They had been together since the Battle of Memphis.

"There was nothing else to do," he said slowly. "We can't defend Yazoo City and the Yanks might have finished the *Arkansas* and used her against us. I burned two more ships on the stocks, the

Republic and the *Mobile*. There is nothing left of our shipyard."
He, too, sat on the ground. None of the men spoke. Granville kept
rubbing his gun. Brown watched him and then said, "Your Dahlgren is all that is left of my command."

"You will stay here and serve the Dolly?" Wyeth asked.

"No. I have been ordered to Mobile to plant torpedoes.[34] I am
leaving today. Do you men care to go with me?"

"Is it an order?" Granville asked quickly.

"No. It is an invitation. We can't move your Dahlgren. It would
have to stay here."

The Englishman looked at his comrades and they nodded. "Then,
sir, we will stay here, too."

Brown arose and shook their hands. "I reckoned you would. You
are the last of the Confederate Navy in these parts. God bless you."

Ves struggled to his feet and leaned gainst the gun. Granville
draped his rag over the carriage and Wyeth blinked his eyes rapidly
as he faced Brown for the last time. "What are your orders, sir?"

"Serve your gun as long as possible. Do not surrender. Blow up
your gun rather than let it fall into the hands of the enemy." He
looked closely at the three ragged sailors. "Woodward, you are in
command. You are a midshipman now."

The men saluted him and watched him walk away over Fort Hill
and down toward Vicksburg to catch a train to Jackson. When he
was out of sight, Granville picked up his rag and resumed his work.
Wyeth said, "I wonder why he put me in charge?"

But they knew. Granville shunned responsibility and Ves, even
had he been well, was not fitted for leadership. The Cajan stretched
out and put a piece of canvas over his eyes, protecting them from
the sun. "And now, Admiral Woodward, what next?"

Wyeth laughed.

The defenders of Vicksburg began living on rumors, and fantastic stories crept in from Jackson, including one that Joe Johnston
was there with a huge army waiting to reinforce Vicksburg and
smash the Yankees again. Actually, Johnston still was at Chattanooga, trying desperately to regain his health. The Confederate
command still was not alarmed. Pemberton had a strong army in
Vicksburg and had checked Sherman on his right flank. True,
Yazoo City was gone and Grierson was on a rampage in middle
Mississippi. But Grant was in no position really to threaten the

fortress. He was across the river and south of Vicksburg, still a long ways from his goal.

As one day followed another in monotonous regularity, the three sailors' biggest problem was to fight boredom and get food. Wyeth spent hours in the woods around Vicksburg hunting fresh game for Ves. He managed to kill a few rabbits and some birds and they caught crawfish in Mint Spring Bayou. Vicksburg was holding its breath, waiting for the storm, when Gar arrived with quinine and news from Natchez.

Ves hugged the Negro and Granville began measuring the powder. It was adulterated and he cursed his English compatriots who were selling such stuff to the South. However, it was better than nothing and he dosed the Cajan and buried the precious quinine after cautioning his comrades not to mention the fact that they had medicine.

Gar had messages for all of them.

Sharon and Laurel were all right and Confederate sympathizers had the upper hand in Natchez now that Youngblood was dead. Wyeth ripped open his letter from Laurel, but Granville put his letter from Sharon aside, trying to affect indifference. Ves had a letter from Sharon, too, and Wyeth read it to him. It was in Laurel's handwriting.

Gar waited until the excitement of his arrival wore away and then brought up the name of Keith Alexander.

"Where is he?" Wyeth asked casually.

"He's looking for you," Gar said.

The Missourian felt tiny bubbles form in his stomach and he gaped at the Negro, then was conscious of the stares of his friends. "What the hell are you talking about?" he said and his throat was dry and his voice was a croak.

"He's looking for you, Mist' Woodward. And he aims to kill you."

"He knows where I am," Wyeth said in an attempt of bravado. "What's eating him?" His face was fiery red. Only then did Gar realize that Wyeth hadn't told his friends all the truth about Morna and he was sorry that he had spoken.

Granville and Ves, however, understood without being told and the Englishman fixed his stare on the Missourian and said slowly, "Let us have the truth, Wyeth. Did you take Morna Alexander to bed?"

"Good God, no!"

"You need not be so emphatic about it," Granville said. "Alexander obviously thinks you did or thinks you tried it."

"Was she any good?" Ves asked.

Wyeth was so angry that he actually spluttered and stammered. "You two make me sick at my belly. I didn't touch that damn woman. That is, I didn't make love to her. . . ."

"You just touched her a little bit, eh?" Granville asked. "I wish I had been in your place. I would have given Alexander something to shoot about. . . ."

Gar felt sorry for Wyeth. "Mis' Laurel don't know nothing much about it. So don't worry. I know you didn't do nothing bad."

"God's eardrum!" Granville was smiling. "We know it, too. Even if he had the chance, which he probably had and didn't know it, our prudish young friend would not dare slip his hand under a lady's stays or hoist her petticoats. . . ."

"Shut up, Mr. Granville." Wyeth's scar was blazing.

"He wouldn't know how," Ves said and was grinning. " 'ygod! Just think of it. I'll bet he had that woman in a corner and then wouldn't take it. 'ygod!"

"It is just as well, Ves," Granville said. "His conscience would have killed him." He still was smiling when he turned to Gar. "Where is this Alexander whose luscious and lonely bride tempts Mr. Woodward?"

"He is a colonel of Scouts," Gar said. "He's som'rs between here and Natchez."

Granville took out his pistol and examined it. The grin disappeared from Ves' face and Wyeth glanced at the pistol, then at Granville. "If I see Alexander first," the Englishman said, "I will challenge him. I am weary of his behavior. I do not like bravos."

"I'll beat out his brains," Ves said. "I'll chew 'em up and spit 'em out."

"You both are very kind," Wyeth said in mock gallantry. "But it seems that I've been selected for the slaughter."

"Let me see you hold this pistol." Granville handed the weapon to Wyeth and shook his head when the Missourian grasped the butt tightly. "We might as well face it," he said. "If Alexander gets to you before I get to him then you will have to defend yourself."

"I can," Wyeth said simply.

"With a rifle, yes. Or a knife. Or your hands. But not with a pistol."

Wyeth balanced the pistol in his palm. "Alexander will challenge me. It is he who seeks revenge. He probably thinks I have sullied his honor and his good name. The Yankee-loving bastard. But he must challenge and that will give me the choice of weapons. I'll choose knives."

Granville took the pistol and held it lightly in his hand. "This is the way, Wyeth. Do not freeze your fingers around the butt. You had better learn this. Alexander will not challenge you. He will provoke you into challenging him and if you duel at all it will be with pistols. I know the type. He will curse you. Perhaps he will insult Laurel to your face. He will do something to trick you into losing your head. Then he will kill you unless you do as I say."

"I can take care of myself," Wyeth said.

"The days here are long," Granville said and handed the gun back to his friend and was delighted when Wyeth's touch was light. "I should have taught you about pistols before this. It will give us something to do to pass the time. Never hurry a pistol shot."

Wyeth pretended he was willing to take instructions only to please Granville and break the monotony. However, he was nervous. The knowledge that Alexander was waiting for him out there and that, should Vicksburg fall, he would come in to avenge his honor made the Missourian nervous. It wasn't trepidation, for Wyeth was not afraid of Keith Alexander. It simply was uncertainty, a vague feeling that someday he must face the deadliest duelist in the South. He wondered just how much Alexander knew. Yet, he really didn't care. Alexander's acute and rather absurd sense of honor had been offended and he would want satisfaction. Well, Wyeth told himself, he would see to it that the Black Knight of Vengeance got his wish.

So he began practicing with Granville's pistol, heeding the directions of his friend. "Never hurry a pistol shot," the Englishman said over and over. "Draw in your breath and hold it. Line up your target and then lower your pistol slowly. Hold your breath. Never jerk the trigger. Squeeze it."

"Alexander shoots from his hip," Wyeth said.

"Nonsense. If he does you can kill him easily. But he does not. No real pistol shot shoots that way. Alexander shoots the same way

I am trying to teach you. Just do not hurry your shot and you will have as good a chance as he has."

Gar took over the duty of caring for Ves and the days began running together and one was exactly as the other. A few provisions were reaching Vicksburg and every day more men rolled into the fortress over the Jackson Railroad. The Privy Navy gave its mornings to the Dolly, polishing it and practicing the manual. The afternoons were given to Wyeth's instruction. Granville selected a flat bit of ground down near Mint Spring Bayou and stepped off the paces and taught Wyeth the routine and fine points of dueling.

Under Gar's devoted attention, Ves began to grow stronger, and with food being issued once a day, life at Vicksburg became almost bearable for the Privy Navy. There was no news from Grant's army down the river and Grierson's Raiders vanished into the wilderness between Jackson and Meridian. Surely that was the limit of the raid. Wirt Adams and his cavalry were on Grierson's flank and to the south, blocking his path. So Grierson was forgot by the rank and file in Vicksburg until, without warning and apparently coming from nowhere, he burst out of the wilderness and slashed his way down the Jackson and New Orleans Railroad, more than half way down the state.

That was dangerously close to Natchez. Granville was frightened by the information and Wyeth was puzzled. "Why don't they head him off?" Wyeth said. "It looks like he's riding for Baton Rouge."

"No," Granville said. "It is as plain as day now. He intends to take Natchez."

Wyeth was stunned. "But Laurel is at Natchez. And Sharon."

"Laurel is safe. Gar says they have not got a thing on her or her father. Besides, Wall MacKenzie can protect his daughter. Even if the Yanks get into Natchez, there is no need to worry about Laurel."

"But Sharon?" Wyeth said. "She has nobody to look after her. And if the Yanks get there and clamp martial law on the town they'll be sure to find out that she took Nate Frome's place." His voice was trembling.

Granville ran his long index finger over his mouth and twisted the ends of the mustache. It dropped below the corners of his mouth. He looked at Wyeth as though he wanted to say something, but, changing his mind, he walked away and over near the Dolly where Gar was reading his Bible to Ves. The Englishman waited until the Wolof finished the chapter, then tapped him on the shoulder and the Negro and Simeon St. Leger Granville walked together down to the Bayou.

"How do you think Ves is?" Granville asked.

"A little bit better."

"No," Granville said and didn't look up. "He is worse. Go to Natchez and bring Miss Sharon back here. You can get her through."

Gar was stroking his beard and smiling.

"Tell her," Granville said, "that her cousin needs her. Tell her there is no room in the hospital for him and that she must nurse him."

"I'll tell her all that, Mist' Granville. But ain't there som'n else you want me to tell her?"

"No. Just tell her that Ves is very sick. And when you come back bring back more quinine."

"I'll leave come sundown. Anything else?"

They were walking back up toward the Dolly. "Yes, Gar. If you happen to run into Keith Alexander, kill him."

"I aim to," Gar said. "I've been watching Mist' Woodward. He just ain't no pistol man. So the first one of us what gets to Mist' Alexander had better kill him."

Granville explained to Wyeth that he was sending the Negro to fetch Sharon, but told Ves that Gar was going for more quinine. The Wolof put his Bowie at his belt and left his snipper with Wyeth. The sun was bowling down behind the Louisiana swamps when Gar walked away, over Fort Hill toward Vicksburg. Granville went as far as the Harwood-Gaines House with him and while he was gone Wyeth told Ves the truth, knowing how it would please the Cajan.

Ves began grinning again. "So you think he's sending for her because he loves her?"

"I know it," Wyeth said.

"She'll come. If he wants her she'll walk up here on her hands and knees. I'm rightly happy, Wyeth. If ol' Sim really loves her, then everything is going to be all right."

A light rain fell that night, breaking the year's first heat wave, and at seven A.M. the next day Porter gave orders for his squadron of ironclads to cast off from the mooring at the village of Hard Times, Louisiana. Confederate lookouts saw the activity and assumed Porter planned to run the batteries at Grand Gulf and then cut into the Red River.

The squadron steamed slowly downstream, but instead of hugging the Louisiana side to escape the wrath of Grand Gulf, the ships wheeled suddenly and bore in toward the Confederate guns that frowned down from the bluff. Before the Rebels were fully aware of the maneuver, the United States Navy trained eighty-one guns on Grand Gulf and blasted out one salvo after another.

Rock Bradford and his *D. A. Elliott* were nestling under the Confederate guns and the first broadside raked the *Elliott* with grape, cutting the ship to pieces. A hunk of grape tore into Rock's chest and the old riverman was hurled aft of his ship. A second broadside blew the *Elliott* to bits and Rock was crushed by falling debris.

Prent Oliver, knowing he didn't have a chance, brought his *Music* out of the Big Black and struggled to swing his one gun into action. Porter's *Benton* sank the little *Music* as though it were a skiff and Prent dived into the river, the last man to leave the last Confederate warship on the Mississippi. Two Union sailors lowered a boat and captured him. It was an inglorious way to finish his fighting. Prent had dreamed of sailing with Semmes on the *Alabama.*

The squadron threw 2500 projectiles into the Confederate fortifications in five hours. Grant watched the battle from a tug in the middle of the river. The Confederates had only thirteen guns to defend Grand Gulf and eight of those were of small calibre.

Goliath was turning on little David. Grand Gulf was smothered by a blanket of iron and every gun of the Confederate battery was silenced temporarily by two P.M. after giving a remarkable demonstration of gunnery. The *Tuscumbia* was struck eighty-one times and was knocked out of the fight. Porter's *Benton* was struck forty-seven times and lost twenty-six men. The Confederates suffered only three casualties, but they lost Grand Gulf.

With the guns on the bluff silent, Grant moved like lightning. His transports, loaded with men, were standing by at Hard Times and had orders to move down the river directly under the battered fortress at Grand Gulf and make a mooring at Rodney, on the Mississippi side.

He didn't want to disembark his army at Rodney. That was too far down; almost to Natchez. The Confederates might awaken to their danger and snip his lines if he went that far south. But Rodney was the only landing place with a road to Port Gibson. Or so Grant thought.

To protect his troops during the danger of disembarkation, Grant was counting on Grierson. Thus far his plans had moved like clockwork and now the time had come for Grierson to veer in from the center of the state and ride for Natchez where Youngblood was to have seized the town and protect Grant's flank.

But Youngblood was dead. Grierson swung in for Natchez expecting Federal soldiers to meet him and escort him triumphantly into a subdued town. Instead of meeting Youngblood's couriers, however, he ran into an advance unit of Wirt Adams' Confederate cavalry. Something had gone wrong somewhere along the line. That's all Grierson knew and all he needed to know. Wirt Adams was between him and Natchez, so he swung in a wide arc, avoiding Adams and missing Natchez, and rode furiously for Baton Rouge.

Grant's Army was ready to float by Grand Gulf when word came that the Nachez coup had failed. There was nothing to do but take a chance on the Rodney landing and leave one flank exposed. Then the gods who had frowned on Grant at Shiloh and who had jeered at him before Vicksburg finally smiled and there came to him a Negro with word that there was a forgotten road to Port Gibson from a landing place at Bruinsburg, up the river from Rodney.

It might be a trap. Many of Grant's officers begged him not to heed the stranger, but Grant questioned the Negro personally and decided to trust his army to an unknown black man. Grant never learned the Negro's name. It was he, however, an unidentified Negro in a Mississippi swamp, who showed Grant the way to Vicksburg, the short cut, the muddy trail that helped save the Union and free such men as the hero whose name history never bothered to record.

The Negro got in the first transport and directed the captain down the river and to a landing at Bruinsburg. There he waited for Grant and took him to the road that led over to Port Gibson, where another road led directly to the rear of Vicksburg.

All that night Grant's Army floated down from Hard Times to Bruinsburg and by sunup of April 30th, the Union Army was on the Mississippi side, on Vicksburg's flank.

Confederate skirmishers, confused by the Bruinsburg landing, eventually found their enemy, but it was too late. Grant was on dry land and his army was off the transports and in battleline. The Southern skirmishers were brushed aside and Grant rolled ahead for Port Gibson. An inadequate but aroused force of Confederate regulars and partisans united on the Port Gibson road to check him. They were crushed. Bewilderment gripped Pemberton at Vicksburg. He needed cavalry. Wirt Adams was off chasing Grierson and Pemberton was wholly in the dark until Grant appeared suddenly on the old road at Bruinsburg and struck out, following the Big Black, heading northeast to the rear of Vicksburg, which was Pemberton's only exit and Grant's only entrance. The Federals, usually bloated with supplies, had only three days' rations. They fanned out along the Big Black, daring to advance away from their base, daring anything. They were between the fortress of Vicksburg and the fortress of Port Hudson. They might have been in a vise. And with food and ammunition for only three days. It was fantastic. Washington was howling that Grant was not a strategist, that he was a thick-headed butcher incapable of lightning strokes and a blundering ox in the shadows of such a galaxy as Lee and Jackson, Forrest and Johnston.

"Live off the land," Grant told his men. "Burn all you can't use."

Grant knew something about the South that most men never grasped. He could have been checked and trapped away down there in Mississippi if Southerners had scorched the earth. But Southerners won't burn their homes. Their homes are their shrines. The military might have lured Grant into a charred wilderness, but the military had no authority to destroy private property. Jefferson Davis was a constitutionalist. He stuck to the letter of the law and lost a war.

Some of Grant's men expected to find a wasted land, but Grant knew better. He found smoke-houses full of meat, and chickens and corn. There was tender fodder for his horses. The South was feeding an enemy that was eating it alive.

Sharon Weatherford, riding with Gar in his light buggy behind his fastest horse, reached Port Gibson a few hours ahead of Grant. Gar didn't waste time in seeking Keith Alexander. He watered his horse in Port Gibson, then they drove on, racing for Vicksburg. They scarcely were across the Big Black before the first unit of Grant's Army thundered into Port Gibson and was ready to apply the torch when their general ordered them to spare the town because it was such a pretty little place.

Sharon wouldn't allow herself to think of all that was happening. Grant had blocked Vicksburg from the north, west and south and now was heading for the eastern gate of the fortress. But Sharon didn't think about all that. She was going to see Simeon St. Leger Granville.

The Spring had turned to May and the land was lush and hot. The sky was a brassy color and the dust was heavy. Summer was sprawling over the South again, smothering it.

Chapter Twenty-Two

GAR drove Sharon to Mrs. Simpson's home in Vicksburg, knowing that the Cajan and her sick cousin would be welcome there. Then he went to Fort Hill and reported to Wyeth that his mission had been completed. He went to Wyeth because the Missourian, as a midshipman, was in command of the battery.

Ves' sunken eyes began sparkling when he learned that Sharon was only a mile or so away. A trace of delight and relief showed on Granville's face. Then he forced away all visible evidence of his feelings and was stony-faced again although his heart was skipping.

Wyeth congratulated Gar and told Granville and the Wolof to take Ves to the Simpson house. "I'll stay with the gun," the midshipman said.

Granville did a childish thing then. He wanted to run over the hill and into Vicksburg to see Sharon and yet he forbade his emotions their freedom. He couldn't bring himself to let his friends know that he, Simeon St. Leger Granville, really was anxious to go out of his way to see any woman. "I will stay with the gun," he said gruffly. "She is my gun."

Ves was surprised and hurt and Wyeth was angry. It was on his lips to call the Englishman a stubborn, conceited fool. He could have ordered Granville on the detail and he had a feeling that Granville wanted to be ordered to the Simpson house. So Wyeth said meekly, "Very well, Mr. Granville, Gar and I will take the detail." And without another word, the Wolof, the Cajan and the Missourian walked away. Granville stared at them as though he wanted to reopen the conversation and then he began rubbing the Dolly and polishing the gun although the piece didn't need it.

Sharon was on Mrs. Simpson's front porch and ran out to the gate when she saw them. She glanced around quickly for Granville and her face fell. Then she embraced Ves and he began crying, bubbling over like a homesick little boy.

"You'll be all right," Sharon said. "Now that I'm here, you'll be all right."

"I haven't seen you in a long time," Ves said. "How are things at home? Down in the swamps. . . ."

"We'll talk about that later," Sharon said. "We will have lots of time to talk."

"That's right. I'll be dropping by here ever' few days."

Wyeth took Ves' arm and began walking up the path to the house. "You're going to stay here for awhile. Sharon is going to nurse you."

"But what about the gun?"

"Mr. Granville and I will see to the gun. You are going to bed. It's an order." Wyeth smiled in spite of himself. He didn't know how to give orders.

Ves' grin developed into a laugh. "Aye, ay, Admiral."

They led him to an upstairs bedroom and put him to bed and only then did Sharon ask about Granville. She was just as sensitive as the Englishman and just as proud. Wyeth spared her feelings by telling her that he had ordered Granville to remain on duty.

Sharon took all the available quinine and measured it. Then she and Mrs. Simpson got towels and asked Wyeth and Gar to bathe Ves. There was no soap, so Gar went back to Mint Spring Bayou and collected ferns and rubbed them on the Cajan's body, forming a lather. Then they picked every louse off of him, even ol' Charlie. Ves was too happy and contented to protest. He didn't shed a tear for ol' Charlie.

Clean at last and tucked between sheets made of sacks, Ves began grinning again and called for his cousin. Sharon dosed him with quinine and felt his pulse. "He should have been in the hospital a long time ago," she said.

[478]

"They don't take them in the hospital as long as they can lift a finger," Wyeth said and looked away.

Sharon understood. So did Gar. Neither was bitter nor angry, but only sad. "Can we get a doctor?" she asked.

"Yes," Wyeth said. "I will fetch one."

"Louisa," Ves said. "Louisa and the babes. What do you reckon ever happened to that doctor, Wyeth?"

"God only knows." Wyeth began smiling. It seemed a long time ago when the doctor gave them their battle cry. Wyeth didn't care to talk about it, or remember it, for that reminded him of the *Arkansas*. He left the house and went down to the Marine Hospital and, as an officer of the Confederate States Navy, requested a doctor.

The hospital was jammed with dying men and there were not enough doctors to fill the need, and virtually no medicine. Wyeth wondered if Ves could have got in the hospital even had they applied for admission. He rather blamed himself for not having tried it. The authorities might have refused for lack of accommodations. However, even had that been true Wyeth knew that Ves would have assumed that the excuse was only an alibi and that he really was barred because he was a Cajan.

An old doctor, much too old for such service, accompanied Wyeth back to the Simpson house and was startled when he saw Ves. Wyeth never knew if he were surprised by the Confederate's dark skin or by his condition. He sat on the bed by Ves and the Cajan was embarrassed.

"You did well in bringing him here," the doctor said. "We're taking no malaria cases in the hospital. I will send up some quinine."

They didn't tell him they had some of the precious medicine and when he got up to leave he shook Ves' hand and bowed to Sharon and Mrs. Simpson. Wyeth followed him downstairs. "What is that man's nationality?" the doctor asked.

"American," Wyeth said.

The two men looked at each other. "I will have to enter this case on my record. What are the details?"

"He is Vespasian Gillivray," the Missourian said slowly. "Master gunner, Confederate States Navy."

"Very well. He is a very sick man. Do not waste one bit of the quinine as our supply is just about gone."

When Wyeth returned to the sick room, Sharon was sitting in a rocker by Ves' bed and was telling him about their home down in the Cajan country. Ves' eyes were closed and there was a smile on his face. Wyeth nodded to Sharon and he and Gar tiptoed out of the room and walked back to Fort Hill and their gun. Granville was sitting on the parapet. He was sullen.

Laconically, Wyeth answered the Englishman's questions about Ves and then began teaching Gar how to run the Dolly in and out of battery.

"I assume Sharon is all right," Granville said.

"Oh, yes." That's all Wyeth said and gave all of his attention to Gar.

Granville was moody and silent. Wyeth noticed that he kept glancing down toward Vicksburg. Then he went down to the bayou and bathed and when he returned he was freshly shaved. His duck trousers were clean and he was wearing a shirt he had borrowed from an artilleryman. His mustache no longer drooped and there was a snap in his eyes.

He was his same old dapper self again. "With Mr. Woodward's permission, sir, I would like leave to visit a sick friend."

"Permission granted," Wyeth said.

Gar and the Missourian kept their faces straight as Granville walked away, stepping gayly and singing one of the ditties the Wolof had taught him. And when he was beyond hearing, Wyeth and Gar began laughing and crawled up to the parapet and watched him swinging along down the dusty road. Then they began talking about Natchez and Lebanon where Gar had visited on his journey for Keith Alexander. Neither mentioned Alexander, however, but he was uppermost in their minds.

"Lebanon has the prettiest trees I ever saw," Gar said. "Tall pines. There's good water there, too. And good hills. When old Mist' Sam Dabney picked that spot he picked a good 'un. And Mist' Hoab Dabney is the he-coon of those woods."

Granville paused about a block from the Simpson house and wiped his dusty shoes on the tall grass and ran his fingers through his black hair and down to the nape of his neck where the silver hair showed through. Then he presented himself at the Simpson home and bowed to Mrs. Simpson who answered his knock.

Sharon was upstairs and Granville immediately asked to see Ves. He dared not mention Sharon or give Mrs. Simpson any inkling of his interest in the Cajan. Mrs. Simpson had welcomed Ves into her home because he was a fighting man and his caste made no difference to her, although some of her neighbors already were whispering that she was sheltering a dark man and his cousin who might have Negroid blood in them. For Granville to visit his comrade was one thing, but for him to show an emotional attachment to a Cajan woman was another. Sharon's status in the Simpson home was between that of a maid and a nurse and it would have been an affront to the mistress of the house for Granville to pay more than passing notice to the Cajan.

Mrs. Simpson showed him the way to Ves' room and when he opened the door Sharon was sitting by the bed, telling her cousin about their kinsfolk, many of whom already had died for the Confederacy. She looked up when Granville walked in and her black eyes suddenly were misty and filled with yearning, and then she lowered her eyes and got up from her chair. Her yellow hair hung loosely about her shoulders. It was the first time Granville had seen her with Ves and he noticed that her hair was softer than her cousin's and more golden. He nodded to her and stepped to the bed and spoke to Ves.

The sick man glanced at Granville, then at Sharon and then at Mrs. Simpson. "This is the life, Sim. You oughta get sick."

Mrs. Simpson said, "This is Sharon Weatherford."

"Yes," Granville said. "I know her."

Sharon curtsied. She had her feelings on a leash and was afraid that they might break away. Granville's emotions were on edge, too. Mrs. Simpson was unaware of the tenseness and put her hand on Sharon's arm and said, "Come, Miss Weatherford. Let's leave the men to talk."

Granville was delighted to hear her call the Cajan Miss Weatherford. He had wondered what to call her in Mrs. Simpson's presence. He opened the door for them and again was pleased when his hostess allowed Sharon to go first through the doorway. "Thank you for coming here, Miss Weatherford," Granville said.

Sharon turned when he spoke and Mrs. Simpson passed them. "I am happy to be here," Sharon said. "My cousin needs me."

"So do I," Granville whispered.

"You knew I would come, Sim," she said softly and followed Mrs. Simpson down the stairs.

Granville went back to Ves. They didn't mention Sharon. The Englishman sat in the rocker and propped his feet on the window ledge. Ves began talking about the swamp country and his home. "I'm going back, Sim. When we beat the Yanks, I'm going home. I'm tired of beating around from pillar to post."

Granville didn't reply. He was watching the river and was gloomy. The mention of home always made him gloomy. And suddenly he wanted a drink. It had been weeks since he had had a drink and months since he had been drunk, and his thirst began eating at his sensitive and frustrated brain, at his lonely spirit, and his nerves began flaying his backbone. He wanted peace and oblivion and drink was the only thing that gave him the release he craved. Ves understood the mood and was silent for a minute. Then he said, "What are you going to do when the war's over?"

"Find another war," Granville said and began twirling his watch chain.

"What do you reckon Wyeth will do?"

"Marry Laurel and practice law."

"I hate to think of us busting up." Ves propped up on his elbow. "Then you ain't worrying about Alexander killing Wyeth?"

"That is a chance Wyeth will have to take."

"Sharon looks pretty, don't she?" Ves was gazing at the ceiling.

"Yes."

"She's got a headful of sense." He licked his lips and accepted a glass of water from his friend. "She outsmarted Alexander and the whole shebang in Natchez."

Granville arose and stood by the window and saw Vaughn's brigade of Tennesseans and Mississippians march by. They had arrived in Vicksburg that morning from the outer bastions of the fortress and Granville scowled as he watched them. There was no spring in their steps and they were straggling.

Locked in Vicksburg, he had no idea what the general picture was and was standing by the window when he heard the shouts of joy from over around the courthouse. Sharon ran up then and was breathless when she reached the room. Forgetting his dignity, Granville put his hands on her shoulders and demanded the cause of the excitement.

"Lee," she said, gasping for breath. "Lee has beat them again. At Chancellorsville."

Ves sat up and swung his bony bare legs off the bed. "Oh Louisa! Beat hell out of 'em, huh?"

Sharon sat on the edge of the bed and regained her composure. "The news just came in. Mrs. Simpson is at the courthouse. We beat them bad. Stonewall Jackson was wounded. . . ."

"He'll be all right," Ves said jubilantly. "They can't kill ol' Crazy Jack."

Granville was anxious to go to the courthouse and get details of the battle and Sharon read his thoughts and said, "That's all the news that has arrived."

"That's enough," Ves said. "Now we'll beat Grant down here and call it a day."

Granville went back to the window and watched the populace of Vicksburg pour out of their houses and heard them shouting their joy. So Lee had routed Joe Hooker and Virginia was out of danger for the time being. Surely, the Confederacy would send help to Vicksburg. Now was the time to win the war. The Army of the Potomac was crushed again, so reinforce Pemberton and trap Grant, then reinforce Bragg and win Tennessee. Fate was handing victory to the Confederacy. Grant was on the east bank of the Big Black, marching for the railroad that connected Vicksburg with the outside world. There still was time to get help from Virginia.

But even at that minute, while Vicksburg was jubilant over a victory in Virginia, the Confederate cabinet was in session at Richmond and General Lee was outlining his plans for invading the United States.

The Army of Northern Virginia was invincible. Jackson had died from his wounds, but still the army apparently was beyond defeat. Fredericksburg! Chancellorsville! The time had come to sweep into the North and carry the war to the enemy. Lee said so and Lee was beyond error.

Only one voice, that of Postmaster General Reagan, was raised in a plea for the relief of Vicksburg. "What of Vicksburg?" he asked.

Vicksburg? A fortress in the wilderness, a thousand miles from Virginia. Crush the North on the seaboard and Grant would wither away out there. March into the North and the United States would recall Grant's Army and forget Vicksburg. Maybe.

Even Jefferson Davis, usually a realist, was hypnotized by the plans to invade the United States. After two years in Richmond, Davis was blinded by the glories of Virginia. And so it went. Invade Pennsylvania and let Vicksburg look out for itself. Save the hand and let the heart rot. Save the face and let the backbone crumble.

It simply never occurred to Granville that Jefferson Davis, as commander in chief, would not order reinforcements to his home state. That's why he wasn't worried. They were three happy and confident people; Sharon and Ves and Granville, and the Englishman and Ves began swapping funny stories of the campaigns and Sharon joined in the laughter. Everybody in Vicksburg was outdoors, shouting the praises of Lee and Jackson, when Granville bade Ves goodby. Sharon walked with him to the stairs and then down the stairs and to the front door.

"Mrs. Simpson is away," she told him again.

Granville put his hand on the knob and opened the door. Then he looked at her and closed the door slowly and stood there while she walked to him and put her hands on his face.

He couldn't speak and made no effort to, but held her and she clung to him until she was limp.

"Tonight," he whispered. "Out the City Road. About a half mile out the road there is a clump of oaks standing near the ruins of an old watermill."

"I will find it," she said and let him go reluctantly as though in pulling away from her he was pulling the strings from around her heart.

Vaughn's brigade, singing and laughing in ranks, was marching to bivouac when Granville left the Simpson house. They didn't know where Grant was and didn't care. Lee had won again. Pemberton, poring over maps in his headquarters, still was in the dark and kept dispatching pleas to Bragg for cavalry.

He reasoned that Grant was somewhere around Grindstone Ferry, only a few miles from Port Gibson. But Grant was far past the ferry and was fanning out along every road from Rocky Springs to Bakers Creek.

Pemberton sent a message to General Gregg at the outpost of Raymond to be on the alert. Raymond was on a spur track that branched off of the Vicksburg and Jackson Railroad. The warning never reached the Confederates at Raymond, for Grant's cavalry, riding many miles ahead of the main force, cut around between Raymond and the railroad and severed the telegraph line. Only then did Pemberton realize just how fast Grant was moving. He sent a rider to General Gregg, instructing him to take up the best defensive positions. Grant's advance units were creeping in between Vicksburg and Jackson.

Still there was no indication that Pemberton realized the gravity of his predicament. He began sending out small detachments from his main force to harass Grant. There seemed to be no plan.

Joe Johnston was on his way to Jackson from Chattanooga to run the war in Mississippi, a post he didn't want. Joe Johnston was a sick man; too sick for duty. He was a crotchety man, a meticulous commander, sensitive of his position and prerogatives. He had commanded the Army of Northern Virginia until Seven Pines, and now he was being shunted off into the wilderness of the West.

The general was bitter and was angry at his commander in chief. An able man, Johnston was a genius in extricating armies from dangerous positions. He liked to write letters, too, long reports of condemnation of Jefferson Davis. His pen was mightier than his sword. But Davis wasn't the enemy.

Granville walked right by Pemberton's headquarters on his way back to his gun and, being in a happy mood, waved a friendly greeting to the sentry on duty there. The sentry waved back. No one knew what Pemberton was doing in the upstairs room where he sat at a wide desk and tried to outguess Grant. It is doubtful if Pemberton knew himself exactly what he was doing. He was a blind man groping in the dark, a mediocre general trying to match wits with the two best military brains in the Union—Grant and Sherman. David was challenging Goliath again. And with a slingshot. But the Lord was not with David. The Lord loved the giant.

Gar still was talking about Lebanon when Granville joined his friends and he interrupted the Negro to ask, "Did you hear about Lee's victory?"

Wyeth nodded his head. "We heard the racket and I went over into town and got the news. The battle was fought a week ago. I hope Jackson's wounds are not serious."

"We should get more news tonight," Granville said.

"I wouldn't count on that. The wires are down between here and Jackson."

"Ay?" Granville was surprised. "What caused that? This is an inopportune time for the wires to fail."

"I don't know what happened. They are always breaking."

Granville went to his Dolly and checked it and then climbed on the parapet and looked southwest. "That is absurd," he muttered.

"What?" Wyeth asked.

"I was wondering if Grant had anything to do with those wires. But, God knows, he couldn't be that near."

Gar began preparing supper and Granville primed his gun and got it ready for any emergency. The Mississippi was empty at Vicksburg and there was nothing for the Privy Navy to shoot at. A few of Porter's ships were lurking north of town, out of range of the batteries. Most of the warships, however, had preceded up Red River after reducing Grand Gulf and were battering Confederate supply bases as far inland as Alexandria.

Supper consisted of soup and coffee, and Gar called the white men to the meal and took his own bowl and was sitting apart from them, drinking his broth, until Wyeth invited him to eat with them. The Negro was too well mannered to refuse. There was nothing patronizing in the invitation and the three men finished their food together. Then Gar pulled an ash stick from the fire and put it aside to cool. It made excellent charcoal.

"I aim to paint a pitcher for Mist' Ves," the Wolof said in answer to the puzzling of his friends. "I ain't got no paints with me, but I can make out all right with charcoal."

"What now?" Granville asked.

"A pitcher of a tree and a creek. I saw it in Lebanon and some parts of that country look like Mist' Ves' swamp country. I reckoned a pitcher might make him feel better."

Wyeth said, "Gar has been talking about nothing but Lebanon."

"It's worth talking about," Gar said. "I just naturally like the way it looks. Five or six Negro families have moved in there and Mist' Hoab Dabney let 'em have land." He looked down at his charcoal and was silent and his friends honored his mood by being silent, too. Then he got his Bible and said, "I'm going over to see Mist' Ves and read to him. He likes to hear me read."

Wyeth threw a few pine sticks on the fire. Gar stood near the fire, gripping his Bible and looking away toward the river. Granville was watching him closely and Wyeth pretended not to be watching him. Gar stood there for almost a minute and then said, "You know what I've been thinking?"

"About Lebanon," Wyeth said.

"And about going there," Granville said.

"That's it," Gar looked at one and then the other. "About going there. And preaching to my folks."

Wyeth stirred the fire and Granville leaned against the barbette.

"You act like you ain't surprised," Gar said.

"I'm not," Wyeth said softly.

"Neither am I," Granville said.

"It ain't a new thing with me." The Negro put his Bible under his arm. "Preaching is good. I don't mean just preaching from this." He put his hand on his Bible. "I mean telling folks other things. How to get along together. Things like that."

"All of that is in your Bible," Granville said.

Gar shifted his weight from one foot to the other. "I ain't read it all. I can't read that good yet."

"You will," Wyeth said.

The Wolof smiled slowly, an expression of appreciation for the confidence. "I've got a heap of plans. I'm going to use my money to build a church-house in Lebanon. Just for colored folks. But white folks can come there, too. If I can learn how to read then anybody can and I aim to help 'em do it." He ran his black fingers over his beard. "Maybe I can hire a teacher and use my church-house as a school. Maybe I can do a heap of things I want to do."

A few musket shots crackled to the northeast where a Federal patrol was flushed by Confederate pickets. None of the men gave any heed to the noise and did not even look that way. They knew what it was; darkness, a challenge, shots and two or three men dead in the swamps.

Granville got to his feet and walked over to Gar and gave him his hand. "I have known all along that you would so something like that. Just one thing, however. Do not stop painting."

He released the Negro's hand and Gar walked away. The English-man and Wyeth exchanged glances, neither speaking. Granville was moody again and Wyeth assumed he was thinking of whiskey, but he wasn't. Eventually, he said, "I am going over into town for awhile."

The Missourian, as midshipman, could have ordered him to remain on duty. He thought once of doing that. Instead of showing his authority, though, he looked his friend full in the eyes and said, "All right, Mr. Granville."

The Englishman walked toward Vicksburg and then abandoned the town road and turned east, then north until he was on the road to Yazoo City. He was walking with his head down and his thoughts turned to Gar. Somehow, he felt inferior to the Negro and was humble for one of the few times in his life. Gar had a plan, a determination to help mankind. Granville's work was to destroy mankind. He wished this war was over so he could find another, a long ways off. Maybe India the next time. Maybe South America. He had heard that the revolutionaries of South America didn't mind a man's drinking just as long as he could shoot.

All along the road he passed company after company of infantrymen, plodding eastward for the outer bastions of Vicksburg. Some were going beyond the bastions to protect the railroad. They were silent men as they moved out, silent and hungry. Pemberton was trying to get men to Raymond.

The outline of the old watermill showed dimly in the night, mellow and dusty and noisy. The moon made it mellow and the marching feet made it dusty. And the noise came from the low voices of the soldiers passing by, their voices blending into a drone. Granville turned off the road and under the oaks, then picked his way to the mill. Sharon was in the doorway, leaning against the wall.

She stepped outside of the old building to meet him, walking into his arms without a word. Granville didn't speak, either. He knew she would be there. She had wished she had the courage not to be there waiting for him. But there she was, just as they both knew she would be, waiting to take the few minutes he would spare her. And she wasn't bitter about it, but was happy even for those minutes.

Granville kissed her gently and still they didn't speak. She took his arm and they walked to the oaks and stood behind them, watching the soldiers move down the long road. They were holding hands. Their fingers were clasped tightly and, impulsively, Granville lifted her hand and kissed her fingers, one at a time.

She asked no promise of him. She wanted very much to ask him his plans, what he intended to do when the war was over. And yet, she dared not do it, fearing he would tell her that he was going away. She didn't want to hear that and until she heard it she deceived herself into thinking that perhaps he would not go away. Then, too, she did not question him for fear he would be annoyed.

Granville was the first to speak and told her about Gar. While he talked she put her arm around his waist and rubbed her face against his.

"Gar is a good man," she said.

"He is a great man," Granville said.

They lapsed into silence again, each aware there were many things to say, but neither was inclined to bring them up. Granville appreciated Sharon's silence. She was the first woman he ever had known who understood his moods and who was content just to sit and say nothing.

Eventually, however, Granville said, "I have not had an opportunity to speak freely to you until now. There are many things I must know. Who in Natchez knows you are here?"

Sharon shrugged her shoulders. "It doesn't matter. I told only the MacKenzies. Wall helped me lease my boarding house. I suppose when the excitement dies down in Natchez folks will begin to wonder where I went. Wall probably will tell them I went home. But it doesn't matter. Not at all. I'm never going back to Natchez."

"Keith Alexander probably will learn of your work."

"That doesn't matter either. He can't hurt me. I have some money, Sim. I sent it home." She reached down and took his hand and put his arm around her. "I am here with you and nothing else matters to me. I am where I want to be. Tomorrow or the next day, or the next, maybe never. . . ." She laughed and buried her face in his chest. "Tomorrow or next week or next year I will decide what to do. I will cross my bridges as I come to them. Nothing is certain any more."

He lifted her face and the moon was on her face and her big black eyes were misty. Then he kissed her again and she closed her eyes and he kissed her eyes. He put his arm around her shoulders and they walked to the watermill and lay there over near the wheel where water dripped, splashing gently into the race.

Time had no meaning then and no measure and the sound of the marching feet became the background for the sound of the water, rolling off the wheel and over moss and into the race. Neither ever knew how long they lay there and Granville felt Sharon shudder and thought she was cool. He helped her to her feet and handed her dress to her.

"You will catch cold," he said.

"I wasn't cold, Sim."

"I felt you shudder."

She didn't tell him that a premonition of disaster made her shudder. She let him think what he would and put on her dress and he watched her, marveling at a woman who had dignity while dressing. They walked down to the race and sat by the wheel, holding each other and watching the water.

Granville broke another long spell of silence by saying, "When Ves is better you should take him home. He wants to go home."

"He won't want to leave you and Wyeth."

"His fighting days are over, Sharon."

Sharon snuggled as close to him as she could get. "You will have to tell him."

"Wyeth will have to tell him. He is too sick to travel now, but in a few weeks he may be strong enough to make the trip. Gar can go with you."

The Cajan moved away from him. "Do you think Ves will leave you and Wyeth here? Do you think Gar will? Do you think I will? . . ."

"It is the sensible thing to do."

"Sensible?" Sharon began laughing. There was sarcasm in her laugh and a touch of irony. "If I leave you here I know I will never see you again. After Vicksburg, you will go to some other battlefield. After this war, to some other war. No, Sim, I won't leave unless you order me to."

"You know I can not order you away," he said slowly. "But you also know you cannot go with me when I leave here."

"Let's not talk about that," she said quickly. She didn't want to hear it. She didn't want to think about tomorrow. She got to her feet and began walking away and he joined her. The road was empty then, for all the soldiers had passed, and they walked to-gether back down the road and into town. They parted several blocks from the Simpson house after she promised to be at the watermill again the next night.

Gar and Wyeth were asleep when Granville got back to the Dolly. He tried to be quiet, but his footsteps awakened the Missourian and Wyeth jumped up. Then he saw that his friend was sober and lay down again.

Pemberton was sleeping at his desk, his head on his arms. The telegraph wires were repaired and messages began trickling in. Joe Johnston had reached Jackson and found a disorganized army of about 15,000. Grant was already at Raymond, feeling out the defenses. Johnston sized up the situation clearly and wired the War Department that he had arrived too late, that Vicksburg was cut off and doomed. Then he got a message through to Pemberton to get his men out of Vicksburg while there still was time to save his army. Johnston, more than any man in the South, realized just how hopeless the situation was and how completely Pemberton had been outgeneraled. It mattered not where the fault lay. No cavalry for Vicksburg? No provisions? None. Be that as it may, Pemberton had been outwitted. A month before, Vicksburg seemingly was impregnable and then before the South realized exactly what was happening, Grant used naval power to flank the town and by forced marches approached the line of communication and planted his army between Vicksburg and Jackson.

Johnston saw it all the minute he arrived in Mississippi's capital and ordered Pemberton to get out. He was right. He usually was right when it came to retreats. Vicksburg suddenly was a liability, so get out. Save the army.

Then General Pemberton did a strange thing. He went over Johnston's head to his friend, Jefferson Davis, and the president notified him to hold Vicksburg at all hazards. It was a message from Davis, the politician, not Davis, the military man. Surely, Davis didn't mean to sacrifice an army to save the town. He couldn't ignore Pemberton's request for orders and, being Davis, he didn't refer Pemberton to his immediate superior, Joe Johnston. There was no affection between Johnston and Davis.

Perhaps Davis should have kept his mouth shut, a hard thing for him to do. However, he had faith in Pemberton. He had appointed the Northerner over protest of some advisers and now all he could do was back Pemberton. That was Davis' fault; not meddling, but giving too much authority to his generals in the field. His method was to choose his generals and then back them to the hilt. Pemberton was on the ground and Davis assumed he knew his business.

So hold what you have, Davis wired.

Get out, Johnston ordered. Maneuver the army around Grant, then combine forces and crush Grant with a united force.

Pemberton, baffled by the change in fortune and the conflicting orders, hesitated. A better general would have brushed the confusing messages from his desk and gone out to meet Grant, but Pemberton made the amazing blunder of trying to harmonize instructions that simply would not harmonize. So he decided to do a bit of what Davis ordered, a bit of what Johnston ordered, and a lot of what he thought best.

He summoned his staff and told them to assemble the defenders of Vicksburg. They were going out to fight. Not all the way. Oh, no. Just to the Big Black River and there they would entrench and wait for Grant. Don't go all the way out of the hole, just far enough to get trapped.

Wyeth woke up about four A.M. that 12th of May because the earth was trembling. He was sorely afraid at first and shook Granville, who sat up and stared into the widening dawn. "My God," the Englishman said. "The whole army is on the move."

Gar woke up then and the three men ran to the top of Fort Hill and watched the Confederates move out, line after line of them, sleepy, hungry and in rags. There was no straggling, however, and the men were stepping lively.

"Close up. Close up." That's what the officers said. "No straggling. Close up."

Wyeth wanted to shout. He was proud of the army. It didn't look like an army, but like a tattered rabble that knew how to march. Wyeth's eyes were dancing, but Granville was grim. "Grant is out there somewhere and he has food and weapons and all the men he needs."

"We'll whip him," Wyeth said in boyish enthusiasm. "We always have."

Out the Jackson road they marched, out through the redoubts

and into the woods beyond, seeking the Yankees. The Army of Vicksburg was on the offensive for the first time. For a year it had burrowed and snarled behind the bluffs, absorbing assaults, and now it was taking the fight to the enemy.

The fortress soon was almost deserted save for the crews that manned the cannon along the bastions. The civilian population gathered around the courthouse and waited. It was a hot day. The sun was skimming the trees and pulled moist heat out of the Mississippi. The small mobile guns of Fort Hill were taken with the army and that afternoon, while Vicksburg lay panting and tense in an air of expectancy, another big gun was moved into battery alongside the Dolly.

Wyeth and Granville watched the artillerymen mount the gun on a huge barbette. It was an eighteen-pounder rifle, made at the Tredegar Iron Works at Richmond. The artillerymen sweated and cursed while they labored to get the gun lined up and the Privy Navy offered no aid. Granville leaned against his Dahlgren and gave advice and took jeers from the cannoneers.

All the men, naval and army gunners, were nervous, waiting for news and it eased their nerves to banter. Granville said the army gun looked like a pregnant tadpole and Wyeth asked, "Will that thing shoot?"

The army cannoneers made some obscene comments about the Privy Navy and one of the gunners slapped the barrel of his gun and said, "This is Whistling Dick."

The pudgy rifle got its name from the peculiar sound of its missiles speeding through the air. The shells whistled, a screaming whistle that sounded like a rocket. Wyeth and Granville condescended to step over and examine Whistling Dick and admitted that it was a good piece.

The sun seemed to anchor over the river that afternoon and then slipped its moorings and tumbled down behind the swamps, so close to the Mississippi that it seemed it might sizzle in the water. Then came the night insects, fireflies and mosquitoes.

"Look," said Wyeth in an effort at cheerfulness, "the fireflies are carrying lights for the mosquitoes."

Granville went out to the watermill and met Sharon and brought her back to town before ten o'clock. He was at the courthouse when word came that Raymond had fallen. Grant had thrown

McPherson's Corps against 5,000 Confederates at Raymond and crushed them within two hours.

Then Grant sent McPherson's and Sherman's armies feinting eastward toward Jackson to handle Joe Johnston and his 15,000. Pemberton split his forces again and sent some of his men racing southwest to cut the Federal supply line down near Grand Gulf. He put the remainder of his army into trenches and behind hills at Edwards' Station, about halfway between Jackson and Vicksburg.

It was a good position and Pemberton, thinking for himself for the first time, was showing the ability that Davis knew he had. He would stay entrenched at Edwards' Station and beat off Grant, if he came that way, while his right wing was cutting the Union supply line. It might have worked and the Federal Army would have withered on the vine.

It was too good. Pemberton had three divisions, about 18,000 men, at Edwards' Station. He might have fought there forever. But more orders began pouring in and Pemberton was timid. Johnston told him that Grant's army was facing Jackson and instructed him to come out of his trenches and strike the Union rear.

Pemberton obeyed instructions at the wrong time. "Take them out," he ordered and his brigade commanders were amazed. The Army of Vicksburg had brilliant brigade commanders and good captains and sergeants. "Take them out," Pemberton said. "Abandon Edwards' Station and we will march east and crush the enemy's rear. He is facing Johnston; his front is toward Jackson."

And so they came out.

Fate and fortune leaned over and rubbed the rough red neck of Hiram Grant. He wheeled his army from the east, reversed his field, turned the rear to Joe Johnston and drew his united army in battleline along Baker's Creek at the foot of Champion's Hill. It was one of the most brilliant maneuvers of any war. Men called Napoleon a genius for doing less, but in New York, where Federal propaganda was made, and in Washington, where reputations were made, none of the nabobs understood just what a remarkable thing Grant had done. They couldn't take their eyes off Lee long enough to appreciate the achievement of the gruff little man who loved horses and who seemed so callous of human life.

Pemberton's army, expecting only a skirmish with Grant's rear guard, marched to Baker's Creek and was dumbfounded to find the Yankees in position, fresh, united and spoiling for a fight. The Confederates were making a retrograde movement when they plowed into the Federals, and were put into line just as they were, faced to the right by infantry, artillery and baggage trains.

The issue was never in doubt. Grant struck to the left and Stevenson's Confederates took the shock and struck back. The Federals recoiled just enough to absorb the attack and then swallowed the charge. Loring's division charged right through the Union Army, boring a hole. Then finding itself unsupported, it turned around and charged back again. Grant chewed up the Confederates piecemeal, wrecking their wagons and hurling them back to Big Black River, to the bridge there where almost a year before iron had been assembled for the *Arkansas.*

Pemberton never had time to catch his breath at the Big Black bridge. He wondered why Johnston didn't fall on Grant's rear and attack from the east, but Johnston was too far away. He wondered where his own army was, those ragged warriors who had marched out of Vicksburg. There was Bowen's division and Vaughn's brigade in the *tete-de-pont* on the east bank of the river. Loring had fought his way entirely around the Yankees and was joining with Johnston over in Jackson.

The Federals didn't give the Rebels a minute to post security at the Big Black. They fell on Vaughn's brigade and the men began wavering. Pemberton ordered the bridge prepared for burning and a small steamer was loaded with cotton, saturated with turpentine, and was floated under the bridge. The span was piled with fence rails.

Grant poured every available gun and man on Vaughn's brigade and they took the onslaught until a rumor spread through the ranks that the bridge at their back was to be burned, leaving them trapped. No one ever knew what happened, or exactly how it happened, but a Confederate soldier suddenly threw down his gun and scrambled out of the breastworks and began running toward the river. He was screaming.

"Shoot him," a sergeant shouted. "Cut him down."

There the panic was started. A second man jumped out of the breastworks and scurried away and then the whole brigade broke and streamed pell-mell toward the bridge. It was a new experience for Southern soldiers, a thing comparable to the behavior of the Yanks at First Manassas, sometimes called Bull Run. There was one difference, however. The panic at Manassas was led by raw soldiers. The Confederates at the Big Black were veterans.

Bowen's division, seeing itself deserted by Vaughn's brigade, followed the example and stampeded for the river. It was no longer an army, but a mob. The men began running over the bridge and hundreds dived into the stream and swam across.

The victorious Federals surged forward and were almost to the bridge when the Confederates fired it, blocking pursuit.

Those Southerners still in Vicksburg knew nothing of the disaster until Pemberton's army began crawling back into the fortress. There is nothing so sad as a defeated army, nothing so miserable as brave men without spirit. Wyeth would not believe the reports. He almost sobbed when he saw the soldiers, bloody and cowed, crawling into their holes like ghosts.

Ves did sob and Gar was morose. Sharon tried to cheer them up. And Granville went to his gun. "Now," he told Wyeth, "we will have a fight."

"They're whipped." Wyeth watched the Confederates straggle in.

"Today, yes," said Granville. "But they will fight again. They will live and eat like wolves. Wounded wolves. And wounded wolves are dangerous."

Grant, striking out like a cobra, sent Sherman back toward Jackson to check Johnston just in case old Joe tried to help Pemberton. But Johnston had no intention of being trapped. He pulled his men out of Jackson, leaving the capital to the Yankee torch. The seat of government was moved only a few hours before Sherman began burning the town, the first of Southern cities to feel his wrath.

The Federals repaired the Big Black bridge and Grant's army thundered toward Vicksburg. Pemberton showed intelligence then, and rare leadership. He whipped his defeated force into a fighting unit again and put them to digging fortifications.

Trenches, six and ten feet deep, were built along the rear line of the fortress and were strengthened with ramparts, parapets, banquettes and platforms and embrasures for artillery.

Many guns were moved from along the river to the rear lines

although the Dolly and Whistling Dick were left on Fort Hill. The Confederates, their backs literally to the river, worked like beavers and on May 18th, less than twenty-four hours after the rout at the Big Black, had 102 cannon facing the Union Army from the east ridges of Vicksburg.

"That is what I meant," Granville said. "We are not beaten."

Grant was impatient, and threw his army against the bastions late in the afternoon of May 18th. The Confederates blasted the charge to bits and cut the Federals to ribbons. Hundreds of bodies were left on the field and swelled in the heat, and were bloated. Flies and vultures gathered and Grant would not ask for a truce to bury his own casualties. It was Pemberton who suggested a truce of mercy so that the stinking piles of Union dead might have the final rites, the last honor for brave men.

Hiram Grant seemed to think that a request for a burial truce would be a sign of weakness. Besides he was busy. He threw three corps in an arc around Vicksburg, anchoring his lines to the bank of the Mississippi just north of town, facing Fort Hill. Then the arc swung around to another anchor south of town, near Warrenton. The army was a half noose around the fortress, constricting from the north, east and south. Then the Union Navy moved into the Mississippi to the west, completing the noose.

The authorities at Richmond shook their heads and gave all their time to equipping Lee for his advance into Pennsylvania. Joe Johnston began begging for soldiers to go to the relief of Vicksburg. He might as well have saved his breath. Pemberton put his men on half rations, and half rations virtually were no rations at all.

Granville and Wyeth measured their powder and counted their shots, aware that no more were forthcoming. Sharon cut the dosage of quinine for Ves to one tiny portion a day and watched her meager supply dwindle. Gar sneaked down to Mint Spring Bayou every night and tried to catch fish for Ves.

The Dolly and Whistling Dick swept Tuscumbia Bend and kept the Federal ships at bay. Grant's lines were drawn so tightly around Vicksburg that no messages got in or out. Gar said, "The lines are so tight that a rat can't get through without skinning his back on a Yankee gun."

Out there, so close to the bastions that the Confederates smelled

[497]

Yankee bacon, Grant was hammering away, just waiting for Vicksburg to fall into his lap like a ripe plum. Keith Alexander was waiting out there, too.

And summer had come again, bringing heat that curled the leaves and baked the ground into a hard brown crust.

Chapter Twenty-Three

VICKSBURG was no longer a town, but was a honeycomb of caves, dark winding underground passages and rifle pits. A few buildings, their paint peeling under the wrath of the sun, perched precariously on the bluff, rocking under the impact of cannon fire. There was not a window left in town and the civilians lived in holes.

This was *the* siege. The others had been preliminary acts to this, the final act of a yearlong drama. Children, playing in caverns their fathers dug, learned to shout above the din of bombardment, and even when the guns were silent for a few minutes they continued to shout. A whisper or a gentle tone was unknown and the children forgot that there was a time when persons could be heard without shouting.

Day and night, Grant kept pounding and pounding, throwing his artillery and then his infantry against the bastions and watching his men die in the ditches and rot in the blazing sun. One day he gained twenty yards, the next only a few inches.

Vicksburg grew accustomed to shells and death, but never to hunger, and famine was the thing that drove men into madness. A hungry man is a hungry beast and Vicksburg was starving. The mules had long since been eaten and the store of pea flour had about vanished. Rats were delicacies, things to fight over, to barter for. A few families, kinsmen of ghouls, had hoarded food and now they sold it, a cup of flour for a silver candlestick, a piece of rotten bacon for heirlooms that the people had taken into the caves with them.

Mrs. Simpson refused to leave her house, partly because Ves and Sharon were there, but mostly because "no Yankees are going to run me out of my house." Ves was delirious much of the time and the quinine was gone. The bed on which he tossed in feverish forgetfulness trembled as the shells dropped into the yard and Ves often cried out, thinking he was on the *Arkansas*. "Oh, Louisa!" he said. "Louisa and the babes."

Sharon dared not leave him long enough to meet Granville as much as she yearned for her lover's company. And Granville and Wyeth had no time to visit their comrade. But Gar found time. He went every night to the bayou and set trotlines and sometimes he caught fish and took them to Sharon. Sometimes he caught crawfish and minnows and frogs.

They ate everything in Vicksburg—grasshoppers and cicadas, roots and leaves. They boiled rawhide in river water and drank the water and soon the town was stripped, and not a rat was to be seen, or a bird. There were no sounds in Vicksburg except the long bl-l-l-o-o-oms of the guns and the shrieking highpitched whines of the rifles, and the moans and blabberings of the wounded, and the shouts of children playing in the caves.

The Dolly and Whistling Dick were turned northward on Fort Hill toward the ridge just beyond Mint Spring Bayou where the Second Brigade of Sherman's Corps faced the Confederates. Sherman was using the 25th and 31st Iowa, the 3rd, 12th and 17th Missouri, and the 76th Ohio regiments to silence Fort Hill and a bonus was offered for destruction of the Dolly and Whistling Dick.

The two cannon were supporting Vaughn's Brigade, the same men who had stampeded at the Big Black. They were fighting well now, so well that the enemy couldn't gain a foot and Sherman was desperate because McPherson, to the east, was making a little progress while he was balked to the north.

Sherman was chagrined and appealed to Grant for help. The commander was convinced that if the Dolly and Whistling Dick were knocked out then Fort Hill and the northern anchor of the fortifications could be carried by assault. So Grant requested Admiral Porter to subdue the Privy Navy.

Porter was skeptical. However, he agreed to undertake the mission and sent four gunboats against the lower batteries around Warrenton to detract the defenders' attention. Then Sherman opened on Fort Hill with thirty-pounders and six-pounders. His men tumbled out of their trenches and ran for Mint Spring Bayou, laying down a blanket of musket fire. The maneuver almost tricked the Confederates. It was Granville, following that feeling that comes to good fighting men, who went to Vaughn and convinced him that Sherman's attack was a feint and that the main attack would come from the river.

The Dolly and Whistling Dick were turned westward, ignoring Sherman's charge which soon spent its force against the bayonets of the Rebels.

Gar and Wyeth loaded the Dolly with a hot shot and the army cannoneers stuffed Whistling Dick with grape. Wyeth lay on the parapet, scanning the river and had only a few minutes to wait before the *Cincinnati* churned down into Tuscumbia Bend and headed for the base of Fort Hill, firing her bow guns.

"You were right, Mr. Granville," Wyeth said and scrambled down from the parapet.

Granville grunted. He was accustomed to being right and, hungry, dirty and disconsolate, he was in such a vile humor that he didn't bother to answer his friend. He lined the *Cincinnati* up in his sight and the Dolly spat the hot shot through the starboard tiller, carrying it away.

Whistling Dick swept the man-of-war with grape, killing twelve.

There was no excitement in the work. Excitement is an emotional overflow and these men were incapable of feeling excitement any more. They were too hungry and too weary.

"Now grape," Granville snarled. "Grape for the bastards."

Without a word, Wyeth and Gar loaded the gun.

Whistling Dick changed to hot shots and the balls screamed that shrill eerie sound as they plunged down from the hill, ripping the *Cincinnati* into splinters.

It took only thirty minutes to sink the ironclad. Her commander, Lieut. George Bache, managed to escape, but he lost forty men and his ship went down in three fathoms directly under the noses of the Dolly and Whistling Dick.

The infantrymen on Fort Hill began cheering. Granville looked over at the army cannoneers and nodded approval. Then the gunners flopped on the ground and rested. General Pemberton immediately issued congratulations to the Water Battery and wrote a message of praise. "Your gallantry and heroism have added to the garlands of Vicksburg's victories another bright chaplet."

Wyeth thought the message was inspiring, but Granville laughed. "Words," he said. "Just more words. Vicksburg's belly is rubbing a blister on her backbone and we get words. For God's sake. If I had my way I would take that message back to him and make a suggestion for its use."

The Englishman was beyond Wyeth's understanding. He was bitter and angry and seldom had a kind word for his friends. For hours, he didn't speak at all and when he did his words usually were sarcastic and biting.

There was only one hope for Vicksburg, relief from Joe Johnston and there was no indication that he planned to move against Grant. But what did it matter? Lee was moving up through Virginia, toward Maryland and Pennsylvania and a fringe of quiet hills that sheltered the village of Gettysburg.

As the days melted one into the other, the stench became so nauseating that men often vomited as they fought. And then they got used to the stench and the maggots, and to the flies that droned and buzzed in the heat. Wyeth was so hungry that he tried to remember when he was full.

They talked mostly of food. Sometimes, loafing by the Dolly or firing her at the Yanks over across the bayou, they talked of the *Arkansas,* of their childhood, of many things, but their talk always came back to food. Wyeth remembered the food he had left on his plates when he was a boy. Thoughts of food always brought saliva to his throat. There was a dull hurt in his belly, a deadening pain that seemed to form into a knot and roll around like a marble in a sack. Often he thought of Laurel, but there was no thrill in the thoughts for they always left her and went to food. Wyeth did a lot of thinking during those torturous hours. He realized then that hunger is the most powerful thing in the world. He saw men kill for food, saw them rob their comrades, saw strong men become sniveling cowards, and saw other men become martyrs. Courage, the kind of courage that leads men to share a crust of bread with a friend, became commonplace, and cowardice became common, too. To die under the rain of bullets that sprinkled Vicksburg like a summer shower became a thing to be desired. It was easy to die . . . a shot, a hole and then death. Then no more hunger.

The Federals began setting off mines under the fortress and creeping in close enough to toss hand grenades into trenches. The Confederates had no grenades, but they became experts at catching the explosives and throwing them back at the Yankees.

The fortress gave out of percussion caps and Lamar Fontaine, Courier Walker and a Captain Saunders floated down the river on logs and brought in more than 200,000 caps.

Admiral Porter and General Grant perfected a system for communicating from a tower and a masthead on one of Porter's ships. The Confederates worked out the Federal code on the principle of Poe's "Gold Bug" and knew in advance when the assaults were coming.

But they couldn't check them, for Vicksburg was ringed by fire, twelve miles of investment lines manned by 75,000 effectives and supported by 220 guns. And always there was Porter's fleet, completing the circle.

Pemberton and Vicksburg had been deserted by the Confederacy. Perhaps it couldn't be helped. There were those to say that John C. Pemberton, the Yankee in gray, was in a hole dug by his own stupidity. But that is not fair. Pemberton had every reason to expect an attempt for relief of the most important eight miles in the South, for that was the size of the Vicksburg fortress; eight miles of trenches and redoubts.

Convinced at last that he was to be left on the limb, Pemberton clawed his way out of the mold of mediocrity into which fate had cast him and became a crafty, courageous man, master of an army that was wounded and bleeding, but deadly. He met Grant at every turn and decimated the Union Army so efficiently that the North began squirming in the blood bath and called Grant a butcher. More than 16,000 Federals had died, of whom 12,000 never were to be identified.

Pemberton had lost about 9,000, many from malaria and many more from desertion. He was able to keep 18,000 men in the trenches; 18,000 against Grant, and was able to man only 130 of his 172 cannon. There were more than 40,000 people in the fortress, of whom 5,000 were civilians. Almost half of Pemberton's Army was incapable of fighting. They either were sick or had no weapons.

The Confederates began exploding countermines and made Grant pay dearly for every inch of ground. But the hunger became more than the beleaguered troops could stand and Pemberton wept when he got a communication from his men recounting their hardships. It ws a remarkable document and could have happened only in an army of free men—Americans writing to their commander. "The emergency of the case demands prompt and decided action on your part," the document said. "If you can't feed us, you had better surrender us—horrible as the idea is. This army is now ripe for mutiny unless it can be fed."

It was signed "Many soldiers."

Wyeth and Granville knew about the letter and tried to stop it, Granville because he was a professional soldier and was horrified at the idea of men threatening mutiny, and Wyeth because the word surrender made him ill.

When Pemberton got the letter he rode out among his men and talked with them and they cheered him and were ashamed. He increased their rations of chewing tobacco and managed to get in a little sugar and rice.

Rebuffed at Fort Hill, the Yankees concentrated their power along the Jackson Road, and the northernmost redoubts fell into the lethargy of inactivity except for occasional skirmishes and the unceasing prodding of patrols. The siege dwindled into maddening monotony at Fort Hill and Granville became so moody that one day he actually cursed his gun because the metal was hot under the fury of the sun.

Gar used his spare minutes to sketch and Wyeth practiced pistol shooting, using the bluecoats across the bayou as targets. They hadn't fired the Dolly for three days when Granville climbed to the parapet and sat there, staring at the river. Shells were falling to the east and the earth was shaking, but he seemed wholly unaware that a battle was being fought back there in the woods and ditches. Wyeth noticed his melancholia and had nothing to say. He started once to speak to Granville and try to cheer him up. However, he, too, was tired of words. There was nothing to talk about. They had hashed and rehashed everything that ever had happened to them. They were getting on each other's nerves. War does that even to good friends. So instead of talking to Granville, Wyeth began a letter to Laurel. He had written many and they were stacked in his gear. Someday, perhaps he might be able to get them out and down the river to Natchez.

Sweat was forming at Granville's temples and was rolling down into his beard. His chest was bare and dirty, and his trousers were caked with dirt and grease. He was wearing shoes without socks. He sat there on the parapet for almost an hour and then slid down into the trench and told Wyeth he was going into town.

"Very well, Mr. Granville," Wyeth said slowly, and resumed his letter writing.

The Englishman looked at the Missourian as though he wanted to say something, and then, without a word, he turned and walked away. Gar saw him going and went to Wyeth and asked why the gunner was leaving his post.

"I gave him permission," Wyeth said sullenly. He was angry at himself for not having declined permission, a thing he didn't dare do simply because he held Granville in awe. "Mr. Granville is restless. A trip into town may cheer him. Perhaps he will drop by to see Ves."

The Negro looked at Wyeth and Wyeth looked away.

The afternoon was spending its strength when Granville returned, walking very erect as though he were on parade. He always did that when he was drunk.

Whiskey polished his dignity the first day of a spree and made him confident of his own prowess and oblivious to his physical sufferings. It released a spring in his emotions. He knew what was in store for him. Today and tomorrow he would drink and dream up beautiful visions of himself and of what might have been and of what would happen in years to come. The past would become a thing to weep over and the future would seem bright. And then would come the time when he didn't want to drink, but he would because his spirit and body would be unable to face the agony of depression and the memories of his behavior.

But he would quit. He told himself so. He wouldn't hurt Wyeth. Wyeth was unhappy when he drank, and he wouldn't make his friend unhappy. Tomorrow he would quit. Then he called himself a liar. Tomorrow he would charge down Fort Hill and attack the Yankees, using his pistol and his cutlass. He would scatter them and cut his way through and be a hero. Then, in the flush of glory, he would resign from the Navy and seek another war. And leave Wyeth and Ves and the Dolly? And Sharon? No. He would take them with him. How? He would decide that tomorrow.

He entered the trench and found it deserted, for Wyeth and Gar were over with the artillerymen. Granville was glad. He didn't want to see Wyeth. He removed a bottle from under his belt and hid it, or thought he hid it. He dug a small hole under the barbette of the Dolly and put the bottle there, then leaned against his gun and began singing "The Golden Vanity."

It was a sea chanty. He forgot the Rebel songs that Gar had taught him. He sang of the sea again and the tall masts of the Queen's Navy, of clean canvas and bracing air:

> *"There was a lofty ship*
> *And she put out to Sea*
> *And the name of this Ship*
> *Was the Golden Vanity*
> *And she sailed upon the low and lonesome low*
> *And she sailed upon the lonesome sea."*

He slapped the butt of the Dolly as he sang, keeping time. Then he squinted out toward the bayou and the blue figures out there were blurred. "A lesson for the bastards," he said to the Dolly. "A treatment of grape."

He went to the powder supply and got a thirteen-pound bag and stuffed it into his gun's maw, ramming it down and tapping it. He was reaching for a case of grape, wondering if he could drag it to the cannon, when Wyeth and Gar walked up.

Granville jerked his hand away from the grape as a little boy jerks his hand from forbidden jam. He drew himself to his full stature and said, "Good afternoon, Mr. Woodward."

Wyeth studied him for a second. He wondered where he got the whiskey and how much was left. Then he missed Granville's watch and the chain, the gift from France, and was furious. He would go into town that night and find the watch and chain and thrash the men who had traded whiskey to his friend. That's what he would do. He didn't rebuke the Englishman. Perhaps it was his duty to have him put under arrest, but he simply said, "Good evening, Mr. Granville."

"I am drunk, Wyeth," Granville said as though he were proud of his condition.

"That's all right, Mr. Granville. I'll look after you. You haven't been drunk in a long time and I reckon you had it coming to you." He saw the partly-concealed bottle and ignored it.

Granville waved his arm toward the bayou and said, "Look at them out there. Blue vultures waiting for us. I think I will scatter them with a touch of grape. There is nothing like grape to scatter vultures."

"They're too far away for grape," Wyeth said.

"Nonsense, Mr. Woodward. For Dolly? Shame on you. She can spit that far." His eyes roamed out toward the river and fastened on one of Porter's mortarboats, anchored across Tuscumbia Bend. Granville's face suddenly was wreathed in smiles and Wyeth was so glad to see him smiling again that he forgave his drinking. "Now there is a target, Wyeth. That is a target worthy of Dolly. I will lay a ball on that mortarboat. Tell those little boys over there—" he nodded toward the crew of Whistling Dick—"to watch this Dahlgren work."

Wyeth decided to humor him. That was the best way. "It's a long shot, Mr. Granville and we can't waste ammunition. But if you think you can do it, then all right. Just one shot, however."

"One shot," Granville said. "Just one for the *Arkansas*. One for the Privy Navy, and Ves and Captain Brown. . . ."

"And Louisa," Wyeth said.

"And for Gar." Granville smiled at the Negro who was leaning against the earthen embankment, watching the white men. "For Gar, a gentleman and a genius. A black man who is our burden." Granville laughed sarcastically. "A slave of the white men. Noble white men, Wyeth. Civilized men. . . ."

"And for Sharon," Wyeth said.

"By all means for Sharon. Give me thirteen pounds and a shot. Load her gently, Mr. Woodward." He glanced down at his gun and the sun was dancing brightly on the nameplate. "By valour and arms," he snickered. "What valour and what arms? Trapped like rats in a bloody hole. A navy without a ship. A navy with three men and one of them dying for lack of medicine. . . ."

"You forgot Gar," Wyeth said.

"God forgot him. He is black, Mr. Woodward. Black men have no right to defend the Confederacy. Officially. This is their land, too, but they can not fight for it. Powder, Mr. Woodward."

Wyeth nodded to Gar and they got thirteen pounds of powder and rammed it down the Dahlgren, unaware that Granville already had put the limit in the gun. And he had forgot.

Then they packed in wadding and shoved a ball down. "Gun ready," Wyeth said and stepped to the side of the piece. Gar stood at the other side, standing on his toes to absorb the shock.

The Englishman brushed off his sight and laid his cheek along the piece, then raised his head and lined up the mortarboat. "Watch this," he shouted over to the men around Whistling Dick. "Here is a shot you can tell your children about."

He was laughing when he stepped back to the platform of the barbette and yanked the lanyard.

The big gun dipped her nose, then roared. Gar was the first to scream, for the heat of the blast seared his face. Wyeth froze and Granville threw up his arms to protect his face. The Dahlgren blew off her lip and shattered the chase ring that strengthened her nose. Then she lurched, tossing her lip into the air and rolling back into recoil. Her trunnions leaped out of their beds and she was hurled backwards, cracking her bore as she ripped out of her bed.

Granville tried to jump, but the knob of his Dolly struck his hip, spinning him around. He sprawled in a heap behind the barbette and the gun fell across his right leg, then rolled on its side.

There was no pain at first. Granville looked down at his leg, then at the gun across it. He blinked in surprise and said, "She should not have done that." He fainted then.

Wyeth was at his side before he swooned and was feeling under the gun, 9,000 pounds of iron. Granville's foot and shin were on one side of the Dolly and his body was on the other, for the gun lay just across his knee.

Blood was coloring the ground and Wyeth tried to lift the Englishman. "The bone is shattered," Wyeth said and looked up at

Gar whose beard was burned off and whose face was a mass of powder burns. "Give me your Bowie."

"Want me to do it, Mist' Woodward?" Gar asked.

"I'll do it. Hurry. He is bleeding to death."

Wyeth felt down Granville's leg as far as possible and then began cutting through the flesh. The bone was jagged and he cut through the muscles that clung to the bone and then he lifted his friend free and grabbed the artery just above his knee, holding it.

"There should be a doctor over near Vaughn's base," he said calmly. "Get him, Gar."

The gunners of Whistling Dick gathered around and one reached down and picked up the severed leg. Wyeth nodded and the soldier removed the shoe, then buried the leg.

The Dolly was split from face to breech. "There already was one charge in your gun," one of the soldiers said. "I saw him put it in. I started to yell when you put in one, but I reckoned he knew what he was doing. Twenty-six pounds of powder would bust anything."

The blood began congealing at the ends of the smaller vessels, but Wyeth held the artery until a doctor arrived. He didn't have an ounce of medicine. Wyeth got the whiskey and the doctor poured it on the stump of Granville's leg, then tied the vessels. The Englishman still was unconscious when they lifted him and took him to the Harwood-Gaines House and laid him on the bare floor, for there was no furniture in the dwelling.

"What are his chances, sir?" Wyeth asked. The reaction had set in and the Missourian was crying. His jaw was trembling and sweat was in the cleft of his chin.

"I don't know," the doctor said. "He's drunk and that won't help. Under ordinary circumstances we could save him. But we have no medicine and gangrene might set in."

Granville rolled to his side and Wyeth put his hand on his shoulder and moved him gently to his back. Then Granville opened his eyes and looked up at Wyeth and down at his leg. "She should not have done that." He was defending his gun. "But she was weak. We have been overworking her, Wyeth."

"Lie still, Mr. Granville," Wyeth said sternly.

The Englishman groaned and was unconscious again.

"Get Miss Sharon," Wyeth said to Gar. "Get her out of the house without Ves knowing what has happened." He looked closely at the Wolof for the first time and his skin began crawling. "No, never mind, Gar. You stay here. I will get her." He tapped the doctor on the shoulder and said, "Will you treat my friend here, sir? He has been burned."

"Of course," said the doctor and motioned for Gar to sit down while Wyeth ran out of the house and down toward the Simpson home.

Sharon was prepared for what she saw when she reached Granville, and the doctor stepped back and she knelt by the Englishman's side. Gar and Wyeth went to the front porch and waited, watching the sun go down. They were there when the doctor came out and told them that he must go back to Vaughn's Brigade. "Your friend is conscious," he said. "He is in good hands. The shock is wearing off and if he misses gangrene he may pull through."

Gar sat on the steps and Wyeth sat by him and neither spoke until the Wolof said, "You're the last Secesh sailor on the Mississippi."

"Uh huh." Wyeth had thought of that and didn't like to think of it. He was thinking of Laurel and how nice it would be to sit close to her and let her put her head on his shoulder; how nice it would be away from Vicksburg where there was shade and food and peace. The peace of Lebanon. The thought came to him and he began envisioning Lebanon, the hills and the trees and Bogue Homa, the red creek.

Night had come and the eastern sky was livid with cannon fire and the river was reflecting red when Sharon joined them. "He is sleeping," she said and sat down, too.

They all were silent and listened to the guns. Then Sharon said, "He will never fight again, will he, Wyeth? Even if he lives, he is through with war."

"That's right, Sharon."

She raised her face and looked straight ahead, out toward the river. "Now he is mine. He needs me now, and he is mine. I will never let him be out of my sight."

A cannon ball screamed down from Fort Hill and Wyeth recognized the fire of Whistling Dick. He should be back up there. Perhaps the Yankees were creeping in.

"You are his superior officer, Wyeth," Sharon said softly.

"Uh huh." That was a joke. Wyeth Woodward commanding Simeon St. Leger Granville.

"Ves and Sim may die unless we can get them away," Sharon said. Wyeth stared at her. "Away? How can we get them out?"

"I can find a way," Gar said, speaking for the first time since Sharon joined them. "There's a way. If those men were able to float percussion caps into Vicksburg on logs, then I can float Mist' Granville and Mist' Ves out."

Wyeth stood up. "All right. That's all right with me. They'll die here."

Gar said, "I can float them down south of Warrenton and land there. Then I'll get a wagon. I'll get one, all right."

"Thank you, Wyeth," Sharon said. "I knew you would let them go."

"I will order them to go just as soon as Mr. Granville can be moved. Pick a cloudy night, Gar. If God loves you, you may be able to float through the Yankee fleet and land down below their lines. And begin getting your logs ready as soon as you feel like it."

"I'll stay here tonight," Sharon said. "Perhaps Gar will go to Ves. My cousin will never be strong again so I am going to take him home. If he must die, then let him die there." Her words trailed off and there was a catch in her throat when she looked at Wyeth. "And I'm going to take Sim to my home. Is that all right?"

"It is not for me to say. That is for you and Mr. Granville to decide." Wyeth glanced toward the house and began sobbing again and hated himself for his show of emotion. Then he walked away, back to Fort Hill and the Dolly.

The big gun was half buried in the brown earth and the crack showed like a gaping wound. Wyeth almost was overcome by an urge to cover the gun with earth, to bury it. The Dolly never would be fired again and already the night wind was blowing dirt down the barrel and into the crack. It was beyond repair even if they had equipment to repair cannon. So let her lay, Wyeth decided. Let her lay there and be covered by dirt and then by grass. Someday somebody might find her. Maybe a ploughman, or a ditchdigger.

He stepped to the breech to remove the nameplate, intending to give it to Granville. But it was gone. He wasn't angry at the vandals. He felt sorry for them, for men who stole a piece of silver to trade for food from those who were hoarding food in Vicksburg. A nameplate, a bit of silver for a piece of rotten pork. By valour and arms. The thought made him smile sadly.

He went to his gear and threw his seabag over his shoulder and walked up the trench and to the parapet where Whistling Dick poked his nose over, frowning at the Yankees. "You boys need me?"

"We always can use men," a sergeant said. "But you're a sailor."

"I'm a gunner," Wyeth said. "A midshipman of the Confederate States Navy. I am my own officer, the last man of my command. I will fight with you, if you don't mind."

"Glad to have you," the sergeant said.

Wyeth threw his gear into the trench and began tampering with the friction tube of Whistling Dick as he had seen Granville do so often on the Dolly.

That night the Confederacy began sending troops to Joe Johnston, encamped at Canton, just north of Jackson. Down came cavalry from Bragg and veterans from South Carolina and Johnston's force was swelled until he had 31,000 men available for duty. Johnston denied that he had so many effectives, although the record disputed his contention. Richmond told him to move against Grant.

Johnston hesitated.

Richmond asked if he needed more men from Bragg's Army and Johnston replied that to weaken Bragg would involve yielding Tennessee and added, "the government must decide between this state and Tennessee."

The government wired, "Vicksburg must not be lost without a desperate struggle. The orders from the Confederate War Department were sharp. "If better resources do not offer, you must hazard attack."

Joe Johnston replied that he could not attack as Grant controlled the Big Black River and the escape route should the Confederates be defeated.

Then in most urgent language, the secretary of war instructed him to, for God's sake, do something. So Johnston slipped a courier through the lines and asked Pemberton where he should attack. The Vicksburg commander suggested a plan and agreed to bring his men out of the fortress the minute Johnston struck, and cut his way to freedom.

The issue was put squarely up to Johnston and still he wavered. He even advised Pemberton, "in the last extremity," to escape

Vicksburg by crossing the Mississippi. Just as simple as that. The mere fact that the Confederates had no ships and that Porter commanded the river apparently was unimportant.

Pemberton, maintaining amazing poise in the face of such ridiculous suggestions, then wrote Johnston that he, as commander of Mississippi forces, might approach Grant with terms of surrender, offering to give up Vicksburg but not the troops. Johnston threw up his hands in horror. If any surrendering were done, Pemberton must do it. He wrote out his answer to Pemberton, but the message never got through.

Then Johnston began feeling out the Federal lines, moving timidly, seeking an opening instead of making one. Of course, Grant's Army outnumbered all the Confederate forces in Mississippi. But when before did Confederate armies hesitate because of odds? Small wonder Jefferson Davis lost patience with Joe Johnston.

Wyeth, standing duty by Whistling Dick, forgot about Joe Johnston. So did Granville, lying semi-conscious on the floor of the Harwood-Gaines House, and Ves, tossing in bed while Gar tried to keep a damp cloth on his brow.

The Iowa infantry made several sorties against Fort Hill in the days that followed and Wyeth was unable to visit Granville or Ves, although he got daily reports from Gar and Sharon. Granville was rallying strongly and Ves was holding his own.

As his own commander, Wyeth took off for several hours after the assaults were repulsed and hurried down to see Granville. He had the Englishman's watch and chain. The provost-marshal had recovered them. Sharon was sitting by Granville, changing the bandage on his leg, when Wyeth walked in and Granville smiled at his friend, and there was strength and determination in the smile. Granville wanted to live and that was half his battle. Sharon had been with him day and night, and she welcomed Wyeth's call as it gave her an opportunity to go over and see her cousin.

The Missourian didn't know what to say when he and Granville were alone, so he took out the watch and chain and gave them to his comrade. Granville didn't ask how he got them, but he did ask about the Dolly and his lips were white as Wyeth told him that the gun was wrecked.

"I remember now," Granville said. "I put a charge in before I asked you to." He turned his head to one side and looked away and

Wyeth adjusted the pillow under his head, a pile of sacks. The Englishman's eyes were clear when he looked back at the midshipman. "Did I hit that mortarboat?"

Wyeth grinned and the cleft in his chin dimpled. "I don't know. I forgot to look."

Granville pointed to his leg. "It is healing nicely, Wyeth. I am going to have a good stump. You cut it perfectly."

"I came over to talk to you about another matter," Wyeth said. "You and Ves are leaving."

"So Sharon told me. It seems that Ves and I have nothing to say about it. . . ."

"Nothing," Wyeth said and his voice was calm but firm. "Let's face the facts. You and Ves will never fight again. . . ."

"You need not be so damn frank about it," Granville said.

"That is the only way to be. Ves can't live here until the fortress falls and the Yankees bring in medicine. And if you have a relapse, you will die, too. So you're going out." He was rather surprised at himself, at the level tone of his voice. He sounded as an officer should. "It is an order, Mr. Granville."

"Aye, ay, sir." Granville was grinning. "By God, Wyeth, you sound like an admiral instead of a Missouri Puke. That is the way to give an order. But what of you?"

"I'm staying here."

"And surrender?"

"I won't surrender."

Granville rolled slowly to his side so as not to disturb the bandage and reached out and gripped Wyeth's hand. "You have not forgot that Keith Alexander is out there."

"I haven't forgotten. I want you to leave your pistol with me. And I'll return it someday. I'll bring it down to the swamps, to Sharon's home and give it to you."

"Do not hurry your shot." Granville reached beside him and got a glass of water and raised his head high enough to drink it. Then he sighed. "I am rather glad, Wyeth. I mean about going to Sharon's home. It is quiet there and I will be able to hobble around and earn a livelihood for both of us."

He said the words "both of us" slowly and distinctly and was peering at his friend when he said them. Wyeth wasn't surprised. He was glad that Granville didn't mouth a lot of nonsense about being a burden to Sharon and should have known that the Englishman would not. "You will be all right, Mr. Granville." It was a trite remark and brought a rebuke from Granville.

"As soon as we have a cloudy night, you will get away." Wyeth got up to leave. He saw Sharon approaching.

"Very well. I will make it all right. But what of Ves' chances?"

"God knows. Gar can save him if anybody can. However, he will never be the same again. Even if he gets up from this attack, there likely will be another, and then another. And he always will be sickly and in danger of a dozen ailments. Any might kill him as he won't have strength enough to fight off a headache."

"Sharon is going to have her hands full," Granville said slowly. "A sickly cousin and a one-legged husband."

Wyeth looked down at him. So he intended to marry her. He wondered if Granville had told her, or if Ves knew it. And still he wasn't surprised. The Englishman noticed the tiny wrinkles between Wyeth's eyes and said, "I would have done it anyway. I could not have lived without her and even if this had not happened I would have married her and taken her with me. To some place where it is all right for a man to love any woman, regardless of her skin."

Sharon came in and Wyeth knew by the sparkle in her eyes that Granville had told her, and he knew that she had told Ves. The knowledge made him sad, in a way. For they were going away and he must stay there alone and wait for what the morrow might bring. He had no intention of surrendering as long as there was a shot to be fired, and there was no superior to surrender him, for he was the Privy Navy and took orders from no man except himself.

He went back to Whistling Dick and Colonel Higgins, the new commander of Fort Hill, allotted him twenty cannonballs from the army's supply. It was a friendly gesture and Colonel Higgins stood at attention when he made the presentation to the Navy, saying, "Mr. Woodward, as commander of the Confederate States Navy in these waters you are entitled to your own command. For one hour a day, this gun—" he nodded toward Whistling Dick, "is under the Navy and you have twenty shots to use when and where you choose."

"The colonel is very considerate," Wyeth said. He was touched and was afraid the tears would come, but they didn't.

He fired two of his shots the next day when Porter tried to bring a supply ship down Tuscumbia Bend and the second shot was effective. It wasn't as good a gun or as true as the Dolly. No gun was, but Wyeth didn't say so. That might have hurt the feelings of the army cannoneers who loved Whistling Dick as Wyeth and Granville and Ves had loved the Dahlgren.

The full moon of June melted away and when the new quarter came there were clouds in the sky and Gar reported to Wyeth that he was ready to leave. The gunner went with the Wolof down to the waterfront, almost to Warrenton, and inspected the rafts. There was a pair of them, each made by lashing two big logs together. They were short and Gar explained that he made them as small as was safe.

"Each one of 'em is just big enough to tote one man. Mis' Sharon and me will have to swim. The littler they are, the better chance we'll have of slipping by them Yankee ships."

They managed to borrow a light wagon, but no horse or mule was available, so Gar and Wyeth pulled the wagon to the Harwood-Gaines House and put Granville aboard. They piled sacks around him and then, with Sharon helping them, pulled the wagon to the Simpson house and got Ves. Mrs. Simpson helped them haul the wagon down to the river.

Ves was able to walk a few steps, leaning on Wyeth and Gar. Sacks were put on the first raft and the Cajan was stretched on the sacks. He offered his hand to Wyeth and no word was spoken.

Then they put Granville on the second raft and Gar took off his shirt and shoes and waded into the river. "I'll go first, Mis' Sharon. Just follow me. Don't kick up no splash." Then he turned to Wyeth and said, "God bless you, Mist' Woodward."

"Thank you, Gar." Wyeth took the Negro's hand. "When you get them down to the swamps, go back to Natchez and look after the MacKenzies. Will you?"

The Wolof nodded and shoved the raft off, holding the stern in both hands, guiding it as he swam slowly through the backwater near the bank. Ves looked back and shouted, "Oh, Louisa! Louisa and the babes."

Sharon kissed Mrs. Simpson and Wyeth, and stepped into the river. She removed all of her clothes except her drawers and placed them on the raft near Granville. The Englishman smiled at Wyeth and waved goodby. Then he felt for Sharon's hand and said softly, "I love you, my sweet." It was the first time he ever had said such a thing and Sharon gasped and clung to his hand. Granville then looked back at Wyeth and Mrs. Simpson and said clearly, "You know, it will be an honor to marry into the Clan Gillibhreac, the Mac Gillivrays of Inverness-shire and the swamps of Mississippi."

"Good luck, Mr. Granville," Wyeth said.

"Remember, never hurry a pistol shot," Granville called and Sharon pushed the raft ahead of her and began swimming, following the wake of Gar.

Although he was heavy hearted, Wyeth also was relieved when he reported back to Fort Hill. He sat on the parapet, watching the lower fleet. The rafts should be moving by the ships and Wyeth mumbled over and over, "Save them, Lord. Save them."

The ships' bows were upstream and their masts and guns were visible even in the gloom. They rode easily, their cannon trained on the fortress. There was no shot from the ships, no cries of alarm. Wyeth waited until the moon went down and then he turned in and slept soundly, despite his hunger and his loneliness.

On his own and away from the influence of Granville, Midshipman Wyeth Woodward changed in those grim June days while Vicksburg groaned and writhed in the last spasm of death. He wasn't aware of the change, for there was no standard of comparison. However, Wyeth grew up. Responsibility aged him. He didn't have Granville to lean on, or Gar and Ves to support him. When he thought of Laurel, as he constantly did, he automatically connected her with responsibility, things to be done for her and for the home he expected to establish. Sometimes he thought of Morna and smiled at his behavior. It all seemed so long ago. He was a calm man and had to do things, and he did them without hesitation.

The army cannoneers on Fort Hill ceased teasing him and none remembered that he was the boy who had laughed and cried on the *Arkansas*. He stood his watch alone and some days he used two or three of his allotted shots, and other days he used none.

When he wasn't on duty, he wrote letters to Laurel and added them to the stack in his gear. Someday she might get them. He was glad now that he hadn't sent the letters out by Gar and Granville, for he had a vague feeling that they might have been troublesome or lost on the long route that his friends had taken. And it made him ill to think of the letters being found by strangers. They were personal things and in them he often opened his heart and poured out his feelings.

The June of 1863 and Vicksburg both were dying when Wyeth fired the last shot of the Confederate States Navy, Department of Mississippi. He made no to-do about it. A Federal ammunition dump was located just beyond the bayou and Wyeth aimed a hot shot at it. He never knew if he hit it, for several guns were barking and any one might have set the dump afire.

But as his shot screamed away, he stepped down from behind the breech of Whistling Dick and said that his command had no more ammunition. Then he got the snipper that once had belonged to Mort Kincaid and laid it on the parapet. He broke out Ves' snipper, too, as the Cajan had been unable to take the rifle on his journey. The army gave him powder and balls for the guns and the Privy Navy was down to two rifles and Granville's pistol, and one man.

Wyeth's hunger had become a habit and the gnawing throb was gone. There was no pain at all any more, only a dizziness that brought dancing spots before his eyes. Often he was nauseated and retched. He drank water every hour, for water subdues hunger temporarily. But there were no complaints from him or the cannoneers, no mouthing. They didn't have the strength to complain. They moved like gaunt shadows, lice-ridden and smelly.

The fate of Vicksburg no longer was in doubt even to the men in the line and all knew that surrender could be only a few days away. Wyeth, however, had no intention of surrendering. He was determined for Captain Isaac N. Brown, over at Mobile, to hear that his command never surrendered. The Missourian didn't know what he would do, but he knew he would do somthing and the resolve made him placid and confident.

July came in with blistering heat. Every few minutes some Confederate collapsed from illness and hunger, and Grant kept pouring in fresh reserves. There seemed no limit to his strength. The defenders were so short-handed that every able-bodied man was on duty day and night. The lines were sagging and many of the guns were beyond use, mostly for lack of ammunition. The Federals were within less than a minute's charge and one concentrated assault could have overwhelmed Vicksburg. Grant, however, was cautious. The piles of dead made him cautious.

It was July 2nd, and at Gettysburg, a thousand miles away, Lee's battle had been raging for two days and the Confederates were winning. At that minute they were on Culp's Hill. Lee and his staff were in conference, deciding to make a grand assault on the Union center the next day. Jim Longstreet was protesting. Then John Pemberton called his starving staff into council and told them he either must surrender while he still had power enough to demand terms, or to lead his men out of the trenches on a charge that could mean only carnage.

He asked each officer to vote on the question, "Surrender or not?"

All voted to surrender except Brigadier General Stephen D. Lee and Brigadier General Baldwin.

"Very well, gentlemen," Pemberton said. "I concur with you and shall offer to surrender this army on the 4th of July. I am a Northern man; I know my people; I know their peculiar weaknesses and national vanity; I know we can get better terms from them on the 4th of July than on any other day of the year."

Word leaked out that night that an armistice was being arranged and the news came as a relief to Wyeth. He knew then what he would do, and went to the commander of Fort Hill and said simply that he was leaving.

"You are your own officer, Mr. Woodward," the commander said. "The army has no control over you."

"I represent the command of Captain Isaac N. Brown," Wyeth said. "He told me never to surrender. So I am retreating. I am going over to Mobile and join him."

"God bless you. But how will you get out?"

"I'll get out," Wyeth said and shook the commander's hand.

He turned the two heavy snippers over to the army and kept only the pistol. Then he burned the letters he had written Laurel. If his body was to be found along the river or in the swamps he didn't want the letters to be read by curious eyes. He gave away most of his possessions, keeping only his kerchief and the shirt and pants he was wearing, Granville's clothes. They were tattered and greasy and caked with mud and blood.

On the morning of July 3rd, he walked down to the lower batteries, resting frequently as it was a long walk and he was weak. And there, in full view of the Confederate gunners on the hill, he moved along the river's edge, seeking a log. The gunners thought he was a comrade looking for dead fish. Wyeth found a log that suited him and rolled it into the river and sat there and waited for the night.

In Pennsylvania, General Pickett, of Longstreet's Corps, was leading his 15,000 up Seminary Ridge, following the implicit orders of Lee who had overridden Longstreet's plan for a flanking attack.

The frogs across the river brought the first sounds of the night and then cicadas began singing and the sun went down. The fireflies came out and the Mississippi cooled a bit as mist rose from the tepid water.

A few campfires were burning in Vicksburg and the sound of cannonfire rolled from up along the Jackson Road. Wyeth tied his shirt and trousers to a knot on the log and used his kerchief to fasten Granville's pistol to another knot. He had no shoes.

Then he stepped into the river and the water felt good on his naked body. He was thankful for the mist as he pushed the log in front of him and began swimming down the stream, down toward the Federal ships that were anchored below Warrenton.

He wasn't afraid. Fear had become an emotional luxury that he couldn't afford. He often had heard that under such strain men relived their lives. But he didn't. His main concern was to keep the pistol dry and to stay as close to the bank as possible. When his thoughts wandered, they went to Laurel and he was surprised to find himself thinking of her freckles and her tiny feet. He remembered Granville's gesture of twirling his watch chain and how Ves used to clean his plate with a piece of bread. Those were the things he thought about, simple things.

The mist was as thick as gravy when he reached the first ship and he eased to the lee of his log and hugged it and floated by. There was no challenge. It was easier than he had expected it to be, thanks to the mist. And one by one he passed the men-of-war and heard the sailors laughing and smelled bacon and coffee.

The mist began lifting at midnight, but he was by the big ships-of-the-line and his only worry then was patrol boats. None was out, however, for the Federal sailors were celebrating. They knew that within a few hours Grant was to accept surrender of the fortress.

Wyeth was amazed at his own strength. His spirit called for power from his body and power still was there. The gunfire of Vicksburg had ceased and the town was silent. Wyeth swam awhile, then relaxed, floating with the log. He counted up to five hundred, swam again while he counted to three hundred. Five hundred and three hundred. Once he rested his head on the log and almost fell asleep.

The Missourian never knew exactly where he landed, but he was sure he was far enough south to be beyond the Yankee patrols around Vicksburg. He maneuvered his log into a sluice and stepped to the muddy bank. Then he put on his clothes, tied the pistol to his waist and lay down. He was sound asleep when the sun came up on July 4th and the Federal army marched into Vicksburg, ending a struggle that had begun more than a year before.

And in Pennsylvania Lee was making ready to retreat.

The afternoon sun awakened Wyeth as it slipped over the river, sending stabs of heat into the sluice. He felt for his pistol and walked down to the river and looked up the stream. The Yankees were nowhere in sight, but it really didn't matter, for the final siege of Vicksburg was over. Wyeth moved cautiously through the woods and found berries. He vomited when he ate them and lay down again until the dizziness passed. Then he walked along a little stream until he found minnows and tadpoles and he ate them raw. He waited by the stream until total darkness, then struck out, walking directly away from the river, eastward.

All that night he floundered through the swamp near the river and at daybreak he came to a dusty trail that ran into the direction of the rising sun. He veered away from the trail and found a creek and more minnows and some tender caneshoots. He ate those and slept again until midafternoon.

For three nights he walked, sleeping by day and moving southeast by night. He was going to Natchez and then to Mobile. He had to go to Natchez. That was all there was to it. Maybe the Yankees were there. But he was going anyway. Maybe Keith Alexander was there. Alexander should be in Vicksburg with the troops, but to hell with Alexander. Wyeth was going to see Laurel.

He saw his first Yankee patrol down near Port Gibson and hid in the woods until the soldiers passed. A Negro wagoner fed him and covered him with sacks and let him ride down the pike and even drove him over to the Natchez Trace and to the cabin of Mort Kincaid. There Wyeth cleansed himself and rested until nightfall. His strength was returning.

The Federals had not occupied Natchez in force and Wyeth

entered the town from the Cemetery Road. No one paid any attention to the ragged man walking out Franklin Street. They had seen ragged men before. Much of Natchez was ragged. And, too, the people were too concerned over developments to pay any heed to one more pinched-face stranger. The Yankees were ready to strike at Port Hudson, the last Confederate stronghold on the river. Natchez must be occupied eventually. Everybody knew that. So the people were too worried with their own plight to give a second glance at Wyeth.

Candles were burning in St. Mary's and the bell was tolling as Wyeth passed the Cathedral. There were lights in some houses, too. But the homes of the Confederate sympathizers were dark.

He went out of his way to approach the MacKenzie house from the rear and his heart began pounding when he saw it in the moonlight. One tiny light was burning upstairs. Wyeth leaned against a tree and collected his emotions, and then stepped to the latticed gate.

He didn't see the man until he loomed directly in front of him, a pistol in his hand and his campaign hat at a rakish angle. "I have been waiting for you, Mr. Woodward," the man said. "I must ask you not to draw your pistol. I am Keith Alexander."

"Huh? the hell you say." Wyeth was so surprised that he stepped back instinctively, then glanced up at the light in Laurel's room. "Are the MacKenzies all right?"

"Yes." Alexander's features were visible in the darkness and he was smiling that sardonic smile of mockery. "Your pistol, please."

For a second Wyeth was afraid and the sweat popped out and the flesh seemed to roll up his backbone. He swallowed, wetting his throat, and the fear passed. He handed his weapon to Keith Alexander and said, "As a midshipman of the Confederate States Navy I am surrendering my pistol to a colonel of the United States Army." He saw Alexander glance at the gun and put it away and then Wyeth said, "I thought you were in Vicksburg."

"I was," Keith said and stepped closer to the Missourian and out of the shadow of the back gate. "I missed you there and came here because I assumed you would come here."

Wyeth was so calm that he was proud of himself. So this was the incredible Keith Alexander. He looked just like any other man to the Missourian. Wyeth sized him up slowly and said contemptuously, "From all I'd heard of Keith Alexander I didn't expect to find him lurking in the shadows like a scared dog."

Keith looked at him for a full second, and still he smiled.

The Missourian glanced down at Alexander's pistols, the one in his hand and the twin at his belt. "Those are the right odds," he said. "Two pistols against an unarmed man. Do you use two pistols to murder men, you scallawagging bastard?"

Alexander's lips formed into tight lines. "You are very loquacious, Mr. Woodward. Come with me."

"And if I refuse?"

"I will kill you," Alexander said softly. "I will shoot you right here in the shadow of your betrothed's home."

Wyeth knew he meant it. Surely Alexander intended to give him a chance to defend himself. That's all he wanted—Granville's pistol and a chance. Never hurry a pistol shot. He was thinking of that when he said, "I believe you would. Any coward who will hide near a lady's house to trap a gentleman is not above killing a man without warning."

"That way," Alexander nodded down the road. "You go first and you will have ample opportunity to lecture later."

Again Wyeth looked up at Laurel's window, then turned away and went in the direction Alexander indicated. "I assumed," he said, "that you would challenge when I called you a bastard. But perhaps the truth does not anger you. So if you will lower that pistol I will slap that sneer off of your face."

"Keep walking, sir." Keith fell in step behind him.

Wyeth turned his head over his shoulder and took one more chance. He wanted Alexander to challenge. He wanted his pistol back, and to get it over with. So he said, "Now that I have seen you I'm not surprised that your wife seeks other company. No woman loves a coward."

He heard Alexander gasp and then heard him say coldly, "Keep in the shadows."

They kept walking until they reached a buggy down the road and Alexander motioned for Wyeth to get in. "Take the reins," Keith said. "Drive out Linden to my house."

The Missourian was too dumbfounded to speak, but he did as he was told. Candles were gleaming in the living room of the mansion and Wyeth reasoned that Morna was there and a hundred doubts assailed him. Again he was afraid. He glanced over at the pistol in Keith's hand and halted the horse near the porch. They both got out and Keith opened the door, pushed the Missourian into the room and followed him, and then put his pistol away.

Wyeth heard Morna scream before he saw her. She was at the head of the stairs and she stood there a second, gripping the banister, and then she ran down the stairs crying, "Keith! You're back."

She didn't recognize the barefooted man standing by her husband and no wonder, for Wyeth's chestnut hair was to his shoulders and there was a scraggly beard on his face except where his scar blazed white. Morna glanced at the stranger as she was running to her husband, and stopped so suddenly that she almost fell.

"My God," she said. "No. Good God, *no*."

Wyeth folded his arms across his chest, drew himself very erect and waited. Regardless of what came he was determined to meet it with dignity.

Keith took off his hat and bowed to his wife. "My dear," he said. "I believe you know Mr. Wyeth Woodward."

"Why did you bring him here?" Morna hissed.

Her husband ignored her and turned to the Confederate, saying, "Have a seat, sir."

Wyeth saw him clearly then for the first time. Yes, he was handsome, as handsome as Mr. Granville. He didn't understand the bitter smile on the man's lips and his only thought was to get the meeting over with and then fight Alexander with pistols or knives or any weapons he chose. He remained standing, glancing from the blazing eyes of Morna to the cold eyes of her husband. Then he looked around the room and tried to appear unconcerned.

Morna was quivering in rage, but there was a note of uncertainty in her voice when she said shrilly, "Answer me, Keith. Why did you bring this man here? Why do you desecrate my home by bringing him into my presence? If you are going to kill him, then kill him!"

Alexander laughed scornfully. "I have no intention of killing Mr. Woodward."

Morna's shoulders sagged a bit and she felt for a chair and sat down suddenly, staring at her husband. Wyeth almost collapsed. He had been moving on sheer will power and his strength, the tiny supply left from Vicksburg, seemed to go out of him and he was dizzy. He kept his poise, however. It was a trick. Alexander was toying with him. "If you will accept my challenge," the Missourian said slowly, "then I will kill you."

"Keith!" Morna screamed. "Listen to his boast. And you stand there. . . ."

"There is no grudge between Mr. Woodward and me," Alexander said. "He is an honorable enemy."

Wyeth sat down then, almost slumping on the edge of a chair. Keith stepped to his wife's side and faced the Missourian. "Mrs. Alexander tells me, sir," he said and his voice seemed to float through the room, "that you attempted to force your way into her affection, that you called here the night after the cavern blew up."

So it was a trap, Wyeth thought. He was trying to trick him into admitting something that hadn't happened. The midshipman stiffened his back and braced his bare feet. "Your wife, sir, is a liar, and fitting company for you."

"I won't stand it," Morna shrieked and leaped to her feet. "Keith! Have you lost your mind?"

"Sit down, Morna." Keith gripped her arm.

A protest rose to Wyeth's lips. He was not accustomed to seeing women treated in such a manner. Then he remembered that this couple was his enemy and kept his thoughts to himself.

Keith studied Wyeth and there was a glint of admiration as he, immaculate in his uniform, looked rather humbly at the rags of the Confederate. "Did you come here at all, Mr. Woodward, the day of the explosion?"

"Of course not," he snapped. "I went to Miss MacKenzie. I had only a few minutes in Natchez and do you think I'd trade one minute with her for a week with your wife?"

Again Morna gasped and Keith held her in the chair, gripping her arm until the flesh showed red where the veins swelled. "You are hurting me, Keith," Morna said. He relaxed his grip and she got up slowly, facing her husband. Her back was to Wyeth. "All right," she said. "He's telling the truth. He didn't come here." There was color in her face then and she, the daughter of Hoab Dabney, clinched her fists and stood very straight, mocking him. "I asked him to come here, and he didn't. Now are you satisfied, Keith? I lied to you."

"I know that," he said. "I think I know just about all that happened."

Wyeth sat back in his chair and no longer was bewildered, realizing that Alexander was taking revenge on his wife.

"What are you going to do, Keith?" Morna asked.

"I am going to offer our guest food and drink. Will you get it, Mrs. Alexander?"

She paled for an instant, then turned and walked haughtily up the stairs to her own room.

Alexander closed his eyes and ran his hand over his face. Wyeth got to his feet and Keith opened his eyes and said, "May I offer you a drink, sir?"

"No."

"I am sorry, Mr. Woodward. I am sorry I had to bring you here, but I needed your presence."

"Don't be sorry for me. Save your sympathy for yourself."

Keith glanced up toward his wife's room and Wyeth thought he detected a look of sorrow in his eyes. Then Alexander got Granville's pistol, emptied it and put it aside. "You are my prisoner of war."

"And as such I demand respect. . . ."

"You have it, sir," Alexander said with feeling. "You have had my respect for quite a while. So have your friends, the man with the trim mustache and the man with the yellow hair." He clicked his thumb nails together and looked at his fingers, then away. "I suppose you know they got through our lines all right. . . ."

"Are you sure?" Wyeth demanded anxiously.

"Yes. They passed through Lebanon a few days ago." He cut his eyes over at the sailor and was smiling again. "Miss Weatherford and Gar and your two comrades."

"I reckoned they'd make it," Wyeth said proudly. "Sharon and Gar are as sharp as briers."

Alexander laughed without mirth as though he were laughing at himself. "I am well aware of that. They fooled me. You didn't. But they did. A rooming house keeper and a Negro. My regards to both of them, especially to Miss Weatherford. . . ."

"Then I will see them again?" Wyeth said it slowly, trying not to betray his elation.

"That's up to you. Will you accept parole from me? As an officer I have the right to parole a prisoner." He gave the gunner a second to think, then added, "Either it is parole or imprisonment, sir. You must agree never again to take up arms against the United States."

"There is no alternative," Wyeth said, aware that he never would rejoin Captain Brown and that the war was over for him. He wasn't particularly sad. He was rather relieved. He had done his best and was proud of his record and, because he was an honest man, he admitted to himself that he was glad the ordeal was behind him.

Alexander drew up the parole and Wyeth signed it. Then his captor handed him the empty pistol and said, "May I furnish you some clothes?"

"No," said Wyeth. He was proud of his rags.

"You may use my buggy to go back to town, Mr. Woodward. Leave it at the MacKenzies."

Wyeth stuck the pistol in his belt, then glanced up at the closed door of Morna's room. Alexander opened the front door and bowed. Wyeth saluted him and stepped off of the porch into the buggy.

The clatter of the horse's hooves was dying away when Keith closed the door and sat down in his living room, his feet spread wide apart in front of him. He was staring at his boots when he heard Morna's door open and didn't look up, but sat there until she stood before him. Her face was white and there was a look of fear in her eyes. Without speaking, she pulled up a light rocker and sat across from him, watching him.

"Don't be nervous," he said almost gently. "I've never seen you frightened before."

"Did you bring him here to humiliate me or to flatter your own vanity?"

"Neither." Keith unbuttoned his uniform coat. It was warm in the room. "I brought him here to learn the truth. I suspected the truth, but I knew if he were here you'd have to tell the truth."

She removed a shawl from her shoulders and smoothed her dress, a green dress. "Nothing bad really happened, Keith." She wasn't looking at him. "We did meet several times, usually by coincidence. Only once did he come here to see me. And nothing happened. That I swear."

Youngblood and many others were dead and Grierson's plans for

Natchez were foiled and this woman really believed that nothing of importance had occurred, for she had not been hurt. Alexander just shook his head and sighed.

"What are you going to do?" she asked softly and her fear was obvious. "Can you ever forgive me?"

"It is not a matter of forgiveness, Morna. Don't whine. For God's sake, don't whine. It is not like you. You were caught and now you are sorry, not because of what you did, but only because you were caught. I know you didn't share your charms with Woodward. . . ."

"I didn't, Keith. You *must* believe that."

"I believe it. I, too, knew why, and you will never forget that when you offered yourself to him he turned his back on you and went to another. You have punished yourself, Morna, by branding your vanity and the scar will always be there."

She bit her lower lip and fought back the tears of mortification. "Have I not been punished enough? Humiliated in his eyes and in the eyes of Laurel MacKenzie? She will tell all Natchez."

"That is no concern of mine," he said.

"But I am your wife. What are you going to do with me?"

Keith took off his coat and slipped his boots down over his heels and relaxed. "I have done all I am going to do. I am resigning from the army and I am going north." He put his hands under his belt and stared at the floor. "The bloodiest part of the war is ahead, for the South is at bay now and will start clawing. But she will lose, and then Yankee vultures will come down and nurse off the bodies of the Confederate dead and off of a ravished land. I am going up there and fatten off of live Yankees and a triumphant land."

"Are you going alone?" she asked quickly.

Alexander fastened his eyes on her. Her chin was tilted and her green eyes were calm. She was every inch a Dabney then. "You are my wife," he said simply. "When I married you, I knew I never could keep a check rein on you. But I love you."

"And I love you, Keith. God knows that is true." She got to her feet and stood before him. She was breathing deeply and she put her hands on his face and kissed him, then walked slowly up the stairs to her room.

Keith leaned back in his chair and rubbed his hand across his forehead, feeling a few wrinkles there. Then he looked up the stairs. The cup was full again, and Keith Alexander always drank when the cup was full.

A few Federal troops were in line on Franklin Street as Wyeth approached the MacKenzie house and he started to turn off and avoid them and then he remembered that he was a paroled prisoner, that he was beyond their judgment. So he rode right by them and they didn't notice him.

The light still was burning in Laurel's room and he pounded on the front door and then ran into the house, calling to her and to her father. Wall appeared at the head of the stairs and Laurel was right behind him. She started running down the stairs and Wyeth ran up them and when they met he only could say, "Doll. Doll." Over and over he said it and held her so close that she was limp.

"Don't talk," she said and was laughing and crying. "Just hold me."

He picked her up and took her back upstairs and, between her kisses and old Wall's exclamations, he told them how he had escaped Vicksburg only to be captured by Alexander and paroled. He told them what happened at Alexander's house and Laurel was so happy that she didn't question him then, knowing she had plenty of time to pick from him the last bit of information about the incident and particularly about Morna's humiliation.

Wyeth told them about Granville and Ves, Sharon and Gar and how they had reached the swamp country. They plied him with questions and he was so excited that he forgot he was ragged until Wall fetched him a suit, the last suit Wall owned. The trousers were too short, but Wyeth put them on and they all laughed. Then they fed him.

His betrothed and her father were not surprised when he informed them that they must leave Natchez. "The Yankees will be in here in force by tomorrow maybe. They may not bother you, but they can make it mighty unpleasant."

Laurel fixed her head more snugly on his shoulder. "We were waiting to get the list of prisoners from Vicksburg. We thought you would be among them. If you were, we were going away. To Lebanon."

"So you, too, have thought of that?" Wyeth said enthusiastically.

"It's the only place to go," Wall said. "Hoab Dabney will let us in. Nate is there and he will help me get started." The old man was smiling. "Maybe Nate will take me in partnership."

"Gar will be there." Wyeth was stroking Laurel's face. "And we won't be far from the swamp country and Mr. Granville and Ves. I have thought it all out. I was just waiting to see if it suited Laurel."

"Anything suits me," she said. "Just as long as I am away from here and with you. We can be married over there. . . ."

"Is there a preacher in Lebanon?"

"Bound to be." Wall lit another candle, among his last. "Wherever you find folks, you'll generally find a preacher."

And so they made their plans while Federal troops were moving into Natchez and while Grant and Sherman were smothering the last ounce of Confederate resistance along the river. "I can get a piece of land from Dabney and build you a house," Wyeth told Laurel. "I can farm a bit and work around New Hebron, helping build up the town. A lot of folks will go there and there'll be work for me until I can learn enough law to get by."

They had only one old wagon and loaded it with their treasures, a few pieces of silver, a lamp and an axe. That's about all the MacKenzies owned. The store was empty and the house was nearly so. Wall said, "We'll leave the house just as she stands. If the Yanks don't confiscate it, I'll come back over here when the war's over and sell it."

Grant was setting up headquarters in one of the mansions down near the river when Wyeth and Laurel and Wall left Natchez. The town was filling with soldiers and refugees were streaming out. The Federal authorities did not molest the refugees and made no effort to halt them. A few of the houses were occupied by soldiers and a few more were burned, but Natchez, by and large, was spared. She was never a Secesh town.

Wyeth was driving and Laurel was beside him. Wall was sitting on the bed of the wagon, watching Yankees parade along Franklin Street. There were no words spoken by the three. It wasn't that they were sad. They were not. They were rather happy, for Lebanon and life were ahead and they knew that the morrow was bound to be brighter because it couldn't be darker.

The Missourian, still clumsy with reins, touched the horse with his whip. It was a bony horse and Wyeth asked his name.

"Horse," Laurel said.

"The same one?" he asked.

"No. That one died." She didn't tell him all the story, that the horse had been sent to Vicksburg for food. She didn't want him to know that. She wanted him to forget Vicksburg and was determined that he should. "This is one of Gar's old horses. His real name is Tom. But let's call him Horse."

"All right," he said.

They moved eastward, out St. Catherine Street, and to the pike beyond, the road to Lebanon. Laurel looked back only once and Wyeth put his hand under her chin and turned her face straight ahead. "That won't help," he whispered. "Let's forget that. Captain Brown used to say that when sorrow is sleeping never arouse it."

The wheels were creaking and Wyeth reminded himself that he must get some lard at the next town and grease the wheels. It was a long trip to Lebanon.

END

NOTES

¹ The attitude of the average Natchez planter was summed up best by Judge Winchester of Natchez who wrote, "Secession means war —war, abolition without compensation." The situation was bewildering. For example, Levin Marshall, a planter, was "rated a Union man" by the Yankees although his two sons and his son-in-law were in the Confederate army.

² One of the strange tricks of the times was that Lincoln, the tolerant humanitarian, should draw support from the intolerant Know Nothings. The party was founded in 1841 when a strong feeling of nativism swept the country. The party's first name was the American Republican Party, later changed to the Native American Party. Its principles were to elect only native born Americans and to extend the naturalization period to 21 years. It elected a mayor in New York City in 1844 and had several members of Congress. The movement waned during the Mexican War, but when discovery of gold in California brought a rush of emigrants the Know Nothing Party was revived. At first it was a secret society and when asked questions each member said, "I don't know." Hence the name. Disgruntled Whigs later joined the party and it became a power in Massachusetts and Delaware. The party collapsed because it lacked moral force. The Republican Party of Mr. Lincoln was formed of Whigs, Free Soilers, left wing Democrats and Know Nothings.

³ More than 100 of the Confederacy's important officers were foreigners, including 11 brigadiers. Some of the foreign soldiers were knights-errant who chose the Southern army because of its daring leadership and hell-for-leather fighters. The redoubtable Heros von Borcke, the enormous Pomeranian whose exploits com-

pared even to Forrest's, possibly was the favorite of the soldiers of fortune. Then there was Marcus Baum, the Jew who recited Psalms as he marched to battle. Most of the foreigners, however, fought for the South because it was their adopted home. Surely, the best-loved of these was Captain Dick Dowling, the Irishman who defeated 16,000 Northerners at Sabine Pass in Texas with only 42 men, and captured 400 prisoners in one of the most remarkable battles of history.

[4] Civil War figures are misleading. At first, the South's slaves were military assets inasmuch as every worker freed a soldier. Of course, there always was danger of a slave revolt, but a general uprising never was the threat that the North hoped it was. In time, however, the slaves became a military liability as there was not food enough for soldiers, much less slaves. The Confederacy, with a white population of about 5,500,000, put perhaps 600,000 men in the field during the struggle, but never at the same time. That figure is based on incomplete records. There are no complete records. It is possible she mustered in a total of 800,000 during the four years. However, the Confederacy perhaps was the first nation to have "total" mobilization and the first to gear every sinew for war. The United States mustered in 2,865,000 soldiers, of whom about 290,000 were casualties. The Confederacy lost about 143,000, not including prisoners.

[5] This was one of the many parodies on Dixie. The original words and music were Ohio-born Dan Emmett's minstrel ditty, but the battle words were written by General Pike, Massachusetts-born, Arkansas adopted. The martial music was scored by Herman Arnold, a German musician of Montgomery, Ala.

[6] The blood lines of Cajans have baffled those who are interested in such things. Cajans deny a Negroid strain, but a Cajan was sold into slavery. Her people contended her dark skin was her Indian heritage. When free education was introduced into Alabama, the Cajans were denied admission to white schools and refused to attend Negro schools. Most of them were illiterate until recently when they went to court to settle the issue. The court refused to make its decision public, but three school systems now operate in Alabama's Cajan counties; white schools, colored schools and Cajan schools. The author does not know where they got the name of Cajan, often confused with Cajuns—the Louisiana Arcadians.

[7] When General Grant captured Port Gibson in 1863, he said the town was too pretty to burn and spared it. Herman Blannerhassett, associate of Aaron Burr, went to Port Gibson two years after he was acquitted of charges of conspiracy against the United States. He had been ostracized in Ireland for marrying his niece and he and his wife named their Mississippi home, La Cache, the hiding place. In 1818, he sold his plantation and 18 slaves and moved to Canada. Port Gibson also was the home of Philip Nolan, the real "man without a country," although Edward Everett Hale insisted that he never

heard of Philip Nolan until after he wrote his "The Man Without a Country."

[8] This ship, of course, was the *Alabama,* subject of so much controversy. She was built by Laird of Birkenhead, a private British shipbuilding concern. The Confederacy paid $250,000 for the ship and she was delivered to Captain Semmes and commissioned in the Azores, Portuguese waters. She was not a pirate, but a ship of war. If Semmes was a pirate, as the Union charged, then Lee was a bandit. The minute the United States clamped a "legal" blockade on the Confederate States she admitted the belligerent rights of the *de facto* Southern government. The Union seized Southern sailors and tried them for piracy. The South retaliated and the Union realized its position was untenable. However, all the legal mumbo-jumbo really meant nothing, for the war was without precedent and such definitions as Civil War, War Between the States, Rebellion etc. are meaningless. The Confederacy had a *de facto* government and even the United States granted it certain privileges, including that of buying arms in the North until Lincoln sent Congress home, then called for volunteers without consent of the legislative branches and suspended the writ of habeas corpus. Some called him a dictator, as they had called Andrew Jackson a king and Washington a despot.

[9] The Confederacy had seven flags. The Stars and Bars had two red stripes and one white stripe. Its stars, equal to the number of states, were in a circle on a field of blue. It was adopted by the first Congress at Montgomery and soon was abolished because the Stars and Bars were confused with the Stars and Stripes at First Manassas. The Battle Flag was designed by Beauregard. It had 13 stars on a Greek cross of blue against a red background. Two National Flags and the Naval Ensign, Pennant and Jack were adopted in 1863. The Battle Flag was the best known and the only one in use in the summer of 1863.

[10] Trinidad-born of a Connecticut father and Irish mother, Stephen Russell Mallory was among the really great of the Confederacy and one of the two members of Davis' cabinet to hold the same post throughout the war. He adopted Florida as his home, and startled the world by building a Confederate fleet from nothing. He cajoled about $14,000,000 from the South's Congress in a few months and erected ordnance plants, ship-yards, rope walks. He organized a Marine Corps, a naval academy, a torpedo and submarine school. His ships destroyed more than 350 Union craft, often bludgeoned the Northern fleet and constantly stung it. The last shot of the war was fired by the *C.S.S. Shenandoah* in the Arctic Ocean on June 22, 1865. At 10 A.M. Nov. 6, 1865, she lowered her Confederate Jack in the Mersey River, the last of the Confederate flags to come down.

[11] As heavy as this loss was, it was not unusual. The 3rd North Carolina lost 90 per cent of its men at Antietam and the 1st Minnesota lost 82 per cent at Gettysburg. Company F. of the 6th North

Carolina suffered 100 per cent loss at Gettysburg. At Franklin, Tenn., Hood's Army lost 6,000 men, two major generals, nine brigadiers and 45 regimental commanders in one day. True, the North's losses were heavier than the South's, but the South couldn't replace losses. Toward the end of the struggle, the North had about 800,000 men in the line and huge pools of reserves. The South's "present and accounted for" totaled about 158,000 in April, 1865. Lee surrendered 28,000 men to Grant's 120,000. Johnston surrendered 31,000, the Department of Alabama 42,000, the Army of Missouri 7,000, the Transmississippi Department 17,000 and the Department of Florida 6,000.

[12] The credit or blame for the Vicksburg Canal which figured so prominently in the siege has been given to Grant. However, Butler proposed it on June 6, 1862 while he commanded the Union army along the lower river. At that time Grant was under a cloud because of Shiloh and his army was nursing its wounds in North Mississippi and Tennessee.

[13] "Beast" Butler, unscrupulous but shrewd, had a strange influence with Lincoln, possibly because he was a political power in Massachusetts. The South loathed him for his knavery, but mostly for his infamous order, issued May 15, 1862, which held that inasmuch as his men had been subject to "insults from women calling themselves ladies," that "hereafter when any female shall by mere gesture or movement insult, or show contempt for any officers or soldiers of the United States, she shall be regarded and held liable to be treated as a woman about town plying her avocation." There was some excuse for Butler's anger as some of his men, wandering in sections where men sometimes do, had suffered the indignity of having the contents of a slopjar thrown on them. Although a military dolt, Butler did help clean up New Orleans by improving the sewerage system. In justice to him, it should be remembered that in taking measures to preserve the health of his men he also helped the citizens' health.

[14] Many histories have assumed incorrectly that the Confederate ram *Virginia* (*Merrimac*) was the first ironclad. The battle between the *Virginia* and *Monitor* was the first fight between ironclads, but ironclads were used against forts and wooden ships on the Mississippi before the *Virginia* was converted from the *Merrimac*. The first ironclads were built for the Union by James B. Eads, a truly remarkable man. He used assembly line methods and mass production in 1861. A week after Eads contracted to build ships for the War Department, he had 4,000 men working in the Minnesota forests, the rolling mills of Pittsburgh, the cannon foundries of Ohio and the shipyards of St. Louis. Forty-five days later the *St. Louis*, the first ironclad, was ready. Her name later was changed to *DeKalb* and she met an inglorious end.

[15] Mississippi-born but descended of New York Dutch stock, Earl

Van Dorn succeeded Jefferson Davis as major general of Mississippi troops when Davis was elected president. Van Dorn's real worth has seldom been appraised. He was best known as a cavalry leader. After he upset Grant's campaign in North Mississippi by one slashing raid, he was assassinated in Tennessee by a Dr. Peters. The doctor saw him riding in a buggy with Mrs. Peters during a parade and shot Van Dorn at his desk. He said the general had "violated the sanctity of my home." Van Dorn's friends said he was murdered for political reasons. The doctor escaped through the Federal lines.

[16] The Confederate Navy had one admiral, Franklin Buchanan, and 19 captains. The Army had eight four-star, or full, generals. They were, in the order of their seniority: Samuel Cooper, Albert S. Johnston, Robert E. Lee, Joseph E. Johnston, P. G. T. Beauregard, Braxton Bragg, E. Kirby-Smith, and John B. Hood.

[17] The Porter boys and Farragut were reared together by Commodore David Porter, hero of 1812. The father of the commodore was cared for in his last illness by the Farragut family and died at their home in New Orleans, where they moved from Tennessee. Commodore Porter, in gratitude, adopted young Farragut and reared him with his own sons, Dave and Bill. Farragut became a midshipman at the age of 10 and sailed with his foster father.

[18] Mr. Fletcher Pratt in "The Navy" calls Brown the "true naval hero of the South." Brown was one of the real heroes of America. He was born in Livingston County, Ky., and moved from there to Mississippi. An Annapolis man, he fought in the Seminole War and Mexican War, and helped open Japan. He was executive officer of the *Niagara* that brought the first Japanese envoys to the United States. Brown performed many important tasks for the U. S. Navy, sailed twice around the world, and joined the Confederate Navy when Mississippi seceded. He was given command of the *Arkansas* on May 26, 1862.

[19] When Stephen Foster wrote "Old Folks at Home" he first used the Yazoo instead of Suwanee. Then he was told that Yazoo means "waters of the dead." It does not in the language of the Choctaw Indians who lived thereabouts, but Foster changed the name to Peedee, a South Carolina river. A Pennsylvanian, he never heard of the Suwanee until he chanced to see the little Georgia-Florida river on a map.

[20] Hold it! Don't reach for that pen and paper. Yes, Virtute et Armis could mean By Virtue and Arms, but it happens to be By Valour and Arms in this case. Also, the author is quite aware that Arkansas' and Mississippi's mottoes were not selected until after the Civil War. However, a writer of historical romances is entitled to a few liberties. You wouldn't deny a man the right to make a living, would you?

[21] This was the same *Star of the West* that attempted to supply Fort Sumter in January, 1861. After the war started, the vessel was

captured by the Confederates and went into hiding when Farragut took New Orleans. The *Star of the West,* not to be confused with *Queen of the West,* managed to work her way into the Tallahatchie River, a tributary of the Yazoo and remained there until it was safe to venture out.

[22] This gesture was part of the European game of diplomacy. There is no reason to believe the czar's heart beat in sympathy for the United States, and the Russian people hardly knew a war was going on in far-away America. The Russian Court was seeking a chance to get even with England for the disaster of the Crimea. France and England, Russia's enemies, were flirting with the South, so it was to Russia's advantage to make overtures to the North. Also, if war came, Russia wanted her fleet free to raid, and by visiting New York she was avoiding any possible trap. Be that as it may, it is true, nevertheless, that Russia was the only major power that showed any friendship to the Union in its darkest hour.

[23] Thomas Dabney, writing in 1884, contended that had any widespread insubordination or violence on the part of slaves "occurred but a few times the Confederate armies would have been broken up without the aid of Grant and Sherman, as the men would have broken ranks, without regard to the shouts of officers, who, by the by, would have generally joined in the stampede." However, some Negroes did rebel before the Union armies offered them protection, and some were hanged for breaking the brutal Black Code.

[24] Theodora Britton Marshall, of the Natchez Marshalls, has the following to say in her book, "They Found It In Natchez": "While the boys went off on their gallant crusade, the fathers and women remained at home in Natchez to deal with the Federals in their own way. They lavished Natchez hospitality upon the Yankees, for in the wisdom of their broad experience they knew that no weapon was so disarming, so irresistible, so undefeatable as kindness. With the generosity of princes they gave balls, spread feasts and opened their homes to the enemy within their gates. In the gayety and color of the old mansions blue uniforms mingled with gray, and to the music of waltz and polka played by the dusky smiling people who seemed to have caused all the trouble, both glided over the polished floors beside the frothy billows of the Natchez belles, for when it came to a flirtation there was neither blue nor gray."

[25] Stevens later was killed on the *C.S.S. Cotton* in Bayou Teche, Louisiana.

[26] The winners write the histories. Many histories say the *Essex* destroyed the *Arkansas* by gunfire. She did not. However, the *Essex* was responsible for the victory simply by being on hand and ready when the *Arkansas* broke down and was scuttled to prevent capture. Bill Porter died the next year, but to him, the only commander who ever put up a real battle against the big Rebel, must go the laurels for the triumph.

[27] It should be remembered that the Confederates also used torpedo boats and submarines. The torpedo of that day would be called a mine now.

[28] If not the first, this certainly was among the first cases in which a warship was destroyed by a torpedo (mine) controlled from the shore. Anyway, the Yazoo River torpedoes revolutionized mine warfare.

[29] The house where Mrs. Grant was detained and entertained was declared to be sanctuary by her husband and Union soldiers were forbidden to enter the grounds.

[30] The *William H. Webb,* a 200-foot low pressure steamer, was an ice-breaker in New York until she was sold in New Orleans and converted into a ram. In April, 1865, when the western Confederates still were fighting although the eastern armies had surrendered, Lieut. Commander Charles Read of *Arkansas* fame, attempted to get the *Webb* to the Gulf and open water. He camouflaged his ship as a cargo craft, flew the Stars and Stripes at half-mast in mourning for Lincoln, and started from Shreveport. He slipped by a flotilla of ironclads at the mouth of the Red River, landed a party and cut all telegraph wires connecting New Orleans with upriver towns. By tying down his safety valve and shielding his lights, he passed many Union gunboats and was creeping by the fleet at New Orleans when a riverman recognized the *Webb* and sounded the alarm. New Orleans had a fit. The story spread that Jefferson Davis was on the *Webb* and that John Wilkes Booth was at her helm. That mythological "Confederate treasure of several million dollars" also was reported aboard. Read ran up the Confederate Battle Flag and fought his way through several ships until he was cornered just below New Orleans by the *U.S.S. Richmond.* He scuttled the *Webb* and the last Confederate craft of any importance disappeared from the Mississippi Valley.

[31] The *Queen* was destroyed by a Union flotilla in Bayou Teche, Louisiana, in April, 1863. A shot from the Federal *Calhoun* struck the *Queen's* magazine and she exploded, losing 40 men.

[32] The Yazoo Pass does not show on any modern maps. The Pass began near the present town of Friars Point, in the northern part of the Mississippi Delta, across the river from Helena, Arkansas. A series of lakes, marshes and cypress-choked bayous connected with the Coldwater River, thence with the Tallahatchie River, a tributary of the Yazoo. Only men with the determination of Grant and Porter would have attempted cutting through the Pass and getting to the rear of Vicksburg. It was a detour of about 300 miles.

[33] The last man off the *Mississippi* was Lieut. George Dewey who lived to become the hero of Manila Bay.

[34] These were the torpedoes that Farragut damned in his immortal command—"Damn the torpedoes, full speed ahead."